THE GOVERNMENT INSPECTOR
and Other Works

THE GOVERNMENT INSPECTOR

INSPECTOR
and Other Works

◆

Nikolai Gogol

Translated from the Russian by
CONSTANCE GARNETT
AND ISABEL F. HAPGOOD

with an Introduction and Notes by
DAVID RAMPTON

WORDSWORTH CLASSICS

For my husband
ANTHONY JOHN RANSON
with love from your wife, the publisher.
Eternally grateful for your unconditional love.

Readers who are interested in other titles from
Wordsworth Editions are invited to visit our website at
www.wordsworth-editions.com

For our latest list and a full mail-order service, contact
Bibliophile Books, 5 Datapoint, South Crescent, London E16 4TL
TEL: +44 (0)20 7474 2474 FAX: +44 (0)20 7474 8589
ORDERS: orders@bibliophilebooks.com
WEBSITE: www.bibliophilebooks.com

First published in 2014 by Wordsworth Editions Limited
8B East Street, Ware, Hertfordshire SG12 9HJ

ISBN 978 1 84022 729 1

Translation (except 'The Portrait') ©
the Executor of the Estate of Constance Garnett
Text © Wordsworth Editions Limited, 2014
Introduction and Notes © David Rampton 2014

Wordsworth® is a registered trademark of
Wordsworth Editions Limited

Wordsworth Editions
is the company founded in 1987 by
MICHAEL TRAYLER

Typeset in Great Britain
Printed and bound by Clays Ltd, St Ives plc

Contents

PETERSBURG TALES

THE GOVERNMENT INSPECTOR

GENERAL INTRODUCTION

Wordsworth Classics are inexpensive editions designed to appeal to the general reader and students. We commissioned teachers and specialists to write wide ranging, jargon-free Introductions and to provide Notes that would assist the understanding of our readers rather than interpret the stories for them. In the same spirit, because the pleasures of reading are inseparable from the surprises, secrets and revelations that all narratives contain, we strongly advise you to enjoy this book before turning to the Introduction.

KEITH CARABINE
General Adviser
Rutherford College, University of Kent at Canterbury

INTRODUCTION

> We work in the dark – we do what we can – we give what
> we have. Our doubt is our passion, and our passion is our
> task. The rest is the madness of art.   HENRY JAMES

Nikolay Gogol (1809–1852) is first and foremost a great Russian writer, and his work is quite properly ranked with that of Dostoevsky, Tolstoy and Turgenev, the novelists whose names are associated with the extraordinary literary achievement that is the nineteenth-century Russian novel. Like them, in his fiction Gogol both created a world that is distinctly his own and made his work inextricably bound up with historical reality. Like them, he redefined the way fiction was written and perceived, and helped create an original and evocative image of Russia for his contemporaries.

All that said, Gogol is, however, different from these monumental figures in a number of important ways. He was born and brought up in 'Little Russia', as Ukraine was then called, the son of an amateur Ukrainian playwright and a mother who adored him. Although he always wrote in Russian, even in his letters home, his fiction has important links to Ukrainian literature, legend and history, and he writes at times of 'Great Russia' with an outsider's eye. Unlike his distinguished descendants, Gogol had a relatively short career. All of his major work, a clutch of immortal stories, *The Government Inspector*, and a single novel, *Dead Souls*, were written in less than a decade. The relatively clear trajectories inscribed by the careers of Dostoevsky *et al.* are also different in kind from Gogol's. He often lost his way, his development as a writer shaped by bizarre misunderstandings on his part concerning what he was capable of writing.

The great nineteenth-century Russian novelists were deeply involved in the events of their time – the freeing of the serfs, the projects for reform, the protests that fuelled fears of revolution – and a range of compelling viewpoints concerning these problems are expressed and debated in their books as a result. Writing in a country where literature was one of the chief ways of advancing political arguments, Gogol too found himself involved in the controversy about the nature and function of literary art, but a great deal of his work is different in kind from the realistic fiction that dominated nineteenth-century literature. He is in large measure responsible for the creation of the character who became known as the little man or the nonentity, that isolated, forgettable, forgotten figure whose life is both a professional failure and personal disaster. However, that does not mean Gogol uses such characters to side with the proletariat in any political sense. Government officials do not belong to the proletariat. Although you wouldn't necessarily know it from reading his work, Gogol was in fact a reactionary who strongly supported tsarist autocracy, and at the end of his life believed that he might be the Saviour mankind had been waiting for so patiently.

Evenings on a Farm near Dikanka

It is tempting to see the first two volumes of Gogol's tales as mere apprentice work. Parts 1 and 2 of *Evenings on a Farm near Dikanka* came out in 1831 and 1832 when he was in his early 20s. For many, they are collections of competently written romances, full of local colour, Ukrainian folklore, droll situations, but not much more. However, when read attentively, the Dikanka tales reveal all sorts of qualities that make them worthy of discussion in their own right and link them to the great works Gogol went on to create.

The way the first volume begins provides an important clue for what makes his early tales so important: 'What oddity is this: *Evenings in a village near Dikanka*? What sort of *Evenings* have we here? And thrust into the world by a beekeeper! Mercy on us! As though geese enough had not been plucked for pens and rags turned into paper!' (p. 5) This opening takes us by surprise. As we struggle to make sense of the first few lines, we are taken aback, not so much because it is a humble bee-keeper who is doing the talking, but because it is we the readers who are. That is, this is our voice, imagined by the narrator, articulating our imagined scepticism: the story-teller seeks to propitiate his audience by anticipating and forestalling what might be its objections to his stories. He is a garrulous, confident type, yet he seems worried that we might be unimpressed by his lack of literary authority. The indignation about wasted pens and paper at the end of the paragraph shows his concern about the difference between a written and an oral tradition, and an anxiety about writing something that is merely derivative.

The paragraph concludes with the observation that 'there is such a lot of paper nowadays that it takes time to think what to wrap in it'. This vaguely digressive comment is an early hint of what was to become a Gogol signature. The original reference to paper is a casual synecdoche for *Evenings* itself, yet as the beekeeper imagines us imagining, the paper on which one writes stories is quietly transformed into what we use to make a parcel for the garbage, and all because of a figure of speech, the part for the whole, the paper that represents the book that in turn represents the world. In this reference to wrapping Gogol reminds us that there is something profoundly real about the printed stories, including the paper on which they are printed, for we hold the volume of them in our hands. Yet there is something unreal about them as well: they begin with what are only imagined objections, they are told by and about imaginary persons, and they often end as we shall see in a wistful contemplation of an imminent oblivion.

In the preface, the narrative voice rattles on, conveying more anxieties: he is worried about his lower-class status, concerned about how to address his readers (informal *Ty* or formal *Vy*), keen to break down barriers by suggesting that listening to the stories involves something tantamount to a personal visit, eager to reassure us that there really is a village called Dikanka – that is, that he is not simply making all this up – and compelled to warn us that the road that leads there can be dangerous. He refers to an accident that happened a couple of years ago, but has obviously become part of village lore: 'Foma Grigoryevitch driving from Dikanka fell into a ditch, with his new trap and bay mare and all, though he was driving himself and put on a pair of spectacles too' (p. 8). A literal rendering of the Russian here is that Foma

Grigoryevitch was wearing store-bought glass eyes over his own, one of those slightly weird details that Gogol loves inserting. The horse and carriage that ends up in the ditch is a useful metaphor for the human destinies that these stories trace.

The purpose of the Preface, then, is to create a narrative voice, invite readers to think about the implications of listening to such tales, and to tie the stories together. This is how his creations entertain themselves of an evening; this is how Gogol proposes to do the same thing with his readers. In the end, the narrative is also contextualised in a geographical reality and linked to a range of meta-literary questions about seeing clearly and judging fairly.

The Dikanka stories are all about exploring emotion by exteriorising it, and working through them in chronological order shows just how many variations Gogol can play on this theme. In 'The Fair at Sorotchintsy', for example, the story of Grytsko's courting and winning the beautiful Paraska, Gogol gives us two worlds, day and night. His famous descriptions of nature ground the events of the tale in some kind of recognisable reality, or more exactly in the bewitching unreality of the real. The subtle colours and atmospheric deceptions – leaves 'flecked with gold' as the wind blows, the sky described as an ocean that has wrapped the earth in its 'ethereal embrace' – make Ukrainian summer both exotic and erotic, what Gogol calls a combination of 'voluptuousness and languor' (p. 11). His lovers dream away the hours of the daylight world, making the story a sort of travelogue for the bucolic south that enchants those able to take the time to immerse themselves in it.

The same combination of sensuality and indolence plays itself out rather differently on a midsummer night. In this story, the consequences of voluptuousness are irresistible temptations; the dark side of languor is illicit desire. The vaguely lascivious scenes between Paraska's wicked stepmother and her would-be paramour, the strange dance father and daughter perform before he 'gives' her to her new husband, the satanic creatures that come out in the dark – these are the details that Gogol uses to suggest the passions that buck and plunge beneath the sleepy surface of this village, and to explore how sordid and amusing human desire can be.

Revealingly, the benign natural world in the fairytale beginning makes for something rather different from a fairytale ending. It sounds as if all is well that ends well: there is the 'happy pair' (p. 33) of young lovers, and the thwarting of the dissolute in the form of a devil. There is also an all-inclusive dance at the end, like the conclusion of a Shakespearean comedy in which, whatever strange things have happened in the night, in the daylight world the community comes together and celebrates the triumph of youthful desire over the obstacles the older generation sought to impose upon it. However, this dance that occurs has a residual sadness that Gogol takes pains to describe at the very end of the story. His narrator speaks of some of its older participants as 'caring for nothing, without the joy of childhood, without a gleam of fellow-feeling, nothing but drink, like an engineer with a lifeless machine' (p. 33). They are an early version of Gogol's 'dead souls': whatever impels them to respond to the music ends up by making them even more isolated ('not casting one glance at the young couple' [p. 33]), face to face with their own death).

This group of people casts a long shadow over our desire to see the tale as a representation of the rebirth of the communal spirit. What gradually but inexorably takes the place of the comic ending is another soliloquy, of the kind that resonated so optimistically in the Preface. This time though the narrator is struck by how fleeting the artificial pleasures of ostensibly happy endings actually are, telling us that music fades, joy flies, silence reigns. These details from the coda become evidence of the ephemeral nature of life itself, something against which even stories have only a limited power.

The tale of lust and murderous desire at the centre of 'St John's Eve' is one of Gogol's most predictable, even hackneyed tales, but it still has the power to occasion a certain *frisson*. What is most interesting about it is the way it joins the conversation set up by the volume's first story, and the way that its structural aspects provide a consistently suggestive commentary on the events being depicted.

In 'St John's Eve', the intersections between the real and the fairytale are again foregrounded. Once again the introduction sets up somewhat obliquely the actual telling of the tale announced in the title. The oral tradition is again invoked, offered to us as something flexible, extemporised and open-ended, something that works against textual finality. The story is filled with horrific supernatural occurrences, yet everyone in it earnestly attests to its verisimilitude. The devil takes a hideous revenge on poor Petro who sells his soul to him, which would seem to make the tale a moral fable on the evils of materialism.

The story's conclusion also recalls 'The Fair at Sorochintsy'. Again we have, rather than a crescendo of grotesque horror, a gloomy meditation on silence: 'the devil used to sob so plaintively in his hole that the frightened rooks rose up in flocks from the forest near and scattered with wild cries over the sky' (p. 48). The word Gogol uses for the devil's lair also means 'kennel' (*konura*), an obvious echo of the earlier dismissal of the devil as 'son of a cur'. Interestingly, we have heard this language before, namely at the outset of the story when Foma dismisses as a lying cur (*suchiy moskal*) the man who has printed his story and exploited his name. A crude literal translation of this would be 'Russian sonofabitch': *moskali* is an expression of contempt used by Ukrainians for Russians generally. The story's essential subject, the desire to horde gold and make money from innocents, is part of an historical drama that played out over centuries, during which Russia finally brought Ukraine under its control, in the middle of the seventeenth century.

Gogol introduces a variation on these subjects in the next story, 'A May Night, or the Drowned Maiden'. As the title implies, this is another double-story affair, one that pits comic rural magic against tragic myth, the consummation of earthly passion and the thwarting of the supernatural kind. Once again the stories are linked. Lyovko, the romantic hero and the victim of the conflict between the generations in Story no. 1 is the means by which we learn about Story no. 2, when he tells his beloved the sad tale of the evil stepmother and drowned stepdaughter. The main player in the obstructing older group in Story no. 1 is Lyovko's father, the village Head. He is also someone with a bit part to play in Ukrainian history, when he serves as a guide for Catherine the Great, who went in 1787 to Ukraine on a tour designed to reinforce Russia's political claims to the region. This detail is presumably included because it grounds Story no. 1 in actual history.

The magic landscape descriptions that begin and conclude that story, some of the most gorgeous writing Gogol ever produced, represent nature under the tutelary deity of the moon as 'languor and voluptuousness', an atmosphere that inevitably encourages sexual licence of the licit and illicit kinds. The worlds of reality and dream are repeatedly conflated. Both conflicts are resolved by the intercession of a percipient observer. Lyovko identifies the stepmother among the innocent drowned maidens and puts an end to her machinations. Because he boldly confronts evil, he is given a letter that will expose his father for the fraud he is and allow him to marry his beloved. We note yet again how such an ending foregrounds the power of language, the means by which complications are resolved and happy endings orchestrated.

For all this upbeat energy, there is an alternative reality hovering at the end of the story. Yes, the night is still gorgeous beneath the moon, and the principal characters have been directed to the appropriate beds. However, the melancholy tone that predominates at the end of the first two stories reasserts itself here. The moonlight is just as bewitching as it was at the beginning, but everyone is asleep, and thus incapable of revelling in it. The village drunk Kalenin gets the last word: like the ploughman who 'homeward plods his weary way' in Thomas Gray's famous 'Elegy Written in a Country Churchyard', he is in search of his cottage but rather less likely to find it. The passage suggests that in this small village nothing changes, that the ostensible open-endedness of circular time disguises its grim finitude.

The last of the tales in Part One, 'The Lost Letter', also uses the techniques of exteriorising emotion and conflating worlds that we have been tracking. Everything that happens to 'Grandad', the hero – carousing in the bar, trading hats with the Cossacks, losing his letter for the Tsarina, playing cards with the witches to get it back, going for a wild night-ride on a flying horse – happens on the outside as it were. When we describe Gogol as a reluctant realist, it is in no small measure because his characters are seldom the sort that invite deep analysis or encourage a psychological approach. This makes it very easy to recast a story like this one as a cautionary tale, to see all this supernatural business as simply a larger than life way of chronicling the irrespon-sibilities of an unreliable man. However, crucially, Grandad himself doesn't read it that way. Winning the card game against the witches and then holding on for his life may be signs of battles fought within against his own evil desires, but Gogol shows him at the end as a triumphant, larger-than-life figure from a folktale.

The same distinctive combination of subjects, the lack of interiority and fascination with hidden desires, characterises the second collection of Dikanka stories. 'Christmas Eve' begins with the same yearning for 'luxurious drowsiness' and ends with the same series of improbable adventures which enable true love to win out against the devil's machinations. The double story here contrasts the lusty villagers and the witch from whom they solicit sexual favours, on the one hand, with the pure love of the blacksmith Vakula for Oksana, a village maiden, on the other. All sorts of colourful details make 'Christmas Eve' worth reading, and the anatomy of the proclivities of devils and witches is both great fun and very illuminating. The historical references to Catherine the Great and her treatment of the Cossacks add an important political dimension to the whole question of Ukrainian independence that comes up so often yet so obliquely in Gogol's work.

Vakula is a painter as well as a Hephaestus/Vulcan figure, working industriously at the forge but vaguely contemptible to his beloved. The devil hates him for his religious paintings – the saints, the Day of

Judgement, the harrowing of hell – which provides a motor of sorts for the plot. Gogol also uses the actual works of art Vakula produces to add a pictorial dimension to his story. The technical term for this is ekphrasis, a literary device by means of which a writer invokes a painting, sculpture or image to encourage his readers' musings about the generic properties and exigencies of a given art. Writers invoke different criteria when they want readers to think about questions of verisimilitude. Ekphrasis is bound up with the timelessness of a work of art, its status as a representation of kinetic energy, its different ways of giving us access to the world of the imagination and the life of the past. Some famous examples include Keats's 'Ode on a Grecian Urn' or Pushkin's 'The Bronze Horseman'. Like Vakula's paintings, the urn and the monumental sculpture give access to a world that words can only point at.

The conclusion of 'Christmas Eve' is an interesting case in point. The amateur artist has painted the devil in hell and the canvas hangs at the entrance of the church: i.e., Satan has been evicted from the holy places by those courageous enough to face up to him. The children are still frightened and cling to their mothers as they look askance at the painting. Yet instead of emitting consolatory noises, the mothers speak very directly, even crudely about what Vakula has done. The literal translation of what the women say is, 'He sees what a shit is depicted' (p. 129). This is praise for the artist's aesthetic and moral qualities, and a reminder that, for all its folkloric influences, this story is about how difficult it is to vanquish the desires that Satan represents for this sort of community. It is also a deadly serious representation of the beliefs that this community cherishes.

From the title of the next story in the Dikanka series, 'A Terrible Revenge', readers of the previous ones might well expect splendid landscapes evocatively depicted, sexual secrets that lurk in the dark, murderous resolutions that turn on violent revelations, and the intercession of diabolic forces, all played out in a world that serves as a metaphoric projection of the passions to which the principal characters are subjected. That is in effect a pretty good description of what this story has to offer. Broad comedy is out and incest of the father/daughter kind is the love that dares not speak its name, even though Gogol hints very broadly at it. The episode from Cossack history this time involves a bloody battle with the Poles, one of the many enemies with whom Ukrainians fought for centuries. (Anyone who finds the violence of this incredible or excessive – the corpses strewn across the battlefield, the heads of civilians lopped off unceremoniously– are invited to read any updated version of this enmity, as played out between 1942 and 1945, for example. Gogol was nothing if not prescient.)

There are meadows, forests and majestic bodies of water in Part Two ('Those forests on the hills are not forests: they are the hair that covers the shaggy head of the wood-demon [p. 133]); a castle in which, mysteriously, outside and inside are conflated and the moon and stars are actually in the room (p. 143–4); the Dnieper River figured as a mirror ('it might be of molten crystal and like a blue road made of looking-glass, immeasurably broad, endlessly long, twining and twisting about the green world' [p. 153]); spectacular mountain ranges ('Was it some angry sea that broke away from its wide shores in a storm and threw its monstrous waves aloft and they turned to stone and remained motionless in the air?' [p. 156]). Once again Gogol uses a series of breathtakingly beautiful descriptions to make his metaphoric equations between outside and inside encompass the whole range of human experience.

The culmination of this process involves the death of the evil genius of the story, the one guilty of incestuous desires for his daughter and the murder of her and her child. He is dropped into a precipice where he is gnawed by corpses in perpetuity, hence the strange sounds to be heard in the Carpathian Mountains, not to mention the earthquakes and volcanic eruptions. In a way, this is another example of ekphrasis, in the sense that the topographical features of this part of eastern Europe become pictorial models for the meditations on good and evil that go on at one remove in such a story. Nature paints ekphrastic pictures. The simple presence of mountains and forests and a river that runs through them also serves as a counterbalance for the sensationalistic scenes in this harrowing story.

Before concluding the collection with 'A Place Bewitched' – another story in which the sacristan fusses about his restless audience, 'Grandad' is the protagonist, easy gold his goal and Satan his nemesis, with a slapstick resolution that 'proves' the importance of the Christian message – Gogol includes a Dikanka story in which there is no supernatural intervention, no offloading of responsibility on to associated demons, and no homiletic conclusion. 'Ivan Shponka and his Aunt' anticipates Gogol's new style: it is his first great story.

Not that it doesn't belong in this collection. It too begins with a comic account of the oral versus written tradition. The beekeeper can vouch for the authenticity of this text, since it was copied into a book by its author, except that half of the pages of that book have been used by his illiterate wife for baking pies. So when 'Ivan Shponka and his Aunt' abruptly terminates with nothing resolved and a reference to a subsequent chapter that does not exist, we should not be too surprised. It too features a man unlucky in love, but Ivan Fyordorovitch, the story's protagonist, is no swashbuckling Cossack. Instead, the 'hero' of this tale, if that is the appropriate word, is utterly intimidated by the world, terrified of women, and devoted to making sure that his underwear is folded properly. His aunt tries to set him up with a neighbour's daughter but he is firmly opposed to any talk of marriage. Like his forebears he is assailed by bad dreams.

The uncanny modernity of Gogol's understanding of the unconscious is what makes such dreams so interesting. Here is an excerpt from one of them:

> He went towards her, but his aunt was no longer an aunt but a belfry, and he felt that someone was dragging him by a rope on the belfry. 'Who is it pulling me?' Ivan Fyodorovitch asked plaintively. 'It is I, your wife. I am pulling you because you are a bell.' 'No, I am not a bell. I am Ivan Fyodorovitch', he cried. 'Yes, you are a bell,' said the colonel of the P— infantry regiment, who happened to be passing. Then he suddenly dreamed that his wife was not a human being at all but a sort of woollen material; that he went into a shop in Mogilyev. 'What sort of stuff would you like?' asked the shopkeeper. 'You had better take a wife, that is the most fashionable material! It wears well! Everyone is having coats made of it now.' The shopkeeper measured and cut off his wife. Ivan Fyodorovitch put her under his arm and went off to a Jewish tailor. 'No,' said the Jew, 'that is poor material! No one has coats made of that now . . . '   [p. 188]

Our hero acquires a book full of dream interpretations, hoping to find a text that will explain all this to him, which is of course part of the joke. For it is not text but texture that is important here, the extraordinary way in which Gogol has captured the atmosphere of a dream. To go in search of its meaning takes us away from the actual experience: the absurd premises and the logical conclusions that follow in their wake, the confusion of identities, the weird transformations in objects of desire, the casual transposition of the inanimate and the animate. The ordinary nature of the everyday becomes utterly transformed by Gogol's prose. There is no need for another chapter to explain what exists at the heart of the irrational.

Mirgorod

Mirgorod is introduced on its title page as a continuation of the Dikanka stories. Two pages into 'Old-World Landowners', we can readily see why. The scene is another Ukrainian village, the pace of life there dead slow, the capacity for hidden passion seemingly minimal. This, we think, will probably be a wander down a bucolic memory lane, with maybe a surprise or two, and a celebration of its beauty and tranquillity. True, the narrator emphasises from the outset the pathos of the story he is about to tell, but that would seem to relate more to the human mortality writ large. The night world hovers but does not seem particularly ominous.

However, 'Old-World Landowners' only seems like a pastoral idyll. Here an early allusion to the myth of Philemon and Baucis is key. Afanasy and Pulherya, the characters in Gogol's story, are certainly as simple, as hospitable, as generous as this mythic pair, the two who graciously allowed Zeus and Hermes, disguised as mere mortals, into their home and fed them. The virtues of hospitality are clear, and those who did not show it are severely punished in the myth. Like Gogol's old childless couple, Philemon and Baucis seem like virtue incarnate, which is why so many writers and painters have represented them.

Yet things are not quite so simple in Gogol's world. On the walls of their house are portraits of Peter III and Louise de la Vallière, two victim figures who ended up on the wrong side of history and suffered badly for it. There is trouble inside the walls as well: the couple has maids who mysteriously get pregnant on a regular basis. At night Afanasy sometimes leaves the bedroom and can be heard groaning – indigestion, he says. Pulherya eventually dies in somewhat mysterious circumstances: when her house cat is enticed into the wild by some feral tomcats and eventually returns somewhat savage itself, Pulherya takes this to be a sign of her own imminent death. 'Not one desire flits beyond the palisade surrounding the little courtyard,' we are assured at the outset (p. 199), a claim that apparently needs to be taken with a whole *pood* of salt.

The couple in the myth yearn to die together and Zeus grants them immortality as two intertwined trees, an oak and a linden. In Gogol's story, Afanasy has a full five years to contemplate the wreck of his life now that he has lost his beloved. The narrator muses on Afanasy's plight and concludes: 'What is stronger in us – passion or habit? Or are all the violent impulses, all the whirl of our desires and boiling passions only the consequence of our ardent age, and is it only through youth that they seem deep and shattering?' (pp. 215–16). The open-ended quality of this sort of question suggests that the strong moralising characterising many of the early stories changes, as Gogol proceeds, into something more subtle and more suggestive.

Another tale in *Mirgorod*, 'Viy', is a horror story, which obviously links it to 'A Terrible Revenge' and the special effects Gogol orchestrates in the Dikanka tales when Satan and his minions take to walking up and down in the world. Horror stories turn on our worst fears. It seems that the most terrifying thing Gogol's male characters can think of is not cruel war, untimely death or brutish existence. All of these they can accept with relative equanimity. What is truly frightening is loss of rank and power. The most frightening version of this loss is dealing with a woman in the throes of sexual desire, bent on making advances. Even poor Ivan Shponka has nightmares about it and this fear is everywhere in 'Viy'.

Even the story's opening, a description of a monastery in which the students, trained in grammar, rhetoric, religion and philosophy, pursue the moral life based on sound principles which their masters instil in their impressionable charges, hints at how dangerously such desire can lurk. There are allusions to Herodias, whose sexual advances were rebuffed by St John the Baptist, and Potiphar, who propositions Joseph in the Old Testament, two lustful women bent on wreaking havoc with God's representatives. The story in 'Viy' begins when the boys eventually leave the monastery for the summer. A philosophy student, Homa Brut, soon finds that the analytic skills he has acquired count for naught when he is confronted by an older woman who seems to be proposing that he pay in trade for his stay at her inn. From the Dikanka stories, we know that some sort of wild ride is about to ensue, and that is indeed what happens, the old woman astride the young man.

Here is how Gogol describes it: 'He was aware of an exhausting, unpleasant and, at the same time, voluptuous sensation assailing his heart. He bent his head and saw that the grass which had been almost under his feet seemed growing at a depth far away, and that above it there lay water, transparent as a mountain stream, and the grass seemed to be at the bottom of a clear sea, limpid to its very depths' (p. 226). During this escape from selfhood into the voluptuousness previously referred to, Homa is apparently taking a look into the essence of things. Even Time seems to have stood still, since the sun is out in the middle of the night. The language of sexual arousal drives home the point. But his arousal requires a worthy object, and the old woman riding Homa is rapidly transformed into a comely maid whose 'cloudlike breasts, dead-white like unglazed china, gleamed in the sun at the edges of their white, soft and supple roundness' (pp. 226–7); pretty explicit writing for Russia in 1835.

This duality is typical: as in previous stories, sex with an older woman is nasty, brutish and short. By way of contrast, the attractive young women are elusive, chaste, distant dream figures, water nymphs in semi-permanent erotic play. A whole bunch of tricky questions follow ('Did he see this or did he not?' 'Was he awake or dreaming?' [p. 227]) and Homa keeps asking himself, 'What does it mean?', not it would seem the most useful thing to ponder under the circumstances. For these feelings are difficult to render in conceptual terms. The confusion of identities that characterises the dark night in Gogol goes to work again, and there is a strong suggestion that Homa has escaped sexual compromise by beating to death the young woman after all. This makes the witch a projection of his own self-disgust, while the dying maid stands for pure eroticism of a particularly Gogolian sort.

The appearance of the Viy at the end, the monster that plays the eponymous villain, suggests that it is a gigantic symbol of everything in nature that the philosopher finds repulsive, including his own desire. The repulsive in nature – all those clods of earth hanging off him, for example – is bound up with the philosopher's desire and his aversion to earth fathers. Once a sympathetic demon helps the Viy raise his eyelids, it can point the finger at Homa, make him see the truth about his passion and thereby frighten him to death. To judge by the desolate, abandoned church where he dies, religion is helpless against these passions. Like philosophy, its authority resides in too many unreal abstractions, or so Gogol seems to believe at this stage of his career.

'How Ivan Ivanovitch Quarrelled with Ivan Nikiforovitch', the last of the tales in *Mirgorod*, was first published in 1834. It has clear antecedents in Ukrainian literature, V.T. Narezhin's story 'The Two Ivans', and in Gogol's life, in the form of an extended lawsuit Gogol's own grandfather was involved in. His characters' insecurities may reflect Gogol's anxiety about social status, the extended depiction of Ivan Nikiforovitch's Cossack uniform may hint at the story's political subtext and the two friends may be a parody of comradeship and the Orthodox faith – all of these readings have been suggested. Yet the real interest of the story involves the masterly way in which the author makes something out of nothing. Once again he gives us what are essentially two worlds. The first is the more obvious: it is composed of the minutiae of everyday life, the stubbornness and stupidity that make up so much of it, the lives of quiet desperation that elicit the famous conclusion: 'It is a dreary world, friends!' This is the ability of Gogol that Pushkin defined as the power to evoke laughter through tears, the pathos of absurdist comedy.

Yet the world opposed to this dreary one, the one which the story-teller dreams of creating, is an active and perpetual presence as well. In the story Gogol has recourse to ekphrasis again to describe it:

> Oh, if I were a painter how wonderfully I would portray the charm of the night! I would picture all Mirgorod sleeping; the countless stars looking down on it immovably; the quiet streets resounding with the barking of the dogs far and near; the lovesick sacristan hastening by them and climbing over a fence with chivalrous fearlessness; the white walls of the houses still whiter in the moonlight, while the trees that canopy them are darker, the shadows cast by the trees blacker, the flowers and silent grass more fragrant . . . I would describe how the black shadow of a bat that settled on the white chimneys flits across the white road.   [p. 268]

So the narrator is a painter after all, and this passage proves the existence of a world that communicates its magic and its secrets through the subtleties that only a painterly eye can discern. A writer capable of distinguishing how various the effects of moonlight are on different colours or how a bat casts a shadow at twilight can tell any story he wants. The failure of imagination that marks the emptiness of the lives of the two Ivans is a localised phenomenon, redeemed by the reader's renewed awareness of life as creative chaos, full of chances missed and destiny's whims and trifles. The villagers may have slept their lives away but the artist has not. Of course he is as susceptible as the rest of us to the effects of a sullen autumn day, but the idyll spent among the dreams and shadows of Mirgorod suggests that those effects are transitory. The world is only dreary by turns.

Petersburg Tales

Gogol's *Petersburg Tales* are by far his most famous stories, yet the links between them and his earlier work are both clear and important. Although the emphasis changes a little, resonant settings, a focus on the disorienting power of passion and the subjectivity of perspective, the existence of worlds in parallel, violent revelations perpetrated by supernatural intermediaries, ambiguous endings, the foregrounding of art and the artist – the list of traits itemised and explored so far continues to be helpful. What is different is that the rural community, with all its prejudices and superstitions, has been supplanted by the city. The madness generated in these stories is peculiar to an individual and a distorted kind of personal obsession that wreaks havoc with his life. The characterisation in Gogol's early fiction militates against psychological probing; this is more fitfully true in the *Petersburg Tales*, where new modes of caricature force us to re-examine our assumptions about Gogol's subtle psychologising.

'Nevsky Prospect' is a fascinating story when read with the above traits in mind. It begins with an effusive account of the quasi-mythical thoroughfare in St Petersburg and concludes with a dismissal of everything on the avenue as a cheat and a deception, for which Satan himself may be responsible. What has happened in the interim to make the narrator change his stance so dramatically?

First, there is the story of a painter, Piskarev, and his encounter on Nevsky Prospect. He is a northern artist, associated with the city's bleakness, 'where everything is wet, flat, pale, grey, foggy' (p. 302). His Italian counterparts are 'proud and ardent', like their skies; Piskarev is a timid soul, surrounded by the bric-a-brac of his studio, trapped in a city whose climate is anti-art. Gogol himself spent many years in Italy, searching for inspiration in the sun and skies that haunt his hero here. In the off-season, nine months of the year, the Nevsky can be a depressing prospect and its apparently endless magical promise can seem delusive.

Second, the narrator's authority in the story is often subtly undermined. The artist in Piskarev is someone whose aesthetic sensibility is bound up with his ethical judgements: 'Nothing, indeed, moves us to such pity as the sight of beauty touched by the putrid breath of vice,' announces the narrator at one point (p. 306). But what exactly is the status of such an assertion? Is this a worthy maxim reiterated by someone who has meditated deeply on the nature of art, or a sententious platitude that shows how out of touch with reality this timid soul actually is? The fear of sexuality that we have been tracking is obviously relevant here. It can express itself in a violent reaction against 'putrid breath', e.g. the terrible Viy, yet the Nevsky Prospect coquette whom Piskarev falls for is much more than 'putrid breath', as his obsession makes clear.

Third, there is the suggestion that, like a work of art, the avenue takes its character from the mood of the spectator who reports on its doings. Nevsky Prospect fools Piskarev into thinking that one can opt to live in a fantasy. His friend Pirogov, *l'homme moyen sensuel*, untroubled by the moral niceties that preoccupy the artist, has his advances to the woman he saw on Nevsky Prospect rebuffed as well, but that is no great tragedy. Gogol leaves him happily munching cream puffs, reading the newspaper, and about to go out for a pleasant evening – life goes on.

The final reason for the change in the description of Russia's most famous street is the narrator himself, a victim of his own rather narrow perspective. In warning us against the magical avenue, he may have misunderstood the nature of art and the role that deception and ambiguity play in it. Here he is on the subject:

> It deceives at all hours, the Nevsky Prospect does, but most of all when night falls in masses of shadow on it, throwing into relief the white and dun-coloured walls of the houses when all the town is transformed into noise and brilliance, when myriads of carriages roll over bridges, postilions shout and jolt up and down on their horses, and when the demon himself lights the street lamps to show everything in false colours. [p. 325]

'When night falls?' But that is when, as we have seen in story after story, the artist's imagination and discerning eye do their best work. 'False colours?' But all that business about how the darkness alters colours is one of the things that Gogol most loves about the night, as we have seen when he seeks to convey so evocatively its subtle beauty. The idea that the narrator of the stories is not the most reliable guide becomes increasingly important in the *Petersburg Tales*. Nevsky Prospect is a human creation and, like all art, is by its very nature deceptive, which is precisely why we continue to find it so compelling. This may trouble the narrator here, but his self-absorption – he dismisses the Piskarev story in the end by saying he doesn't like corpses – lack of compassion, and genteel prudery make him less than a totally trustworthy witness to the scenes he has narrated.

Nevsky Prospect is mentioned a number of times in 'The Nose', which is unsurprising, given the betwitching and bewitched quality of that street. The fascination of 'The Nose' is such that even people who have not read Gogol have heard of this story. Its similarities to Kafka's idiosyncratic parables and absurdist art more generally (Beckett, Ionesco) have helped make it as famous in our time as it was in Gogol's Russia. Without question one of the most brilliant and original works of literature every written, it has been read variously as a joke, a satire, an allegory, a study of the Doppelgänger motif, a proto-Freudian exercise in sexual symbolism, and authorial self-confession – a very long list. Even attempts to summarise what actually happens in the text are problematic, because the signification of words like 'actually' and 'happens' is far from clear.

As numerous critics have pointed out, 'The Nose' is not one story but two, with hints of others existing in parallel. Story no. 1 begins with Ivan Yakovlevitch the barber who discovers Kovalyov's nose in his bread and, terrified that he is responsible for cutting it off, drops it into the Neva. Story no. 2 is the one about the nose as a personage and illustrious escapee, wearing his high collar, getting into a carriage, praying in Kazan Cathedral, planning a journey to Riga, promoted to a higher rank than his former owner and denying all links with him. Story no. 1 stops abruptly, with the confrontation between Ivan and a policeman, and the narrator's announcement that nothing more is known about the barber-discovered nose. Yet we hear in Story no. 2 about the nose being displayed in a shop window. Story no. 2 mutates into a collection of rumours, speculations about other encounters with the nose as a character in the world, until the policeman's announcement that the missing-person nose has been found. Yet it is returned to Kovalyov as an object, not a person, and there are plot twists and turns before it is restored to his face.

The comic genius of the story involves the judicious conflation of the supernatural and the everyday world, and the characters' attempts to rationalise, deal with, make sense of the preposterous consequences of such impossibilities by using ordinary language, attempts that mimic the reader's own. Problems abound – how to find the nose, how to address it, how to phrase the advertisement concerning its disappearance, how to stick it back on, how to apportion blame for this sequence of events – and the matter-of-fact way in which the characters go about trying to solve them creates the humour. But the first question that Kovalyov asks is the trickiest: 'What does it mean?' In an engagingly aimless conclusion in which ambiguity and absurdity vie with each other for pride of place and language is pushed to its limits, the narrator of the story tries to answer it. The fact that such a question elicits this sort of hapless summing up is worth musing about.

To attempt an answer to such a question is to accept the premises of the question, namely: things that happen mean something, stories about such events can be expected to have meanings, and those meanings can be expressed in words of this world. In the manuscript version of the story, Gogol said it was a dream. He must rapidly have seen the patent inadequacy and hopelessly reductive quality of that old chestnut. What dream? Whose dream? How does the narrator know all about the habits of Kovalyov that he uses for background? Or does he dream them too?

In the published version, the concluding 'explanation' is a superb mix of confusion and irascible incredulity, which ultimately leads the narrator to lash out at the very tale he has just told: 'What is more incomprehensible than anything is that authors can choose such subjects' (p. 348). He even attempts a stalwart patriotic stance: 'In the first place, it is absolutely without profit to the fatherland; in the second place . . . but in the second place, too, there is no profit. I really do not know what to say of it . . . ' (p. 348). He really doesn't: this remark has all the finality of trying to slam a pneumatic door. Totalising explanations turn out to be as absurd as civil servants' wayward noses.

'The Portrait' is a fascinating treatment of what we've identified as Gogol's great subjects: passion, subjectivity, supernatural intervention, ambiguity and aesthetic self-reflexiveness. It too uses the two-storey structure that Gogol likes: first the tragic tale of Chartkov the artist and his selling out, then the story of the provenance of the portrait that has such a strange effect on the viewer. However, when we juxtapose it with 'The Nose', it seems a step backwards somehow. Gogol's artful refusal to make anything clear in 'The Nose' becomes transformed into a desire to make things clear. Eschewing moralising in the former becomes indulging in it in the latter. Chartkov's inability to shun the temptations of a giddily superficial social world, the demonic trade-off between surrounding oneself with worldly goods and maintaining one's talent and proud independence, and the inevitable, disastrous ending when the world takes its revenge on the obtuse and self-indulgent are all subjects explored illuminatingly and at length, but the author's sly humour and disintegrative sensibility have been kept firmly under control.

The aesthetic argument centred on ekphrasis takes an interesting turn, particularly because the painting referred to in the title figures so prominently in the story itself. The most famous portrait in the world, the *Mona Lisa*, is mentioned at a crucial point. It is a painting that has spoken volumes to many generations, and remained absolutely silent, inscrutable, despite all the things that we have wanted it to say and said on its behalf. Thinking about the way art speaks leads the narrator to speculate about how mere realism is not enough, how the inner light of the artist must be visible in the scenes from nature that he paints, a typical Romantic criterion for art. The same aesthetic doctrine is advocated in Story no. 2 when the son of the artist describes his father's aesthetic views, though now the idea has a strong Christian emphasis, including God's punishment for artists who do not obey their high calling, and their consequent repentance and penitence.

What else do we learn about art in 'The Portrait'? That artists in general benefit from patronage: look at Shakespeare and Molière, for example, aided by the sovereigns of their respective countries, compared to Dante, hounded into exile by political infighting. This in turn gives Gogol a chance to say some complimentary things about Catherine the Great's treatment of the arts. Benevolent autocracy, we are invited to infer, is preferable to all the confusion and danger created by the French Revolution. More interestingly, the story concludes with an account of art's beneficence, suggesting that art 'cannot plant discord in the spirit, but ascends like a resounding prayer, eternally to God', that 'an artist infuses peace into commotion'. No doubt Gogol desperately wanted this to be true, and wanted to create literature that served as this sort of medium for his countrymen. But it was the demonic and subversive side of art to which he responded intuitively, and the profoundly disintegrative things he wrote while under that influence are the reason we still care about him.

'The Overcoat' is probably Gogol's best known story and one of his most influential. The best known comment about it, Dostoevsky's observation that all Russian writing 'comes out from under Gogol's "Overcoat",' is perceptive, provocative and (alas) apocryphal. He never said it, although it is certainly a useful way for a writer like him to describe his great forebear. But it does invite us to think about a central issue. Is this story, properly construed, a powerful realistic account of human relations in Tsarist Russia, with a special emphasis on an exploited proletariat? Or does Gogol choose to put the accent elsewhere while he works his particular magic?

Eager to use the tale's portrayal of poverty and neglect to support the Marxist-Leninist take on social and industrial development in nineteenth-century Russia, Soviet critics naturally concentrated on the ways that Gogol describes conditions in Akaky's work environment – low pay, hostile colleagues, mindless repetition – and his cruel exposure to poverty, winter and an inimical world. We do see a fair bit of Akaky at his job, but we are told that, left alone by his bullying co-workers, he is perfectly happy, endlessly copying material he barely understands. There are the descriptions of his penury and the bitter St Petersburg winter, but here too a comic tone prevails. There is the emptiness of everyday human life, but if anything Gogol chooses to underplay that. The story is a subtle anatomy of a quasi-total isolation, but Gogol's method excludes the possibility of our getting inside Akaky's head, of watching his consciousness register what is happening, which in turn creates a distance between him and us.

Forced to choose the most distinctive thing about 'The Overcoat', I would opt for aesthetic self-reflexiveness, Gogol's interest in foregrounding the art of narrative. Even the opening paragraph is a riff on names and naming, as the narrator abruptly decides not to tell us in the very first sentence what government office his hero works for. The figure of speech here is aposiopoesis, and it effectively draws attention to the language of the introduction and the gaps it leaves. So too with the next few pages of the tale, which contain a zany summary of how Akaky Bashmatchkin came to have such a strange name. A bashmak is a shoe, the narrator reminds us, but Akaky's father and grandfather wore boots. So far, so unhelpful. Then the Gogolian comic signature: Akaky's brother-in-law also wore boots, which is interesting to know but firmly locates us in a world where causal links are lacking. When we learn in the same paragraph that his mother chose Akaky as a name because she didn't want Moky, Sossy or Hozdazat, we can feel the same sort of strange thing happening.

Once again Gogol uses the tale's ending to make readers think about conclusions and the conventions they invoke. Certainly the idea of making eminent people pay for their dismissive hauteur by having one of their victims arise from his grave and boldly assert his claims to their property is a revolutionary one. Readers of the tale should pay attention to it, yet it is harder to keep in focus given what follows Akaky's proto-revolutionary uprising.

In the third sentence from the end of the tale Gogol mentions the appearance of another ghost, not one that is keen to take from the rich and appropriate for the poor:

> One sentry in Kolomna, for instance, saw with his own eyes a ghost appear from behind a house; but, being by natural constitution somewhat feeble – so much so that on one occasion an ordinary, well-grown pig, making a sudden dash out of some building, knocked him off his feet, to the vast entertainment of the cabmen standing round, from whom he exacted two kopecks each for snuff for such rudeness – he did not dare to stop it, and so followed it in the dark until the ghost suddenly looked round, and, stopping, asked him: 'What do you want?' displaying a fist such as you never see among the living.
>
> [pp. 420–1]

The whole story trails off into irrelevancy: this ghost is taller than the others and, besides, it is a ghost (*privedenie*) as opposed to a corpse (*mertvets*), the word used for Akaky's appearances, so it is not he after all. Although this inconclusive conclusion is not particularly surprising, the pig is. We have met a number of them in Gogol, in the Dikanka tales, for example, where they occasionally sit in for demons. But this one sounds more like the one in the story of the two Ivans, the pig who bolts into the courtroom and makes off with an important piece of evidence. This sudden entrance by a pig is another example of what we have been calling the Gogol signature, the final, gorgeous, inconsequential, superfluous detail, the last word in the story, if we insist that it have one.

Before taking up the story which concludes *Petersburg Tales*, 'A Madman's Diary', just a word about 'The Carriage', a story that Tolstoy called Gogol's best and Chekhov described as worth 200,000 rubles. It consists of an anecdote about a man, the personification of craven hypocrisy and servile sycophancy, who is exposed when he forgets that he has invited the staff of a local regiment to lunch. It takes place in an out-of-the-way Russian town, not St Petersburg, yet because it was published in 1835 and represents another brilliant facet of Gogol's art, it is usually grouped with the *Petersburg Tales*. Its simplicity and directness threaten to make commentary on it seem irrelevant. It also shows quite dramatically just how extensive Gogol's range actually is.

'A Madman's Diary' is also unique, in the sense that it is the only story in which Gogol surrenders the narrative voice to an actual character. Popristchin's plight resembles those of his counterparts in the *Petersburg Tales*: professionally stymied, personally frustrated, the victims of repressed desires that refuse to be sublimated, Piskarev, Bashmatchkin *et al.* are the embodiment of an isolation so profound that it grades into paranoia and solipsism.

The story might be usefully characterised as an examination of the mad logic of insanity. G. K. Chesterton argues that a madman is not someone 'who has lost his reason' but someone 'who has lost everything except his reason', his judgement, his emotional balance, his sense of self. Chesterton explains that this is why it is so hard to win an argument with an insane person:

> If a man says (for instance) that men have a conspiracy against him, you cannot dispute it except by saying that all the men deny that they are conspirators; which is exactly what conspirators would do. His explanation covers the facts as much as yours. Or if a man says that he is the rightful King of England, it is no complete answer to say that the existing authorities call him mad; for if he were King of England that might be the wisest thing for the existing authorities to do.

So too for the King of Spain. The 'complete answer' to Popristchin's claim that he is Ferdinand VIII is the sum total of our responses to his strange tale. The compassion that Gogol seeks to evoke is for the stifling quality of his hero's existence, for the way that monomania makes the world so small and the self so large that it takes over everything. The conviction that there are a myriad links between Popristchin and everything he encounters denies the ultimate isolation of every human soul even while it offers a moving example of such isolation. His view of the world has all the inevitability of his idiosyncratic logic: if we can't see our noses, they must all be in the moon; if there is no King of Spain, I must be he; if Polignac is scheming to keep Charles X in power, he is no doubt responsible for the problems I'm encountering when I try to claim my throne. Because he has neither been to the moon, nor been a party to the political machinations that led to the Carlist Wars or the events surrounding the July Monarchy, he insists that his reading of the world is as plausible as any other.

We leave Popristchin at the height of his discomfort, in one of those ambiguous conclusions that Gogol loves. First a troika is invoked to take the madman away, the same one that is so memorably identified with Russia's tumultuous journey into the unknown at the end of *Dead Souls*. He dreams of heading into the darkness, characterised by the limited gradations of colour in a black and white world, the vision that arrives at the end of so many of Gogol's stories. Popristchin imagines himself racing over the planet and simultaneously going home to mother, and his maudlin plea for succour in her lap sounds the sentimental note Gogol often strikes in such circumstances. The Gogol signature, though, undermining anything as saccharine as collapsing on the bosom of the sympathetic family, is the last sentence about the King of France having a boil just under his nose. Having gone so carefully through Gogol's major works we know that this is no time to ask what this means, but rather another delightful opportunity to revel in the extraordinary power of his creative nonsense.

The Government Inspector

In addition to being the author of some of the most innovative and compelling Russian fiction ever written, Gogol also distinguished himself as a playwright. *The Gamblers*, a play about a cardsharp deceived by a bunch of cardsharps, enjoyed considerable success when it was first performed in 1843. *Marriage* is a consummate farce that represented a new departure in Russian theatrical tradition and makes for good theatre even today. *The Government Inspector*, the only other work for the stage that Gogol completed, is without question the greatest Russian play ever written. Its depiction of folly, hypocrisy, fecklessness, greed and incompetence have made it a national institution, famous for its characters, their crazy names, their cleverly scripted confrontations and a series of rapid-fire exchanges that have found their way into everyday Russian speech. Although Gogol's prose is in many ways the key to his extraordinary artistry, he shows in this play how his exquisite comic sense, keen ear for a range of tonalities, capacity for vivid dramatisation and ability to create a superbly varied range of caricatures more than make up for the limitations that the genre imposed upon him. The theatrical tradition Gogol inherited was in large measure composed of hundreds of competent imitations of the French classical style, with its aristocratic characters and didactic emphasis. He changed all that, by giving playgoers something distinctively Russian and original.

Like everything Gogol wrote, *The Government Inspector* has been read in very diverse ways. The play contains enough slapstick to make it work superbly as vaudeville. The rampant corruption revealed in it, along with Gogol's professed intention to laugh at all that was bad in Russia, made nineteenth-century progressive critics applaud it. Soviet commentators were particularly keen to explain the play as a devastating critique of Tsarist Russia, and some of its most famous productions have emphasised its satiric power. Any play that features a postmaster who opens other people's letters, a policeman who deals out black eyes to innocent citizens, a schoolteacher accused of radicalism for grimacing, a Charity Commissioner who is advised to release most of his charges, a doctor who cannot speak his patients' language and a mayor who manipulates the whole rotten system to pursue his own ends constitutes a fairly broad canvas for such an approach. Tsar Nicholas I, present at opening night, 19 April 1836, seems to have seen *The Government Inspector* this way too. In light of its varied and impressive stage history, Gogol's play seems almost infinitely adaptable in this regard.

Gogol's own take on his play is itself of great interest. He is very precise in the stage directions he provides concerning how the characters should look and act, and he was unhappy with the way certain scenes were acted and directed at the Moscow premiere. Ten years later, Gogol published a play about *The Government Inspector* to clarify various points. In this strange sketch, which the censors refused to allow on the stage, various actors, men of letters and theatregoers debate the *The Government Inspector*'s much discussed qualities. They raise a range of issues. Some of the characters argue for its striking lack of social utility and its potential for actually damaging the Russian spirit. Others dispute the significance of various scenes and comments, the proper role of the spectator, the question of the playwright's intelligence, the inevitably beneficent effects of art whether it is praising beauty or revealing the repellent quality of monstrosity, the play's lack of moral clarity ('we cannot see the good in the good'), the destructive effect of the play's scepticism and its ostensible acceptance of chaos and disorder.

Having reached a sort of critical nadir, *The Government Inspector* is then the subject of a commentary by the premiere's lead actor. He insists that its secret meaning is allegorical. What if the town where all these selfish monsters live and flourish is ourselves, he suggests. That would make the confrontation with the real Government Inspector a representation of true conscience and our confrontation with it on Judgement Day, at which there will be no flinching away from the truth. Aligned with the mocking laughter of those who hate themselves and mankind, our passions are as hypocritical as Khlestakov's, and more dangerous. The play is ultimately an invitation extended to Russia to become a watchword for people who strive for eternal truth and beauty.

This is the 'last word' in Gogol's appended explanatory playlet, but how are we to take it? It is tempting but too easy to accuse Gogol of retrospectively striking a moral pose, and *ex post factum* attempting to impose a moral, occasioned by an outburst of the Christian zealousness that characterised the last decade of his life. There is, after all, a moment that anticipates this ending, that strange encounter in the play at which Khlestakov and the Major see each other for the first time, where there seems to be some deeper level of recognition at work. Even one of the Mayor's desperate last cries, 'I see nothing; nothing but pigs' snouts instead of faces . . . ' (p. 525), could be taken as a reference to the demonic forces assembled to bustle the wayward off to hell.

Nevertheless, there are problems with wholeheartedly embracing Gogol's reading as the key that unlocks all the play's mysteries. One of the most important is the ending that Gogol so adroitly enlists in making his case. Surely the lack of a moral message at the conclusion can be used to argue against any allegorical reading. It concludes with a famous tableau, but that can be not only the frozen moment in which all the amoral characters are apprehended but the sealing up of the play in its own imaginative universe. If we think back to the ways Gogol uses ekphrasis in his stories, a number of elements assert themselves in this scene. First there is the silence of the tableau: what was a bustle of human activity suddenly becomes an aesthetic object. It says whatever we want it to say, but it does not say it in words, hence its ambiguity. That silence or immutability takes us out of time, and out of the world of abstractions too. The audience's applause, particularly if the tableau lasts more than a minute, as Gogol in his stage directions insists it should, releases actors and audience, as the variegated humdrum world reasserts itself.

We also need to be wary whenever a critical voice, even if it belongs to the author, ends up sounding humourless and unbending, particularly when it is discussing one of the funniest plays ever written. As we saw in 'The Overcoat', this might be called the 'pig' problem. For the reappearance of pigs at the end of *The Government Inspector* when the Mayor looks around reminds us of the disconnect between the soaring rhetoric of religious apotheosis and the words used to describe messy, earthbound, comic encounters. For many spectators, the manic stream of zany confrontation in *The Government Inspector* diminishes the convincingness of any sort of solemn or abstract response.

A tentative conclusion might be that any reading that enables the playgoer to savour the distinctively Gogolian details of the *The Government Inspector* deserves a hearing. On practically the first page, the Mayor reads aloud a letter announcing the imminent arrival of the Government Inspector. Everyone is instantly apprehensive, but then he rambles on, quoting apparently irrelevant details from the letter, things like, ' "Ivan Kirillovitch has grown much stouter, and is always playing the fiddle" ' (pp. 459–60). These charming asides are the mark of a master. In a different way, Gogol creates an intriguing variation on the self-reflexiveness theme by including the Mayor's prescient fear that some literary type will come along and stick them all into a comedy. The same character's final confrontation with the audience ('What are you laughing at?' [p. 525]) as his time on stage gradually runs out constitutes another self-reflexive moment to savour, whatever we conclude about the large questions that the play raises.

Then there is the extraordinary suggestiveness of Khlestakov's pre-posterous fabrications concerning his life in St Petersburg. He claims to be responsible for three hugely popular operas, Bellini's *Norma*, Meyerbeer's *Robert le Diable* and Mozart's *Marriage of Figaro*. It is difficult to think of three works that combine a more suggestive mix of tragic and comic renditions of the fantastic, legendary and melo-dramatic, always with an emphasis on the human penchant for duplicity and intrigue. The links with Gogol's invented worlds go deep. When Khlestakov confesses to being Baron Brambeus, the pseudonym of a journalist and orientalist named Osip Senkovsky, the plot thickens. Under this name Senkovsky wrote in the early 1830s about a number of fantastic imaginary voyages taken by his invented baron, a low-level civil servant with ambition to rise in the ranks. The conclusions of these excursions are ambiguous and, in them, the supernatural and the natural are conflated. Mistaken identities also abound: in Turkey, for example, the baron is mistakenly assumed to be a representative of the Russian government.

In other words, in some ways Brambeus is a character right out of Gogol's fiction, and Khlestakov becomes Gogol's refashioning of Senkovsky's strange invention. Khlestakov also claims to be the author of *Yuri Miroslavsky*, a romantic tale about true love's tribulations at the time of an early seventeenth-century conflict between Russia and Poland. The actual author of this bestseller was Mikhail Zagoskin, the man who directed the premiere of *The Inspector General*. So there are wheels within wheels here. When Khlestakov announces that he is responsible for all of these works of art, in an intriguing way he is, since in him are subsumed a whole range of creative impulses that constitute a sustained exercise in lying and duplicity. One of the purposes of the play is to force us to see reality and fiction as existing on a spectrum rather than as words that define discrete entities.

Shakespeare's great comic character Falstaff famously says that he is not only witty himself but the cause of wit in others. So too Gogol and his extraordinary genius: he makes his audience smarter, he uses intricacy and ambiguity to help us see more profoundly into what makes humanity so enviable and laughable. He encourages his audience's imagination to expand. A case in point is Vladimir Nabokov's commentary on *The Government Inspector*. He claims that the play 'begins with a blinding flash of lightning and ends in a thunderclap' and that it is 'wholly placed in the tense gap between the flash and the crash'. In his book on Gogol, Nabokov tells his story backwards, from his hideous death to his birth on April Fool's Day. Nabokov even singles out the much discussed characters' names for special treatment:

> Khlestakov's very name is a stroke of genius, for it conveys to the Russian reader an effect of lightness and rashness, a prattling tongue, the swish of a slim walking cane, the slapping sound of playing cards, the braggadocio of a nincompoop and the dashing ways of a lady-killer (minus the capacity for completing this or any other action).

It is this sort of wit and insight, this sensitivity to subtle effects, this kind of savouring that best represents the tribute that we owe Gogol.

Select Bibliography

Chesterton, G. K., *Orthodoxy*, New York, 2012

Chizhevsky, Dmitri, 'Gogol: Artist and Thinker', *Annals of the Ukrainian Academy of Arts and Sciences in the US*, 2 (Summer 1952), pp. 261–78

_____ , 'The Unknown Gogol', *Slavonic and Eastern European Review*, 30 (1952), pp. 476–93

Debreczeny, Paul, *Nikolay Gogol and his Contemporary Critics*, Philadelphia, 1966

Driessen, F. C., *Gogol as a Short-Story Writer: A Study of his Technique of Composition*, Finlay, Ian F. (trans.), London, 1965

Ehre, Milton and Gottschalk, Fruma (eds and trans.), *The Theatre of Nikolai Gogol: Plays and Selected Writings*, Chicago, 1980

English, Christopher (ed. and trans.), *Village Evenings near Dikanka and Mirgorod*, Oxford, 1994

_____ , (ed. and trans.), *Nikolai Gogol: Plays and Petersburg Tales*, Oxford, 1998

Erlich, Victor, *Gogol*, New Haven, 1969

Evreinoff, Nicolas, *Histoire du théâtre russe*, Paris, 1947

Fanger, Donald, *The Creation of Nikolai Gogol*, Cambridge, Mass., 1979

Grayson, Jane and Wigsell, Faith (eds), *Nikolay Gogol: Text and Context*, London, 1989

Karlinsky, Simon, *The Sexual Labyrinth of Nikolai Gogol*, Cambridge, Mass., 1976

Kent, Leonard J. (ed.), *The Collected Tales and Plays of Nikolai Gogol*, New York, 1969

Lindstrom, Thais S., *Nikolai Gogol*, New York, 1974

Magarshack, David, *Gogol: A Life*, London, 1957

Maguire, Robert A. (ed. and trans.), *Gogol from the Twentieth Century: Eleven Essays*, Princeton, 1974

Mirsky, D. S., *A History of Russian Literature*, New York, 1949

Nabokov, Vladimir, *Nikolai Gogol*, Norfolk, Conn., 1944

Peace, Richard (ed.), *The Enigma of Gogol: An Examination of the Writings of N. V. Gogol and their Place in the Russian Literary Tradition*, Cambridge, 1981

Pevear, Richard and Volokhonsky, Larissa (trans.), *The Collected Tales of Nikolai Gogol*, New York, 1998

Rowe, William Woodin, *Through Gogol's Looking Glass: Reverse Vision, False Focus, and Precarious Logic*, New York, 1976

Setschkareff, Vsevolod, *Gogol: His Life and Works*, London, 1965

Shapiro, Gavriel, *Nikolai Gogol and the Baroque Cultural Heritage*, University Park, Penn., 1993

Tertz, Abram [Andrei Sinyavsky], *In the Shadow of Gogol*, London, 1975

Troyat, Henri, *Divided Soul: The Life of Gogol*, Amphoux, Nancy (trans.), Garden City, NY, 1973

Wilson, Edmund, 'Gogol: The Demon in the Overgrown Garden', *The Nation* (1952), pp. 520–4

Woodward, James B., *The Symbolic Art of Gogol: Essays on his Short Fiction*, Columbus, Ohio, 1982

Abbreviated Table of Civil, Court and Military Ranks

CIVIL RANKS	COURT RANKS	MILITARY RANKS
1 Chancellor of the Empire		Field Marshal
2 Actual Privy Councillor	Chief Chamberlain	General
3 Privy Councillor	Marshal	Lieutenant-General
4 Actual Councillor of State	Chamberlain	Major-General
5 Councillor of State	Master of Ceremonies	Brigadier
6 Collegiate Councillor	Gentleman of the Bedchamber (ranks 5–8)	Colonel
7 Court Councillor		Lieutenant-Colonel
8 Collegiate Assessor		Major
9 Titular Councillor		Captain
10 Collegiate Secretary		Staff-Captain
11 Naval Secretary		Lieutenant
12 County Secretary		Second-Lieutenant
13 Provincial Secretary		Ensign
14 Collegiate Registrar		

EVENINGS ON A FARM NEAR DIKANKA

Part One

Translator's Note

The following tales are the earliest of Gogol's writings that have come down to us. They appeared in various magazines, and the first four ['The Fair at Sorotchintsy', 'St John's Eve', 'A May Night or The Drowned Maiden' and 'The Lost Letter'] were published in book form in 1831, when Gogol was twenty-two, the others ['Christmas Eve', 'A Terrible Revenge', 'Ivan Fyodorovitch Shponka and his Aunt' and 'A Place Bewitched'] a year later. They were at first accepted by the public as tales told by a village sacristan and written down by a beekeeper, Rudy Panko. Nothing like them had been seen in Russian before, and their freshness, spirit, and picturesque setting attracted attention at once.

To many Petersburg readers of that date the Ukraine must have been a country as unfamiliar as to us today. The beautiful scenery, the glorious summer, hot and sunny as in Italy, the exuberant fertility of the soil, the villages of neat white cottages and well-kept gardens, and the liveliness, sturdy independence and rollicking gaiety of the free peasants of the South make up a picture in striking contrast to the grey skies, the rows of thatched mud-coloured huts huddled together without a flower or a fruit bush, and the mournful apathy of the serfs of Great Russia, as we see them, for instance, in some of Turgenev's *Sportman's Sketches*.

Gogol had spent his life in the Ukraine up to the age of nineteen and he put the impressions and memories of childhood into these pictures of peasant life. In letters to his mother he appealed to her for descriptions of village customs, merry-makings and old-fashioned dress, as well as for the words of popular songs and ballads, and we find the details sent him in many passages, for example, in the account of the wedding in 'St John's Eve'. The popular superstitions are almost always treated, as by the peasants themselves, with a comic levity, free from all trace of scepticism. The devil, while a danger to be reckoned with, is always an object of derision and is usually made a fool of, as in 'Christmas Eve', a story based on the popular legend 'The Blacksmith and the Devil'. The one exception is the tale 'A Terrible Revenge', which is written in a high-flown romantic style, curiously different from the humorous realism of the others.

Preface

'What oddity is this: *Evenings in a village near Dikanka*? What sort of *Evenings* have we here? And thrust into the world by a beekeeper! Mercy on us! As though geese enough had not been plucked for pens and rags turned into paper! As though folks enough of all classes had not covered their fingers with inkstains! The whim must take a beekeeper to follow their example! Really, there is such a lot of paper nowadays that it takes time to think what to wrap in it.'

I had a foreboding in my heart of all this talk a month ago. In fact, for a villager like me to poke his nose out of his hole into the great world – is, merciful heavens, just like what happens if you go into the apartments of some great lord: they all come round you and make you feel like a fool; it would not matter so much if it were only the upper servants, but no, some wretched little whipper-snapper loitering in the backyard pesters you too; and on all sides they begin stamping at you and asking: 'Where are you going? Where? What for? Get out, peasant, out you go!' I can tell you . . . But what's the use of talking! I would rather go twice a year into Mirgorod where the district court assessor and the reverend Father have not seen me for the last five years, than show myself in the great world; still, if you do it, whether you regret it or not, you must face the consequences.

At home, dear readers – no offence meant (you may be annoyed at a beekeeper like me addressing you so simply, as though I were speaking to some old friend or crony) – at home in the village it has always been the peasants' habit, as soon as the work in the fields is over, to climb up on the stove[1] and rest there all the winter, and we beekeepers put our bees away in a dark cellar. At the season when you see no cranes in the sky nor pears on the trees, there is sure to be a light burning somewhere at the end of the village as soon as evening comes on, laughter and singing is heard in the distance, there is the twang of the balalaika and at times of the fiddle, talk and noise . . . Those are our *evening parties!* As you see they are like your balls, though not altogether so, I must say. If you go to balls, it is to move your legs and yawn with your hand over your mouth; while with us the girls gather together into one cottage, not for a ball, but with their distaff and carding-comb. And at first one may say they do work; the distaffs hum, there is a constant flow of song, and no one looks up from her work; but as soon as the lads burst into the cottage with the fiddler, there is an uproar at once, fun begins, they set off dancing, and I could not tell you all the pranks that are played.

But best of all is when they crowd together and fall to guessing riddles or simply babble. Goodness, what stories they tell! What tales of old times they unearth! What terrible things they describe! But nowhere are such stories told as in the cottage of the beekeeper Rudy Panko. Why the villagers call me Rudy Panko, I really cannot say. My hair, I fancy, is more grey nowadays than red. But think what you like of it, it is our habit – when a nickname has once been given, it sticks to a man all his life. Good people meet together at the beekeeper's on the eve of a holiday, sit down to the table – and then you have only to listen! And I may say, the guests are by no means of the humbler sort, mere peasants; their visit would be an honour for someone of more consequence than a beekeeper. For instance, do you know the sacristan of the Dikanka church, Foma Grigoryevitch? Ah, he has a head! What stories he can reel off! You will find two of them in this book. He never wears one of those homespun dressing-gowns that you so often see on village sacristans; no, if you go to see him, even on working days he will always receive you in a gaberdine of fine cloth of the colour of cold potato mash, for which he paid almost six roubles a yard at Poltava. As for his high boots, no one in the village has ever said that they smelt of tar; every one knows that he rubs them with the very best fat, such as I believe many a peasant would be glad to put in his porridge. Nor would any one ever say that he wipes his nose on the skirt of his gaberdine, as many men of his calling do; no, he takes from his bosom a clean, neatly folded white handkerchief embroidered on the hem with red cotton, and after putting it to its proper use, folds it up in twelve as his habit is, and puts it back in his bosom.

And one of the visitors . . . Well, he is such a fine young gentleman that you might take him for an assessor or a kammerherr[2] any minute. Sometimes he would hold up his finger, and looking at the tip of it, begin telling a story – as choicely and cleverly as though it were printed in a book! Sometimes you listen and listen and begin to be puzzled. You can't make head or tail of it, not if you were to hang for it. Where did he pick up such words? Foma Grigoryevitch once told him a funny story in mockery of this. He told him how a student who had been having lessons from a deacon came back to his father such a Latin scholar that he had forgotten our orthodox tongue: he put *us* on the end of all the words; a spade was *spadus*, a female was *femalus*. It happened one day that he went with his father in the fields. The Latin scholar saw a rake and asked his father: 'What do you call that, father?' And without looking what he was doing he stepped on the teeth of the rake. Before the father had time to answer the handle flew up and hit the lad on the head. 'The damned rake!' he cried, putting his hand to his forehead and jumping half a yard into the air, 'may the devil shove its father off a bridge, how it can hit one!' So he remembered the name, you see, poor fellow!

Such a tale was not to the taste of our ingenious storyteller. He rose from his seat without speaking, stood in the middle of the room with his legs apart, craned his head forward a little, thrust his hand into the back pocket of his pea-green coat, took out his round lacquer snuffbox, flipped on the face of some Mussulman general, and taking a good pinch of snuff powdered with wood-ash and leaves of lovage,[3] crooked his elbow, lifted it to his nose and sniffed the whole pinch up with no help from his thumb – and still without a word. And it was only when he felt in another pocket and brought out a checked blue cotton hand-kerchief that he muttered the saying. I believe it was, 'Cast not thy pearls before swine.'[4] 'There's bound to be a quarrel,' I thought, seeing that Foma Grigoryevitch's fingers seemed moving as though to make a long nose. Fortunately my old woman chose the moment to set butter and hot rolls on the table. We all set to work upon it. Foma Grigorye-vitch's hand instead of forming a rude gesture stretched out for the hot roll, and as always happened they all began praising the skill of my wife.

We have another storyteller, but he (night is not the time to think of him!) has such a store of terrible stories that it makes the hair stand up on one's head. I have purposely omitted them; good people might be so scared that they would be afraid of the beekeeper, as though he were the devil, God forgive me. If, please God, I live to the New Year and bring out another volume, then I might frighten my readers with the ghosts and marvels that were seen in old days in our Christian country. Among them, maybe, you will find some tales told by the beekeeper himself to his grandchildren. If only people will read and listen I have enough of them stored away for ten volumes, I dare say, if only I am not too damned lazy to rack my brains for them.

But there, I have forgotten what is most important: when you come to see me, gentlemen, take the high road straight to Dikanka. I have put the name on my title-page on purpose that our village may be more easily found. You have heard enough about Dikanka, I have no doubt, and indeed there is a house there finer than the beekeeper's cottage: and, I need say nothing about the park: I don't suppose you would find anything like it in your Petersburg. When you reach Dikanka you need only ask any little boy in a dirty shirt minding geese: 'Where does the beekeeper, Rudy Panko, live?' 'Yonder,' he will say, pointing with his finger, and if you like he will lead you to the village. But there is one thing I must ask you, not to walk here lost in thought, nor to be too clever, in fact, for our village roads are not so smooth as those before your mansions. The year before last Foma Grigoryevitch driving from Dikanka fell into a ditch, with his new trap and bay mare and all, though he was driving himself and put on a pair of spectacles too.

But, when you do arrive, we will give you melons such as you have never tasted in your life, I expect; and you will find no better honey in any village, I will take my oath on that. Just fancy, when you bring in the comb the scent in the room is something you can't imagine; it is clear as a tear or a costly crystal such as you see in ear-rings. And what pies my old woman will feed you on! What pies, if only you knew: simply sugar, perfect sugar! And the butter fairly melts on your lips when you begin to eat them. Really, when one comes to think of it, what can't these women do! Have you, friends, ever tasted pear kvass[5] flavoured with sloes,[6] or raisin and plum vodka? Or frumenty[7] with milk? Good heavens, what dainties there are in the world! As soon as you begin eating them, it is a treat and no mistake: too good for words! Last year . . . But how I am running on! Only come, make haste and come; and we will give you such good things that you will talk about them to every one you meet.

RUDY PANKO
Beekeeper

THE FAIR AT SOROTCHINTSY

I am weary of the cottage,
Oie, take me from my home,
To where there's noise and bustle,
To where the girls are dancing gaily,
Where the lads are making merry!

from an old ballad

HOW INTOXICATING, how magnificent is a summer day in Little Russia![8] How luxuriously warm the hours when midday glitters in stillness and sultry heat and the blue fathomless ocean arching like a voluptuous cupola over the plain seems to be slumbering, bathed in languor, clasping the fair earth and holding it close in its ethereal embrace! Upon it, not a cloud; in the plain, not a sound. Everything might be dead; only above in the heavenly depths a lark is trilling and from the airy heights the silvery notes drop down upon adoring earth, and from time to time the cry of a gull or the ringing note of a quail sounds in the steppe. The towering oaks stand, idle and apathetic, like aimless wayfarers, and the dazzling gleams of sunshine light up picturesque masses of leaves, casting on to others a shadow black as night, only flecked with gold when the wind blows. The insects of the air flit like sparks of emerald, topaz and ruby about the gay kitchen gardens, topped by stately sunflowers. Grey haystacks and golden sheaves of corn are ranged like tents on the plain and stray over its immensity. The broad branches of cherries, of plums, apples and pears bent under their load of fruit, the sky with its pure mirror – the river in its green proudly erect frame . . . how full of voluptuousness and languor is the Little Russian Summer!

Such was the splendour of a day in the hot August of eighteen hundred . . . eighteen hundred . . . yes, it will be thirty years ago, while the road eight miles beyond the village of Sorotchintsy bustled with people hurrying to the fair from all the farms, far and near. From early morning waggons full of fish and salt had trailed in an endless chain along the road. Mountains of pots wrapped in hay moved along slowly, as though weary of being shut up in the dark; only here and there a brightly-painted tureen or crock boastfully peeped out from behind the hurdle that held the high pile on the waggon, and attracted longing glances from the devotees of such luxury. Many of the passers-by looked enviously at the tall potter, the owner of these treasures, who walked slowly behind his goods, carefully wrapping his flaunting and coquettish crocks in the detestable hay.

On one side of the road, apart from all the rest, a team of weary oxen dragged a waggon, piled up with sacks, hemp, linen and various homely goods, and followed by their owner, in a clean linen shirt and dirty linen trousers. With a lazy hand he wiped from his swarthy face the streaming perspiration that even trickled from his long moustaches, powdered by the relentless barber who uninvited visits fair and foul alike and has for thousands of years forcibly powdered all mankind. Beside him, tied to the waggon, walked a mare, whose meek air betrayed her advancing years.

Many of the passers-by, especially the young men, took off their caps as they met our peasant. But it was not his grey moustaches or his dignified step which led them to do so; one had but to raise one's eyes a little to discover the explanation of this deference: on the waggon was sitting a pretty daughter, with a round face, black eyebrows arching evenly above her clear brown eyes, carelessly smiling rosy lips, with red and blue ribbons twisted in the long plaits which with a bunch of wild flowers crowned her charming head. Everything seemed to interest her; everything was new and wonderful . . . and her pretty eyes were racing all the time from one object to another. She might well be diverted! It was her first visit to a fair! A girl of eighteen for the first time at a fair! . . . But none of the passers-by knew what it had cost her to persuade her father to bring her, though he would have been ready enough but for her spiteful stepmother, who had learned to manage him as cleverly as he drove his old mare, now as a reward for long years of service being taken to be sold. The irrepressible woman . . . But we are forgetting that she, too, was sitting on the top of the load dressed in a smart green woollen pelisse,[9] adorned with little tails, to imitate ermine, though they were red in colour, in a gorgeous *plahta*[10] checked like a chessboard, and a flowered chintz cap that gave a particularly majestic air to her fat red face, the expression of which betrayed something so unpleasant and savage that every one hastened in alarm to turn from her to the bright face of her daughter.

The river Psyol gradually came into our traveller's view; already in the distance they felt its cool freshness the more welcome after the exhausting, wearisome heat. Through the dark and light green foliage of the birches and poplars, carelessly scattered over the plain, there were glimpses of the cold glitter of the water, and the lovely river unveiled its shining silvery bosom, over which the green tresses of the trees drooped luxuriantly. Wilful as a beauty in those enchanting hours when her faithful mirror so jealously frames her brow full of pride and dazzling splendour, her lily shoulders and her marble neck, shrouded by the dark waves of her hair, when with disdain she flings aside one ornament to replace it by another and there is no end to her whims – the river almost every year changes its course, picks out a new channel and surrounds itself with new and varied scenes. Rows of watermills tossed up great waves with their heavy wheels, and flung them violently down again, churning them into foam, scattering froth and making a great clatter. At that moment the waggon with the persons we have described reached the bridge, and the river lay before them in all its beauty and grandeur like a sheet of glass. Sky, green and dark blue forest, men, waggons of pots, watermills – all were standing or walking upside-down, and not sinking into the lovely blue depths.

Our fair maiden mused gazing at the glorious view, and even forgot to crack the sunflower seeds with which she had been busily engaged all the way, when all at once the words, 'I say what a girl!' caught her ear. Looking round she saw a group of lads standing on the bridge, of whom one, dressed rather more smartly than the others in a white jacket and grey astrakhan cap, was jauntily looking at the passers-by with his arms akimbo. The girl could not but notice his sunburnt but pleasing face and glowing eyes, which seemed striving to look right through her, and she dropped her eyes at the thought that he might have uttered those words.

'A fine girl!' the young man in the white jacket went on, keeping his eyes fixed on her. 'I'd give all I have to kiss her. And there's a devil sitting in front!'

There were peals of laughter all round; but the slow-moving peasant's gaily dressed wife was not pleased at such a greeting: her red cheeks blazed and a torrent of choice language fell like rain on the head of the wanton youth.

'Plague take you, you rascally bargee![11] May your father crack his head on a pot! May he slip down on the ice, the confounded antichrist! May the devil singe his beard in the next world!'

'I say, isn't she swearing!' said the young man staring at her, as though puzzled at such a sharp volley of unexpected greetings, 'and she can bring her tongue to utter words like that, the witch! She is a hundred if she is a day!'

'A hundred!' the elderly charmer caught him up. 'You infidel! Go and wash your face! You worthless scamp! I've never seen your mother, but I know she's good for nothing. And your father is good for nothing, and your aunt is good for nothing! A hundred, indeed! Why, the milk is scarcely dry on his . . .'

At that moment the waggon began to go down from the bridge and the last words could not be heard; but without stopping to think he picked up a handful of mud and threw it at her. The throw achieved more than he could have hoped: the new chintz cap was spattered all over and the laughter of the rowdy scamps was louder than ever. The buxom charmer was boiling with rage; but by this time the waggon was far away, and she wreaked her vengeance on her innocent step-daughter and her slow husband, who, long since accustomed to such onslaughts, preserved a stubborn silence and received the tempestuous language of his wrathful spouse with indifference. In spite of that her indefatigable tongue went on clacking until they reached the house of their old friend and crony the Cossack Tsybulya on the outskirts of the village. The meeting of the old friends, who had not seen each other for a long time, put this unpleasant incident out of their minds for a while, as our travellers talked of the fair and rested after their long journey.

2

Good gracious me! What isn't there at that fair! Wheels, window-panes, tar, tobacco, straps, onions, all sorts of haberdashery . . . so that even if you had thirty roubles in your purse you could not buy up all the fair.   *from a Little Russian farce*

You have no doubt heard a rushing waterfall when everything is quivering and filled with uproar, and a chaos of strange vague sounds floats like a whirlwind round you. Are you not instantly overcome by the same feelings in the turmoil of the village fair, when all the people are melted into one huge monster all of whose body is stirring in the marketplace and the narrow streets, with shouting, laughing and clatter? Noise, swearing, bellowing, bleating, roaring – all blend into one discordant uproar. Oxen, sacks, hay, gypsies, pots, peasant-women, cakes, caps – everything is bright, gaudy, discordant, flitting in groups, shifting to and fro before your eyes. The different voices drown one another, and not a single word can be caught, can be saved from the deluge; not one cry is distinct. Only the clapping of hands after each bargain is heard on all sides. A waggon breaks down, there is the clank of iron, the thud of boards thrown on to the ground, and one's head is so dizzy one does not know which way to turn.

The peasant whose acquaintance we have already made had been for some time elbowing his way through the crowd with his black-browed daughter; he went up to one waggonload, fingered another, enquired the prices; and meanwhile his thoughts kept revolving round his ten sacks of wheat and the old mare he had brought to sell. From his daughter's face it could be seen that she was not over pleased to be dawdling by the waggons of flour and wheat. She longed to be where red ribbons, ear-rings, crosses made of copper and pewter and coins were smartly displayed under linen awnings. But even where she was she found many objects worthy of notice: she was much diverted at the sight of a gypsy and a peasant, who clapped hands so that they both cried out with pain; of a drunken Jew slapping a woman on the back; of huckster-women quarrelling with words of abuse and gestures of contempt; of a Great Russian with one hand stroking his goat's beard, with another . . . But at that moment she felt someone pull her by the embroidered sleeve of her smock. She looked round – and the bright-eyed young man in the white jacket stood before her. She started and her heart throbbed, as it had never done before at any joy or grief; it seemed strange and delightful, and she could not make out what had happened to her.

'Don't be frightened, dear heart, don't be frightened!' he said to her in a low voice, taking her hand. 'I'll say nothing to hurt you!'

'Perhaps it is true that you will say nothing to hurt me,' the girl thought to herself; 'only it is strange . . . it might be the Evil One! One knows that it is not right . . . but I haven't the strength to take away my hand.'

The peasant looked round and was about to say something to his daughter, but on the other side he heard the word 'wheat.' That magic word instantly made him join two dealers who were talking loudly, and riveted his attention upon them so that nothing could have distracted it. This is what the corn-dealers were saying.

3

Do you see what a fellow he is?
Not many such as he in the world.
Tosses off vodka like beer!

KOTLYAREVSKY, *Aeneid* [12]

'So you think, neighbour, that our wheat won't sell well?' said a man, who looked like an artisan of some big village, in dirty tar-stained trousers of coarse homespun material, to another, with a big swelling on his forehead, wearing a dark blue jacket patched in parts.

'It's not a matter of thinking: I am ready to put a halter round my neck and hang from that tree like a sausage in the cottage before Christmas, if we sell a single bushel.'

'What nonsense are you talking, neighbour? No wheat has been brought except ours,' answered the man in the homespun trousers.

'Yes, you may say what you like,' thought the father of our beauty, who had not missed a single word of the dealers' conversation. 'I have ten sacks here in reserve.'

'Well, you see it's like this, if there is any devilry mixed up in a thing, you will get no more profit from it than a hungry soldier,' the man with the swelling on his forehead said significantly.

'What do you mean by devilry?' retorted the man in the homespun trousers.

'Did you hear what people are saying?' went on he of the swelled forehead, giving him a sidelong look out of his morose eyes.

'Well?'

'Ah, you may say, well! The assessor, may he never wipe his lips again after the gentry's plum brandy, has set aside an evil spot for the fair, where you may burst before you get rid of a single grain. Do you see that old tumbledown barn which stands yonder, see, under the hill?' (At this point the inquisitive peasant went closer and was all attention.) 'All manner of devilish tricks go on in that barn, and not a single fair has taken place in this spot without trouble. The parish clerk passed it late last night and all of a sudden a pig's snout looked out at the window of the loft, and grunted so that it sent a shiver down his back. You may be sure that the *red jacket* will be seen again!'

'What's that about a red jacket?'

Our attentive listener's hair stood up on his head at these words. He looked round in alarm and saw that his daughter and the young man were calmly standing in each other's arms, murmuring soft nothings to each other and oblivious of every coloured jacket in the world. This dispelled his terror and restored his equanimity.

'Aha–ha–ha, neighbour! You know how to hug a girl, it seems! I had been married three days before I learned to hug my poor dear Hveska, and I owed that to a friend who was my best man: he gave me a hint.'

The youth saw at once that his fair one's father was not very quick-witted, and began making a plan for disposing him in his favour.

'I believe you don't know me, good friend, but I recognised you at once.'

'Maybe you did.'

'If you like I'll tell you your name and your surname and everything about you: your name is Solopy Tcherevik.'

'Yes, Solopy Tcherevik.'

'Well, have a good look: don't you know me?'

'No, I don't know you. No offence meant: I've seen so many faces of all sorts in my day, how the devil can one remember them all?'

'I am sorry you don't remember Golopupenko's son!'

'Why, is Ohrim your father?'

'Who else? The bald grandad, maybe, if he's not!'

At this the friends took off their caps and proceeded to kiss each other; our Golopupenko's son made up his mind, however, to attack his new acquaintance without loss of time.

'Well, Solopy, you see, your daughter and I have so taken to each other that we are ready to spend our lives together.'

'Well, Paraska,' said Tcherevik, laughing and turning to his daughter; 'maybe you really might, as they say . . . you and he . . . graze on the same grass! Come, shall we shake hands on it? And now, my new son-in-law, stand me a glass!'

And all three found themselves in the famous refreshment-bar of the fair – a Jewess's booth, adorned with a numerous flotilla of stoups, bottles and flasks of every kind and description.

'Well, you are a smart fellow! I like you for that,' said Tcherevik a little exhilarated, seeing how his intended son-in-law filled a pint mug and, without winking an eyelash, tossed it off at a gulp, flinging down the mug afterwards and smashing it to bits. 'What do you say, Paraska? Haven't I found you a fine husband? Look, look how smartly he takes his drink!'

And laughing and staggering he went with her towards his waggon; while our young man made his way to the booths where fancy goods were displayed, where there were even dealers from Gadyatch and

Mirgorod, the two famous towns of the province of Poltava, to pick out the best wooden pipe in a smart copper setting, a flowered red kerchief and cap, for wedding presents to his father-in-law and every one else who must have one.

4

> If it's a man, it's no matter,
> But if there's a woman, you see
> There is need to please her.
>
> KOTLYAREVSKY

'Well wife, I have found a husband for my daughter!'

'This is a moment to look for husbands, I must say! You are a fool – a fool! It must have been ordained at your birth that you should remain one! Whoever has seen, whoever has heard of such a thing as a decent man running after husbands at a time like this? You had much better be thinking how to get your corn off your hands. A nice young man he must be, too! I expect he is the shabbiest scarecrow in the place!'

'Oh, not a bit of it! You should see what a lad he is! His jacket alone is worth more than your pelisse and red boots. And how he takes his vodka! The devil confound me and you too if ever I have seen a lad before toss off a pint without winking!'

'To be sure, if he is a drunkard and a vagabond he is a man after your own heart. I wouldn't mind betting it's the very same rascal who pestered us on the bridge. I am sorry I haven't come across him yet: I'd let him know.'

'Well, Hivrya, what if it were the same: why is he a rascal?'

'Eh! Why is he a rascal? Ah, you addle-pate! Do you hear? Why is he a rascal? Where were your stupid eyes when we were driving past the mills? They might insult his wife here, right before his snuffy nose, and he would not care a hang!'

'I see no harm in him, anyway: he is a fine fellow! Only maybe, that he plastered your face with dung.'

'Aha! I see you won't let me say a word! What's the meaning of it? It's not like you! You must have managed to get a drop before you have sold anything.'

Here Tcherevik himself realised that he had said too much and instantly put his hands over his head doubtless expecting that his wrathful spouse would promptly seize his hair in her wifely claws.

'Go to the devil! So much for our wedding!' he thought to himself, retreating before his wife's attack. 'I shall have to refuse a good fellow for no rhyme or reason. Merciful God! Why didst Thou send such a plague on us poor sinners? With so many nasty things in the world, Thou must needs go and create women!'

5

Droop not, plane tree,
Still art thou green.
Fret not, little Cossack,
Still art thou young.

Little Russian song

The lad in the white jacket sitting by his waggon gazed absent-mindedly at the crowd that moved noisily about him. The weary sun after blazing through morning and noon was tranquilly withdrawing from the earth, and the daylight was going out in a bright seductive glow. The tops of the white booths and tents stood out with dazzling brightness, suffused in a faint rosy tint of fiery light. The panes in the window-frames piled up for sale glittered; the green goblets and bottles on the tables in the drinking-booths flashed like fire; the heaps of melons and pumpkins looked as though they were cast in gold and dark copper. There was less talk, and the weary tongues of hagglers,[13] peasants and gypsies moved more slowly and deliberately. Here and there lights began gleaming, and savoury steam from boiling dumplings floated over the hushed streets.

'What are you grieving over, Grytsko?' a tall sunburnt gypsy cried, slapping our young friend on the shoulder. 'Come, let me have your oxen for twenty roubles!'

'It's naught but oxen and oxen with you. All that you gypsies care for is gain; cheating and deceiving honest folk!'

'Tfoo, the devil! You do seem to be in trouble! You are vexed at having tied yourself up with a girl maybe?'

'No, that's not my way: I keep my word; what I have once done stands for ever. But it seems that old screw Tcherevik has not a half-pint of conscience: he gave his word, but he has taken it back . . . Well, it is no good blaming him: he is a blockhead and that's the fact. It's all the doing of that old witch whom we lads jeered at on the bridge today! Ah, if I were the Tsar or some great lord I would first hang all the fools who let themselves be saddled by women . . .'

'Well, will you let the oxen go for twenty, if we make Tcherevik give you Paraska?'

Grytsko stared at him in surprise. There was a look spiteful, malicious, ignoble and at the same time haughty in the gypsy's swarthy face: any man looking at him would have recognised that there were great qualities in that strange soul, though their only reward on earth would be the gallows. The mouth, completely sunken between the nose and the pointed chin and for ever curved in a mocking smile, the little eyes that gleamed like fire and the lightning flashes of intrigue and enterprise for ever flitting over his face – all this seemed in keeping with the strange costume he wore. The dark brown full coat, which looked as though it would drop into dust at a touch; the long black hair that fell in tangled tresses on his shoulders; the shoes on his bare sunburnt feet, all seemed to be in character and part of him.

'I'll let you have them for fifteen, not twenty, if only you don't deceive me!' the young man answered, keeping his searching gaze fixed on the gypsy.

'Fifteen? Done! Mind you don't forget; fifteen! Here is a blue note[14] as a pledge!'

'But if you deceive me?'

'If I do, the pledge is yours!'

'Right! Well, let us shake hands on the bargain!'

'Let us!'

6

What a misfortune! Roman is coming; here he is, he'll give me
a drubbing in a minute; and you, too, master Homo, will not
get off without trouble.   *from a Little Russian comedy*

'This way, Afanassy Ivanovitch! The fence is lower here, put your foot up and don't be afraid: my fool has gone off for the night with his crony to the waggons to see that the Great Russians don't filch anything but ill-luck.'

So Tcherevik's formidable spouse fondly encouraged the priest's son who was faint-heartedly clinging to the fence. He soon climbed on to the top and stood there for some time in hesitation, like a long terrible phantom, looking where he could best jump and at last coming down with a crash among the rank weeds.

'How dreadful! I hope you have not hurt yourself? Please God, you've not broken your neck!' Hivrya faltered anxiously.

'Sh! It's all right, it's all right, dear Havronya Nikiforovna,' the priest's son brought out in a painful whisper, getting on to his feet, 'except for being afflicted by the nettles, that serpent-like weed, to use the words of our late head priest.'

'Let us go into the house; there is nobody there. I was beginning to think you were ill or asleep, Afanassy Ivanovitch: you did not come and did not come. How are you? I hear that your honoured father has had a run of good luck!'

'Nothing to speak of, Havronya Nikiforovna: during the whole fast father has received nothing but fifteen sacks of spring corn, four sacks of millet, a hundred buns; and as for fowls they don't run up to fifty, and the eggs were mostly rotten. But the truly sweet offerings, so to say, can only come from you Havronya Nikiforovna!' the priest's son continued with a tender glance at her as he edged nearer.

'Here is an offering for you, Afanassy Ivanovitch!' she said, setting some bowls on the table and coyly fastening the buttons of her jacket as though they had not been undone on purpose, 'curd doughnuts, wheaten dumplings, buns and cakes!'

'I bet they have been made by the cleverest hands of any daughter of Eve!' said the priest's son, setting to work upon the cakes and with the other hand drawing the curd doughnuts towards him. 'Though indeed, Havronya Nikiforovna, my heart thirsts for a gift from you sweeter than any buns or dumplings!'

'Well, I don't know what dainty you will ask for next, Afanassy Ivano-vitch!' answered the buxom beauty, pretending not to understand.

'Your love, of course, incomparable Havronya Nikiforovna!' the priest's son whispered, holding a curd doughnut in one hand and encircling her ample waist with his arm.

'Goodness knows what you are thinking about, Afanassy Ivanovitch!' said Hivrya, bashfully casting down her eyes. 'Why, you will be trying to kiss me next, I shouldn't wonder!'

'As for that, I must tell you,' the young man went on. 'When I was still at the seminary, I remember as though it were today . . .'

At that moment there was a sound of barking and a knock at the gate. Hivrya ran out quickly and came back looking pale.

'Afanassy Ivanovitch, we are caught: there are a lot of people knocking, and I fancy I heard Tsybulya's voice . . .'

The doughnut stuck in the young man's throat . . . His eyes almost started out of his head, as though someone had just come from the other world to visit him.

'Climb up here!' cried the panic-stricken Hivrya, pointing to some boards that lay across the rafter just below the ceiling, loaded with all sorts of domestic odds and ends.

Danger gave our hero courage. Recovering a little, he clambered on the stove and from there clambered cautiously on to the boards, while Hivrya ran headlong to the gate, as the knocking was getting louder and more insistent.

7

But here are miracles, gentlemen!

from a Little Russian comedy

A strange incident had taken place at the fair: there were rumours all over the place that the *red jacket* had been seen somewhere among the wares. The old woman who sold bread-rings fancied she saw the devil in the shape of a pig, bending over the waggons as though looking for something. The news soon flew to every corner of the now resting camp, and every one would have thought it a crime to disbelieve it, in spite of the fact that the bread-ring seller, whose stall was next to the drinking-booth, had been staggering about all day and could not walk straight. To this was added the story – by now greatly exaggerated – of the marvel seen by the district clerk in the tumbledown barn; so towards night people were all huddling together; their peace of mind was destroyed, and every one was too terrified to close an eye; while those who were not cast in an heroic mould and had secured a night's lodging in a cottage, made their way homewards. Among the latter were Tcherevik with his daughter and his friend Tsybulya, and they, together with the friends who had offered to keep them company, were responsible for the loud knocking that had so alarmed Hivrya. Tsybulya was already a little exhilarated. This could be seen from his twice driving round the yard with his waggon before he could find the cottage. His guests, too, were all rather merry, and they unceremoniously pushed into the cottage before their host. Our Tcherevik's wife sat as though on thorns, when they began rummaging in every corner of the cottage.

'Well, gossip,' cried Tsybulya as he entered, 'you are still shaking with fever?'

'Yes, I am not well,' answered Hivrya, looking uneasily towards the boards on the rafters.

'Come, wife, get the bottle out of the waggon!' said Tsybulya to his wife, who came in with him, 'we will empty it with these good folk, for the damned women have given us such a scare that one is ashamed to own it. Yes, mates, there was really no sense in our coming here!' he went on, taking a pull out of an earthenware jug. 'I don't mind betting a new cap that the women thought they would have a laugh at us. Why, if it were Satan – who's Satan? Spit on him! If he stood here before me this very minute, I'll be damned if I wouldn't make a long nose at him!'

'Why did you turn so pale, then?' cried one of the visitors, who was a head taller than any of the rest and tried on every occasion to display his valour.

'I? . . . Lord bless you! Are you dreaming?'

The visitors laughed; the boastful hero smiled complacently.

'As though he could turn pale now!' put in another; 'his cheeks are as red as a poppy; he is not a *tsybulya*[15] now, but a beetroot – or, rather, the *red jacket* itself that frightened us all so.'

The bottle went the round of the table, and made the visitors more exhilarated than ever. At this point Tcherevik, greatly exercised about the *red jacket* which would not let his inquisitive mind rest, appealed to his friend: 'Come, mate, kindly tell me! I keep asking about this damned *jacket* and can get no answer from any one!'

'Eh, mate, it's not a thing to talk about at night; however, to satisfy you and these good friends' (saying this he turned towards his guests), 'who want, I see, to know about these strange doings as much as you do. Well, so be it. Listen!'

Here he scratched his shoulder, mopped his face with the skirt of his coat, leaned both arms on the table, and began: 'Once upon a time a devil was kicked out of hell, what for I cannot say . . .'

'How so, mate?' Tcherevik interrupted. 'How could it come about that a devil was turned out of hell?'

'I can't help it, mate, if he was turned out, he was – as a peasant turns a dog out of his cottage. Perhaps a whim came over him to do a good deed – and so they showed him the door. And the poor devil was so homesick, so homesick for hell that he was ready to hang himself. Well, there was nothing for it. In his trouble he took to drink. He settled in the tumbledown barn which you have seen at the bottom of the hill and which no good man will pass now without making the sign of the cross as a safeguard; and the devil became such a rake you would not find another like him among the lads: he sat day and night in the pot-house!'

At this point the severe Tcherevik interrupted again: 'Goodness knows what you are saying, mate! How could any one let a devil into a pot-house? Why, thank God, he has claws on his paws and horns on his head.'

'Ah, that was just it – he had a cap and gloves on. Who could recognise him? Well, he kept it up till he drank away all he had with him. They gave him credit for a long time, but at last they would give no more. The devil had to pawn his red jacket for less than a third of its value to the Jew who sold vodka in those days at Sorotchintsy. He pawned it and said to him: "Mind now, Jew, I shall come to you for my jacket in a year's time; take care of it!" And he disappeared and no more was seen of him. The Jew examined the coat thoroughly: the cloth was better than anything you could get in Mirgorod, and the red of it glowed like fire, so that one could not take one's eyes off it! And it seemed to the Jew a long time to wait till the end of the year. He scratched his curls and got nearly five gold pieces for it from a gentleman who was passing by. The Jew forgot all about the date fixed. But all of a sudden one evening a man turns up: "Come, Jew, hand me over my jacket!" At first the Jew did not know him, but afterwards when he had had a good look at him, he pretended he had never seen him before. "What jacket? I have no jacket. I know nothing about your jacket!" The other walked away; only, when the Jew locked himself up in his room and, after counting over the money in his chests, flung a sheet round his shoulders and began saying his prayers in Jewish fashion, all at once he heard a rustle . . . And there were pigs' snouts looking in at every window.'

At that moment an indistinct sound not unlike the grunt of a pig was audible; every one turned pale. Drops of sweat stood out on Tsybulya's face.

'What was it?' cried the panic-stricken Tcherevik.

'Nothing,' answered Tsybulya, trembling all over

'Eh?' responded one of the guests.

'Did you speak?'

'No!'

'Who was it grunted?'

'God knows why we are in such a fluster! It's nothing!'

They all looked about fearfully and began rummaging in the corners. Hivrya was more dead than alive.

'Oh, you are a set of women!' she brought out aloud. 'You are not fit to be Cossacks and men! You ought to sit spinning and heckling[16] yarn! Maybe someone misbehaved, God forgive me, or someone's bench creaked, and you are all in a fluster as though you were crazy!'

This put our heroes to shame and made them pull themselves together. Tsybulya took a pull at the jug and went on with his story.

'The Jew fainted with terror; but the pigs with legs as long as stilts climbed in at the windows and so revived him in a trice with plaited thongs, making him skip higher than this ceiling. The Jew fell at their feet and confessed everything . . . Only the jacket could not be restored in a hurry. The gentleman had been robbed of it on the road by a gypsy who sold it to a pedlar-woman, and she brought it back again to the fair at Sorotchintsy; but no one would buy anything from her after that. The woman wondered and wondered and at last saw what it was: there was no doubt the red jacket was at the bottom of it; it was not for nothing that she had felt stifled when she put it on. Without stopping to think she flung it in the fire – the devilish thing would not burn! . . . "Ah, that's a gift for the devil!" she thought. The woman managed to thrust it into the waggon of a peasant who had come to the fair to sell his butter. The silly fellow was delighted; only no one would ask for his butter. "Ah, it's an evil hand foisted that red jacket on me!" He took his axe and chopped it into bits; he looked at it – and each bit joined up to the next till the jacket was whole again! Crossing himself, he went at it with the axe again, he flung the bits all over the place and went away. Only ever since then, just at the time of the fair, the devil walks all over the marketplace with the face of a pig, grunting and collecting the scraps of his jacket. Now they say there is only the left sleeve missing. Folk have fought shy of the place ever since, and it is ten years since the fair has been held on it. But in an evil hour the assessor . . . '

The rest of the sentence died away on the speaker's lips: there was a loud rattle at the window, the panes fell tinkling on the floor, and a terrible pig's face looked in at the window rolling its eyes as though asking, 'What are you doing here, good people?'

8

> His tail between his legs like a dog,
> Like Cain, trembling all over;
> The snuff dropped from his nose.
>
> KOTLYAREVSKY, *Aeneid*

Every one in the room was numb with horror. Tsybulya sat petrified with his mouth open; his eyes were almost flying out of his head like bullets; his outspread fingers stood motionless in the air. The valiant giant in overwhelming terror leapt up and struck his head against the rafter; the boards shifted, and with a thud and a crash the priest's son fell to the floor.

'Aïe, aïe, aïe!' one of the party screamed desperately, flopping on the locker in alarm, and waving his arms and legs.

'Save me!' wailed another, hiding his head under a sheepskin.

Tsybulya, roused from the stupefaction by this second horror, crept shuddering under his wife's skirts. The valiant giant climbed into the oven in spite of the narrowness of the opening, and closed the oven door on himself. And Tcherevik, clapping a basin on his head instead of a cap, dashed to the door as though he had been scalded, and ran through the streets like a lunatic, not knowing where he was going; only weariness caused him to slacken his pace. His heart was thumping like an oil press; streams of perspiration rolled down him. He was on the point of sinking to the ground in exhaustion when all at once he heard someone running after him . . . His breath failed him.

'The devil! The devil!' he cried frantically, redoubling his efforts, and a minute later he fell unconscious on the ground.

'The devil! The devil!' came a shout behind him, and all he felt was something falling with a thud on the top of him. Then his senses deserted him and, like the dread inmate of a narrow coffin, he remained lying dumb and motionless in the middle of the road.

9

In front, like any one else;
Behind, upon my soul, like a devil!

from a folk tale

'Do you hear, Vlas?' one of the crowd asleep in the street said, sitting up, 'someone spoke of the devil near us!'

'What is it to me?' the gypsy near him grumbled, stretching, 'they may talk of all their kindred for aught I care!'

'But he bawled, you know, as though he were being strangled!'

'A man will cry out anything in his sleep!'

'Say what you like, we must have a look. Strike a light!'

The other gypsy, grumbling to himself, rose to his feet, sent a shower of sparks flying like lightning flashes, blew the tinder with his lips, and with a *kaganets* in his hands – the usual Little Russian lamp consisting of a broken pot full of mutton fat – set off, lighting the way before him.

'Stop! There is something lying here! Show a light this way!'

Here they were joined by several others.

'What's lying there, Vlas?'

'Why, it looks like two men: one on top, the other under. Which of them is the devil I can't make out yet!'

'Why, who is on top?'

'A woman!'

'Oh, well, then that's the devil!'

A general shout of laughter roused almost the whole street.

'A woman astride of a man! I suppose she knows how to ride!' one of the bystanders exclaimed.

'Look, lads!' said another, picking up a broken piece of the basin of which only one half still remained on Tcherevik's head, 'what a cap this fine fellow put on!'

The growing noise and laughter brought our corpses to life, and Tcherevik and his spouse, full of the panic they had passed through, gazed with staring eyes in terror at the swarthy faces of the gypsies; in the dim and flickering light they looked like a wild horde of gnomes bathed in the heavy fumes of the underworld, in the darkness of everslumbering night.

10

Fie upon you, out upon you, image of Satan!

from a Little Russian comedy

The freshness of morning breathed over the awakening folk of Sorotchintsy. Clouds of smoke from all the chimneys floated to meet the rising sun. The fair began to hum with life. Sheep were bleating, horses neighing; the cackle of geese and pedlar-women sounded all over the encampment again – and terrible tales of the red jacket, which had roused such alarm in the mysterious hours of darkness, vanished with the return of morning.

Stretching and yawning, Tcherevik lay drowsily under his friend Tsybulya's thatched barn among oxen and sacks of flour and wheat. And apparently he had no desire to part with his dreams, when all at once he heard a voice, familiar as his own stove, the blessed refuge of his lazy hours, or as the pothouse kept by his cousin not ten paces from his own door.

'Get up, get up!' his tender spouse squeaked in his ear, tugging at his arm with all her might.

Tcherevik, instead of answering, blew out his cheeks and began waving his hands, as though beating a drum.

'Idiot!' she shouted, retreating out of reach of his arms, which almost struck her in the face.

Tcherevik sat up, rubbed his eyes and looked about him.

'The devil take me, my dear, if I didn't fancy your face was a drum on which I was forced to beat an alarm, like a soldier, by those pig-faces that Tsybulya was telling us about . . .'

'Give over talking nonsense, do! Go, make haste and take the mare to market! We are a laughing-stock, upon my word: we've come to the fair and not sold a handful of hemp . . .'

'Of course, wife,' Tcherevik assented, 'they will laugh at us now, to be sure.'

'Go along, go along! They are laughing at you as it is!'

'You see, I haven't washed yet,' Tcherevik went on, yawning, scratching his back and trying to gain time.

'What a moment to be fussy about cleanliness! When have you cared about that? Here's the towel, wipe your ugly face.'

Here she snatched up something that lay crumpled up – and darted back in horror: it was the cuff of a red jacket!

'Go along and get to work,' she repeated, recovering herself, on seeing that her husband was motionless with terror and his teeth were chattering.

'A fine sale there will be now!' he muttered to himself as he untied the mare and led her to the marketplace. 'It was not for nothing that, while I was getting ready for this cursed fair, my heart was as heavy as though someone had put a dead cow on my back, and twice the oxen turned homewards of their own accord. And now I come to think of it, I do believe it was Monday when we started.[17] And so everything has gone wrong! . . . And the cursed devil can never be satisfied: he might have worn his jacket without one sleeve – but no, he can't let honest folk rest in peace. Now if I were the devil – God forbid – do you suppose I'd go hanging around at night after a lot of damned rags?'

Here our Tcherevik's meditations were interrupted by a thick harsh voice. Before him stood a tall gypsy.

'What have you for sale, good man?'

Tcherevik was silent for a moment; he looked at the gypsy from head to foot and said with unruffled composure, neither stopping nor letting go the bridle: 'You can see for yourself what I am selling.'

'Harness?' said the gypsy, looking at the bridle which the other had in his hand.

'Yes, harness, if a mare is the same thing as harness.'

'But devil take it, neighbour, one would think you had fed her on straw!'

'Straw?'

Here Tcherevik would have pulled at the bridle to lead his mare forward and convict the shameless slanderer of his lie; but his hand moved with extraordinary ease and struck his own chin. He looked – in it was a severed bridle, and tied to the bridle – oh horror! His hair stood up on his head – a piece of a red sleeve! . . . Spitting, crossing himself and brandishing his arms he ran away from the unexpected gift and, running faster than a young man, vanished in the crowd.

11

For my own corn I have been beaten.

Proverb

'Catch him! Catch him!' cried several lads at a narrow street-corner, and Tcherevik felt himself suddenly seized by stalwart hands.

'Bind him! That's the fellow who stole an honest man's mare.'

'God bless you! What are you binding me for?'

'Fancy his asking! Why did you want to steal a mare from a peasant at the fair, Tcherevik?'

'You're out of your wits, lads! Who has ever heard of a man stealing from himself?'

'That's an old trick! An old trick! Why were you running your hardest, as though the devil were on your heels?'

'Any one would run when the devil's garment . . .'

'Aïe, my good soul, try that on others! You'll catch it yet from the court assessor, to teach you to go scaring people with tales of the devil.'

'Catch him! Catch him!' came a shout from the other end of the street. 'There he is, there is the runaway!'

And Tcherevik beheld his friend Tsybulya in the most pitiful plight with his hands tied behind him, led along by several lads.

'Queer things are happening!' said one of them. 'You should hear what this scoundrel says! You have only to look at his face to see he is a thief. When we set to asking him why he was running like one possessed, he says he put his hand in his pocket and instead of his snuff pulled out a bit of the devil's jacket and it burst into a red flame – and he took to his heels!'

'Aha! Why, these two are birds of a feather! We had better tie them together!'

12

'In what am I to blame, good folks?

'Why are you beating me?' said our poor wretch.

'Why are you falling upon me?

'What for, what for?' he said, bursting into tears,

Streams of bitter tears, and clutching at his sides.

ARTEMOVSKY-GULAK, *Pan Ta Sobaka* [18]

'Maybe you really have picked up something, mate?' Tcherevik asked, as he lay bound beside Tsybulya in a thatched shanty.

'You too, mate! May my arms and legs wither if ever I stole anything in my life, except maybe buns and cream from my mother, and that only before I was ten years old.'

'Why has this trouble come upon us, mate? It's not so bad for you: you are charged, anyway, with stealing from somebody else; but what have I, unlucky wretch, done to deserve such a foul slander, as stealing my mare from myself? It seems, mate, it was written at our birth that we should have no luck!'

'Woe to us, forlorn and forsaken!'

At this point the two friends fell to weeping violently.

'What's the matter with you, Tcherevik?' said Grytsko, entering at that moment. 'Who tied you up like that?'

'Ah, Golopupenko, Golopupenko!' cried Tcherevik, delighted. 'Here, mate, this is the lad I was telling you about. Ah, he is a smart one! God strike me dead on the spot if he did not toss off a whole jug, almost as big as your head, and never turned a hair!'

'What made you put a slight on such a fine lad, then, mate?'

'Here, you see,' Tcherevik went on, addressing Grytsko, 'God has punished me, it seems, for having wronged you. Forgive me, good lad! Upon my soul, I'd be glad to do anything for you . . . But what would you have me do? There's the devil in my old woman!'

'I am not one to remember evil, Tcherevik! If you like, I'll set you free!'

Here he made a sign to the other lads, and the very ones who were guarding them ran to untie them.

'Then you must do your part, too: a wedding! And let us keep it up so that our legs ache with dancing for a year afterwards!'

'Good, good!' said Tcherevik, striking his hands together. 'I feel as pleased as though the soldiers had carried off my old woman! Why give it another thought? Whether she likes it or not, the wedding shall be today – and that's all about it!'

'Mind now, Solopy: in an hour's time I will be with you; but now go home – there you will find purchasers for your mare and your wheat.'

'What! Has the mare been found?'

'Yes.'

Tcherevik was struck dumb with joy and stood still, gazing after Grytsko.

'Well, Grytsko, have we mishandled the job?' said the tall gypsy to the hurrying lad. 'The oxen are mine now, aren't they?'

'Yours! Yours!'

13

Fear not, fear not, little mother,
Put on your red boots.
Trample your foes
Under foot
So that your ironshod
Heels may clang,
So that your foes
May be hushed and still.   *A wedding song*

Paraska mused sitting alone in the cottage with her pretty chin propped on her hand. Many dreams hovered about her little head. At times a faint smile stirred her crimson lips and some joyful feeling lifted her dark brows, while at times a cloud of pensiveness set them frowning above her clear brown eyes.

'But what if it does not come true as he said?' she whispered with an expression of doubt. 'What if they don't let me marry him? If . . . No, no; that will not be! My stepmother does just as she likes; why mayn't I do as I like? I've plenty of obstinacy too. How handsome he is! How wonderfully his black eyes glow! How delightfully he says, "Paraska darling!" How his white jacket suits him! But his belt ought to be a bit brighter! . . . I will weave him one when we settle in a new cottage. I can't help being pleased when I think,' she went on, taking from her bosom a little red paper-framed looking-glass bought at the fair and gazing into it, 'how I shall meet her one day somewhere and she may burst before I bow to her, nothing will induce me. No, stepmother, you've beaten your stepdaughter for the last time. The sand will rise up on the rocks and the oak bend down to the water like a willow, before I bow down before you. But I was forgetting . . . let me try on a cap, if it has to be my stepmother's, and see how it suits me to look like a wife?'

Then she got up, holding the looking-glass in her hand and bending her head down to it, walked in excitement about the room, as though in dread of falling, seeing below her, instead of the floor, the ceiling with the boards laid on the rafters from which the priest's son had so lately dropped, and the shelves set with pots.

'Why, I am like a child,' she cried, 'afraid to take a step!'

And she began tapping with her feet – growing bolder as she went on; at last she laid her left hand on her hip and went off into a dance, clinking with her metalled heels, holding the looking-glass before her and singing her favourite song:

> 'Little green periwinkle,
>   Twine lower to me!
> And you, black-browed dear one,
>   Come nearer to me!
> Little green periwinkle,
>   Twine lower to me!
> And you, black-browed dear one,
>   Come nearer to me!'

At that moment Tcherevik peeped in at the door, and seeing his daughter dancing before the looking-glass, he stood still. For a long time he looked, laughing at the innocent prank of his daughter, who was apparently so absorbed that she noticed nothing; but when he heard the familiar notes of the song, his muscles began working: he stepped forward, his arms jauntily akimbo, and forgetting all he had to do, set to dancing. A loud shout of laughter from his friend Tsybulya startled both of them.

'Here is a pretty thing! The dad and his daughter getting up a wedding on their own account! Make haste and come along: the bridegroom has arrived!'

At the last words Paraska flushed a deeper crimson than the ribbon which bound her head, and her light-hearted parent remembered his errand.

'Well, daughter, let us make haste! Hivrya is so pleased that I have sold the mare,' he went on, looking timorously about him, 'that she has run off to buy herself aprons and all sorts of rags, so we must get it all over before she is back.'

Paraska had no sooner stepped over the threshold than she felt herself caught in the arms of the lad in the white jacket, who with a crowd of people was waiting for her in the street.

'God bless you!' said Tcherevik, joining their hands. 'May their lives together cleave as the wreaths of flowers they weave.'

At this point a hubbub was heard in the crowd.

'I'd burst before I'd allow it!' screamed Tcherevik's helpmate, who was being shoved back by the laughing crowd.

'Don't excite yourself, wife!' Tcherevik said coolly, seeing that two sturdy gypsies held her hands, 'what is done can't be undone: I don't like going back on a bargain!'

'No, no, that shall never be!' screamed Hivrya, but no one heeded her; several couples surrounded the happy pair and formed an impenetrable dancing wall around them.

A strange feeling, hard to put into words, would have overcome any one watching how the whole crowd was willy-nilly transformed into a scene of unity and harmony, at one stroke of the bow of the fiddler, who had long twisted moustaches and wore a homespun jacket. Men whose sullen faces seemed to have known no gleam of a smile for years were tapping with their feet and wriggling their shoulders; everything was heaving, everything was dancing. But an even stranger and more enigmatic feeling would have been stirred in the heart at the sight of old women, whose ancient faces breathed the indifference of the tomb, shoving their way between the young, laughing, living human beings. Caring for nothing, without the joy of childhood, without a gleam of fellow-feeling, nothing but drink, like an engineer with a lifeless machine, makes them perform actions that seem human; yet they slowly wag their drunken heads, dancing after the rejoicing crowd, not casting one glance at the young couple.

The sounds of laughter, song and uproar grew fainter and fainter. The strains of the fiddle were lost in vague and feeble notes, and died away in the wind. In the distance there was still the sound of dancing feet, something like the far-away murmur of the sea, and soon all was stillness and emptiness again.

Is it not thus that joy, lovely and inconstant guest, flies from us? In vain the last solitary note tries to express gaiety. In its own echo it hears melancholy and emptiness and listens to it, bewildered. Is it not thus that those who have been sportive friends in free and stormy youth, one by one stray, lost, about the world and leave their old comrade lonely and forlorn at last? Sad is the lot of one left behind! Heavy and sorrowful is his heart and naught can aid him!

1829

ST JOHN'S EVE

A True Story told by the Sacristan

IT WAS A SPECIAL PECULIARITY of Foma Grigoryevitch's that he had a mortal aversion for repeating the same story. It sometimes happened that one persuaded him to tell a story over again, but then he would be bound to add something fresh, or would tell it so differently that you hardly knew it for the same. It chanced that one of those people – it is hard for us, simple folk, to know what to call them, for scriveners they are not, but they are like the dealers at our fairs: they beg, they grab, they filch all sorts of things and bring out a little book, no thicker than a child's reader, every month or every week – well, one of these gentry got this story out of Foma Grigoryevitch, though he quite forgot all about it. And then that young gentleman in the pea-green coat of whom I have told you already and whose story, I believe, you have read, arrives from Poltava, brings with him a little book and, opening it in the middle, shows it to us. Foma Grigoryevitch was just about to put his spectacles astride his nose, but recollecting that he had forgotten to mend them with thread and wax, handed it to me. As I know how to read after a fashion and do not wear spectacles, I set to reading it aloud. I had hardly turned over two pages when Foma Grigoryevitch suddenly nudged my arm.

'Wait a minute: tell me first what it is you are reading?'

I must own I was a little taken aback by such a question.

'What I am reading, Foma Grigoryevitch? Your story, your own words.'

'Who told you it was my story?'

'What better proof do you want – it is printed here, "Told by the sacristan of So-and-so." '

'Hang the fellow who printed that! He's lying, the cur! Is that how I told it? What is one to do when a man has a screw loose in his head? Listen, I'll tell it to you now.'

We moved up to the table and he began:

My grandfather (the kingdom of Heaven be his! May he have nothing but rolls made of fine wheat and poppy-cakes with honey to eat in the other world!) was a great hand at telling stories. Sometimes when he talked one could sit listening all day without stirring. He was not like the gabblers nowadays who drive you to pick up your cap and go out as soon as they begin spinning their yarns in a voice which sounds as though they had had nothing to eat for three days. I remember as though it were today – the old lady, my mother, was living then – how on a long winter evening when frost crackled outside and sealed up the narrow window of our cottage, she would sit with her distaff[19] pulling out a long thread with one hand, rocking the cradle with her foot and singing a song which I can hear now. Spluttering and trembling as though it were afraid of something, the lamp lighted up the cottage. The distaff hummed while we children clustered together listening to Grandad, who was so old that he had hardly climbed down from the stove for five years past. But not even his marvellous accounts of the old days, of the raids of the Cossacks, of the Poles, of the gallant deeds of Podkova,[20] of Poltor-Kozhuh[21] and Sagaidatchny[22] interested us so much as stories of strange things that had happened long ago; they always made our hair stand on end and set us shuddering. Sometimes we were so terrified by them that in the evening you can't think how queer everything looked. Sometimes you would step out of the cottage for something at night and fancy that some visitor from the other world had got into your bed. And, may I never live to tell this tale again, if I did not often take my coat rolled up by way of pillow for the devil huddling there. But the chief thing about my Grandad's stories was that he never in his life told a lie and everything he told us had really happened.

One of his wonderful stories I am going to tell you now. I know there are lots of smart fellows who scribble in law-courts and read even modern print, though if you put in their hands a simple prayer-book they could not make out a letter of it, and yet they are clever enough at grinning and mocking! Whatever you tell them, they turn it all into ridicule. Such unbelief is spreading all over the world! Why – may God and the Holy Virgin look ill upon me! – you will hardly believe me: I dropped a word about witches one day, and there was a mad fellow – didn't believe in witches! Here, thank God, I have lived all these long years and have met unbelievers who would tell a lie at confession as easily as I'd take a pinch of snuff, but even they made the sign of the cross in terror of witches. May they dream of . . . but I won't say what I would like them to dream of . . . Better not speak of them.

How many years ago! Over a hundred, my Grandad told us, no one would have known our village: it was a hamlet, the poorest of hamlets! A dozen huts or so, without plaster, or proper roofs, stood up here and there in the middle of the fields. No fences, no real barns where cattle or carts could be housed. And it was only the rich lived as well as that – you should have seen the likes of us poor ones: we used to dig a hole in the ground, and that was our hut! You could only tell from the smoke that Christians were living there. You will ask why did they live like that? It was not that they were poor: for in those days almost every one was a Cossack and brought home plenty of good things from other lands; but more because it was no use to have a good hut. All sorts of folk were roaming about the country then: Crimeans, Poles, Lithuanians! And sometimes even fellow-countrymen came in gangs and robbed us. All sorts of things used to happen.

In this village there often appeared a man, or rather a devil in human form. Why he came and where he came from nobody knew. He drank and made merry and then vanished, as though he had sunk into the water, and they heard no news of him. Then all at once he seemed to drop from the sky and was prowling about the streets of the village which was hardly more than a hundred paces from Dikanka, though there is no trace of it now . . . He would pick up with any stray Cossacks, and then there was laughter and singing, the money would fly and vodka would flow like water . . . Sometimes he'd set upon the girls, heap ribbons, ear-rings, necklaces on them, till they did not know what to do with them. To be sure, the girls did think twice before they took his presents: who knows, they might really come from the devil. My own grandfather's aunt, who used to keep a tavern on what is now the Oposhnyansky Road where Basavryuk (that was the name of this devil of a fellow) often went for a drink, said she wouldn't take a present from him for all the riches in the world. And yet how could they refuse? Everybody was terrified when he scowled with his shaggy eyebrows and gave a look from under them that might make the stoutest take to his heels; and if a girl did accept, the very next night a friend of his from the bog with horns on his head might pay her a visit and try to strangle her with the necklace round her neck, or bite her finger if she had a ring, or pull her hair if she had a ribbon in it. A plague take them then, his fine presents! And the worst of it was, there was no getting rid of them: if you threw them into the water, the devilish necklace or ring would float on the top and come back straight into your hands.

In the village there was a church, and I fancy, if I remember right, it was St Panteley's.[23] The priest there in those days was Father Afanassy of blessed memory. Noticing that Basavryuk did not come to church even on Easter Sunday, he thought to reprimand him and threaten him with a church penance. But no such thing! It was he that caught it! 'Look here, my good sir,' Basavryuk bellowed in reply to him, 'you mind your own business and don't meddle with other people's, unless you want your billy-goat's gullet choked with hot frumenty!' What was to be done with the cursed fellow? Father Afanassy merely declared that he should reckon any one who associated with Basayryuk a Catholic, an enemy of the Church of Christ and of the human race.

In the same village a Cossack called Korzh had a workman who was always known as Petro the Kinless – perhaps because no one remembered his parents. It is true that the churchwarden used to say that they had died of the plague when he was a year old, but my grandfather's aunt would not hear of that and did her very utmost to provide him with relations, though poor Petro cared no more about them than we do about last year's snow. She used to say that his father was still in Zaporozhye, that he had been taken prisoner by the Turks and suffered goodness knows what tortures, and that in some marvellous way he had escaped, disguised as a eunuch. The black-browed girls and young women cared nothing about his relations. All they said was that if he put on a new tunic, a black astrakhan cap with a smart blue top to it, hung a Turkish sword at his side and carried a whip in one hand and a handsome pipe in the other, he would outshine all the lads of the place. But the pity was that poor Petro had only one grey jacket with more holes in it than gold pieces in a Jew's pocket. And that was not what mattered; what did matter was that old Korzh had a daughter, a beauty – such as I fancy you have never seen. My grandfather's aunt used to say – and women, you know, would rather kiss the devil, saving your presence, than call any girl a beauty – that the girl's plump cheeks were as fresh and bright as a poppy of the most delicate shade of pink when it glows, washed by God's dew, unfolds its leaves and preens itself in the rising sun; that her brows, like black strings such as our girls buy nowadays to hang crosses or coins on from travelling Russian pedlars, were evenly arched and seemed to gaze into her clear eyes; that her little mouth at which the young men stared greedily looked as though it had been created to utter the notes of a nightingale; that her hair, black as a raven's wings and soft as young flax, fell in rich curls on her gold-embroidered jacket (in those days our girls did not do their hair in plaits and twine them with bright-coloured ribbons). Ah, may God never grant me to sing 'Alleluia' again in the choir, if I could not kiss her on the spot now, in spite of the grey which is spreading all over the old stubble on my head, and of my old woman, always at hand when she is not wanted. Well, if a lad and a girl live near each other . . . you all know what is bound to happen. Before the sun had fully risen, the footprints of the little red boots could be seen on the spot where Pidorka had been talking to her Petro. But Korzh would never have had an inkling that anything was amiss if – clearly it was the devil's prompting – one day Petro had not been so unwary as to imprint, as they say, a hearty kiss on Pidorka's rosy lips in the outer room without taking a good look round; and the same devil – may he dream of the Holy Cross, the son of a cur! – prompted the old chap to open the door. Korzh stood petrified, clutching at the door, with his mouth wide open. The accursed kiss seemed to overwhelm him completely. It seemed to him louder than the thud against the wall of the pestle with which in our day the peasants used to make a bang for lack of musket and gunpowder.

Recovering himself, he took his grandfather's whip from the wall and was about to flick it on Petro's back, when all of a sudden Pidorka's six-year-old brother Ivas ran in and threw his arms round the old man's legs in terror, shouting 'Father, father, don't beat Petro!'

There was no help for it: the father's heart was not made of stone: hanging the whip on the wall, he quietly led Petro out of the hut. 'If you ever show yourself again in my hut, or even under the windows, then listen: you will lose your black moustaches, and your forelock, too – it is long enough to go twice round your ear – will take leave of your head, or my name is not Terenty Korzh!'

Saying this he dealt him a light blow on the back of the neck, and Petro, caught unawares, flew headlong. So that was what his kisses brought him!

Our cooing doves were overwhelmed with sadness; and then there was a rumour in the village that a new visitor was continually seen at Korzh's – a Pole, all in gold lace, with moustaches, a sabre, spurs and pockets jingling like the bell on the bag that our sexton Taras carries about the church with him every day. Well, we all know why people visit a father when he has a black-browed daughter. So one day Pidorka bathed in tears took her little brother in her arms: 'Ivas my dear, Ivas my darling, run fast as an arrow from the bow, my golden little one, to Petro, tell him everything: I would love his brown eyes. I would kiss his fair face, but my fate says nay. More than one towel I have soaked with my bitter tears. I am sick and sad at heart. My own father is my foe: he is forcing me to marry the detested Pole. Tell him that they are making ready the wedding, only there will be no music at our wedding, the deacons will chant instead of the pipe and the lute. I will not walk out to dance with my bridegroom: they will carry me. Dark, dark will be my dwelling, of maple wood, and instead of a chimney a cross will stand over it!'

Standing stock-still, as though turned to stone, Petro heard Pidorka's words lisped by the innocent child.

'And I, poor luckless fool, was thinking of going to the Crimea or Turkey to win gold in war, and, when I had money, to come to you, my beauty. But it is not to be! An evil eye has looked upon us! I, too, will have a wedding, my dear little fish; but there will be no clergy at that wedding – a black raven will croak over me instead of a priest; the open plain will be my dwelling, the grey storm-clouds will be my roof; an eagle will peck out my brown eyes; the rains will wash my Cossack bones and the whirlwind will dry them. But what am I saying? To whom, of whom am I complaining? It is God's will, seemingly. If I must perish, then perish!' and he walked straight away to the tavern.

My grandfather's aunt was rather surprised when she saw Petro at the tavern and at an hour when a good Christian is at matins, and she stared at him open-eyed as though half awake when he asked for a mug of vodka, almost half a pailful. But in vain the poor fellow thought to drown his sorrow. The vodka stung his tongue like a nettle and seemed to him bitterer than wormwood. He flung the mug upon the ground.

'Give over grieving, Cossack!' something boomed out in a bass voice above him.

He turned round: it was Basavryuk! Ugh, what a figure he looked! Hair like bristles, eyes like a bullock's.

'I know what it is you lack: it's this!' And then with a fiendish laugh he jingled the leather pouch he carried at his belt.

Petro started.

'Aha! Look how it glitters!' yelled the other, pouring the gold pieces into his hand. 'Aha! How it rings! And you know, only one thing is asked for a whole pile of such baubles.'

'The devil!' cried Petro. 'Very well, I am ready for anything!' They shook hands on it.

'Mind, Petro, you are just in time: tomorrow is St John the Baptist's Day. This is the only night in the year in which the bracken blossoms.[24] Don't miss your chance! I will wait for you at midnight in the Bear's Ravine.'

I don't think the hens are as eager for the minute when the goodwife brings their corn as Petro was for evening to come. He was continually looking whether the shadow from the tree were longer, whether the setting sun were not flushing red, and as the hours went on he grew more impatient. Ah, how slowly they went ! It seemed as though God's day had lost its end somewhere. At last the sun was gone. There was only a streak of red on one side of the sky. And that, too, was fading. It turned colder. The light grew dimmer and dimmer till it was quite dark. At last! With his heart almost leaping out of his breast, he set off on his way and carefully went down through the thick forest to a deep hollow, which was known as the Bear's Ravine. Basavryuk was there already. It was so dark that you could not see your hand before your face. Hand in hand, they made their way over a muddy bog, caught at by the thorns that grew over it and stumbling almost at every step. At last they reached a level place. Petro looked round – he had never chanced to come there before. Here Basavryuk stopped.

'You see there are three hillocks before you? There will be all sorts of flowers on them, but may the powers from yonder keep you from picking one of them. But as soon as the bracken blossoms, pick it and do not look round, whatever you may fancy is behind you.'

Petro wanted to question him further . . . but behold, he was gone. He went up to the three hillocks: where were the flowers? He saw nothing. Rank weeds overshadowed everything and smothered all else with their dense growth. But there came a flash of summer lightning in the sky, and he saw before him a whole bed of flowers, all marvellous, all new to him; and there, too, were the simple plumes of bracken. Petro was puzzled and he stood in perplexity – with his arms akimbo.

'What is there marvellous in this? One sees that green stuff a dozen times a day – what is there strange in it? Didn't the devil mean to make a mock of me?'

All at once a little flower began to turn red and to move as though it were alive. It really was marvellous! It moved and grew bigger and bigger and turned red like a burning coal. A little star suddenly shone out, something snapped – and the flower opened before his eyes, shedding light on the others about it like a flame.

'Now is the time!' thought Petro, and stretched out his hand. He saw hundreds of shaggy hands were stretched from behind him towards it, and something seemed to be flitting to and fro behind his back. Shutting his eyes, he pulled at the stalk and the flower was left in his hand. Everything was hushed. Basavryuk, looking blue like a corpse, appeared sitting on a stump. He did not stir a finger. His eyes were fastened on something which only he could see; his mouth was half open, and no answer came from it. Nothing stirred all around. Ugh, it was terrible! . . . But at last a whistle sounded, which turned Petro cold all over, and it seemed to him as though the grass were murmuring, and the flowers were talking among themselves with a voice as delicate and sweet as silver bells: the trees resounded with angry gusts. Basavryuk's face suddenly came to life, his eyes sparkled. 'At last, you are back, old hag!' he growled through his teeth. 'Look, Petro, a beauty will appear before you: do whatever she tells you, or you will be lost for ever!'

Then with a gnarled stick he parted a thornbush and a little hut – on hen's legs, as they say in fairy tales – stood before them. Basavryuk struck it with his fist and the wall tottered. A big black dog ran out to meet him, and changing into a cat, with a squeal flew at their eyes.

'Don't be angry, don't be angry, old devil!' said Basavryuk, spicing his words with an oath which would make a good man stop his ears. In a trice where the cat had stood was an old woman wrinkled like a baked apple and bent double, her nose and chin meeting like nutcrackers.

'A fine beauty!' thought Petro, and a shudder ran down his back.

The witch snatched the flower out of his hands, bent over it and spent a long time muttering something and sprinkling it with water of some sort. Sparks flew out of her mouth, there were flecks of foam on her lips. 'Throw it!' she said, giving him back the flower. Petro threw it and, marvellous to relate, the flower did not fall at once, but stayed for a long time like a ball of fire in the darkness, and floated in the air like a boat; at last it began slowly descending and fell so far away that it looked like a little star no bigger than a poppy-seed. 'Here!' the old woman wheezed in a hollow voice, and Basavryuk, giving him a spade, added: 'Dig here, Petro, here you will see more gold than you or Korzh ever dreamed of.'

Petro, spitting into his hands, took the spade, thrust at it with his foot and threw out the earth, a second spadeful, a third, another . . . Something hard! . . . The spade clanked against something and would go no further. Then his eyes could distinguish clearly a small iron-bound box. He tried to get hold of it, but the box seemed to sink deeper and deeper into the earth; and behind him he heard laughter more like the hissing of snakes.

'No, you will never see the gold till you have shed human blood!' said the witch, and brought him a child about six years old covered with a white sheet, signing to him to cut off its head. Petro was dumb-foundered. A mere trifle! For no rhyme or reason to murder a human being, and an innocent child, too! Angrily he pulled the sheet off the child, and what did he see? Before him stood Ivas. The poor child crossed its arms and hung its head . . . Like one possessed, Petro flew at the witch, knife in hand, and was just lifting his hand to strike . . .

'And what did you promise for the sake of the girl?' thundered Basavryuk, and his words went through Petro like a bullet. The witch stamped her foot; a blue flame shot out of the earth and shed light down into its centre, so that it all looked as though made of crystal; and everything under the surface could be seen clearly. Gold pieces, precious stones in chests and in cauldrons were piled up in heaps under the very spot on which they were standing. His eyes glowed . . . his brain reeled. Frantic, he seized the knife and the innocent blood spurted into his eyes . . . Devilish laughter broke out all round him. Hideous monsters galloped in herds before him. Clutching the headless corpse in her hands, the witch drank the blood like a wolf . . . His head was in a whirl! With a desperate effort he set off running. Everything about him was lost in a red light. The trees all bathed in blood seemed to be burning and moaning. The red-hot sky quivered . . . Gleams of fire like lightning flashed before his eyes. At his last gasp he ran into his hut and fell on the ground like a sheaf of corn. He sank into a deathlike sleep

For two days and two nights he slept without waking. Waking on the third day, he stared for a long time into the corners of the hut. But he tried in vain to remember what had happened; his memory was like an old miser's pocket out of which you can't entice a penny. Stretching a little, he heard something clink at his feet. He looked: two sacks of gold. Only then he remembered as though it were a dream that he had been looking for a treasure, that he had been frightened alone in the forest . . . But at what price, how he had obtained it – that he could not recall.

Korzh saw the sacks and – was softened. Petro was this and Petro was that, and he could not say enough for him. 'And wasn't I always fond of him, and wasn't he like my own son to me?' And the old fox carried on so incredibly that Petro was moved to tears. Pidorka began telling him how Ivas had been stolen by some passing gypsies, but Petro could not even remember the child: that cursed devilry had so confounded him!

There was no reason for delay. They sent the Pole away with a flea in his ear and began preparing the wedding. They baked wedding cakes, they hemmed towels and kerchiefs, rolled out a barrel of vodka, set the young people down at the table, cut the wedding-loaf, played the lute, the pipe, the bandura[25] and the cymbals – and the merry-making began . . .

You can't compare weddings nowadays with what they used to be.

My grandfather's aunt used to tell about them – it was a treat! How the girls in a smart headdress of yellow, blue and pink ribbons, with gold braid tied over it, in fine smocks embroidered with red silk on every seam and adorned with little silver flowers, in morocco boots with high iron heels, danced round the room as gracefully as peacocks, swishing like a whirlwind. How the married women in a boat-shaped headdress, the whole top of which was made of gold brocade with a little slit at the back showing a peep of the gold cap below, with two little horns of the very finest black astrakhan, one in front and one behind, in blue coats of the very best silk with red lappets, holding their arms with dignity akimbo, stepped out one by one and rhythmically danced the *gopak*! How the lads in high Cossack hats, in fine cloth jerkins girt with silver embroidered belts, with a pipe in their teeth danced attendance on them and cut all sorts of capers! Korzh himself looking at the young couple could not refrain from recalling his young days: with a bandura in his hand, smoking his pipe and singing, at the same time balancing a goblet on his head, the old man fell to dancing in a half-squatting position. What won't people think of when they are making merry? They would begin, for instance, putting on masks – my goodness, they looked like monsters! Ah, it was a very different thing from dressing up at weddings nowadays. What do they do now? Only rig themselves out like gypsies or soldiers. Why, in old days one would be a Jew and another a devil, first they would kiss each other and then pull each other's forelocks. . . . Upon my soul! One laughed till one held one's sides. They would put on Turkish and Tatar dresses, all glittering like fire . . . And was soon as they began fooling and playing tricks . . . there were no bounds to what they would do! An amusing incident happened to my grandfather's aunt who was at that wedding herself: she was wearing a full Tatar dress and with a goblet in her hand she was treating the company. The devil prompted someone to splash vodka over her from behind; another one, it seems, was just as clever, at the same moment he struck a light and set fire to her . . . The flame flared up: poor aunt, terrified, began flinging off all her clothes before everybody. . . . The din, the laughter, the hubbub that arose – it was like a fair. In fact, the old people never remembered such a merry wedding.

Pidorka and Petro began to live like lady and gentleman. They had plenty of everything, it was all spick and span . . . But good people shook their heads a little as they watched the way they went on. 'No good comes from the devil,' all said with one voice. 'From whom had his wealth come, if not from the tempter of good Christians? Where could he have got such a pile of gold? Why had Basavryuk vanished on the very day that Petro had grown rich?'

You may say that people invent things! But really, before a month was out, no one would have known Petro. What had happened to him, God only knows. He would sit still without stirring and not say a word to anyone; he was always brooding and seemed trying to remember something. When Pidorka did succeed in making him talk, he would seem to forget and keep up a conversation and even be merry, but if by chance his eye fell on the bags, 'Stay, stay, I have forgotten,' he would say, and again he would sink into thought and again try to remember something. Sometimes after he had been sitting still for a long time it seemed that in another moment he would recall it all . . . and then it would pass away again. He fancied he had been sitting in a tavern; they brought him vodka; the vodka burnt him; the vodka was nasty; someone came up, slapped him on the shoulder; he . . . but after that everything seemed shrouded in a fog. The sweat dropped down his face and he sat down again, feeling helpless.

What did not Pidorka do! She consulted wizards, poured wax into water and burnt a bit of hemp – nothing was of any use. So the summer passed. Many of the Cossacks had finished their mowing and harvesting; many of the more reckless ones had gone off fighting. Flocks of ducks were still plentiful on our marshes, but there was not a nettle-wren to be seen. The steppes turned red. Stacks of corn, like Cossacks' caps, were dotted about the field here and there. Waggons laden with faggots and logs were to be met on the roads. The ground was firmer and in places it was frozen. Snow began falling and the twigs on the trees were decked in hoar-frost like hare-fur. Already one bright frosty day the red-breasted bullfinch was strutting about like a smart Polish gentleman, looking for seeds in the heaps of snow, and the children were whipping wooden stops on the ice with huge sticks while their fathers lay quietly on the stove, coming out from time to time with a lighted pipe between their teeth to swear roundly at the good orthodox frost, or to get a breath of air and thrash the corn stored in the outer room.

At last the snow began to melt and 'the pike smashed the ice with its tail,' but Petro was still the same, and as time went on he was gloomier still. He would sit in the middle of the hut, as though riveted to the spot, with the bags of gold at his feet. He shunned company, let his hair grow, began to look dreadful and thought only about one thing: he kept trying to remember something and was vexed and angry that he could not remember it. Often he would get up from his seat wildly, wave his arms, fix his eyes on something as though he wanted to catch it; his lips would move as though trying to utter some long-forgotten word – and then would remain motionless . . . He was overcome by fury; he would gnaw and bite his hands as though he were mad, and tear out his hair in handfuls in his vexation, until he would grow quiet again and seem to sink into forgetfulness; and then he would begin to remember again, and again there would be fury and torment . . . It was, indeed, a heaven-sent infliction.

Pidorka's life was not worth living. At first she was afraid to remain alone in her hut, but afterwards she grew used to her trouble, poor thing. But no one would have known her for the Pidorka of earlier days. No colour, no smile; she was pining and wasting away, she was crying her bright eyes out. Once someone must have taken pity on her and advised her to go to the witch in the Bear's Ravine, who was reputed able to cure all the diseases in the world. She made up her mind to try this last resource; little by little, she persuaded the old woman to go home with her. It was after sunset, on St John's Eve. Petro was lying on the bench lost in forgetfulness and did not notice the visitor come in. But little by little he began to sit up and look at her. All at once he trembled, as though he were on the scaffold; his hair stood on end . . . and he broke into a laugh that cut Pidorka to the heart with terror. 'I remember, I remember!' he cried with a fearful joy and, snatching up an axe, flung it with all his might at the old woman. The axe made a cut two inches deep in the oak door. The old woman vanished and a child about seven in a white shirt, with its head covered, was standing in the middle of the hut . . . The veil flew off. 'Ivas!' cried Pidorka and rushed up to him, but the phantom was covered from head to foot with blood and shed a red light all over the hut . . . She ran into the outer room in terror, but, coming to herself, wanted to help her brother; in vain! The door had slammed behind her so that she could not open it. Neighbours ran up: they began knocking, broke open the door: not a living soul within! The whole hut was full of smoke, and only in the middle where Petro had stood was a heap of ashes from which smoke was still rising. They rushed to the bags: they were full of broken potsherds instead of gold pieces. The Cossacks stood as though rooted to the spot with their mouths open and their eyes starting out of their heads, not daring to move an eyelash. This miracle threw them into such a panic.

What happened afterwards I don't remember. Pidorka took a vow to go on a pilgrimage. She gathered together all the goods left her by her father, and a few days later she vanished from the village. No one could say where she had gone. Some old women were so obliging as to declare that she had followed Petro where he had gone; but a Cossack who came from Kiev said he had seen in the convent there a nun wasted to a skeleton, who never ceased praying, and in her by every token the villagers recognised Pidorka; he told them that no one had ever heard her say a word; that she had come on foot and brought a setting for the ikon of the Mother of God with such bright jewels in it that it dazzled everyone who looked at it.

But let me tell you, this was not the end of it all. The very day that the devil carried off Petro, Basavryuk turned up again: but every one ran away from him. They knew now the kind of bird he was: no one but Satan himself disguised in human form in order to unearth buried treasure; and since unclean hands cannot touch the treasure he entices young men to help him. The same year every one deserted their old huts and moved into a new village, but even there they had no peace from that cursed Basavryuk. My grandfather's aunt used to say that he was particularly angry with her for having given up her old tavern on the Oposhnyansky Road and did his utmost to pay her out. One day the elders of the village were gathered at her tavern and were conversing according to their rank, as the saying is, at the table, in the middle of which was stood a whole roast sheep, and it would be a lie to call it a small one. They chatted of one thing and another; of marvels and strange happenings. And all at once they fancied – and of course it would be nothing if it were one of them, but they all saw it at once – that the sheep raised its head, its sly black eyes gleamed and came to life; it suddenly grew a black bristly moustache and significantly twitched it at the company. They all recognised at once in the sheep's head the face of Basavryuk; my grandfather's aunt even thought that in another minute he would ask for vodka . . . The worthy elders picked up their caps and hurried home. Another day, the churchwarden himself, who liked at times a quiet half-hour with the family goblet, had not drained it twice when he saw the goblet bow down to him. 'The devil take you!' and he set to crossing himself . . . And at the same time a strange thing happened to his better-half: she had only just mixed the dough in a huge tub when suddenly the tub jumped away. 'Stop, stop!' Not a bit of it! Its arms akimbo, the tub went solemnly pirouetting about all over the hut . . . You may laugh; but it was no laughing matter to our forefathers. And in spite of Father Afanassy's going all over the village with holy water and driving the devil out of every street with the sprinkler, my grandfather's aunt complained for a long time that as soon as evening came on someone knocked on the roof and scratched on the wall.

But there! In this place where our village is standing you would think everything was quiet nowadays; but you know it is not so long ago, within my father's memory – and indeed I remember it – that no good man would pass the ruined tavern which the unclean race repaired long afterwards at their own expense. Smoke came out in clouds from the grimy chimney and, rising so high that one's cap dropped off if one looked at it, scattered hot embers all over the steppe, and the devil – no need to mention him, son of a cur – used to sob so plaintively in his hole that the frightened rooks rose up in flocks from the forest near and scattered with wild cries over the sky.

A MAY NIGHT

or

THE DROWNED MAIDEN

> The devil only knows what to make of it! If Christian folk
> begin any task, they fret and fret themselves like dogs after a
> hare, and all to no purpose; but as soon as the devil comes into
> it – in a jiffy – lo and behold, the thing's done!

1

Ganna

A RINGING SONG flowed like a river down the streets of the
village. It was the hour when, weary from the cares and labours of
the day, the lads and girls gather together in a ring in the glow
of the clear evening to pour out their gaiety in strains never far removed
from melancholy. And the brooding evening dreamily embraced the
dark-blue sky, transforming everything into vagueness and distance. It
was already dusk, yet still the singing did not cease. Lyovko, a young
Cossack, the son of the village Head, slipped away from the singers
with a bandura in his hands. He was wearing an astrakhan cap.
The Cossack walked down the street thrumming on the strings of his
instrument and dancing to it. At last he stopped quietly before the
door of a cottage surrounded with low-growing cherry trees. Whose
cottage was it? Whose door was it? After a few moments of silence, he
began playing and singing:

> 'The sun is low, the evening's nigh,
> Come out to me, my little heart!'

'No, it seems my bright-eyed beauty is sound asleep,' said the Cossack when he had finished the song, and he went nearer to the window. 'Galya! Galya, are you asleep, or don't you want to come out to me? You are afraid, I suppose, that someone will see us, or perhaps you don't want to put your fair little face out into the cold? Don't be afraid, there is no one about, and the evening is warm. And if any one should appear, I will cover you with my jacket, wrap my sash round you or hide you in my arms – and no one will see us. And if there is a breath of cold, I'll press you warmer to my heart, I'll warm you with my kisses, I'll put my cap over your little white feet. My heart, my little fish, my necklace! Look out for a minute. Put your little white hand at least out of the window . . . No, you are not asleep, proud maiden!' he brought out more loudly, in the voice of one ashamed at having for a moment demeaned himself; 'you are pleased to mock at me; farewell!'

At this point he turned away, thrust his cap rakishly to one side, and walked haughtily away from the window, softly thrumming the strings of the bandura. At that moment the wooden handle turned: the door was flung open with a creak, and a girl in her seventeenth spring looked about her timidly, shrouded in the dusk, and, without leaving hold of the handle, stepped over the threshold. Her bright eyes shone with welcome like stars in the semi-darkness; her red coral necklace gleamed, and even the modest blush that suffused her cheeks could not escape the lad's eagle eye.

'How impatient you are!' she said to him in a low voice. 'You are angry already! Why did you choose this time? Crowds of people are strolling up and down the street . . . I keep trembling . . . '

'Oh, do not tremble, my lovely willow! Cling closer to me!' said the lad, putting his arms round her, and casting aside his bandura, which hung on a long strap round his neck, he sat down with her at the door of the cottage. 'You know it's pain to me to pass an hour without seeing you.'

'Do you know what I am thinking?' the girl broke in, pensively gazing at him. 'Something seems whispering in my ear that henceforth we shall not meet so often. People here are not good: the girls all look so enviously, and the lads . . . I even notice that of late my mother has taken to watching me more strictly. I must own, it was pleasanter for me with strangers.'

A look of sadness passed over her face at these last words.

'Only two months at home and already you are weary of it! Perhaps you are tired of me, too?'

'Oh, I am not tired of you,' she replied, laughing. 'I love you, my black-browed Cossack! I love you because you have brown eyes, and when you look at me with them, it seems as though there were laughter in my heart; and it is gay and happy; because you twitch your black moustache so charmingly, because you walk along the streets singing and playing the bandura, and it's sweet to listen to you.'

'Oh, my Galya!' cried the lad, kissing her and pressing her warmly to his heart.

'Stop! Enough, Lyovko! Tell me first, have you told your father?'

'Told him what?' he said, as though waking up from sleep. 'That I want to marry and that you will be my wife? Yes, I have told him.' But the words 'I have told him' had a despondent sound upon his lips.

'Well?'

'What's one to do with him? He pretended to be deaf, the old rogue, as he always does; he wouldn't hear anything, and then began scolding me for strolling about all over the place, and playing pranks in the streets with the boys. But don't grieve, my Galya! I give you the word of a Cossack that I will get round him.'

'Well, you have only to say the word, Lyovko, and you will have everything your own way. I know that from myself, sometimes I wouldn't obey you, but you have only to say a word – and I can't help doing what you want. Look, look!' she went on, laying her head on his shoulder and turning her eyes upward to the warm Ukrainian sky that showed dark blue, unfathomable through the leafy branches of the cherry trees that stood in front of them. 'Look, yonder; far away, the stars are twinkling, one, two, three, four, five . . . It's the angels of God, opening the windows of their bright dwellings in the sky and looking out at us, isn't it? Yes, Lyovko! They are looking at our earth, aren't they? If only people had wings like birds, so they could fly thither, high up, high up . . . Oh, it's dreadful! Not one oak here reaches to the sky. But they do say there is some tree in a distant land the top of which reaches right to heaven and God comes down by it to the earth on the night before Easter.'

'No, Galya, God has a ladder reaching from heaven right down to earth. The holy archangels put it up before Easter Sunday, and as soon as God steps on the first rung of it, all the evil spirits fall headlong and sink in heaps down to hell. And that is how it is that at Christ's festival there isn't one evil spirit on earth.'

'How softly the water murmurs, like a child lying in its cradle!' Ganna went on, pointing to the pond in its gloomy setting of a wood of maple trees and weeping willows, whose drooping boughs dipped into it. Like a feeble old man, it held the dark distant sky in its cold embrace, covering with its icy kisses the flashing stars, which gleamed dimly in the warm ocean of the night air as though they felt the approach of the brilliant sovereign of the night. An old wooden house lay slumbering with closed shutters on the hill by the copse; its roof was covered with moss and weeds; leafy apple trees grew in all directions under the windows; the wood, wrapping it in its shade, threw an uncanny gloom over it; a thicket of nut trees lay at its foot and sloped down to the pond.

'I remember as though it were a dream,' said Ganna, not taking her eyes off him, 'long, long ago when I was little and lived with mother, they used to tell some dreadful story about that house. Lyovko, you must know it, tell it me . . .'

'Never mind about it, my beauty! The women and silly folk tell all sorts of stories. You will only upset yourself, you'll be frightened and won't sleep soundly.'

'Tell me, tell me, dear black-browed lad!' she said, pressing her face against his cheek and putting her arm around him. 'No, I see you don't love me; you have some other girl. I won't be frightened; I will sleep sound at night. Now I shan't sleep if you don't tell me. I shall be worried and thinking . . . Tell me, Lyovko . . . !'

'It seems folk are right when they say that there is a devil of curiosity in girls, egging them on. Well, listen then. Long ago, my little heart, there was a Cossack officer used to live in that house. He had a daughter, a fair maiden, white as snow, white as your little face. His wife had long been dead; he took it into his head to marry again. "Will you care for me the same, father, when you take another wife?" "Yes, I shall, my daughter, I shall press you to my heart more warmly than ever! I shall, my daughter. I shall give you ear-rings and necklaces brighter than ever!"

'The father brought his young wife to her new home. The new wife was fair of face. All red and white was the young wife; only she gave her stepdaughter such a dreadful look that the girl uttered a shriek when she saw her, and the harsh stepmother did not say a word to her all day. Night came on. The father went with his young wife to his sleeping chamber, and the fair maiden shut herself up in her little room. She felt sad at heart, she began to weep. She looked round, and a dreadful black cat was stealing up to her; there were sparks in her fur and her steely claws scratched on the floor. In terror she jumped on a bench, the cat followed her; she jumped on the oven-step, the cat jumped after her, and suddenly leapt on her neck and was stifling her. Tearing herself away with a shriek she flung it on the floor. Again the dreadful cat stole up. She was overcome with terror. Her father's sword was hanging on the wall. She snatched it up and brought it down with a crash on the floor, one paw with its steely claws flew off and the cat with a squeal disappeared into a dark corner. All day the young wife did not come out of her room; two days afterwards she came out with her arm bandaged. The poor maiden guessed that her stepmother was a witch and that she had cut off her hand. On the fourth day the father bade his daughter fetch the water, sweep the house like a humble peasant-girl and not show herself in her father's apartments. It was a hard lot for the poor girl, but there was no help for it; she obeyed her father's will. On the fifth day the father turned his daughter, barefoot, out of the house and did not give her a bit of bread to take with her. Then only the maiden fell to sobbing, hiding her white face in her hands. "You have sent your own daughter to perish, father! The witch has ruined your sinful soul! God forgive you; and it seems it is not His will that I should live in this fair world . . . " And yonder do you see . . . ?' At this point Lyovko turned to Ganna, pointing towards the house, 'Look this way, yonder, on the very highest part of the bank! From that bank the maiden threw herself into the water. And from that hour she was seen no more . . . '

'And the witch?' Ganna asked in a frightened voice, fastening her tearful eyes on him.

'The witch? The old women make out that ever since then all the maidens drowned in the pond have come out on moonlight nights into that garden to warm themselves, and the officer's daughter is leader among them. One night she saw her stepmother beside the pond; she pounced upon her, and with a shriek dragged her into the water. But the witch saved herself even then: she changed under water into one of the drowned girls, and so escaped the scourge of green reeds with which the maidens meant to beat her. Trust a woman! They say, too, that the maiden assembles all the drowned girls every night and looks into the face of each, trying to find out the witch, but hitherto has not found her. And if she comes across any living man she makes him guess which it is; or else she threatens to drown him in the water. So, my Galya, that's how old people tell the story! . . . The present master wants to set up a distillery there and has sent a distiller here to see to it . . . But, I hear voices. It's our fellows coming back from singing. Good-night, Galya! Sleep well and don't think about these old women's tales.'

Saying this, he embraced her warmly, kissed her and walked away.

'Good-night, Lyovko,' said Ganna, gazing dreamily at the dark wood.

At that moment a huge fiery moon began majestically rising from the earth. Half of it was still below the horizon, yet all the world was already flooded with its solemn light. The pond was covered with gleaming ripples. The shadow of the trees began to stand out clearly against the dark green grass.

'Good-night, Ganna!' the words uttered behind her were accompanied by a kiss.

'You have come back,' she said, looking round, but seeing a lad she did not know, she turned away.

'Good-night, Ganna!' she heard again, and again she felt a kiss on her cheek.

'Here the Evil One has brought another!' she said angrily.

'Good-night, dear Ganna!'

'That's the third one!'

'Good-night, good-night, good-night, Ganna,' and kisses were showered upon her from all sides.

'Why, there is a regular gang of them!' cried Ganna, tearing herself away from the crowd of lads, who vied with each other in trying to embrace her. 'I wonder they are not sick of this everlasting kissing! Upon my word, one won't be able to show oneself in the street soon!'

The door slammed upon these words and nothing more was heard but the iron bolt squeaking in its socket.

2

The Head

Do you know the Ukrainian night? Oh, you do not know the Ukrainian night! Look at it: the moon looks out from the centre of the sky; the immense dome of heaven stretches further, more inconceivably immense than ever; it glows and breathes; the earth is all bathed in a silvery light; and the exquisite air is refreshing and warm and full of voluptuousness, and an ocean of fragrance is stirring. Divine night! Enchanting night! The woods stand motionless, mysterious, full of gloom, and cast huge shadow. Calm and still lie the ponds. The cold and darkness of their waters are gloomily walled in by the dark green gardens. The virginal thickets of wild cherry timidly stretch their roots into the cold of the water and from time to time murmur in their leaves, as though angry and indignant when the sweet rogue – the night wind – steals up suddenly and kisses them. All the countryside is sleeping. But overhead all is breathing; all is marvellous, triumphal. And the soul is full of the immensity and the marvel; and silvery visions rise up in harmonious multitudes from its depths. Divine night! Enchanting night!

And suddenly it all springs into life: the woods, the ponds and the stones. The glorious clamour of the Ukrainian nightingale bursts upon the night and one fancies the moon itself is listening in mid-heaven . . . The hamlet on the upland sleeps as though spellbound. The groups of cottages gleam whiter, fairer than ever in the moonlight; their low walls stand out more dazzlingly in the darkness. The singing has ceased. All is still. God-fearing people are asleep. Only here and there is a light in the narrow windows. Here and there before the doorway of a cottage a belated family is still at supper.

'But that's not the way to dance the *gopak*.[26] I feel that it won't come right somehow. What was that my crony was saying . . . ? Oh yes: hop, tra–la! hop, tra–la! hop, hop, hop!' So a middle-aged peasant, who had been drinking and was dancing down the street, talked to himself. 'I swear, that's not the way to dance the *gopak*. Why should I tell a lie about it? I swear it's not right. Come: hop, tra–la! hop, tra–la! hop, hop, hop!'

'There's a man tipsy! And it's not as though it were a lad, but an old fool like that, enough to make the children laugh, dancing in the street at night!' cried an elderly woman who passed by, carrying an armful of straw. 'Go to your cottage! You ought to have been asleep long ago!'

'I am going,' said the peasant, stopping. 'I am going. I don't care about any Head. He thinks, the Old One flay his father, that because he is the Head, because he pours cold water over folks in the frost, he can turn up his nose at every one! Head indeed! I am my own Head. God strike me dead! Strike me dead, God! I am my own Head. That's how it is and nohow else,' he went on, and going up to the first cottage he reached and standing before the window, he passed his fingers over the window pane and tried to find the door handle. 'Wife, open! Look alive, I tell you open! It's time the Cossack was asleep!'

'Where are you going, Kalenik? You are at somebody else's cottage,' some girls on their way home from the merry singing, shouted from behind him, laughing. 'Shall we show you your cottage?'

'Show me the way, kind maidens fair!'

'Maidens fair! Do you hear,' said one of them, 'how polite Kalenik is? We must show him the way to his cottage for that . . . but no, you dance on in front.'

'Dance . . . ? ah, you tricky girls!' Kalenik drawled, laughing and shaking his finger at them, and he lurched forward because his legs were not steady enough to stand still. 'Come, give me a kiss. I'll kiss you all, every one of you . . . !' And with staggering steps he fell to running after them. The girls set up a shriek and huddled together;

then, growing bolder, ran over to the other side of the street, seeing that Kalenik was not very rapid on his feet.

'Yonder is your cottage!' they shouted to him, pointing, as they walked away, to a cottage, much larger than his own, which belonged to the Head of the village. Kalenik obediently turned in that direction, beginning to abuse the Head again.

But who was this village Head who aroused such unfavourable opinions and criticisms? Oh, he was an important person in the village. While Kalenik is on his way we shall certainly have time to say something about him. All the villagers took off their caps when they saw him, and the girls, even the youngest, wished him good-day. Which of the lads would not have liked to be Head? He was free to help himself to every one's snuff, and the sturdy peasant would stand respectfully, cap in hand, all the time while the Head fumbled with his fat, coarse fingers in the peasant's birch-bark snuffbox. At the village council, although his power was limited to a few votes, he always took the upper hand and almost on his own authority sent whom he pleased to level and repair the roads or dig the ditches. He was austere, forbidding of aspect, and not fond of wasting words. Long very long ago when the great Tsaritsa Catherine, of blessed memory, was going to the Crimea,[27] he had been chosen to act as a guide. For two whole days he had performed this duty, and had even been deemed worthy to sit on the box beside the Tsaritsa's coachman. It was from that time that he had taken to bowing his head with a dignified and meditative air, to stroking his long, drooping moustaches, and to shooting hawk-like glances from under his brows. And from that time, too, whatever subject was broached, the Head always cleverly turned the conversation to the way in which he had guided the Tsaritsa, and sat on the box of the Tsaritsa's carriage. He liked at times to pretend to be deaf, especially when he heard something that he did not want to hear. He could not endure foppishness: he always wore a long tunic of black homespun cloth, always girt with a coloured woollen sash, and no one had ever seen him in any other costume, except on the occasion of the Tsaritsa's visit to the Crimea when he wore a dark blue Cossack tunic. But hardly any one in the village can remember that time; the tunic he still kept locked up in a chest. He was a widower, but he had living in the house with him his sister-in-law, who cooked the dinner and the supper, washed the benches, whitewashed the cottage, wove him shirts, and looked after the house. They did say in the village that she was not his sister-in-law at all, but we have seen already that there were many who bore no good-will to the Head and were glad to circulate any scandal about him.

Though, perhaps, what did give colour to the story was the fact that the sister-in-law was displeased if he went out into a field that was full of girls reaping, or visited a Cossack who had a young daughter. The Head had but one eye, but that eye was a shrewd villain and could see a pretty village girl a long way off. He does not, however, fix it upon a prepossessing face before he has taken a good look around to see whether his sister-in-law is watching him. But we have said almost all that we need about the Head, while tipsy Kalenik was on his way there still continuing to bestow on the Head the choicest epithets his slow and halting tongue could pitch upon.

3

An Unexpected Rival

A Plot

'No, lads, no, I won't! What pranks you are up to! I wonder you are not sick of mischief. Goodness knows, people call us scamps enough already. You had better go to bed!' So said Lyovko to his rollicking companions who were persuading him to join in some fresh pranks. 'Farewell, lads! Good-night to you!' and with rapid steps he walked away from them down the street.

'Is my bright-eyed Ganna asleep?' he wondered, as he approached the cottage with the cherry trees known to us already. Subdued voices could be heard in the stillness. Lyovko stood still. He could see the whiteness of a shirt through the trees . . . 'What does it mean?' he wondered, and stealing up a little nearer, hid behind a tree, The face of the girl who stood before him gleamed in the moonlight . . . It was Ganna! But who was the tall man standing with his back towards him? In vain he gazed at him; the shadow covered him from head to foot. Only a little light fell upon him in front, but the slightest step forward would have exposed Lyovko to the unpleasant risk of being discovered. Quietly leaning against the tree he resolved to remain where he was. The girl distinctly pronounced his name.

'Lyovko? Lyovko is a milksop,' the tall man brought out huskily and in a low voice. 'If I ever meet him here, I'll pull him out by his top-knot.'[28]

'I should like to know what scoundrel it is, boasting that he will pull me away by my topknot!' murmured Lyovko softly, and he craned his neck, trying not to miss one word. But the intruder went on speaking so softly that he could not hear what was said.

'I wonder you are not ashamed!' said Ganna, when he had finished speaking. 'You are lying, you are deceiving me; you don't love me; I shall never believe that you love me!'

'I know,' the tall man went on, 'Lyovko has talked a lot of nonsense to you and has turned your head.' (At this point the boy fancied that the voice was not quite unknown to him, it seemed as though he had heard it before.) 'I'll show Lyovko what I am made of!' the unknown went on in the same way. 'He thinks I don't see all his wanton tricks. He shall find out, the young cur, what my fists are like!'

At those words Lyovko could not restrain his rage. Taking three steps towards him, he swung his fist to give him a clout on the ear which might have sent him flying, for all his apparent strength; but at that instant the moonlight fell on his face, and Lyovko was stupefied to see standing before him – his father. An unconscious jerk of the head and a faint whistle were the only expression of his amazement. A rustle was heard. Ganna hurriedly flew into the cottage, slamming the door after her.

'Good-night, Ganna!' one of the lads cried at that moment, stealing up and putting his arm round the Head, and skipped back with horror, meeting his stiff moustache.

'Good-night, my beauty!' cried another; but this one was sent flying by a violent push from the Head.

'Good-night, good-night Ganna!' called several lads, hanging on his neck.

'Be off, you cursed scamps!' cried the Head, pushing them off and kicking them. 'Ganna indeed! Go and be hanged like your fathers, you brood of Satan! They come round one like flies after honey! I'll teach you . . . !'

'The Head, the Head, it's the Head,' shouted the lads and scattered in all directions.

'Aha, father!' said Lyovko, recovering from his amazement and looking after the Head as he walked away swearing. 'So these are the tricks you are up to! A nice thing! And I have been brooding and wondering what was the meaning of his always pretending to be deaf when one begins speaking about it. Wait a bit, old fellow, I'll teach you to hang about under young girls' windows. I'll teach you to lure away other men's sweethearts! Hey, lads! Come here, come here, this way!' he shouted, waving his hands to the lads who had gathered into a group again. 'Come here! I advised you to go to bed, but now I have changed my mind and am ready to make merry with you all right.'

'That's the way to talk!' said a stout, broad-shouldered lad who was reckoned the merriest and most mischievous in the village. 'It always makes me sick when we can't manage to have a decent bit of fun and play some prank. I always feel as though I had missed something, as though I had lost my cap or my pipe; not like a Cossack, in fact.'

'What do you say to our giving the Head a good stir up?'

'The Head?'

'Yes. What's he thinking about? He rules us as though he were a hetman.[29] He is not satisfied with treating us as though we were his serfs, but he must needs go after our girls, too. I do believe there is not a nice-looking girl in the whole village that he has not made up to.'

'That's true, that's true!' cried all the lads with one voice.

'What's wrong with us, lads? Aren't we the same sort as he is? Thank God, we are free Cossacks! Let us show him, lads, that we are free Cossacks!'

'We'll show him,' shouted the lads. 'And if we give it to the Head, we won't spare his clerk either!'

'We won't spare the clerk! And I have just made up a splendid song, it's the very thing for him. Come along, I will teach it you,' Lyovko went on, striking the strings of his bandura. 'But I say, dress up in anything that comes handy!'

'Go it, brave Cossacks!' said the sturdy scamp, striking his feet together and clapping his hands. 'How glorious! What fun. When you go in for a frolic you feel as though you were celebrating bygone years. Your heart is light and free and your soul might be in paradise. Hey, lads! Hey, now for some fun . . . !'

And the crowd moved noisily down the street, and God-fearing old women, awakened from their sleep by the shouts, pulled up their windows and crossed themselves with drowsy hands, saying: 'Well, the lads are enjoying themselves now!'

4

The Lads Make Merry

Only one cottage at the end of the village was still lighted up. It was the Head's. He had finished his supper long ago, and would no doubt have been asleep by this time, but he had a visitor, the man who had been sent to set up a distillery by the landowner who had a small piece of land among the free Cossacks. The visitor, a short, fat little man with little eyes that were always laughing, and seeming to express the pleasure he took in smoking, sat in the place of honour under the ikons, continually spitting and catching with his finger the tobacco ash that kept dropping out of his short pipe. Clouds of smoke were spreading rapidly over him and enveloping him in a dark blue fog. It seemed as though a big chimney of some distillery, weary of sitting on its roof, had thought it would like a change, and was sitting decorously in the Head's cottage. Short thick moustaches stuck out below his nose; but they so indistinctly appeared and disappeared in the smoky atmosphere that they seemed like a mouse that the distiller, infringing the monopoly of the granary cat, had caught and held in his mouth. The Head, being in his own house, was sitting in his shirt and linen trousers. His eagle eye was beginning little by little to close and grow dim like the setting sun. One of the village constables who made up the Head's staff was smoking a pipe at the end of the table, and out of respect to his host still kept on his tunic.

'Are you thinking of setting up your distillery soon?' the Head asked, addressing the distiller and making the sign of the cross over his mouth as he yawned.

'With the Lord's help, maybe by the autumn we shall begin distilling. I'll bet that by Intercession[30] our honoured Head will be drawing German bread-rings with his feet on the road.'

As he uttered these words, the distiller's eyes disappeared; where they had been were gleams of light stretching to his ears; his whole frame began to quiver with laughter, and for an instant his mirthful lips abandoned the pipe that poured forth clouds of smoke.

'Please God I may,' said his host, twisting his face into a semblance of a smile. 'Now, thank God, distilleries are doing better. But years ago, when I was guiding the Tsaritsa by the Pereyaslav Road, Bezborodko,[31] now deceased . . .'

'Well, old friend, that was a time! In those days there were only two distilleries all the way from Krementchug to Romny. But now . . . Have you heard what the damned Germans are going to do? They say that instead of burning wood in distilleries like all decent Christians, they are soon going to use some kind of devilish steam . . . ' As he said this the distiller looked thoughtfully at the table and at his hands lying on it. 'How it is done with steam – upon my soul, I don't know!'

'What fools they are, those Germans, God forgive me!' said the Head. 'I'd thrash them, the brood of Satan! Did any one ever hear the like of boiling anything by steam? According to that, you couldn't take a spoonful of soup without boiling your lips like a young sucking pig.'

'And you, friend,' the sister-in-law, who was sitting on the bed with her feet tucked under her, interposed, 'are you going to stay with us all that time without your wife?'

'Why, what do I want with her? It would be different if she were something worth having.'

'Isn't she good-looking?' asked the Head, fixing his eye upon him.

'Good-looking, indeed! Old as the devil. Her face all wrinkles like an empty purse.' And the stubby frame of the distiller shook with laughter again.

At that moment something began fumbling at the door; the door opened – and a peasant crossed the threshold without taking off his cap, and stood in the middle of the cottage as though in hesitation, gaping and staring at the ceiling. This was our friend Kalenik.

'Here I am home at last,' he said, sitting down on the bench near the door, and taking no notice of the company present. 'I say, how the son of evil, Satan, did lengthen out the road! You went on and on, and no end to it! I feel as though someone had broken my legs. Woman, get the sheepskin to put down for me. I am not coming up beside you on the stove, that I am not, my legs ache! Fetch it, it's lying there under the ikons; only mind you don't upset the pot with the snuff. Or no, don't touch it, don't touch it! Maybe you are drunk today . . . Let me get it myself.'

Kalenik tried to get up, but an overmastering force riveted him to his seat.

'I like that,' said the Head. 'Walks into another man's cottage and gives orders as though he were at home! Throw him out, neck and crop . . .'

'Let him stay and rest, friend!' said the distiller, holding him back by the arm. 'He is a useful man; I wish there were more folk like him, and our distillery would do finely . . .'

It was not good-nature, however, that dictated this remark. The distiller believed in omens of all sorts, and to turn a man out who had already sat down on the bench would have meant provoking misfortune.

'It seems as though age is creeping on me . . . ' muttered Kalenik, lying down on the bench. 'It would be all right if I were drunk, but I am not drunk. No, indeed, I am not drunk. Why tell a lie about it? I am ready to tell the Head himself so. What do I care for the Head. May he choke, the cur! I spit on him. I wish a waggon would run over him, the one-eyed devil! Why does he drench people in the frost?'

'Aha, the pig has made its way into the cottage, and is putting its feet on the table,' said the Head, wrathfully rising from his seat; but at that moment a heavy stone, smashing the window to shivers, fell at their feet. He stopped short. 'If I knew,' he said, picking up the stone, 'if I knew what gallows-bird flung in that stone I'd teach him to throw stones! What tricks!' he went on, looking with flashing eyes at the stone in his hand. 'May he choke with this stone . . . !'

'Stay, stay, God preserve you, friend!' cried the distiller, turning pale. 'God preserve you in this world and the next from blessing any one with such abuse!'

'Here's a champion! Confound him!'

'Don't think of it, friend! I suppose you don't know what happened to my late mother-in-law?'

'Your mother-in-law?'

'Yes, my mother-in-law. One evening, a little earlier it may be than it is now, they sat down to supper: my mother-in-law and father-in-law and their hired man and their hired girl and their five children. My mother-in-law shook some dumplings out of a big cauldron into a bowl to cool them. They were all hungry after their work and did not want to wait for the dumplings to get cool. Picking them up on long wooden skewers they began eating them. All at once a man appeared: where he came from no one can say, who he was, God only knows. He asks them to let him sit down to table. Well, there is no refusing a hungry man food. They gave him a skewer, too. Only the visitor stowed away the dumplings like a cow eating hay. While the others had eaten one each, and were prodding after more with their skewers, the bowl was as clean as a gentleman's floor. My mother-in-law put out some more; she thought the visitor had had enough and would take less. Nothing of the sort: he began gulping them down faster than ever and emptied the second bowl. "And may you choke with the dumplings!" thought my hungry mother-in-law, when all of a sudden the man choked and fell on the floor. They rushed up to him, but the spirit had fled. He was choked.'

'And serve him right, the damned glutton!' said the Head.

'Quite so, but it didn't end with that: from that time forward my mother-in-law had no rest. As soon as night came on the dead man climbed up. He sat astride on the chimney, the cursed fellow, holding a dumpling in his teeth. In the daytime all was quiet and they didn't hear a sound of him, but as soon as it began to get dusk, look at the roof and there you would see him, sitting on the chimney, the son of a cur.'

'And a dumpling in his teeth?'

'And a dumpling in his teeth.'

'How marvellous, friend! I had heard something of the sort about your mother-in-law . . .'

The speaker stopped short. Under the window they heard an uproar and the thud of dancing feet. First there was the soft thrumming of the bandura strings, then a voice joined in with it. The strings twanged more loudly, several voices joined in and the singing rose up like a whirlwind.

> 'Laddies, have you heard the news now!
> Heads it seems are none too sound!
> Our one-eyed Head's a barrel-head
> Whose staves have come unbound!
> Come, cooper, knock upon it hard,
> And bind with hoops of steel!
> Come hammer, cooper, on the head
> And hit with right good will!
> Our Head is grey and has one eye;
> Old as sin, and what a blockhead!
> Full of whims and wanton fancies;
> Makes up to the girls . . . the blockhead!
> You must try to ape the young ones!
> When you should be in your coffin,
> Flung in by the scruff and whiskers!
> By the topknot you're so proud of!'

'A fine song, friend!' said the distiller, inclining his head a little on one side and turning towards his host, who was struck dumb with amazement at such insolence. 'Fine! It's only a pity that they refer to the Head in rather disrespectful terms . . . '

And again he put his hands on the table with a sort of gleeful delight in his eyes, preparing himself to hear more, for from below came peals of laughter and shouts of 'Again! Again!' However, a penetrating eye could have seen at once that it was not astonishment that kept the Head from moving. An old experienced cat will sometimes in the same way let an inexperienced mouse run round his tail while he is rapidly making a plan to cut off its way back to its hole. The Head's solitary eye was still fixed on the window, and already his hand, after making a sign to the constable, was on the wooden door-handle, when all at once a shout rose from the street . . . The distiller, among whose characteristics curiosity was one, hurriedly filled his pipe and ran out into the street; but the rogues had already scattered in all directions.

'No, you won't get away from me!' cried the Head, dragging by the arm a man in a black sheepskin, put on inside out. The distiller, seizing the opportunity, ran to have a look at this disturber of the peace, but he staggered back in alarm at seeing a long beard and a horribly painted face. 'No, you won't escape me!' shouted the Head, still dragging straight into the outer room his prisoner, who offered no resistance but followed him quietly, as though going into his own cottage. 'Karpo, open the storeroom!' said the Head to the constable; 'we'll put him in the dark storeroom. And then we will wake the clerk, get the constables together, catch all these brawlers, and today we will pass judgment on them all.'

The constable clanked a small padlock in the outer room and opened the storeroom. At that instant his captive, taking advantage of the dark storeroom, wrenched himself out of his hands with a violent effort.

'Where are you off to?' cried the Head, clutching him more tightly than ever by the collar.

'Let go, it's me!' cried a thin shrill voice.

'That won't help you, that won't help you, my lad. You may squeal like a devil, as well as a woman, you won't take me in,' and he shoved him into the dark storeroom, so that the poor prisoner uttered a moan as he fell on the floor, while, accompanied by the constable and followed by the distiller, puffing like a steamer, he went off to the clerk's cottage.

They walked along all three with their eyes on the ground, lost in meditation, when, at a turning into a dark lane, all of them at once uttered a shriek, from a violent bang on their foreheads, and a similar cry of pain echoed in response. The Head, screwing up his eye, saw with surprise the clerk and two constables.

'I was coming to see you, worthy clerk!'

'And I was coming to your worship, honoured Head.'

'Strange things have been happening, worthy clerk.'

'Very strange things, honoured Head!'

'Why, what?'

'The lads have gone crazy! They are going on disgracefully in the street, whole gangs of them. They describe your honour in language . . . I should be ashamed to repeat it. A drunken soldier couldn't bring his dirty tongue to utter such words.' (All this the lanky clerk, in striped linen breeches and a waistcoat the colour of wine dregs, accompanied by craning his neck forward and dragging it back again to its former position.) 'I had just dropped into a doze, when the cursed scamps roused me from my bed with their shameful songs and knocking! I meant to take stern measures with them, but while I was putting on my breeches and waistcoat, they all ran away in different directions. The ringleader did not get away, though. He is singing now in the cottage where we keep prisoners. I was all eagerness to find out what bird it was we'd caught, but his face is all black like the devils who forge nails for sinners.'

'And how is he dressed, worthy clerk?'

'In a black sheepskin put on inside out, honoured Head.'

'Aren't you lying, clerk? What if that rascal is sitting now in my storeroom?'

'No, honoured Head! You yourself, not in anger be it said, are a little in error!'

'Give me a light! We will have a look at him!'

The light was brought, the door unlocked, and the Head uttered a groan of amazement when he saw facing him – his sister-in-law!

'Tell me, please,' with these words she pounced upon him, 'have you lost what little wits you ever had? Was there a grain of sense in your thick head, you one-eyed fool, when you pushed me into the dark storeroom? It was lucky I did not hit my head against the iron hook. Didn't I scream out to you that it was me? The cursed bear seizes me in his iron paws and shoves me in! May the devils treat you the same in the other world . . . !'

The last words were uttered in the street where she had gone for some purpose of her own.

'Yes, I see that it's you,' said the Head, recovering himself. 'What do you say, worthy clerk? Isn't this scamp a cunning rogue?'

'He is a cunning rogue, honoured Head.'

'Isn't it high time that we gave all these rascals a good lesson and set them to work?'

'It's high time, high time, honoured Head!'

'They have taken it into their heads, the fools . . . What the devil? I thought I heard my sister-in-law scream in the street . . . They have taken it into their heads, the fools, that they are as good as I am. They think I am one of them, a simple Cossack! . . . ' The little cough that followed this, and the way he looked round from under his brows indicated that the Head was about to speak of something important. 'In the year eighteen . . . I never can bring out these confounded dates – Ledatchy, who was then Commissar, was given orders to pick out from the Cossacks the most intelligent of them all. Oh!' (that 'Oh!' he pronounced with his finger in the air) 'the most intelligent! to act, as guide to the Tsaritsa. At that time I . . . '

'What need to tell us! We all know that, honoured Head! We all know how you won the royal favour. Own now that I was right. You took a sin upon your soul when you said that you had caught that rogue in the black sheepskin.'

'Well, as for that devil in the black sheepskin, we'll put him in fetters and punish him severely as an example to others! Let him know what authority means! By whom is the Head appointed if not by the Tsar?

Then we'll get hold of the other fellows: I have not forgotten how the confounded scamps drove a herd of pigs into my kitchen garden that ate up all my cabbages and cucumbers; I have not forgotten how the sons of Satan refused to thrash my corn; I have not forgotten . . . But plague take them, I must find out who that rascal is, wearing a sheepskin inside out.'

'He's a wily bird, it seems!' said the distiller, whose cheeks during the whole of this conversation were continually being charged with smoke, like a siege cannon, and his lips, abandoning the short pipe, were ejecting a perfect fountain of smoke. 'It wouldn't be amiss, anyway, to keep the fellow for working in the distillery; or better still, hang him from the top of an oak tree like a church candlestick.'

Such a witticism did not seem quite foolish to the distiller, and he at once decided, without waiting for the approval of the others, to reward himself with a husky laugh.

At that moment they drew near a small cottage that had almost sunk into the earth. Our friends' curiosity grew keener: they all crowded round the door. The clerk took out a key and jingled it about the lock; but it was the key of his chest. The impatience became acute. Thrusting his hand into his pocket he began fumbling for it, and swearing because he could not find it.

'Here!' he said at last, bending down and taking it from the depths of the roomy pocket with which his full striped trousers were provided.

At that word the hearts of all our heroes seemed melted into one, and that huger heart beat so violently that the sound of its uneven throb was not lost even in the creaking of the lock. The door was opened, and . . . The Head turned white as a sheet, the distiller was aware of a cold chill, and the hair of his head seemed rising up towards heaven; horror was depicted on the countenance of the clerk; the constables were rooted to the spot, and were incapable of closing their mouths, which had fallen open simultaneously: before them stood the sister-in-law.

No less amazed than they, she, however, pulled herself together, and made a movement as though to approach them.

'Stop!' cried the Head in an unnatural voice, and slammed the door in her face. 'Oh Lord, it is Satan!' he went on. 'A light! Quick, a light! I won't spare the cottage, though it is Crown property. Set fire to it, set fire to it, that the devil's bones may not be left on earth!'

The sister-in-law screamed terribly, hearing through the door this sinister decision.

'What are you about, friends!' said the distiller. 'Your hair, thank God, is almost white, but you have not gained sense yet: a witch won't burn with ordinary fire! Only a light from a pipe can burn a changeling of the devil's! Wait a bit, I will manage it in a minute!'

Saying this, he scattered some burning ash out of his pipe on to a wisp of straw, and began blowing on it. The poor sister-in-law was meanwhile overwhelmed with despair; she began loudly imploring and beseeching them.

'Stay, friends! Why take a sin upon us in vain? Perhaps it is not Satan!' said the clerk. 'If it, whatever it may be that is sitting there, consents to make the sign of the cross, that's a sure token that it is not a devil.'

The proposition was approved.

'Get thee behind me, Satan!' said the clerk, putting his lips to the keyhole. 'If you don't stir from your place we will open the door.'

The door was opened.

'Cross yourself!' said the Head, looking behind him as though seeking a safe place in case of retreat.

The sister-in-law crossed herself.

'The devil! It really is my sister-in-law! What evil spirit dragged you to this hole?'

And the sister-in-law, sobbing, told them that the lads had seized her in the street and, in spite of her resistance, had bundled her in at the wide window of the cottage and had nailed up the shutter. The clerk glanced: the staples of the broad shutter had been pulled out, and it was only fixed on by a board at the top.

'All right, you one-eyed Satan!' she screamed, stepping up to the Head, who staggered back and still scanned her with his solitary eye. 'I know your design – you wanted, you would have been glad to do for me, to be more free to go after the girls, to have no one to see the grey-headed old grandad playing the fool. You think I don't know what you were saying this evening to Ganna? Oh, I know all about it. It's hard to deceive me, let alone for a numskull like you. I am long-suffering, but when I do lose patience, you'll have something to put up with.'

Saying this, she shook her fist at him and walked away quickly, leaving him completely stupefied.

'Well, Satan has certainly had a hand in it this time,' he thought, scratching his head vigorously.

'We've caught him,' cried the constables, coming in at that instant.

'Caught whom?' asked the Head.

'The devil with his sheepskin inside out.'

'Give him here!' shouted the Head, seizing the prisoner by the arm. 'You are mad! This is the drunkard, Kalenik.'

'What a queer thing! We had him in our hands, honoured Head!' answered the constables. 'The confounded lads came round us in the lane, began dancing and capering, tugging at us, putting out their tongues and snatching him out of our hands . . . Damnation take it! . . . And how we hit on this crow instead of him the devil only knows!'

'By my authority and that of all the members of the parish council the command is given,' said the Head, 'to catch that rascal this minute, and in the same way all whom you find in the street, and to bring them to me to be questioned! . . . '

'Upon my word, honoured Head . . . !' cried some of them, bowing down to his feet. 'You should have seen what ugly faces; strike us dead, we have been born and been christened but have never seen such horrid faces. Mischief may come of it, honoured Head. They may give a simple man such a fright that there isn't a woman in the place who would undertake to cure him of his panic.'

'Panic, indeed! Why? Are you refusing to obey? I expect you are hand in glove with them? You are mutinying! What's this . . . ! What's the meaning of it . . . ? You are getting up a rebellion . . . ! You . . . you . . . I'll report it to the Commissar. This minute, do you hear, this minute! Run, fly like a bird! I'll show you . . . You'll show me . . . '

They all ran off in different directions.

5

The Drowned Maiden

The instigator of all this turmoil, undisturbed by anything and untroubled by the search-parties that were being sent in all directions, walked slowly towards the old house and the pond. I think that I need hardly say that it was Lyovko. His black sheepskin was unbuttoned; he held his cap in his hand; the sweat ran down his face in streams. The maple wood stood majestic and gloomily black, only sprinkled with delicate silver on the side facing the moon. A refreshing coolness from the motionless pond breathed on the tired wanderer and lured him to rest for a while on the bank. All was still. The only sound was the trilling of the nightingale in the deepest recesses of the wood. An overpowering drowsiness soon made his eyes close; his tired limbs were almost sinking into sleep and forgetfulness; his head drooped . . . 'No, if I go on like this I shall fall asleep here!' he said, getting on to his feet and rubbing his eyes.

He looked round and the night seemed even more brilliant. A strange enchanting radiance was mingled with the light of the moon. He had never seen anything like it before. A silvery mist had fallen over everything around him. The fragrance of the apple blossom and the night-scented flowers flooded the whole earth. He gazed with amazement at the motionless water of the pond: the old manor-house, upside down in the water, was distinct and looked serenely dignified. Instead of gloomy shutters there were bright glass windows and doors. There was a glitter of gilt through the clean panes. And then it seemed as though a window opened. Holding his breath, not stirring, nor taking his eyes from the pond, he seemed to pass into its depths and saw – first, a white elbow appeared in the window, then a charming little head with sparkling eyes, softly shining through her dark brown locks, peeped out and rested on the elbow, and he saw her slightly nod her head. She beckoned, she smiled . . . His heart suddenly began throbbing . . . The water quivered and the window was closed again. He moved slowly away from the pond and looked at the house: the gloomy shutters were open; the window panes gleamed in the moonlight. 'See how little one can trust what people say,' he thought to himself. 'It's a new house; the paint is as fresh as though it had been painted today. Someone is living there.' And in silence he went up closer to it, but all was still in the house. The glorious singing of the nightingales rang out loud and melodious, and when it seemed to die away in languor and voluptuousness, there was heard the rustle and churr of the grass-hoppers, or the deep note of some marsh bird, striking his slippery beak on the broad mirror of the water. There was a sense of sweet stillness and space and freedom in Lyovko's heart. Tuning his bandura, he began playing it and singing:

'Oh, thou moon, my darling moon!
    And thou, glowing clear sunrise!
Oh, shine brightly o'er the cottage,
    Where my lovely maiden lies!'

The window slowly opened and the head, the reflection of which he had seen in the pond, looked out listening intently to the singing. Her long eyelashes half hid her eyes. She was white all over, like a sheet, like the moonlight; but how exquisite, how lovely! She laughed . . . ! Lyovko started.

'Sing me a song, young Cossack!' she said softly, bending her head on one side and veiling her eyes completely with her thick eyelashes.

'What song shall I sing you, my fair lady?'

Tears rolled slowly down her pale face. 'Youth,' she said, and there was something inexpressibly touching in her speech, 'Youth, find me my stepmother! I will grudge you nothing. I will reward you. I will reward you richly, sumptuously. I have sleeves embroidered with silk, corals, necklaces. I will give you a girdle adorned with pearls. I have gold. Youth, find me my stepmother! She is a terrible witch, I had no peace in life because of her. She tormented me, she made me work like a simple peasant-girl. Look at my face. By her foul spells she drew the roses from my cheeks. Look at my white neck: they will not wash off, they will not wash off, they never will be washed away, those dark blue marks left by her claws of steel! Look at my white feet, far have they trodden – not on carpets only – but on the hot sand, on the damp earth, on sharp thorns have they trodden! And at my eyes, look at my eyes; they have grown dim with weeping! Find her, youth, find me my stepmother . . . !'

Her voice, which had risen, sank into silence. Tears streamed down her pale face. The young man's heart was oppressed by a painful feeling of pity and sadness.

'I am ready to do anything for you, my fair lady!' he said with heartfelt emotion, 'but how can I, where can I find her?'

'Look, look!' she said quickly, 'she is here, she is on the bank, playing games among my maidens, and warming herself in the moonlight. She is sly and cunning, she has taken the form of a drowned maiden; but I know, I feel that she is here. I am oppressed, I am stifled by her. I cannot swim lightly and easily like a fish, because of her. I drown and sink to the bottom like a key. Find her, youth!'

Lyovko looked towards the bank: in the delicate silvery mist there were maidens glimmering, light as shadows, in smocks white as a meadow dotted with lilies-of-the-valley; gold necklaces, strings of beads, coins glittered on their necks; but they were pale; their bodies looked as though moulded out of transparent clouds, and it seemed as though the moonlight shone through them. The maidens singing and playing drew nearer to him. He heard their voices.

'Let us play raven and chickens,' they murmured, like river reeds kissed by the ethereal lips of the wind at the quiet hour of twilight.

'Who will be raven?'

They cast lots, and one of the girls stepped out of the group. Lyovko scrutinised her. Her face, her dress, all was exactly like the rest. The only thing he noticed was that she did not like to play her part. The group drew out in a chain, it raced rapidly away from the pursuit of the rapacious enemy.

'No, I don't want to be the raven,' said the maiden, weary and exhausted, 'I am sorry to snatch the chickens from their poor mother.'

'You are not the witch!' thought Lyovko.

'Who will be raven?' The maidens made ready to cast lots again.

'I will be raven!' One in the centre of the group offered herself.

Lyovko began looking intently at her face. Boldly and swiftly she pursued the chain, and darted from side to side to capture her victim. At that point Lyovko noticed that her body was not so translucent as the others, something black could be seen in the inside. Suddenly there was a shrieking; the raven had pounced on one of the chain, seized her, and Lyovko fancied that she put out her claws, and that there was a spiteful gleam of joy in her face.

'The witch!' he said suddenly, pointing his finger at her and turning towards the house.

The maiden at the window laughed, and the girls, shouting, led away the one who had played raven.

'How am I to reward you, youth? I know you have no need of gold: you love Ganna, but your harsh father will not let you marry her. Now he will not hinder it: take this note and give it him . . . '

Her white hand was outstretched, her face seemed in a marvellous way full of light and radiance . . . With his heart beating painfully, overwhelmed with agitation, he clutched the note, and . . . woke up.

6

The Awakening

'Can I have been asleep?' Lyovko wondered, getting up from the little hillock. 'It was as living as though it were real . . . ! Strange, strange!' he said, looking about him. The moon standing right over his head showed that it was midnight; everywhere all was still, and a chill air rose from the pond; above him stood the old house with its shutters closed. The moss and high grass showed that it had been abandoned long ago. Then he opened his hand, which had been tightly closed all the time he had been asleep, and cried out with astonishment, feeling a note in it. 'Oh, if I could only read!' he thought, turning it over, and looking at it on all sides. At that moment he heard a noise behind him.

'Don't be afraid, seize him straight away! Why are you so scared? There are a dozen of us. I bet you anything it is a man and not a devil . . . !' So the village Head shouted to his companions and Lyovko felt himself seized by several hands, some of which were shaking with fear.

'Throw off your dreadful mask, friend! Leave off making fools of folk,' said the Head, seizing him by the collar; but he was astounded when he turned his eye upon him. 'Lyovko! Son!' he cried, stepping back in amazement and dropping his hands. 'It's you, son of a cur! Oh, you devil's brood! I was wondering who could be the rascal, what devil turned inside out was playing these tricks. And it seems it is all your doing – you half-cooked pudding sticking in your father's throat! You are pleased to get up rows in the street, compose songs . . . ! Ah, ah, Lyovko! What's the meaning of it? It seems your back is itching for the rod! Seize him!'

'Stay, father! I was told to give you this letter,' said Lyovko.

'This is not the time for letters, my dear! Bind him.'

'Stay, honoured Head,' said the clerk, opening the note, 'it is the Commissar's handwriting.'

'The Commissar's?'

'The Commissar's,' the constable repeated mechanically.

'The Commissar's? Strange! It is more incomprehensible than ever!' Lyovko thought to himself.

'Read it, read it!' said the Head. 'What does the Commissar write?'

'We shall hear what the Commissar writes,' said the distiller, holding his pipe in his teeth and striking a light.

The clerk cleared his throat and began reading:

'Instruction to the Head, Yevtuh Makogonenko. The news has reached us that you, old fool, instead of collecting past arrears and setting the village in order, have gone silly and been behaving disgracefully . . . '

'Upon my soul,' the Head interrupted, 'I don't hear a word!'

The clerk began over again: 'Instruction to the Head, Yevtuh Makogonenko. The news has reached us that you, old foo . . . '

'Stop, stop! You needn't go on,' cried the Head. 'Though I can't hear it, I know that what matters isn't that. Read what comes later!'

'And therefore I command you to marry your son Lyovko Makogonenko to Ganna Petrychenkov, a Cossack maiden of your village, and also to mend the bridges on the high road, and do not without my authorisation give the villagers' horses to the law-court gentry, even if they have come straight from the government office. If on my coming I find these my commands not carried out, I shall hold you alone responsible. Commissar, retired Lieutenant, Kozma Derkatch-Drishpanovsky.'

'Well, upon my word!' said the Head, gaping with wonder. 'Do you hear that, do you hear? The Head is responsible for it all, and so you must obey me unconditionally, or you will catch it! . . . As for you,' he went on, turning to Lyovko, 'since it's the Commissar's orders, though I can't understand how it came to his ears, I'll marry you: only first you shall have a taste of my whip! You know the one that hangs on the wall near the ikons. I'll repair it tomorrow . . . Where did you get that note . . . ?'

In spite of Lyovko's astonishment at this unexpected turn of events, he had the wit to get ready in his mind an answer and to conceal the true explanation of the way he had received the letter.

'I was in the town yesterday evening,' he said, 'and met the Commissar getting out of his chaise.[32] Learning that I came from this village, he gave me the letter and told me to give you the message, father, that on his way back he will come and dine with us.'

'He told you that?'

'Yes.'

'Do you hear,' said the Head with an air of dignity, turning to his companions, 'the Commissar is coming in person to the likes of us, that is to me, to dinner. Oh . . . ' Here he held up his finger and lifted up his head as though he were listening to something. 'The Commissar, do you hear, the Commissar is coming to dine with me! What do you think, worthy clerk, and you, friend? That's an honour not to be sniffed at! Isn't it?'

'To the best of my recollection,' chimed in the clerk, 'no village Head has ever yet entertained the Commissar to dinner.'

'There are Heads and Heads,' said the Head with a self-satisfied air. His mouth twisted and something in the nature of a husky laugh more like the rumbling of distant thunder came from his lips. 'What do you think, worthy clerk? Oughtn't we for this distinguished visitor to give orders that every cottage should send at least a chicken and, well, some linen and anything else . . . Eh?'

'We ought to, we ought to, honoured Head.'

'And when is the wedding to be, father?' asked Lyovko.

'Wedding? I'll teach you to talk about weddings . . . ! Oh well, for the sake of our distinguished visitor . . . tomorrow the priest shall marry you. Confound you! Let the Commissar see what punctual discharge of duty means! Well, lads, now it is bedtime! Go home . . . ! What has happened today reminds me of the time when I . . . ' At these words the Head glanced from under his brows with his habitual air of importance and dignity.

'Now the Head's going to tell us how he guided the Tsaritsa,' said Lyovko, and with rapid steps he made his way joyfully towards the familiar cottage, surrounded by low-growing cherry trees. 'God give you the kingdom of Heaven, kind and lovely lady!' he thought to himself. 'May you in the other world be smiling for ever among the holy angels. I shall tell no one of the marvel that has happened this night; to you only Galya, I will tell it. Only you will believe me and together we will pray for the peace of the soul of the luckless drowned maiden!'

Here he drew near the cottage: the window was open, the moonlight shone through it upon Ganna as she lay asleep with her head upon her arm, a soft glow on her cheeks: her lips moved faintly murmuring his name. 'Sleep, my beauty, dream of all that is fairest in the world, though that will not be better than our awakening.'

Making the sign of the cross over her he closed the window and gently moved away.

And in a few minutes all the village was asleep; only the moon floated as radiant and marvellous in the infinite spaces of the glorious Ukrainian sky. There was the same triumphal splendour on high, and the night, the divine night glowed with the same solemn grandeur. The earth was as lovely in the marvellous silvery light, but no one was enchanted by it; all were sunk in sleep. Only from time to time the silence was broken for a moment by the bark of a dog, and for a long while drunken Kalenik was still staggering along the slumbering street looking for his cottage.

THE LOST LETTER

A Tale Told by the Sacristan

SO YOU want me to tell you another story about Grandad? Certainly, why not amuse you with some more . . . ? Ah, the old days, the old days! What joy, what gladness it brings to the heart when one hears of what was done in the world so long, long ago, that the year and the month are forgotten! And when some kinsman of one's own is mixed up in it, a grandfather or great-grandfather – then I'm done for: may I be taken with a cough at the Anthem to the Holy Martyr Varvara[33] if I don't fancy that I'm doing it all myself, as though I had crept into my great-grandfather's soul, or my great-grandfather's soul were playing tricks in me . . . But there, our girls and young women are the worst for plaguing me; if I only let them catch a glimpse of me, it's 'Foma Grigoryevitch! Foma Grigoryevitch! Come now, some terrible tale! Come now, come now . . . !' Tara–ta–ta, ta–ta–ta and they keep on and on . . . I don't grudge telling them a story, of course, but you should see what happens to them when they are in bed. Why, I know every one of them is trembling under the quilt as though she were in a fever and would be glad to creep under her sheepskin, head and all. If a rat scratches against a pot, or she herself touches the oven-fork with her foot – it's 'Lord preserve us!' and her heart's in her heels. But it's no matter next day; she'll pester me over again to tell her a terrible story, and that's all about it. Well, what am I to tell you? Nothing comes into my mind at the minute . . . oh yes, I'll tell you how the witches played 'Fools'[34] with my grandfather. But I must beg you first, good friends, not to interrupt me or it will make a hash of it not fit to put to one's lips. My Grandad, I must tell you, was a leading Cossack in his day. He knew t-o to, and where to put the mark of abbreviation. On a saint's day, he would boom out the Acts of the Apostles, in a voice that would make a priest's son of today feel small. Well, you know without my telling you that in those days if you collected all who could read and write from the whole of Baturin[35] you'd not need your cap to hold them in, there wouldn't be a handful altogether. So it's no wonder that every one who met my Grandad made him a bow, and a low one too.

One day our noble Hetman took it into his head to send a writing to the Tsaritsa about something. The secretary of the regiment in those days – there, I can't remember his name, the devil take him . . . Viskryak, no, that's not it, Motuzotchka, that's not it, Goloputsek – no, not Goloputsek . . . all I know is that it was a queer name that began in an odd way – he sent for my Grandad and told him that the Hetman himself had named him as messenger to the Tsaritsa. My Grandad never liked to waste time getting ready: he sewed the writing up in his cap, led out his horse, kissed his wife and his two sucking-pigs, as he used to call them, of whom one was my own father, and Grandad made the dust fly that day as though fifteen lads had been playing a rowdy game in the middle of the street. The cock had not crowed for the fourth time next morning before Grandad had already reached Konotop. There used to be a fair there in those days: there were such crowds moving up and down the streets that it made one giddy to watch them. But as it was early the people were all stretched out on the ground asleep. Beside a cow would be lying a rakish lad with a nose as red as a bullfinch; a little further a pedlar-woman with flints, packets of blue, small shot and bread-rings was snoring where she sat; a gypsy lay under a cart, a dealer on a waggon of fish; while a Great Russian with a big beard, carrying belts and sleeves for sale, sprawled with his legs stuck out in the middle of the road . . . In fact, there was a rabble of all sorts, as there always is at fairs. My Grandad stopped to have a good look round. Meanwhile, little by little, there began to be a stir in the booths: the Jewesses made a clatter with the bottles; smoke rolled up in rings here and there, and the smell of hot doughnuts floated all over the encampment. It came into my Grandad's mind that he had no steel and tinder, nor tobacco with him; so he began sauntering about the fair. He had not gone twenty paces when he met a Zaporozhets. A gay spark, and you could see it at once from his face! Breeches red as fire, a full-skirted blue coat and bright-flowered girdle, a sabre at his side and a pipe with a fine brass chain right down to his heels – a regular Zaporozhets Cossack, that's all you can say! Ah, they were folk! One would stand up, stretch himself, stroke his gallant moustaches, clink with his iron heels – and off he would go! And how he would go! His legs would whirl round like a distaff in a woman's hands: his fingers would pluck at all the strings of the bandura like a whirlwind, and then pressing it to his side he would set off dancing, burst into song – his whole soul rejoicing . . . ! Yes, the good old days are over; you don't see such Cossacks nowadays! No. So they met. One word leads to another, it doesn't take long to make friends. They fell to chatting and chatting, so that Grandad quite forgot about his journey. They had a drinking bout, as at a wedding before Lent. Only at last I suppose they got tired of smashing the pots and flinging money to the crowd, and, indeed, one can't stay for ever at a fair! So the new friends agreed not to part, but to travel on together. It was getting on for evening when they rode out into the open country. The sun had set; here and there streaks of red glowed in the sky where it had been; the country was gay with different coloured fields like the checked petticoats our black-browed peasant wives wear on holidays.

Our Zaporozhets talked away like mad. Grandad and another jaunty fellow who had joined them began to think that there was a devil in him. Where did it all come from? Tales and stories of such marvels that sometimes Grandad held his sides and almost split his stomach with laughing. But the further they went the darker it grew and with it the gay talk grew more disconnected. At last our storyteller was altogether silent and started at the slightest rustle.

'Aha, neighbour!' they said to him, 'you have set to nodding in earnest: you are wishing now that you were at home and on the stove!'

'It's no use to have secrets from you,' he said, suddenly turning round and fixing his eyes upon them. 'Do you know that I sold my soul to the devil long ago?'

'As though that were something unheard of! Who hasn't had dealings with the devil in his day? That's why you must drain the cup of pleasure to the dregs, as the saying is.'

'Ah, lads! I would, but this night the fatal hour has come! Hey, brothers!' he said, clasping their hands, 'do not give me up! Watch over me one night! Never will I forget your friendship!'

Why not help a man in such trouble? Grandad vowed straight off he'd sooner have the forelock cut off his own head than let the devil sniff with his dog-nose at a Christian soul.

Our Cossacks would perhaps have ridden on further, if the whole sky had not clouded over as though with black homespun and it had not turned as dark as under a sheepskin. But there was a light twinkling in the distance and the horses, feeling that a stall was near, quickened their pace, pricking up their ears and staring into the darkness. It seemed as though the light flew to meet them, and the Cossacks saw before them a tavern, lurching over on one side like a peasant woman on her way home from a merry christening party. In those days taverns were not what they are now. There was nowhere for a good man to turn round or dance a jig – indeed, he had nowhere to lie down, even if the drink had got into his head and his legs began drawing rings all over the floor. The yard was all blocked up with dealers' waggons; under the sheds, in the mangers, in the barns men were snoring like tom-cats, one curled up and another sprawling. Only the tavern-keeper before his little pot-lamp was making cuts in a stick to mark the number of quarts and pints the dealers had drained.

Grandad after ordering a third of a pailful for the three of them went off to the barn. They lay down side by side. But before he had time to turn round he saw that his friends were already sleeping like the dead. Waking the third Cossack, the one who had joined them, Grandad reminded him of the promise given to their comrade. The man sat up, rubbed his eyes and fell asleep again. There was nothing for it, he had to watch alone. To drive away sleep in some way, he examined all the waggons, looked at the horses, lighted his pipe, came back and sat down again beside his comrades. All was still, it seemed as though not a fly were moving. Then he fancied something grey poked out its horns from a waggon close by . . . Then his eyes began to close, so that he was obliged to rub them every minute with his fist and to keep them open with the rest of the vodka. But soon, when they were a little clearer, everything had vanished. At last a little later something queer showed itself again under the waggon . . . Grandad opened his eyes as wide as he could, but the cursed sleepiness made everything misty before them; his hands felt numb, his head rolled back and he fell into such a sound sleep that he lay as though he were dead. Grandad slept for hours, and he only sprang up on his feet when the sun was baking his shaven head. After stretching twice and scratching his back, he noticed that there were no longer so many waggons standing there as in the evening. The dealers, it seemed, had trailed off before dawn. He looked for his companions – the Cossack was still asleep, but the Zaporozhets was gone. No one could tell him anything when he asked; only his topcoat was still lying in the same place. Grandad was frightened and didn't know what to think. He went to look for the horses – no sign of his or the Zaporozhets'! What could that mean? Supposing the Evil One had taken the Zaporozhets, who had taken the horses? Thinking it over, Grandad concluded that probably the devil had come on foot, and as it's a good journey to hell he had carried off his horse. He was terribly upset at not having kept his Cossack word.

'Well,' he thought, 'there is nothing to be done, I will go on foot. Maybe I shall come across some horse-dealer on his way from the fair. I shall manage somehow to buy a horse.' But when he reached for his cap, his cap was not there either. Grandad wrung his hands when he remembered that the day before he had changed caps for a time with the Zaporozhets. Who else could have carried it off if not the devil himself! A nice mess with the Hetman's favour! A nice job he'd made of taking the writing for the Tsaritsa! At this point my Grandad fell to bestowing such names on the devil as I fancy must have set him sneezing more than once in hell. But scolding is not much use, and however often my Grandad scratched his head, he could not think of any plan. What was he to do? He turned to take counsel from others: he got together all the good folk who were in the tavern at the time, dealers and simple wayfarers, told them how it all happened and what a misfortune had befallen him. A long time the dealers pondered. Leaning their chins on their whips, they shook their heads and said that they had never heard of such a marvel in Christendom as a devil carrying off a Hetman's letter. Others added that when the devil or a Great Russian stole anything, you might whistle for it. Only the tavern-keeper sat silent in the corner. Grandad went up to him, too. When a man says nothing, you may be sure he thinks the more. But the tavern-keeper was sparing of his words, and if Grandad had not felt in his pocket for five silver coins, he might have gone on standing before him to no purpose.

'I will tell you how to find the writing,' said the tavern-keeper, leading him aside. His words lifted a weight from Grandad's heart. 'I see from your eyes that you are a Cossack and not a woman. Mind now! Near the tavern you will find a turning on the right into the forest. As soon as it begins to grow dark you must be ready to start. There are gypsies living in the forest and they come out of their dens to forge iron on nights on which none but witches go abroad on their oven-rakes. What their real trade is you had best not enquire. There will be much knocking in the forest, only do not you go where you hear the knocking; there'll be a little path facing you near a burnt tree, go by that little path, go on and on . . . The thorns may scratch you, the thick nut bushes may block the path, but you still go on; and when you come to a little stream, only then you may stop. There you will see whom you need. But forget not to take in your pockets that for which pockets are made . . . You understand, both devils and men prize that.' Saying this the tavern-keeper went off to his corner and would not say another word.

My Grandad was by no means one of the fainthearted brigade; if he met a wolf, he would take him by the tail straight away; if he used his fist among the Cossacks, they would fall to the ground like pears. But a shudder ran down him when he stepped into the forest on such a dark night. Not one little star in the sky. Dark and dim as a wine-cellar; there was no sound except far, far overhead a cold wind sporting in the treetops, and the trees like the heads of drunken Cossacks wagged recklessly while their leaves whispered a tipsy song. And there was such a cold blast that Grandad thought of his sheepskin, and all at once it was as though a hundred hammers began tapping in the forest with a noise that set his ears ringing. And the whole forest was lit up for a moment as though by summer lightning. At once Grandad caught sight of a little path winding between the bushes. And here was the burnt tree and here were the thorn bushes! So everything was as he had been told; no, the tavern-keeper had not deceived him. It was not altogether pleasant tearing his way through the prickly bushes; he had never in his life known the damned thorns and twigs scratch so badly. He was almost crying out at every step. Little by little he came out into an open place, and as far as he could see the trees seemed wider apart, and as he went on he came upon bigger trees than he had ever seen on the further side of Poland. And behold, among the trees gleamed a little stream, dark like tempered steel. For a long time Grandad stopped on the bank, looking in all directions. On the other bank a light was twinkling; it seemed every minute on the point of going out, and then was reflected again in the stream, trembling like a Pole in the hands of Cossacks. And here was the little bridge!

'Well, maybe none but the devil's chariot crosses by it.' Grandad stepped out boldly, however, and before another man would have had time to get out his horn and take a pinch of snuff he was on the other side. Only now he discerned that there were people sitting round a fire, and such charming pig-faces that at any other time God knows what he would not have given to escape their acquaintance. But now there was no help for it, he had to make friends with them. So Grandad swung off a low bow, saying: 'God help you, good people!'

Not one nodded his head; they all sat in silence and kept dropping something into the fire. Seeing one place empty Grandad without more ado sat down. The charming pig-faces said nothing. Grandad said nothing either. For a long time they sat in silence. Grandad was already beginning to be bored; he fumbled in his pocket, pulled out his pipe, looked round – not one of them glanced at him.

'Well, your worships, will you be so kind; as a matter of fact, in a manner of speaking . . . ' (Grandad had knocked about the world a good bit and knew how to turn a phrase, and maybe even if he had been before the Tsar he would not have been at a loss.)

'In a manner of speaking, not to forget myself nor to slight you – a pipe I have, but that with which to light it I lack.' To this speech, too, there was not a word. Only one of the pig-faces thrust a hot brand straight in Grandad's face, so that if he had not turned aside a little, he might have parted with one eye for ever. At last, seeing that time was being wasted, he made up his mind to tell his story whether the unclean race would listen or not. They pricked up their ears and stretched out their paws. Grandad guessed what that meant; he pulled out all the money he had with him and flung it to them as though to dogs. As soon as he had flung the money, everything was in a turmoil before him, the earth shook and all at once – he never knew how to explain this part – he found himself almost in hell itself.

'Merciful heavens!' groaned my Grandad when he had taken a good look round. What marvels were here! One ugly face after another, as the saying is. The witches were as many as the snowflakes that fall sometimes at Christmas. They were all dressed up and painted like fine ladies at a fair. And all the lot of them were dancing some sort of devil's jig as though they were drunk. What a dust they raised, God help us! Any Christian would have shuddered to see how high the devils skipped. In spite of his terror, my Grandad fell a-laughing when he saw the devils with their dogs' faces on their little German legs, wag their tails, twist and turn about the witches, like our lads about the pretty girls, while the musicians beat on their cheeks with their fists as though they were tambourines and whistled with their noses as though they were horns. As soon as they saw Grandad, they pressed round him in a crowd. Pig-faces, dog-faces, goat-faces, bustard[36]-faces and horse-faces – all craned forward, and here they were actually trying to kiss him. Grandad could not help spitting, he was so disgusted! At last they caught hold of him and made him sit down at a table, as long, maybe, as the road from Konotop to Baturin.[37]

'Well, this is not altogether so bad!' thought Grandad, seeing on the table pork, sausages, onion minced with cabbage and many other dainties. 'The hellish rabble doesn't keep the fasts, it seems.'

My Grandad, I may as well tell you, was by no means averse to good fare on occasion. He ate with good appetite, the dear man, and so without wasting words he pulled towards him a bowl of sliced bacon fat and a smoked ham, took up a fork not much smaller than those with which a peasant pitches hay, picked out the most solid piece, laid it on a piece of bread – and lo and behold! – put it in another mouth just close beside his very ear, and, indeed, there was the sound of another fellow's jaws chewing it and clacking with his teeth, so that all the table could hear. Grandad didn't mind; he took up another piece, and this time it seemed as though he had caught it with his lips, but again it did not go down his gullet. A third time he tried – again he missed it. Grandad flew into a rage; he forgot his fright and in whose claws he was, and ran up to the witches: 'Do you mean to laugh at me, you brood of Herod?[38] If you don't this very minute give me back my Cossack cap – may I be a Catholic if I don't twist your pig-snouts to the wrong side of your heads!'

He had finished the last word when the monsters grinned and set up such a roar of laughter that it sent a chill to my Grandad's heart.

'Good!' shrieked one of the witches, whom my Grandad took to be the leader among them because she was almost the greatest beauty of the lot, 'we will give you back your cap, but not until you win it back from us in three games of "Fools"!'

What was he to do? For a Cossack to sit down and play 'Fools' with a lot of women! Grandad kept refusing and refusing, but in the end sat down. They brought the cards, a greasy pack such as we only see used by priests' wives to tell the girls their fortunes and what their husbands will be like.

'Listen!' barked the witch again: 'if you win one game, the cap is yours; if you are left "Fool" in every one of the three games, it's no use your fuming, you'll never see your cap nor maybe the world again!'

'Deal, deal, you old witch! What will be, will be.'

Well, the cards were dealt. Grandad picked up his – he couldn't bear to look at them; they were such rubbish; as though to mock him, not a single trump. Of the other suits the highest was a ten and he hadn't even a pair; while the witch kept giving him five at once. It was his fate to be left 'Fool'! As soon as Grandad was left 'Fool,' the monsters began neighing, barking, and grunting on all sides: 'Fool, fool, fool!'

'Shout till you split, you devils,' cried Grandad, putting his fingers to his ears.

'Well,' he thought, 'the witch didn't play fair, now I am going to deal myself.' He dealt; he turned up the trump and looked at his cards; they were first-rate, he had trumps. And at first things could not have gone better; till the witch put down five cards with kings among them.

Grandad had nothing in his hand but trumps! Quick as thought he beat all the kings with trumps!

'Ha–ha! but that's not like a Cossack! What are you covering them with, neighbour?'

'What with? With trumps!'

'Maybe to your thinking they are trumps, but to our thinking they are not!'

Lo and behold! The cards were really of another suit! What devilry was this? A second time he was 'Fool' and the devils set off splitting their throats again: 'Fool! fool!' so that the table rocked and the cards danced upon it.

Grandad flew into a passion; he dealt for the last time. Again he had a good hand. The witch put down five again; Grandad covered them and took from the pack a handful of trumps.

'Trump!' he shouted, flinging a card on the table so that it spun round like a basket; without saying a word she covered it with the eight of another suit.

'What are you beating my trump with, old devil?'

The witch lifted her card and under it was the six of another suit not trumps.

'What devilish trickery!' said Grandad, and in his vexation he struck the table with his fist as hard as he could. Luckily the witch had a poor hand; this time as luck would have it Grandad had pairs. He began drawing cards out of the pack, but it was of no use; such rubbish came that Grandad let his hands fall. There was not one good card in the pack. So he just played anything – a six. The witch had to take it, she could not cover it. 'So there! What do you say to that? Ay, ay! there is something wrong, I'll be bound!' Then on the sly under the table Grandad made the sign of the cross over the cards, and behold – he had in his hand the ace, king, and knave of trumps, and the card he had just played was not a six, but the queen!

'Well, I've been the fool! King of trumps! Well, have you taken it? Ay, you brood of cats! Would you like the ace too? The ace! The knave . . . !'

A tumult arose in hell; the witch went into convulsions and all of a sudden the cap flew flop into Grandad's face.

'No, no, that's not enough!' shouted Grandad, plucking up his courage and putting on his cap. 'If my gallant horse is not standing before me at once, may a thunderbolt strike me dead in this foul place, if I do not make the sign of the holy cross over all of you!' And he was just raising his hand to do it when the horse's bones rattled before him.

'Here is your horse!'

The poor man burst out crying like a silly child as he looked at them. He grieved for his old comrade!

'Give me some sort of a horse,' he said, 'to get out of your den!' A devil cracked a whip – a horse like fire rose up under him and Grandad flew upwards like a bird.

Terror came over him, however, when the horse, heeding neither shout nor rein, galloped over ditches and bogs. The places he went through were such that it made him shudder at the mere telling of it. He looked down and was more terrified than ever: an abyss, a fearful precipice! But that was nought to the satanic beast; he leapt straight over it. Grandad tried to hold on; he could not. Over tree-stumps, over hillocks he flew headlong into a ditch, and fell so hard on the ground at the bottom that it seemed he had breathed his last. Anyway, he could remember nothing of what happened to him then; and when he came to himself a little and looked about him it was broad daylight; he caught glimpses of familiar places and found himself lying on the roof of his own hut.

Grandad crossed himself as he climbed down. What devils' tricks! Damn it all! What marvellous things befall a man! He looked at his hands, they were all bathed in blood; he looked into a butt of water – and his face was the same. Washing himself thoroughly that he might not scare the children, he went quietly into the hut, and what did he see! The children staggered back towards him and pointed in alarm, saying: 'Look! Look! Mother's jumping like mad!' And, indeed, his wife was sitting asleep before her wool-comb, holding her distaff in her hands and in her sleep was bouncing up and down on the bench. Grandad, taking her gently by the hand, woke her. 'Good-morning, wife! Are you quite well?' For a long while she gazed at him with staring eyes, but at last recognised Grandad and told him that she had dreamed that the stove was riding round the hut shovelling out with a spade the pots and tubs . . . and devil knows what else.

'Well,' said Grandad, 'you have had it asleep, I have had it awake, I see I must have our hut blessed; but I cannot linger now.'

Saying this Grandad rested a little, then got out his horse and did not stop by day or by night till he arrived and gave the writing to the Tsaritsa herself. There Grandad beheld such wonderful things that for long after he used to tell the tale: how they brought him to the palace, and it so high that if you were to set ten huts one on top of another then they maybe would not be high enough; how he glanced into one room – nothing, into another – nothing, into a third still nothing, into a fourth even, nothing, but in the fifth there she was sitting in her golden crown, in a new grey gown and red boots, eating golden dumplings; how she had bade them fill a whole cap with five-rouble notes for him; how . . . I can't remember it all! As for all his bobbery with the devils, Grandad forgot even to think about it, and, if it happened that someone reminded him of it, Grandad would say nothing, as though the matter did not concern him, and we had the greatest pains to persuade him to tell us how it had all happened. And seemingly to punish him for not rushing out at once after that to have the hut blessed, every year just at that same time a strange thing happened to his wife – she would dance and nothing would stop her. Whatever they did, her legs would go their own way and something seemed nudging her to dance.

EVENINGS ON A FARM
NEAR DIKANKA

Part Two

Preface

Here is a second part for you, and I had better say the last one! I did not want, I did not at all want to bring it out. One ought not to outstay one's welcome. I must tell you they are already beginning to laugh at me in the village. 'The old fellow has gone silly,' they say, 'he is amusing himself with children's toys in his old age!' And, indeed, it is high time to rest. I expect you imagine, dear readers, that I am only pretending to be old. Pretend, indeed, when I have no teeth left in my mouth! Now if anything soft comes my way I manage to chew it, but I can't tackle anything hard. So here is another book for you! Only don't scold me! It is not nice to scold at parting, especially when God only knows whether one will soon meet again. In this book you will find stories told by people you do not know at all, except, perhaps, Foma Grigoryevitch. That gentleman in the pea-green coat who talked in such fine language that many of the wits even from Great Russia could not understand him, has not been here for a long time. He never looked in upon us since he quarrelled with us all. I did not tell you about it, did I? It was a regular comedy. Last year, some time in the summer, I believe it was on my Saint's Day, I had visitors to see me . . . (I must tell you, dear readers, that my neighbours, God give them good health, do not forget the old man.) It is fifty years since I began keeping my name-day; but just how old I am neither I nor my old woman could say. It must be somewhere about seventy. The priest at Dikanka, Father Harlampy, knew when I was born, but I am sorry to say he has been dead these fifty years. So I had visitors to see me: Zahar Kirilovitch Tchuhopupenko, Stepan Ivanovitch Kurotchka, Taras Ivanovitch Smachnenky, the assessor Harlampy Kirilovitch Hlosta; there was another one . . . I forget his name . . . Osip . . . Osip . . . Upon my soul, every one in Mirgorod knows him! Whenever he begins speaking he snaps his fingers and put his arms akimbo . . . Well, bless the man! I shall think of it presently. The gentleman from Poltava whom you know already came too. Foma Grigoryevitch I do not count, he is one of ourselves. Everybody talked (I must tell you that our conversation is never about trifles; I always like seemly conversation, so as to combine pleasure and profit, as the saying is) – we discussed how to pickle apples. My old woman began saying that first you had to wash the apples thoroughly, then put them to soak in kvass and then . . . 'All that is no use whatever!' the gentleman from

Poltava interrupted, thrusting his hand into his pea-green coat and pacing about the room majestically, 'not the slightest use! First you must sprinkle them with tansy[39] and then . . . ' Well, I ask you, dear readers, did you ever hear of apples being sprinkled with tansy? It is true, people do use blackcurrant leaves, swine-herb,[40] trefoil;[41] but to put in tansy . . . I have never heard of such a thing! And I fancy no one knows more about these things than my old woman. But there you are! I quietly drew him aside, as a good neighbour: 'Come now, Makar Nazarovitch, don't make people laugh! You are a man of some consequence; you have dined at the same table with the governor, as you told us yourself. Well, if you were to say anything like this there, you would set them all laughing at you!' And what do you imagine he said to that? Nothing! He spat on the floor, picked up his cap and went out. He might have said goodbye to somebody, he might have given us a nod; all we heard was his chaise with a bell on it drive up to the gate; he got into it and drove off. And a good thing too! We don't want guests like that. I tell you what, dear readers, there is nothing in the world worse than these high-class people. Because his uncle was a commissar once, he turns up his nose at every one. As though there were no rank in the world higher than a commissar! Thank God, there are people greater than commissars. No, I don't like these high-class people. Now Foma Grigoryevitch, for instance – he is not a high-class man, but just look at him: there is a serene dignity in his face. Even when he takes a pinch of ordinary snuff you can't help feeling respect for him. When he sings in the choir in the church there is no describing how touching it is. You feel as though you were melting . . . ! While that other . . . But there, God bless the man. He thinks we cannot do without his tales. But here, you see, is a book of them without him.

I promised you, I remember, that in this book there should be my story too. And I did mean to put it in. But I found that for my story I should need three books of this size, at least. I did think of printing it separately, but I thought better of it. I know you: you would be laughing at the old man. No, I shall not! Goodbye. It will be a long time before we meet again, if we ever do. But there, it would not matter to you if I never existed at all. One year will pass and then another – and none of you will remember or regret the old beekeeper,

RUDY PANKO

CHRISTMAS EVE

T HE LAST DAY before Christmas had passed. A clear winter
night had come; the stars peeped out; the moon rose majestically in
the sky to light good people and all the world so that all might
enjoy singing *kolyadki* and praising the Lord. It was freezing harder
than in the morning; but it was so still that the crunch of the snow
under the boot could be heard half a mile away. Not one group of lads
had appeared under the cottage windows yet; only the moon peeped in
at them stealthily as though calling to the girls who were dressing up in
their best to make haste and run out on the crunching snow. At that
moment the smoke rose in puffs from a cottage chimney and passed like
a cloud over the sky, and a witch, astride a broomstick, rose up in the air
together with the smoke.

If the assessor of Sorotchintsy, in his cap edged with lambskin
and cut like an Uhlan's,[42] in his dark blue greatcoat lined with black
astrakhan, had driven by at that minute with his three hired horses and
the fiendishly plaited whip with which it is his habit to urge on his
coachman, he would certainly have noticed her, for there is not a witch
in the world who could elude the eyes of the Sorotchintsy assessor. He
can count on his fingers how many little pigs every peasant-woman's
sow has farrowed and how much linen is lying in her chest and just
which of her clothes and household belongings her goodman pawns
on Sunday at the tavern. But the Sorotchintsy assessor did not drive
by, and, indeed, what business is it of his? He has his own district.
Meanwhile, the witch rose so high in the air that she was only a little
black patch gleaming up aloft. But wherever that little patch appeared,
there the stars one after another vanished. Soon the witch had gathered
a whole sleeveful of them. Three or four were still shining. All at once
from the opposite side another little patch appeared, grew larger, began
to lengthen out and was no longer a little patch. A short-sighted man
would never have made out what it was, even if he had put the wheels of
the Commissar's chaise on his nose by way of spectacles. At first it

looked like a regular German; the narrow little face, continually twisting and turning and sniffing at everything, ended in a little round heel, like our pigs' snouts; the legs were so thin, that if the mayor of Yareskovo had had legs like that, he would certainly have broken them in the first Cossack dance. But behind he was for all the world a district attorney in uniform, for he had a tail as long and pointed as the uniform coat-tails are nowadays. It was only from the goat-beard under his chin, from the little horns sticking upon his forehead, and from his being no whiter than a chimney-sweep, that one could tell that he was not a German or a district attorney, but simply the devil, who had one last night left him to wander about the wide world and teach good folk to sin. On the morrow when the first bells rang for matins, he would run with his tail between his legs straight off to his lair.

Meanwhile the devil stole silently up to the moon and stretched his hand out to seize it, but drew it back quickly as though he were scorched, sucked his fingers and danced about, then ran up from the other side and again skipped away and drew back his hand. But in spite of all his failures the sly devil did not give up his tricks. Running up, he suddenly seized the moon with both hands; grimacing and blowing, he kept flinging it from one hand to the other, like a peasant who has picked up an ember for his pipe with bare fingers; at last, he hurriedly put it in his pocket and ran on as though nothing had happened.

No one in Dikanka noticed that the devil had stolen the moon. It is true the district clerk, coming out of the tavern on all fours, saw the moon for no reason whatever dancing in the sky and swore he had to the whole village; but people shook their heads and even made fun of him. But what motive led the devil to this lawless act? Why, this was how it was; he knew that the rich Cossack, Tchub, had been invited by the sacristan to a supper of frumenty at which a kinsman of the sacristan's, who had come from the bishop's choir, wore a dark blue coat and could take the very lowest bass-note, the mayor, the Cossack Sverbyguz and some others were to be present, and at which besides the Christmas frumenty there were to be mulled vodka, saffron vodka and good things of all sorts. And meanwhile his daughter, the greatest beauty in the village, was left at home, and there was no doubt that the black-smith, a very strong and fine young fellow, would pay her a visit, and him the devil hated more than Father Kondrat's sermons. In his spare time the blacksmith had taken up painting and was reckoned the finest artist in the whole countryside. Even the Cossack officer L—ko, who was still strong and hearty in those days, sent for him to Poltava expressly to paint a paling fence round his house. All the bowls from which the Cossacks of Dikanka supped their beetroot soup had been painted by the blacksmith. He was a God-fearing man and often painted ikons of the saints: even now you may find his Luke the Evangelist in the church of T. But the triumph of his art was a picture painted on the church wall in the chapel on the right. In it he depicted St Peter on the Day of Judgement with the keys in his hand driving the Evil Spirit out of hell; the frightened devil was running in all directions, foreseeing his doom, while the sinners, who had been imprisoned before, were chasing him and striking him with whips, blocks of wood and anything they could get hold of. While the artist was working at this picture and painting it on a big wooden board, the devil did all he could to hinder him; he gave him a nudge on the arm, unseen, blew some ashes from the forge in the smithy and scattered them on the picture; but, in spite of it all, the work was finished, the picture was brought into the church and let into the wall of the side-chapel, and from that day the devil has sworn to revenge himself on the blacksmith.

He had only one night left to wander upon earth; but he was looking for some means of venting his wrath on the blacksmith that night. And that was why he made up his mind to steal the moon, reckoning that old Tchub was lazy and slow to move, and the sacristan's cottage a good long step away: the road passed by cross paths beside the mills and the graveyard and went round a ravine. On a moonlight night mulled vodka and saffron vodka might have tempted Tchub; but in such darkness it was doubtful whether any one could drag him from the stove and bring him out of the cottage. And the blacksmith, who had for a long time been on bad terms with him, would on no account have ventured, strong as he was, to visit the daughter when the father was at home.

And so, as soon as the devil had hidden the moon in his pocket, it was at once so dark all over the world that not every one could have found the way to the tavern, let alone to the sacristan's. The witch gave a shriek when she suddenly found herself in darkness. Then the devil running up, all bows and smiles, put his arm round her and began whispering in her ear the sort of thing that is usually whispered to all the female sex. Things are queerly arranged in our world! All who live in it are always trying to outdo and imitate one another. In old days the judge and the police-captain were the only ones in Mirgorod who used to wear cloth overcoats lined with sheepskin in the winter, while all the petty officials wore plain sheepskin; but nowadays the assessor and the chamberlain have managed to get themselves new cloth greatcoats lined with astrakhan. The year before last the treasury clerk and the district clerk bought dark blue duck at sixty kopecks the yard. The sexton has got himself nankeen trousers for the summer and a striped waistcoat of camel's hair. In fact every one tries to be somebody! When will folks give up being vain! I am ready to bet that many would be surprised to see the devil carrying on in that way. What is most annoying is that, no doubt, he fancies himself a handsome fellow, though his figure is a shameful sight. With a face, as Foma Grigoryevitch used to say, the abomination of abominations, yet even he plays the gallant! But in the sky and under the sky it was growing so dark that there was no seeing what followed between them.

'So you have not been to see the sacristan in his new cottage, mate?' said the Cossack Tchub coming out at his door to a tall lean peasant in a short sheepskin, whose stubby beard showed that for at least a fort-night it had not been touched by the broken piece of scythe with which for lack of a razor peasants usually shave their beards. 'There will be a fine drinking-party there tonight!' Tchub went on, grinning as he spoke. 'If only we are not late!'

Hereupon Tchub set straight the belt that closely girt his sheepskin, pulled his cap more firmly on his head, and gripped his whip, the terror and the menace of tiresome dogs; but glancing upwards, he stopped. 'What the devil! Look! Look, Panas . . . !'

'What?' articulated his friend, and he too turned his face upwards.

'What, indeed! There is no moon!'

'What a nuisance! There really is no moon.'

'That's just it, there isn't!' Tchub brought out with some annoyance at his friend's imperturbable indifference. 'You don't care, I'll be bound.'

'Well, what can I do about it?'

'Some devil,' Tchub went on, wiping his moustaches with his sleeve, 'must needs go and meddle – may he never have a glass of vodka to drink in the mornings, the dog! Upon my word, it's as though to mock us . . . As I sat indoors I looked out of the window and the night was lovely! It was light, the snow was sparkling in the moonlight; you could see everything as though it were day. And here before I'm out of the door, you can't see your hand before your face! May he break his teeth on a crust of buckwheat bread!'

Tchub went on grumbling and scolding for a long while, and at the same time he was hesitating what to decide. He had a desperate longing to gossip over all sorts of nonsense at the sacristan's, where no doubt the mayor was already sitting, as well as the bass choir-singer, and Mikita, the tar-dealer, who used to come once a fortnight on his way to

Poltava, and who cracked such jokes that all the village worthies held their sides with laughing. Already in his mind's eye Tchub saw the mulled vodka on the table. All this was alluring, it is true, but the darkness of the night recalled the charms of laziness, so dear to every Cossack. How nice it would be now to lie on the oven-step with his legs tucked under him, quietly smoking his pipe and listening through a luxurious drowsiness to the songs and carols of the light-hearted lads and lasses who gathered in groups under the windows! He would undoubtedly have decided on the latter course had he been alone; but for the two together, it was not so dreary and terrible to go through the dark night; besides he did not care to seem sluggish and cowardly to others. When he had finished scolding he turned again to his friend.

'So there is no moon, mate?'

'No!'

'It's strange really! Let me have a pinch of snuff! You have splendid snuff, mate! Where do you get it?'

'Splendid! Devil a bit of it!' answered the friend, shutting the birch-bark snuffbox with patterns pricked out upon it. 'It wouldn't make an old hen sneeze!'

'I remember,' Tchub still went on, 'the inn-keeper, Zuzulya, once brought me some snuff from Nyezhin. Ah, that was snuff! It was good snuff! So how is it to be, mate? It's dark, you know!'

'So maybe we'll stay at home,' his friend brought out, taking hold of the door-handle.

If his friend had not said that, Tchub would certainly have made up his mind to stay at home; but now something seemed egging him on to oppose it. 'No, mate, let us go! It won't do, we must go!'

Even as he was saying it, he was vexed with himself that he had said it. He very much disliked turning out on such a night, but it was a comfort to him that he was acting on his own decision and not following advice.

His friend looked round and scratched his shoulders with the handle of his whip, without the slightest sign of vexation on his face, like a man to whom it is a matter of complete indifference whether he sits at home or turns out – and the two friends set off on their road.

Now let us see what Tchub's daughter, the beauty, was doing all by herself. Before Oksana was seventeen, people were talking about nothing but her in almost the whole world, both on this side of Dikanka and on the other side of Dikanka. The lads were all at one in declaring that there never had been and never would be a finer girl in the village. Oksana heard and knew all that was said about her and, like a beauty, was full of caprices. If, instead of a checked skirt and an apron, she had been dressed as a lady, she could never have kept a servant. The lads ran after her in crowds, but, losing patience, by degrees forsook the wilful beauty, and turned to others who were not so spoilt. Only the black-smith was persistent and would not abandon his courtship, although he was treated not a whit better than the rest. When her father went out, Oksana spent a long while yet dressing herself in her best and prinking before a little looking-glass in a pewter frame; she could not tear herself away from admiring herself.

'What put it into folks' heads to spread it abroad that I am pretty?' she said, as it were without thinking, simply to talk to herself about something. 'Folks lie, I am not pretty at all!'

But the fresh living face reflected in the looking-glass, in its childish youthfulness, with its sparkling black eyes and inexpressibly charming smile that stirred the soul, at once proved the contrary.

'Can my black eyebrows and my eyes,' the beauty went on, still holding the mirror, 'be so beautiful that there are none like them in the world? What is there pretty in that turned-up nose, and in the cheeks and the lips? Is my black hair pretty? Ough, my curls might frighten one in the evening, they twist and twine round my head like long snakes! I see now that I am not pretty at all!' And, moving the looking-glass a little further away, she cried out: 'No, I am pretty! Ah, how pretty! Wonderful! What a joy I shall be to the man whose wife I become! How my husband will admire me! He'll be wild with joy. He will kiss me to death!'

'Wonderful girl!' whispered the blacksmith, coming in softly. 'And hasn't she a little conceit! She's been standing looking in the mirror for an hour and can't tear herself away, and praising herself aloud, too!'

'Yes, lads, I am a match for you? Just look at me!' The pretty coquette went on: 'how gracefully I step: my shift is embroidered with red silk. And the ribbons on my head! You will never see richer braid! My father bought me all this that the finest young man in the world may marry me.' And, laughing, she turned round and saw the blacksmith . . .

She uttered a shriek and stood still, coldly facing him.

The blacksmith's hands dropped helplessly to his sides.

It is hard to describe what the dark face of the lovely girl expressed. There was sternness in it, and through the sternness a sort of defiance of the embarrassed blacksmith, and at the same time a hardly perceptible flush of vexation delicately suffused her face; and all this was so mingled and so indescribably pretty that to give her a million kisses was the best thing that could have been done at the moment.

'Why have you come here?' was how Oksana began. 'Do you want me to shove you out of the door with a spade? You are all very clever at coming to see us. You sniff out in a minute when there are no fathers in the house. Oh, I know you! Well, is my chest ready!'

'It will be ready, my little heart, it will be ready after Christmas. If only you knew how I have worked at it; for two nights I didn't leave the smithy. But, there, no priest's wife will have a chest like it. The iron I bound it with is better than what I put on the officer's chariot, when I worked at Poltava. And how it will be painted! You won't find one like it if you wander over the whole neighbourhood with your little white feet! Red and blue flowers will be scattered over the whole ground. It will glow like fire. Don't be angry with me! Allow me at least to speak to you, to look at you!'

'Who's forbidding you? Speak and look!'

Hereupon she sat down on the bench, glanced again at the looking-glass and began arranging her hair. She looked at her neck, at her shift, embroidered in red silk, and a subtle feeling of complacency could be read on her lips and fresh cheeks, and was reflected in her eyes.

'Allow me to sit beside you,' said the blacksmith.

'Sit down,' said Oksana, with the same emotion still perceptible on her lips and in her gratified eyes.

'Wonderful, lovely Oksana, allow me to kiss you!' ventured the blacksmith, growing bolder, and he drew her towards him with the intention of snatching a kiss. But Oksana turned away her cheek, which had been exceeding close to the blacksmith's lips, and pushed him away.

'What more do you want? When there's honey he must have a spoonful! Go away, your hands are harder than iron. And you smell of smoke. I believe you have smeared me all over with your soot.'

Then she picked up the looking-glass and began prinking again.

'She does not love me!' the blacksmith thought to himself, hanging his head. 'It's all play to her while I stand before her like a fool and cannot take my eyes off her. And I should like to stand before her always and never to take my eyes off her! Wonderful girl! What would I not give to know what is in her heart, and whom she loves. But no, she cares for nobody. She is admiring herself; she is tormenting poor me, while I am so sad that everything is darkness to me. I love her as no man in the world ever has loved or ever will.'

'Is it true that your mother's a witch?' Oksana brought out, and she laughed. And the blacksmith felt that everything within him was laughing. That laugh echoed as it were at once in his heart and in his softly thrilling veins, and for all that his soul was vexed that he had not the right to kiss that sweetly laughing face.

'What care I for mother? You are father and mother to me and all that is precious in the world. If the Tsar summoned me and said: "Smith Vakula, ask me for all that is best in my kingdom, I will give you anything. I will bid them make you a golden forge and you shall work with silver hammers." "I don't care," I should say to the Tsar, "for precious stones or a golden forge nor for all your kingdom: give me rather my Oksana." '

'You see, what a fellow you are! Only my father's no fool either. You'll see that, when he doesn't marry your mother!' Oksana said, smiling slily. 'But the girls are not here . . . What's the meaning of it? We ought to have been singing long ago, I am getting tired of waiting.'

'Let them stay away, my beauty!'

'I should hope not! I expect the lads will come with them. And then there will be dances. I can fancy what funny stories they will tell!'

'So you'll be merry with them?'

'Yes, merrier than with you. Ah! Someone knocked; I expect it is the girls and the lads.'

'What's the use of my staying longer?' the blacksmith said to himself. 'She is jeering at me. I am no more to her than an old rusty horseshoe. But if that's so, anyway I won't let another man laugh at me. If only I see for certain that she likes someone better than me, I'll teach him to keep off . . .'

A knock at the door and a cry of 'Open!' ringing out sharply in the frost interrupted his reflections.

'Stay, I'll open the door,' said the blacksmith, and he went out intending in his vexation to break the ribs of any one who might be there.

The frost grew sharper, and up aloft it turned so cold that the devil kept hopping from one hoof to the other and blowing into his fists, trying to warm his frozen hands. And indeed it is small wonder that he should be cold, being used day after day to knocking about in hell, where, as we all know, it is not as cold as it is with us in winter, and where, putting on his cap and standing before the hearth, like a real cook, he fries sinners with as much satisfaction as a peasant-woman fries a sausage at Christmas.

The witch herself felt that it was cold, although she was warmly clad; and so, throwing her arms upwards, she stood with one foot out, and putting herself into the attitude of a man flying along on skates, without moving a single muscle, she dropped through the air, as though on an ice-slope, and straight into her chimney.

The devil set off after her in the same way. But as the creature is nimbler than any dandy in stockings, there is no wonder that he reached the top of the chimney almost on the neck of his mistress, and both found themselves in a roomy oven among the pots.

The witch stealthily moved back the oven door to see whether her son, Vakula, had invited visitors to the cottage; but seeing that there was no one, except the sacks that lay in the middle of the floor, she crept out of the oven, flung off her warm pelisse, set herself to rights, and no one could have told that she had been riding on a broom the minute before.

Vakula's mother was not more than forty years old. She was neither handsome nor ugly. Indeed, it is hard to be handsome at such an age. However, she was so clever at alluring even the steadiest Cossacks (who, it may not be amiss to observe, do not care much about beauty) that the mayor and the sacristan, Osip Nikiforovitch (if his wife were not at home, of course), and the Cossack, Korny Tchub, and the Cossack, Kassian Sverbyguz, were all dancing attendance on her. And it must be said to her credit that she was very skilful in managing them: not one of them dreamed that he had a rival. If a God-fearing peasant or a gentleman (as the Cossacks call themselves) wearing a cape with a hood went to church on Sunday or, if the weather was bad, to the tavern, how could he fail to look in on Soloha, eat curd dumplings with sour cream, and gossip in the warm cottage with its chatty and agreeable mistress? And the Cossack would purposely go a long way round before reaching the tavern, and would call that 'looking in on his way.' And when Soloha went to church on a holiday, dressed in a bright-checked *plahta* with a cotton *zapaska*,* and above it a dark blue overskirt on the back of which gold flourishes were embroidered, and took up her stand close to the right side of the choir, the sacristan would be sure to begin coughing and unconsciously screw up his eyes in her direction; the mayor would smooth his moustaches, begin twisting the curl behind his ear, and say to the man standing next to him: 'Ah, a nice woman, a devil of a woman!' Soloha would bow to each one of them, and each one would think that she was bowing to him alone.

But any one fond of meddling in other people's business would notice at once that Soloha was most gracious to the Cossack Tchub. Tchub was a widower. Eight stacks of corn always stood before his cottage. Two pairs of stalwart oxen poked their heads out of the wattled barn by

---

* A Little Russian garment consisting of two separate pieces of material, like two aprons, one worn in front and one at the back, making a skirt slit to the waist and there held together with a girdle. (*Translator's Note*)

the roadside and mooed every time they saw their crony, the cow, or their uncle, the stout bull, pass. A bearded billy-goat used to clamber on to the very roof, from which he would bleat in a harsh voice like the police-captain's, taunting the turkeys when they came out into the yard, and turning his back when he saw his enemies, the boys, who used to jeer at his beard. In Tchub's trunks there was plenty of linen and many full coats and old-fashioned over-dresses with gold lace on them; his wife had been fond of fine clothes. In his vegetable patch, besides poppies, cabbages and sunflowers, two fields were sown every year with tobacco. All this Soloha thought that it would not be amiss to join to her own farm, and, already reckoning in what good order it would be when it passed into her hands, she felt doubly well-disposed to old Tchub. And to prevent her son Vakula from courting Tchub's daughter and succeeding in getting possession of it all himself (then he would very likely not let her interfere in anything), she had recourse to the common manoeuvre of all dames of forty – that is, setting Tchub at loggerheads with the blacksmith as often as she could. Possibly these sly tricks and subtlety were the reason that the old women were beginning here and there, particularly when they had drunk a drop too much at some merry gathering, to say that Soloha was certainly a witch, that the lad Kizyakolupenko had seen a tail on her back no bigger than a peasant-woman's distaff; that, no longer ago than the Thursday before last, she had run across the road in the form of a black cat; that on one occasion a sow had run up to the priest's wife, had crowed like a cock, put Father Kondrat's cap on her head and run away again . . .

It happened that just when the old women were talking about this, a cowherd, Tymish Korostyavy, came up. He did not fail to tell them how in the summer, just before St Peter's Feast,[43] when he had lain down to sleep in the stable, putting some straw under his head, he saw with his own eyes a witch, with her hair down, in nothing but her shift, begin milking the cows, and he could not stir he was so spellbound, and she had smeared his lips with something so nasty that he was spitting the whole day afterwards. But all that was somewhat doubtful, for the only one who can see a witch is the assessor of Sorotchintsy. And so all the notable Cossacks waved their hands impatiently when they heard such tales. 'They are lying, the bitches!' was their usual answer.

After she had crept out of the stove and set herself to rights, Soloha, like a good housewife, began tidying up and putting everything in its place; but she did not touch the sacks. 'Vakula brought those in, let him take them out himself!' she thought. Meanwhile the devil, who had chanced to turn round just as he was flying into the chimney, had caught sight of Tchub arm-in-arm with his neighbour already a long way from home. Instantly he flew out of the chimney, cut across their road and began flinging up heaps of frozen snow in all directions. A blizzard sprang up. All was whiteness in the air. The snow zigzagged like network behind and in front and threatened to plaster up the eyes, the mouth and the ears of the friends. And the devil flew back to the chimney again in the firm conviction that Tchub would go back home with his neighbour, would find the blacksmith there and probably give him such a dressing-down that it would be a long time before he would be able to handle a brush and paint offensive caricatures.

As a matter of fact, as soon as the blizzard began and the wind blew straight in their faces, Tchub expressed his regret, and pulling his hood further down on his head showered abuse on himself, the devil and his friend. His annoyance was feigned, however. Tchub was really glad of the snowstorm. They had still eight times as far to go as they had gone already before they would reach the sacristan's. They turned round. The wind blew on the back of their heads, but they could see nothing through the whirling snow.

'Stay, mate! I fancy we are going wrong,' said Tchub, after walking on a little. 'I do not see a single cottage. Oh, what a snowstorm! You go a little that way, mate, and see whether you find the road, and meanwhile I'll look this way. It was the foul fiend put it into my head to go trudging out in such a storm! Don't forget to shout when you find the road. Oh what a heap of snow Satan has driven into my eyes!'

The road was not to be seen, however. Tchub's friend, turning off, wandered up and down in his long boots, and at last came straight upon the tavern. This lucky find so cheered him that he forgot everything and, shaking the snow off, walked straight in, not worrying himself in the least about the friend he had left on the road. Meanwhile Tchub fancied that he had found the road. Standing still, he fell to shouting at the top of his voice, but, seeing that his friend did not appear, he made up his mind to go on alone. After walking on a little he saw his own cottage. Snowdrifts lay all about it and on the roof. Clapping his frozen hands together, he began knocking at the door and shouting peremptorily to his daughter to open it.

'What do you want here?' the blacksmith called grimly, as he came out.

Tchub, recognising the blacksmith's voice, stepped back a little. 'Ah, no, it's not my cottage,' he said to himself. 'The blacksmith doesn't come into my cottage. Though, as I come to look well, it is not the blacksmith's either. Whose cottage can it be? I know! I didn't recognise it! It's where lame Levtchenko lives, who has lately married a young wife. His is the only cottage that is like mine. I did think it was a little queer that I had reached home so soon. But Levtchenko is at the sacristan's now, I know that. Why is the blacksmith here . . . ? Ah, a–ha! He comes to see his young wife. So that's it! Good . . . ! Now I understand it all.'

'Who are you and what are you hanging about at people's doors for?' said the blacksmith more grimly than before, coming closer up to him.

'No, I am not going to tell him who I am,' thought Tchub. 'He'll give me a good drubbing, I shouldn't wonder, the damned brute.' And, disguising his voice, he answered: 'It's I, good man! I have come for your diversion to sing carols under your windows.'

'Go to the devil with your carols!' Vakula shouted angrily. 'Why are you standing there? Do you hear! Be off with you.'

Tchub already had that prudent intention; but it annoyed him to be forced to obey the blacksmith's orders. It seemed as though some evil spirit nudged his arm and compelled him to say something contradictory. 'Why are you bawling like that?' he said in the same voice. 'I want to sing carols and that's enough!'

'A–ha! I see words aren't enough for you!' And upon that Tchub felt a very painful blow on his shoulder.

'So I see you are beginning to fight now!' he said, stepping back a little.

'Be off, be off!' shouted the blacksmith, giving Tchub another shove.

'Well, you are!' said Tchub in a voice that betrayed pain, annoyance and timidity. 'You are fighting in earnest, I see, and hitting pretty hard, too.'

'Be off, be off!' shouted the blacksmith, and slammed the door.

'Look, how he swaggered!' said Tchub when he was left alone in the road. 'Just try going near him! What a fellow! He's a somebody! Do you suppose I won't have the law of you? No, my dear lad, I am going straight to the Commissar. I'll teach you! I don't care if you are a blacksmith and a painter. But I must look at my back and shoulders; I believe they are black and blue. The devil's son must have hit hard. It's a pity that it is cold, and I don't want to take off my pelisse. You wait, you fiend of a blacksmith; may the devil give you a drubbing and your smithy, too; I'll make you dance! Ah, the damned rascal! But, I say, he is not at home, now. I expect Soloha is all alone. H'm . . . it's not far off, I might go! It's such weather now that no one will come in on us. There's no saying what may happen . . . Oh dear, how hard that damned blacksmith did whack!'

Here Tchub, rubbing his back, set off in a different direction. The agreeable possibilities awaiting him in a tryst with Soloha took off the pain a little and made him insensible even to the frost, the crackling of which could be heard on all the roads in spite of the howling of the storm. At moments a look of mawkish sweetness came into his face, though the blizzard soaped his beard and moustaches with snow more briskly than any barber who tyrannically holds his victim by the nose. But if everything had not been hidden by the criss-cross of the snow, Tchub might have been seen long afterwards stopping and rubbing his back as he brought out: 'The damned blacksmith did whack hard!' and then going on his way again.

While the nimble dandy with the tail and goat-beard was flying out of the chimney and back again into the chimney, the pouch which hung on a shoulder-belt at his side and in which he had put the stolen moon chanced to catch in something in the stove and came open – and the moon took advantage of this accident to fly up through the chimney of Soloha's cottage and to float smoothly through the sky. Everything was flooded with light. It was as though there had been no snowstorm. The snow sparkled, a broad silvery plain, studded with crystal stars. The frost seemed less cold. Groups of lads and girls appeared with sacks. Songs rang out, and under almost every cottage window were crowds of carol-singers.

How wonderful is the light of the moon! It is hard to put into words how pleasant it is on such a night to mingle in a group of singing, laughing girls and among lads ready for every jest and sport which the gaily smiling night can suggest. It is warm under the thick pelisse; the cheeks glow brighter than ever from the frost and Old Sly himself prompts to mischief.

Groups of girls with sacks burst into Tchub's cottage and gathered round Oksana. The blacksmith was deafened by the shouts, the laughter, the stories. They vied with one another in telling the beauty some bit of news, in emptying their sacks and boasting of the little loaves, the sausages and curd dumplings of which they had already gathered a fair harvest from their singing. Oksana seemed to be highly pleased and delighted, she chatted first with one and then with another and laughed without ceasing.

With what envy and vexation the blacksmith looked at this gaiety, and this time he cursed the carol-singing, though he was passionately fond of it himself.

'Oh, Odarka!' said the light-hearted beauty, turning to one of the girls, 'you have some new slippers. Ah, how pretty! And with gold on them! It's nice for you, Odarka, you have a man who will buy you anything, but I have no one to get me such splendid slippers.'

'Don't grieve, my precious Oksana!' put in the blacksmith. 'I will get you slippers such as not many a lady wears.'

'You!' said Oksana, with a rapid and haughty glance at him. 'I should like to know where you'll get hold of slippers such as I could put on my feet. Perhaps you will bring me the very ones the Tsaritsa wears?'

'You see the sort she wants!' cried the crowd of girls, laughing.

'Yes!' the beauty went on proudly, 'all of you be my witnesses: if the blacksmith Vakula brings me the very slippers the Tsaritsa wears, here's my word on it, I'll marry him that very day.'

The girls carried off the capricious beauty with them.

'Laugh away! laugh away!' thought the blacksmith as he followed them out. 'I laugh at myself! I wonder and can't think what I have done with my senses! She does not love me – well, let her go! As though there were no one in the world but Oksana. Thank God, there are lots of fine girls besides her in the village. And what is Oksana? She'll never make a good housewife; the only thing she is good at is dressing up. No, it's enough! It's time I gave up playing the fool!'

But at the very time when the blacksmith was making up his mind to be resolute, some evil spirit set floating before him the laughing image of Oksana saying mockingly, 'Get me the Tsaritsa's slippers, blacksmith, and I will marry you!' Everything within him was stirred and he could think of nothing but Oksana.

The crowds of carol-singers, the lads in one party and the girls in another, hurried from one street to the next. But the blacksmith went on and saw nothing, and took no part in the merrymaking which he had once loved more than any.

Meanwhile the devil was making love in earnest at Soloha's: kissed her hand with the same airs and graces as the assessor does the priest's daughter's, put his hand on his heart, sighed and said bluntly that, if she would not consent to gratify his passion and reward his devotion in the usual way, he was ready for anything: would fling himself in the water and let his soul go straight to hell. Soloha was not so cruel; besides, the devil as we know was alone with her. She was fond of seeing a crowd hanging about her and was rarely without company. That evening, however, she was expecting to spend alone, because all the noteworthy inhabitants of the village had been invited to keep Christmas Eve at the sacristan's. But it turned out otherwise: the devil had only just urged his suit, when suddenly they heard a knock and the voice of the stalwart mayor. Soloha ran to open the door, while the nimble devil crept into a sack that was lying on the floor.

The mayor, after shaking the snow off his cap and drinking a glass of vodka from Soloha's hand, told her that he had not gone to the sacristan's because it had begun to snow; and, seeing a light in her cottage, had dropped in, meaning to spend the evening with her.

The mayor had hardly had time to say this when they heard a knock at the door and the voice of the sacristan. 'Hide me somewhere,' whispered the mayor. 'I don't want to meet the sacristan now.'

Soloha thought for some time where to hide so bulky a visitor; at last she selected the biggest coal-sack. She shot the coal out into a barrel, and the stalwart mayor, moustaches, head, pelisse and all, crept into the sack.

The sacristan walked in, clearing his throat and rubbing his hands, and told her that no one had come to his party and that he was heartily glad of this opportunity to enjoy a visit to her and was not afraid of the snowstorm. Then he went closer to her and, with a cough and a smirk, touched her plump bare arm with his long fingers and said with an air expressive both of slyness and satisfaction: 'And what have you here, magnificent Soloha?' and saying this he stepped back a little.

'How do you mean? My arm, Osip Nikiforovitch!' answered Soloha.

'H'm! Your arm! He – he – he!' cried the sacristan, highly delighted with his opening. And he paced up and down the room.

'And what have you here, incomparable Soloha . . . ?' he said with the same air, going up to her again, lightly touching her neck and skipping back again in the same way.

'As though you don't see, Osip Nikiforovitch!' answered Soloha; 'my neck and my necklace on my neck.'

'H'm! A necklace on your neck! He – he – he!' and the sacristan walked again up and down the room, rubbing his hands.

'And what have you here, incomparable Soloha . . . ?' There's no telling what the sacristan (a carnal-minded man) might have touched next with his long fingers, when suddenly they heard a knock at the door and the voice of the Cossack Tchub.

'Oh dear, someone who's not wanted!' cried the sacristan in alarm. 'What now if I am caught here, a person of my position . . . ! It will come to Father Kondrat's ears . . .'

But the sacristan's apprehensions were really of a different nature; he was more afraid that his doings might come to the knowledge of his better-half, whose terrible hand had already turned his thick mane into a very scanty one. 'For God's sake, virtuous Soloha!' he said, trembling all over, 'your loving-kindness, as it says in the Gospel of St Luke, chapter thirt . . . thirt . . .[44] What a knocking, oh dear, what a knocking! Ough, hide me somewhere!'

Soloha turned the coal out of another sack, and the sacristan, whose proportions were not too ample, crept into it and settled at the very bottom, so that another half-sack of coal might have been put in on the top of him.

'Good-evening, Soloha!' said Tchub, as he came into the cottage. 'Maybe you didn't expect me, eh? You didn't, did you? Perhaps I am in the way . . . ?' Tchub went on with a good-humoured and significant expression on his face, which betrayed that his slow-moving mind was at work and preparing to utter some sarcastic and amusing jest.

'Maybe you had some entertaining companion here . . . ! Maybe you have someone in hiding already? Eh?' And enchanted by this observation of his, Tchub laughed, inwardly triumphant at being the only man who enjoyed Soloha's favour. 'Come, Soloha, let me have a drink of vodka now. I believe my throat's frozen stiff with this damned frost. God has sent us weather for Christmas Eve! How it has come on, do you hear, Soloha, how it has come on . . . ? Ah, my hands are stiff, I can't unbutton my sheepskin! How the storm has come on . . . '

'Open the door!' a voice rang out in the street accompanied by a thump on the door.

'Someone is knocking,' said Tchub standing still.

'Open!' the shout rang out louder still.

'It's the blacksmith!' cried Tchub, catching up his pelisse. 'I say, Sohola, put me where you like; for nothing in the world will I show myself to that damned brute. May he have a pimple as big as a haycock[45] under each of his eyes, the devil's son!'

Soloha, herself alarmed, flew about like one distraught and, forgetting what she was doing, signed to Tchub to creep into the very same sack in which the sacristan was already sitting. The poor sacristan dared not betray his pain by a cough or a groan when the heavy Cossack sat down almost on his head and put a frozen boot on each side of his face.

The blacksmith walked in, not saying a word nor removing his cap, and almost fell down on the bench. It could be seen that he was in a very bad humour.

At the very moment when Soloha was shutting the door after him, someone knocked at the door again. This was the Cossack Sverbyguz. He could not be hidden in the sack, because no sack big enough could be found anywhere. He was more corpulent than the mayor and taller than Tchub's neighbour Panas. And so Soloha led him into the kitchen-garden to hear from him there all that he had to tell her.

The blacksmith looked absent-mindedly at the corners of his cottage, listening from time to time to the voices of the carol-singers floating far away through the village. At last his eyes rested on the sacks. 'Why are those sacks lying there? They ought to have been cleared away long ago. This foolish love has turned me quite silly. Tomorrow's Christmas and rubbish of all sorts is still lying about the cottage. I'll carry them to the smithy!'

Hereupon the blacksmith stooped down to the huge sacks, tied them up more tightly and prepared to hoist them on his shoulders. But it was evident that his thoughts were straying, God knows where; or he would have heard how Tchub gasped when the hair of his head was twisted in the string that tied the sack and the stalwart mayor began hiccupping quite distinctly.

'Can nothing drive that wretched Oksana out of my head?' the black-smith was saying. 'I don't want to think about her; but I keep thinking and thinking and, as luck will have it, of her and nothing else. How is it that thoughts creep into the mind against the will? The devil! The sacks seem to have grown heavier than they were! Something besides coal must have been put into them. I am a fool! I forget that now everything seems heavier to me. In old days I could bend and unbend again a copper coin or a horseshoe with one hand, and now I can't lift sacks of coal. I shall be blown over by the wind next . . . No!' he cried, pulling himself together after a pause, 'I am not a weak woman! I won't let any one make a mock of me! If there were ten such sacks, I would lift them all.' And he briskly hoisted on his shoulders the sacks which two stalwart men could not have carried. 'I'll take this one too,' he went on, picking up the little one at the bottom of which the devil lay curled up. 'I believe I put my tools in this one.' Saying this he went out of the hut whistling the song: 'I can't be bothered with a wife.'

The singing, laughter and shouts sounded louder and louder in the streets. The crowds of jostling people were reinforced by newcomers from neighbouring villages. The lads were full of mischief and mad pranks. Often among the carols some gay song was heard which one of the young Cossacks had made up on the spot. All at once one of the crowd would let out a begging New Year's song instead of a carol and bawl at the top of his voice:

> 'Christmas faring!
> Be not sparing!
> A tart or pie, please!

Bowl of porridge!
String of sausage!'

A roar of laughter rewarded the wag. Little windows were thrown up and the withered hand of an old woman (the old women, together with the sedate fathers, were the only people left indoors) was thrust out with a sausage or a piece of pie.

The lads and the girls vied with one another in holding out their sacks and catching their booty. In one place the lads, coming together from all sides, surrounded a group of girls. There was loud noise and clamour; one flung a snowball, another pulled away a sack full of all sorts of good things. In another place, the girls caught a lad, gave him a kick and sent him flying headlong with his sack into the snow. It seemed as though they were ready to make merry the whole night through. And, as though of design, the night was so splendidly warm. And the light of the moon seemed brighter still from the glitter of the snow.

The blacksmith stood still with his sacks. He fancied he heard among the crowd of girls the voice and shrill laugh of Oksana. Every vein in his body throbbed; flinging the sacks on the ground so that the sacristan at the bottom groaned over the bruise he received, and the mayor gave a loud hiccup, he strolled with the little sack on his shoulders together with a group of lads after a crowd of girls, among whom he heard the voice of Oksana.

'Yes, it is she! She stands like a queen, her black eyes sparkling. A handsome lad is telling her something. It must be amusing, for she is laughing. But she is always laughing.' As it were unconsciously, he could not say how, the blacksmith squeezed his way through the crowd and stood beside her.

'Oh, Vakula, you here! Good-evening!' said the beauty, with the smile which almost drove Vakula mad. 'Well, have you sung many carols? Oh, but what a little sack! And have you got the slippers that the Tsaritsa wears? Get me the slippers and I will marry you . . . !' And laughing she ran off with the other girls.

The blacksmith stood as though rooted to the spot. 'No, I cannot bear it; it's too much for me . . . ' he brought out at last. 'But, my God, why is she so fiendishly beautiful? Her eyes, her words and everything, well, they scorch me, they fairly scorch me . . . No, I cannot master myself. It's time to put an end to it all. Damn my soul, I'll go and drown myself in the hole in the ice and it will all be over!'

Then with a resolute step he walked on, caught up the group of girls, overtook Oksana and said in a firm voice: 'Farewell, Oksana! Find any lover you like, make a fool of whom you like; but me you will not see again in this world.'

The beauty seemed amazed and would have said something, but with a wave of his hand the blacksmith ran away.

'Where are you off to, Vakula?' said the lads, seeing the blacksmith running.

'Goodbye, mates!' the blacksmith shouted in answer. 'Please God we shall meet again in the other world, but we shall not walk together again in this. Farewell! Do not remember evil against me! Tell Father Kondrat to sing a requiem service for my sinful soul. Sinner that I am, for the sake of worldly things, I did not finish painting the candles for the ikons of the Wonder-worker and the Mother of God. All the goods which will be found in my chest are for the church. Farewell!'

Saying this, the blacksmith fell to running again with the sack upon his back.

'He is gone crazy!' said the lads.

'A lost soul!' an old woman, who was passing, muttered devoutly. 'I must go and tell them that the blacksmith has hanged himself!'

Meanwhile, after running through several streets Vakula stopped to take breath. 'Where am I running?' he thought, 'as though everything were over already. I'll try one way more: I'll go to the Zaporozhets, Paunchy Patsyuk; they say he knows all the devils and can do anything he likes. I'll go to him, for my soul is lost anyway!'

At that the devil, who had lain for a long while without moving, skipped for joy in the sack; but the blacksmith, fancying that he had somehow twitched the sack with his hand and caused the movement himself, gave the sack a punch with his stalwart fist and, shaking it on his shoulders, set off to Paunchy Patsyuk.

This Paunchy Patsyuk certainly at one time had been a Zaporozhets; but no one knew whether he had been turned out of the camp or whether he had run away from Zaporozhye of his own accord.

For a long time, ten years or perhaps fifteen, he had been living in Dikanka. At first he had lived like a true Zaporozhets: he had done no work, slept three-quarters of the day, ate as much as six mowers and drank almost a whole pailful at a time. He had somewhere to put it all, however, for though Patsyuk was not very tall he was fairly bulky in width. Moreover, the trousers he used to wear were so full that, however long a step he took, no trace of his leg was visible, and it seemed as though a wine-distiller's butt were moving down the street. Perhaps it was just this that gave rise to his nickname, Paunchy. Before many

weeks had passed after his coming to the village, every one had found
out that he was a wizard. If any one were ill, he called in Patsyuk at
once: Patsyuk had only to whisper a few words and it was as though the
ailment had been lifted off by his hand. If it happened that a hungry
gentleman was choked by a fishbone, Patsyuk could punch him so
skilfully on the back that the bone went the proper way without causing
any harm to the gentleman's throat. Of late years he was rarely seen
anywhere. The reason of that was perhaps sloth, though possibly also
the fact that it was every year becoming increasingly difficult for him to
pass through a doorway. People had of late been obliged to go to him if
they had need of him.

Not without some timidity, the blacksmith opened the door and saw
Patsyuk sitting Turkish-fashion on the floor before a little tub on which
stood a bowl of dumplings. This bowl stood as though purposely on a
level with his mouth. Without moving a single finger, he bent his head
a little towards the bowl and sipped the soup, from time to time catching
the dumplings with his teeth.

'Well,' thought Vakula to himself, 'this fellow's even lazier than
Tchub: he does eat with a spoon, anyway, while this fellow won't even
lift his hand!'

Patsyuk must have been entirely engrossed with the dumplings, for
he seemed to be quite unaware of the entrance of the blacksmith, who
made him a very low bow as soon as he stepped on the threshold.

'I have come to ask you a favour, Patsyuk!' said Vakula, bowing
again.

Fat Patsyuk lifted his head and again began swallowing dumplings.

'They say that you – no offence meant . . . ' the blacksmith said,
taking heart, 'I speak of this not by way of any insult to you – that you
are a little akin to the devil.'

When he had uttered these words, Vakula was alarmed, thinking
that he had expressed himself too bluntly and had not sufficiently
softened his language, and, expecting that Patsyuk would pick up the
tub together with the bowl and fling them straight at his head, he
turned aside a little and covered his face with his sleeve that the hot
dumpling soup might not spatter it. But Patsyuk looked up and again
began swallowing the dumplings.

The blacksmith, reassured, made up his mind to go on. 'I have come
to you, Patsyuk. God give you everything, goods of all sorts in
abundance and bread in proportion!' (The blacksmith would sometimes throw in a fashionable word: he had got into the way of it during
his stay in Poltava when he was painting the paling-fence for the

officer.) 'There is nothing but ruin before me, a sinner! Nothing in the world will help! What will be, will be. I have to ask help from the devil himself. Well, Patsyuk,' the blacksmith brought out, seeing his unchanged silence, 'what am I to do?'

'If you need the devil, then go to the devil,' answered Patsyuk, not lifting his eyes to him, but still making away with the dumplings.

'It is for that that I have come to you,' answered the blacksmith, dropping another bow to him. 'I suppose that nobody in the world but you knows the way to him!'

Patsyuk answered not a word, but ate up the remaining dumplings. 'Do me a kindness, good man, do not refuse me!' persisted the blacksmith. 'Whether it is pork or sausage or buckwheat flour or linen, say – millet or anything else in case of need . . . as is usual between good people . . . we will not grudge it. Tell me at least how, for instance, to get on the road to him.'

'He need not go far who has the devil on his shoulders!' Patsyuk pronounced carelessly, without changing his position.

Vakula fastened his eyes upon him as though the interpretation of those words were written on his brow. 'What does he mean?' his face asked dumbly, while his mouth stood half-open ready to swallow the first word like a dumpling.

But Patsyuk was still silent.

Then Vakula noticed that there were neither dumplings nor a tub before him; but two wooden bowls were standing on the floor instead – one was filled with turnovers, the other with some cream. His thoughts and his eyes unconsciously fastened on these dainties. 'Let us see,' he said to himself, 'how Patsyuk will eat the turnovers. He certainly won't want to bend down to lap them up like the dumplings; besides he couldn't – he must first dip the turnovers in the cream.'

He had hardly time to think this when Patsyuk opened his mouth, looked at the turnovers and opened his mouth wider still. At that moment a turnover popped out of the bowl, splashed into the cream, turned over on the other side, leapt upwards and flew straight into his mouth. Patsyuk ate it up and opened his mouth again, and another turnover went through the same performance. The only trouble he took was to munch it up and swallow it.

'My word, what a miracle!' thought the blacksmith, his mouth dropping open with surprise, and at the same moment he was aware that a turnover was creeping towards him and was already smearing his mouth with cream. Pushing away the turnover and wiping his lips, the blacksmith began to reflect what marvels there are in the world and to what subtle devices the evil spirit may lead a man, saying to himself at the same time that no one but Patsyuk could help him.

'I'll bow to him once more, maybe he will explain properly . . . The devil, though! Why, today is a fast day and he is eating turnovers with meat in them! What a fool I am really. I am standing here and making ready to sin! Back . . . !' And the pious blacksmith ran headlong out of the cottage.

But the devil sitting in the sack and already gloating over his prey could not endure to let such a glorious capture slip through his fingers. As soon as the blacksmith put down the sack the devil skipped out of it and mounted astride on his neck.

A cold shudder ran over the blacksmith's skin; pale and scared, he did not know what to do; he was on the point of crossing himself . . . But the devil, putting his dog's nose down to Vakula's right ear, said: 'It's I, your friend; I'll do anything for a friend and comrade! I'll give you as much money as you like,' he squeaked into his left ear. 'Oksana shall be yours this very day,' he whispered, turning his nose again to the right ear. The blacksmith stood still, hesitating.

'Very well,' he said at last; 'for such a price I am ready to be yours!'

The devil clasped his hands in delight and began galloping up and down on the blacksmith's neck. 'Now the blacksmith is done for!' he thought to himself: 'now I'll pay you out, my dear, for all your paintings and false tales thrown up at the devils! What will my comrades say now when they learn that the most pious man of the whole village is in my hands!'

Here the devil laughed with joy, thinking how he would taunt all the long-tailed crew in hell, how furious the lame devil, who was reckoned the most resourceful among them, would be.

'Well, Vakula!' piped the devil, not dismounting from his neck, as though afraid he might escape, 'you know nothing is done without a contract.'

'I am ready!' said the blacksmith. 'I have heard that among you contracts are signed with blood. Stay, I'll get a nail out of my pocket!'

Here he put his hand behind him and caught the devil by the tail.

'What a man you are for a joke!' cried the devil, laughing. 'Come, let go, that's enough mischief!'

'Wait a bit, friend!' cried the blacksmith, 'and what do you think of this?' As he said that he made the sign of the cross and the devil became as meek as a lamb. 'Wait a bit,' said the blacksmith, pulling him by the tail to the ground: 'I'll teach you to entice good men and honest Christians into sin.'

Here the blacksmith leaped astride on the devil and lifted his hand to make the sign of the cross.

'Have mercy, Vakula!' the devil moaned piteously; 'I will do anything you want, anything; only let me off with my life: do not lay the terrible cross upon me!'

'Ah, so that's your note now, you damned German! Now I know what to do. Carry me at once on yourself! Do you hear? And fly like a bird!'

'Whither?' asked the melancholy devil.

'To Petersburg, straight to the Tsaritsa!' And the blacksmith almost swooned with terror, as he felt himself mounting into the air.

Oksana stood for a long time pondering on the strange sayings of the blacksmith. Already an inner voice was telling her that she had treated him too cruelly. 'What if he really does make up his mind to do something dreadful! I shouldn't wonder! Perhaps his sorrow will make him fall in love with another girl, and in his vexation he will begin calling her the greatest beauty in the village. But no, he loves me. I am so beautiful! He will not give me up for anything; he is playing, he is pretending. In ten minutes he will come back to look at me, for certain. I really was cross. I must, as though it were against my will, let him kiss me. Won't he be delighted!' And the frivolous beauty went back to jesting with her companions.

'Stay,' said one of them, 'the blacksmith has forgotten his sacks: look what terrible great sacks! He has made more by his carol-singing than we have. I fancy they must have put here quite a quarter of a sheep, and I am sure that there are no end of sausages and loaves in them. Glorious! We shall have enough to feast on for all Christmas week!'

'Are they the blacksmith's sacks?' asked Oksana. 'We had better drag them to my cottage and have a good look at what he has put in them.'

All the girls laughingly approved of this proposal.

'But we can't lift them!' the whole group cried, trying to move the sacks.

'Wait a minute,' said Oksana; 'let us run for a sledge and take them away on it!'

And the crowd of girls ran out to get a sledge.

The captives were dreadfully bored with staying in the sacks, although the sacristan had poked a fair-sized hole to peep through. If there had been no one about, he might have found a way to creep out; but to creep out of a sack before everybody, to be a laughing stock . . . that thought restrained him, and he made up his mind to wait, only uttering a slight groan under Tchub's ill-mannered boots.

Tchub himself was no less desirous of freedom, feeling that there was something under him that was terribly uncomfortable to sit upon. But as soon as he heard his daughter's plan, he felt relieved and did not want to creep out, reflecting that it must be at least a hundred paces and perhaps two hundred to his hut; if he crept out, he would have to set himself to rights, button up his sheepskin, fasten his belt – such a lot of trouble! Besides, his winter cap had been left at Soloha's. Let the girls drag him in the sledge.

But things turned out not at all as Tchub was expecting. Just when the girls were running to fetch the sledge, his lean neighbour, Panas, came out of the tavern, upset and ill-humoured. The woman who kept the tavern could not be persuaded to serve him on credit. He thought to sit on in the tavern in the hope that some godly gentleman would come along and stand him treat; but as ill-luck would have it, all the gentlefolk were staying at home and like good Christians were eating rice and honey in the bosom of their families. Meditating on the degeneration of manners and the hard heart of the Jewess who kept the tavern, Panas made his way up to the sacks and stopped in amazement. 'My word, what sacks somebody has flung down in the road!' he said, looking about him in all directions. 'I'll be bound there is pork in them. Some carol-singer is in luck to get so many gifts of all sorts! What terrible great sacks! Suppose they are only stuffed full of buckwheat cake and biscuits, that's worth having; if there should be nothing but flat-cakes in them, that would be welcome, too; the Jewess would give me a dram of vodka for each cake. Let's make haste and get them away before any one sees.'

Here he flung on his shoulder the sack with Tchub and the sacristan in it, but felt it was too heavy. 'No, it'll be too heavy for one to carry,' he said; 'and here by good luck comes the weaver Shapuvalenko. Good-evening, Ostap!'

'Good-evening!' said the weaver, stopping.

'Where are you going?'

'Oh, nowhere in particular.'

'Help me carry these sacks, good man! Someone has been singing carols, and has dropped them in the middle of the road. We'll go halves over the things.'

'Sacks? Sacks of what? White loaves or flat-cakes?'

'Oh, all sorts of things, I expect.'

They hurriedly pulled some sticks out of the fence, laid the sack on them and carried it on their shoulders.

'Where shall we take it? To the tavern?' the weaver asked on the way.

'That's just what I was thinking; but, you know, the damned Jewess won't trust us, she'll think we have stolen it somewhere; besides, I have only just come from the tavern. We'll take it to my hut. No one will hinder us there, the wife's not at home.'

'Are you sure she is not at home?' the prudent weaver enquired.

'Thank God that I am not quite a fool yet,' said Panas; 'the devil would hardly take me where she is. I expect she will be trailing round with the other women till daybreak.'

'Who is there?' shouted Panas's wife, opening the door of the hut as she heard the noise in the porch made by the two friends with the sack. Panas was dumb-foundered.

'Here's a go!' articulated the weaver, letting his hands fall.

Panas's wife was a treasure of a kind that is not uncommon in this world. Like her husband, she hardly ever stayed at home, but almost every day visited various cronies and well-to-do old women, flattered them and ate with good appetite at their expense; she only quarrelled with her husband in the mornings, as it was only then that she sometimes saw him. Their hut was twice as old as the district clerk's trousers; there was no straw in places on their thatched roof. Only the remnants of a fence could be seen, for every one, as he went out of his house, thought it unnecessary to take a stick for the dogs, relying on passing by Panas's kitchen garden and pulling one out of his fence. The stove was not heated for three days at a time. Whatever the tender wife managed to beg from good Christians she hid as far as possible out of her husband's reach, and often wantonly robbed him of his gains if he had not had time to spend them on drink. In spite of his habitual imperturbability Panas did not like to give way to her, and consequently left his house every day with both eyes blackened, while his better-half, sighing and groaning, waddled off to tell her old friends of her husband's unmannerliness and the blows she had to put up with from him.

Now you can imagine how disconcerted were the weaver and Panas by this unexpected apparition. Dropping the sack, they stood before it, and concealed it with their skirts, but it was already too late; Panas's wife, though she did not see well with her old eyes, had observed the sack.

'Well, that's good!' she said, with a face which betrayed the joy of a vulture. 'That's good, that you have gained so much, singing carols! That's how it always is with good Christians; but no, I expect you have filched it somewhere. Show me your sack at once, do you hear, show me this very minute!'

'The bald devil may show you, but we won't,' said Panas, assuming a dignified air.

'What's it to do with you?' said the weaver. 'We've sung the carols, not you.'

'Yes, you will show me, you wretched drunkard!' screamed the wife, striking her tall husband on the chin with her fist and forcing her way towards the sack. But the weaver and Panas manfully defended the sack and compelled her to beat a retreat. Before they recovered themselves the wife ran out again with an oven-fork in her hands. She nimbly caught her husband a thwack on the arms and the weaver one on his back and reached the sack.

'Why did we let her pass?' said the weaver, coming to himself.

'Ay, we let her pass! Why did you let her pass?' said Panas coolly.

'Your oven-fork is made of iron, seemingly!' said the weaver after a brief silence, rubbing his back. 'My wife bought one last year at the fair, gave twenty-five kopecks; that one's all right . . . it doesn't hurt . . .'

Meanwhile the triumphant wife, setting the pot-lamp on the floor, untied the sack and peeped into it.

But her old eyes, which had so well described the sack, this time certainly deceived her.

'Oh, but there is a whole pig lying here!' she shrieked, clapping her hands in glee.

'A pig! Do you hear, a whole pig!' The weaver nudged Panas. 'And it's all your fault.'

'It can't be helped!' replied Panas, shrugging his shoulders.

'Can't be helped! Why are we standing still? Let us take away the sack! Here, come on! Go away, go away, it's our pig!' shouted the weaver, stepping forward.

'Go along, go along, you devilish woman! It's not your property!' said Panas, approaching.

His spouse picked up the oven-fork again, but at that moment Tchub crawled out of the sack and stood in the middle of the room, stretching like a man who has just woken up from a long sleep. Panas's wife shrieked, slapping her skirts, and they all stood with open mouths.

'Why did she say it was a pig, the silly! It's not a pig!' said Panas, gazing open-eyed.

'My word! What a man has been dropped into a sack!' said the weaver, staggering back in alarm. 'You may say what you please, you can burst if you like, but the foul fiend has had a hand in it. Why, he would not go through a window!'

'It's Tchub!' cried Panas, looking more closely.

'Why, who did you think it was?' said Tchub, laughing. 'Well, haven't I played you a fine trick? I'll be bound you meant to eat me by way of pork! Wait a bit, I'll console you: there is something in the sack, if not a whole pig, it's certainly a little porker or some live beast. Something was continually moving under me.'

The weaver and Panas flew to the sack, the lady of the house clutched at the other side of it, and the battle would have been renewed, had not the sacristan, seeing that now he had no chance of concealment, scrambled out of the sack of his own accord.

The woman, astounded, let go of the leg by which she was beginning to drag the sacristan out of the sack.

'Here's another of them!' cried the weaver in horror, 'the devil knows what has happened to the world . . . My head's going round . . . Men are put into sacks instead of cakes or sausages!'

'It's the sacristan!' said Tchub, more surprised than any of them. 'Well, there! You're a nice one, Soloha! To put one in a sack . . . I thought at the time her hut was very full of sacks . . . Now I understand it all: she had a couple of men hidden in each sack. While I thought it was only me she . . . So there you have her!'

The girls were a little surprised on finding that one sack was missing.

'Well, there is nothing for it, we must be content with this one,' murmured Oksana.

The mayor made up his mind to keep quiet, reasoning that if he called out to them to untie the sack and let him out, the silly girls would run away in all directions; they would think that the devil was in the sack – and he would be left in the street till next day. Meanwhile the girls, linking arms together, flew like a whirlwind with the sledge over the crunching snow. Many of them sat on the sledge for fun; others even clambered on to the top of the mayor. The mayor made up his mind to endure everything.

At last they arrived, threw open the door into the outer room of the hut and dragged in the sack amid laughter.

'Let us see what is in it,' they all cried, hastening to untie it.

At this point the hiccup which had tormented the mayor became so much worse that he began hiccupping and coughing loudly.

'Ah, there is someone in it!' they all shrieked, and rushed out of doors in horror.

'What the devil is it? Where are you tearing off to as though you were all possessed?' said Tchub, walking in at the door.

'Oh, daddy!' cried Oksana, 'there is someone in the sack!'

'In the sack? Where did you get this sack?'

'The blacksmith threw it in the middle of the road,' they all said at once.

'So that's it; didn't I say so?' Tchub thought to himself. 'What are you frightened at? Let us look. Come now, my man – I beg you won't be offended at our not addressing you by your proper name – crawl out of the sack!'

The mayor did crawl out.

'Oh!' shrieked the girls.

'So the mayor got into one, too,' Tchub thought to himself in bewilderment, scanning him from head to foot. 'Well, I'm blessed!' He could say nothing more.

The mayor himself was no less confused and did not know how to begin. 'I expect it is a cold night,' he said, addressing Tchub.

'There is a bit of a frost,' answered Tchub. 'Allow me to ask you what you rub your boots with, goose-fat or tar?' He had not meant to say that; he had meant to ask: 'How did you get into that sack, mayor?' and he did not himself understand how he came to say something utterly different.

'Tar is better,' said the mayor. 'Well, good-night, Tchub!' and, pulling his winter cap down over his head, he walked out of the hut.

'Why was I such a fool as to ask him what he rubbed his boots with?' said Tchub, looking towards the door by which the mayor had gone out.

'Well, Soloha is a fine one! To put a man like that in a sack . . . ! My word, she is a devil of a woman! While I, poor fool . . . But where is that damned sack?'

'I flung it in the corner, there is nothing more in it,' said Oksana.

'I know all about that; nothing in it, indeed! Give it here; there is another one in it! Shake it well . . . What, nothing? My word, the cursed woman! And to look at her she is like a saint, as though she had never tasted anything but lenten fare . . . !'

But we will leave Tchub to pour out his vexation at leisure and will go back to the blacksmith, for it must be past eight o'clock.

At first it seemed dreadful to Vakula, particularly when he rose up from the earth to such a height that he could see nothing below, and flew like a fly so close under the moon that if he had not bent down he would have caught his cap in it. But in a little while he gained confidence and even began mocking at the devil. (He was extremely amused by the way the devil sneezed and coughed when he took the little cyprus-wood cross off his neck and held it down to him. He purposely raised his hand to scratch his head, and the devil, thinking he was going to make the sign of the cross over him, flew along more swiftly than ever.) It was quite light at that height. The air was transparent, bathed in a light silvery mist. Everything was visible, and he could even see a wizard whisk by them like a hurricane, sitting in a pot, and the stars gathering together to play hide-and-seek, a whole swarm of spirits whirling away in a cloud, a devil dancing in the light of the moon and taking off his cap at the sight of the blacksmith galloping by, a broom flying back home, from which evidently a witch had just alighted at her destination . . . And many nasty things besides they met. They all stopped at the sight of the blacksmith to stare at him for a moment, and then whirled off and went on their way again. The blacksmith flew on till all at once Petersburg flashed before him, glittering with lights. (There happened to be an illumination that day.) The devil, flying over the city gate, turned into a horse and the blacksmith found himself mounted on a fiery steed in the middle of the street.

My goodness! The clatter, the uproar, the brilliant light; the walls rose up, four storeys on each side; the thud of the horses' hoofs and the rumble of the wheels echoed and resounded from every quarter; houses seemed to start up out of the ground at every step; the bridges trembled; carriages raced along; sledge-drivers and postilions shouted; the snow crunched under the thousand sledges flying from all parts; people passing along on foot huddled together, crowded under the houses which were studded with little lamps, and their immense shadows flitted over the walls with their heads reaching the roofs and the chimneys.

The blacksmith looked about him in amazement. It seemed to him as though all the houses had fixed their innumerable fiery eyes upon him, watching. Good Lord! He saw so many gentlemen in cloth fur-lined overcoats that he did not know whom to take off his cap to. 'Good gracious, what a lot of gentry here!' thought the blacksmith. 'I fancy every one who comes along the street in a fur coat is the assessor and again the assessor! And those who are driving about in such wonderful chaises with glass windows, if they are not police-captains they certainly must be commissars or perhaps something grander still.' His words were cut short by a question from the devil: 'Am I to go straight to the Tsaritsa?'

'No, I'm frightened,' thought the blacksmith. 'The Zaporozhtsy, who marched in the autumn through Dikanka, are stationed here, where I don't know. They came from the camp with papers for the Tsaritsa;

anyway I might ask their advice. Hey, Satan! Creep into my pocket and take me to the Zaporozhtsy!'

And in one minute the devil became so thin and small that he had no difficulty in creeping into the blacksmith's pocket. And before Vakula had time to look round he found himself in front of a big house, went up a staircase, hardly knowing what he was doing, opened a door and drew back a little from the brilliant light on seeing the smartly furnished room; but he regained confidence a little when he recognised the Zaporozhtsy who had ridden through Dikanka and now, sitting on silk-covered sofas, their tar-smeared boots tucked under them, were smoking the strongest tobacco, usually called 'root'.

'Good-day to you, gentlemen! God be with you, this is where we meet again,' said the blacksmith, going up to them and swinging off a low bow.

'What man is that?' the one who was sitting just in front of the blacksmith asked another who was further away.

'You don't know me?' said the blacksmith. 'It's I, Vakula, the blacksmith! When you rode through Dikanka in the autumn you stayed nearly two days with me. God give you all health and long years! And I put a new iron hoop on the front wheel of your chaise!'

'Oh!' said the same Zaporozhets, 'it's that blacksmith who paints so well. Good-day to you, neighbour! How has God brought you here?'

'Oh, I just wanted to have a look round. I was told . . .'

'Well, neighbour,' said the Zaporozhets, drawing himself up with dignity and wishing to show he could speak Russian too, 'well, it's a big city.'

The blacksmith, too, wanted to keep up his credit and not to seem like a novice. Moreover, as we have had occasion to see before, he too could speak like a book.

'A considerable town!' he answered carelessly. 'There is no denying the houses are very large, the pictures that are hanging up are uncommonly good. Many of the houses are painted with letters in gold leaf to exuberance. The configuration is superb, there is no other word for it!'

The Zaporozhtsy, hearing the blacksmith express himself so freely, drew the most flattering conclusions in regard to him.

'We will have a little more talk with you, neighbour; now we are going at once to the Tsaritsa.'

'To the Tsaritsa? Oh, be so kind, gentlemen, as to take me with you!'

'You?' a Zaporozhets pronounced in the tone in which an old man speaks to his four-year-old charge when the latter asks to be sat on a real, big horse. 'What would you do there? No, we can't do that. We are going to talk about our own affairs to the Tsaritsa.' And his face assumed an expression of great significance.

'Do take me!' the blacksmith persisted.

'Ask them to!' he whispered softly to the devil, banging on the pocket with his fist.

He had hardly said this, when another Zaporozhets brought out: 'Do let us take him, mates!'

'Yes, do let us take him!' others joined in.

'Put on the same dress as we are wearing, then.'

The blacksmith was hastily putting on a green tunic when all at once the door opened and a man covered with gold lace said it was time to go.

Again the blacksmith was moved to wonder, as he was whisked along in an immense coach swaying on springs, as four-storeyed houses raced by him on both sides and the rumbling pavement seemed to be moving under the horses' hoofs.

'My goodness, how light it is!' thought the blacksmith to himself. 'At home it is not so light as this in the daytime.'

The coaches stopped in front of the palace. The Zaporozhtsy got out, went into a magnificent vestibule and began ascending a brilliantly lighted staircase.

'What a staircase!' the blacksmith murmured to himself, 'it's a pity to trample it with one's feet. What decorations! They say the stories tell lies! The devil a bit they do! My goodness! What banisters, what workmanship! Quite fifty roubles must have gone on the iron alone!'

When they had mounted the stairs, the Zaporozhtsy walked through the first drawing-room. The blacksmith followed them timidly, afraid of slipping on the parquet at every footstep. They walked through three drawing-rooms, the blacksmith still overwhelmed with admiration. On entering the fourth, he could not help going up to a picture hanging on the wall. It was the Holy Virgin with the Child in her arms.

'What a picture! What a wonderful painting!' he thought. 'It seems to be speaking! It seems to be alive! And the Holy Child! It's pressing its little hands together and laughing, poor thing! And the colours! My goodness, what colours! I fancy there is not a kopeck-worth of ochre on it, it's all emerald green and crimson lake. And the blue simply glows! A fine piece of work! I expect the background was put in with the most expensive white lead. Wonderful as that painting is, though, this copper handle,' he went on, going up to the door and fingering the lock, 'is even more wonderful. Ah, what a fine finish! That's all done, I expect, by German blacksmiths and most expensive.'

Perhaps the blacksmith would have gone on reflecting for a long time, if a flunkey in livery had not nudged his arm and reminded him not to lag behind the others. The Zaporozhtsy passed through two more rooms and then stopped. They were told to wait in the third, in which there was a group of several generals in gold-laced uniforms. The Zaporozhtsy bowed in all directions and stood all together.

A minute later, a rather thick-set man of majestic stature, wearing the uniform of a Hetman and yellow boots, walked in, accompanied by a regular suite. His hair was in disorder, he squinted a little, his face wore an expression of haughty dignity and the habit of command could be seen in every movement. All the generals, who had been walking up and down rather superciliously in their gold uniforms, bustled about and seemed with low bows to be hanging on every word he uttered and even on his slightest gesture, so as to fly at once to carry out his wishes. But the Hetman did not even notice all that: he barely nodded to them and went up to the Zaporozhtsy.

The Zaporozhtsy all bowed down to the ground.

'Are you all here?' he asked deliberately, speaking a little through his nose.

'All, little father!' answered the Zaporozhtsy, bowing again.

'Don't forget to speak as I have told you!'

'No, little father, we will not forget.'

'Is that the Tsar?' asked the blacksmith of one of the Zaporozhtsy.

'Tsar, indeed! It's Potyomkin[46] himself,' answered the other.

Voices were heard in the other room, and the blacksmith did not know which way to look for the number of ladies who walked in, wearing satin gowns with long trains, and courtiers in gold-laced coats with their hair tied in a tail at the back. He could see a blur of brilliance and nothing more.

The Zaporozhtsy all bowed down at once to the floor and cried out with one voice: 'Have mercy, little mother, mercy!'

The blacksmith, too, though seeing nothing, stretched himself very zealously on the floor.

'Get up!' An imperious and at the same time pleasant voice sounded above them. Some of the courtiers bustled about and nudged the Zaporozhtsy.

'We will not get up, little mother! We will not get up! We will die, but we will not get up!' shouted the Zaporozhtsy.

Potyomkin bit his lips. At last he went up himself and whispered peremptorily to one of the Zaporozhtsy. They rose to their feet.

Then the blacksmith, too, ventured to raise his head, and saw standing before him a short and, indeed, rather stout woman with blue eyes, and at the same time with that majestically smiling air which was so well able to subdue everything and could only belong to a queen.

'His Excellency has promised to make me acquainted today with my people whom I have not hitherto seen,' said the lady with the blue eyes, scrutinising the Zaporozhtsy with curiosity.

'Are you well cared for here?' she went on, going nearer to them.

'Thanks, little mother! The provisions they give us are excellent, though the mutton here is not at all like what we have in Zaporozhye . . . What does our daily fare matter . . . ?'

Potyomkin frowned, seeing that the Zaporozhtsy were saying something quite different from what he had taught them . . .

One of the Zaporozhtsy, drawing himself up with dignity, stepped forward: 'Be gracious, little mother! How have your faithful people angered you? Have we taken the hand of the vile Tatar? Have we come to agreement with the Turk? Have we been false to you in deed or in thought? How have we lost your favour? First we heard that you were commanding fortresses to be built everywhere against us; then we heard you mean to turn us into carbineers;[47] now we hear of new oppressions. Wherein are your Zaporozhye troops in fault? In having brought your army across the Perekop and helped your generals to slaughter the Tatars in the Crimea . . . ?'[48]

Potyomkin carelessly rubbed with a little brush the diamonds with which his hands were studded and said nothing.

'What is it you want?' Catherine asked anxiously.

The Zaporozhtsy looked meaningly at one another.

'Now is the time! The Tsaritsa asks what we want!' the blacksmith said to himself, and he suddenly flopped down on the floor.

'Your Imperial Majesty, do not command me to be punished! Show me mercy! Of what, be it said without offence to your Imperial Graciousness, are the little slippers made that are on your feet? I fancy there is no Swede nor a shoemaker in any kingdom in the world can make them like that. Merciful heavens, if only my wife could wear slippers like that!'

The Empress laughed. The courtiers laughed too. Potyomkin frowned and smiled both together. The Zaporozhtsy began nudging the blacksmith under the arm, wondering whether he had not gone out of his mind.

'Stand up!' the Empress said graciously. 'If you wish to have slippers like these, it is very easy to arrange it. Bring him at once the very best slippers with gold on them! Indeed, this simple-heartedness greatly pleases me! Here you have a subject worthy of your witty pen!' the Empress went on, turning to a gentleman with a full but rather pale face, who stood a little apart from the others and whose modest coat with big mother-of-pearl buttons on it showed that he was not one of the courtiers.

'You are too gracious, your Imperial Majesty. It needs a La Fontaine [49] at least to do justice to it!' answered the man with the mother-of-pearl buttons, bowing.

'I tell you sincerely, I have not yet got over my delight at your *Brigadier*.[50] You read so wonderfully well! I have heard, though,' the Empress went on, turning again to the Zaporozhtsy, 'that none of you are married in the Syetch.'

'What next, little mother! Why, you know yourself, a man cannot live without a wife,' answered the same Zaporozhets who had talked to the blacksmith, and the blacksmith wondered, hearing him address the Tsaritsa as though purposely in coarse language, speaking like a peasant, at it is commonly called, though he could speak like a book.

'They are sly fellows!' he thought to himself. 'I'll be bound he does not do that for nothing.'

'We are not monks,' the Zaporozhets went on, 'but sinful folk. Ready like all honest Christians to fall into sin. There are among us many who have wives, but do not live with them in the Syetch. There are some who have wives in Poland; there are some who have wives in Ukraine; there are some who have wives even in Turkey.'

At that moment they brought the blacksmith the slippers.

'My goodness, what fine embroidery!' he cried joyfully, taking the slippers. 'Your Imperial Majesty! If the slippers on your feet are like this – and in them your Honour, I expect, goes sliding on the ice – what must the feet themselves be like! They must be made of pure sugar at least, I should think!'

The Empress, who had in fact very well-shaped and charming feet, could not help smiling at hearing such a compliment from the lips of a simple-hearted blacksmith, who in his Zaporozhets dress might be reckoned a handsome fellow in spite of his swarthy face.

Delighted with such gracious attention, the blacksmith would have liked to have cross-questioned the pretty Tsaritsa thoroughly about everything: whether it was true that tsars eat nothing but honey, fat bacon and suchlike; but, feeling that the Zaporozhtsy were digging him in the ribs, he made up his mind to keep quiet. And when the Empress, turning to the older men, began questioning them about their manner of life and customs in the Syetch, he, stepping back, stooped down to his pocket and said softly: 'Hurry me away from here and make haste!' And at once he found himself outside the city gates.

'He is drowned! On my word he is drowned! May I never leave this spot if he is not drowned!' lisped the weaver's fat wife, standing with a group of Dikanka women in the middle of the street.

'Why, am I a liar then? Have I stolen any one's cow? Have I put the evil eye on someone, that I am not to be believed?' shouted a purple-nosed woman in a Cossack tunic, waving her arms. 'May I never want to drink water again if old Dame Perepertchih didn't see with her own eyes the blacksmith hanging himself!'

'Has the blacksmith hanged himself? Well, I never!' said the mayor, coming out of Tchub's hut, and he stopped and pressed closer to the group.

'You had better say, may you never want to drink vodka, you old drunkard!' answered the weaver's wife. 'He had need to be as mad as you to hang himself! He drowned himself! He drowned himself in the hole in the ice! I know that as well as I know that you were in the tavern just now.'

'You disgrace! See what she throws up against me!' the woman with the purple nose retorted wrathfully. 'You had better hold your tongue, you wretch! Do you think I don't know that the sacristan comes to see you every evening?'

The weaver's wife flared up.

'What about the sacristan? Whom does the sacristan go to? What lies are you telling?'

'The sacristan?' piped the sacristan's wife, squeezing her way up to the combatants, in an old blue cotton coat lined with hare-skin. 'I'll let the sacristan know! Who was it said the sacristan?'

'Well, this is the lady the sacristan visits!' said the woman with the purple nose, pointing to the weaver's wife.

'So it's you, you bitch!' said the sacristan's wife, stepping up to the weaver's wife. 'So it's you, is it, witch, who cast a spell over him and gave him a foul poison to make him come to you!'

'Get thee behind me, Satan!'[51] said the weaver's wife, staggering back.

'Oh, you cursed witch, may you never live to see your children! Wretched creature! Tfoo!'

Here the sacristan's wife spat straight into the other woman's face.

The weaver's wife endeavoured to do the same, but spat instead on the unshaven chin of the mayor, who had come close up to the combatants that he might hear the quarrel better.

'Ah, nasty woman!' cried the mayor, wiping his face with the skirt of his coat and lifting his whip.

This gesture sent them all flying in different directions, scolding loudly.

'How disgusting!' repeated the mayor, still wiping his face. 'So the blacksmith is drowned! My goodness! What a fine painter he was! What good knives and reaping-hooks and ploughs he could forge! What a strong man he was! Yes,' he went on musing; 'there are not many fellows like that in our village. To be sure, I did notice while I was in that damned sack that the poor fellow was very much depressed. So that is the end of the blacksmith! He was and is not! And I was meaning to have my dapple mare shod . . . !' And filled with such Christian reflections, the mayor quietly made his way to his own cottage.

Oksana was much troubled when the news reached her. She put little faith in Dame Perepertchih's having seen it and in the women's talk; she knew that the blacksmith was rather too pious a man to bring himself to send his soul to perdition. But what if he really had gone away, intending never to return to the village? And, indeed, in any place it would be hard to find as fine a fellow as the blacksmith. And how he loved her! He had borne with her caprices longer than any one of them . . . All night long the beauty turned over from her right side to her left and her left to her right, and could not go to sleep. Now tossing in bewitching nakedness which the darkness concealed even from herself, she reviled herself almost aloud; now growing quieter, made up her mind to think of nothing – and kept thinking all the time. She was in a perfect fever, and by the morning head over ears in love with the blacksmith.

Tchub expressed neither pleasure nor sorrow at Vakula's fate. His thoughts were absorbed by one subject: he could not forget the treachery of Soloha and never left off abusing her even in his sleep.

Morning came. Even before daybreak the church was full of people. Elderly women in white linen wimples, in white cloth tunics, crossed themselves piously at the church porch. Ladies in green and yellow blouses, some even in dark blue overdresses with gold streamers behind, stood in front of them. Girls who had a whole shopful of ribbons twined on their heads, and necklaces, crosses, and coins round their necks, tried to make their way closer to the ikon-stand. But in front of all stood the gentlemen and humble peasants with moustaches, with forelocks, with thick necks and newly-shaven chins, for the most part wearing hooded cloaks, below which peeped a white or sometimes a dark blue jacket. Wherever one looked every face had a festive air. The mayor was licking his lips in anticipation of the sausage with which he would break his fast; the girls were thinking how they would slide with the lads on the ice; the old woman murmured prayers more zealously than ever. All over the church one could hear the Cossack Sverbyguz bowing to the ground. Only Oksana stood feeling unlike herself: she prayed without praying. So many different feelings, each more amazing, each more distressing than the other, crowded upon her heart that her face expressed nothing but overwhelming confusion; tears quivered in her eyes. The girls could not think why it was and did not suspect that the blacksmith was responsible. However, not only Oksana was concerned about the blacksmith. All the villagers observed that the holiday did not seem like a holiday, that something was lacking. To make things worse, the sacristan was hoarse after his travels in the sack and he wheezed scarcely audibly; it is true that the chorister who was on a visit to the village sang the bass splendidly, but how much better it would have been if they had had the blacksmith too, who used always when they were singing *Our Father* or the *Holy Cherubim* to step up into the choir and from there sing it with the same chant with which it is sung in Poltava. Moreover, he alone performed the duty of a churchwarden. Matins were already over; after matins mass was over . . . Where indeed could the blacksmith have vanished to?

It was still night as the devil flew even more swiftly back with the blacksmith, and in a trice Vakula found himself inside his own cottage. At that moment the cock crowed.

'Where are you off to?' cried the blacksmith, catching the devil by his tail as he was about to run away. 'Wait a bit, friend, that's not all: I haven't thanked you yet.' Then, seizing a switch, he gave him three lashes and the poor devil set to running like a peasant who has just had a hiding from the tax-assessor. And so, instead of tricking, tempting and fooling others, the enemy of mankind was fooled himself. After that Vakula went into the outer room, made himself a hole in the hay and slept till dinner-time. When he woke up he was frightened at seeing that the sun was already high. 'I've overslept myself and missed matins and mass!'

Then the worthy blacksmith was overwhelmed with distress, thinking that no doubt God, as a punishment for his sinful intention of damning his soul, had sent this heavy sleep, which had prevented him from even being in church on this solemn holiday. However, comforting himself with the thought that next week he would confess all this to the priest and that from that day he would begin making fifty bows a day for a whole year, he glanced into the cottage; but there was no one there. Apparently Soloha had not yet returned.

Carefully he drew out from the breast of his coat the slippers and again marvelled at the costly workmanship and wonderful adventure of the previous night. He washed and dressed himself in his best, put on the very clothes which he had got from the Zaporozhtsy, took out of a chest a new cap of good astrakhan with a dark blue top not once worn since he had bought it while staying in Poltava; he also took out a new girdle of rainbow colours; he put all this together with a whip in a kerchief and set off straight to see Tchub.

Tchub opened his eyes wide when the blacksmith walked into his cottage, and did not know what to wonder at most, the blacksmith's having risen from the dead, the blacksmith's having dared to come to see him, or the blacksmith's being dressed up such a dandy, like a Zaporozhets. But he was even more astonished when Vakula untied the kerchief and laid before him a new cap and a girdle such as had never been seen in the village, and then plumped down on his knees before him, and said in a tone of entreaty: 'Have mercy, father! Be not wroth! Here is a whip; beat me as much as your heart may desire. I give myself up, I repent of everything! Beat, but only be not wroth. You were once a comrade of my father's, you ate bread and salt together and drank the cup of goodwill.'

It was not without secret satisfaction that Tchub saw the blacksmith, who had never knocked under to any one in the village and who could twist five-kopeck pieces and horseshoes in his hands like pancakes, lying now at his feet. In order to keep up his dignity still further, Tchub took the whip and gave him three strokes on the back. 'Well, that's enough; get up! Always obey the old! Let us forget everything that has passed between us. Come, tell me now what is it that you want?'

'Give me Oksana to wife, father!'

Tchub thought a little, looked at the cap and the girdle. The cap was delightful and the girdle, too, was not inferior to it; he thought of the treacherous Soloha and said resolutely: 'Good! Send the matchmakers!'

'Aïe!' shrieked Oksana, as she crossed the threshold and saw the blacksmith, and she gazed at him with astonishment and delight.

'Look, what slippers I have brought you!' said Vakula, 'they are the same as the Tsaritsa wears!'

'No, no! I don't want slippers!' she said, waving her arms and keeping her eyes fixed upon him. 'I am ready without slippers . . . ' She blushed and could say no more.

The blacksmith went up to her and took her by the hand; the beauty looked down. Never before had she looked so exquisitely lovely. The enchanted blacksmith gently kissed her; her face flushed crimson and she was even lovelier still.

The bishop of blessed memory was driving through Dikanka. He admired the site on which the village stands, and as he drove down the street stopped before a new cottage.

'And whose is this cottage so gaily painted?' asked his reverence of a beautiful woman, who was standing near the door with a baby in her arms.

'The blacksmith Vakula's!' Oksana, for it was she, told him, bowing.

'Splendid! Splendid work!' said his reverence, examining the doors and windows. The windows were all outlined with a ring of red paint; everywhere on the doors there were Cossacks on horseback with pipes in their teeth.

But his reverence was even warmer in his praise of Vakula when he learned that by way of church penance he had painted free of charge the whole of the left choir green with red flowers.

But that was not all. On the wall, to one side as you go in at the church, Vakula had painted the devil in hell – such a loathsome figure that every one spat as he passed. And the women would take a child up to the picture, if it would go on crying in their arms, and would say: 'There, look! What a fright!'[52] And the child, restraining its tears, would steal a glance at the picture and nestle closer to its mother.

A TERRIBLE REVENGE

1

THERE was a bustle and an uproar in a quarter of Kiev: the Esaul Gorobets was celebrating his son's wedding. A great many people had come as guests to the wedding. In old days they liked good fare, better still liked drinking, and best of all they liked merry-making. Among others the Zaporozhets Mikitka came on his sorrel horse straight from a riotous feast at the Pereshlay Plain where for seven days and seven nights he had been giving the Polish king's soldiers red wine to drink. The Esaul's adopted brother, Danilo Burulbash, came too, with his young wife Katerina and his twelve-months-old son, from beyond the Dnieper where his homestead lay between two mountains. The guests marvelled at the fair face of the young wife Katerina, her eyebrows as black as German velvet, her smart cloth dress and under-skirt of blue silk and her boots with silver heels; but they marvelled still more that her old father had not come with her. He had been living in that region for scarcely a year, and for twenty-one years before nothing had been heard of him and he had only come back to his daughter when she was married and had borne a son. No doubt he would have many strange stories to tell. How could he fail to have them, after being so long in foreign parts! Everything there is different: the people are not the same and there are no Christian churches . . . But he had not come.

They brought the guests mulled vodka with raisins and plums in it and a wedding loaf on a big dish. The musicians fell to upon the bottom crust in which coins had been baked and put their fiddles, cymbals and tambourines down for a brief rest. Meanwhile the girls and young women, after wiping their mouths with embroidered handkerchiefs, stepped out again; and the lads, putting their arms akimbo and looking haughtily about them, were on the point of going to meet them, when the old Esaul brought out two ikons to bless the young couple. These ikons had come to him from the venerable hermit, Father Varfolomey.

They had no rich setting, there was no gleam of gold or silver on them, but no evil power dare approach the man in whose house they stand. Raising the ikons on high the Esaul was about to deliver a brief prayer . . . when all at once the children playing on the ground cried out in terror, and the people drew back, and every one pointed with their fingers in alarm at a Cossack who was standing in their midst. Who he was nobody knew. But he had already danced splendidly and had diverted the people standing round him. But when the Esaul lifted up the ikons at once the Cossack's face completely changed: his nose grew bigger and twisted to one side, his dancing eyes turned from brown to green, his lips turned blue, his chin quivered and grew pointed like a spear, a tusk peeped out of his mouth, a hump appeared behind his head, and the Cossack turned into an old man.

'It is he! It is he!' shouted the crowd, huddling close together.

'The wizard has appeared again!' cried the mothers, snatching up their children.

Majestically and with dignity the Esaul stepped forward and, turning the ikons towards him, said in a loud voice: 'Avaunt, image of Satan! This is no place for you!' And, hissing and clacking his teeth like a wolf, the strange old man vanished.

Talk and conjecture arose among the people and the hubbub was like the roar of the sea in bad weather.

'What is this wizard?' asked the young people who knew nothing about him.

'There will be trouble!' muttered their elders, shaking their heads. And everywhere about the spacious courtyard folks gathered in groups listening to the story of the dreadful wizard. But almost every one told it differently and no one could tell anything certain about him.

A barrel of mead was rolled out and many gallons of Greek wine were brought into the yard. The guests regained their light-heartedness. The orchestra struck up – the girls, the young women, the gallant Cossacks in their gay-coloured coats flew round in the dance. After a glass, old folks of ninety, of a hundred, fell to dancing too, remembering the years that had not passed in vain. They feasted till late into the night and feasted as none feast nowadays. The guests began to disperse, but only a few made their way home: many of them stayed to spend the night in the Esaul's wide courtyard; and even more Cossacks dropped to sleep uninvited under the benches, on the floor, by their horses, by the stables; wherever the tipplers stumbled there they lay, snoring for the whole town to hear.

There was a soft light all over the earth: the moon had come up from behind the mountain. It covered the steep bank of the Dnieper as with a costly damask muslin, white as snow, and the shadows drew back further into the pine forest.

A boat, hollowed out of an oak tree, was floating in the Dnieper. Two lads were sitting in the bow; their black Cossack caps were cocked on one side, and the drops flew in all directions from their oars like sparks from a flint.

Why were the Cossacks not singing? Why were they not telling of the Polish priests who go about the Ukraine forcing the Cossack people to turn Catholic, or of the two days' fight with the Tatars at the Salt Lake?[53] How could they sing, how could they tell of gallant deeds? Their lord, Danilo, was plunged in thought, and the sleeve of his crimson tunic hung out of the boat and was dipped in the water; their mistress, Katerina, was softly rocking her child and keeping her eyes fixed upon it, while her gala cloth gown was splashed by the spray like fine grey dust and unguarded by the linen cover.

Sweet it is to look from mid-Dnieper at the lofty mountains, at the broad meadows, at the green forests! Those mountains are not mountains: they end in peaks below, as above, and both under and above them lie the high heavens. Those forests on the hills are not forests: they are the hair that covers the shaggy head of the wood-demon. Down below he washes his beard in the water, and under his beard and over his head lie the high heavens. Those meadows are not meadows: they are a green girdle encircling the round sky; and above and below the moon hovers over them.

Lord Danilo looks not about him; he looks at his young wife. 'Why are you plunged in sadness, my young wife, my golden Katerina?'

'I am not plunged in sadness, my lord Danilo! I am full of dread at the strange tales of the wizard. They say he was born so terrible to look at . . . and not one of the children would play with him. Listen, my lord Danilo, what dreadful things they say: he fancied all were mocking at him. If he met a man in the dark he thought that he opened his mouth and grinned at him; and next day they found that man dead. I marvelled and was frightened hearing those tales,' said Katerina, taking out a kerchief and wiping the face of the sleeping child. The kerchief had been embroidered by her with leaves and fruits in red silk.

Lord Danilo said not a word, but looked into the darkness where far away beyond the forest there was the dark ridge of an earthern wall and beyond the wall rose an old castle. Three lines furrowed his brow; his left hand stroked his gallant moustaches.

'It is not that he is a wizard that is cause for fear,' he said, 'but that he is an evil guest. What whim has brought him hither? I have heard say that the Poles mean to build a fort to cut off our way to the Zaporozhtsy. That may be true . . . I will scatter that devil's nest if any rumour reaches me that he harbours our foes there. I will burn the old wizard so that even the crows will find nought to peck at. Moreover, I fancy he lacks not store of gold and wealth of all kinds. 'Tis there the devil lives! If he has gold . . . We shall soon row by the crosses – that's the graveyard! There lie his evil forefathers. I am told they were all ready to sell themselves to Satan for a brass farthing – soul and threadbare coat and all. If truly he has gold, there is no need to tarry: there is not always booty to be won in war . . . '

'I know what you are planning: my heart bodes no good from your meeting him. But you are breathing so hard, you are looking so fierce, your brows are knitted so angrily above your eyes . . . '

'Hold your peace, woman!' said Danilo wrathfully. 'If one has dealings with you, one will turn woman oneself. Lad, give me a light for my pipe!' Here he turned to one of the rowers who, knocking some hot ash from his pipe, began putting it into his master's. 'She would scare me with the wizard!' Danilo went on. 'A Cossack, thank God, fears neither devil nor Polish priest. What should we come to if we listened to women? No good, should we, lads? The best wife for us is a pipe and a sharp sword!'

Katerina sat silent, looking down into the slumbering river; and the wind ruffled the water into eddies and all Dnieper shimmered with silver like a wolf's skin in the night.

The boat turned and hugged the wooded bank. A graveyard came into sight; tumbledown crosses stood huddled together. No guelder-rose grows among them, no grass is green there; only the moon warms them from the heavenly heights.

'Do you hear the shouts, lads? Someone is calling for our help!' said Danilo, turning to his oarsmen.

'We hear shouts, and seemingly from that bank,' the two lads cried together, pointing to the graveyard.

But all was still again. The boat turned, following the curve of the projecting bank. All at once the rowers dropped their oars and stared before them without moving. Danilo stopped too: a chill of horror ran through the Cossack's veins.

A cross on one of the graves tottered and a withered corpse rose up out of the earth. Its beard reached to the waist; the nails on its fingers were longer than the fingers themselves. It slowly raised its hands upwards. Its face was all twisted and distorted. One could see it was suffering terrible torments. 'I am stifling, stifling!' it moaned in a strange, unhuman voice. Its voice seemed to scrape on the heart like a knife, and suddenly it disappeared under the earth. Another cross tottered and again a dead body came forth, more terrible and taller than the one before; it was all hairy, with a beard to its knees and even longer claws. Still more terribly it shouted: 'I am stifling,' and vanished into the earth. A third cross tottered, a third corpse appeared. It seemed like a skeleton rising from the earth; its beard reached to its heels; the nails on its fingers pierced the ground. Terribly it raised its hands towards the sky as though it would seize the moon, and shrieked as though someone were sawing its yellow bones . . .

The child asleep on Katerina's lap screamed and woke up; the lady screamed too; the oarsmen let their caps fall in the river; even their master shuddered.

Suddenly it all vanished as though it had never been; but it was a long time before the rowers took up their oars again. Burulbash looked anxiously at his young wife who, panic-stricken, was rocking the screaming child in her arms; he pressed her to his heart and kissed her on the forehead.

'Fear not, Katerina! Look, there is nought!' he said, pointing around. ''Tis the wizard who would frighten folk, that none may dare break into his foul nest. He will but scare women by that! Let me hold my son!'

With those words Danilo lifted up his son and kissed him. 'Why, Ivan, you are not afraid of wizards, are you? Say: "Nay, daddy, I'm a Cossack!" Stop, give over crying! soon we shall be home! Then mother will give you your porridge, put you to bed in your cradle, and sing:

> "Lullaby, my little son,
> Lullaby to sleep!
> Play about and grow a man!
> To the glory of the Cossacks
> And confusion of our foes."

Listen, Katerina! I fancy that your father will not live at peace with us. He was sullen, gloomy, as though angry when he came . . . If he doesn't like it, why come? He would not drink to Cossack freedom! He has never dandled the child! At first I would have trusted him with all that lay in my heart, but I could not do it, the words stuck in my throat. No, he has not a Cossack heart! When Cossack hearts meet, they almost leap out of the breast to greet each other! Well, my dear lads, is the bank near? I will give you new caps. You, Stetsko, I will give one made of velvet and gold. I took it from a Tatar with his head; all his trappings came to me; I let nothing go but his soul. Well, land here! Here, we are home, Ivan, but still you cry! Take him, Katerina . . . !'

They all got out. A thatched roof came into sight behind the mountain: it was Danilo's ancestral home. Beyond it was another mountain, and then the open plain, and there you might travel a hundred miles and not see a single Cossack.

3

Danilo's house lay between two mountains in a narrow valley that ran down to the Dnieper. It was a low-pitched house like a humble Cossack's hut and there was only one large room in it; but he and his wife and their old serving-woman and a dozen picked lads all had their places in it. There were oak shelves running round the walls at the top. Bowls and cooking-pots were piled upon them. Among them were silver goblets and drinking-cups mounted in gold, gifts or booty brought from the war. Lower down hung costly swords, muskets, arquebusses, spears; willingly or unwillingly, they had come from the Tatars, the Turks and the Poles, and many a dent there was in them. Looking at them, Danilo was reminded as by tokens of his encounters. At the bottom of the wall were smooth-planed oak benches; beside them, in front of the oven-step, the cradle hung on cords from a ring fixed in the ceiling. The whole floor of the room was beaten hard and plastered with clay. On the benches slept Danilo and his wife; on the oven-step the old serving-woman; the child played and was lulled to sleep in the cradle; and on the floor the serving-men slept in a row. But a Cossack likes best to sleep on the flat earth in the open air; he needs no feather bed nor pillow; he piles fresh hay under his head and stretches at his ease upon the grass. It rejoices his heart to wake up in the night and look up at the lofty sky spangled with stars and to shiver at the chill of night which refreshes his Cossack bones; stretching and muttering through his sleep, he lights his pipe and wraps himself more closely in his sheepskin.

Burulbash did not wake early after the merry-making of the day before; when he woke he sat on a bench in a corner and began sharpening a new Turkish sabre, for which he had just bartered something; and Katerina set to work embroidering a silken towel with gold thread.

All at once Katerina's father came in, angry and frowning, with a foreign pipe in his teeth; he went up to his daughter and began questioning her sternly, asking what was the reason she had come home so late the night before.

'It is not her, but me you should question about that, father-in-law! Not the wife but the husband is responsible. That's our way here, don't put yourself out about it,' said Danilo, going on with his work, 'perhaps in infidel lands it is not so – I don't know.'

The colour came into the father-in-law's face, there was a wild gleam in his eye. 'Who, if not a father, should watch over his daughter!' he muttered to himself. 'Well, I ask you: where were you gadding till late at night?'

'Ah, that's it at last, dear father-in-law! To that I will answer that I have left swaddling-clothes behind me long ago. I can ride a horse, I can wield a sharp sword, and there are other things I can do . . . I can refuse to answer to any one for what I do.'

'I know, I see, Danilo, you seek a quarrel! A man who is not open has some evil in his mind.'

'You may think as you please,' said Danilo, 'and I will think as I please. Thank God, I've had no part in any dishonourable deed so far; I have always stood for the orthodox faith and my fatherland, not like some vagrants who go tramping God knows whither while good Christians are fighting to the death, and afterwards come back to reap the harvest they have not sown. They are worse than the Uniats:[54] they never look into the church of God. It is such men that should be strictly questioned where they have been gadding.'

'Hey, Cossack! Do you know . . . I am no great shot: my bullet pierces the heart at seven hundred feet; I am nought to boast of at swordplay either: my man is left in bits smaller than the grains you use for porridge.'

'I am ready,' said Danilo jauntily, making the sign of the cross in the air with the sabre, as though he knew what he had sharpened it for.

'Danilo!' Katerina cried aloud, seizing him by the arm and hanging on it, 'think what you are doing, madman, see against whom you are lifting your hand! Father, your hair is white as snow, but you have flown into a rage like a senseless lad!'

'Wife!' Danilo cried menacingly, 'you know I don't like that; you mind your woman's business!'

There was a terrible clatter of swords; steel hacked steel and the Cossacks sent sparks flying like dust. Katerina went out weeping into a room apart, flung herself on the bed and covered her ears that she might not hear the clash of the swords. But the Cossacks did not fight so faint-heartedly that she could smother the sound of their blows. Her heart was ready to break; she seemed to hear all over her the clank of the swords. 'No, I cannot bear it, I cannot bear it . . . Perhaps the crimson blood is already flowing out of the white body; maybe by now my dear one is helpless and I am lying here!' And pale all over, scarcely breathing, she went back.

A terrible and even fight it was; neither of the Cossacks was winning the day. At one moment Katerina's father attacked and Danilo seemed to give way; then Danilo attacked and the sullen father seemed to yield, and again they were equal. They boiled with rage, they swung their swords . . . Ough! The swords clashed . . . and with a clatter the blades flew out of the handles.

'Thank God!' said Katerina, but she screamed again when she saw that the Cossacks had picked up their muskets. They put in the flints and drew the triggers.

Danilo fired and missed. Her father took aim . . . He was old, he did not see so well as the younger man, but his hand did not tremble. A shot rang out . . . Danilo staggered; the crimson blood stained the left sleeve of his Cossack tunic.

'No!' he cried, 'I will not yield so easily. Not the left but the right hand is ataman. I have a Turkish pistol hanging on the wall: never yet has it failed me. Come down from the wall, old comrade! Do your friend a service!' Danilo stretched out his hand.

'Danilo!' cried Katerina in despair, clutching his hands and falling at his feet. 'Not for myself I beseech you. There is but one end for me: unworthy is the wife who will outlive her husband; Dnieper, the cold Dnieper will be my grave . . . But look at your son, Danilo, look at your son! Who will cherish the poor child? Who will be kind to him? Who will teach him to race on the raven steed, to fight for faith and freedom, to drink and carouse like a Cossack? You must perish, my son, you must perish! Your father will not think of you! See how he turns away his head. Oh, I know you now! You are a wild beast and not a man! You have the heart of a wolf and the mind of a crafty reptile! I thought there was a drop of pity in you, that there was human feeling in your breast of stone. Terribly have I been deceived! This will be a delight to you. Your bones will dance in the grave with joy when they hear the foul brutes of Poles throwing your son into the flames, when your son shrieks under the knife or the scalding water. Oh, I know you! You would be glad to rise up from the grave and fan the flames under him with your cap!'

'Stay, Katerina! Come, my precious Ivan, let me kiss you! No, my child, no one shall touch a hair of your head. You shall grow up to the glory of your fatherland; like a whirlwind you shall fly at the head of the Cossacks with a velvet cap on your head and a sharp sword in your hand. Give me your hand, father! Let us forget what has been between us! For what wrong I have done you I ask pardon. Why do you not give me your hand?' said Danilo to Katerina's father, who stood without moving, with no sign of anger nor of reconciliation on his face.

'Father!' cried Katerina, embracing and kissing him, 'don't be merciless, forgive Danilo: he will never offend you again!'

'For your sake only, my daughter, I forgive him!' he answered, kissing her with a strange glitter in his eyes.

Katerina shuddered faintly: the kiss and the strange glitter seemed uncanny to her. She leaned her elbows on the table, at which Danilo was bandaging his wounded hand, while he mused that he had acted ill and unlike a Cossack in asking pardon when he had done no wrong.

4

The day broke, but without sunshine: the sky was overcast and a fine rain was falling on the plains, on the forest and on the broad Dnieper. Katerina woke up, but not joyfully: her eyes were tear-stained, and she was restless and uneasy.

'My dear husband, my precious husband! I have had a strange dream!'

'What dream, my sweet wife Katerina?'

'I had a strange dream, and as vivid as though it were real, that my father was that very monster whom we saw at the Esaul's. But I entreat you, do not put faith in the dream: one dreams all manner of foolishness. I dreamed that I was standing before him, was trembling and frightened and all my veins moaned at every word he said. If only you had heard what he said . . . '

'What did he say, my golden Katerina?'

'He said: "Look at me, Katerina, how handsome I am! People are wrong in saying I am ugly. I should make you a splendid husband. See what a look there is in my eyes!" Then he turned his eyes full of fire upon me, I cried out and woke up . . . '

'Yes, dreams tell many a true thing. But do you know that all is not quiet beyond the mountain? I fancy the Poles have begun to show themselves again. Gorobets sent me a message to keep awake; but he need not have troubled – I am not asleep as it is. My lads have piled up a dozen barricades during the night. The common soldiers we will regale with leaden plums and the gentry shall dance to the whips.'

'And father, does he know of this?'

'Your father is a burden on my back! I cannot make him out. He has committed many sins in foreign parts, I'll be bound. What other reason can there be? Here he has lived with us more than a month and not once has he made merry like a true Cossack! He would not drink mead! Do you hear, Katerina, he would not drink the mead which I wrung out of the Jews at Brest. Hey, lad!' cried Danilo, 'run to the cellar, boy, and bring me the Jews' mead! He won't even drink vodka! What do you make of that? I verily believe, my lady Katerina, that he does not believe in Christ. Eh, what do you think?'

'God knows what you are saying, my lord Danilo!'

'Strange, wife!' Danilo went on, taking the earthenware mug from the Cossack, 'even the unclean Catholics have a weakness for vodka; it is only the Turks who do not drink. Well, Stetsko, have you had a good sip of mead in the cellar?'

'I just tried it, master.'

'You are lying, you son of a dog! See how the flies have settled on your moustache! I can see from your eyes that you have gulped down half a pailful. Oh, you Cossacks! What reckless fellows! Ready to give all else to a comrade, but he keeps his drink to himself. It is a long time, my lady Katerina, since I have been drunk. Eh?'

'A long time indeed! Why, last . . .'

'Don't be afraid, don't be afraid, I won't drink more than a mugful! And here is the Turkish abbot at the door!' he muttered through his teeth, seeing his father-in-law stooping to come in.

'What's this, my daughter!' said the father, taking his cap off his head and setting straight his girdle where hung a sabre set with precious stones, 'the sun is already high and your dinner is not ready.'

'Dinner is ready, my lord and father, we will serve it at once! Bring out the pot of dumplings!' said the young mistress to the old serving-woman who was wiping the wooden bowls. 'Stay, I had better get it out myself, while you call the men.'

They all sat down on the floor in a ring; facing the ikons sat the father, on his left Danilo, on his right Katerina, and ten of the trustiest servants in blue and yellow tunics.

'I don't like these dumplings!' said the father, laying down his spoon after eating a little, 'there is no flavour in them!'

'I know you like Jewish noodles better,' thought Danilo. 'Why do you say there is no flavour in the dumplings, father-in-law? Are they badly made or what? My Katerina makes dumplings such as the Hetman does not often taste. And there is no need to despise them: it is a Christian food! All holy people and godly saints have eaten dumplings!'

Not a word from the father; Danilo, too, said no more.

They served roast boar with cabbage and plums.

'I don't like pork,' said Katerina's father, picking out a spoonful of cabbage.

'Why don't you like pork?' said Danilo, 'it is only Turks and Jews who won't eat pork.'

The father frowned more angrily than ever.

He ate nothing but some baked flour-pudding with milk over it, and instead of vodka drank some black liquid from a bottle he took out of his bosom.

After dinner Danilo slept like a hero and only woke towards evening. He sat down to write to the Cossack troops, while his young wife sat on the oven-step, rocking the cradle with her foot. The lord Danilo sat there, his left eye on his writing while his right eye looked out of the window. From the window far away he could see the shining mountains and the Dnieper; beyond the Dnieper lay the dark-blue forest; overhead glimmered the clear night-sky. But the lord Danilo was not gazing at the far-away sky and the blue forest; he was watching the projecting tongue of land on which stood the old castle. He fancied that a light gleamed at a narrow little window in the castle. But everything was still; it must have been his fancy. All he could hear was from three sides the hollow murmur of the Dnieper down below and the resounding splash of the waves for a moment awakening one after the other. It was not in a turmoil; like an old man, it muttered and grumbled and found nothing to its taste. Everything has changed about it; it keeps up a feud with the mountains, wood and meadows on its banks and carries its complaints against them to the Black Sea.

And now on the wide expanse of the Dnieper he descried the black speck of a boat, and again there was a gleam of light in the castle. Danilo gave a low whistle and the faithful serving-man ran in at the sound.

'Make haste, Stetsko, bring with you a sharp sword and a musket, and follow me!'

'Are you going out?' asked Katerina.

'I am, wife. I must look everywhere and see that all is in order.'

'But I am fearful to be left alone. I am weighed down with sleep: what if I should have the same dream again? And, indeed, I am not sure it was a dream – it was all so living.'

'The old woman will stay with you, and there are Cossacks sleeping in the porch and in the courtyard.'

'The old woman is asleep already, and somehow I put no trust in the Cossacks. Listen, my lord Danilo; lock me in the room and take the key with you. Then I shall not be so fearful; and let the Cossacks lie before the door.'

'So be it!' said Danilo, wiping the dust off his musket and loading it with powder.

The faithful Stetsko stood already equipped with all the Cossack's accoutrements. Danilo put on his astrakhan cap, closed the window, bolted and locked the door, and, stepping between his sleeping Cossacks, went out from the courtyard towards the mountains.

The sky was almost completely clear again. A fresh breeze blew lightly from the Dnieper. But for the wail of a gull in the distance all was silent. But a faint rustle stirred . . . Burulbash and his faithful servant stealthily hid behind the brambles that screened a barricade of felled trunks. Someone in a red tunic, with two pistols, and a sword at his side came down the mountain-side. ''Tis my father-in-law,' said Danilo, scanning him from behind the bushes. 'Whither goes he at this hour, and with what design? Mind, Stetsko, keep a sharp watch which road your mistress's father takes.'

The man in the red tunic went down to the riverbank and turned towards the jutting tongue of land.

'Ah, so that is where he is going,' said Danilo. 'Why, Stetsko, hasn't he gone to the wizard's den?'

'Nowhere else, for certain, my lord Danilo! Or we should have seen him on the other side; but he disappeared near the castle.'

'Wait a minute, let us get out, and follow his track. There is some secret in this. Yes, Katerina, I told you your father was an evil man; he did nothing like a good Christian.'

Danilo and his faithful servant leaped out on the headland. Soon they were out of sight; the slumbering forest around the castle hid them. A gleam of light came into an upper window; the Cossacks stood below wondering how to climb to it; no gate nor door was to be seen; doubtless there was a door in the courtyard, but how could they climb in? They could hear in the distance the clanking of chains and the stirring of dogs.

'Why am I wasting time?' said Danilo, seeing a big oak tree by the window. 'Stay here, lad! I will climb up the oak; from it I can look straight into the window.'

With this he took off his girdle, put down his sword that it might not jingle, and gripping the branches lifted himself up. There was still a light at the window. Sitting on a branch close to the window, he held on to the tree and looked in: it was light in the room but there was no candle. On the wall were mysterious symbols; weapons were hanging there, but all were strange – not such as are worn by Turks or Tatars or Poles or Christians or the noble Swedish people. Bats flitted to and fro under the ceiling and their shadows flitted to and fro over the floor, the doors and the walls. Then the door noiselessly opened. Someone in a red tunic walked in and went straight up to the table, which was covered with a white cloth. 'It is he, it is my father-in-law!' Danilo crept a little lower down and huddled closer to the tree.

But his father-in-law had no time to look whether any one were peeping in at the window. He came in, morose and ill-humoured; he drew the cloth off the table, and at once the room was filled with transparent blue light; but the waves of pale golden light with which the room had been filled, eddied and dived, as in a blue sea, without mingling with it, and ran through it in streaks like the lines in marble. Then he set a pot upon the table and began scattering some herbs in it.

Danilo looked more attentively and saw that he was no longer wearing the red tunic; and that now he had on full trousers, such as Turks wear, with pistols in his girdle and on his head a queer cap embroidered all over with letters that were neither Russian nor Polish. As he looked at his face the face began to change; his nose grew longer and hung right down over his lips; in one instant his mouth stretched to his ears; a crooked tooth stood out beyond his lips; and he saw before him the same wizard who had appeared at the Esaul's wedding feast. 'Your dream told truth, Katerina!' thought Burulbash.

The wizard began pacing round the table; the symbols on the wall began changing more rapidly, the bats flitted more swiftly up and down and to and fro. The blue light grew dimmer and dimmer and at last seemed to fade away. And now there was only a dim pinkish light in the room. With a faint ringing sound this marvellous light seemed to flood every corner, and suddenly it vanished and all was darkness. Nothing was heard but a murmur like the wind in the quiet evening hour when hovering over the mirrorlike water it bows the silvery willows lower into its depths. And it seemed to Danilo as though the moon were shining in the room, the stars were moving, there were vague glimpses of the bright blue sky within it, and he even felt the chill of night coming from it. And Danilo fancied (he began fingering his moustaches to make sure he was not dreaming) that it was no longer the sky but his own hut he was seeing through the window; his Tatar and Turkish swords were hanging on the walls; round the walls were the shelves with pots and pans; on the table stood bread and salt; the cradle hung from the ceiling . . . but terrible faces looked out where the ikons should have been; on the oven-step . . . but a thick mist hid all and it was dark again. And with a wonderful sound the rosy light flooded the room again, and again the wizard stood motionless in his strange turban. The sounds grew louder and deeper, the delicate rosy light shone more brilliant and something white like a cloud hovered in the middle of the room; and it seemed to lord Danilo that the cloud was not a cloud, that a woman was standing there; but what was she made of? Of air, surely? Why did she stand not touching the floor, not leaning on anything, why did the rosy light and the magic symbols on the wall show through her? And now she moved her transparent head; a soft light shone in her pale blue eyes; her hair curled and fell over her shoulders like a pale grey mist; a faint flush coloured her lips like the scarcely perceptible crimson glimmer of dawn glowing through the white transparent sky of morning; the brows darkened a little . . . Ah, it was Katerina! Danilo felt his limbs turned to stone; he tried to speak, but his lips moved without uttering a sound.

The wizard stood without moving. 'Where have you been?' he asked, and the figure standing before him trembled.

'Oh, why did you call me up?' she moaned softly. 'I was so happy. I was in the place where I was born and lived for fifteen years. Ah, how good it was there! How green and fragrant was the meadow where I used to play in childhood! The darling wild flowers were the same as ever, and our hut and the garden! Oh, how my dear mother embraced me! How much love there was in her eyes! She caressed me, she kissed my lips and my cheeks, combed out my fair hair with a fine comb . . . Father!' Then she bent her pale eyes on the wizard. 'Why did you slay my mother?'

The wizard shook his finger at her menacingly. 'Did I ask you to speak of that?' And the ethereal beauty trembled. 'Where is your mistress now?'

'My mistress Katerina has fallen asleep and I was glad of it: I flew up and darted off. For long years I have longed to see my mother. I am suddenly fifteen again, I feel light as a bird. Why have you sent for me?'

'You remember all I said to you yesterday?' the wizard said, so softly that it was hard to catch the words.

'I remember, I remember! But what would I not give to forget them. Poor Katerina, there is much she knows not that her spirit knows!'

'It is Katerina's spirit,' thought Danilo, but still he dared not stir.

'Repent, father! Is it not dreadful that after every murder you commit the dead rise up from their graves?'

'You are at your old tune again!' said the wizard menacingly. 'I will have my way, I will make you do as I will, Katerina shall love me . . .'

'Oh, you are a monster and not my father!' she moaned. 'No, your will shall not be done! It is true that by your foul spells you have power to call up and torture her spirit; but only God can make her do what He wills. No, never shall Katerina, so long as I am living in her body, bring herself to so ungodly a deed. Father, a terrible judgment is at hand! Even if you were not my father, you would never make me false to my faithful and beloved husband. Even if my husband were not true and dear to me, I would not betray him, for God loves not souls that are faithless and false to their vows.'

Then she fixed her pale eyes on the window under which Danilo was sitting and stood stock-still . . .

'What are you looking at? Whom do you see there . . . ?' cried the wizard.

The wraith of Katerina trembled. But already Danilo was on the ground and with his faithful Stetsko making his way to his mountain home. 'Terrible, terrible!' he murmured to himself, feeling a thrill of fear in his Cossack heart, and he rapidly crossed his courtyard, in which the Cossacks slept as soundly as ever, all but one who sat on guard smoking a pipe.

The sky was all spangled with stars.

5

'How glad I am you have awakened me!' said Katerina, wiping her eyes with the embroidered sleeve of her smock and looking her husband up and down as he stood facing her. 'What a terrible dream I have had! I could hardly breathe! Ough . . . ! I thought I was dying . . .'

'What was your dream? Was it like this?' And Burulbash told his wife all that he had seen.

'How did you know it, husband?' asked Katerina in amazement. 'But no, many things you tell me I did not know. No, I did not dream that my father murdered my mother; I did not dream of the dead. No, Danilo, you have not told the dream right. Oh, what a fearful man my father is!'

'And it is no wonder that you have not dreamed of that. You do not know a tenth part of what your spirit knows. Do you know your father is the Antichrist? Only last year when I was getting ready to go with the

Poles against the Crimean Tatars (I was still allied with that faithless people then), the Father Superior of the Bratsky Monastery (he is a holy man, wife) told me that the Antichrist has the power to call up every man's spirit; for the spirit wanders at its own will when the body is asleep and flies with the archangels about the dwelling of God. I disliked your father's face from the first. I would not have married you had I known you had such a father; I would have given you up and not have taken upon myself the sin of being allied to the brood of Antichrist.'

'Danilo!' cried Katerina, hiding her face in her hands and bursting into tears. 'In what have I been to blame? Have I been false to you, my beloved husband? How have I roused your wrath? Have I not served you truly? Do I say a word to cross you when you come back merry from a drinking bout? Have I not borne you a black-browed son?'

'Do not weep, Katerina; now I know you and nothing would make me abandon you. The sin all lies at your father's door.'

'No, do not call him my father! He is not my father. God is my witness I disown him, I disown my father! He is Antichrist, a rebel against God! If he were perishing, if he were drowning, I would not hold out a hand to save him; if his throat were parched by some magic herb I would not give him a drop of water. You are my father!'

6

In a deep underground cellar at lord Danilo's the wizard lay bound in iron chains and locked in with three locks; while his devilish castle above the Dnieper was on fire and the waves, glowing red as blood, splashed and surged round the ancestral walls. It was not for sorcery, it was not for ungodly deeds that the wizard lay in the underground cellar – for his wickedness God was his judge; it was for secret treachery that he was imprisoned, for plotting with the foes of Orthodox Russia to sell to the Catholics the Ukrainian people and burn Christian churches. The wizard was gloomy; thoughts black as night strayed through his mind; he had but one day left to live and on the morrow he would take leave of the world; his punishment was awaiting him on the morrow. It was no light one: it would be an act of mercy if he were boiled alive in a cauldron or his sinful skin were flayed from him. The wizard was melancholy, his head was bowed. Perhaps he was already repenting on the eve of death; but his sins were not such as God would forgive. Above him was a little window covered with an iron grating. Clanking his chains he stood to look out of the window and see whether his daughter were passing. She was gentle and forgiving as a dove; would she not have mercy on her father . . . ? But there was no one. The road ran below the window, no one passed along it. Beneath it rippled the Dnieper, it cared for no one; it murmured, and its monotonous splash sounded dreary to the captive.

Then someone appeared upon the road – it was a Cossack! And the prisoner heaved a deep sigh. Again it was empty. Yonder someone was coming down the hill . . . a green overskirt flapped in the wind . . . a golden headdress glittered on her head . . . It was she! He pressed still closer to the window. Now she was coming nearer . . .

'Katerina, daughter! Have pity on me, be merciful!'

She was dumb, she would not listen, she did not turn her eyes towards the prison, and had already passed, already vanished. The whole world was empty; dismally the Dnieper murmured; it lays a load of sadness on the heart; but did the wizard know aught of such sadness?

The day was drawing to a close. Now the sun was setting; now it had vanished. Now it was evening, it was cool; an ox was lowing somewhere; sounds of voices floated from afar; people doubtless going home from their work and making merry; a boat flashed into sight on the Dnieper . . . no one thought of the prisoner. A silver crescent gleamed in the sky; now someone came along the road in the opposite direction; it was hard to tell the figure in the darkness; it was Katerina coming back.

'Daughter, for Christ's sake! even the savage wolf-whelps will not tear their mother in pieces – daughter, give one look at least to your guilty father!'

She heeded not but walked on.

'Daughter, for the sake of your unhappy mother . . . '

She stopped.

'Come close and hear my last words!'

'Why do you call me, enemy of God? Do not call me daughter! There is no kinship between us. What do you want of me for the sake of my unhappy mother?'

'Katerina, my end is nigh; I know that your husband means to tie me to the tail of a wild mare and send it racing in the open country, and maybe he will invent an end more dreadful yet . . . '

'But is there in the world a punishment bad enough for your sins? You may be sure no one will plead for you.'

'Katerina! It is not punishment in this world that I fear but in the next . . . You are innocent, Katerina; your soul will fly about God in paradise; but your ungodly father's soul will burn in a fire everlasting and never will that fire be quenched; it will burn more and more hotly; no drop of dew will fall upon it, nor will the wind breathe on it . . . '

'I can do nought to ease that punishment,' said Katerina, turning away.

'Katerina, stay for one word! You can save my soul! You know not yet how good and merciful is God. Have you heard of the Apostle Paul, what a sinful man he was – but afterwards he repented and became a saint?'

'What can I do to save your soul?' said Katerina. 'It is not for a weak woman like me to think of that.'

'If I could but get out, I would abandon everything. I will repent, I will go into a cave, I will wear a hair shirt next my skin and will spend day and night in prayer. I will give up not only meat, but even fish I will not taste! I will lay nothing under me when I lie down to sleep! And I will pray without ceasing, pray without ceasing! And if God's mercy does not release me from at least a hundredth part of my sins, I will bury myself up to the neck in the earth or build myself up in a wall of stone; I will take neither food nor drink and perish; and I will give all my goods to the monks that they may sing a requiem for me for forty days and forty nights.'

Katerina pondered. 'If I were to unlock you I could not undo your fetters.'

'I do not fear chains,' he said. 'You say that they have fettered my hands and feet? No, I threw a mist over their eyes and held out a dry tree instead of hands. Here, see: I have not a chain upon me now!' he said, walking into the middle of the cellar. 'I should not fear these walls either and should pass them; but your husband does not know what walls these are: they were built by a holy hermit, and no evil power can deliver a prisoner from them without the very key with which the hermit used to lock his cell. Just such a cell will I build for myself, incredible sinner as I have been, when I am free again.'

'Listen, I will let you out; but what if you deceive me?' said Katerina, standing still at the door, 'and instead of repenting, again become the devil's comrade?'

'No, Katerina, I have not long left to live; my end is near even if I am not put to death. Can you believe that I will give myself up to eternal punishment?'

The key grated in the lock.

'Farewell! God in His mercy keep you, my child!' said the wizard, kissing her.

'Do not touch me, you fearful sinner; make haste and go . . . ' said Katerina.

But he was gone.

'I let him out!' she said to herself, terror-stricken, looking wildly at the walls. 'What answer shall I give my husband now? I am undone. There is nothing left but to bury myself alive!' and sobbing she almost fell upon the block on which the prisoner had been sitting. 'But I have saved a soul,' she said softly. 'I have done a godly deed; but my husband . . . I have deceived him for the first time. Oh, how terrible, how hard it will be for me to lie to him! Someone is coming! It is he! My husband!' she uttered a desperate shriek and fell senseless on the ground.

7

'It is I, my daughter! It is I, my darling!' Katerina heard, as she revived and saw the old serving-woman before her. The woman bent down and seemed to whisper to her, and stretching out her withered old hand sprinkled her with water.

'Where am I?' said Katerina, sitting up and looking round her. 'The Dnieper is splashing before me, behind me are the mountains . . . Where have you taken me, granny?'

'I have taken you out; I have carried you in my arms from the stifling cellar; I locked up the cellar again that you might not be in trouble with my lord Danilo.'

'Where is the key?' asked Katerina, looking at her girdle. 'I don't see it.'

'Your husband has taken it, to have a look at the wizard, my child.'

'To look! Granny, I am lost!' cried Katerina.

'God mercifully preserve us from that, my child! Only hold your peace, my little lady, no one will know anything.'

'He has escaped, the cursed Antichrist! Do you hear, Katerina, he has escaped!' said Danilo, coming up to his wife. His eyes flashed fire; his sword hung clanking at his side. His wife was like one dead.

'Has someone let him out, dear husband?' she brought out trembling.

'Yes, someone has – you are right: the devil. Look, where he was is a log covered with chains. It is God's pleasure, it seems, that the devil should not fear a Cossack's hands! If any one of my Cossacks had dreamed of such a thing and I knew of it . . . I could find no punishment bad enough for him!'

'And if it had been I?' Katerina could not resist saying, and she stopped, panic-stricken.

'If you had done it you would be no wife to me. I would sew you up in a sack and drown you in mid-Dnieper . . . !'

Katerina could hardly breathe and she felt the hair stand up on her head.

8

On the frontier road the Poles had gathered at a tavern and feasted there for two days. There were not a few of the rabble. They had doubtless met for some raid: some had muskets; there was jingling of spurs and clanking of swords. The nobles made merry and boasted, they talked of their marvellous deeds, they mocked at the Orthodox Christians, calling the Ukrainian people their serfs, and insolently twirled their moustaches and sprawled on the benches. There was a priest among them, too; but he was like themselves and had not even the semblance of a Christian priest: he drank and caroused with them and uttered shameful words with his unclean tongue. The servants were no better than their masters: tucking up the sleeves of their tattered tunics, they walked about with a swagger as though they were of consequence. They played cards, struck each other on the nose with cards; they had brought with them other men's wives; there was shouting, quarrelling . . . ! Their masters were at the height of their revelry, playing all sorts of tricks, pulling the Jewish tavern-keeper by the beard, painting a cross on his impious brow, shooting blank charges at the women and dancing the Cracovienne[55] with their impious priest. Such sinfulness had never been seen on Russian soil even among the Tatars; it was God's chastisement, seemingly, for the sins of Russia that she should be put to so great a shame! In the midst of the bedlam, talk could be heard of lord Danilo's homestead above the Dnieper, of his lovely wife . . . The gang of thieves was plotting foul deeds!

9

The lord Danilo sat at the table in his house leaning on his elbow, thinking. The lady Katerina sat on the oven-step, singing.

'I am sad, my wife!' said lord Danilo. 'My head aches and my heart aches. I feel weighed down. It seems my death is hovering not far away.'

'Oh, my precious husband! Lean your head upon me! Why do you cherish such black thoughts?' thought Katerina, but dared not utter the words. It was bitter to her, feeling her guilt, to receive her husband's caresses.

'Listen, wife!' said Danilo, 'do not desert our son when I am no more. God will give you no happiness either in this world or the next if you forsake him. Sad it will be for my bones to rot in the damp earth, sadder still it will be for my soul!'

'What are you saying, my husband? Was it not you who mocked at us weak women? And now you are talking like a weak woman yourself. You must live long years yet.'

'No, Katerina, my heart feels death near at hand. The world grows a sad place; cruel days are coming. Ah, I remember, I remember the years – they will not return for sure! He was living then, the honour and glory of our army, old Konashevitch! The Cossack regiments pass before my eyes as though it were today. Those were golden days, Katerina! The old Hetman sat on a raven steed; his mace shone in his hand; the soldiers stood around him, and on each side moved the red sea of the Zaporozhtsy. The Hetman began to speak – and all stood as though turned to stone. The old man wept when he told us of old days and battles long ago. Ah, Katerina, if only you knew how we fought in those days with the Turks! The scar on my head shows even now. Four bullets pierced me in four places and not one of the wounds has quite healed. How much gold we took in those days! The Cossacks filled their caps with precious stones. What horses, Katerina! If you only knew, what horses, Katerina, we drove away with us! Ah, I shall never fight like that! One would think I am not old and I am strong in body, yet the sword drops out of my hand, I live doing nothing and know not what I live for. There is no order in the Ukraine: the colonels and the esauls quarrel like dogs: there is no chief over them all. Our gentry have changed everything after the Polish style, they have copied their sly ways . . . they have sold their souls, accepting the Uniat faith. The Jews are oppressing the poor. Oh, those days, those days! Those days that are past! Whither have you fled, my years? Go to the cellar, boy, and bring me a jug of mead! I will drink to the life of the past and to the years that have gone!'

'How shall we receive our guests, lord Danilo? The Poles are coming from the side of the meadow,' said Stetsko, coming into the hut.

'I know what they are coming for,' said Danilo. 'Saddle the horses, my faithful men! Put on your harness! Bare your swords! Don't forget to take your rations of lead: we must do honour to our guests!'

But before the Cossacks had time to saddle their horses and load their guns, the Poles covered the mountain-side as leaves cover the ground in autumn.

'Ah, here we have foes to try our strength with!' said Danilo, looking at the stout Poles swaying majestically on their gold-harnessed steeds in the front ranks. 'It seems it is my lot to have one more glorious jaunt! Take your pleasure, Cossack soul, for the last time! Go ahead, lads, our festival has come!'

And the festival was kept on the mountains and great was the merry-making: swords were playing, bullets flying, horses neighing and stamping. The shouting dazed the brain; the smoke blinded the eye. All was confusion, but the Cossack felt where was friend, where was foe; whenever a bullet whistled a gallant rider dropped from the saddle, whenever a sword flashed – a head fell to the ground, muttering wild words.

But the red crest of lord Danilo's Cossack cap could always be seen in the crowd; the gold girdle of his dark blue tunic gleamed bright, the mane on his raven steed fluttered in the breeze. Like a bird he flew hither and thither, shouting and waving his Damascus sword and hacking to right and to left. Hack away, Cossack, make merry! Comfort your gallant heart; but look not at the gold trappings and tunics: trample under foot the gold and jewels! Stab, Cossack! Wreak your will, Cossack! But look back: already the godless Poles are setting fire to the huts and driving away the frightened cattle. And like a whirlwind Danilo turned round, and the cap with the red crest gleamed now by the huts while the crowd about him scattered.

Hour after hour the Poles fought with the Cossacks; there were not many left of either; but lord Danilo did not slacken; with his long spear he thrust Poles from the saddle and his spirited steed trampled them under foot. Already his yard was almost cleared, already the Poles were flying in all directions; already the Cossacks were stripping the golden tunics and rich trappings from the slain; already lord Danilo was setting off in pursuit, when he looked round to call his men together . . . and was overwhelmed with fury: he saw Katerina's father. There he stood on the hillside aiming his musket at him. Danilo urged his horse straight upon him . . . Cossack, you go to your ruin! Then came the crack of a shot – and the wizard vanished behind the hill. Only the faithful Stetsko caught a glimpse of the red tunic and the strange hat. The Cossack staggered and fell to the ground. The faithful Stetsko flew to his master's aid: his lord lay stretched on the ground with his bright eyes closed while the crimson blood spurted from his breast. But he was aware of his faithful servant's presence; slowly he raised his eyelids and his eyes gleamed: 'Farewell, Stetsko! Tell Katerina not to forsake her son! And do not you, my faithful servants, forsake him either!' and he ceased. His gallant soul flew from his noble body; his lips turned blue; the Cossack slept, never to wake again.

His faithful servant sobbed and beckoned to Katerina: 'Come, lady, come! Deeply has your lord been carousing; in drunken sleep he lies on the damp earth; and long will it be ere he awakens!'

Katerina wrung her hand and fell like a sheaf of corn on the dead body: 'Husband, is it you lying here with closed eyes? Rise up, my peerless falcon, stretch out your hand! Stand up! Look, if only once, at your Katerina, move your lips, utter one word . . . ! But you are mute, you are mute, my noble lord! You have turned blue as the Black Sea. Your heart is not beating! Why are you so cold, my lord? It seems my tears are not scalding, they have no power to warm you! It seems my weeping is not loud, it will not waken you! Who will lead your regiments now? Who will gallop on your raven steed, loudly calling, and lead the Cossacks, waving your sword? Cossacks, Cossacks, where is your honour and glory? Your honour and glory is lying with closed eyes on the damp earth. Bury me, bury me with him! Throw earth upon my eyes! Press the maple boards upon my white bosom! My beauty is useless to me now!'

Katerina grieved and wept; while the distant horizon was covered with dust: the old Esaul Gorobets was galloping to the rescue.

10

Lovely is the Dnieper in still weather when, freely and smoothly, its waters glide through forests and mountains. Not a sound, not a ripple is stirring. You look and cannot tell whether its majestic expanse moves or moves not; and it might be of molten crystal and like a blue road made of looking-glass, immeasurably broad, endlessly long, twining and twisting about the green world. Sweet it is then for the burning sun to peep at itself from the heights and to plunge its beams in the cool of its glassy waves, and for the forests on the banks to watch their bright reflections in the water. Wreathed in green, they press with the wild flowers close to the river's edge, and bending over look in and are never tired of gazing and admiring their bright reflection, and smile and greet it with nodding branches. In mid-Dnieper they dare not look: none but the sun and the blue sky gaze into it; rarely a bird flies to the middle of the river. Glorious it is! No river like it in the world! Lovely too is the Dnieper on a warm summer night when all are sleeping – man, beast and bird, while God alone majestically surveys earth and heaven and majestically shakes His garment. The stars are scattered from His garment; they glow and shine above the world, and all are reflected together in the Dnieper. All of them the Dnieper holds in its dark bosom; not one escapes it till quenched in the sky. The black forests dotted with sleeping crows and the mountains cleft asunder in ages past strive, hanging over, to conceal the river in their long shadows, but in vain! There is nought in the world could hide the Dnieper. Deep, deep blue it flows, spreading its waters far and wide at midnight as at midday; it is seen far, far away, as far as the eye of man can see. Shrinking from the cold of night and huddling closer to the bank, it leaves behind a silver trail gleaming like the blade of a Damascus sword, while the deep blue water slumbers again. Lovely then, too, is the Dnieper, and no river is like it in the world! When dark blue storm-clouds pile in masses over the sky, the dark forest totters to its roots, the oaks creak, and the lightning zigzagging through the storm-clouds suddenly lights up the whole world – terrible then is the Dnieper! Then its mountainous billows roar flinging themselves against the hillside, and flashing and moaning rush back and wail and lament in the distance. So the old mother laments as she lets her Cossack son go to the war. Bold and reckless, he rides his raven steed, arms akimbo and jaunty cap on one side, while she, sobbing, runs after him, seizes him by the stirrup, catches the bridle and wrings her hands over him, bathed in bitter tears.

Strange and black are the burnt tree-stumps and stones on the jutting bank between the warring waves. And the landing boat is beaten against the bank, thrown upwards and flung back again. What Cossack dared row out in a boat when old Dnieper was raging? Surely he knew not that the river swallows men like flies.

The boat reached the bank, out of it stepped the wizard. He was in no happy mood: bitter to him was the funeral feast which the Cossacks had kept over their slain master. Heavily had the Poles paid for it: forty-four of them in all their harness and accoutrements and thirty-three servants were hacked to pieces, while the others were captured with their horses to be sold to the Tatars.

He went down stone steps between the burnt stumps to a place where he had a cave dug deep in the earth. He went in softly, not letting the door creak, put a pot on the table that was covered with a cloth and began with his long hands strewing into it some strange herbs; he took a ladle made of some rare wood, scooped up some water with it and poured it out, moving his lips and repeating an incantation. The cave was flooded with rosy light and his face was terrible to look upon: it seemed covered with blood, only the deep wrinkles showed up black upon it and his eyes were as though on fire. Foul sinner! His beard was grey, his face was lined with wrinkles, he was shrivelled with age, and still he persisted in his godless design. A white cloud began to hover in the cave and something like joy gleamed in his face; but why did he suddenly stand motionless with his mouth open, not daring to stir, why did his hair rise up on his head? The features of a strange face gleamed upon him from the cloud. Unbidden, uninvited it had come to visit him; it grew more distinct and fastened its eyes immovably upon him. The features, eyebrows, eyes, lips – all were unfamiliar; never in his life had he seen them. And there was nothing terrible, seemingly, about it, but he was overwhelmed with horror. The strange marvellous face still looked fixedly at him from the cloud. Then the cloud vanished, but the unfamiliar face was more distinct than ever and the piercing eyes were still riveted on him. The wizard turned white as a sheet; he shrieked in a wild unnatural voice and overturned the pot . . . All was over.

11

'Take comfort, my dear sister!' said the old Esaul Gorobets, 'rarely do dreams come true!'

'Lie down, sister,' said his young daughter-in-law, 'I will fetch an old dame, a wise woman; no evil spirit can stand against her, she will help you.'

'Fear nothing!' said his son, touching his sword, 'no one shall wrong you!'

Dully and with dim eyes Katerina looked at them all and found no word to say.

'I myself brought about my ruin: I let him out!' she said at last. 'He gives me no peace! Here I have been ten days with you in Kiev and my sorrow is no less. I thought that at least I could bring up my son to avenge . . . I dreamed of him, looking terrible! God forbid that you should ever see him like that! My heart is still throbbing. "I will kill your child, Katerina," he shouted, "if you do not marry me . . . " ' And she flung herself sobbing on the cradle; and the frightened child stretched out its little hands and cried.

The Esaul's son was boiling with anger as he heard such words.

The Esaul Gorobets himself was roused. 'Let him try coming here, the accursed Antichrist; he will learn whether there is still strength in the old Cossack's arm. God sees,' he said, turning his keen eyes to heaven, 'whether I did not hasten to give a hand to brother Danilo. It was His holy will! I found him lying on the cold bed upon which so many, many Cossacks have been laid. But what a funeral feast we had for him! We did not leave a single Pole alive! Be comforted, my child! No one shall dare to harm you, so long as I am alive or my son.'

As he finished speaking the old Cossack captain approached the cradle and the child saw hanging from a strap his red pipe set in silver and the pouch with the flashing steel, and stretched out its arms towards him and laughed. 'He takes after his father,' said the old Esaul, unfastening the pipe and giving it to the child, 'he is not out of the cradle, but he is thinking of a pipe already!'

Katerina heaved a sigh and fell to rocking the cradle. They agreed to spend the night together and soon afterwards they were all asleep; Katerina, too, dropped asleep.

All was still in the courtyard and the house; every one slept but the Cossacks who were keeping watch. Suddenly Katerina woke with a scream, and the others woke too. 'He is slain, he is murdered!' she cried, and flew to the cradle. All surrounded the cradle and were numb with horror when they saw that the child in it was dead. None uttered a sound, not knowing what to think of this unheard-of crime.

12

Far from the Ukraine, beyond Poland and the populous town of Lemberg,[56] run ranges of high mountains. Mountain after mountain, like chains of stone flung to right and to left over the land, they fetter it with layers of rock to keep out the resounding turbulent sea. These stony chains stretch into Wallachia[57] and the Sedmigradsky region[58] and stand like a huge horseshoe between the Galician and Hungarian peoples. There are no such mountains in our country. The eye shrinks from viewing them and no human foot has climbed to their tops. They are a wonderful sight. Was it some angry sea that broke away from its wide shores in a storm and threw its monstrous waves aloft and they turned to stone and remained motionless in the air? Or did heavy storm-clouds fall from heaven and cumber up the earth? For they have the same grey colour and their white crests flash and sparkle in the sun.

Up to the Carpathian Mountains one may hear Russian speech, and just beyond the mountain there are still here and there echoes of our native tongue; but further beyond, faith and speech are different. The numerous Hungarian people live there; they ride, fight and drink like any Cossack, and do not grudge gold pieces from their pockets for their horses' trappings and costly tunics. There are great wide lakes among the mountains. They are still as glass and as mirrors reflect bare mountain tops and the green slopes below.

But who rides through the night on a huge raven steed whether stars shine or not? What hero of superhuman stature gallops under the mountains, above the lakes, is mirrored with his gigantic horse in the still waters and throws his vast reflection on the mountains? His plated armour glitters, his sabre rattles by the saddle; his helmet is tilted forward; his moustaches are black; his eyes are closed; his eyelashes are drooping – he is asleep and drowsily holds the reins; and on the same horse sits with him a young child, and he, too, is asleep and drowsily holds on to the hero. Who is he, whither goes he, and why? Who knows. Not one day nor two has he been travelling over the mountains. Day breaks, the sun shines and he is seen no more; only from time to time the mountaineers behold a long shadow flitting over the mountains though the sky is bright and there is no cloud upon it. But as soon as night brings back the darkness, he appears again and is reflected in the lakes and his shadow follows him quivering. Already he has crossed many mountains and at last he reaches Krivan.[59] There is no mountain in the Carpathians higher than this one; it towers like a monarch above the others. There the horse and his rider halted and sank into even deeper slumber and the lowering clouds hid them from view.

13

'Hush . . . don't knock like that, nurse: my child is asleep. My baby cried a long time, now he is asleep. I am going to the forest, nurse! But why do you look at me like this? You are terrible: there are iron pincers coming out of your eyes . . . ugh, how long they are, and they glow like fire! You must be a witch! Oh, if you are a witch, go away! You will steal my son. How absurd the Esaul is; he thinks it is gay for me to live in Kiev. No, my husband and my son are here. Who will look after the house? I went out so quietly that even the dog and the cat did not hear me. Do you want to grow young again, nurse? That's not hard at all; you have but to dance. Look, how I dance.'

And uttering these incoherent sentences Katerina set to dancing, looking wildly about her and putting her arms akimbo. With a shriek she tapped with her feet, her silver heels clanked regardless of time or tune. Her black tresses floated loose about her white neck. Like a bird she flew round without resting, waving her hands and nodding her head, and it seemed as though she must either fall helpless to the ground or soar away from earth altogether.

The old nurse stood mournfully, her wrinkled face wet with tears; the trusty Cossacks had a load of sorrow on their hearts as they looked at their mistress. At last she was exhausted and languidly tapped with her feet on the same spot, fancying she was dancing a round. 'I have a necklace, lads,' she said, stopping at last, 'and you have not . . . ! Where is my husband?' she cried suddenly, drawing a Turkish dagger out of her girdle. 'Oh, this is not the knife I need.' With that, tears of grief came into her eyes. 'My father's heart is far away; it will not reach it. His heart is wrought of iron; it was forged by a witch in the furnace of hell. Why does not my father come? Does not he know that it is time to stab him? He wants me to come myself, it seems . . . ' and breaking off she laughed uncannily. 'A funny story came into my mind: I remembered how my husband was buried. He was buried alive, you know . . . It did make me laugh . . . ! Listen, listen!' and instead of speaking she began to sing:

> 'A blood-stained chariot races on,
> A Cossack lies upon it
> Shot through the breast, stabbed to the heart,
> In his right hand he holds an arrow
> And blood is trickling from it,
> A stream of blood is flowing.
> A plane tree stands over the river,
> Above the tree a raven croaks.
> A mother is weeping for the Cossack.
> Weep not, mother, do not grieve!
> For your son is married.
> He chose a lady for his bride,
> A mound of earth in the bare fields
> Without a door or window.
> And this is how my story ends.
> A fish was dancing with a crab,
> And may an ague take his mother,
> If he will not love me!'

This was how she muddled lines from different songs together. She had been living two days already in her own house and would not hear of Kiev. She would not say her prayers, refused to see any one, and wandered from morning till night in the dark oak thickets. Sharp twigs scratched her white face and shoulders; the wind fluttered her loose hair; the autumn leaves rustled under her feet – she looked at nothing. At the hour when the glow of sunset dies away and before the stars come out or the moon shines, it is fearful to walk in the forest; unbaptised infants scratch in the trees and clutch at the branches, sobbing and laughing, they hover over the road and the wastes of nettles; maidens who have lost their souls rise up one after the other from the depths of the Dnieper, their green tresses stream over their shoulders, the water drips splashing to the ground from their long hair; and a maiden shines through the water as through a veil of crystal; her lips smile mysteriously, her cheeks glow, her eyes bewitch the soul . . . as though she might burn with love, as though she might kiss one to death. Flee, Christian! Her lips are ice, her bed – the cold water; she will tickle you to death and drag you under water. Katerina looked at no one, in her frenzy she had no fear of the water-witches; she wandered at night with her knife, seeking her father.

In the early morning a visitor arrived of handsome appearance in a red tunic, and enquired for the lord Danilo; he heard all the story, wiped his tear-stained eyes with his sleeves and shrugged his shoulders. He said that he had fought side by side with Barulbash; side by side they had done battle with the Turks and the Crimeans; never had he thought that the lord Danilo would meet with such an end. The visitor told them many other things and wanted to see the lady Katerina.

At first Katerina heeded nothing of what the guest said; but afterwards she began to listen to his words as though understanding. He told her how Danilo and he had lived together like brothers; how once they had hidden under a dam from the Crimeans . . . Katerina listened and kept her eyes fixed upon him.

'She will recover,' the Cossacks thought, looking at her, 'this guest will heal her! She is listening like one who understands!'

The visitor began meanwhile describing how Danilo had once in a confidential conversation said to him: 'Mind, brother Kopryan, when it is God's will that I am gone, you take Katerina, take her for your wife . . .'

Katerina looked piercingly at him: 'Ah!' she shrieked, 'it is he, it is my father!' and she flew at him with her knife.

For a long time he struggled trying to snatch the knife from her; at last he snatched it away, raised it to strike – and a terrible deed was done: the father killed his frantic daughter.

The astounded Cossacks dashed at him, but the wizard had already leapt upon his horse and was gone.

14

An unheard-of marvel appeared beyond Kiev. All the nobles and the Hetmans assembled to see the marvel: in all directions the far distance had become visible. Far off was the dark blue of the mouth of the Dnieper and beyond that the Black Sea. Men who had travelled recognised the Crimea rising mountainous out of the sea and the marshy Sivash.[60] On the right could be seen the Galician land.[61]

'And what is that?' people asked the old men, pointing to white and grey crests looming far away in the sky, looking more like clouds.

'Those are the Carpathian Mountains!' said the old men, 'among them are some that are for ever covered with snow, and the clouds cling to them and hover there at night.'

Then a new miracle happened: the clouds vanished from the highest peak and on the top of it appeared a horseman, in full knightly accoutrements, with his eyes closed, and he was distinctly seen as though he had been standing close to them.

Then among the marvelling and fearful people, one leapt on a horse, and looking wildly about him as though to see whether he were pursued, hurriedly set his horse galloping at its utmost speed. It was the wizard. Why was he so panic-stricken? Looking in terror at the marvellous knight, he recognised the face which had appeared to him when he was working his spells. He could not have said why his whole soul was thrown into confusion at this sight, and, looking fearfully about him, he raced till he was overtaken by night and the stars began to come out. Then he turned homewards, perhaps to ask the Evil One what was meant by this marvel. He was just about to leap with his horse over a stream which lay across his path when his horse suddenly stopped in full gallop, looked round at him – and, marvellous to relate! laughed aloud! Two rows of white teeth gleamed horribly in the darkness. The wizard's hair stood up on his head. He uttered a wild scream – wept like one frantic and turned his horse straight for Kiev. He felt as though he were being pursued on all sides: the trees that surrounded him in the dark forest strove to strangle him, nodding their black beards and stretching out their long branches; the stars seemed to be racing ahead of him and pointing to the sinner; the very road seemed to be flying after him.

The despairing wizard fled to the holy places in Kiev.

15

A holy hermit sat alone in his cave before a little lamp and did not take his eyes off the holy book. It was many years since he had first shut himself up in his cave; he had already made himself a coffin in which he lay down to sleep instead of a bed. The holy man closed his book and fell to praying . . . Suddenly there ran in a man of a strange and terrible aspect. At first the holy hermit was astounded and stepped back seeing such a man. He was trembling all over like an aspen leaf; his eyes looked from side to side in panic, a light of terror gleamed in them; his hideous face made one shudder.

'Father, pray! pray!' he shouted desperately, 'pray for a lost soul!' and he sank to the ground.

The holy hermit crossed himself, took up his book, opened it and stepped back in horror, dropping the book: 'No, incredible sinner! There is no mercy for you! Avaunt! I cannot pray for you!'

'No?' the wizard cried frantically.

'Look! The letters in the holy book are dripping with blood . . . There has never been such a great sinner in the world!'

'Father! You are mocking me!'

'Hence, accursed sinner! I am not mocking you. I am overcome with fear. It is not good for a man to be with you!'

'No, no! You are mocking, say not so . . . I see that your lips are smiling and the rows of your old teeth are gleaming white!'

And like one possessed he flew at the holy hermit and killed him.

A terrible moan was heard and echoed through the forest and the fields. Dry withered arms with long claws rose up from beyond the forest; they trembled and disappeared.

And now he felt no fear nor anything. All was confusion: there was a noise in his ears, a noise in his head as though he were drunk, and everything before his eyes was veiled as though by spiders' webs. Leaping on to his horse he rode straight to Kanev, thinking thence to go through Tcherkassy[62] direct to the Crimean Tatars, though he knew not why he went. He rode one day and a second and still Kanev was not in sight. The road was the same, he ought to have reached it long before, but there was no sign of Kanev. Far away there gleamed the cupolas of churches; but that was not Kanev but Shumsk.[63] The wizard was amazed to find that he had travelled quite the wrong way. He turned back towards Kiev, and a day later a town appeared – not Kiev but Galitch,[64] a town further from Kiev than Shumsk and not far from Hungary. At a loss what to do he turned back, but felt again that he was going backwards as he went on. No one in the world could tell what was in the wizard's soul; and had any one seen and known, he would not have slept at night or laughed again in his life. It was not malice, not terror and not fierce anger. There is no word in the world to say what it was. He was burning, scalding, he would have liked to trample the whole country from Kiev to Galitch with all the people and everything in it and drown it in the Black Sea. But it was not from malice he would do it: no, he knew not why he wanted it. He shuddered when he saw the Carpathian Mountains and lofty Krivan, its crest capped with a grey cloud; the horse still galloped on and now was racing among the mountains. The clouds suddenly lifted, and facing him appeared the horseman in his terrible immensity . . . The wizard tried to halt, he tugged at the rein; the horse neighed wildly, tossed its mane and dashed towards the horseman. Then the wizard felt everything swoon within him, while the motionless horseman stirred and suddenly opened his eyes, saw the wizard flying towards him and laughed. The wild laugh echoed through the mountains like a clap of thunder and resounded in the wizard's heart, setting his whole body throbbing. He felt that some mighty being had taken possession of him and was moving within him, hammering on his heart and his veins . . . so fearfully that laugh resounded within him!

The horseman stretched out his fearful hand, seized the wizard and lifted him into the air. The wizard died instantly and he opened his eyes after his death: but he was dead and looked out of dead eyes. Neither the living nor the risen from the dead have such a terrible look in their eyes. He turned his dead eyes from side to side and saw dead men rising up from Kiev, from Galicia and the Carpathian Mountains, exactly like him.

Pale, very pale, one taller than another, one bonier than another, they thronged round the horseman who held this awful prey in his hand. The horseman laughed once more and dropped the wizard down a precipice. And all the corpses leapt into the precipice and fastened their teeth in the dead man's flesh. Another, taller and more terrible than all the rest, tried to rise from the ground but could not – he had not the power, he had grown so immense underground; and if he had risen out of the earth he would have overturned the Carpathians and the whole of the Sedmigradsky and the Turkish lands. He only stirred slightly, but that set the whole earth quaking, and overturned many houses and crushed many people.

And often in the Carpathians a sound is heard as though a thousand mills were churning up the water with their wheels: it is the sound of the dead men gnawing a corpse in the fatal abyss which no man has seen yet, for none dare pass it. It sometimes happens that the earth trembles from one end to another: that is said by the learned men to be due to a mountain near the sea from which flames issue and hot streams flow. But the old men who live in Hungary and Galicia know better, and say that it is the dead man who has grown so immense in the earth trying to rise that makes the earth quake.

16

A crowd had gathered round an old bandura-player in the town of Gluhov and had been listening for an hour to the blind man's playing. No bandura-player sang so well and such marvellous songs. First he sang of the rule of the Hetmans in the old days, of Sagaidatchny[65] and Hmelnitsky.[66] Times were different then: the Cossacks were at the height of their glory, they trampled their foes underfoot and no one dared to mock at them. The old man sang merry songs too, and looked about at the crowd as though his eyes could see, and his fingers with little plates of bone fixed on them danced like flies over the strings, and it seemed that the strings themselves were playing; and the crowd, the old people looking down and the young staring at the singer, dared not even whisper together.

'Stay,' said the old man, 'I will sing to you of what happened long ago.' The people pressed closer and the blind man sang:

'In the days of Stepan, prince of Sedmigrad (the prince of Sedmigrad was also King of the Poles[67]), there lived two Cossacks: Ivan and Petro. They lived together like brothers: "See here, Ivan," said Petro, "whatever you gain, let us go halves; when one is merry, the other is merry too; when one is sad, the other is sad too; when one wins booty, we share it; when one gets taken prisoner, the other sells everything to ransom him or else goes himself into captivity." And, indeed, whatever the Cossacks gained they shared equally: if they drove away herds of cattle or horses – they shared them.

'King Stepan made war on the Turks. He had been fighting with the Turks three weeks and could not drive them out. And the Turks had a Pasha who with a few janissaries could slaughter a whole regiment. So King Stepan proclaimed that if a brave warrior could be found to bring him the Pasha dead or alive he would give him a reward equal to the pay of the whole army.

' "Let us go and catch the Pasha, brother," said Ivan to Petro. And the two Cossacks set off, one one way, one the other.

'Whether Petro would have been successful or not there is no telling; but Ivan led the Pasha with a lasso round his neck to the King. "Brave fellow!" said King Stepan, and he commanded that he should be given a sum equal to the pay of the whole army, and that he should be given land wherever he chose and cattle as many as he pleased. As soon as Ivan received the reward from the King, he shared the money that very day with Petro. Petro took half of the King's money, but could not bear the thought that Ivan had been so honoured by the King, and he hid deep in his heart desire for vengeance.

'The two Cossacks were journeying to the land beyond the Carpathians that the King had granted to Ivan. Ivan had set his son on the horse behind him, tying the child to himself. The boy had fallen asleep; Ivan, too, began to doze. A Cossack should not sleep, the mountain paths are perilous . . . ! But the Cossack had a horse who knew the way; it would not stumble or step aside. There is a precipice between the mountains; no one has ever seen the bottom of it; it is deep as the sky is high. The road passed just above the precipice; two men could ride abreast on it, but for three it was too narrow. The horse began stepping cautiously with the slumbering Cossack on its back. Petro rode beside him; he trembled all over and was breathless with joy. He looked round and thrust his adopted brother into the precipice; and the horse with the Cossack and the baby fell into the abyss.

'But Ivan caught at a branch and only the horse dropped to the bottom. He began scrambling up with his son upon his back. He looked up when he was nearly at the top and saw that Petro was holding a lance ready to thrust him back. "Merciful God! better I had never raised my eyes again than I should see my own brother holding a lance ready to thrust me back . . . ! Dear brother, stab me if that is my fate, but take my son: what has the innocent child done that he should be doomed to so cruel a death?" Petro laughed and thrust at him with the lance; the Cossack fell with his child to the bottom. Petro took all his goods and began to live like a Pasha. No one had such droves of horses as Petro; no one had such flocks of sheep. And Petro died.

'After he was dead, God summoned the two brothers, Ivan and Petro, to the judgement-seat. "This man is a great sinner," said God. "Ivan, it will take me long to find a punishment for him; you choose him a punishment!" For a long time Ivan pondered what punishment to fix and at last he said: "That man did me a great injury: he betrayed his brother like a Judas and robbed me of my honourable name and offspring. And a man without honourable name and offspring is like a seed of corn dropped into the earth and wasted in vain. If it does not sprout, no one knows that the seed has been dropped into the earth.

' "Let it be, O Lord, that none of his descendants may be happy upon earth; that the last of his race may be the worst criminal that has ever been seen, and that at every crime he commits, his ancestors, unable to rest in their graves and suffering torments unknown to the world of the living, should rise from the tomb! And that the Judas, Petro, should be unable to rise and that hence he should suffer pain all the more intense; that he should bite the earth like one possessed and writhe underground!

' "And when the time comes that that man's wickedness has reached its full measure, let me, O Lord God, rise on my horse from the precipice to the highest peak of the mountains, and let him come to me and I will throw him from that mountain into the deepest abyss. And let all his dead ancestors, wherever they lived in their lifetime, come from various parts of the earth to gnaw him for the sufferings he inflicted upon them, and let them gnaw him for ever, and I should rejoice looking at his sufferings. And let the Judas, Petro, be unable to rise out of the earth, that he should lust to gnaw but be forced to gnaw himself, and that his bones should grow bigger and bigger as time goes on, so that his pain may be the greater. That torture will be worse for him than any other, for there is no greater torture for a man than to long for revenge and be unable to take it."

' "A terrible punishment thou hast devised, O man . . . !" God said. "All shall be as thou hast said; but thou shalt sit for ever on thy horse there and shalt not enter the Kingdom of Heaven!" And so it all was fulfilled accordingly; the strange horseman still sits on his steed in the Carpathians and sees the dead men gnawing the corpse in the bottomless abyss and feels how the dead Petro grows larger underground, gnaws his bones in dreadful agony and sets the earth quaking fearfully.'

The blind man had finished his song; he began thrumming the strings again and singing amusing ballads about Homa and Yeryoma, and Stklyar Stokoza . . . But his listeners, old and young, could not rouse themselves from reverie; they still stood with bowed heads, pondering on the terrible story of long ago.

IVAN FYODOROVITCH SHPONKA
AND HIS AUNT

THERE IS A STORY about this story: we were told it by Stepan Ivanovitch Kurotchka, who came over from Gadyatch. You must know that my memory is incredibly poor: you may tell me a thing or not tell it, it is all the same. It is just pouring water into a sieve. Being aware of this failing, I purposely begged him to write the story down in an exercise-book. Well, God give him good health, he was always a kind man to me, he set to work and wrote it down. I put it in the little table; I expect you know it; it stands in the corner as you come in by the door . . . But there, I forgot that you had never been in my house. My old woman, with whom I have lived thirty years, has never learnt to read – no use hiding one's shortcomings. Well, I noticed that she baked the pies on paper of some sort. She bakes pies beautifully, dear readers; you will never taste better pies anywhere. I happened to look on the underside of a pie – what do I see? Written words! My heart seemed to tell me at once: I went to the table, only half the book was there! All the other pages she had carried off for the pies! What could I do? There is no fighting at our age! Last year I happened to be passing through Gadyatch. Before I reached the town I purposely tied a knot in my handkerchief that I might not forget to ask Stepan Ivanovitch about it. That was not all, I vowed to myself that as soon as ever I sneezed in the town I would be sure to think of it. It was all no use. I drove through the town and sneezed and blew my nose too, but still I forgot it; and I only thought of it nearly five miles after I had passed through the town-gate. There was no help for it, I had to print it without the end. How-ever, if any one particularly wants to know what happened later on in the story, he need only go on purpose to Gadyatch and ask Stepan Ivanovitch. He will be glad to tell the story, I dare say, all over again from the beginning. He lives not far from the brick church. There is a little lane close by, and as soon as you turn into the lane it is the second or third gate. Or better still, when you see a big post with a quail on it in the yard and coming to meet you a stout peasant woman in a green petticoat (it may be as well to mention that he is a bachelor), that is his yard. Though indeed you may meet him in the market, where he is to be seen every morning before nine o'clock, choosing fish and vegetables for his table and talking to Father Antip or the Jewish contractor. You will know him at once, for there is no one else who has trousers of flowered linen and a yellow cotton coat. And another thing you may know him by – he always swings his arms as he walks. Denis Petrovitch, the assessor, now deceased, always used to say when he saw him in the distance, 'Look, look, here comes our windmill!'

1

Ivan Fyodorovitch Shponka

It is four years since Ivan Fyodorovitch retired from the army and came to live on his farm Vytrebenki. When he was still Vanyusha, he was at the Gadyatch district school, and I must say he was a very well-behaved and industrious boy. Nikifor Timofyevitch Dyepritchastie, the teacher of Russian grammar, used to say that if all the boys had been as anxious to do their best as Shponka, he would not have brought into the class-room the maple-wood ruler with which, as he owned himself, he was tired of hitting the lazy and mischievous boys' hands. His exercise-book was always neat, with a ruled margin, and not the tiniest blot anywhere. He always sat quietly with his arms folded and his eyes fixed on the teacher, and he never used to stick scraps of paper on the back of the boy sitting in front of him, never cut the form and never played at shoving the other boys off the form[68] before the master came in. If any one wanted a penknife to mend his pen, he immediately applied to Ivan Fyodorovitch knowing that he always had a penknife, and Ivan Fyodorovitch, at that time simply Vanyusha, would take it out of a little leather case attached to a buttonhole of his grey coat, and would only request that the sharp edge should not be used for scraping the pen, pointing out that there was a blunt side for the purpose. Such good conduct soon attracted the attention of the Latin master, whose cough in the passage was enough to reduce the class to terror, even before his frieze coat and pockmarked countenance had appeared in the doorway. This terrible master, who always had two birches lying on his desk and half of whose pupils were always on their knees, made Ivan Fyodorovitch monitor, although there were many boys in the class of much greater ability. Here I cannot omit an incident which had an influence on the whole of his future life. One of the boys entrusted to his charge tried to induce his monitor to write *scit* [69] on his report, though he had not learnt his lesson, by bringing into class a pancake soaked in butter and wrapped in paper. Though Ivan Fyodorovitch was usually conscientious, on this occasion he was hungry and could not resist the temptation: he took the pancake, held a book up before him and began eating it, and he was so absorbed in this occupation that he did not observe that a deathly silence had fallen upon the classroom. He only woke up with horror when a terrible hand protruding from a frieze overcoat seized him by the ear and dragged him into the middle of the room. 'Hand over that pancake! Hand it over, I tell you, you rascal!' said the terrible master; he seized the buttery pancake in his fingers and flung it out of window, sternly forbidding the boys running about in the yard to pick it up. Then he proceeded on the spot to whack Ivan Fyodorovitch very painfully on the hands; and quite rightly – the hands were responsible for taking it and no other part of the body. Anyway, the timidity which had always been characteristic of him was more marked from that time forward. Possibly the same incident was the explanation of his feeling no desire to enter the civil service, having learnt by experience that one is not always successful in hiding one's misdeeds.

He was very nearly fifteen when he moved up into the second class, where instead of the four rules of arithmetic and the abridged catechism, he went on to the longer one, the book of the duties of man, and fractions. But seeing that the further you went into the forest the thicker the wood became, and receiving the news that his father had departed this life, he stayed only two years longer at school, and with his mother's consent went into the P— infantry regiment.

The P— infantry regiment was not at all of the class to which many infantry regiments belong, and, although it was for the most part stationed in country places, it was in no way inferior to many cavalry regiments. The majority of the officers drank neat spirit and were quite as good at dragging about Jews by their curls as any Hussars; some of them even danced the mazurka,[70] and the colonel of the regiment never missed an opportunity of mentioning the fact when he was talking to any one in company. 'Among my officers,' he used to say, patting himself on the belly after every word, 'a number dance the mazurka, quite a number of them, really a great number of them indeed.' To show our readers the degree of culture of the P— infantry regiment, we must add that two of the officers were passionately fond of the game of bank and used to gamble away their uniforms, caps, overcoats, sword-knots and even their underclothes, which is more than you could find in every cavalry regiment.

Contact with such comrades did not, however, diminish Ivan Fyodorovitch's timidity; and as he did not drink neat spirit, preferring to it a wineglassful of ordinary vodka before dinner and supper, did not dance the mazurka or play bank, naturally he was bound to be always left alone. And so it came to pass that while the others were driving about with hired horses, visiting the less important landowners, he sitting at home spent his time in pursuits peculiar to a mild and gentle soul: he either polished his buttons, or read a dream-book or set mousetraps in the corners of his room, or failing everything he would take off his uniform and lie on his bed.

On the other hand, no one in the regiment was more punctual in his duties than Ivan Fyodorovitch, and he drilled his platoon in such a way that the commander of the company always held him up as a model to the others. Consequently in a short time, eleven years after becoming an ensign, he was promoted to be a second lieutenant.

During that time he had received the news that his mother was dead, and his aunt, his mother's sister, whom he only knew from her bringing him in his childhood – and even sending him when he was at Gadyatch – dried pears and extremely nice honey cakes which she made herself (she was on bad terms with his mother and so Ivan Fyodorovitch had not seen her in later years), this aunt, in the goodness of her heart, undertook to look after his little estate and in due time informed him of the fact by letter.

Ivan Fyodorovitch, having the fullest confidence in his aunt's good sense, continued to perform his duties as before. Some men in his position would have grown conceited at such promotion, but pride was a feeling of which he knew nothing, and as lieutenant he was the same Ivan Fyodorovitch as he had been when an ensign. He spent another four years in the regiment after the event of so much consequence to him, and was about to leave the Mogilyev[71] district for Great Russia with his regiment when he received a letter as follows:

MY DEAR NEPHEW, IVAN FYODOROVITCH – I am sending you some linen: five pairs of thread socks and four shirts of fine linen; and what is more I want to talk to you of something serious; since you have already a rank of some importance, as I suppose you are aware, and have reached a time of life when it is fitting to take up the management of your land, there is no reason for you to remain longer

in military service. I am getting old and can no longer see to everything on your farm; and in fact there is a great deal that I want to talk
to you about in person.

Come, Vanyusha! Looking forward to the real pleasure of seeing
you, I remain your very affectionate Aunt.

VASSILISSA TSUPTCHEVSKA

PS – There is a wonderful turnip in our kitchen garden, more like a
potato than a turnip.

A week after receiving this letter Ivan Fyodorovitch wrote an answer
as follows:

HONOURED MADAM, AUNTIE, VASSILISSA KASHPAROVNA – Thank
you very much for sending the linen. My socks especially are very
old, my orderly has darned them four times and that has made them
very tight. As to your views in regard to my service in the army, I
completely agree with you, and the day before yesterday I sent in my
papers. As soon as I get my discharge I will engage a chaise. As to
your commission in regard to the seed wheat and Siberian corn I
cannot carry it out; there is none in all the Mogilyev province. About
here pigs are mostly fed on brewers' grains together with a little beer
when it has grown flat. With the greatest respect, honoured madam
and auntie, I remain your nephew

IVAN SHPONKA

At last Ivan Fyodorovitch received his discharge with the grade of
lieutenant, hired for forty roubles a Jew to drive from Mogilyev to
Gadyatch, and set off in the chaise just at the time when the trees are
clothed with young and still scanty leaves, the whole earth is bright with
fresh green, and there is the fragrance of spring over all the fields.

2

The Journey

Nothing of great interest occurred on the journey. They were travelling
a little over a fortnight. Ivan Fyodorovitch might have arrived a little
sooner than that, but the devout Jew kept the Sabbath on the Saturdays
and, putting his horse-cloth over his head, prayed the whole day. Ivan
Fyodorovitch, however, as I have had occasion to mention already, was
a man who did not give way to being bored. During these intervals he
undid his trunk, took out his underclothes, inspected them thoroughly

to see whether they were properly washed and folded; carefully removed the fluff from his new uniform, which had been made without epaulettes, and repacked it all in the best possible way. He was not fond of reading in general; and if he did sometimes look into a dream-book, it was because he liked to meet again what he had already read several times. In the same way one who lives in the town goes every day to the club, not for the sake of hearing anything new there, but in order to meet there friends with whom it has been his habit to chat at the club from time immemorial. In the same way a government clerk will read a directory of addresses with immense satisfaction several times a day with no ulterior object, he is simply entertained by the printed list of names. 'Ah! Ivan Gavrilovitch So-and-so . . . ' he murmurs mutely to himself. 'And here again am I! H'm . . . !' and next time he reads it over again with exactly the same exclamations.

After a fortnight's journey Ivan Fyodorovitch reached a little village some eighty miles from Gadyatch. This was on Friday. The sun had long set when with the chaise and the Jew he reached an inn.

This inn differed in no respects from other little village inns. As a rule the traveller is zealously regaled in them with hay and oats, as though he were a post-horse. But should he want to lunch as decent people do lunch, he keeps his appetite intact for some future opportunity. Ivan Fyodorovitch, knowing all this, had provided himself beforehand with two bundles of bread-rings and a sausage, and asking for a glass of vodka, of which there is never a shortage in any inn, he began his supper, sitting down on a bench before an oak table which was fixed immovably in the clay floor.

Meanwhile he heard the rattle of a chaise. The gates creaked but it was a long while before the chaise drove into the yard. A loud voice was engaged in scolding the old woman who kept the inn. 'I will drive in,' Ivan Fyodorovitch heard, 'but if I am bitten by a single bug in your inn, I will beat you, on my soul I will, you old witch! And I will give you nothing for your hay!'

A minute later the door opened and there walked – or rather squeezed himself – in a stout man in a green frock-coat. His head rested immovably on his short neck, which seemed even thicker, from a double chin. To judge from his appearance, he belonged to that class of men who do not trouble their heads about trifles and whose whole life has passed easily.

'I wish you good day, honoured sir!' he pronounced on seeing Ivan Fyodorovitch.

Ivan Fyodorovitch bowed in silence.

'Allow me to ask, to whom have I the honour of speaking?' the stout newcomer continued.

At such an examination Ivan Fyodorovitch involuntarily got up and stood at attention as he usually did when the colonel asked him a question. 'Retired Lieutenant Ivan Fyodorovitch Shponka,' he answered.

'And may I ask what place you are bound for?'

'My own farm Vytrebenki.'

'Vytrebenki!' cried the stern examiner. 'Allow me, honoured sir, allow me!' he said, going towards him, and waving his arms as though someone were hindering him or as though he were making his way through a crowd, he folded Ivan Fyodorovitch in an embrace and kissed him first on the right cheek and then on the left and then on the right again. Ivan Fyodorovitch was much gratified by this kiss, for his lips were pressed against the stranger's fat cheeks as though against soft cushions.

'Allow me to make your acquaintance, my dear sir!' the fat man continued: 'I am a landowner of the same district of Gadyatch and your neighbour; I live not more than four miles from your Vytrebenki in the village of Hortyshtche; and my name is Grigory Grigoryevitch Stortchenko. You really must, sir, you really must pay me a visit at Hortyshtche. I won't speak to you if you don't. I am in haste now on business . . . Why, what's this?' he said in a mild voice to his postilion, a boy in a Cossack tunic with patched elbows and a bewildered expression, who came in and put bags and boxes on the table. 'What's this, what's the meaning of it?' and by degrees Grigory Grigoryevitch's voice grew more and more threatening. 'Did I tell you to put them here, my good lad? Did I tell you to put them here, you rascal? Didn't I tell you to heat the chicken up first, you scoundrel? Be off!' he shouted, stamping. 'Stay, you fright! Where's the basket with the bottles? Ivan Fyodorovitch!' he said, pouring out a glass of liqueur, 'I beg you take some cordial!'

'Oh, really, I cannot . . . I have already had occasion . . . ' Ivan Fyodorovitch began hesitatingly.

'I won't hear a word, sir!' the gentleman raised his voice, 'I won't hear a word! I won't budge till you drink it . . . '

Ivan Fyodorovitch, seeing that it was impossible to refuse, not without gratification emptied the glass.

'This is a fowl, sir,' said the fat Grigory Grigoryevitch, carving it in a wooden box. 'I must tell you that my cook Yavdoha is fond of a drop at times and so she often dries up things. Hey, lad!' here he turned to the boy in the Cossack tunic who was bringing in a feather-bed and pillows, 'make my bed on the floor in the middle of the room! Mind you put plenty of hay under the pillow! And pull a bit of hemp from the woman's distaff to stop up my ears for the night! I must tell you, sir, that I have the habit of stopping up my ears at night ever since the damnable occasion when a cockroach crawled into my left ear in a Great Russian inn. The confounded long-beards, as I found out afterwards, eat their soup with beetles in it. Impossible to describe what happened to me; there was such a tickling, such a tickling in my ear . . . I was downright crazy! I was cured by a simple old woman in our district, and by what do you suppose? Simply by whispering to it. What do you think, my dear sir, about doctors? What I think is that they simply hoax us and make fools of us: some old women know a dozen times as much as all these doctors.'

'Indeed, what you say is perfectly true, sir. There certainly are cases . . . ' Here Ivan Fyodorovitch paused as though he could not find the right word. It may not be amiss to mention here that he was at no time lavish of words. This may have been due to timidity, or it may have been due to a desire to express himself elegantly.

'Shake up the hay properly, shake it up properly!' said Grigory Grigoryevitch to his servant. 'The hay is so bad about here that you may come upon a twig in it any minute. Allow me, sir, to wish you a good-night! We shall not see each other tomorrow. I am setting off before dawn. Your Jew will keep the Sabbath because tomorrow is Saturday, so it is no good for you to get up early. Don't forget my invitation; I won't speak to you if you don't come to see me at Hortyshtche.'

At this point Grigory Grigoryevitch's servant pulled off his coat and high boots and gave him his dressing-gown instead, and Grigory Grigoryevitch stretched on his bed, and it looked as though one huge feather-bed were lying on another.

'Hey, lad! where are you, rascal? Come here and arrange my quilt. Hey, lad, prop up my head with hay! Have you watered the horses yet? Some more hay! here, under this side! And do arrange the quilt properly, you rascal! That's right, more! Ough . . . !'

Then Grigory Grigoryevitch heaved two sighs and filled the whole room with a terrible whistling through his nose, snoring so loudly at times that the old woman who was snoozing on the settle, suddenly waking up, looked about her in all directions, but, seeing nothing, subsided and went to sleep again.

When Ivan Fyodorovitch woke up next morning, the fat gentleman was no longer there. This was the only noteworthy incident that occurred on the journey. Two days later he drew near his little farm.

He felt his heart begin to throb when the windmill waving its sails peeped out and, as the Jew drove his nag up the hill, the row of willows came into sight below. The pond gleamed bright and shining through them and a breath of freshness rose from it. Here he used to bathe in old days; in that pond he used to wade with the peasant lads up to his neck after crayfish. The covered cart mounted the dam and Ivan Fyodorovitch saw the little old-fashioned house thatched with reeds, and the apple trees and cherry trees which he used to climb on the sly. He had no sooner driven into the yard than dogs of all kinds, brown, black, grey, spotted, ran up from every side. Some flew under the horse's hoofs, barking, others ran behind the cart, noticing that the axle was smeared with bacon fat; one, standing near the kitchen and keeping his paw on a bone, uttered a volley of shrill barks; and another gave tongue in the distance, running to and fro wagging his tail and seeming to say: 'Look, good Christians! what a fine young fellow I am!' Boys in grubby shirts ran out to stare. A sow who was promenading in the yard with sixteen little pigs lifted her snout with an inquisitive air and grunted louder than usual. In the yard a number of hempen sheets were lying on the ground covered with wheat, millet and barley drying in the sun. A good many different kinds of herbs, such as wild chicory and swine-herb, were drying on the roof.

Ivan Fyodorovitch was so occupied in scrutinising all this that he was only roused when a spotted dog bit the Jew on the calf of his leg as he was getting down from the box. The servants who ran out, that is the cook and another woman and two girls in woollen petticoats, after the first exclamations: 'It's our young master!' informed him that his aunt was sowing sweet corn together with the girl Palashka and Omelko the coachman, who often performed the duties of a gardener and watchman also. But his aunt, who had seen the sack-covered cart in the distance, was already on the spot. And Ivan Fyodorovitch was astonished when she almost lifted him from the ground in her arms, hardly able to believe that this could be the aunt who had written to him of her old age and infirmities.

3

Auntie

Auntie Vassilissa Kashparovna was at this time about fifty. She had never been married, and commonly declared that she valued her maiden state above everything. Though, indeed, to the best of my memory, no one ever courted her. This was due to the fact that all men were sensible of a certain timidity in her presence, and never had the spirit to make her an offer. 'A girl of great character, Vassilissa Kashparovna!' all the young men used to say, and they were quite right, too, for there was no one Vassilissa Kashparovna could not get the whip hand of. With her own manly hand, tugging every day at his topknot of curls, she could, unaided, turn the drunken miller, a worthless fellow, into a perfect treasure. She was of almost gigantic stature and her breadth and strength were fully in proportion. It seemed as though nature had made an unpardonable mistake in condemning her to wear a dark brown gown with little flounces on weekdays and a red cashmere shawl on Sunday and on her name-day, though a dragoon's moustaches and high top-boots would have suited her better than anything. On the other hand, her pursuits completely corresponded with her appearance: she rowed the boat herself and was more skilful with the oars than any fisherman; shot game; stood over the mowers all the while they were at work; knew the exact number of the melons, of all kinds, in the kitchen garden; took a toll of five kopecks from every waggon that crossed her dam; climbed the trees and shook down the pears; beat lazy vassals with her terrible hand and with the same menacing hand bestowed a glass of vodka on the deserving. Almost at the same moment she was scolding, dyeing yarn, racing to the kitchen, brewing kvass, making jam with honey; she was busy all day long and everywhere in the nick of time. The result of all this was that Ivan Fyodorovitch's little property, which had consisted of eighteen souls at the last census, was flourishing in the fullest sense of the word. Moreover, she had a very warm affection for her nephew and carefully accumulated kopecks for him.

From the time of his arrival at his home Ivan Fyodorovitch's life was completely transformed and took an entirely different turn. It seemed as though nature had designed him expressly for looking after an estate of eighteen souls. Auntie herself observed that he would make an excellent farmer, though she did not yet permit him to meddle in every branch of the management. 'He's but a young child yet,' she used commonly to say, though Ivan Fyodorovitch was as a fact not far off forty. 'How should he know it all!'

However, he was always in the fields with the reapers and mowers, and this was a source of unutterable pleasure to his gentle heart. The sweep of a dozen or more gleaming scythes in unison; the sound of the grass falling in even swathes; the carolling songs of the reapers at intervals, at one time joyous as the welcoming of a guest, at another mournful as parting; the calm pure evening – and what an evening! How free and fresh the air! How everything revived; the steppe flushed red then turned dark blue and gleamed with flowers; quails, bustards, gulls, grasshoppers, thousands of insects and all of them whistling, buzzing, churring, calling and suddenly blending into a harmonious chorus; nothing silent for an instant, while the sun sets and is hidden. Oh, how fresh and delightful it was! Here and there about the fields camp-fires are built and cauldrons set over them, and round the fires the mowers sit down; the steam from the dumplings floats upwards; the twilight turns greyer . . . It is hard to say what passed in Ivan Fyodorovitch at such times. When he joined the mowers, he forgot to try their dumplings, though he liked them particularly, and stood motionless, watching a gull disappear in the sky or counting the sheaves of corn dotted over the field.

In a short time Ivan Fyodorovitch was spoken of as a great farmer. Auntie was never tired of rejoicing over her nephew and never lost an opportunity of boasting of him. One day – it was just after the end of the harvest, that is at the end of July – Vassilissa Kashparovna took Ivan Fyodorovitch by the arm with a mysterious air, and said she wanted now to speak to him of a matter which had long been on her mind.

'You are aware, dear Ivan Fyodorovitch,' she began, 'that there are eighteen souls on your farm, though, indeed, that is by the census register, and in reality they may reckon up to more, they may be twenty-four. But that is not the point. You know the copse that lies behind our vegetable ground, and no doubt you know the broad meadow behind it; there are very nearly sixty acres in it; and the grass is so good that it is worth a hundred roubles every year, especially if, as they say, a cavalry regiment is to be stationed at Gadyatch.'

'To be sure, Auntie, I know: the grass is very good.'

'You needn't tell me the grass is very good, I know it; but do you know that all that land is by rights yours? Why do you look so surprised? Listen, Ivan Fyodorovitch! You remember Stepan Kuzmitch? What am I saying: "you remember"! You were so little that you could not even pronounce his name. Yes, indeed! How could you remember! When I came on the very eve of St Philip's Fast and took you in my arms, you almost ruined my dress; luckily I was just in time to hand you to your nurse, Matryona; you were such a horrid little thing then . . . ! But that is not the point. All the land beyond our farm, and the village of Hortyshtche itself belonged to Stepan Kuzmitch. I must tell you that before you were in this world he used to visit your mamma – though, indeed, only when your father was not at home. Not that I say it in blame of her – God rest her soul! – though your poor mother was always unfair to me! But that is not the point. Be that as it may, Stepan Kuzmitch made a deed of gift to you of that same estate of which I have been speaking. But your poor mamma, between ourselves, was a very strange character. The devil himself (God forgive me for the nasty word!) would have been puzzled to understand her. What she did with that deed of gift – God only knows. It's my opinion that it is in the hands of that old bachelor, Grigory Grigoryevitch Stortchenko. That pot-bellied rascal has got hold of the whole estate. I'd bet anything you like that he has hidden that deed.'

'Allow me to ask, Auntie: isn't he the Stortchenko whose acquaintance I made at the inn?' Hereupon Ivan Fyodorovitch described his meeting with Stortchenko.

'Who knows,' said his aunt after a moment's thought, 'perhaps he is not a rascal. It's true that it's only six months since he came to live among us; there's no finding out what a man is in that time. The old lady, his mother, is a very sensible woman, so I hear, and they say she is a great hand at salting cucumbers; her own serf-girls can make capital rugs. But as you say he gave you such a friendly welcome, go and see him, perhaps the old sinner will listen to his conscience and will give up what is not his. If you like you can go in the chaise, only those confounded brats have pulled out all the nails at the back; you must tell the coachman, Omelko, to nail the leather on better everywhere.'

'What for, Auntie? I will take the trap that you sometimes go out shooting in.'

With that the conversation ended.

4

The Dinner

It was about dinner-time when Ivan Fyodorovitch drove into the hamlet of Hortyshtche and he felt a little timid as he approached the manor-house. It was a long house, not thatched with reeds like the houses of many of the neighbouring landowners, but with a wooden roof. Two barns in the yard also had wooden roofs: the gate was of oak. Ivan Fyodorovitch felt like a dandy who, on arriving at a ball, sees every one more smartly dressed than himself. He stopped his trap by the barn as a sign of respect and went on foot towards the front door.

'Ah, Ivan Fyodorovitch!' cried the fat man Grigory Grigoryevitch, who was crossing the yard in his coat but without cravat, waistcoat and braces. But apparently this attire weighed oppressively on his bulky person, for the perspiration was streaming down him.

'Why, you said you would come as soon as you had seen your aunt, and all this time you have not been here?' After these words Ivan Fyodorovitch's lips found themselves again in contact with the same cushions.

'Chiefly being busy looking after the land . . . I have come just for a minute to see you on business . . . '

'For a minute? Well, that won't do. Hey, lad!' shouted the fat gentleman, and the same boy in the Cossack tunic ran out of the kitchen. 'Tell Kassyan to shut the gate tight, do you hear! Make it fast! And take this gentleman's horse out of the shafts this minute. Please come indoors; it is so hot out here that my shirt's soaked.'

On going indoors Ivan Fyodorovitch made up his mind to lose no time and in spite of his shyness to act with decision.

'My aunt had the honour . . . she told me that a deed of gift of the late Stepan Kuzmitch . . . '

It is difficult to describe the unpleasant grimace made by the broad countenance of Grigory Grigoryevitch at these words.

'Oh dear, I hear nothing!' he responded. 'I must tell you that a cockroach got into my left ear (those bearded Russians breed cockroaches in all their huts); no pen can describe what agony it was, it kept tickling and tickling. An old woman cured me by the simplest means . . . '

'I meant to say . . . ' Ivan Fyodorovitch ventured to interrupt, seeing that Grigory Grigoryevitch was intentionally changing the subject; 'that in the late Stepan Kuzmitch's will mention is made, so to speak, of a deed of gift . . . According to it I ought . . . '

'I know; so your aunt has told you that story already. It's a lie, upon my soul it is! My uncle made no deed of gift. Though, indeed, some such deed is referred to in the will. But where is it? No one has produced it. I tell you this because I sincerely wish you well. Upon my soul it is a lie!'

Ivan Fyodorovitch said nothing, reflecting that possibly his aunt really might be mistaken.

'Ah, here comes mother with my sisters!' said Grigory Grigoryevitch, 'so dinner is ready. Let us go!'

Thereupon he drew Ivan Fyodorovitch by the hand into a room in which vodka and savouries were standing on the table.

At the same time a short little old lady, a regular coffeepot in a

cap, with two young ladies, one fair and one dark, came in. Ivan
Fyodorovitch, like a well-bred gentleman, went up to kiss the old
lady's hand and then to kiss the hands of the two young ladies.

'This is our neighbour, Ivan Fyodorovitch Shponka, mother,' said
Grigory Grigoryevitch.

The old lady looked intently at Ivan Fyodorovitch, or perhaps it
only seemed that she looked intently at him. She was good-natured
simplicity itself, though; she looked as though she would like to ask
Ivan Fyodorovitch: 'How many cucumbers have you salted for the
winter?'

'Have you had some vodka?' the old lady asked.

'You can't have had your sleep out, mother,' said Grigory Grigoryevitch. 'Who asks a visitor whether he has had anything. You offer it to
him, that's all: whether we have had any or not, that is our business.
Ivan Fyodorovitch! The centaury-flavoured vodka or the Trofimov
brand? Which do you prefer? And you, Ivan Ivanovitch, why are you
standing there?' Grigory Grigoryevitch brought out, turning round,
and Ivan Fyodorovitch saw the gentleman so addressed approaching
the vodka, in a frock-coat with long skirts and an immense stand-up
collar, which covered the whole back of his head, so that his head sat
in it, as though it were a chaise.

Ivan Ivanovitch went up to the vodka and rubbed his hands, carefully
examined the wineglass, filled it, held it up to the light, and poured all
the vodka at once into his mouth. He did not, however, swallow it at
once, but rinsed his mouth thoroughly with it first before finally
swallowing it, and then after eating some bread and salted mushrooms,
he turned to Ivan Fyodorovitch.

'Is it not Ivan Fyodorovitch, Mr Shponka, I have the honour of
addressing?'

'Yes, certainly,' answered Ivan Fyodorovitch.

'You have changed a great deal, sir, since I saw you last. Why!' he
continued, 'I remember you that high!' As he spoke he held his hand a
yard from the floor. 'Your poor father, God grant him the kingdom of
Heaven, was a rare man. He used to have melons such as you never see
anywhere now. Here, for instance,' he went on, drawing him aside,
'they'll set melons before you on the table – such melons! You won't care
to look at them! Would you believe it, sir, he used to have water melons,'
he pronounced with a mysterious air, flinging out his arms as if he were
about to embrace a stout tree-trunk, 'upon my soul as big as this!'

'Come to dinner!' said Grigory Grigoryevitch, taking Ivan Fyodorovitch by the arm.

Grigory Grigoryevitch sat down in his usual place at the end of the table, draped with an enormous table-napkin which made him resemble the Greek heroes depicted by barbers on their signs. Ivan Fyodorovitch, blushing, sat down in the place assigned to him, facing the two young ladies; and Ivan Ivanovitch did not let slip the chance of sitting down beside him, inwardly rejoicing that he had someone to whom he could impart his various items of information.

'You shouldn't take the bishop's nose, Ivan Fyodorovitch! It's a turkey!' said the old lady, addressing Ivan Fyodorovitch, to whom the rustic waiter in a grey swallowtail patched with black was offering a dish. 'Take the back!'

'Mother! no one asked you to interfere!' commented Grigory Grigoryevitch. 'You may be sure our visitor knows what to take himself! Ivan Fyodorovitch! Take a wing, the other one there with the gizzard! But why have you taken so little? Take a leg! Why do you stand gaping with the dish? Ask him! Go down on your knees, rascal! Say, at once, "Ivan Fyodorovitch, take a leg!" '

'Ivan Fyodorovitch, take a leg!' the waiter with the dish bawled, kneeling down.

'H'm! Do you call this a turkey?' Ivan Ivanovitch muttered in a low voice, turning to his neighbour with an air of disdain. 'Is that what a turkey ought to look like? If you could see my turkeys! I assure you there is more fat on one of them than on a dozen of these. Would you believe me, sir, they are really a repulsive sight when they walk about my yard, they are so fat . . . !'

'Ivan Ivanovitch, you are telling lies!' said Grigory Grigoryevitch, overhearing these remarks.

'I tell you,' Ivan Ivanovitch went on talking to his neighbour, affecting not to hear what Grigory Grigoryevitch had said, 'last year when I sent them to Gadyatch, they offered me fifty kopecks apiece for them, and I wouldn't take even that.'

'Ivan Ivanovitch! I tell you, you are lying!' observed Grigory Grigoryevitch, dwelling on each syllable for greater distinctness and speaking more loudly than before.

But Ivan Ivanovitch behaved as though the words could not possibly refer to him; he went on as before, but in a much lower voice: 'Yes, sir, I would not take it. There is not a gentleman in Gadyatch . . . '

'Ivan Ivanovitch! you are a fool, and that's the truth,' Grigory Grigoryevitch said in a loud voice. 'Ivan Fyodorovitch knows all about it better than you do, and doesn't believe you.'

At this Ivan Ivanovitch was really offended: he said no more, but fell to putting away the turkey, even though it was not so fat as those that were a repulsive sight.

The clatter of knives, spoons and plates took the place of conversation for a time, but loudest of all was the sound made by Grigory Grigoryevitch, smacking his lips over the marrow out of the mutton bones.

'Have you,' enquired Ivan Ivanovitch after an interval of silence, poking his head out of the chaise, 'read the *Travels of Korobeynikov in the Holy Land*?[72] It's a real delight to heart and soul! Such books aren't published nowadays. I very much regret that I did not notice in what year it was written.'

Ivan Fyodorovitch, hearing mention of a book, applied himself diligently to taking sauce.

'It is truly marvellous, sir, when you think that a humble artisan visited all those places: over two thousand miles, sir! Over two thousand miles! Truly, it was by divine grace that it was vouchsafed him to reach Palestine and Jerusalem.'

'So you say,' said Ivan Fyodorovitch, who had heard a great deal about Jerusalem from his orderly, 'that he visited Jerusalem.'

'What are you saying, Ivan Fyodorovitch?' Grigory Grigoryevitch enquired from the end of the table.

'I had occasion to observe what distant lands there are in the world!' said Ivan Fyodorovitch, genuinely gratified that he had succeeded in uttering so long and difficult a sentence.

'Don't you believe him, Ivan Fyodorovitch!' said Grigory Grigoryevitch, who had not quite caught what he said, 'he always tells fibs!'

Meanwhile dinner was over. Grigory Grigoryevitch went to his own room, as his habit was, for a little nap; and the visitors followed their aged hostess and the young ladies into the drawing-room, where the same table on which they had left vodka when they went out to dinner was now as though by some magical transformation covered with little saucers of jam of various sorts and dishes of cherries and different kinds of melons.

The absence of Grigory Grigoryevitch was perceptible in everything: the old lady became more disposed to talk and, of her own accord, without being asked, revealed several secrets in regard to the making of apple cheese, and the drying of pears. Even the young ladies began talking; though the fair one, who looked some six years younger than her sister and who was apparently about five-and-twenty, was rather silent.

But Ivan Ivanovitch was more talkative and livelier than any one. Feeling secure that no one would snub or contradict him, he talked of cucumbers and of planting potatoes and of how much more sensible people were in old days – no comparison with what people are now! – and of how as time goes on everything improves and the most intricate inventions are discovered. He was, indeed, one of those persons who take great pleasure in relieving their souls by conversation and will talk of anything that possibly can be talked about. If the conversation touched upon grave and solemn subjects, Ivan Ivanovitch sighed after each word and nodded his head slightly: if the subject were of a more homely character, he would pop his head out of his chaise and make faces from which one could almost, it seemed, read how to make pear kvass, how large were the melons of which he was speaking and how fat were the geese that were running about in his yard.

At last, with great difficulty and not before evening, Ivan Fyodoro-vitch succeeded in taking his leave, and although he was usually ready to give way and they almost kept him for the night by force, he persisted in his intention of going – and went.

5

Auntie's New Plans

'Well, did you get the deed of gift out of the old reprobate?' Such was the question with which Ivan Fyodorovitch was greeted by his aunt, who had been expecting him for some hours in the porch and had at last been unable to resist going out to the gate.

'No, Auntie,' said Ivan Fyodorovitch, getting out of the trap: 'Grigory Grigoryevitch has no deed of gift!'

'And you believed him? He was lying, the confounded fellow! Some day I shall come across him and I will give him a drubbing with my own hands. Oh, I'd get rid of some of his fat for him! Though perhaps we ought first to consult our court assessor and see if we couldn't get the law of him . . . But that's not the point now. Well, was the dinner good?'

'Very . . . yes, excellent, Auntie!'

'Well, what did you have? Tell me. The old lady, I know, is a great hand at looking after the cooking.'

'Curd fritters with sour cream, Auntie: a stew of stuffed pigeons . . .'

'And a turkey with pickled plums?' asked his aunt, for she was herself very skilful in the preparation of that dish.

'Yes, there was a turkey, too . . . ! Very handsome young ladies Grigory Grigoryevitch's sisters, especially the fair one!'

'Ah!' said Auntie, and she looked intently at Ivan Fyodorovitch, who dropped his eyes, blushing. A new idea flashed into her mind. 'Come, tell me,' she said eagerly and with curiosity, 'what are her eyebrows like?' It may not be amiss to observe that Auntie considered fine eyebrows as the most important item in a woman's looks.

'Her eyebrows, Auntie, are exactly like what you described yours as being when you were young. And there are little freckles all over her face.'

'Ah,' commented his aunt, well pleased with Ivan Fyodorovitch's observation, though he had had no idea of paying her a compliment. 'What sort of dress was she wearing? Though, indeed, it's hard to get good material nowadays, such as I have here, for instance, in this gown. But that's not the point. Well, did you talk to her about anything?'

'Talk . . . how do you mean, Auntie? Perhaps you are imagining . . . '

'Well, what of it, there would be nothing strange in that? Such is God's will! It may have been ordained at your birth that you should make a match of it.'

'I don't know how you can say such a thing, Auntie. That shows that you don't know me at all . . . '

'Well, well, now he is offended,' said his aunt. 'He's still only a child!' she thought to herself: 'he knows nothing! We must bring them together – let them get to know each other!'

Hereupon Auntie went to have a look at the kitchen and left Ivan Fyodorovitch alone. But from that time forward she thought of nothing but seeing her nephew married as soon as possible and fondling his little ones. Her brain was absorbed in making preparations for the wedding, and it was noticeable that she bustled about more busily than ever, though the work was the worse rather than the better for it. Often when she was making the pies, a job which she never left to the cook, she would forget everything, and imagining that a tiny great-nephew was standing by her asking for some pie, would absently hold out her hands with the nicest bit for him, and the yard-dog taking advantage of this would snatch the dainty morsel and by its loud munching rouse her from her reverie, for which it was always beaten with the oven fork. She even abandoned her favourite pursuits and did not go out shooting, especially after she shot a crow by mistake for a partridge, a thing which had never happened to her before.

At last, four days later, every one saw the chaise brought out of the carriage house into the yard. The coachman Omelko (he was also the gardener and the watchman) had been hammering from early morning, nailing on the leather and continually chasing away the dogs who licked the wheels. I think it my duty to inform my readers that this was the very chaise in which Adam used to drive; and therefore, if any one gives out that some other chaise was Adam's, it is an absolute lie, and his chaise is certainly not the genuine article. It is impossible to say how it survived the Deluge. It must be supposed that there was a special coach-house for it in Noah's Ark. I am very sorry that I cannot give a living picture of it for my readers. It is enough to say that Vassilissa Kashparovna was very well satisfied with its structure and always expressed regret that the old style of carriages had gone out of fashion. The chaise had been constructed a little on one side, so that the right half stood much higher than the left, and this pleased her particularly, because, as she said, a stout person could sit on one side and a tall person on the other. Inside the chaise, however, there was room for five small persons or three such as Auntie herself.

About midday Omelko, having finished with the chaise, brought out of the stable three horses which were a little younger than the chaise, and began harnessing them with cord to the magnificent equipage. Ivan Fyodorovitch and his aunt, one on the left side and the other on the right, stepped in and the chaise drove off. The peasants they met on the road seeing this sumptuous turn-out (Vassilissa Kashparovna rarely drove out in it) stopped respectfully, taking off their caps and bowing low.

Two hours later the chaise stopped at the front door – I think I need not say – of Stortchenko's house. Grigory Grigoryevitch was not at home. His old mother and the two young ladies came into the dining-room to receive the guests. Auntie walked in with a majestic step, with a great air stopped short with one foot in front, and said in a loud voice: 'I am delighted, dear madam, to have the honour to offer you my respects in person; and at the same time to thank you for your hospitality to my nephew, who has been warm in his praises of it. Your buckwheat is very good, madam – I saw it as we drove into the village. May I ask how many sheaves you get to the acre?'

After that followed kisses all round. As soon as they were seated in the drawing-room, the old lady began: 'About the buckwheat I cannot tell you: that's Grigory Grigoryevitch's department: it's long since I have had anything to do with the farming; indeed, I am not equal to it, I am old now! In old days I remember the buckwheat stood up to my waist; now goodness knows what it is like, though they do say everything is better now.' At that point the old lady heaved a sigh, and some observers would have heard in that sigh the sigh of a past age, of the eighteenth century.

'I have heard, madam, that your own maids can make excellent carpets,' said Vassilissa Kashparovna, and with that touched on the old lady's most sensitive chord: at those words she seemed to brighten up, and she talked readily of the way to dye the yarn and prepare the thread.

From carpets the conversation passed easily to the salting of cucumbers and drying of pears. In short, before the end of an hour the two ladies were talking together as though they had been friends all their lives. Vassilissa Kashparovna had already said a great deal to her in such a low voice that Ivan Fyodorovitch could not hear what she was saying.

'Yes, would not you like to have a look at them?' said the old lady, getting up.

The young ladies and Vassilissa Kashparovna also got up and all moved towards the maids' room. Auntie made a sign, however, to Ivan Fyodorovitch to remain and said something in an undertone to the old lady.

'Mashenka,' said the latter, addressing the fair-haired young lady, 'stay with our visitor and talk with him, that he may not be dull!'

The fair-haired young lady remained and sat down on the sofa. Ivan Fyodorovitch sat on his chair as though on thorns, blushed and cast down his eyes; but the young lady appeared not to notice this and sat unconcernedly on the sofa, carefully scrutinising the windows and the walls, or watching the cat timorously running round under the chairs.

Ivan Fyodorovitch grew a little bolder and would have begun a conversation; but it seemed as though he had lost all his words on the way. Not a single idea came into his mind.

The silence lasted for nearly a quarter of an hour. The young lady went on sitting as before.

At last Ivan Fyodorovitch plucked up his courage. 'There are a great many flies in summer, madam!' he brought out in a half-trembling voice.

'A very great many!' answered the young lady. 'My brother has made a flapper out of an old slipper of mamma's on purpose to kill them, but there are lots of them still.'

Here the conversation dropped again, and Ivan Fyodorovitch was utterly unable to find anything to say.

At last the old lady together with his aunt and the dark-haired young lady came back again. After a little more conversation, Vassilissa Kashparovna took leave of the old lady and her daughters in spite of their entreaties that they would stay the night. The three ladies came out on the steps to see their visitors off, and continued for some time nodding to the aunt and nephew, as they looked out of the chaise.

'Well, Ivan Fyodorovitch, what did you talk about when you were alone with the young lady?' Auntie asked him on the way home.

'A very discreet and well-behaved young lady, Marya Grigoryevna!' said Ivan Fyodorovitch.

'Listen, Ivan Fyodorovitch, I want to talk seriously to you. Here you are thirty-eight, thank God; you have obtained a good rank in the service – it's time to think about children! You must have a wife . . . '

'What, Auntie!' cried Ivan Fyodorovitch panic-stricken, 'a wife! No, Auntie, for goodness' sake . . . You make me quite ashamed . . . I've never had a wife . . . I shouldn't know what to do with her!'

'You'll find out, Ivan Fyodorovitch, you'll find out,' said his aunt, smiling, and she thought to herself: 'what next, he is a perfect baby, he knows nothing!' 'Yes, Ivan Fyodorovitch!' she went on aloud, 'we could not find a better wife for you than Marya Grigoryevna. Besides, you are very much attracted by her. I have had a good talk with the old lady about it: she'll be delighted to see you her son-in-law. It's true that we don't know what that reprobate Grigoryevitch will say to it; but we won't consider him, and if he takes it into his head not to give her a dowry, we'll have the law of him . . . '

At that moment the chaise drove into the yard and the ancient nags grew more lively, feeling that their stable was not far off.

'Mind, Omelko! Let the horses have a good rest first, and don't take them down to drink the minute they are unharnessed; they are over-heated.'

'Well, Ivan Fyodorovitch,' his aunt went on as she got out of the chaise, 'I advise you to think it over well. I must run to the kitchen: I forgot to tell Soloha what to get for supper, and I expect the wretched girl won't have thought of it herself.'

But Ivan Fyodorovitch stood as though thunderstruck. It was true that Marya Grigoryevna was a very nice-looking young lady; but to get married . . . ! It seemed to him so strange, so peculiar, he couldn't think of it without horror. Living with a wife . . . ! Unthinkable! He would not be alone in his own room, but they would always have to be two together . . . ! Perspiration came out on his face as he sank more deeply into meditation.

He went to bed earlier than usual but in spite of all his efforts he could not go to sleep. But at last sleep, that universal comforter, came to him; but such sleep! He had never had such incoherent dreams. First, he dreamed that everything was whirling with a noise around him, and he was running and running, as fast as his legs could carry him . . . Now he was at his last gasp . . . All at once someone caught him by the

ear. 'Aie! who is it?' 'It is I, your wife!' a voice resounded loudly in his
ear – and he woke up. Then he imagined that he was married, that
everything in their little house was so peculiar, so strange: a double bed
stood in his room instead of a single one; his wife was sitting on a chair.
He felt queer: he did not know how to approach her, what to say to her,
and then he noticed that she had the face of a goose. He happened to
turn aside and saw another wife, also with the face of a goose. Turning
in another direction, he saw yet a third wife; and behind him was still
another. Then he was seized by panic: he dashed away into the garden:
but there it was hot, he took off his hat, and – saw a wife sitting in his
hat. Drops of sweat came out on his face. He put his hand in his pocket
for his handkerchief and in his pocket too there was a wife; he took
some cotton-wool out of his ear – and there too sat a wife . . . Then he
suddenly began hopping on one leg, and Auntie, looking at him, said
with a dignified air: 'Yes, you must hop on one leg now, for you are a
married man.' He went towards her, but his aunt was no longer an aunt
but a belfry, and he felt that someone was dragging him by a rope on
the belfry. 'Who is it pulling me?' Ivan Fyodorovitch asked plaintively.
'It is I, your wife. I am pulling you because you are a bell.' 'No, I am not
a bell, I am Ivan Fyodorovitch,' he cried. 'Yes, you are a bell,' said the
colonel of the P— infantry regiment, who happened to be passing.
Then he suddenly dreamed that his wife was not a human being at all
but a sort of woollen material; that he went into a shop in Mogilyev.
'What sort of stuff would you like?' asked the shopkeeper. 'You had
better take a wife, that is the most fashionable material! It wears well!
Everyone is having coats made of it now.' The shopkeeper measured
and cut off his wife. Ivan Fyodorovitch put her under his arm and went
off to a Jewish tailor. 'No,' said the Jew, 'that is poor material! No one
has coats made of that now . . . '

Ivan Fyodorovitch woke up in terror, not knowing where he was; he
was dripping with cold perspiration.

As soon as he got up in the morning, he went at once to his fortune-
teller's book, at the end of which a virtuous bookseller had in the
goodness of his heart and disinterestedness inserted an abridged dream-
book. But there was absolutely nothing in it that remotely resembled
this incoherent dream.

Meanwhile a quite new design, of which you shall hear more in the
following chapter, was being matured in Auntie's brain.

A PLACE BEWITCHED

A True Story told by the Sacristan

UPON MY WORD, I am sick of telling stories! Why, what would you expect? It really is tiresome; one goes on telling stories and there is no getting out of it! Oh, very well, I will tell you a story then; only, mind, it is for the last time. Well, we were talking about a man's being able to get the better, as the saying is, of the Unclean Spirit. To be sure, if you come to that, all sorts of things do happen in this world . . . Better not say so, though: if the devil wants to bamboozle you he will, upon my soul he will . . . Here you see my father had the four of us; I was only a silly child then, I wasn't more than eleven, no, not eleven. I remember as though it were today when I was running on all fours and set to barking like a dog, my Dad shouted at me, shaking his head: 'Ay, Foma, Foma, you are almost old enough to be married and you are as foolish as a young mule.'

My Grandfather was still living then and fairly – may his hiccough be easier in the other world – strong on his legs. At times he would take a fancy . . . But how am I to tell a story like this? Here one of you has been for the last hour raking an ember for his pipe out of the stove and the other has run behind the cupboard for something. It's too much . . . ! It would be all very well if you didn't want to hear me, but you kept worrying me for a story . . . If you want to listen, then listen!

Just at the beginning of spring Dad went with the waggons to the Crimea to sell tobacco; but I don't remember whether he loaded two or three waggons; tobacco fetched a good price in those days. He took my three-year-old brother with him to train him betimes as a dealer. Grandfather, Mother and I and a brother and another brother were left at home. Grandfather had sown melons on a bit of ground by the roadway and went to stay at the shanty there; he took us with him, too, to scare the sparrows and the magpies off the garden. I can't say it came amiss to us: sometimes we'd eat so many cucumbers, melons, turnips, onions and peas that upon my word, you would have thought there were cocks crowing in our stomachs. Well, to be sure it was profitable too: travellers jog along the road, every one wants to treat himself to a melon, and, besides that, from the neighbouring farms they would often bring us fowls, turkeys, eggs, to exchange for our vegetables. We did very well.

But what pleased Grandfather more than anything was that some fifty dealers would pass with their waggonloads every day. They are people, you know, who have seen life: if one of them will tell you anything, you may well prick up your ears, and to Grandfather it was like dumplings to a hungry man. Sometimes there would be a meeting with old acquaintances – every one knew Grandfather – and you know yourself how it is when old folks get together: it is this and that, and so then and so then, and so this happened and that happened . . . Well, they just run on. They remember things that happened, God knows when.

One evening – why, it seems as though it might have happened today – the sun had begun to set. Grandfather was walking about the garden taking off the leaves with which he covered the water melons in the day to save their being scorched by the sun.

'Look, Ostap,' I said to my brother, 'yonder come some waggoners!'

'Where are the waggoners?' said Grandfather, as he put a mark on the big melon that the lads mightn't eat it by accident.

There were, as a fact, six waggons trailing along the road, a waggoner, whose moustache had gone grey, was walking ahead of them. He was still – what shall I say? ten paces off, when he stopped.

'Good day, Maxim, so it has pleased God we should meet here.'

Grandfather screwed up his eyes. 'Ah, good day, good day! Where do you come from? And Bolyatchka here, too! Good day, good day, brother! What the devil! Why, they are all here: Krutotryshtchenko too! And Petcherytsya! And Kovelyok and Stetsko! Good day! Ha, ha, ho, ho . . . !' And they fell to kissing each other.

They took the oxen out of the shafts and let them graze on the grass; they left the waggons on the road and all sat down in a circle in front of the shanty and lighted their pipes. Though they had no thoughts for their pipes; what with telling stories and chattering, I don't believe they smoked a pipe apiece.

After supper Grandfather began regaling his visitors with melons. So, taking a melon each, they trimmed it neatly with a knife (they were all old hands, had been about a good bit and knew how to eat in company – I dare say they would have been ready to sit down even at a gentleman's table); after cleaning the melon well, every one made a hole with his finger in it, drank the juice, began cutting it up into pieces and putting them into his mouth.

'Why are you standing there gaping, lads?' said my grandfather. 'Dance, you puppies! where's your pipe, Ostap? Now then, the Cossack dance! Foma, arms akimbo! Come, that's it, hey, hop!'

I was a brisk lad in those days. Cursed old age! Now I can't step out like that; instead of cutting capers, my legs can only trip and stumble. For a long time Grandad watched us as he sat with the dealers. I noticed that his legs wouldn't keep still, it was as though something was tugging at them.

'Look, Foma,' said Ostap, 'if the old chap isn't going to dance.'

What do you think, he had hardly uttered the words when the old man could resist it no longer! He longed, you know, to show off before the dealers.

'I say, you little devils, is that the way to dance! This is the way to dance!' he said, getting up on to his feet, stretching out his arms and tapping with his heels.

Well, there is no denying he did dance, he couldn't have danced better if it had been with the Hetman's wife. We stood aside and the old man went twirling his legs all over the flat place beside the cucumber beds. But as soon as he had got halfway through the dance and wanted to do his best and cut some capers with his legs in a whirl – his feet wouldn't rise from the ground, whatever he did! 'What a plague!' He moved backwards and forwards again, got to the middle of the dance – it wouldn't go! Whatever he did – he couldn't do it and he didn't do it! His legs stood still as though made of wood. 'Look you, the place is bewitched, look you, it is a visitation of Satan! The Herod, the enemy of mankind has a hand in it!' Well, he couldn't disgrace himself before the dealers like that, could he? He made a fresh start and began cutting tiny trifling capers, a joy to see; up to the middle – then no! It wouldn't be danced, and that is all about it!

'Ah, you rascally Satan! I hope you may choke with a rotten melon, that you may perish when you are little, son of a bitch. See what shame he has brought me to in my old age . . . !' And indeed someone did laugh behind his back.

He looked round; no melon garden, no dealers, nothing; behind, in front, on both sides was a flat field. 'Ay! Sss! . . . Well, I never!' he began screwing up his eyes – the place doesn't seem quite unfamiliar: on one side a copse, behind the copse some sort of post sticking up which can be seen far away against the sky. Dash it all! But that's the dovecote in the priest's garden! On the other side, too, there is something greyish; he looked closer: it was the district clerk's threshing barn. So this was where the unclean power had dragged him! Going round in a ring, he hit upon a little path. There was no moon: instead of it a white blur glimmered through a dark cloud.

'There will be a high wind tomorrow,' thought Grandad. All at once there was the gleam of a light on a little grave to one side of the path. 'Well, I never!' Grandad stood still, put his arms akimbo and stared at it. The light went out; far away and a little further yet, another twinkled. 'A treasure!' cried Grandad. 'I'll bet anything if it's not a treasure!' And he was just about spitting on his hands to begin digging when he remembered that he had no spade nor shovel with him. 'Oh what a pity! Well – who knows? – maybe I've only to lift the turf and there it lies, the precious dear! Well, there's nothing for it, I'll mark the place anyway so as not to forget it afterwards.'

So pulling along a good-sized branch that must have been broken off by a high wind, he laid it on the little grave where the light gleamed and went along the path. The young oak copse grew thinner; he caught a glimpse of a fence. 'There, didn't I say that it was the priest's garden?' thought Grandad. 'Here's his fence; now it is not three-quarters of a mile to the melon patch.'

It was pretty late, though, when he came home, and he wouldn't have any dumplings. Waking my brother Ostap, he only asked him whether it was long since the dealers had gone, and then rolled himself up in his sheepskin. And when Ostap was beginning to ask him: 'And what did the devils do with you today, Grandad?' 'Don't ask,' he said, wrapping himself up tighter than ever, 'don't ask, Ostap, or your hair will turn grey!'

And he began snoring so that the sparrows who had been flocking together to the melon patch rose up into the air in a fright. But how was it he could sleep? There's no denying, he was a sly beast. God give him the kingdom of Heaven, he could always get out of any scrape; sometimes he would pitch such a yarn that you would have to bite your lips.

Next day as soon as ever it began to get light Grandad put on his smock, fastened his belt, took a spade and shovel under his arm, put on his cap, drank a mug of kvass, wiped his lips with his skirt and went straight to the priest's kitchen garden. He passed both the hedges and the low oak copse and there was a path winding out between the trees and coming out into the open country; it seemed like the same. He came out of the copse and the place seemed exactly the same as yesterday: yonder he saw the dovecote sticking out, but he could not see the threshing barn. 'No, this isn't the place, it must be a little further; it seems I must turn a little towards the threshing barn!' He turned back a little and began going along another path – then he could see the barn but not the dovecote. Again he turned, and a little nearer to the dovecote the barn was hidden. As though to spite him it began drizzling with rain. He ran again towards the barn – the dovecote vanished; towards the dovecote – the barn vanished.

'You damned Satan, may you never live to see your children!' he cried. And the rain came down in bucketfuls.

So taking off his new boots and wrapping them in a handkerchief, that they might not be warped by the rain, he ran off at a trot like some gentleman's saddle-horse. He crept into the shanty, drenched through, covered himself with his sheepskin and set to grumbling between his teeth, and reviling the devil with words such as I had never heard in my life. I must own I should really have blushed if it had happened in broad daylight.

Next day I woke up and looked; Grandad was walking about the melon patch as though nothing had happened, covering the melons with burdock leaves. At dinner the old chap got talking again and began scaring my young brother, saying he would swop him for a fowl instead of a melon; and after dinner he made a pipe out of a bit of wood and began playing on it; and to amuse us gave us a melon which was twisted in three coils like a snake; he called it a Turkish one. I don't see such melons anywhere nowadays; it is true he got the seed from somewhere far away. In the evening, after supper, Grandad went with the spade to dig a new bed for late pumpkins. He began passing that betwitched place and he couldn't resist saying, 'Cursed place!' He went into the middle of it, to the spot where he could not finish the dance the day before, and in his anger struck it a blow with his spade. In a flash – that same field was all around him again: on one side he saw the dovecote standing up, and on the other – the threshing barn. 'Well, it's a good thing I bethought me to bring my spade. And yonder's the path, and there stands the little grave! And there's the branch lying on it, and yonder, see yonder, is the light! If only I have made no mistake!'

He ran up stealthily, holding the spade in the air as though he were going to hit a hog that had poked its nose into a melon patch, and stopped before the grave. The light went out. On the grave lay a stone overgrown with weeds. 'I must lift up that stone,' thought Grandad, and tried to dig round it on all sides. The damned stone was huge! But planting his feet on the ground he shoved it off the grave. 'Goo!' it rolled down the slope. 'That's the right road for you to take! Now things will go more briskly!'

At this point Grandad stopped, took out his horn, sprinkled a little snuff in his hand, and was about to raise it to his nose when all at once, 'Tchee-hee,' something sneezed above his head so that the trees shook and all Grandad's face was spattered. 'You might at least turn aside when you want to sneeze,' said Grandad, wiping his eyes. He looked round – there was no one there. 'No, it seems the devil doesn't like the snuff,' he went on, putting back the horn in his bosom and picking up his spade. 'He's a fool! Neither his grandfather nor his father ever had a pinch of snuff like that!' He began digging, the ground was soft, the spade simply went down into it. Then something clanked. Putting aside the earth he saw a cauldron.

'Ah, you precious dear, here you are!' cried Grandad, thrusting the spade under it.

'Ah, you precious dear, here you are!' piped a bird's beak, pecking the cauldron.

Grandad looked round and dropped the spade.

'Ah, you precious dear, here you are!' bleated a sheep's head from the top of the trees.

'Ah, you precious dear, here you are!' roared a bear, poking its snout out from behind a tree. A shudder ran down Grandad's back.

'Why, one is afraid to say a word here!' he muttered to himself.

'One is afraid to say a word here!' piped the bird's beak.

'Afraid to say a word here!' bleated the sheep's head.

'To say a word here!' roared the bear.

'Hm!' said Grandad, and he felt terrified.

'Hm!' piped the beak.

'Hm!' bleated the sheep.

'Hm!' roared the bear.

Grandad turned round in a fright. Mercy on us, what a night! No stars nor moon; pits all round him, a bottomless precipice at his feet and a crag hanging over his head and looking every minute as though it would break off and come down on him. And Grandad fancied that a horrible face peeped out from behind it. 'Oo! Oo!' A nose like a black-smith's bellows. You could pour a bucket of water into each nostril! Lips like two hogs! Red eyes seemed starting out above and a tongue was thrust out too, and jeering. 'The devil take you!' said Grandad, flinging down the cauldron. 'Damn you and your treasure! What a loathsome snout!' And he was just going to cut and run, but he looked round and stopped, seeing that everything was as before. 'It's only the unclean powers trying to frighten me!'

He set to work at the cauldron again. No, it was too heavy! What was he to do? He couldn't leave it now! So exerting himself to his utmost he clutched at it. 'Come, heave ho! Again, again!' And he dragged it out. 'Ough, now for a pinch of snuff!'

He took out his horn. Before shaking any out though, he took a good look round to be sure there was no one there. He fancied there was no one; but then it seemed to him that the trunk of the tree was gasping and blowing, ears made their appearance, there were red eyes, puffing nostrils, a wrinkled nose and it seemed on the point of sneezing. 'No, I won't have a pinch of snuff!' thought Grandad, putting away the horn. 'Satan will be spitting in my eyes again!' He made haste to snatch up the cauldron and set off running as fast as his legs could carry him; only he felt something behind him scratching on his legs with twigs ... 'Aïe, aïe, aïe!' was all that Grandad could cry as he ran his utmost; and it was not till he reached the priest's kitchen garden that he took breath a little.

'Where can Grandad be gone?' we wondered, waiting three hours for him. Mother had come from the farm long ago and brought a pot of hot dumplings. Still no sign of Grandad! Again we had supper without him. After supper mother washed the pot and was looking where to throw the dishwater because there were melon beds all round, when she sees coming straight towards her a barrel! It was rather dark. She felt sure one of the lads was hiding behind it in mischief and shoving it towards her. 'That's just right, I'll throw the water at him,' she said, and flung the hot dishwater out.

'Aïe!' shouted a bass voice. Only fancy, Grandad! Well, who would have known him! Upon my word we thought it was a barrel coming up! I must own, though it was rather a sin, we really thought it funny when Grandad's grey head was all drenched in the dishwater and decked with melon peelings.

'I say, you devil of a woman!' said Grandad, wiping his head with the skirt of his smock. 'What a hot bath she has given me, as though I were a pig before Christmas! Well, lads, now you will have something for bread-rings! You'll go about dressed in gold tunics, you puppies! Look what I have brought you!' said Grandad, and opened the cauldron.

What do you suppose there was in it? Come, think well, and make a guess? Eh? Gold? Well now, it wasn't gold – it was dirt, filth, I am ashamed to say what it was. Grandad spat, dropped the cauldron and washed his hands after it.

And from that time forward Grandad made us two swear never

to trust the devil. 'Don't you believe it!' he would often say to us. 'Whatever the foe of our Lord Christ says, he is always lying, the son of a bitch! There isn't a ha'p'orth of truth in him!' And if ever the old man heard that things were not right in some place: 'Come, lads, let's cross ourselves! That's it! That's it! Properly!' and he would begin making the sign of the cross. And that accursed place where he couldn't finish the dance he fenced in and bade us fling there all the rubbish, all the weeds and litter which he raked off the melon patch.

So you see how the unclean powers take a man in. I know that bit of ground well; later on some neighbouring Cossacks hired it from Dad for a melon patch. It's capital ground and there is always a wonderful crop on it; but there has never been anything good grown on that bewitched place. They may sow it properly, but there's no saying what it is that comes up: not a melon – not a pumpkin – not a cucumber, the devil only knows what to make of it.

MIRGOROD[73]

Mirgorod is a particularly small town on the River Horol. It has one ropewalk, one brickyard, four watermills and forty-five windmills.

from Zyablovsky's *Geography*[74]

Though in Mirgorod the bread-rings are made of black dough, they are rather nice.

from *The Notes of a Traveller*

OLD-WORLD LANDOWNERS

I AM VERY FOND of the modest manner of life of those solitary owners of remote villages, who in Little Russia are commonly called 'old-fashioned', who are like tumbledown picturesque little houses, delightful in their simplicity and complete unlikeness to the new smooth buildings whose walls have not yet been discoloured by the rain, whose roofs are not yet covered with green lichen, and whose porch does not display its red bricks through the peeling stucco. I like sometimes to enter for a moment into that extraordinarily secluded life in which not one desire flits beyond the palisade surrounding the little courtyard, beyond the hurdle of the orchard filled with plum and apple trees, beyond the village huts surrounding it, lying all aslant under the shade of willows, elders and pear trees. The life of their modest owners is so quiet, so quiet, that for a moment one is lost in forgetfulness and imagines that those passions, desires and restless promptings of the evil spirit that trouble the world have no real existence, and that you have only beheld them in some lurid dazzling dream. I can see now the low-pitched little house with the gallery of little blackened wooden posts running right round it, so that in hail or storm they could close the shutters without being wetted by the rain. Behind it a fragrant bird-cherry, rows of dwarf fruit trees, drowned in a sea of red cherries and amethyst plums, covered with lead-coloured bloom; a spreading maple in the shade of which a rug is laid to rest on; before the house a spacious courtyard of short fresh grass with a little pathway trodden from the storehouse to the kitchen and from the kitchen to the master's apartments; a long-necked goose drinking water with young goslings soft as down around her; a palisade hung with strings of dried pears and apples and rugs put out to air; a cartful of melons standing by the storehouse; an unharnessed ox lying lazily beside it – they all have an inexpressible charm for me, perhaps because I no longer see them and because everything from which we are parted is dear to us.

Be that as it may, at the very moment when my chaise was driving up to the steps of that little house, my soul passed into a wonderfully sweet and serene mood; the horses galloped merrily up to the steps; the coachman very tranquilly clambered down from the box and filled his pipe as though he had reached home; even the barking set up by phlegmatic Rovers, Pontos and Neros was pleasant to my ears. But more than all I liked the owners of these modest little nooks – the little old men and women who came out solicitously to meet me. I can see their faces sometimes even now among fashionable dress-coats in the noise and crowd, and then I sink into a half-dreaming state, and the past rises up before me. Their faces always betray such kindness, such hospitality and single-heartedness that unconsciously one renounces, for a brief spell at least, all ambitious dreams, and imperceptibly passes with all one's heart into this humble bucolic life.

To this day I cannot forget two old people of a past age, now, alas! no more. To this day I am full of regret, and it sends a strange pang to my heart when I imagine myself going some time again to their old now deserted dwelling, and seeing the heap of ruined huts, the pond choked with weeds, an overgrown ditch on the spot where the little house stood – and nothing more. It is sad! I am sad at the thought! But let me turn to my story.

Afanasy Ivanovitch Tovstogub and his wife Pulherya Ivanovna Tovstogubiha, as the surrounding peasants called her, were the old people of whom I was beginning to tell you. If I were a painter and wanted to portray Philemon and Baucis[75] on canvas, I could choose no other models. Afanasy Ivanovitch was sixty. Pulherya Ivanovna was fifty-five. Afanasy Ivanovitch was tall, always wore a camlet[76]-covered sheepskin, used to sit bent up, and was invariably almost smiling, even though he were telling a story or simply listening. Pulherya Ivanovna was rather grave and scarcely ever laughed; but in her face and eyes there was so much kindness, so much readiness to regale you with the best of all they had, that you would certainly have found a smile superfluously sweet for her kind face. The faint wrinkles on their faces were drawn so charmingly that an artist would surely have stolen them; it seemed as though one could read in them their whole life, clear and serene – the life led by the old typically Little Russian, simple-hearted and at the same time wealthy families, always such a contrast to the meaner sort of Little Russians who, struggling up from making tar and petty trading, swarm like locusts in the law courts and public offices, fleece their fellow-villagers of their last farthing, inundate Petersburg with pettifogging attorneys, make their pile at last and solemnly add v to surnames ending in o.[77] No, they, like all the old-fashioned primitive Little Russian families, were utterly different from such paltry contemptible creatures.

One could not look without sympathy at their mutual love. They never addressed each other familiarly, but always with formality. 'Was it you who broke the chair, Afanasy Ivanovitch?' 'Never mind, don't be cross, Pulherya Ivanovna, it was I.' They had had no children, and so all their affection was concentrated on each other. At one time in his youth Afanasy Ivanovitch was in the service and had been lieutenant-major; but that was very long ago, that was all over, Afanasy Ivanovitch himself scarcely ever recalled it. Afanasy Ivanovitch was married at thirty when he was a fine young fellow and wore an embroidered waistcoat; he even eloped rather neatly with Pulherya Ivanovna, whose relations opposed their marriage; but he thought very little about that either now, at any rate he never spoke of it.

All these far-away extraordinary adventures had been followed by a peaceful and secluded life, by the soothing and harmonious dreams that you enjoy when you sit on a wooden balcony overlooking the garden, while a delicious rain keeps up a luxurious sound pattering on the leaves, flowing in gurgling streams and inducing a drowsiness in your limbs, while a rainbow hides behind the trees and in the form of a half-broken arch gleams in the sky with seven soft colours – or when you are swayed in a carriage that drives between green bushes while the quail of the steppes calls and the fragrant grass mingled with ears of corn and wild flowers thrusts itself in at the carriage doors, flicking you pleasantly on the hands and face.

Afanasy Ivanovitch always listened with a pleasant smile to the guests who visited him; sometimes he talked himself, but more often he asked questions. He was not one of those old people who bore one with everlasting praises of old days or denunciations of the new: on the contrary, as he questioned you, he showed great interest and curiosity about the circumstances of your own life, your failures and successes, in which all kind-hearted old people show an interest, though it is a little like the curiosity of a child who examines the seal on your watch at the same time as he talks to you. Then his face, one may say, was breathing with kindliness.

The rooms of the little house in which our old people lived were small and low-pitched, as they usually are in the houses of old-world folk. In each room there was an immense stove which covered nearly a third of the floor space. These rooms were terribly hot, for both Afanasy Ivanovitch and Pulherya Ivanovna liked warmth. The stoves were all heated from the outer room, which was always filled almost up to the ceiling with straw, commonly used in Little Russia instead of firewood. The crackle and flare of this burning straw made the outer room exceedingly pleasant on a winter's evening when ardent young men, chilled with the pursuit of some sunburnt charmer, run in, clapping their hands. The walls of the room were adorned with a few pictures in old-fashioned narrow frames. I am convinced that their owners had themselves long ago forgotten what they represented, and if some of them had been taken away they would probably not have noticed it. There were two big portraits painted in oils. One depicted a bishop, the other Peter III;[78] a fly-blown Duchesse de La Vallière[79] looked out from a narrow frame. Round the windows and above the doors there were numbers of little pictures which one grew used to looking upon as spots on the wall and so never examined them. In almost all the rooms the floor was of clay, but cleanly painted and kept with a neatness with which probably no parquet floor in a wealthy house, lazily swept by sleepy gentlemen in livery, has ever been kept.

Pulherya Ivanovna's room was all surrounded with chests and boxes, big and little. Numbers of little bags and sacks of flower seeds, vegetable seeds, and melon seeds hung on the walls. Numbers of balls of different coloured wools and rags of old-fashioned gowns made half a century ago were stored in the little chests and between the little chests in the corners. Pulherya Ivanovna was a notable housewife and stored everything, though sometimes she could not herself have said to what use it could be put afterwards.

But the most remarkable thing in the house was the singing of the doors. As soon as morning came the singing of the doors could be heard all over the house, I cannot say why it was they sang: whether the rusty hinges were to blame for it or whether the mechanic who made them had concealed some secret in them; but it was remarkable that each door had its own voice; the door leading to the bedroom sang in the thinnest falsetto and the door into the dining-room in a husky bass; but the one on the outer room gave out a strange cracked and at the same time moaning sound, so that as one listened to it one heard distinctly: 'Holy Saints! I am freezing!' I know that many people very much dislike this sound; but I am very fond of it, and if here I sometimes happen to hear a door creak, it seems at once to bring me a whiff of the country: the low-pitched little room lighted by a candle in an old-fashioned candlestick; supper already on the table; a dark May night peeping in from the garden through the open window at the table laid with knives and forks; the nightingale flooding garden, house, and far-away river with its trilling song; the tremor and rustle of branches and, my God! what a long string of memories stretches before me then! . . .

The chairs in the room were massive wooden ones such as were common in old days; they all had high carved backs and were without any kind of varnish or stain; they were not even upholstered, and were rather like the chairs on which bishops sit to this day. Little triangular tables in the corners and square ones before the sofa, and the mirror in its thin gold frame carved with leaves which the flies had covered with black spots; in front of the sofa a rug with birds on it that looked like flowers and flowers that looked like birds: that was almost all the furnishing of the unpretentious little house in which my old people lived. The maids' room was packed full of young girls, and girls who were not young, in striped petticoats; Pulherya Ivanovna sometimes gave them some trifling sewing or set them to prepare the fruit, but for the most part they ran off to the kitchen and slept. Pulherya Ivanovna thought it necessary to keep them in the house and looked strictly after their morals; but to her great surprise many months never passed without the waist of some girl or other growing much larger than usual. This seemed the more surprising as there was scarcely a bachelor in the house with the exception of the houseboy, who used to go about barefoot in a grey tail coat, and if he were not eating was sure to be asleep. Pulherya Ivanovna usually scolded the erring damsel and punished her severely that it might not happen again.

A terrible number of flies were always buzzing on the window-panes, above whose notes rose the deep bass of a bumble bee, sometimes accompanied by the shrill plaint of a wasp; then as soon as candles were brought all the swarm went to bed and covered the whole ceiling with a black cloud.

Afanasy Ivanovitch took very little interest in farming his land, though he did drive out sometimes to the mowers and reapers and watched their labours rather attentively; the whole burden of management rested upon Pulherya Ivanovna. Pulherya Ivanovna's housekeeping consisted in continually locking up and unlocking the storeroom, and in salting, drying and preserving countless masses of fruits and vegetables. Her house was quite like a chemical laboratory. There was everlastingly a fire built under an apple tree; and a cauldron or a copper pan of jam, jelly,[80] or fruit cheese made with honey, sugar and I don't remember what else, was scarcely ever taken off the iron tripod on which it stood. Under another tree the coachman was for ever distilling in a copper retort vodka with peach leaves, or bird-cherry flowers or centaury or cherry stones, and at the end of the process was utterly unable to control his tongue, jabbered such nonsense that Pulherya Ivanovna could make nothing of it, and had to go away to sleep it off in the kitchen. Such a quantity of all this stuff was boiled, salted and dried that the whole courtyard would probably have been drowned in it at last (for Pulherya Ivanovna always liked to prepare a store for the future in addition to all that was reckoned necessary for use), if the larger half of it had not been eaten up by the serf-girls who, stealing into the storeroom, would overeat themselves so frightfully that they were moaning and complaining of stomach ache all day. Pulherya Ivanovna had little chance of looking after the tilling of the fields or other branches of husbandry. The steward, in conjunction with the village elder, robbed them in a merciless fashion. They had adopted the habit of treating their master's forest-land as though it were their own; they made numbers of sledges and sold them at the nearest fair; moreover, all the thick oaks they sold to the neighbouring Cossacks to be cut down for building mills. Only on one occasion Pulherya Ivanovna had desired to inspect her forests. For this purpose a chaise was brought out with immense leather aprons which, as soon as the coachman shook the reins and the horses, who had served in the militia, set off, filled the air with strange sounds, so that a flute and a tambourine and a drum all seemed suddenly audible; every nail and iron bolt clanked so loudly that even at the mill it could be heard that the mistress was driving out of the yard, though the distance was fully a mile and a half. Pulherya Ivanovna could not help noticing the terrible devastation in the forest and the loss of the oaks, which even in childhood she had known to be a hundred years old.

'Why is it, Nitchipor,' she said, addressing her steward who was on the spot, 'that the oaks have been so thinned? Mind that the hair on your head does not grow as thin.'

'Why is it?' the steward said. 'They have fallen down! They have simply fallen: struck by lightning, gnawed by maggots – they have fallen, lady.' Pulherya Ivanovna was completely satisfied with this answer, and on arriving home merely gave orders that the watch should be doubled in the garden near the Spanish cherry trees and the big winter pears.

These worthy rulers, the steward and the elder, considered it quite superfluous to take all the flour to their master's granaries; they thought that the latter would have quite enough with half, and what is more they took to the granaries the half that had begun to grow mouldy or had got wet and been rejected at the fair. But however much the steward and the elder stole; however gluttonously everyone on the place ate, from the housekeeper to the pigs, who guzzled an immense number of plums and apples and often pushed the tree with their snouts to shake a perfect rain of fruit down from it; however much the sparrows and crows pecked; however many presents all the servants carried to their friends in other villages, even hauling off old linen and yarn from the storerooms, all of which went into the ever-flowing stream, that is, to the pot-house; however much was stolen by visitors, phlegmatic coachmen and flunkeys, yet the blessed earth produced everything in such abundance, and Afanasy Ivanovitch and Pulherya Ivanovna wanted so little, that all this terrible robbery made no perceptible impression on their prosperity.

Both the old people were very fond of good fare, as was the old-fashioned tradition of old-world landowners. As soon as the sun had risen (they always got up early) and as soon as the doors set up their varied concert, they were sitting down to a little table, drinking coffee. When he had finished his coffee Afanasy Ivanovitch would go out into the porch and, shaking his handkerchief, say 'Kish, kish! Get off the steps, geese!' In the yard he usually came across the steward. As a rule he entered into conversation with him, questioned him about the field labours with the greatest minuteness, made observations and gave orders which would have impressed anyone with his extraordinary knowledge of farming; and no novice would have dared to dream that he could steal from such a sharp-eyed master. But the steward was a wily old bird: he knew how he must answer, and, what is more, he knew how to manage the land.

After this Afanasy Ivanovitch would go back indoors, and going up to his wife would say: 'Well, Pulherya Ivanovna, isn't it time perhaps for a snack of something?'

'What would you like to have now, Afanasy Ivanovitch? Would you like lardy-cakes or poppy-seed pies, or perhaps salted mushrooms?'

'Perhaps mushrooms or pies,' answered Afanasy Ivanovitch; and the table would at once be laid with a cloth, pies and mushrooms.

An hour before dinner Afanasy Ivanovitch would have another snack, would empty an old-fashioned silver goblet of vodka, would eat mushrooms, various sorts of dried fish and so on. They sat down to dinner at twelve o'clock. Besides the dishes and sauce-boats, there stood on the table numbers of pots with closely-covered lids that no appetising masterpiece of old-fashioned cookery might be spoilt. At dinner the conversation usually turned on subjects closely related to the dinner. 'I fancy this porridge,' Afanasy Ivanovitch would say, 'is a little bit burnt. Don't you think so, Pulherya Ivanovna?' 'No, Afanasy Ivanovitch. You put a little more butter to it, then it won't taste burnt, or have some of this mushroom sauce; pour that over it!' 'Perhaps,' said Afanasy Ivanovitch, passing his plate: 'Let us try how it would be.'

After dinner Afanasy Ivanovitch went to lie down for an hour, after which Pulherya Ivanovna would take a sliced water melon and say: 'Taste what a nice melon, Afanasy Ivanovitch.'

'Don't you be so sure of it, Pulherya Ivanovna, because it is red in the middle,' Afanasy Ivanovitch would say, taking a good slice. 'There are some that are red and are not nice.'

But the melon quickly disappeared. After that Afanasy Ivanovitch would eat a few pears and go for a walk in the garden with Pulherya Ivanovna. On returning home Pulherya Ivanovna would go to look after household affairs, while he sat under an awning turned towards the courtyard and watched the storeroom continually displaying and concealing its interior and the serf-girls pushing one another as they brought in or carried out heaps of trifles of all sorts in wooden boxes, sieves, trays and other receptacles for holding fruit. A little afterwards he sent for Pulherya Ivanovna, or went himself to her and said: 'What shall I have to eat, Pulherya Ivanovna?'

'What would you like?' Pulherya Ivanovna would say. 'Shall I go and tell them to bring you the fruit-dumpling I ordered them to keep on purpose for you?'

'That would be nice,' Afanasy Ivanovitch answered.

'Or perhaps you would like some jelly?'

'That would be good too,' Afanasy Ivanovitch would answer. Then all this was promptly brought him and duly eaten.

Before supper Afanasy Ivanovitch would have another snack of something. At half-past nine they sat down to supper. After supper they at once went to bed, and a universal stillness reigned in this active and at the same time tranquil home.

The room in which Afanasy Ivanovitch and Pulherya Ivanovna slept was so hot that not many people could have stayed in it for several hours; but Afanasy Ivanovitch, in order to be even hotter, used to sleep on the platform of the stove, though the intense heat made him get up several times in the night and walk about the room. Sometimes Afanasy Ivanovitch would moan as he walked about the room. Then Pulherya Ivanovna would ask: 'What are you groaning for, Afanasy Ivanovitch?'

'Goodness only knows, Pulherya Ivanovna; I feel as though I had a little stomach ache,' said Afanasy Ivanovitch.

'Hadn't you better eat something, Afanasy Ivanovitch?'

'I don't know whether it would be good, Pulherya Ivanovna! What should I eat, though?'

'Sour milk or some dried pears stewed.'

'Perhaps I might try it, anyway,' said Afanasy Ivanovitch.

A sleepy serf-girl went off to rummage in the cupboards, and Afanasy Ivanovitch would eat a plateful, after which he commonly said: 'Now it does seem to be better.'

Sometimes, if it was fine weather and rather warm indoors, Afanasy Ivanovitch being in good spirits liked to make fun of Pulherya Ivanovna and talk of something.

'Pulherya Ivanovna,' he would say, 'what if our house were suddenly burnt down, where should we go?'

'Heaven forbid!' Pulherya Ivanovna would say crossing herself.

'But suppose our house were burnt down, where should we go then?'

'God knows what you are saying, Afanasy Ivanovitch! How is it possible that our house could be burnt down? God will not permit it.'

'Well, but if it were burnt down?'

'Oh, then we would move into the kitchen. You should have for the time the little room that the housekeeper has now.'

'But if the kitchen were burnt too?'

'What next! God will preserve us from such a calamity as both house and kitchen burnt down all at once! Well, then we would move into the storeroom while a new house was being built.'

'And if the storeroom were burnt?'

'God knows what you are saying! I don't want to listen to you! It's a sin to say it, and God will punish you for saying such things!'

And Afanasy Ivanovitch, pleased at having made fun of Pulherya Ivanovna, sat smiling in his chair.

But the old couple seemed most of all interesting to me on the occasions when they had guests. Then everything in their house assumed a different aspect. These good-natured people lived, one may say, for visitors. The best of everything they had was all brought out. They vied with each other in trying to regale you with everything their husbandry produced. But what pleased me most of all was that in their solicitude there was no trace of unctuousness. This hospitality and readiness to please was so gently expressed in their faces, was so in keeping with them, that the guests could not help falling in with their wishes, which were the expression of the pure serene simplicity of their kindly guileless souls. This hospitality was something quite different from the way in which a clerk of some government office who has been helped in his career by your efforts entertains you, calling you his benefactor and cringing at your feet. The visitor was on no account to leave on the same day: he absolutely had to stay the night. 'How could you set off on such a long journey at so late an hour!' Pulherya Ivanovna always said. (The guest usually lived two or three miles away.)

'Of course not,' Afanasy Ivanovitch said. 'You never know what may happen: robbers or other evil-minded men may attack you.'

'God preserve us from robbers!' said Pulherya Ivanovna. 'And why talk of such things at night? It's not a question of robbers, but it's dark, it's not fit for driving at all. Besides, your coachman . . . I know your coachman, he is so frail, and such a little man, any horse would be too much for him; and besides he has probably had a drop by now and is asleep somewhere.' And the guest was forced to remain; but the evening spent in the low-pitched hot room, the kindly, warming and soporific talk, the steam rising from the food on the table, always nourishing and cooked in first-class fashion, was compensation for him. I can see as though it were today Afanasy Ivanovitch sitting bent in his chair with his invariable smile, listening to his visitor with attention and even delight! Often the talk touched on politics. The guest, who also very rarely left his village, would often with a significant air and a mysterious expression trot out his conjectures, telling them that the French had a secret agreement with the English to let Bonaparte out again in order to attack Russia,[81] or would simply prophesy war in the near future; and then Afanasy Ivanovitch, pretending not to look at Pulherya Ivanovna, would often say: 'I think I shall go to the war myself; why shouldn't I go to the war?'

'There he goes again!' Pulherya Ivanovna interrupted. 'Don't you believe him,' she said, turning to the guest. 'How could an old man like him go to the war! The first soldier would shoot him! Yes, indeed he would! He'd simply take aim and shoot him.'

'Well,' said Afanasy Ivanovitch, 'and I'll shoot him.'

'Just hear how he talks!' Pulherya Ivanovna caught him up. 'How could he go to the war! And his pistols have been rusty for years and are lying in the cupboard. You should just see them: why, they'd explode with the gunpowder before they'd fire a shot. And he'd blow off his hands and disfigure his face and be wretched for the rest of his days!'

'Well,' said Afanasy Ivanovitch, 'I'd buy myself new weapons; I'll take my sabre or a Cossack lance.'

'That's all nonsense. An idea comes into his head and he begins talking!' Pulherya Ivanovna interrupted with vexation. 'I know he is only joking, but yet I don't like to hear it. That's the way he always talks; sometimes one listens and listens till it frightens one.'

But Afanasy Ivanovitch, pleased at having scared Pulherya Ivanovna a little, laughed sitting bent up in his chair. Pulherya Ivanovna was most attractive to me when she was taking a guest in to lunch. 'This,' she would say, taking a cork out of a bottle, 'is vodka distilled with milfoil and sage – if anyone has a pain in the shoulder blades or loins, it is very good; now this is distilled with centaury – if anyone has a ringing in the ears or a rash on the face, it is very good; and this now is distilled with peach stones – take a glass, isn't it a delicious smell? If anyone getting up in the morning knocks his head against a corner of the cupboard or a table and a bump comes up on his forehead, he has only to drink one glass of it before dinner and it takes it away entirely; it all passes off that very minute, as though it had never been there at all.' Then followed a similar account of the other bottles, which all had some healing properties. After burdening the guest with all these remedies she would lead him up to a number of dishes. 'These are mushrooms with wild thyme! These are with cloves and hazelnuts! A Turkish woman taught me to salt them in the days when we still had Turkish prisoners here. She was such a nice woman, and it was not noticeable at all that she professed the Turkish religion: she went about almost exactly as we do; only she wouldn't eat pork; she said it was forbidden somewhere in their law. And these are mushrooms prepared with black currant leaves and nutmeg! And these are big pumpkins: it's the first time I have pickled them in vinegar; I don't know what they'll be like! I learnt the secret from Father Ivan; first of all you must lay some oak leaves in a tub and then sprinkle with pepper and saltpetre and then put in the flower of the hawkweed, take the flowers and strew them in with stalks uppermost. And here are the little pies; these are cheese pies. And those are the ones Afanasy Ivanovitch is very fond of, made with cabbage and buckwheat.'

'Yes,' Afanasy Ivanovitch would add, 'I am very fond of them; they are soft and a little sourish.'

As a rule Pulherya Ivanovna was in the best of spirits when she had guests. Dear old woman! She was entirely given up to her visitors. I liked staying with them, and although I overate fearfully, as indeed all their visitors did, and though that was very bad for me, I was always glad to go and see them. But I wonder whether the very air of Little Russia has not some peculiar property that promotes digestion; for if anyone were to venture to eat in that way here, there is no doubt he would find himself lying in his coffin instead of his bed.

Good old people! But my account of them is approaching a very melancholy incident which transformed for ever the life of that peaceful nook. This incident is the more impressive because it arose from such an insignificant cause. But such is the strange order of things; trifling causes have always given rise to great events, and on the other hand great undertakings frequently end in insignificant results. Some military leader rallies all the forces of his state, carries on a war for several years, his generals cover themselves with glory, and in the end it all results in gaining a bit of land in which there is not room to plant a potato; while sometimes two sausage-makers of two towns quarrel over some nonsense, and in the end the towns are drawn into the quarrel, then villages, and then the whole kingdom. But let us abandon these reflections: they are out of keeping here; besides I am not fond of reflections, so long as they get no further than being reflections.

Pulherya Ivanovna had a little grey cat, which almost always lay curled up at her feet. Pulherya Ivanovna sometimes stroked her and with one finger scratched her neck, which the spoilt cat stretched as high as she could. I cannot say that Pulherya Ivanovna was excessively fond of her, she was simply attached to her from being used to seeing her about. Afanasy Ivanovitch, however, often teased her about her affection for it.

'I don't know, Pulherya Ivanovna, what you find in the cat: what use is she? If you had a dog, then it would be a different matter: one can take a dog out shooting, but what use is a cat?'

'Oh, be quiet, Afanasy Ivanovitch,' said Pulherya Ivanovna. 'You are simply fond of talking and nothing else. A dog is not clean, a dog makes a mess, a dog breaks everything, while a cat is a quiet creature: she does no harm to anyone.'

Cats and dogs were all the same to Afanasy Ivanovitch, however; he only said it to tease Pulherya Ivanovna a little.

Beyond their garden they had a big forest which had been completely spared by the enterprising steward, perhaps because the sound of the axe would have reached the ears of Pulherya Ivanovna. It was wild and neglected, the old tree-stumps were covered with overgrown nut bushes and looked like the feathered legs of trumpeter pigeons. Wild cats lived in this forest. Wild forest cats must not be confounded with the bold rascals who run about on the roofs of houses; in spite of their fierce disposition the latter, being in cities, are far more civilised than the inhabitants of the forest. Unlike the town cats the latter are for the most part shy and gloomy creatures; they are always gaunt and lean, they mew in a coarse uncultured voice. They sometimes scratch their way underground into the very storehouses and steal bacon; they even penetrate into the kitchen, springing suddenly in at the open window when they see that the cook has gone off into the high grass.

In fact they are unacquainted with any noble sentiments; they live by plunder, and murder little sparrows in their nests. These cats had for a long time past sniffed through a hole under the storehouse at Pulherya Ivanovna's gentle little cat and at last they enticed her away, as a company of soldiers entices a silly peasant girl. Pulherya Ivanovna noticed the disappearance of the cat and sent to look for her; but the cat was not found. Three days passed; Pulherya Ivanovna was sorry to lose her, but at last forgot her. One day when she was inspecting her vegetable garden and was returning with fresh green cucumbers plucked by her own hand for Afanasy Ivanovitch, her ear was caught by a most pitiful mew. As though by instinct she called: 'Puss, puss!' and all at once her grey cat, lean and skinny, came out from the high grass; it was evident that she had not tasted food for several days. Pulherya Ivanovna went on calling her, but the cat stood mewing and did not venture to come close; it was clear that she had grown very wild during her absence. Pulherya Ivanovna went on still calling the cat, who timidly followed her right up to the fence. At last, seeing the old familiar places, she even went indoors. Pulherya Ivanovna at once ordered milk and meat to be brought her and, sitting before her, enjoyed the greediness with which her poor little favourite swallowed piece after piece and lapped up the milk. The little grey fugitive grew fatter almost before her eyes and soon did not eat so greedily. Pulherya Ivanovna stretched out her hand to stroke her, but the ungrateful creature had evidently grown too much accustomed to the ways of wild cats, or had adopted the romantic principle that poverty with love is better than a palace, and, indeed, the wild cats were as poor as church mice; anyway, she sprang out of a window and no one of the house-serfs could catch her.

The old lady sank into thought. 'It was my death coming for me!' she said to herself, and nothing could distract her mind. All day she was sad. In vain Afanasy Ivanovitch joked and tried to find out why she was so melancholy all of a sudden. Pulherya Ivanovna made no answer, or answered in a way that could not possibly satisfy Afanasy Ivanovitch. Next day she was perceptibly thinner.

'What is the matter with you, Pulherya Ivanovna? You must be ill.'

'No, I am not ill, Afanasy Ivanovitch! I want to tell you something strange; I know that I shall die this summer: my death has already come to fetch me!'

Afanasy Ivanovitch's lips twitched painfully. He tried, however, to overcome his gloomy feeling and with a smile said: 'God knows what you are saying, Pulherya Ivanovna! You must have drunk some peach vodka instead of the concoction you usually drink.'

'No, Afanasy Ivanovitch, I have not drunk peach vodka,' said Pulherya

Ivanovna. And Afanasy Ivanovitch was sorry that he had so teased her;
he looked at her and a tear hung on his eyelash.

'I beg you, Afanasy Ivanovitch, to carry out my wishes,' said Pulherya
Ivanovna; 'when I die, bury me by the church fence. Put my grey dress
on me, the one with the little flowers on a brown ground. Don't put on
me my satin dress with the crimson stripes: a dead woman has no need
of a dress – what use is it to her? – while it will be of use to you: have a
fine dressing-gown made of it, so that when visitors are here you can
show yourself and welcome them, looking decent.'

'God knows what you are saying, Pulherya Ivanovna!' said Afanasy
Ivanovitch. 'Death may be a long way off, but you are frightening me
already with such sayings.'

'No, Afanasy Ivanovitch, I know now when my death will come.
Don't grieve for me, though: I am an old woman and have lived long
enough, and you are old, too; we shall soon meet in the other world.'

But Afanasy Ivanovitch was sobbing like a child.

'It's a sin to weep, Afanasy Ivanovitch! Do not be sinful and anger
God by your sorrow. I am not sorry that I am dying; there is only one
thing I am sorry about' – a heavy sigh interrupted her words for a
minute – 'I am sorry that I do not know in whose care to leave you, who
will look after you when I am dead. You are like a little child. You need
somebody who loves you to look after you.'

At these words there was an expression of such deep, such distressed
heartfelt pity on her face that I doubt whether anyone could have looked
at her at that moment unmoved.

'Mind, Yavdoha,' she said, turning to the housekeeper for whom she
had purposely sent, 'that when I die you look after your master, watch
over him like the apple of your eye, like your own child. Mind that what
he likes is always cooked for him in the kitchen; that you always give
him clean linen and clothes; that when visitors come you dress him in
his best, or else maybe he will sometimes come out in his old dressing-
gown, because even now he often forgets when it's a holiday and when
it's a working day. Don't take your eyes off him, Yavdoha; I will pray for
you in the next world and God will reward you. Do not forget, Yavdoha,
you are old, you have not long to live – do not take a sin upon your soul.
If you do not look after him you will have no happiness in life. I myself
will beseech God not to give you a happy end. And you will be unhappy
yourself and your children will be unhappy, and all your family will not
have the blessing of God in anything.'

Poor old woman! At that minute she was not thinking of the great
moment awaiting her, nor of her soul, nor of her own future life: she

was thinking only of her poor companion with whom she had spent her life and whom she was leaving helpless and forlorn. With extraordinary efficiency she arranged everything, so that Afanasy Ivanovitch should not notice her absence when she was gone. Her conviction that her end was at hand was so strong, and her state of mind was so attuned to it, that she did in fact take to her bed a few days later and could eat nothing. Afanasy Ivanovitch never left her bedside and was all solicitude. 'Perhaps you would eat a little of something, Pulherya Ivanovna,' he said, looking with anxiety into her eyes. But Pulherya Ivanovna said nothing. At last, after a long silence she seemed trying to say something, her lips stirred – and her breathing ceased.

Afanasy Ivanovitch was absolutely overwhelmed. It seemed to him so uncanny that he did not even weep; he looked at her with dull eyes as though not grasping the significance of the corpse.

The dead woman was laid on the table dressed in the gown she had herself fixed upon, her arms were crossed and a wax candle put in her hand – he looked at all this apathetically. Numbers of people of all kinds filled the courtyard; numbers of guests came to the funeral; long tables were laid out in the courtyard; they were covered with masses of funeral rice, of home-made beverages and pies. The guests talked and wept, gazed at the dead woman, discussed her qualities and looked at him; but he himself looked queerly at it all. The coffin was carried out at last, the people crowded after it and he followed it. The priests were in full vestments, the sun was shining, babies were crying in their mothers' arms, larks were singing and children raced and skipped about the road. At last the coffin was put down above the grave, he was bidden approach and kiss the dead woman for the last time. He went up and kissed her; there were tears in his eyes, but they were somehow apathetic tears. The coffin was lowered, the priest took the spade and first threw in a handful of earth; the deep rich voices of the deacon and the two sacristans sang 'Eternal Memory' under the pure cloudless sky; the labourers took up their spades and soon the earth covered the grave and made it level. At that moment he pressed forward, everyone stepped aside and made way for him, anxious to know what he meant to do. He raised his eyes, looked at them vacantly and said: 'So you have buried her already! What for?' He broke off and said no more.

But when he was home again, when he saw that his room was empty, that even the chair Pulherya Ivanovna used to sit on had been taken away – he sobbed, sobbed violently, inconsolably, and tears flowed from his lustreless eyes like a river.

Five years have passed since then. What grief does not time bear away? What passion survives in the unequal combat with it? I knew a man in the flower of his youth and strength, full of true nobility of character. I knew him in love, tenderly, passionately, madly, fiercely, humbly; and before me, and before my eyes almost, the object of his passion, a tender creature, lovely as an angel, was struck down by merciless death. I have never seen such awful depths of spiritual suffering, such frenzied poignant grief, such devouring despair as overwhelmed the luckless lover. I had never imagined that a man could create for himself such a hell with no shadow, no shape, no semblance of hope . . . People tried not to leave him alone; all weapons with which he might have killed himself were hidden from him. A fortnight later he suddenly mastered himself, and began laughing and jesting; he was given his freedom, and the first use he made of it was to buy a pistol. One day his family were terrified by the sudden sound of a shot; they ran into the room and saw him stretched on the floor with a shattered skull. A doctor, who happened to be there at the time and whose skill was famous, saw signs of life in him, found that the wound was not absolutely fatal and, to the amazement of everyone, the young man recovered. The watch kept on him was stricter than ever. Even at dinner a knife was not laid for him and everything was removed with which he could have hurt himself; but in a short time he found another opportunity and threw himself under the wheels of a passing carriage. An arm and a leg were broken; but again he recovered. A year after that I saw him in a roomful of people: he was sitting at a table saying gaily 'petit ouvert',[82] as he covered a card, and behind him, with her elbows on the back of his chair, was standing his young wife, turning over his counters.

At the end of the five years after Pulherya Ivanovna's death I was in those parts and drove to Afanasy Ivanovitch's little farm to visit my old neighbour, in whose house I used at one time to spend the day pleasantly and always to overeat myself with the choicest masterpieces of its hospitable mistress.

As I approached the courtyard the house seemed to me twice as old as it had been: the peasants' huts were lying completely on one side, as no doubt their owners were too; the palisade and the hurdle round the yard were completely broken down, and I myself saw the cook pull sticks out of it to heat the stove, though she need have only taken two steps further to reach the faggot-stack. Sadly I drove up to the steps; the same old Neros and Trustys, by now blind or lame, barked, wagging their fluffy tails covered with burdocks. An old man came out to greet me. Yes, it was he! I knew him at once; but he stooped twice as much as before. He knew me and greeted me with the old familiar smile. I followed him indoors. It seemed as though everything was as before. But I noticed a strange disorder in everything, an unmistakable absence of something. In fact I experienced the strange feelings which come upon us when for the first time we enter the house of a widower whom we have known in old days inseparable from the wife who has shared his life. The feeling is the same when we see a man crippled whom we have always known in health. In everything the absence of careful Pulherya Ivanovna was visible: at table a knife was laid without a handle; the dishes were not cooked with the same skill. I did not want to ask about the farm, I was afraid even to look at the farm buildings. When we sat down to dinner, a maid tied a napkin round Afanasy Ivanovitch, and it was well she did so, as without it he would have spilt sauce all over his dressing-gown. I tried to entertain him and told him various items of news; he listened with the same smile, but from time to time his eyes were completely vacant, and his thoughts did not stray, but vanished. Often he lifted a spoonful of porridge and instead of putting it to his mouth put it to his nose; instead of sticking his fork into a piece of chicken, he prodded the decanter, and then the maid, taking his hand, brought it back to the chicken. We sometimes waited several minutes for the next course.

Afanasy Ivanovitch himself noticed it and said: 'Why is it they are so long bringing the food?' But I saw through the crack of the door that the boy who carried away our plates was asleep and nodding on a bench, not thinking of his duties at all.

'This is the dish,' said Afanasy Ivanovitch, when we were handed curd-cakes with sour cream; 'this is the dish,' he went on, and I noticed that his voice began quivering and a tear was ready to drop from his leaden eyes, but he did his utmost to restrain it: 'This is the dish which my . . . my . . . dear . . . my dear . . . ' And all at once he burst into tears; his hand fell on the plate, the plate turned upside down, slipped and was smashed, and the sauce was spilt all over him. He sat vacantly, vacantly held the spoon; and tears like a stream, like a ceaselessly flowing fountain, flowed and flowed on the napkin that covered him.

'My God!' I thought, looking at him, 'five years of all-destroying time – an old man already apathetic, an old man whose life one would have thought had never once been stirred by a strong feeling, whose whole life seemed to consist in sitting on a high chair, in eating dried fish and pears, in telling good-natured stories – and such long, such bitter grief! What is stronger in us – passion or habit? Or are all the violent impulses, all the whirl of our desires and boiling passions only the consequence of our ardent age, and is it only through youth that they seem deep and shattering?'

Be that as it may, at that moment all our passions seemed like child's play beside this effect of long, slow, almost insensible habit. Several times he struggled to utter his wife's name, but, halfway through the word, his quiet and ordinary face worked convulsively and his childish weeping cut me to the very heart. No, those were not the tears of which old men are usually so lavish, as they complain of their pitiful position and their troubles; they were not the tears which they drop over a glass of punch either. No! They were tears which brimmed over uninvited from the accumulated rankling pain of a heart already turning cold.

He did not live long after that. I heard lately of his death. It is strange, though, that the circumstances of his end had some resemblance to those of Pulherya Ivanovna's death. One day Afanasy Ivanovitch ventured to take a little walk in the garden. As he was pacing slowly along a path with his usual absent-mindedness, without a thought of any kind in his head, he had a strange adventure. He suddenly heard someone behind him pronounce in a fairly distinct voice: 'Afanasy Ivanovitch!' He turned round but there was absolutely nobody there; he looked in all directions, he peered into the bushes – no one anywhere. It was a still day and the sun was shining. He pondered for a minute; his face seemed to brighten and he brought out at last: 'It's Pulherya Ivanovna calling me!'

It has happened to you doubtless some time or other to hear a voice calling you by name, which simple people explain as a soul grieving for a human being and calling him, and after that, they say, death follows inevitably. I must own I was always frightened by that mysterious call. I remember that in childhood I often heard it. Sometimes suddenly someone behind me distinctly uttered my name. Usually on such occasions it was a very bright and sunny day; not one leaf in the garden was stirring; the stillness was deathlike; even the grasshopper left off churring for the moment; there was not a soul in the garden. But I confess that if the wildest and most tempestuous night had lashed me with all the fury of the elements, alone in the middle of an impenetrable forest, I should not have been so terrified as by that awful stillness in the midst of a cloudless day. I usually ran out of the garden in a great panic, hardly able to breathe, and was only reassured when I met some person, the sight of whom dispelled the terrible spiritual loneliness.

Afanasy Ivanovitch surrendered completely to his inner conviction that Pulherya Ivanovna was calling him; he submitted with the readiness of an obedient child, wasted away, coughed, melted like a candle and at last flickered out, as it does when there is nothing left to sustain its feeble flame. 'Lay me beside Pulherya Ivanovna' was all he said before his end.

His desire was carried out and he was buried near the church beside Pulherya Ivanovna's grave. The guests were fewer at the funeral, but there were just as many beggars and peasants. The little house was now completely emptied. The enterprising steward and the elder hauled away to their huts all that were left of the old-fashioned goods and furniture, which the housekeeper had not been able to carry off. Soon there arrived, I cannot say from where, a distant kinsman, the heir to the estate, who had been a lieutenant, I don't know in what regiment, and was a terrible reformer. He saw at once the great slackness and disorganisation in the management of the land; he made up his mind to change all that radically, to improve things and bring everything into order. He bought six splendid English sickles, pinned a special number on each hut, and managed so well that within six months his estate was put under the supervision of a board of trustees.

The sage trustees (consisting of an ex-assessor and a lieutenant in a faded uniform) had within a very short time left no fowls and eggs. The huts, which were almost lying on the earth, fell down completely; the peasants gave themselves up to drunkenness and most of them ran away. The real owner, who got on, however, pretty comfortably with his trustees and used to drink punch with them, very rarely visited his estate and never stayed long. To this day he drives about to all the fairs in Little Russia, carefully enquiring the prices of all sorts of produce sold wholesale, such as flour, hemp, honey and so on; but he only buys small trifles such as flints, a nail to clean out his pipe, in fact nothing which exceeds at the utmost a rouble in price.

VIY

AS SOON AS the rather musical seminary bell which hung at the gate of the Bratsky Monastery rang out every morning in Kiev, schoolboys and students hurried thither in crowds from all parts of the town. Students of grammar, rhetoric, philosophy and theology trudged to their classrooms with exercise-books under their arms. The grammarians were quite small boys: they shoved each other as they went along and quarrelled in a shrill alto; they almost all wore muddy or tattered clothes, and their pockets were full of all manner of rubbish, such as knucklebones, whistles made of feathers, or a half-eaten pie, sometimes even little sparrows, one of whom suddenly chirruping at an exceptionally quiet moment in the classroom would cost its owner some sound whacks on both hands and sometimes a thrashing. The rhetoricians walked with more dignity; their clothes were often quite free from holes; on the other hand, their countenances almost all bore some decoration, after the style of a figure of rhetoric; either one eye had sunk right under the forehead, or there was a monstrous swelling in place of a lip, or some other disfigurement. They talked and swore among themselves in tenor voices. The philosophers conversed an octave lower in the scale; they had nothing in their pockets but strong, cheap tobacco. They laid in no stores of any sort, but ate on the spot anything they came across; they smelt of pipes and vodka to such a distance that a passing workman would sometimes stop a long way off and sniff the air like a setter dog.

As a rule the market was just beginning to stir at that hour, and the women with bread-rings, rolls, melon seeds, and poppy cakes would tug at the skirts of those whose coats were of fine cloth or some cotton material.

'This way, young gentlemen, this way!' they kept saying from all sides: 'here are bread-rings, poppy cakes, twists, good white rolls; they are really good! Made with honey! I baked them myself.'

Another woman lifting up a sort of long twist made of dough would cry: 'Here's a bread-stick! Buy my bread-stick, young gentlemen!'

'Don't buy anything off her; see what a horrid woman she is, her nose is nasty and her hands are dirty . . . '

But the women were afraid to worry the philosophers and the theologians, for the latter were fond of taking things to taste and always a good handful.

On reaching the seminary, the crowd dispersed to their various classes, which were held in low-pitched but fairly large rooms, with little windows, wide doorways, and dirty benches. The classroom was at once filled with all sorts of buzzing sounds: the 'auditors' heard their pupils repeat their lessons; the shrill alto of a grammarian rang out, and the window-pane responded with almost the same note; in a corner a rhetorician, whose mouth and thick lips should have belonged at least to a student of philosophy, was droning something in a bass voice, and all that could be heard at a distance was 'Boo, boo, boo . . . ' The 'auditors', as they heard the lesson, kept glancing with one eye under the bench, where a roll or a cheese-cake or some pumpkin seeds were peeping out of a scholar's pocket.

When this learned crowd managed to arrive a little too early, or when they knew that the professors would be later than usual, then by general consent they got up a fight, and everyone had to take part in it, even the monitors whose duty it was to maintain discipline and look after the morals of all the students. Two theologians usually settled the arrangements for the battle: whether each class was to defend itself individually, or whether all were to be divided into two parties, the bursars and the seminarists. In any case the grammarians first began the attack, and, as soon as the rhetoricians entered the fray, they ran away and stood at points of vantage to watch the contest. Then the devotees of philosophy, with long black moustaches, joined in, and finally those of theology, very thick in the neck and attired in shocking trousers, took part. It commonly ended in theology beating all the rest, and the philosophers, rubbing their ribs, would be forced into the classroom and sat down on the benches to rest. The professor, who had himself at one time taken part in such battles, could, on entering the class, see in a minute from the flushed faces of his audience that the battle had been a good one and, while he was caning a rhetorician on the fingers, in another classroom another professor would be smacking philosophy's hands with a wooden bat. The theologians were dealt with in quite a different way: they received, to use the expression of a professor of theology, 'a peck of peas apiece,' in other words, a liberal drubbing with short leather thongs.

On holidays and ceremonial occasions the bursars and the seminarists went from house to house as mummers. Sometimes they acted a play, and then the most distinguished figure was always some theologian, almost as tall as the belfry of Kiev, who took the part of Herodias[83] or Potiphar's wife.[84] They received in payment a piece of linen, or a sack of millet or half a boiled goose, or something of the sort. All this crowd of students – the seminarists as well as the bursars, with whom they maintain an hereditary feud – were exceedingly badly off for means of subsistence, and at the same time had extraordinary appetites, so that to reckon how many dumplings each of them tucked away at supper would be utterly impossible, and therefore the voluntary offerings of prosperous citizens could not be sufficient for them. Then the 'senate' of the philosophers and theologians despatched the grammarians and rhetoricians, under the supervision of a philosopher (who sometimes took part in the raid himself), with sacks on their shoulders to plunder the kitchen gardens – and pumpkin porridge was made in the bursars' quarters. The members of the 'senate' ate such masses of melons that next day their 'auditors' heard two lessons from them instead of one, one coming from their lips, another muttering in their stomachs. Both the bursars and the seminarists wore long garments resembling frock-coats, 'prolonged to the utmost limit', a technical expression signifying below their heels.

The most important event for the seminarists was the coming of the vacation: it began in June, when they usually dispersed to their homes. Then the whole highroad was dotted with philosophers, grammarians and theologians. Those who had nowhere to go went to stay with some comrade. The philosophers and theologians took a situation, that is, undertook the tuition of the children in some prosperous family, and received in payment a pair of new boots or sometimes even a coat. The whole crowd trailed along together like a gypsy encampment, boiled their porridge, and slept in the fields. Everyone hauled along a sack in which he had a shirt and a pair of leg-wrappers. The theologians were particularly careful and precise: to avoid wearing out their boots, they took them off, hung them on sticks and carried them on their shoulders, particularly if it was muddy; then, tucking their trousers up above their knees, they splashed fearlessly through the puddles. When they saw a village they turned off the highroad and, going up to any house which seemed a little better looking than the rest, stood in a row before the windows and began singing a chant at the top of their voices. The master of the house, some old Cossack villager, would listen to them for a long time, his head propped on his hands, then he would sob bitterly and say, turning to his wife: 'Wife! What the scholars are singing must be very deep; bring them fat bacon and anything else that we have.' And a whole bowl of dumplings was emptied into the sack, a good-sized piece of bacon, several flat loaves, and sometimes a trussed hen would go into it too. Fortified with such stores, the grammarians, rhetoricians, philosophers and theologians went on their way again. Their numbers lessened, however, the further they went. Almost all wandered off towards their homes, and only those were left whose parental abodes were further away.

Once, at the time of such a migration, three students turned off the highroad in order to replenish their store of provisions at the first homestead they could find, for their sacks had long been empty. They were the theologian, Halyava; the philosopher, Homa Brut; and the rhetorician, Tibery Gorobets.

The theologian was a well-grown broad-shouldered fellow; he had an extremely odd habit – anything that lay within his reach he invariably stole. In other circumstances, he was of an excessively gloomy temper, and when he was drunk he used to hide in the rank grass, and the seminarists had a lot of trouble to find him there.

The philosopher, Homa Brut, was of a cheerful temper, he was very fond of lying on his back, smoking a pipe; when he was drinking he always engaged musicians and danced the trepak.[85] He often had a taste of the 'peck of peas,' but took it with perfect philosophical indifference, saying that there is no escaping what has to be. The rhetorician, Tibery Gorobets, had not yet the right to wear a moustache, to drink vodka, and to smoke a pipe. He only wore a curl round his ear, and so his character was as yet hardly formed; but, judging from the big bumps on the forehead, with which he often appeared in class, it might be presumed that he would make a good fighter. The theologian, Halyava, and the philosopher, Homa, often pulled him by the forelock as a sign of their favour, and employed him as their messenger.

It was evening when they turned off the highroad; the sun had only just set and the warmth of the day still lingered in the air. The theologian and the philosopher walked along in silence smoking their pipes; the rhetorician, Tibery Gorobets, kept knocking off the heads of the wayside thistles with his stick. The road ran between scattered groups of oak and nut trees standing here and there in the meadows. Sloping uplands and little hills, green and round as cupolas, were interspersed here and there about the plain. The cornfields of ripening wheat, which came into view in two places, showed that some village must soon be seen. It was more than an hour, however, since they had passed the cornfields, yet they had come upon no dwelling. The sky was now completely wrapped in darkness, and only in the west there was a pale streak left of the glow of sunset.

'What the devil does it mean?' said the philosopher, Homa Brut. 'It looked as though there must be a village in a minute.'

The theologian did not speak, he gazed at the surrounding country, then put his pipe back in his mouth, and they continued on their way.

'Upon my soul!' the philosopher said, stopping again, 'not a devil's fist to be seen.'

'Maybe some village will turn up further on,' said the theologian, not removing his pipe.

But meantime night had come on, and a rather dark night. Small storm-clouds increased the gloom, and by every token they could expect neither stars nor moon. The students noticed that they had lost their way and for a long time had been walking off the road.

The philosopher, after feeling about with his feet in all directions, said at last, abruptly: 'I say, where's the road?'

The theologian did not speak for a while, then after pondering, he brought out: 'Yes, it is a dark night.'

The rhetorician walked off to one side and tried on his hands and knees to feel for the road, but his hands came upon nothing but foxes' holes. On all sides of them there was the steppe, which, it seemed, no one had ever crossed.

The travellers made another effort to press on a little, but there was the same wilderness in all directions. The philosopher tried shouting, but his voice seemed completely lost on the steppe, and met with no reply. All they heard was, a little afterwards, a faint moaning like the howl of a wolf.

'I say, what's to be done?' said the philosopher.

'Why, halt and sleep in the open!' said the theologian, and he felt in his pocket for flint and tinder to light his pipe again. But the philosopher could not agree to this: it was always his habit at night to put away a quarter loaf of bread and four pounds of fat bacon, and he was conscious on this occasion of an insufferable sense of loneliness in his stomach. Besides, in spite of his cheerful temper, the philosopher was rather afraid of wolves.

'No, Halyava, we can't,' he said. 'What, stretch out and lie down like a dog, without a bite or a sup of anything? Let's make another try for it;

maybe we shall stumble on some dwelling-place and get at least a drink of vodka for supper.'

At the word 'vodka' the theologian spat to one side and brought out: 'Well, of course, it's no use staying in the open.'

The students walked on, and to their intense delight caught the sound of barking in the distance. Listening which way it came from, they walked on more boldly and a little later saw a light.

'A village! It really is a village!' said the philosopher.

He was not mistaken in his supposition; in a little while they actually saw a little homestead consisting of only two cottages looking into the same farmyard. There was a light in the windows; a dozen plum trees stood up by the fence. Looking through the cracks in the paling-gate the students saw a yard filled with carriers' waggons. Stars peeped out here and there in the sky at the moment.

'Look, mates, don't let's be put off! We must get a night's lodging somehow!'

The three learned gentlemen banged on the gates with one accord and shouted, 'Open!'

The door of one of the cottages creaked, and a minute later they saw before them an old woman in sheepskin.

'Who is there?' she cried, with a hollow cough.

'Give us a night's lodging, granny; we have lost our way; a night in the open is as bad as a hungry belly.'

'What manner of folks may you be?'

'Oh, harmless folks: Halyava, a theologian; Brut, a philosopher; and Gorobets, a rhetorician.'

'I can't,' grumbled the old woman. 'The yard is crowded with folk and every corner in the cottage is full. Where am I to put you? And such great hulking fellows, too! Why, it would knock my cottage to pieces if I put such fellows in it. I know these philosophers and theologians; if one began taking in these drunken fellows, there'd soon be no home left. Be off, be off! There's no place for you here!'

'Have pity on us, granny! How can you let Christian souls perish for no rhyme or reason? Put us where you please; and if we do aught amiss or anything else, may our arms be withered, and God only knows what befall us – so there!'

The old woman seemed somewhat softened.

'Very well,' she said, as though reconsidering, 'I'll let you in, but I'll put you all in different places; for my mind won't be at rest if you are all together.'

'That's as you please; we'll make no objection,' answered the students.

The gate creaked and they went into the yard.

'Well, granny,' said the philosopher, following the old woman, 'how would it be, as they say . . . upon my soul I feel as though somebody were driving a cart in my stomach: not a morsel has passed my lips all day.'

'What next will he want!' said the old woman. 'No, I've nothing to give you, and the oven's not been heated today.'

'But we'd pay for it all,' the philosopher went on, 'tomorrow morning, in hard cash. Yes!' he added in an undertone, 'the devil a bit you'll get!'

'Go in, go in! And you must be satisfied with what you're given. Fine young gentlemen the devil has brought us!'

Homa the philosopher was thrown into utter dejection by these words, but his nose was suddenly aware of the odour of dried fish; he glanced towards the trousers of the theologian who was walking at his side, and saw a huge fishtail sticking out of his pocket. The theologian had already succeeded in filching a whole carp from a waggon. And as he had done this from no interested motive but simply from habit, and, quite forgetting his carp, was already looking about for anything else he could carry off, having no mind to miss even a broken wheel, the philosopher slipped his hand into his friend's pocket, as though it were his own, and pulled out the carp.

The old woman put the students in their several places: the rhetorician she kept in the cottage, the theologian she locked in an empty closet, the philosopher she assigned a sheep's pen, also empty.

The latter, on finding himself alone, instantly devoured the carp, examined the hurdle-walls of the pen, kicked an inquisitive pig that woke up and thrust its snout in from the next pen, and turned over on his right side to fall into a sound sleep. All at once the low door opened, and the old woman bending down stepped into the pen.

'What is it, granny, what do you want?' said the philosopher.

But the old woman came towards him with outstretched arms.

'Aha, ha!' thought the philosopher. 'No, my dear, you are too old!'

He turned a little away, but the old woman unceremoniously approached him again.

'Listen, granny!' said the philosopher. 'It's a fast time now; and I am a man who wouldn't sin in a fast for a thousand golden pieces.'

But the old woman opened her arms and tried to catch him without saying a word.

The philosopher was frightened, especially when he noticed a strange glitter in her eyes. 'Granny, what is it? Go – go away – God bless you!' he cried.

The old woman said not a word, but tried to clutch him in her arms.

He leapt on to his feet, intending to escape; but the old woman stood in the doorway, fixed her glittering eyes on him and again began approaching him.

The philosopher tried to push her back with his hands, but to his surprise found that his arms would not rise, his legs would not move, and he perceived with horror that even his voice would not obey him; words hovered on his lips without a sound. He heard nothing but the beating of his heart. He saw the old woman approach him. She folded his arms, bent his head down, leapt with the swiftness of a cat upon his back, and struck him with a broom on the side; and he, prancing like a horse, carried her on his shoulders. All this happened so quickly that the philosopher scarcely knew what he was doing. He clutched his knees in both hands, trying to stop his legs from moving, but to his extreme amazement they were lifted against his will and executed capers more swiftly than a Circassian racer.[86] Only when they had left the farm, and the wide plain lay stretched before them with a forest black as coal on one side, he said to himself: 'Aha! She's a witch!'

The waning crescent of the moon was shining in the sky. The timid radiance of midnight lay mistily over the earth, light as a transparent veil. The forests, the meadows, the sky, the dales, all seemed as though slumbering with open eyes; not a breeze fluttered anywhere; there was a damp warmth in the freshness of the night; the shadows of the trees and bushes fell on the sloping plain in pointed wedge shapes like comets. Such was the night when Homa Brut, the philosopher, set off galloping with a mysterious rider on his back. He was aware of an exhausting, unpleasant, and at the same time, voluptuous sensation assailing his heart. He bent his head and saw that the grass which had been almost under his feet seemed growing at a depth far away, and that above it there lay water, transparent as a mountain stream, and the grass seemed to be at the bottom of a clear sea, limpid to its very depths; anyway, he saw clearly in it his own reflection with the old woman sitting on his back. He saw shining there a sun instead of the moon; he heard the bluebells ringing as they bent their little heads; he saw a water-nymph float out from behind the reeds, there was the gleam of her leg and back, rounded and supple, all brightness and shimmering. She turned towards him and now her face came nearer, with eyes clear, sparkling, keen, with singing that pierced to the heart; now it was on the surface, and shaking with sparkling laughter it moved away; and now she turned on her back, and her cloudlike breasts, dead-white like unglazed china, gleamed in the sun at the edges of their white, soft and supple roundness. Little bubbles of water like beads bedewed them. She was all quivering and laughing in the water . . .

Did he see this or did he not? Was he awake or dreaming? But what was that? The wind or music? It is ringing and ringing and eddying and coming closer and piercing to his heart with an insufferable thrill . . .

'What does it mean?' the philosopher wondered, looking down as he flew along, full speed. The sweat was streaming from him. He was aware of a fiendishly voluptuous feeling, he felt a stabbing, exhaustingly terrible delight. It often seemed to him as though his heart had melted away, and with terror he clutched at it. Worn out, desperate, he began trying to recall all the prayers he knew. He went through all the exorcisms against evil spirits, and all at once felt somewhat refreshed; he felt that his step was growing slower, the witch's hold upon his back seemed feebler, thick grass touched him, and now he saw nothing extraordinary in it. The clear, crescent moon was shining in the sky.

'Good!' the philosopher Homa thought to himself, and he began repeating the exorcisms almost aloud. At last, quick as lightning, he sprang from under the old woman and in his turn leapt on her back. The old woman, with a tiny tripping step, ran so fast that her rider could scarcely breathe. The earth flashed by under him; everything was clear in the moonlight, though the moon was not full; the ground was smooth, but everything flashed by so rapidly that it was confused and indistinct. He snatched up a piece of wood that lay on the road and began whacking the old woman with all his might. She uttered wild howls; at first they were angry and menacing, then they grew fainter, sweeter, clearer, then rang out gently like delicate silver bells that stabbed him to the heart; and the thought flashed through his mind: was it really an old woman?

'Oh, I can do no more!' she murmured, and sank exhausted on the ground.

He stood up and looked into her face (there was the glow of sunrise, and the golden domes of the Kiev churches were gleaming in the distance): before him lay a lovely creature with luxuriant tresses all in disorder and eyelashes as long as arrows. Senseless she tossed her bare white arms and moaned, looking upwards with eyes full of tears.

Homa trembled like a leaf on a tree; he was overcome by pity and a strange emotion and timidity, feelings he could not himself explain. He set off running, full speed. His heart throbbed uneasily as he went, and he could not account for the strange new feeling that had taken possession of it. He did not want to go back to the farm; he hastened to Kiev, pondering all the way on this incomprehensible adventure.

There was scarcely a student left in the town. All had dispersed about the countryside, either to situations, or simply without them; because in the villages of Little Russia they could get dumplings, cheese, sour cream, and puddings as big as a hat without paying a kopeck for them. The big rambling house in which the students were lodged was absolutely empty, and although the philosopher rummaged in every corner, and even felt in all the holes and cracks in the roof, he could not find a bit of bacon or even a stale roll such as were commonly hidden there by the students.

The philosopher, however, soon found means to improve his lot: he walked whistling three times through the market, finally winked at a young widow in a yellow bonnet who was selling ribbons, shot and wheels – and was that very day regaled with wheat dumplings, a chicken . . . in short, there is no telling what was on the table laid for him in a little mud house in the middle of a cherry orchard.

That same evening the philosopher was seen in a tavern: he was lying on the bench, smoking a pipe as his habit was, and in the sight of all he flung the Jew who kept the house a gold coin. A mug stood before him. He looked at all that came in and went out with eyes full of cool satisfaction, and thought no more of his extraordinary adventure.

Meanwhile rumours were circulating everywhere that the daughter of one of the richest Cossack *sotniks*,* who lived nearly forty miles from Kiev, had returned one day from a walk, terribly injured, hardly able to crawl home to her father's house, was lying at the point of death, and had expressed a wish that one of the Kiev seminarists, Homa Brut, should read the prayers over her and the psalms for three days after her death. The philosopher heard of this from the rector himself, who summoned him to his room and informed him that he was to set off on the journey without any delay, that the noble *sotnik* had sent servants and a carriage to fetch him.

The philosopher shuddered from an unaccountable feeling which he could not have explained to himself. A dark presentiment told him that something evil was awaiting him. Without knowing why, he bluntly declared that he would not go.

'Listen, Domine Homa!' said the rector. (On some occasions he expressed himself very courteously with those under his authority.) 'Who the devil is asking you whether you want to go or not? All I have

---

* An officer in command of a company of Cossaks, consisting originally of a hundred, but in later times of a larger number. (*Translator's Note*)

to tell you is that if you go on jibbing and making difficulties, I'll order you such a whacking with a young birch tree, on your back and the rest of you, that there will be no need for you to go to the bath after.'

The philosopher, scratching behind his ear, went out without uttering a word, proposing at the first suitable opportunity to put his trust in his heels. Plunged in thought he went down the steep staircase that led into a yard shut in by poplars, and stood still for a minute, hearing quite distinctly the voice of the rector giving orders to his butler and someone else – probably one of the servants sent to fetch him by the *sotnik*.

'Thank his honour for the grain and the eggs,' the rector was saying: 'and tell him that as soon as the books about which he writes are ready I will send them at once, I have already given them to a scribe to be copied, and don't forget, my good man, to mention to his honour that I know there are excellent fish at his place, especially sturgeon, and he might on occasion send some; here in the market it's bad and dear. And you, Yavtuh, give the young fellows a cup of vodka each, and bind the philosopher or he'll be off directly.'

'There, the devil's son!' the philosopher thought to himself. 'He scented it out, the wily long-legs!' He went down and saw a covered chaise, which he almost took at first for a baker's oven on wheels. It was, indeed, as deep as the oven in which bricks are baked. It was only the ordinary Cracow carriage in which Jews travel fifty together with their wares to all the towns where they smell out a fair. Six healthy and stalwart Cossacks, no longer young, were waiting for him. Their tunics of fine cloth, with tassels, showed that they belonged to a rather important and wealthy master; some small scars proved that they had at some time been in battle, not ingloriously.

'What's to be done? What is to be must be!' the philosopher thought to himself and, turning to the Cossacks, he said aloud: 'Good day to you, comrades!'

'Good health to you, master philosopher,' some of the Cossacks replied.

'So I am to get in with you? It's a goodly chaise!' he went on, as he clambered in, 'we need only hire some musicians and we might dance here.'

'Yes, it's a carriage of ample proportions,' said one of the Cossacks, seating himself on the box beside the coachman, who had tied a rag over his head to replace the cap which he had managed to leave behind at a pot-house. The other five and the philosopher crawled into the recesses of the chaise and settled themselves on sacks filled with various purchases they had made in the town. 'It would be interesting to know,' said the philosopher, 'if this chaise were loaded up with goods of some sort, salt for instance, or iron wedges, how many horses would be needed then?'

'Yes,' the Cossack, sitting on the box, said after a pause, 'it would need a sufficient number of horses.'

After this satisfactory reply the Cossack thought himself entitled to hold his tongue for the remainder of the journey.

The philosopher was extremely desirous of learning more in detail, who this *sotnik* was, what he was like, what had been heard about his daughter who in such a strange way returned home and was found on the point of death, and whose story was now connected with his own, what was being done in the house, and how things were there. He addressed the Cossacks with enquiries, but no doubt they too were philosophers, for by way of a reply they remained silent, smoking their pipes and lying on their backs. Only one of them turned to the driver on the box with a brief order. 'Mind, Overko, you old booby, when you are near the tavern on the Tchuhraylovo road, don't forget to stop and wake me and the other chaps, if any should chance to drop asleep.'

After this he fell asleep rather audibly. These instructions were, however, quite unnecessary for, as soon as the gigantic chaise drew near the pot-house, all the Cossacks with one voice shouted: 'Stop!' Moreover, Overko's horses were already trained to stop of themselves at every pot-house.

In spite of the hot July day, they all got out of the chaise and went into the low-pitched dirty room, where the Jew who kept the house hastened to receive his old friends with every sign of delight. The Jew brought from under the skirt of his coat some ham sausages, and, putting them on the table, turned his back at once on this food forbidden by the Talmud. All the Cossacks sat down round the table; earthenware mugs were set for each of the guests. Homa had to take part in the general festivity, and, as Little Russians infallibly begin kissing each other or weeping when they are drunk, soon the whole room resounded with smacks. 'I say, Spirid, a kiss.' 'Come here, Dorosh, I want to embrace you!'

One Cossack with grey moustaches, a little older than the rest, propped his cheek on his hand and began sobbing bitterly at the thought that he had no father nor mother and was all alone in the world. Another one, much given to moralising, persisted in consoling him, saying: 'Don't cry; upon my soul, don't cry! What is there in it . . . ? The Lord knows best, you know.'

The one whose name was Dorosh became extremely inquisitive, and, turning to the philosopher Homa, kept asking him: 'I should like to know what they teach you in the college. Is it the same as what the deacon reads in church, or something different?'

'Don't ask!' the sermonising Cossack said emphatically: 'let it be as it is, God knows what is wanted, God knows everything.'

'No, I want to know,' said Dorosh, 'what is written there in those books? Maybe it is quite different from what the deacon reads.'

'Oh, my goodness, my goodness!' said the sermonising worthy, 'and why say such a thing; it's as the Lord wills. There is no changing what the Lord has willed!'

'I want to know all that's written. I'll go to college, upon my word, I will. Do you suppose I can't learn? I'll learn it all, all!'

'Oh my goodness . . . !' said the sermonising Cossack, and he dropped his head on the table, because he was utterly incapable of supporting it any longer on his shoulders. The other Cossacks were discussing their masters and the question why the moon shone in the sky. The philosopher, seeing the state of their minds, resolved to seize his opportunity and make his escape. To begin with he turned to the grey-headed Cossack who was grieving for his father and mother.

'Why are you blubbering, uncle?' he said, 'I am an orphan myself! Let me go in freedom, lads! What do you want with me?'

'Let him go!' several responded, 'why, he is an orphan, let him go where he likes.'

'Oh, my goodness, my goodness!' the moralising Cossack articulated, lifting his head. 'Let him go!'

'Let him go where he likes!'

And the Cossacks meant to lead him out into the open air themselves, but the one who had displayed his curiosity stopped them, saying: 'Don't touch him. I want to talk to him about college: I am going to college myself . . . '

It is doubtful, however, whether the escape could have taken place, for when the philosopher tried to get up from the table his legs seemed to have become wooden, and he began to perceive such a number of doors in the room that he could hardly discover the real one.

It was evening before the Cossacks bethought themselves that they had further to go. Clambering into the chaise, they trailed along the road, urging on the horses and singing a song of which nobody could have made out the words or the sense. After trundling on for the greater part of the night, continually straying off the road, though they knew every inch of the way, they drove at last down a steep hill into a valley, and the philosopher noticed a paling or hurdle that ran alongside, low trees and roofs peeping out behind it. This was a big village belonging to the *sotnik*. By now it was long past midnight; the sky was dark, but there were little stars twinkling here and there. No light was to be seen in a single cottage. To the accompaniment of the barking of dogs, they drove into the courtyard. Thatched barns and little houses came into sight on both sides; one of the latter, which stood exactly in the middle opposite the gates, was larger than the others, and was apparently the *sotnik*'s residence. The chaise drew up before a little shed that did duty for a barn, and our travellers went off to bed. The philosopher, however, wanted to inspect the outside of the *sotnik*'s house; but, though he stared his hardest, nothing could be seen distinctly; the house looked to him like a bear; the chimney turned into the rector. The philosopher gave it up and went to sleep.

When he woke up, the whole house was in commotion: the *sotnik*'s daughter had died in the night. Servants were running hurriedly to and fro; some old women were crying; an inquisitive crowd was looking through the fence at the house, as though something might be seen there. The philosopher began examining at his leisure the objects he could not make out in the night. The *sotnik*'s house was a little, low-pitched building, such as was usual in Little Russia in old days; its roof was of thatch; a small, high, pointed gable with a little window that looked like an eye turned upwards, was painted in blue and yellow flowers and red crescents; it was supported on oak posts, rounded above and hexagonal below, with carving at the top. Under the gable was a little porch with seats on each side. There were verandahs round the house resting on similar posts, some of them carved in spirals. A tall pyramidal pear tree, with trembling leaves, made a patch of green in front of the house. Two rows of barns for storing grain stood in the middle of the yard, forming a sort of wide street leading to the house. Beyond the barns, close to the gate, stood facing each other two three-cornered storehouses, also thatched. Each triangular wall was painted in various designs and had a little door in it. On one of them was depicted a Cossack sitting on a barrel, holding a mug above his head with the inscription: 'I'll drink it all!' On the other, there was a bottle, flagons, and at the sides, by way of ornament, a horse upside down, a pipe, a tambourine, and the inscription: 'Wine is the Cossack's comfort!' A drum and brass trumpets could be seen through the huge window in the loft of one of the barns. At the gates stood two cannons. Everything showed that the master of the house was fond of merrymaking, and that the yard often resounded with the shouts of revellers. There were two windmills outside the gate. Behind the house stretched gardens,

and through the treetops the dark caps of chimneys were all that could
be seen of cottages smothered in green bushes. The whole village lay
on the broad sloping side of a hill. The steep side, at the very foot of
which lay the courtyard, made a screen from the north. Looked at from
below, it seemed even steeper, and here and there on its tall top uneven
stalks of rough grass stood up black against the clear sky; its bare aspect
was somehow depressing; its clay soil was hollowed out by the fall and
trickle of rain. Two cottages stood at some distance from each other on
its steep slope; one of them was overshadowed by the branches of a
spreading apple tree, banked up with soil and supported by short stakes
near the root. The apples, knocked down by the wind, were falling right
into the master's courtyard. The road, coiling about the hill from
the very top, ran down beside the courtyard to the village. When the
philosopher scanned its terrific steepness and recalled their journey
down it the previous night, he came to the conclusion that either the
sotnik had very clever horses or that the Cossacks had very strong heads
to have managed, even when drunk, to escape flying head over heels
with the immense chaise and baggage. The philosopher was standing
on the very highest point in the yard. When he turned and looked in
the opposite direction he saw quite a different view. The village sloped
away into a plain. Meadows stretched as far as the eye could see; their
brilliant verdure was deeper in the distance, and whole rows of villages
looked like dark patches in it, though they must have been more than
fifteen miles away. On the right of the meadowlands was a line of hills,
and a hardly perceptible streak of flashing light and darkness showed
where the Dnieper ran.

'Ah, a splendid spot!' said the philosopher, 'this would be the place to
live, fishing in the Dnieper and the ponds, bird-catching with nets, or
shooting king snipe and little bustard. Though I do believe there would
be a few great bustards too in those meadows! One could dry lots of
fruit, too, and sell it in the town, or, better still, make vodka of it, for
there's no drink to compare with fruit-vodka. But it would be just as
well to consider how to slip away from here.'

He noticed outside the fence a little path completely overgrown with
weeds; he was mechanically setting his foot on it with the idea of simply
going first out for a walk, and then stealthily passing between the
cottages and dashing out into the open country, when he suddenly felt a
rather strong hand on his shoulder.

Behind him stood the old Cossack who had on the previous evening
so bitterly bewailed the death of his father and mother and his own
solitary state.

'It's no good your thinking of making off, Mr Philosopher!' he said: 'this isn't the sort of establishment you can run away from; and the roads are bad, too, for anyone on foot; you had better come to the master: he's been expecting you this long time in the parlour.'

'Let us go! To be sure . . . I'm delighted,' said the philosopher, and he followed the Cossack.

The *sotnik*, an elderly man with grey moustaches and an expression of gloomy sadness, was sitting at a table in the parlour, his head propped on his hands. He was about fifty; but the deep despondency on his face and its wan pallor showed that his soul had been crushed and shattered at one blow, and all his old gaiety and noisy merrymaking had gone for ever. When Homa went in with the old Cossack, he removed one hand from his face and gave a slight nod in response to their low bows.

Homa and the Cossack stood respectfully at the door.

'Who are you, where do you come from, and what is your calling, good man?' said the *sotnik*, in a voice neither friendly nor ill-humoured.

'A bursar, student in philosophy, Homa Brut . . .'

'Who was your father?'

'I don't know, honoured sir.'

'Your mother?'

'I don't know my mother either. It is reasonable to suppose, of course, that I had a mother; but who she was and where she came from, and when she lived – upon my soul, good sir, I don't know.'

The old man paused and seemed to sink into a reverie for a minute.

'How did you come to know my daughter?'

'I didn't know her, honoured sir, upon my word, I didn't. I have never had anything to do with young ladies, never in my life. Bless them, saving your presence!'

'Why did she fix on you and no other to read the psalms over her?'

The philosopher shrugged his shoulders. 'God knows how to make that out. It's a well-known thing, the gentry are for ever taking fancies that the most learned man couldn't explain, and the proverb says: "The devil himself must dance at the master's bidding." '

'Are you telling the truth, philosopher?'

'May I be struck down by thunder on the spot if I'm not.'

'If you had but lived one brief moment longer,' the *sotnik* said to himself mournfully, 'I should have learned all about it. "Let no one else read over me, but send, father, at once to the Kiev Seminary and fetch the bursar, Homa Brut; let him pray three nights for my sinful soul. He knows . . . !" But what he knows, I did not hear: she, poor darling, could say no more before she died. You, good man, are no doubt well known for your holy life and pious works, and she, maybe, heard tell of you.'

'Who? I?' said the philosopher, stepping back in amazement. 'I – holy life!' he articulated, looking straight in the *sotnik*'s face. 'God be with you, sir! What are you talking about! Why – though it's not a seemly thing to speak of – I paid the baker's wife a visit on Maundy Thursday.'

'Well . . . I suppose there must be some reason for fixing on you. You must begin your duties this very day.'

'As to that, I would tell your honour . . . Of course, any man versed in holy scripture may, as far as in him lies . . . but a deacon or a sacristan would be better fitted for it. They are men of understanding, and know how it is all done; while I . . . Besides I haven't the right voice for it, and I myself am good for nothing. I'm not the figure for it.'

'Well, say what you like, I shall carry out all my darling's wishes, I will spare nothing. And if for three nights from today you duly recite the prayers over her, I will reward you, if not . . . I don't advise the devil himself to anger me.'

The last words were uttered by the *sotnik* so vigorously that the philosopher fully grasped their significance.

'Follow me!' said the *sotnik*.

They went out into the hall. The *sotnik* opened the door into another room, opposite the first. The philosopher paused a minute in the hall to blow his nose and crossed the threshold with unaccountable apprehension.

The whole floor was covered with red cotton stuff. On a high table in the corner under the holy images lay the body of the dead girl on a coverlet of dark blue velvet adorned with gold fringe and tassels. Tall wax candles, entwined with sprigs of guelder rose, stood at her feet and head, shedding a dim light that was lost in the brightness of daylight. The dead girl's face was hidden from him by the inconsolable father, who sat down facing her with his back to the door. The philosopher was impressed by the words he heard: 'I am grieving, my dearly beloved daughter, not that in the flower of your age you have left the earth, to my sorrow and mourning, without living your allotted span; I grieve, my darling, that I know not him, my bitter foe, who was the cause of your death. And if I knew the man who could but dream of hurting you, or even saying anything unkind of you, I swear to God he should not see his children again, if he be old as I, nor his father and mother, if he be of that time of life, and his body should be cast out to be devoured by the birds and beasts of the steppe! But my grief it is, my wild marigold, my birdie, light of my eyes, that I must live out my days without comfort, wiping with the skirt of my coat the trickling tears that flow from my old eyes, while my enemy will be making merry and secretly mocking at the feeble old man . . .'

He came to a standstill, due to an outburst of sorrow, which found vent in a flood of tears.

The philosopher was touched by such inconsolable sadness; he coughed, uttering a hollow sound in the effort to clear his throat. The *sotnik* turned round and pointed him to a place at the dead girl's head, before a small lectern with books on it.

'I shall get through three nights somehow,' thought the philosopher: 'and the old man will stuff both my pockets with gold pieces for it.'

He drew near, and clearing his throat once more, began reading, paying no attention to anything else and not venturing to glance at the face of the dead girl. A profound stillness reigned in the apartment. He noticed that the *sotnik* had withdrawn. Slowly he turned his head to look at the dead, and . . .

A shudder ran through his veins: before him lay a beauty whose like had surely never been on earth before. Never, it seemed, could features have been formed in such striking yet harmonious beauty. She lay as though living: the lovely forehead, fair as snow, as silver, looked deep in thought; the even brows – dark as night in the midst of sunshine – rose proudly above the closed eyes; the eye-lashes, that fell like arrows on the cheeks, glowed with the warmth of secret desires; the lips were rubies, ready to break into the laugh of bliss, the flood of joy . . . But in them, in those very features, he saw something terrible and poignant. He felt a sickening ache stirring in his heart, as though, in the midst of a whirl of gaiety and dancing crowds, someone had begun singing a funeral dirge. The rubies of her lips looked like blood surging up from her heart. All at once he was aware of something dreadfully familiar in her face. 'The witch!' he cried in a voice not his own, as, turning pale, he looked away and fell to repeating his prayers. It was the witch that he had killed!

When the sun was setting, they carried the corpse to the church. The philosopher supported the coffin swathed in black on his shoulder, and felt something cold as ice on it. The *sotnik* walked in front, with his hand on the right side of the dead girl's narrow resting home. The wooden church, blackened by age and overgrown with green lichen, stood disconsolately, with its three cone-shaped domes, at the very end of the village. It was evident that no service had been performed in it for a long time. Candles had been lighted before almost every image. The coffin was set down in the centre opposite the altar. The old *sotnik* kissed the dead girl once more, bowed down to the ground, and went out together with the coffin-bearers, giving orders that the philosopher should have a good supper and then be taken to the church. On reaching the kitchen all the men who had carried the coffin began putting their hands on the stove, as the custom is with Little Russians, after seeing a dead body.

The hunger, of which the philosopher began at that moment to be conscious, made him for some minutes entirely oblivious of the dead girl. Soon all the servants began gradually assembling in the kitchen, which in the *sotnik*'s house was something like a club, where all the inhabitants of the yard gathered together, including even the dogs, who wagging their tails, came to the door for bones and slops. Wherever anybody might be sent, and with whatever duty he might be charged, he always went first to the kitchen to rest for at least a minute on the bench and smoke a pipe. All the unmarried men in their smart Cossack tunics lay there almost all day long, on the bench, under the bench, or on the stove – anywhere, in fact, where a comfortable place could be found to lie on. Then everybody invariably left behind in the kitchen either his cap or a whip to keep stray dogs off or some such thing. But the biggest crowd always gathered at supper-time, when the drover who had taken the horses to the paddock, and the herdsman who had brought the cows in to be milked, and all the others who were not to be seen during the day, came in. At supper, even the most taciturn tongues were moved to loquacity. It was then that all the news was talked over: who had got himself new breeches, and what was hidden in the bowels of the earth, and who had seen a wolf. There were witty talkers among them; indeed, there is no lack of them anywhere among the Little Russians.

The philosopher sat down with the rest in a big circle in the open air before the kitchen door. Soon a peasant-woman in a red bonnet popped out, holding in both hands a steaming bowl of dumplings, which she set down in their midst. Each pulled out a wooden spoon from his pocket, or, for lack of a spoon, a wooden stick. As soon as their jaws began moving more slowly, and the wolfish hunger of the whole party was somewhat assuaged, many of them began talking. The conversation naturally turned on the dead maiden.

'Is it true,' said a young shepherd who had put so many buttons and copper discs on the leather strap on which his pipe hung that he looked like a small haberdasher's shop, 'is it true that the young lady, saving your presence, was on friendly terms with the Evil One?'

'Who? The young mistress?' said Dorosh, a man our philosopher already knew, 'why, she was a regular witch! I'll take my oath she was a witch!'

'Hush, hush, Dorosh,' said another man, who had shown a great disposition to soothe the others on the journey, 'that's no business of ours, God bless it! It's no good talking about it.'

But Dorosh was not at all inclined to hold his tongue; he had just been to the cellar on some job with the butler, and, having applied his lips to two or three barrels, he had come out extremely merry and talked away without ceasing.

'What do you want? Me to be quiet?' he said, 'why, I've been ridden by her myself! Upon my soul, I have!'

'Tell us, uncle,' said the young shepherd with the buttons, 'are there signs by which you can tell a witch?'

'No, you can't,' answered Dorosh, 'there's no way of telling: you might read through all the psalm-books and you couldn't tell.'

'Yes, you can, Dorosh, you can; don't say that,' the former comforter objected; 'it's with good purpose God has given every creature its peculiar habit; folks that have studied say that a witch has a little tail.'

'When a woman's old, she's a witch,' the grey-headed Cossack said coolly.

'Oh! You're a nice set!' retorted the peasant-woman, who was at that instant pouring a fresh lot of dumplings into the empty pot; 'regular fat hogs!'

The old Cossack, whose name was Yavtuh and nickname Kovtun, gave a smile of satisfaction seeing that his words had cut the old woman to the quick; while the herdsman gave vent to a guffaw, like the bellowing of two bulls as they stand facing each other.

The beginning of the conversation had aroused the philosopher's curiosity and made him intensely anxious to learn more details about the *sotnik*'s daughter, and so, wishing to bring the talk back to that subject, he turned to his neighbour with the words: 'I should like to ask why all the folk sitting at supper here look upon the young mistress as a witch? Did she do a mischief to anybody or bring anybody to harm?'

'There were all sorts of doings,' answered one of the company, a man with a flat face strikingly resembling a spade. 'Everybody remembers the dog-boy Mikita and the . . .'

'What about the dog-boy Mikita?' said the philosopher.

'Stop! I'll tell about the dog-boy Mikita,' said Dorosh.

'I'll tell about him,' said the drover, 'for he was a great crony of mine.'

'I'll tell about Mikita,' said Spirid.

'Let him, let Spirid tell it!' shouted the company.

Spirid began: 'You didn't know Mikita, Mr Philosopher Homa. Ah, he was a man! He knew every dog as well as he knew his own father. The dog-boy we've got now, Mikola, who's sitting next but one from me, isn't worth the sole of his shoe. Though he knows his job, too, but beside the other he's trash, slops.'

'You tell the story well, very well!' said Dorosh, nodding his head approvingly.

Spirid went on: 'He'd see a hare quicker than you'd wipe the snuff from your nose. He'd whistle: "Here, Breaker! Here Swift-foot!" and he in full gallop on his horse; and there was no saying which would out-race the other, he the dog, or the dog him. He'd toss off a mug of vodka without winking. He was a fine dog-boy! Only a little time back he began to be always staring at the young mistress. Whether he had fallen in love with her, or whether she had simply bewitched him, anyway the man was done for, he went fairly silly; the devil only knows what he turned into . . . pfoo! No decent word for it . . . '

'That's good,' said Dorosh.

'As soon as the young mistress looks at him, he drops the bridle out of his hand, calls Breaker Bushybrow, is all of a fluster and doesn't know what he's doing. One day the young mistress comes into the stable where he is rubbing down a horse.

' "I say, Mikita," says she, "let me put my foot on you." And he, silly fellow, is pleased at that. "Not your foot only," says he, "you may sit on me altogether." The young mistress lifted her foot, and, as soon as he saw her bare, plump, white leg, he went fairly crazy, so he said. He bent his back, silly fellow, and, clasping her bare legs in his hands, ran galloping like a horse all over the countryside. And he couldn't say where he was driven, but he came back more dead than alive, and from that time he withered up like a chip of wood; and one day when they went into the stable, instead of him they found a heap of ashes lying there and an empty pail; he had burnt up entirely, burnt up of himself. And he was a dog-boy such as you couldn't find another all the world over.'

When Spirid had finished his story, reflections upon the rare qualities of the deceased dog-boy followed from all sides.

'And haven't you heard tell of Sheptun's wife?' said Dorosh, addressing Homa.

'No.'

'Well, well! You are not taught with too much sense, it seems, in the seminary. Listen, then. There's a Cossack called Sheptun in our village – a good Cossack! He is given to stealing at times, and telling lies when there's no occasion, but . . . he's a good Cossack. His cottage is not so far from here. Just about the very hour that we sat down this evening to table, Sheptun and his wife finished their supper and lay down to sleep, and, as it was fine weather, his wife lay down in the yard, and Sheptun in the cottage on the bench; or no . . . it was the wife lay indoors on the bench and Sheptun in the yard . . .'

'Not on the bench, she was lying on the floor,' put in a peasant-woman, who stood in the doorway with her cheek propped in her hand.

Dorosh looked at her, then looked down, then looked at her again, and after a brief pause, said: 'When I strip off your petticoat before everybody, you won't be pleased.'

This warning had its effect; the old woman held her tongue and did not interrupt the story again.

Dorosh went on: 'And in the cradle hanging in the middle of the cottage lay a baby a year old – whether of the male or female sex I can't say. Sheptun's wife was lying there when she heard a dog scratching at the door and howling fit to make you run out of the cottage. She was scared, for women are such foolish creatures that, if towards evening you put your tongue out at one from behind a door, her heart's in her mouth. However, she thought: "Well, I'll go and give that damned dog a whack on its nose, and maybe it will stop howling," and taking the oven-fork she went to open the door. She had hardly opened it when a dog dashed in between her legs and straight to the baby's cradle. She saw that it was no longer a dog, but the young mistress, and, if it had been the young lady in her own shape as she knew her, it would not have been so bad. But the peculiar thing is that she was all blue and her eyes glowing like coals. She snatched up the child, bit its throat, and began sucking its blood. Sheptun's wife could only scream: "Oh, horror!" and rushed towards the door. But she sees the door's locked in the passage; she flies up to the loft and there she sits all of a shake, silly woman; and then she sees the young mistress coming up to her in the loft; she pounced on her, and began biting the silly woman. When Sheptun pulled his wife down from the loft in the morning she was bitten all over and had turned black and blue; and next day the silly woman died. So you see what uncanny and wicked doings happen in the world! Though it is of the gentry's breed, a witch is a witch.'

After telling the story, Dorosh looked about him complacently and thrust his finger into his pipe, preparing to fill it with tobacco. The subject of the witch seemed inexhaustible. Each in turn hastened to tell some tale of her. One had seen the witch in the form of a haystack come right up to the door of his cottage; another had had his cap or his pipe stolen by her; many of the girls in the village had had their hair cut off by her; others had lost several quarts of blood sucked by her.

At last the company pulled themselves together and saw that they had been chattering too long, for it was quite dark in the yard. They all began wandering off to their several sleeping places, which were either in the kitchen, or the barns, or the middle of the courtyard.

'Well, Mr Homa! Now it's time for us to go to the deceased lady,' said the grey-headed Cossack, addressing the philosopher; and together with Spirid and Dorosh they set off to the church, lashing with their whips at the dogs, of which there were a great number in the road, and which gnawed their sticks angrily.

Though the philosopher had managed to fortify himself with a good mugful of vodka, he felt a fearfulness creeping stealthily over him as they approached the lighted church. The stories and strange tales he had heard helped to work upon his imagination. The darkness under the fence and trees grew less thick as they came into the more open place. At last they went into the church enclosure and found a little yard, beyond which there was not a tree to be seen, nothing but open country and meadows swallowed up in the darkness of night. The three Cossacks and Homa mounted the steep steps to the porch and went into the church. Here they left the philosopher with the best wishes that he might carry out his duties satisfactorily, and locked the door after them, as their master had bidden them.

The philosopher was left alone. First he yawned, then he stretched, then he blew into both hands, and at last he looked about him. In the middle of the church stood the black coffin; candles were gleaming under the dark images; the light from them only lit up the ikon-stand and shed a faint glimmer in the middle of the church; the distant corners were wrapped in darkness. The tall, old-fashioned ikon-stand showed traces of great antiquity; its carved fretwork, once gilt, only glistened here and there with splashes of gold; the gilt had peeled off in one place, and was completely tarnished in another; the faces of the saints, blackened by age, had a gloomy look. The philosopher looked round him again. 'Well,' he said, 'what is there to be afraid of here? No living man can come in here, and to guard me from the dead and ghosts from the other world I have prayers that I have but to read aloud to keep them from laying a finger on me. It's all right!' he repeated with a wave of his hand, 'let's read.' Going up to the lectern he saw some bundles of candles. 'That's good,' thought the philosopher; 'I must light up the whole church so that it may be as bright as by daylight. Oh, it is a pity that one must not smoke a pipe in the temple of God!'

And he proceeded to stick up wax candles at all the cornices, lecterns and images, not stinting them at all, and soon the whole church was flooded with light. Only overhead the darkness seemed somehow more profound, and the gloomy ikons looked even more sullenly out of their antique carved frames, which glistened here and there with specks of gilt. He went up to the coffin, looked timidly at the face of the dead – and could not help closing his eyelids with a faint shudder: such terrible, brilliant beauty!

He turned and tried to move away; but with the strange curiosity, the self-contradictory feeling, which dogs a man especially in times of terror, he could not, as he withdrew, resist taking another look. And then, after the same shudder, he looked again. The striking beauty of the dead maiden certainly seemed terrible. Possibly, indeed, she would not have overwhelmed him with such panic fear if she had been a little less lovely. But there was in her features nothing faded, tarnished, dead; her face was living, and it seemed to the philosopher that she was looking at him with closed eyes. He even fancied that a tear was oozing from under her right eyelid, and, when it rested on her cheek, he saw distinctly that it was a drop of blood.

He walked hastily away to the lectern, opened the book, and to give himself more confidence began reading in a very loud voice. His voice smote upon the wooden church walls, which had so long been deaf and silent; it rang out, forlorn, unechoed, in a deep bass in the absolutely dead stillness, and seemed somehow uncanny even to the reader himself. 'What is there to be afraid of?' he was saying meanwhile to himself. 'She won't rise up out of her coffin, for she will fear the word of God. Let her lie there! And a fine Cossack I am, if I should be scared. Well, I've drunk a drop too much – that's why it seems dreadful. I'll have a pinch of snuff. Ah, the good snuff! Fine snuff, good snuff!' However, as he turned over the pages, he kept taking sidelong glances at the coffin, and an involuntary feeling seemed whispering to him: 'Look, look, she is going to get up! See, she'll sit up, she'll look out from the coffin!'

But the silence was deathlike; the coffin stood motionless; the candles shed a perfect flood of light. A church lighted up at night with a dead body in it and no living soul near is full of terror!

Raising his voice, he began singing in various keys, trying to drown the fears that still lurked in him, but every minute he turned his eyes to the coffin, as though asking, in spite of himself: 'What if she does sit up, if she gets up?'

But the coffin did not stir. If there had but been some sound! Some living creature! There was not so much as a cricket churring in the corner! There was nothing but the faint splutter of a far-away candle, the light tap of a drop of wax falling on the floor.

'What if she were to get up . . . ?'

She was raising her head . . .

He looked at her wildly and rubbed his eyes. She was, indeed, not lying down now, but sitting up in the coffin. He looked away, and again turned his eyes with horror on the coffin. She stood up . . . she was walking about the church with her eyes shut, moving her arms to and fro as though trying to catch someone.

She was coming straight towards him. In terror he drew a circle round him; with an effort he began reading the prayers and pronouncing the exorcisms which had been taught him by a monk who had all his life seen witches and evil spirits.

She stood almost on the very line; but it was clear that she had not the power to cross it, and she turned livid all over like one who has been dead for several days. Homa had not the courage to look at her; she was terrifying. She ground her teeth and opened her dead eyes; but, seeing nothing, turned with fury – that was apparent in her quivering face – in another direction, and, flinging her arms, clutched in them each column and corner, trying to catch Homa. At last she stood still, holding up a menacing finger, and lay down again in her coffin.

The philosopher could not recover his self-possession, but kept gazing at the narrow dwelling-place of the witch. At last the coffin suddenly sprang up from its place and with a hissing sound began flying all over the church, zigzagging through the air in all directions.

The philosopher saw it almost over his head, but at the same time he saw that it could not cross the circle he had drawn, and he redoubled his exorcisms. The coffin dropped down in the middle of the church and stayed there without moving. The corpse got up out of it, livid and greenish. But at that instant the crow of the cock was heard in the distance; the corpse sank back in the coffin and closed the lid.

The philosopher's heart was throbbing and the sweat was streaming down him; but, emboldened by the cock's crowing, he read on more rapidly the pages he ought to have read through before. At the first streak of dawn the sacristan came to relieve him, together with old Yavtuh, who was at that time performing the duties of a beadle.

On reaching his distant sleeping-place, the philosopher could not for a long time get to sleep; but weariness gained the upper hand at last and he slept on till dinner-time. When he woke up, all the events of the night seemed to him to have happened in a dream. To keep up his strength he was given at dinner a mug of vodka.

Over dinner he soon grew lively, made a remark or two, and devoured a rather large sucking pig almost unaided; but some feeling he could not have explained made him unable to bring himself to speak of his adventures in the church, and to the enquiries of the inquisitive he replied: 'Yes, all sorts of strange things happened.' The philosopher was one of those people who, if they are well fed, are moved to extraordinary benevolence. Lying down with his pipe in his teeth he watched them all with a honied look in his eyes and kept spitting to one side.

After dinner the philosopher was in excellent spirits. He went round the whole village and made friends with almost everybody; he was kicked out of two cottages, indeed; one good-looking young woman caught him a good smack on the back with a spade when he took it into his head to try her shift and skirt, and enquire what stuff they were made of. But as evening approached the philosopher grew more pensive. An hour before supper almost all the servants gathered together to play *kragli* – a sort of skittles in which long sticks are used instead of balls, and the winner has the right to ride on the loser's back. This game became very entertaining for the spectators; often the drover, a man as broad as a pancake, was mounted on the swineherd, a feeble little man, who was nothing but wrinkles. Another time it was the drover who had to bow his back, and Dorosh, leaping on it, always said: 'What a fine bull!' The more dignified of the company sat in the kitchen doorway. They looked on very gravely, smoking their pipes, even when the young people roared with laughter at some witty remark from the drover or Spirid. Homa tried in vain to give himself up to this game; some gloomy thought stuck in his head like a nail. At supper, in spite of his efforts to be merry, terror grew within him as the darkness spread over the sky.

'Come, it's time to set off, Mr Seminarist!' said his friend, the grey-headed Cossack, getting up from the table, together with Dorosh; 'let us go to our task.'

Homa was taken to the church again in the same way; again he was left there alone and the door was locked upon him. As soon as he was alone, fear began to take possession of him again. Again he saw the dark ikons, the gleaming frames, and the familiar black coffin standing in menacing stillness and immobility in the middle of the church.

'Well,' he said to himself, 'now there's nothing marvellous to me in this marvel. It was only alarming the first time. Yes, it was only rather alarming the first time, and even then it wasn't so alarming; now it's not alarming at all.'

He made haste to take his stand at the lectern, drew a circle round him, pronounced some exorcisms, and began reading aloud, resolving not to raise his eyes from the book and not to pay attention to anything. He had been reading for about an hour and was beginning to cough and feel rather tired; he took his horn out of his pocket and, before putting the snuff to his nose, stole a timid look at the coffin. His heart turned cold; the corpse was already standing before him on the very edge of the circle, and her dead, greenish eyes were fixed upon him. The philosopher shuddered, and a cold chill ran through his veins. Dropping his eyes to the book, he began reading the prayers and exorcisms more loudly, and heard the corpse again grinding her teeth and waving her arms trying to catch him. But, with a sidelong glance out of one eye, he saw that the corpse was feeling for him where he was not standing, and that she evidently could not see him. He heard a hollow mutter, and she began pronouncing terrible words with her dead lips; they gurgled hoarsely like the bubbling of boiling pitch. He could not have said what they meant; but there was something fearful in them. The philosopher understood with horror that she was making an incantation.

A wind blew through the church at her words, and there was a sound as of multitudes of flying wings. He heard the beating of wings on the panes of the church windows and on the iron window-frames, the dull scratching of claws upon the iron, and an immense troop thundering on the doors and trying to break in. His heart was throbbing violently all this time; closing his eyes, he kept reading prayers and exorcisms. At last there was a sudden shrill sound in the distance; it was a distant cock crowing. The philosopher, utterly spent, stopped and took breath.

When they came in to fetch him, they found him more dead than alive; he was leaning with his back against the wall while, with his eyes almost starting out of his head, he stared at the Cossacks as they came in. They could scarcely get him along and had to support him all the way back. On reaching the courtyard, he pulled himself together and bade them give him a mug of vodka. When he had drunk it, he stroked down the hair on his head and said: 'There are lots of foul things of all sorts in the world! And the panics they give one, there . . . ' With that the philosopher waved his hand in despair.

The company sitting round him bowed their heads, hearing such sayings. Even a small boy, whom everybody in the servants' quarters felt himself entitled to depute in his place when it was a question of cleaning the stables or fetching water, even this poor youngster stared open-mouthed at the philosopher.

At that moment the old cook's assistant, a peasant-woman, not yet past middle age, a terrible coquette, who always found something to pin to her cap – a bit of ribbon, a pink, or even a scrap of coloured paper, if she had nothing better – passed by, in a tightly girt apron, which displayed her round, sturdy figure.

'Good day, Homa!' she said, seeing the philosopher. 'Aïe, aïe, aïe! What's the matter with you?' she shrieked, clasping her hands.

'Why, what is it, silly woman?'

'Oh, my goodness! Why, you've gone quite grey!'

'Aha! why, she's right!' Spirid pronounced, looking attentively at the philosopher. 'Why, you have really gone as grey as our old Yavtuh.'

The philosopher, hearing this, ran headlong to the kitchen, where he had noticed on the wall a fly-blown triangular bit of looking-glass before which were stuck forget-me-nots, periwinkles and even wreaths of marigolds, testifying to its importance for the toilet of the finery-loving coquette. With horror he saw the truth of their words: half of his hair had in fact turned white.

Homa Brut hung his head and abandoned himself to reflection. 'I will go to the master,' he said at last. 'I'll tell him all about it and explain that I cannot go on reading. Let him send me back to Kiev straight away.'

With these thoughts in his mind he bent his steps towards the porch of the house.

The *sotnik* was sitting almost motionless in his parlour. The same hopeless grief which the philosopher had seen in his face before was still apparent. Only his cheeks were more sunken. It was evident that he had taken very little food, or perhaps had not eaten at all. The extraordinary pallor of his face gave it a look of stony immobility.

'Good day!' he pronounced on seeing Homa, who stood, cap in hand, at the door. 'Well, how goes it with you? All satisfactory?'

'It's satisfactory, all right; such devilish doings, that one can but pick up one's cap and take to one's heels.'

'How's that?'

'Why, your daughter, your honour . . . Looking at it reasonably, she is, to be sure, of noble birth, nobody is going to gainsay it; only, saving your presence, God rest her soul . . . '

'What of my daughter?'

'She had dealings with Satan. She gives one such horrors that there's no reading scripture at all.'

'Read away! Read away! She did well to send for you; she took much care, poor darling, about her soul and tried to drive away all evil thoughts with prayers.'

'That's as you like to say, your honour; upon my soul, I cannot go on with it!'

'Read away!' the *sotnik* persisted in the same persuasive voice, 'you have only one night left; you will do a Christian deed and I will reward you.'

'But whatever rewards . . . Do as you please, your honour, but I will not read!' Homa declared resolutely.

'Listen, philosopher!' said the *sotnik*, and his voice grew firm and menacing. 'I don't like these pranks. You can behave like that in your seminary; but with me it is different. When I flog, it's not the same as your rector's flogging. Do you know what good leather whips are like?'

'I should think I do!' said the philosopher, dropping his voice; 'everybody knows what leather whips are like: in a large dose, it's quite unendurable.'

'Yes, but you don't know yet how my lads can lay them on!' said the *sotnik*, menacingly, rising to his feet, and his face assumed an imperious and ferocious expression that betrayed the unbridled violence of his character, only subdued for the time by sorrow.

'Here they first give a sound flogging, then sprinkle with vodka, and begin over again. Go along, go along, finish your task! If you don't – you'll never get up again. If you do – a thousand gold pieces!'

'Oho, ho! He's a stiff one!' thought the philosopher as he went out: 'he's not to be trifled with. Wait a bit, friend; I'll cut and run, so that you and your hounds will never catch me.'

And Homa made up his mind to run away. He only waited for the hour after dinner when all the servants were accustomed to lie about in the hay in the barns and to give vent to such snores and wheezing that the backyard sounded like a factory.

The time came at last. Even Yavtuh closed his eyes as he lay stretched out in the sun. With fear and trembling, the philosopher stealthily made his way into the pleasure garden, from which he fancied he could more easily escape into the open country without being observed. As is usual with such gardens, it was dreadfully neglected and overgrown, and so made an extremely suitable setting for any secret enterprise. Except for one little path, trodden by the servants on their tasks, it was entirely hidden in a dense thicket of cherry trees, elders and burdock, which thrust up their tall stems covered with clinging pinkish burs. A network of wild hop was flung over this medley of trees and bushes of varied hues, forming a roof over them, clinging to the fence and falling, mingled with wild bell-flowers, from it in coiling snakes. Beyond the fence, which formed the boundary of the garden, there came a perfect forest of rank grass and weeds, which looked as though no one cared to peep enviously into it, and as though any scythe would be broken to bits trying to mow down the stout stubbly stalks.

When the philosopher tried to get over the fence, his teeth chattered and his heart beat so violently that he was frightened at it. The skirts of his long coat seemed to stick to the ground as though someone had nailed them down. As he climbed over, he fancied he heard a voice shout in his ears with a deafening hiss: 'Where are you off to?' The philosopher dived into the long grass and fell to running, frequently stumbling over old roots and trampling upon moles. He saw that when he came out of the rank weeds he would have to cross a field, and that beyond it lay a dark thicket of blackthorn, in which he thought he would be safe. He expected after making his way through it to find the road leading straight to Kiev. He ran across the field at once and found himself in the thicket.

He crawled through the prickly bushes, paying a toll of rags from his coat on every thorn, and came out into a little hollow. A willow with spreading branches bent down almost to the earth. A little brook sparkled pure as silver. The first thing the philosopher did was to lie down and drink, for he was insufferably thirsty. 'Good water!' he said, wiping his lips; 'I might rest here!'

'No, we had better go straight ahead; they'll be coming to look for you!'

These words rang out above his ears. He looked round – before him was standing Yavtuh. 'Curse Yavtuh!' the philosopher thought in his wrath; 'I could take you and fling you . . . And I could batter in your ugly face and all of you with an oak post.'

'You needn't have gone such a long way round,' Yavtuh went on, 'you'd have done better to keep to the road I have come by, straight by the stable. And it's a pity about your coat. It's good cloth. What did you pay a yard for it? But we've walked far enough; it's time to go home.'

The philosopher trudged after Yavtuh, scratching himself. 'Now the cursed witch will give it to me!' he thought. 'Though, after all, what am I thinking about? What am I afraid of? Am I not a Cossack? Why, I've been through two nights, God will succour me the third also. The cursed witch committed a fine lot of sins, it seems, since the Evil One makes such a fight for her.'

Such were the reflections that absorbed him as he walked into the courtyard. Keeping up his spirits with these thoughts, he asked Dorosh, who through the patronage of the butler sometimes had access to the cellars, to pull out a keg of vodka; and the two friends, sitting in the barn, put away not much less than half a pailful, so that the philosopher, getting on his feet, shouted: 'Musicians! I must have musicians!' and without waiting for the latter fell to dancing a jig in a clear space in the middle of the yard. He danced till it was time for the afternoon snack, and the servants who stood round him in a circle, as is the custom on such occasions, at last spat on the ground and walked away, saying: 'Good gracious, what a time the fellow keeps it up!' At last the philosopher lay down to sleep on the spot, and a good sousing of cold water was needed to wake him up for supper. At supper he talked of what it meant to be a Cossack, and how he should not be afraid of anything in the world.

'Time is up,' said Yavtuh, 'let us go.'

'A splinter through your tongue, you damned hog!' thought the philosopher, and getting to his feet he said: 'Come along.'

On the way the philosopher kept glancing from side to side and made faint attempts at conversation with his companions. But Yavtuh said nothing; and even Dorosh was disinclined to talk. It was a hellish night. A whole pack of wolves was howling in the distance, and even the barking of the dogs had a dreadful sound.

'I fancy something else is howling; that's not a wolf,' said Dorosh. Yavtuh was silent. The philosopher could find nothing to say.

They drew near the church and stepped under the decaying wooden domes that showed how little the owner of the place thought about God and his own soul. Yavtuh and Dorosh withdrew as before, and the philosopher was left alone.

Everything was the same, everything wore the same sinister familiar aspect. He stood still for a minute. The horrible witch's coffin was still standing motionless in the middle of the church.

'I won't be afraid; by God, I will not!' he said, and, drawing a circle around himself as before, he began recalling all his spells and exorcisms. There was an awful stillness; the candles spluttered and flooded the whole church with light. The philosopher turned one page, then turned another and noticed that he was not reading what was written in the book. With horror he crossed himself and began chanting. This gave him a little more courage; the reading made progress, and the pages turned rapidly one after the other.

All of a sudden . . . in the midst of the stillness . . . the iron lid of the coffin burst with a crash and the corpse rose up. It was more terrible than the first time. Its teeth clacked horribly against each other, its lips twitched convulsively, and incantations came from them in wild shrieks. A whirlwind swept through the church, the ikons fell to the ground, broken glass came flying down from the windows. The doors were burst from their hinges and a countless multitude of monstrous beings trooped into the church of God. A terrible noise of wings and scratching claws filled the church. All flew and raced about looking for the philosopher.

All trace of drink had disappeared, and Homa's head was quite clear now. He kept crossing himself and repeating prayers at random. And all the while he heard the unclean horde whirring round him, almost touching him with their loathsome tails and the tips of their wings. He had not the courage to look at them; he only saw a huge monster, the whole width of the wall, standing in the shade of its matted locks as of a forest; through the tangle of hair two eyes glared horribly with eyebrows slightly lifted. Above it something was hanging in the air like an immense bubble with a thousand claws and scorpion-stings stretching from the centre; black earth hung in clods on them. They were all looking at him, seeking him, but could not see him, surrounded by his mysterious circle. 'Bring Viy! Fetch Viy!' he heard the corpse cry.

And suddenly a stillness fell upon the church; the wolves' howling was heard in the distance, and soon there was the thud of heavy footsteps resounding through the church. With a sidelong glance he saw they were bringing a squat, thick-set, bandy-legged figure. He was covered all over with black earth. His arms and legs grew out like strong sinewy roots. He trod heavily, stumbling at every step. His long eyelids hung down to the very ground. Homa saw with horror that his face was of iron. He was supported under the arms and led straight to the spot where Homa was standing.

'Lift up my eyelids. I do not see!' said Viy in a voice that seemed to come from underground – and all the company flew to raise his eyelids.

'Do not look!' an inner voice whispered to the philosopher. He could not restrain himself, and he looked.

'There he is!' shouted Viy, and thrust an iron finger at him. And all pounced upon the philosopher together. He fell expiring to the ground, and his soul fled from his body in terror.

There was the sound of a cock crowing. It was the second cock-crow; the first had been missed by the gnomes. In panic they rushed pell-mell to the doors and windows to fly out in utmost haste; but they could not; and so they remained there, stuck in the doors and windows.

When the priest went in, he stopped short at the sight of this defamation of God's holy place, and dared not serve the requiem on such a spot. And so the church was left for ever, with monsters stuck in the doors and windows, was overgrown with forest trees, roots, rough grass and wild thorns, and no one can now find the way to it.

When the rumours of this reached Kiev, and the theologian, Halyava, heard at last of the fate of the philosopher Homa, he spent a whole hour plunged in thought. Great changes had befallen him during that time. Fortune had smiled on him; on the conclusion of his course of study, he was made bell-ringer of the very highest belfry, and he was almost always to be seen with a damaged nose, as the wooden staircase to the belfry had been extremely carelessly made.

'Have you heard what has happened to Homa?' Tibery Gorobets, who by now was a philosopher and had a newly-grown moustache, asked, coming up to him.

'Such was the lot God sent him,' said Halyava the bell-ringer. 'Let us go to the pot-house and drink to his memory!'

The young philosopher, who was beginning to enjoy his privileges with the ardour of an enthusiast, so that his full trousers and his coat and even his cap reeked of spirits and coarse tobacco, instantly signified his readiness.

'He was a fine fellow, Homa!' said the bell-ringer, as the lame inn-keeper set the third mug before him. 'He was a fine man! And he came to grief for nothing.'

'I know why he came to grief: it was because he was afraid; if he had not been afraid, the witch could not have done anything to him. You have only to cross yourself and spit just on her tail, and nothing will happen. I know all about it. Why, all the old women who sit in our market in Kiev are all witches.'

To this the bell-ringer bowed his head in token of agreement. But, observing that his tongue was incapable of uttering a single word, he cautiously got up from the table, and, lurching to right and to left, went to hide in a remote spot in the rough grass; from the force of habit, however, he did not forget to carry off the sole of an old boot that was lying about on the bench.

THE TALE OF HOW IVAN IVANOVITCH
QUARRELLED WITH
IVAN NIKIFOROVITCH

1

Ivan Ivanovitch and Ivan Nikiforovitch

IVAN IVANOVITCH has a splendid bekesh!* Superb! And what astrakhan! Phew, damn it all, what astrakhan! Purplish-grey with a frost on it! I'll bet anything you please that nobody can be found with one like it! Now do just look at it – particularly when he is standing talking to somebody – look from the side: isn't it delicious? There is no finding words for it. Velvet! Silver! Fire! Merciful Lord! Nikolay the Wonder-worker, Holy Saint! Why have not I a bekesh like that! He had it made before Agafya Fedosyevna went to Kiev. You know Agafya Fedosyevna, who bit off the tax assessor's ear?

An excellent man is Ivan Ivanovitch! What a house he has in Mirgorod! There's a porch all round it on oak posts, and there are seats under the porch everywhere. When the weather is too hot, Ivan Ivanovitch casts off his bekesh and his nether garments, remaining in nothing but his shirt, and rests under his porch watching what is passing in the yard and in the street. What apple trees and pear trees he has under his very windows! You only open the window – and the branches fairly thrust themselves into the room. That is all in the front of the house; but you should just see what he has in the garden at the back! What has he not there? Plums, cherries white and black, vegetables of all sorts, sunflowers, cucumbers, melons, peas, even a threshing barn and a forge.

An excellent man is Ivan Ivanovitch! He is very fond of a melon: it is

* A short coat made of fur or astrakhan. (*Translator's Note*)

his favourite dish. As soon as he has dined and come out into the porch, wearing nothing but his shirt, he at once bids Gapka bring him two melons, and with his own hands cuts them into slices, collects the seeds in a special piece of paper, and begins eating them. And then he tells Gapka to bring the inkstand, and with his own hand writes an inscription on the paper containing the seeds: 'This melon was eaten on such and such a date.' If some visitor happens to be there, he adds: 'So and so was present.'

The late Mirgorod judge always looked at Ivan Ivanovitch's house with admiration. Yes, the little house is very nice. What I like is that barns and sheds have been built on every side of it so that, if you look at it from a distance, there is nothing to be seen but roofs, lying one over another, very much like a plateful of pancakes or even more like those funguses that grow upon a tree. All the roofs are thatched with reeds, however; a willow, an oak tree and two apple trees lean their spreading branches on them. Little windows with carved and whitewashed shutters peep through the trees and run out even into the street.

An excellent man is Ivan Ivanovitch! The Poltava Commissar, Dorosh Tarasovitch Puhivotchka, knows him too; when he comes from Horol, he always goes to see him. And whenever the chief priest, Father Pyotr, who lives at Koliberda,[87] has half a dozen visitors, he always says that he knows no one who fulfils the duty of a Christian and knows how to live as Ivan Ivanovitch does.

Goodness, how time flies! He had been a widower ten years even then. He had no children. Gapka has children and they often run about the yard. Ivan Ivanovitch always gives each of them a bread-ring, a slice of melon, or a pear. His Gapka carries the keys of the cupboards and cellars; but the key of the big chest standing in his bedroom, and of the middle cupboard, Ivan Ivanovitch keeps himself, and he does not like anyone to go to them. Gapka is a sturdy wench, she goes about in a zapaska, with fine healthy calves and fresh cheeks.

And what a devout man Ivan Ivanovitch is! Every Sunday he puts on his bekesh and goes to church. When he goes in Ivan Ivanovitch bows in all directions and then usually instals himself in the choir and sings a very good bass. When the service is over, Ivan Ivanovitch cannot bear to go away without making the round of the beggars. He would, perhaps, not care to go through this tedious task, if he were not impelled to it by his innate kindliness. 'Good morrow, poor woman!' he commonly says, seeking out the most crippled beggar-woman in a tattered gown made up of patches. 'Where do you come from, poor thing?'

'I've come from the hamlet, kind sir; I've not had a drop to drink or a morsel to eat for three days; my own children turned me out.'

'Poor creature! What made you come here?'

'Well, kind sir, I came to ask alms, in case anyone would give me a copper for bread.'

'Hm! Then I suppose you want bread?' Ivan Ivanovitch usually enquires.

'Indeed and I do! I am as hungry as a dog.'

'Hm!' Ivan Ivanovitch usually replies, 'so perhaps you would like meat too?'

'Indeed and I'll be glad of anything your honour may be giving me.'

'Hm! Is meat better than bread?'

'Is it for a hungry beggar to be choosing? Whatever you kindly give, sure, it's all good.' With this the old woman usually holds out her hand.

'Well, go along and God be with you,' says Ivan Ivanovitch. 'What are you staying for? I am not beating you, am I?'

And after addressing similar enquiries to a second and a third, he at last returns home or goes to drink a glass of vodka with his neighbour, Ivan Nikiforovitch, or to see the judge or the police-captain.

Ivan Ivanovitch is very much pleased if anyone gives him a present, or any little offering. He likes that very much.

Ivan Nikiforovitch is a very good man, too. His garden is next door to Ivan Ivanovitch's. They are such friends as the world has never seen. Anton Prokofyevitch Golopuz, who goes about to this day in his cinnamon-coloured coat with light blue sleeves, and dines on Sundays at the judge's, used frequently to say that the devil himself had tied Ivan Nikiforovitch and Ivan Ivanovitch together with a string; where the one went the other would turn up also.

Ivan Nikiforovitch has never been married. Though people used to say he was going to be married, it was an absolute falsehood. I know Ivan Nikiforovitch very well and can say that he has never had the faintest idea of getting married. What does all this gossip spring from? For instance, it used to be rumoured that Ivan Nikiforovitch was born with a tail. But this invention is so absurd, and at the same time disgusting and improper, that I do not even think it necessary to disprove it to enlightened readers, who must doubtless be aware that none but witches, and only very few of them, in fact, have a tail. Besides, witches belong rather to the female than to the male sex.

In spite of their great affection, these rare friends were not at all alike. Their characters can be best understood by comparison. Ivan Ivanovitch has a marvellous gift for speaking extremely pleasantly. Goodness! How he speaks! Listening to him can only be compared with the sensation you have when someone is searching your head, or gently passing a finger over your heel. One listens and listens and hangs one's head. It is pleasant! Extremely pleasant! Like a nap after bathing. Ivan Nikiforovitch, on the other hand, is rather silent. But if he does rap out a word, one must look out, that's all! He is more cutting than any razor. Ivan Ivanovitch is spare and tall; Ivan Nikiforovitch is a little shorter, but makes up for it in breadth. Ivan Ivanovitch's head is like a radish, tail downwards; Ivan Nikiforovitch's head is like a radish, tail upwards. Ivan Ivanovitch only lies in the porch in his shirt after dinner; in the evening he puts on his bekesh and goes off somewhere, either to the town shop which he supplies with flour, or into the country to catch quail. Ivan Nikiforovitch lies all day long on his steps usually with his back to the sun – if it is not too hot a day – and he does not care to go anywhere. If the whim takes him in the morning, he will walk about the yard, see how things are going in the garden and the house, and then go back to rest again. In old days he used to go round to Ivan Ivanovitch sometimes. Ivan Ivanovitch is an exceedingly refined man, he never utters an improper word in gentlemanly conversation, and takes offence at once if he hears one. Ivan Nikiforovitch is sometimes not so circumspect. Then Ivan Ivanovitch usually gets up from his seat and says: 'That's enough, that's enough, Ivan Nikiforovitch; we had better make haste out into the sun instead of uttering such ungodly words.' Ivan Ivanovitch is very angry if a fly gets into his beetroot soup: he is quite beside himself then – he will leave the plateful, and his host will catch it. Ivan Nikiforovitch is exceedingly fond of bathing and, when he is sitting up to his neck in water, he orders the table and the samovar to be set in the water too, and is very fond of drinking tea in such refreshing coolness. Ivan Ivanovitch shaves his beard twice a week; Ivan Nikiforovitch only once. Ivan Ivanovitch is exceedingly inquisitive. God forbid that you should begin to tell him about something and not finish the story! If he is displeased with anything, he lets you know it. It is extremely difficult to tell from Ivan Nikiforovitch's face whether he is pleased or angry; even if he is delighted at something he will not show it. Ivan Ivanovitch is rather of a timorous character. Ivan Nikiforovitch, on the other hand, wears trousers with such ample folds that if they were blown out you could put the whole courtyard with the barns and barn-buildings into them. Ivan Ivanovitch has big expressive snuff-coloured eyes and a mouth rather like the letter V; Ivan Nikiforovitch has little yellowish eyes completely lost between his thick eyebrows and chubby cheeks, and a nose that looks like a ripe plum. If Ivan Ivanovitch offers you snuff, he always first licks the lid of the snuffbox, then taps on it with his finger, and, offering it to you, says, if you are someone he knows: 'May I make so bold as to ask you to help yourself, sir?' Or if you are someone he does not know: 'May I make so bold as to ask you to help yourself, sir, though I have not the honour of knowing your name and your father's and your rank in the service?'

Ivan Nikiforovitch puts his horn of snuff straight into your hands and merely adds: 'Help yourself.' Both Ivan Ivanovitch and Ivan Nikiforovitch greatly dislike fleas, and so neither Ivan Ivanovitch nor Ivan Nikiforovitch ever let a Jew dealer pass without buying from him various little bottles of an elixir protecting them from those insects, though they abuse him soundly for professing the Jewish faith. In spite of some dissimilarities, however, both Ivan Ivanovitch and Ivan Nikiforovitch are excellent persons.

2

From which may be learned the object of Ivan Ivanovitch's desire, the subject of a conversation between Ivan Ivanovitch and Ivan Nikiforovitch, and in what way it ended

One morning – it was in July – Ivan Ivanovitch was lying under his porch. The day was hot, the air was dry and quivering. Ivan Ivanovitch had already been out into the country to see the mowers and the farm, had already questioned the peasants and the women he met whence they had come, where they were going, how, and when, and why; he was terribly tired and lay down to rest. As he lay down, he looked round at the storehouses, the yard, the barns, the hens running about the yard, and thought to himself: 'Good Lord, what a manager I am! What is there that I have not got? Fowls, buildings, barns, everything I want, herb and berry vodka; pears and plum trees in my orchard; poppies, cabbage, peas in my kitchen-garden . . . What is there that I have not got? . . . I should like to know what there is I have not got?'

After putting so profound a question to himself, Ivan Ivanovitch sank into thought; meanwhile, his eyes were in search of a new object, and, passing over the fence into Ivan Nikiforovitch's yard, were involuntarily caught by a curious spectacle. A lean peasant-woman was carrying out disused clothes that had been stored away, and hanging them out on a line to air. Soon an old uniform with frayed facings stretched its sleeves out in the air and embraced a brocade blouse; after it, a gentleman's dress-coat with a crest on the buttons and a moth-eaten collar displayed itself behind it; white cashmere trousers, covered with stains, which had once been drawn over the legs of Ivan Nikiforovitch, though now they could scarcely have been drawn on his fingers. After them other garments in the shape of an inverted V were suspended, then a dark blue Cossack tunic which Ivan Nikiforovitch had had made twenty years before when he had been preparing to enter the militia and was already letting his moustaches grow. At last, to put the finishing touch, a sword was displayed that looked like a spire sticking up in the air. Then the skirts of something resembling a full-coat fluttered, grass-green in colour and with copper buttons as big as a five-kopeck piece. From behind peeped a waistcoat trimmed with gold lace and cut low in front. The waistcoat was soon concealed by the old petticoat of a deceased grandmother with pockets in which one could have stowed a water melon. All this taken together made up a very interesting spectacle for Ivan Ivanovitch, while the sunbeams, catching here and there a blue or a green sleeve, a red facing or a bit of gold brocade, or playing on the sword-spire, turned it into something extra-ordinary, like the show played in the villages by strolling vagrants, when a crowd of people closely packed looks at King Herod in his golden crown or at Anton leading the goat. Behind the scenes the fiddle squeaks; a gypsy claps his hands on his lips by way of a drum, while the sun is setting and the fresh coolness of the southern night imperceptibly creeps closer to the fresh shoulders and bosoms of the plump village-women.

Soon the old woman emerged from the storeroom, sighing and groaning as she hauled along an old-fashioned saddle with broken stirrups, with shabby leather cases for pistols, and a saddle-cloth that had once been crimson embroidered in gold and with copper discs. 'She is a silly woman!' thought Ivan Ivanovitch, 'she'll pull out Ivan Nikiforovitch himself to air next!'

And indeed Ivan Ivanovitch was not entirely mistaken in this surmise. Five minutes later Ivan Nikiforovitch's nankeen trousers were swung up, and filled almost half of the courtyard. After that she brought out his cap and his gun.

'What is the meaning of it?' thought Ivan Ivanovitch. 'I have never seen a gun at Ivan Nikiforovitch's. What does he want with that? He never shoots, but keeps a gun! What use is it to him? But it is a nice thing! I have been wanting to get one like that for a long time past.

I should very much like to have that nice gun; I like to amuse myself with a gun. Hey, woman!' Ivan Ivanovitch shouted, beckoning to her.

The old woman went up to the fence.

'What's that you have got there, granny?'

'You see yourself – a gun.'

'What sort of gun?'

'Who can say what sort! If it were mine, I might know, maybe, what it is made of; but it is the master's.'

Ivan Ivanovitch got up and began examining the gun from every point of view, and even forgot to scold the old woman for hanging it and the sword to air.

'It's made of iron, one would think,' the old woman went on.

'Hm! Made of iron. Why is it made of iron?' Ivan Ivanovitch said to himself. 'Has your master had it long?'

'Maybe he has.'

'It's a fine thing!' Ivan Ivanovitch went on. 'I'll ask him for it. What can he do with it? Or I'll swop something for it. I say, granny, is your master at home?'

'Yes.'

'What is he doing, lying down?'

'Yes.'

'Well, that's all right, I'll come and see him.'

Ivan Ivanovitch dressed, took his gnarled stick to keep off the dogs, for there are many more dogs in the streets of Mirgorod than there are men, and went out.

Though Ivan Nikiforovitch's courtyard was next to Ivan Ivanovitch's and one could climb over the fence from one into the other, yet Ivan Ivanovitch went by the street. From the street he had to pass into a by-lane which was so narrow that, if two one-horse carts happened to meet in it, they could not pass, but had to remain in that position until they were each dragged by their back wheels in the opposite direction into the street; as for anyone on foot, he was as apt to be adorned with burdocks as with flowers. Ivan Ivanovitch's cart-shed looked into this lane on the one side, and Ivan Nikiforovitch's barn, gates, and dovecot on the other. Ivan Ivanovitch went up to the gate and rattled with the latch. Dogs began barking from within, but soon a crowd of various colours ran up, wagging their tails on seeing that it was a person they knew. Ivan Ivanovitch crossed the courtyard in which Indian pigeons, fed by Ivan Nikiforovitch with his own hand, melon rinds, with here and there green stuff or a broken wheel or hoop off a barrel, or a boy sprawling in a muddy smock – made up a picture such as painters love!

The shadow cast by the garments on the clothesline covered almost the whole courtyard and gave it some degree of coolness. The woman met him with a bow and stood still gaping. Before the house a little porch was adorned with a roof on two oak posts – an unreliable shelter from the sun which at that season in Little Russia shines in deadly earnest and bathes a pedestrian from head to foot in scalding sweat. From this can be seen how strong was Ivan Ivanovitch's desire to obtain the indispensable article, since he had even brought himself to break his invariable rule of walking only in the evening by going out at this hour in such weather!

The room into which Ivan Ivanovitch stepped was quite dark, because the shutters were closed and the sunbeam that penetrated through a hole in the shutter was broken into rainbow hues and painted upon the opposite wall a garish landscape of thatched roofs, trees and clothes hanging in the yard, but all the other way round. This made an uncanny twilight in the whole room.

'God's blessing!' said Ivan Ivanovitch.

'Ah, good day, Ivan Ivanovitch!' answered a voice from the corner of the room. Only then Ivan Ivanovitch observed Ivan Nikiforovitch lying on a rug spread out upon the floor.

'You must excuse my being in a state of nature.' Ivan Nikoforovitch was lying without anything on, even his shirt.

'Never mind. Have you slept well today, Ivan Nikiforovitch?'

'I have. And have you slept, Ivan Ivanovitch?'

'I have.'

'So now you have just got up?'

'Just got up? Good gracious, Ivan Nikiforovitch! How could I sleep till now! I have just come from the farm. The cornfields along the roadside are splendid! Magnificent! And the hay is so high and soft and golden!'

'Gorpina!' shouted Ivan Nikiforovitch, 'bring Ivan Ivanovitch some vodka and some pies with sour cream.'

'It's a very fine day.'

'Don't praise the weather, Ivan Ivanovitch. The devil take it! There's no doing anything for the heat!'

'So you must bring the devil in. Aïe, Ivan Nikiforovitch! You will remember my words, but then it will be too late; you will suffer in the next world for your ungodly language.'

'What have I done to offend you, Ivan Ivanovitch? I've not referred to your father or your mother. I don't know in what way I have offended you!'

'That's enough, that's enough, Ivan Nikiforovitch!'

'Upon my soul I have done nothing to offend you, Ivan Ivanovitch!'

'It's strange that the quails still don't come at the bird-call.'

'You may think what you like, but I have done nothing to offend you.'

'I don't know why it is they don't come,' said Ivan Ivanovitch as though he did not hear Ivan Nikiforovitch; 'whether it is not quite time yet . . . though the weather one would think is just right.'

'You say the cornfields are good . . . '

'Magnificent! Magnificent!'

Then followed a silence.

'How is it you are hanging the clothes out, Ivan Nikiforovitch?' Ivan Ivanovitch said at last.

'Yes, that damned woman has let splendid clothes almost new get mildewy; now I am airing them; it's excellent fine cloth, they only need turning and I can wear them again.'

'I liked one thing there, Ivan Nikiforovitch.'

'What's that?'

'Tell me, please, what do you want that gun for that's been hung out to air with the clothes?' At this point Ivan Ivanovitch held out a snuffbox. 'May I beg you to help yourself?'

'Not at all, you help yourself. I'll take a pinch of my own.' With this Ivan Nikiforovitch felt about him and got hold of his horn. 'There's a silly woman! So she has hung the gun out, too, has she? Capital snuff the Jew makes in Sorotchintsy. I don't know what he puts in it, but it's so fragrant! It's a little like balsam. Here, take some, chew a little in your mouth. Isn't it like balsam? Do take some, help yourself!'

'Please tell me, Ivan Nikiforovitch, I am still harping on the gun: what are you going to do with it? It's no use to you, you know.'

'No use to me, but what if I go shooting?'

'Lord bless you, Ivan Nikiforovitch, whenever will you go shooting? At the Second Coming perhaps? You have never yet killed a single duck as far as I know and as others tell me, and you have not been created by the Lord for shooting. You have a dignified figure and deportment. How could you go trailing about the bogs when that article of your apparel which it is not quite seemly to mention is in holes on every occasion as it is? What would it be like then? No, what you want is rest and peace.' (Ivan Ivanovitch as we have mentioned already was extremely picturesque in his speech when he wanted to persuade anyone. How he talked! Goodness, how he talked!) 'Yes, you must behave accordingly. Listen, give it to me!'

'What an idea! It's an expensive gun. You can't get guns like that nowadays. I bought it from a Turk when I was going into the militia;

and to think of giving it away now all of a sudden! Impossible! It's an indispensable thing!'

'What is it indispensable for?'

'What for? Why if burglars should break into the house . . . Not indispensable, indeed! Now, thank God, my mind is at rest and I am afraid of nobody. And why? Because I know I have a gun in my cupboard.'

'A fine gun! Why, Ivan Nikiforovitch, the lock is spoilt.'

'What if it is spoilt? It can be repaired; it only needs a little hemp oil to get the rust off.'

'I see no kind feeling for me in your words, Ivan Nikiforovitch. You won't do anything to show your goodwill.'

'What do you mean, Ivan Ivanovitch, saying I show you no goodwill? Aren't you ashamed? Your oxen graze on my meadow and I have never once interfered with them. When you go to Poltava you always ask me for my trap, and have I ever refused it? Your little boys climb over the fence into my yard and play with my dogs – I say nothing. Let them play, so long as they don't touch anything! Let them play!'

'Since you don't care to give it me, perhaps you might exchange it for something?'

'What will you give me for it?'

With this Ivan Nikiforovitch sat up, leaning on his elbow, and looked at Ivan Ivanovitch.

'I'll give you the grey sow, the one that I fed up in the sty. A splendid sow! You'll see if she won't give you a litter of suckling-pigs next year.'

'I don't know how you can suggest that, Ivan Ivanovitch. What use is your sow to me? Am I going to give a wake for the devil?'

'Again! You must keep bringing the devil in! It's a sin, it really is a sin, Ivan Nikiforovitch!'

'How could you really, Ivan Ivanovitch, give me for the gun the devil knows what – a sow?'

'Why is she the devil knows what, Ivan Nikiforovitch?'

'Why is she? I should think you might know that for yourself. This is a gun, a thing everyone knows; while that – the devil only knows what to call it – is a sow! If it had not been you speaking, I might have taken it as an insult.'

'What fault have you found in the sow?'

'What do you take me for? That I should take a pig . . . ?'

'Sit still, sit still! I will say no more . . . You may keep your gun, let it rust and rot standing in the corner of the cupboard – I don't want to speak of it again.'

A silence followed upon that.

'They say,' began Ivan Ivanovitch, 'that three kings have declared war on our Tsar.'

'Yes, Pyotr Fyodorovitch told me so. What does it mean? And what's the war about?'

'There is no saying for certain, Ivan Nikiforovitch, what it's about. I imagine that the kings want us all to accept the Turkish faith.'

'My word, the fools, what a thing to want!' Ivan Nikiforovitch commented, raising his head.

'So you see, and our Tsar has declared war on them for that. "No," he says, "you accept the Christian faith!"'

'Well, our fellows will beat them, Ivan Ivanovitch, won't they?'

'They certainly will. So you won't exchange the gun, Ivan Nikiforovitch?'

'I wonder at you, Ivan Ivanovitch: I believe you are a man noted for your culture and education, but you talk like a boy. Why should I be such a fool . . . ?'

'Sit still, sit still. God bless the thing! Plague take it; I won't speak of it again.'

At that moment some lunch was brought in. Ivan Ivanovitch drank a glass of vodka and ate a pie with sour cream.

'I say, Ivan Nikiforovitch, I'll give you two sacks of oats besides the sow; you have not sown any oats, you know. You would have to buy oats this year, anyway.'

'Upon my soul, Ivan Ivanovitch, one wants one's belly full of peas to talk to you.' (That was nothing; Ivan Nikiforovitch would let off phrases worse than that.) 'Who has ever heard of swopping a gun for two sacks of oats? I'll be bound you won't offer your bekesh.'

'But you forget, Ivan Nikiforovitch, I am giving you the sow, too.'

'What, two sacks of oats and a sow for a gun!'

'Why, isn't it enough?'

'For the gun?'

'Of course for the gun!'

'Two sacks for a gun?'

'Two sacks, not empty, but full of oats; and have you forgotten the sow?'

'You can go and kiss your sow or the devil, if you prefer him!'

'Oh! You'll see, your tongue will be pierced with red hot needles for such ungodly sayings. One has to wash one's face and hands and fumigate oneself after talking to you.'

'Excuse me, Ivan Ivanovitch: a gun is a gentlemanly thing, a very interesting entertainment, besides being a very agreeable ornament to a room . . .'

'You go on about your gun, Ivan Nikiforovitch, like a fool with a gaudy bag,' said Ivan Ivanovitch with annoyance, for he was really beginning to feel cross.

'And you, Ivan Ivanovitch, are a regular gander.'

If Ivan Nikiforovitch had not uttered that word, they would have quarrelled and have parted friends as they always did; but now something quite different happened. Ivan Ivanovitch turned crimson.

'What was that you said, Ivan Nikiforovitch?' he asked, raising his voice.

'I said you were like a gander, Ivan Ivanovitch!'

'How dare you, sir, forget propriety and respect for a man's rank and family and insult him with such an infamous name?'

'What is there infamous about it? And why are you waving your hands about like that, Ivan Ivanovitch?'

'I repeat, how dare you, regardless of every rule of propriety, call me a gander?'

'Hoity-toity! Ivan Ivanovitch. What are you in such a cackle about?'

Ivan Ivanovitch could no longer control himself; his lips were quivering; his mouth lost its usual resemblance to the letter V and was transformed into an O; his eyes blinked until it was positively alarming. This was extremely rare with Ivan Ivanovitch; he had to be greatly exasperated to be brought to this pass. 'Then I beg to inform you,' Ivan Ivanovitch articulated, 'that I do not want to know you.'

'No great loss! Upon my word, I shan't weep for that!' answered Ivan Nikiforovitch.

He was lying, upon my soul he was! He was very much upset by it.

'I will never set foot in your house again.'

'Aha, ah!' said Ivan Nikiforovitch, so vexed that he did not know what he was doing, and, contrary to his habit, he rose to his feet. 'Hey, woman, lad!' At this the same lean old woman and a small boy muffled in a long and full coat appeared in the doorway.

'Take Ivan Ivanovitch by the arms and lead him out of the door!'

'What! A gentleman!' Ivan Ivanovitch cried out indignantly, full of a sense of injured dignity. 'You only dare! You approach! I will annihilate you together with your stupid master! The very crows will not find your place!' (Ivan Ivanovitch used to speak with extraordinary force when his soul was agitated.)

The whole group presented a striking picture: Ivan Nikiforovitch, standing in the middle of the room in full beauty completely unadorned!

The serving-woman, with her mouth wide open and an utterly senseless terror-stricken expression on her face! Ivan Ivanovitch, as the Roman tribunes are depicted, with one arm raised! It was an extraordinary moment, a magnificent spectacle! And meanwhile there was but one spectator: that was the boy in an enormous overcoat, who stood very tranquilly picking his nose.

At last Ivan Ivanovitch took his cap.

'Very nice behaviour on your part, Ivan Nikiforovitch! Excellent! I will not let you forget it!'

'Go along, Ivan Ivanovitch, go along! And mind you don't cross my path. If you do, I will smash your ugly face, Ivan Ivanovitch!'

'So much for that, Ivan Nikiforovitch,' answered Ivan Ivanovitch, putting his thumb to his nose and slamming the door, which squeaked huskily and sprang open again.

Ivan Nikiforovitch appeared in the doorway and tried to add something, but Ivan Ivanovitch flew out of the yard without looking back.

3

What happened after the quarrel of Ivan Ivanovitch and Ivan Nikiforovitch

And so two worthy men, the honour and ornament of Mirgorod, had quarrelled! And over what? Over a trifle, over a gander. They refused to see each other, and broke off all relations, though they had hitherto been known as the most inseparable friends! Hitherto Ivan Ivanovitch and Ivan Nikiforovitch had sent every day to enquire after each other's health, and used often to converse together from their respective balconies and would say such agreeable things to each other that it warmed the heart to hear them.

On Sundays, Ivan Ivanovitch in his cloth bekesh, and Ivan Nikiforovitch in his yellowish-brown nankeen Cossack tunic, used to set off to church almost arm in arm. And if Ivan Ivanovitch, who had extremely sharp eyes, first noticed a puddle or filth of any sort in the middle of the street – a thing which sometimes does happen in Mirgorod – he would always say to Ivan Nikiforovitch: 'Be careful, don't put your foot down here, for it is unpleasant.' Ivan Nikiforovitch for his part, too, showed the most touching signs of affection, and, however far off he might be standing, always stretched out his hand with his horn of snuff and said: 'Help yourself!' And how capitally they both managed their lands . . . ! And now these two friends . . . I was thunderstruck when I heard of it! For a long time I refused to believe it. Merciful Heavens! Ivan Ivanovitch has quarrelled with Ivan Nikiforovitch! Such estimable men! Is there anything in this world one can depend on after that?

When Ivan Ivanovitch reached home he was for a long time in a state of violent agitation. It was his habit to go first of all to the stable to see whether the mare was eating her oats (Ivan Ivanovitch had a roan mare with a bald patch on her forehead, a very good little beast); then to feed the turkeys and sucking-pigs with his own hand, and only then to go indoors, where he either made wooden bowls (he was very skilful, as good as a turner, at carving things out of wood), or would read a book published by Lyubiy, Gariy and Popov[88] (Ivan Ivanovitch did not remember the title of it, because the servant had long ago torn off the upper part of the title-page to amuse a child with it), or would rest in the porch. Now he paid no heed to any of his usual occupations. Instead of doing so, on meeting Gapka he began scolding her for dawdling about doing nothing, though she was dragging grain into the kitchen; he shook his stick at the cock which came to the front steps for its usual tribute; and when a grubby little boy in a tattered shirt ran up to him, shouting 'Daddy, daddy! Give me a cake!' he threatened him and stamped his foot so alarmingly that the terrified boy fled.

At last, however, he recovered himself and began to follow his usual pursuits. He sat down to dinner late, and it was almost evening when he lay down to rest under the porch. The good beetroot soup with pigeons in it which Gapka had cooked completely effaced the incident of the morning. Ivan Ivanovitch began to look after his garden and household with pleasure again. At last his eyes rested on the neighbouring court-yard and he said to himself: 'I haven't been to see Ivan Nikiforovitch today: I'll go round to him.' Saying this, Ivan Ivanovitch took his stick and his cap and was going out into the street; but he had scarcely walked out of the gate when he remembered the quarrel, spat on the ground, and turned back. Almost the same action took place in Ivan Nikiforovitch's yard. Ivan Ivanovitch saw the serving-woman put her foot on the fence with the intention of climbing over into his yard, when suddenly the voice of Ivan Nikiforovitch was audible, shouting: 'Come back, come back! No need!'

Ivan Ivanovitch felt very dreary, however. It might very well have happened that these worthy men would have been reconciled the very next day, had not a particular event in the house of Ivan Nikiforovitch destroyed every hope of reconciliation and poured oil on the fire of resentment when it was on the point of going out.

On the evening of the very same day Agafya Fedosyevna arrived on a visit to Ivan Nikiforovitch. Agafya Fedosyevna was neither a relative nor a sister-in-law, nor, indeed, any connection of Ivan Nikiforovitch's. One would have thought that she had absolutely no reason to visit him, and he was, indeed, not particularly pleased to see her. She did visit him, however, and used to stay with him for whole weeks at a time and occasionally longer, indeed. Then she carried off the keys and took the whole housekeeping into her own hands. This was very disagreeable to Ivan Nikiforovitch, but, strange to say, he obeyed her like a child and, though he attempted sometimes to quarrel with her, Agafya Fedosyevna always got the best of it.

I must own I do not understand why it has been ordained that women should take us by the nose as easily as they take hold of the handle of the teapot: either their hands are so created or our noses are fit for nothing better. And, although Ivan Nikiforovitch's nose was rather like a plum, she took him by that nose and made him follow her about like a little dog. Indeed, he reluctantly changed his whole manner of life when she was there: he did not lie so long in the sun, and, when he did lie there, it was not in a state of nature; he always put on his shirt and his trousers, though Agafya Fedosyevna was far from insisting upon it. She was not one to stand on ceremony and, when Ivan Nikiforovitch had a feverish attack, she used to rub him herself with her own hands from head to foot with vinegar and turpentine. Agafya Fedosyevna wore a cap on her head, three warts on her nose, and a coffee-coloured dressing-jacket with yellow flowers on it. Her whole figure resembled a tub, and so it was as hard to find her waist as to see one's nose without a looking-glass. Her legs were very short and shaped on the pattern of two cushions. She used to talk scandal and eat pickled beetroot in the mornings, and was a wonderful hand at scolding; and, through all these varied pursuits, her face never for one moment changed its expression, a strange peculiarity only found as a rule in women.

As soon as she arrived, everything was turned upside down. 'Don't you be reconciled with him, Ivan Nikiforovitch, and don't you beg his pardon; he wants to be your ruin; he is that sort of man! You don't know him!' The damned woman went on whispering and whispering, till she brought Ivan Nikiforovitch to such a state that he would not hear Ivan Ivanovitch's name.

Everything assumed a different aspect. If the neighbour's dog ran into the yard, it was whacked with whatever was handy; if the children climbed over the fence, they came back howling with their little grubby shirts held up and marks of a switch on their backs. Even the very serving-woman, when Ivan Ivanovitch would have asked her some question, was so rude that Ivan Ivanovitch, a man of extreme refinement, could only spit and say: 'What a nasty woman! Worse than her master!'

At last to put the finishing touches to all his offences, the detested neighbour put up directly opposite, at the spot where the fence was usually climbed, a goose-pen, as though with special design to emphasise the insult. This revolting pen was put up with diabolical rapidity in a single day.

This excited fury and a desire for revenge in Ivan Ivanovitch. He did not, however, show any sign of annoyance, although part of the pen was actually on his land; but his heart throbbed so violently that it was extremely hard for him to maintain this outward composure.

So he spent the day. Night came on . . . Oh, if I were a painter how wonderfully I would portray the charm of the night! I would picture all Mirgorod sleeping; the countless stars looking down on it immovably; the quiet streets resounding with the barking of the dogs far and near; the lovesick sacristan hastening by them and climbing over a fence with chivalrous fearlessness; the white walls of the houses still whiter in the moonlight, while the trees that canopy them are darker, the shadows cast by the trees blacker, the flowers and silent grass more fragrant; while from every corner the crickets, the indefatigable minstrels of the night, set up their churring song in unison. I would describe how in one of those low-pitched clay houses a black-browed maiden, tossing on her solitary bed, dreams with her young breast heaving of a hussar's spurs and moustache, while the moonlight smiles on her cheeks. I would describe how the black shadow of a bat that settled on the white chimneys flits across the white road . . . But even so I could hardly have depicted Ivan Ivanovitch as he went out that night with a saw in his hand, so many were the different emotions written on his countenance! Quietly, stealthily, he slunk up and crept under the goose-pen. Ivan Nikiforovitch's dogs knew nothing as yet of the quarrel between them, and so allowed him as a friend to approach the pen, which stood firmly on four oak posts. Creeping up to the nearest post, he put the saw to it and began sawing. The noise of the saw made him look round every minute, but the thought of the insult revived his courage. The first post was sawn through; Ivan Ivanovitch set to work on the second. His eyes were burning and could see nothing for terror. All at once he uttered a cry and almost fainted; he thought he saw a corpse, but soon he recovered on perceiving that it was the goose, craning its neck at him. Ivan Ivanovitch spat with indignation and went on with his work again. The second post, too, was sawn through; the goose-house tottered.

Ivan Ivanovitch's heart began beating so violently as he attacked the third post, that several times he had to stop. More than half of the post was sawn through when all at once the tottering pen gave a violent lurch . . . Ivan Ivanovitch barely had time to leap aside when it came down with a crash. Snatching up the saw in a terrible panic he ran home and flung himself on his bed, without even courage to look out of the window at the results of his terrible act. He fancied that all Ivan Nikiforovitch's household were assembled: the old serving-woman, Ivan Nikiforovitch, the boy in the immense overcoat, were all led by Agafya Fedosyevna, coming with cudgels to break down and smash his house.

Ivan Ivanovitch passed all the following day in a kind of fever. He kept fancying that in revenge his detested neighbour would set fire to his house at least; and so he gave Gapka orders to keep a continual lookout to see whether dry straw had been put down anywhere. At last, to anticipate Ivan Nikiforovitch, he made up his mind to be ahead of him and to lodge a complaint against him in the Mirgorod district court. What this meant the reader may learn from the following chapter.

4

Of what took place in the Mirgorod District Court

A delightful town is Mirgorod! There are all sorts of buildings in it. Some thatched with straw and some with reeds, some even with a wooden roof. A street to the right, a street to the left, everywhere an excellent fence; over it twines the hop, upon it hang pots and pans, behind it the sunflower displays its sun-like head and one catches glimpses of red poppies and fat pumpkins . . . Splendid! The fence is always adorned with objects which make it still more picturesque – a check petticoat stretched out on it or a smock or trousers. There is no thieving nor robbery in Mirgorod, and so everyone hangs on his fence what he thinks fit. If you come from the square, you will certainly stop for a moment to admire the view. There is a pool in it – a wonderful pool! You have never seen one like it! It fills up almost the whole square. A lovely pool! The houses, which might in the distance be taken for haystacks, stand round admiring its beauty.

But to my thinking there is no better house than the district court. Whether it is built of oak or birch wood does not matter to me, but, honoured friends, there are eight windows in it! Eight windows in a row, looking straight on the square and on to that stretch of water of which I have spoken already and which the police-captain calls the lake! It is the only one painted the colour of granite; all the other houses in Mirgorod are simply whitewashed. Its roof is all made of wood, and would, indeed, have been painted red, if the oil intended for that purpose had not been eaten by the office clerks with onions, for, as luck would have it, it was Lent, and so the roof was left unpainted. There are steps leading out to the square, and the hens often run up them, because there are almost always grains or other things eatable scattered on the steps; this is not done on purpose, however, but simply from the carelessness of the petitioners coming to the court. The building is divided into two parts: in the one is the court, in the other is the lock-up. In the first part, there are two clean, whitewashed rooms; one the outer room for petitioners to wait in, while in the other there is a table adorned with five inkstands; on the table stands the image of the two-headed eagle, the symbol of office; there are four oak chairs with high backs, and along the walls stand iron-bound chests in which the records of the lawsuits of the district are piled up. On one of these chests a boot polished with blacking was standing at the moment.

The court had been sitting since early morning. The judge, a rather stout man, though considerably thinner than Ivan Nikiforovitch, with a good-natured face and a greasy waistcoat, was talking over a pipe and a cup of tea with the court assessor. The judge's lips were close under his nose, and so his nose could sniff his upper lip to his heart's content. This upper lip served him instead of a snuffbox, for the snuff aimed at his nose almost always settled upon it. And so the judge was talking to the court assessor. At one side a barefooted wench was holding a trayful of cups. At the end of the table the secretary was reading the summing up of a case, but in such a monotonous and depressing tone that the very man whose case it was would have fallen asleep listening to him. The judge would no doubt have been the first to do so if he had not been engaged in an interesting conversation.

'I purposely tried to find out,' said the judge, taking a sip of tea, though the cup was by now cold, 'how they manage to make them sing so well. I had a capital blackbird two years ago. And do you know, it suddenly went off completely and began singing all anyhow; and the longer it went on, the worse it got; it took to lisping, wheezing – good for nothing! And you know it was the merest trifle! I'll tell you how it's done. A little pimple no bigger than a pea grows under the throat, this must be pricked with a needle. I was told that by Zahar Prokofye-vitch, and if you like I'll tell you just how it happened: I was going to see him . . .'

'Am I to read the second, Demyan Demyanovitch?' the secretary, who had finished reading some minutes before, broke in.

'Oh, have you finished it already? Fancy, how quick you have been! I haven't heard a word of it! But where is it? Give it here! I'll sign it! What else have you got there?'

'The case of the Cossack Bokitko's stolen cow.'

'Very good, read away! Well, so I arrived at his house . . . I can even tell you exactly what he gave me. With the vodka some sturgeon was served, unique! Yes, not like the sturgeon . . . ' (At this the judge put out his tongue and smiled, while his nose sniffed his invariable snuffbox) ' . . . to which our Mirgorod shop treats us. I didn't taste the herring because, as you are aware, it gives me heartburn; but I tried the caviare – splendid caviare! There can be no two words about it, superb! Then I drank peach-vodka distilled with centaury. There was saffron-vodka, too; but, as you are aware, I never touch it. It's very nice you know; it whets the appetite before a meal they say, and puts a finishing touch afterwards . . . Ah! What do my ears hear, what do my eyes behold . . . !' the judge cried out all at once on seeing Ivan Ivanovitch walk in.

'God be with you! I wish you good health!' Ivan Ivanovitch pronounced, bowing in all directions with the urbanity which was his peculiar characteristic. My goodness, how he could fascinate us all with his manners! I have never seen such refinement anywhere. He was very well aware of his own consequence, and so looked upon the universal respect in which he was held as his due. The judge himself handed Ivan Ivanovitch a chair; his nose drew in all the snuff from his upper lip, which was always a sign with him of great satisfaction.

'What may I offer you, Ivan Ivanovitch?' he enquired. 'Will you take a cup of tea?'

'No, thank you very much!' answered Ivan Ivanovitch; and he bowed and sat down.

'Oh, pray do, just a cup!' repeated the judge.

'No, thank you. Very grateful for your hospitality!' answered Ivan Ivanovitch. He bowed and sat down.

'Just one cup!' repeated the judge.

'Oh, do not trouble, Demyan Demyanovitch!' At this Ivan Ivanovitch bowed and sat down.

'One little cup?'

'Well, perhaps just one cup!' pronounced Ivan Ivanovitch, and he put out his hand to the tray.

Merciful heavens! The height of refinement in that man! There is no describing the pleasing impression made by such manners!

'Mayn't I offer you another cup?'

'No, thank you very much!' answered Ivan Ivanovitch, putting the cup turned upside down upon the tray and bowing.

'To please me, Ivan Ivanovitch!'

'I cannot; I thank you!' With this Ivan Ivanovitch bowed and sat down.

'Ivan Ivanovitch! Come now, as a friend, just one cup!'

'No, very much obliged for your kindness!' Saying this, Ivan Ivanovitch bowed and sat down.

'Just one cup! One cup!'

Ivan Ivanovitch put out his hand to the tray and took a cup.

Well, I am blessed! How that man could keep up his dignity; how ready he was!

'I have,' said Ivan Ivanovitch, after drinking the last drop, 'urgent business with you, Demyan Demyanovitch: I wish to lodge a complaint.' With this Ivan Ivanovitch put down his cup and took from his pocket a sheet of stamped paper covered with writing. 'A complaint against my enemy, my sworn foe.'

'Against whom is that?'

'Against Ivan Nikiforovitch Dovgotchun!'

At these words the judge almost fell off his chair. 'What are you saying!' he articulated, flinging up his hands; 'Ivan Ivanovitch! Is this you?'

'You see for yourself it is I!'

'The Lord be with you and all the Holy Saints! What! You, Ivan Ivanovitch, have become the enemy of Ivan Nikiforovitch! Was it your lips uttered those words? Say it again! Was not someone hiding behind you and speaking with your voice . . . ?'

'What is there so incredible in it? I cannot bear the sight of him: he has done me a deadly injury, he has insulted my honour!'

'Holy Trinity! How shall I ever tell my mother? She, poor old dear, says every day when my sister and I quarrel: "You live like cats and dogs, children. If only you would take example from Ivan Ivanovitch and Ivan Nikiforovitch: once friends, always friends! To be sure they are friends! To be sure they are excellent people!" Fine friends after all! Tell me what's it all about? How is it?'

'It's a delicate matter, Demyan Demyanovitch! It cannot be told by word of mouth: better bid your secretary read my petition. Take it in that way; it would be more proper here.'

'Read it aloud, Taras Tihonovitch!' said the judge, turning to the secretary. Taras Tihonovitch took the petition and, blowing his nose as all secretaries in district courts do blow their noses, that is, with the help of two fingers, began reading:

'From Ivan, son of Ivan, Pererepenko, gentleman and landowner of the Mirgorod district, a petition; whereof the following points ensue:

'(1) Whereas the gentleman Ivan, son of Nikifor, Dovgotchun, notorious to all the world for his godless lawfully-criminal actions which overstep all bounds and provoke aversion, did, on the seventh day of July of the present year 1810, perpetrate a deadly insult upon me, both personally affecting my honour and likewise for the humiliation and confusion of my rank and family. The said gentleman is, moreover, of loathsome appearance, has a quarrelsome temper, and abounds with blasphemous and abusive words of every description . . . '

Here the reader made a slight pause to blow his nose again, while the judge folded his arms with a feeling of reverence and said to himself: 'What a smart pen! Lord have mercy on us! How the man does write!'

Ivan Ivanovitch begged the secretary to read on, and Taras Tihonovitch continued:

'The said gentleman, Ivan, son of Nikifor, Dovgotchun, when I went to him with friendly propositions called me publicly by an insulting name derogatory to my honour, to wit, "gander", though it is well known to all the district of Mirgorod that I have never had the name of that disgusting animal and do not intend to be so named in the future. The proof of my gentle origin is the fact that in the register in the church of the Three Holy Bishops, there is recorded both the day of my birth and likewise the name given me in baptism. A "gander", as all who have any knowledge whatever of science are aware, cannot be inscribed in the register, seeing that "a gander" is not a man but a bird, a fact thoroughly well known to everyone, even though he may not have been to a seminary. But the aforesaid pernicious gentleman, though fully aware of all this, abused me with the aforesaid foul name for no other purpose than to inflict a deadly insult to my rank and station.

'(2) This same unmannerly and ungentlemanly gentleman has inflicted damage, moreover, upon my private property, inherited by me from my father of the clerical calling, Ivan of blessed memory, son of Onisim Pererepenko, inasmuch as in contravention of every law he has moved a goose-pen precisely opposite my front entrance, which was done with no other design but to emphasise the insult paid me, forasmuch as the said goose-pen had till then been standing in a suitable place and was fairly solid. But the abominable design of the aforesaid gentleman was solely to compel me to witness unseemly incidents: forasmuch as it is well known that no man goes into a pen, above all a goose-pen, for any seemly purpose. In carrying out this illegal action the two foremost posts have trespassed upon my private property, which passed into my possession in the lifetime of my father, Ivan of blessed memory, son of Onisim Pererepenko, which runs in a straight line from the barn to the place where the women wash their pots.

'(3) The gentleman described above, whose very name inspires aversion, cherishes in his heart the wicked design of setting fire to me in my own house. Whereof unmistakable signs are manifest from what follows: in the first place, the said pernicious gentleman has taken to emerging frequently from his apartments, which he never did in the past by reason of his slothfulness and the repulsive corpulence of his person; in the second place, in the servants' quarters adjoining the very fence which is the boundary of my land inherited by me from my late father, Ivan of blessed memory, son of Onisim Pererepenko, there is a light burning every day and for an exceptional length of time, which same is manifest proof thereof; inasmuch as hitherto through his niggardly stinginess not only the tallow candle but even the little oil-lamp was always put out.

'And therefore I petition that the said gentleman, Ivan, son of Nikifor, Dovgotchun, as being guilty of arson, of insulting my rank, name and family, and of covetously appropriating my property, and above all for the vulgar and reprehensible coupling with my name the title of "gander", be condemned to the payment of a fine together with all costs and expenses, and himself be thrown into fetters as a law-breaker, and put in the prison of the town, and that this my petition may meet with prompt and immediate attention. Written and composed by Ivan, son of Ivan, Pererepenko, gentleman and landowner of Mirgorod.'

When the petition had been read, the judge drew nearer to Ivan Ivanovitch, took him by a button and began addressing him in somewhat this fashion: 'What are you about, Ivan Ivanovitch? Have some fear of God! Drop the petition, deuce take it! (Satan bedevil it!) Much better shake hands with Ivan Nikiforovitch and kiss him, and buy some santurin or nikopol[89] wine or simply make some punch and invite me! We'll have a good drink together and forget it all!'

'No, Demyan Demyanovitch, this is not a matter,' said Ivan Ivanovitch with the dignity which always suited him so well, 'this is not a matter which admits of an amicable settlement. Goodbye! Goodbye to you, too, gentlemen!' he continued with the same dignity, turning to the rest of the company: 'I trust that the necessary steps will in due course be taken in accordance with my petition.' And he went out leaving everyone present in amazement.

The judge sat without saying a word; the secretary took a pinch of snuff; the clerks upset the broken bottle which served them for an inkstand, and the judge himself was so absent-minded that he enlarged the pool of ink on the table with his finger.

'What do you say to this, Dorofy Trofimovitch?' said the judge after a brief silence, turning to the assessor.

'I say nothing,' said the assessor.

'What things people do!' the judge went on. He had hardly uttered the words when the door creaked and the foremost half of Ivan Nikiforovitch landed in the office – the remainder of him was still in the hall. That Ivan Nikiforovitch should appear, and in the court, too, seemed so extraordinary that the judge cried out, the secretary interrupted his reading, one clerk, in a frieze semblance of a dress-coat, put his pen in his lips, while another swallowed a fly. Even the veteran with a stripe on his shoulder who discharged the duties of messenger and house-porter, and who had hitherto been standing at the door scratching himself under his dirty shirt – even he gaped and trod on somebody's foot.

'What fate has brought you? How and why? How are you, Ivan Nikiforovitch?'

But Ivan Nikiforovitch was more dead than alive, for he had stuck in the doorway and could not take a step backwards or forwards. In vain the judge shouted to anyone who might be in the waiting-room to shove Ivan Nikiforovitch from behind into the court. There was nobody in the waiting-room but an old woman who had come with a petition, and in spite of all her efforts she could do nothing with her bony hands. Then one of the clerks, a broad-shouldered fellow with thick lips and a thick nose, with a drunken look in his squinting eyes, and ragged elbows, approached the foremost half of Ivan Nikiforovitch, folded the latter's arms across his chest as though he were a baby, and winked to the veteran, who shoved with his knee in Ivan Nikiforovitch's belly, and in spite of the latter's piteous moans he was squeezed out into the waiting-room. Then they drew back the bolts and opened the second half of the door, during which operation the united efforts and heavy breathing of the clerk and his assistant, the veteran, diffused such a powerful odour about the room that the court seemed transformed for a time into a pot-house.

'I hope you are not hurt, Ivan Nikiforovitch? I'll tell my mother and she'll send you a lotion; you only rub it on your back and it will all pass off.'

But Ivan Nikiforovitch flopped into a chair, and except for prolonged sighs and groans could say nothing. At last in a faint voice hardly audible from exhaustion he brought out: 'Would you like some?' and taking his snuff-horn from his pocket added: 'take some, help yourself!'

'Delighted to see you,' answered the judge, 'but still I cannot imagine what has led you to take so much trouble and to oblige us with such an agreeable surprise.'

'A petition . . . ' was all Ivan Nikiforovitch could articulate.

'A petition? What sort of petition?'

'A complaint . . . ' (Here breathlessness led to a prolonged pause.) 'Oh! . . . a complaint against that scoundrel . . . Ivan Ivanovitch Pererepenko!'

'Good Lord! You at it too! Such rare friends! A complaint against such an exemplary man . . . !'

'He is the devil himself!' Ivan Nikiforovitch pronounced abruptly.

The judge crossed himself.

'Take my petition, read it!'

'There is no help for it, read it aloud, Taras Tihonovitch,' said the judge, addressing the secretary with an expression of displeasure, though his nose unconsciously sniffed his upper lip, which it commonly did only from great satisfaction. Such perversity on the part of his nose caused the judge even more vexation: he took out his handkerchief and swept from his upper lip all the snuff, to punish its insolence.

The secretary, after going through his usual performance, which he invariably did before beginning to read, that is, blowing his nose without the assistance of a pocket-handkerchief, began in his ordinary voice, as follows:

'The petition of Ivan, son of Nikifor, Dovgotchun, gentleman of the Mirgorod district, whereof the following points ensue:

'(1) Whereas by his spiteful hatred and undisguised ill-will, the self-styled gentleman, Ivan, son of Ivan, Pererepenko, is committing all sorts of mean, injurious, malicious and shocking actions against me, and yesterday, like a robber and a thief, broke – with axes, saws, screwdrivers and all sorts of carpenter's tools – at night into my yard and into my private pen situate therein, and with his own hand, and infamously hacked it to pieces, whereas on my side I had given no cause whatever for so lawless and burglarious a proceeding.

'(2) The said gentleman Pererepenko has designs upon my life, and, concealing the said design until the seventh of last month, came to me and began in cunning and friendly fashion begging from me a gun, which stands in my room, and with his characteristic meanness offered me for it many worthless things such as a grey sow and two measures of oats. But, guessing his criminal design at the time, I tried in every way to dissuade him therefrom; but the aforesaid blackguard and scoundrel, Ivan, son of Ivan, Pererepenko, swore at me like a peasant and from that day has cherished an implacable hostility towards me. Moreover, the often afore-mentioned ferocious gentleman and brigand, Ivan, son of Ivan, Pererepenko, is of a very ignoble origin: his sister was known to all the world as a strumpet, and left the place with the regiment of light cavalry stationed five years ago at Mirgorod and registered her husband as a peasant; his father and mother, too, were exceedingly lawless people, and both were incredible drunkards. But the aforementioned gentleman and robber, Pererepenko, has surpassed all his family in his beastly and reprehensible behaviour, and under a show of piety is guilty of the most profligate conduct: he does not keep the fasts, seeing that on St Philip's Eve[90] the godless man bought a sheep and next day bade his illegitimate wench Gapka slaughter it, alleging that he had need at once for tallow for lamps and candles.

'Wherefore I petition that the said gentleman may, as guilty of robbery, sacrilege and cheating, and caught in the act of theft and burglary, be thrown into fetters and cast into the lock-up of the town or prison of the province, and there as may seem best, after being deprived of his grades and nobility, be soundly flogged and be sent to hard labour in Siberia if need be, and be ordered to pay all costs and expenses, and that this my petition may receive immediate attention. To this petition Ivan, son of Nikifor, Dovgotchun, gentleman of the Mirgorod district, herewith puts his hand.'

As soon as the secretary had finished reading, Ivan Nikiforovitch picked up his cap and bowed with the intention of going away.

'Where are you off to, Ivan Nikiforovitch?' the judge called after him. 'Do stay a little! Have some tea! Oryshko! Why are you standing there, silly girl, winking at the clerks? Go and bring some tea!'

But Ivan Nikiforovitch, terrified at having come so far from home and having endured so dangerous a quarantine, was already through the doorway saying: 'Don't put yourself out, with pleasure I'll . . .' and he shut the door after him, leaving all the court in amazement.

There was no help for it. Both petitions had been received and the case seemed likely to awaken considerable interest, when an unforeseen circumstance gave it an even more remarkable character. When the judge had gone out of the court, accompanied by the assessor and the secretary, and the clerks were stowing away into a sack the various fowls, eggs, pies, rolls and other trifles brought by the petitioners, the grey sow ran into the room and, to the surprise of all present, seized – not a pie or a crust of bread, but Ivan Nikiforovitch's petition, which was lying at the end of the table with its pages hanging over the edge. Snatching up the petition, the grey grunter ran out so quickly that not one of the clerks could overtake her, in spite of the rulers and inkpots that were thrown after her.

This extraordinary incident caused a terrible commotion, because they had not taken a copy of the petition. The judge, his secretary, and the assessor spent a long time arguing over this unprecedented event; at last it was decided to write a report on it to the police-captain, since proceedings in this matter were more the concern of the city police. The report, No. 389, was sent to him the same day and led to rather an interesting explanation, of which the reader may learn from the next chapter.

5

In which is described a Consultation between two
Personages highly respected in Mirgorod

Ivan Ivanovitch had only just seen after his household duties and gone out, as his habit was, to lie down in the porch, when to his unutterable surprise he saw something red at the garden gate. It was the police-captain's red cuff which, like his collar, had acquired a glaze, and at the edges was being transformed into polished leather. Ivan Ivanovitch thought to himself: 'It's just as well that Pyotr Fyodorovitch has come for a little talk'; but he was much surprised to see the police-captain walking extremely fast and waving his hands, which he did not do as a rule. There were eight buttons on the police-captain's uniform; the ninth had been torn off during the procession at the consecration of the church two years before, and the police-constables had not yet been able to find it; though when the superintendents presented the police-captain with their daily reports he invariably enquired whether the button had been found. These eight buttons had been sewn on as peasant-women sow beans, one to the right and the next to the left. His left leg had been struck by a bullet in his last campaign, and so, as he limped along, he flung it so far to one side that it almost cancelled all the work done by the right leg. The more rapidly the police-captain forced the march the less he advanced, and so, while he was approaching the porch, Ivan Ivanovitch had time enough to lose himself in conjecture why the police-captain was waving his arms so vigorously. This interested him the more as he thought the latter's business must be of exceptional importance, since he was actually wearing his new sword.

'Good day, Pyotr Fyodorovitch!' cried Ivan Ivanovitch, who, as we have said already, was very inquisitive and could not restrain his impatience at the sight of the police-captain attacking the step, still not raising his eyes, but struggling with his unruly members which were utterly unable to take the step at one assault.

'A very good day to my dear friend and benefactor, Ivan Ivanovitch!' answered the police-captain.

'Pray be seated. You are tired I see, for your wounded leg hinders . . .'

'My leg!' cried the police-captain, casting upon Ivan Ivanovitch a glance such as a giant casts on a pigmy or a learned pedant on a dancing-master. With this he stretched out his foot and stamped on the floor with it. This display of valour, however, cost him dear, for his whole person lurched forward and his nose pecked the railing; but the sage guardian of order, to preserve appearances, at once righted himself and felt in his pocket as though to get out his snuffbox.

'I can assure you, my dearest friend and benefactor, Ivan Ivanovitch, that I have made worse marches in my time. Yes, seriously I have. For instance during the campaign of 1807 . . .[91] Ah, I'll tell you how I climbed over a fence to visit a pretty German.' With this the police-captain screwed up one eye and gave a fiendishly sly smile.

'Where have you been today?' asked Ivan Ivanovitch, desirous of cutting the police-captain short and bringing him as quickly as possible to the occasion of his visit. He would very much have liked to ask what it was the police-captain intended to tell him; but a refined *savoir faire* made him feel the impropriety of such a question, and Ivan Ivanovitch was obliged to control himself and to wait for the solution of the mystery, though his heart was throbbing with unusual violence.

'By all means, I will tell you where I have been,' answered the police-captain; 'in the first place I must tell you that it is beautiful weather today . . .'

The last words were almost too much for Ivan Ivanovitch.

'But excuse me,' the police-captain went on, 'I've come to you today about an important matter.' Here the police-captain's face and deportment resumed the anxious expression with which he had attacked the steps. Ivan Ivanovitch revived, and trembled as though he were in a fever, though as his habit was, he promptly asked: 'What is it? Important? Is it really important?'

'Well, you will see: first of all, I must hasten to inform you, dear friend and benefactor, Ivan Ivanovitch, that you . . . for my part kindly observe I say nothing, but the forms of government, the forms of government demand it: you have committed a breach of public order!'

'What are you saying, Pyotr Fyodorovitch? I don't understand a word of it.'

'Upon my soul, Ivan Ivanovitch! How can you say you don't understand a word of it? Your own beast has carried off a very important legal document, and after that you say you don't understand a word of it!'

'What beast?'

'Saving your presence, your own grey sow.'

'And how am I to blame? Why did the court porter open the door?'

'But, Ivan Ivanovitch, the beast is your property; so you are to blame.'

'I am very much obliged to you for putting me on a level with a sow.'

'Come, I did not say that, Ivan Ivanovitch! Dear me, I did not say that! Kindly consider the question yourself with an open mind. You are undoubtedly aware that, in accordance with the forms of government, unclean animals are prohibited from walking about in the town, especially in the principal streets. You must admit that that's prohibited.'

'God knows what you are talking about. As though it mattered a sow going out into the street!'

'Allow me to put to you, allow me, allow me, Ivan Ivanovitch; it's utterly impossible. What can we do? It's the will of the government, we must obey. I do not dispute the fact that fowls and geese sometimes run into the street and even into the square – fowls and geese, mind; but even last year I issued a proclamation that pigs and goats were not to be allowed in public squares, and I ordered that proclamation to be read aloud before the assembled people.'

'Well, Pyotr Fyodorovitch, I see nothing in all this but that you are trying to insult me in every way possible.'

'Oh, you can't say that, my dear friend and benefactor, you can't say that I am trying to insult you! Think yourself: I didn't say a word to you last year when you put up a roof of fully a yard higher than the legal height. On the contrary, I pretended I hadn't noticed it at all. Believe me, dearest friend, on this occasion, too, I would absolutely, so to speak . . . but my duty, my office, in fact, requires me to look after public cleanliness. Only consider when all at once there rushes into the principal street . . . '

'Your principal street, indeed! Why, every peasant-woman goes there to fling away what she does not want.'

'Allow me to say, Ivan Ivanovitch, that it's you who are insulting me! It is true it does happen at times, but mostly under a fence, or behind barns or sheds; but that a sow in farrow should run into the principal street, the square, is a thing that . . . '

'Good gracious, Pyotr Fyodorovitch! Why, a sow is God's creation!'

'Agreed. All the world knows that you are a learned man, that you are versed in the sciences and all manner of subjects. Of course, I have never studied any sciences at all. I began to learn to write only when I was thirty. You see I rose from the ranks, as you are aware.'

'Hm!' said Ivan Ivanovitch.

'Yes,' the police-captain went on, 'in 1801 I was in the 42nd regiment of light cavalry,[92] an ensign in the 4th company. Our company commander was – if you will allow me to say so – Captain Yeremyeyev.' At this the police-captain put his finger into the snuffbox which Ivan Ivanovitch held open and fiddled with the snuff.

Ivan Ivanovitch answered: 'Hm.'

'But my duty,' the police-captain went on, 'is to obey the commands of government. Are you aware, Ivan Ivanovitch, that anyone who purloins a legal document in a court of law is liable like any other criminal to be tried in a criminal court?'

'I am so well aware of it that if you like I will teach you. That applies to human beings; for instance, if you were to steal a document; but a sow is an animal, God's creation.'

'Quite so, but the law says one guilty of purloining . . . I beg you to note attentively, *one guilty!* Nothing is here defined as to species, sex or calling; therefore an animal, too, may be guilty. Say what you like, but until sentence is passed on it, the animal ought to be handed over to the police, as guilty of a breach of order.'

'No, Pyotr Fyodorovitch,' retorted Ivan Ivanovitch coolly, 'that will not be so!'

'As you like, but I am bound to follow the regulations of government.'

'Why are you threatening me? I suppose you mean to send the one-armed soldier for her? I'll bid my servant-girl show him out with the oven-fork; his remaining arm will be broken.'

'I will not venture to argue with you. In that case, if you will not hand her over to the police, make what use you like of her; cut her up, if you like, for Christmas, and make her into ham or eat her as fresh pork. Only I should like to ask you, if you will be making sausages, to send me just a couple of those your Gapka makes so nicely of the blood and fat. My Agrafena Trofimovna is very fond of them.'

'Certainly I'll send you a couple of sausages.'

'I shall be very grateful to you, dear friend and benefactor. Now allow me to say just one more word. I am charged by the judge and, indeed, by all our acquaintances, so to speak, to reconcile you with your friend, Ivan Nikiforovitch.'

'What! That boor! Reconcile me with that ruffian! Never! That will never be! Never!' Ivan Ivanovitch was in an extremely resolute mood.

'Have it your own way,' answered the police-captain, regaling both nostrils with snuff. 'I will not venture to advise you; however, allow me to put it to you; here you are now on bad terms, while if you are reconciled . . . '

But Ivan Ivanovitch began talking about catching quails, which was his usual resource when he wanted to change the subject.

And so the police-captain was obliged to go about his business without having achieved any success whatever.

6

From which the Reader may easily learn all that is contained therein

In spite of all the efforts of the court to conceal the affair, the very next day all Mirgorod knew that Ivan Ivanovitch's sow had carried off Ivan Nikiforovitch's petition. The police-captain himself, in a moment of forgetfulness, first let slip a word. When Ivan Nikiforovitch was told of it, he made no comment; he only asked: 'Wasn't it the grey one?'

But Agaya Fedosyevna, who was present at the time, began setting upon Ivan Nikiforovitch again: 'What are you thinking about, Ivan Nikiforovitch? You'll be laughed at as a fool if you let it pass! A fine gentleman you'll be after this! You'll be lower than the peasant-woman who sells the doughnuts you are so fond of.'

And the pertinacious woman talked him round! She picked up a swarthy middle-aged man with pimples all over his face, in a dark blue coat with patches on the elbows, a typical scribbling pettifogger! He smeared his high-boots with tar, wore three pens in his ear and a glass bottle by way of an inkpot tied on a string to a button. He would eat nine pies at a sitting and put the tenth in his pocket, and would write so much of all manner of legal chicanery on a single sheet of stamped paper that nobody could read it aloud straight off without intervals of coughing and sneezing. This little image of a man rummaged about, racked his brains and wrote, and at last concocted the following document:

'To the Mirgorod district court from the gentleman, Ivan, son of Nikifor, Dovgotchun.

'Concerning the aforesaid my petition the which was from me, the gentleman Ivan, son of Nikifor, Dovgotchun, relating to the gentleman Ivan, son of Ivan, Pererepenko, wherein which the district court of Mirgorod has manifested its partiality. And the same wanton insolence of the grey sow which was kept a secret and has reached our ears from persons in no way concerned therewith. Whereto the partiality and connivance, as of evil intention, falls within the jurisdiction of the law; inasmuch as the aforesaid sow is a foolish creature and thereby the more apt for the purloining of papers. Wherefrom it is evidently apparent that the sow frequently aforementioned, could not otherwise than have been incited to the same by the opposing party, the self-styled gentleman, Ivan, son of Ivan, Pererepenko, the same having been already detected in housebreaking, attempted murder and sacrilege. But the aforesaid Mirgorod court with its characteristic partiality manifested its tacit connivance; without the which connivance the aforesaid sow could by no manner of means have been admitted to the purloining of the paper, inasmuch as the Mirgorod district court is well provided with service; to which intent it is sufficient to name one soldier present on all occasions in the reception-room, who, though he has a cross-eye and a somewhat invalidated arm, is yet fully capable of driving out a sow and striking her with a stick. Wherefrom the connivance of the aforesaid Mirgorod court thereto is proven and the partition of the ill-gotten profits therefrom on mutual terms is abundantly evident. The aforesaid robber and gentleman, Ivan, son of Ivan, Pererepenko, is manifestly the scoundrelly accomplice therein. Wherefore I, the gentleman Ivan, son of Nikifor, Dovgotchun, do herewith inform the said district court that if the petition above-mentioned shall not be recovered from the aforesaid grey sow, or from the gentleman Pererepenko, her accomplice, and if proceedings shall not be taken upon it in accordance with justice and in my favour, then I, the gentleman, Ivan, son of Nikifor,

Dovgotchun, will lodge a complaint with the higher court concerning such illegal connivance of the aforesaid district court, transferring the case thereto with all due formalities.

'Ivan, son of Nikifor, Dovgotchun, gentleman of the Mirgorod district.'

This petition produced its effect. The judge, like good-natured people as a rule, was a man of cowardly disposition. He appealed to the secretary. But the secretary emitted a bass 'Hm' through his lips, while his countenance wore the expression of unconcern and diabolical ambiguity which appears only on the face of Satan when he sees the victim who has appealed to him lying at his feet. One resource only was left: to reconcile the two friends. But how approach that when all attempts had hitherto been unsuccessful? However, they decided to try again; but Ivan Ivanovitch declared point-blank that he would not hear of it, and was, indeed, very much incensed. Ivan Nikiforovitch turned his back instead of answering, and did not utter a word. Then the case went forward with the extraordinary rapidity for which our courts of justice are so famous. A document was registered, inscribed, docketed, filed, copied, all in one and the same day; and then the case was laid on a shelf, where it lay and lay and lay for one year and a second and a third. Numbers of young girls had time to get married; a new street was laid down in Mirgorod, the judge lost one molar tooth and two side ones; more small children were running about Ivan Ivanovitch's yard than before (goodness only knows where they sprang from); to spite Ivan Ivanovitch, Ivan Nikiforovitch built a new goose-pen, though a little further away than the first, and so completely screened himself from Ivan Ivanovitch that these worthy gentlemen scarcely ever saw each other's faces – and still the case lay in perfect order, in the cupboard which had been turned to marble by ink-stains.

Meanwhile there occurred an event of the greatest importance in Mirgorod. The police-captain was giving a ball! Where can I find brushes and colours to paint the variety of the assembly and the magnificence of the entertainment? Take a clock, open it, and look what is going on there! A terrible to-do, isn't it? Now imagine as many if not more wheels standing in the police-captain's courtyard. What chaises and travelling carriages were not there! One had a wide back and a narrow front; another a narrow back but a wide front. One was a chaise and a covered trap both at once; another was neither chaise nor trap; one was like a huge haystack or a fat merchant's wife; another was like a dishevelled Jew or a skeleton that had not quite got rid of its skin.

One was in profile exactly like a pipe with a long mouthpiece; another a strange creation, utterly shapeless and fantastic, was unlike anything in the world. From the midst of this chaos of wheels and box-seats rose the semblance of a carriage with a window like that of a room, with a thick bar right across it. The coachmen in grey Cossack coats, tunics and grey jerkins, in sheepskin hats and caps of all patterns, with pipes in their hands, led the unharnessed horses about the courtyards. What a ball it was that the police-captain gave! Allow me, I will count over all who were there. Taras Tarasovitch, Yevil Akinfovitch, Yevtihy Yevtihiyevitch, Ivan Ivanovitch – not *the* Ivan Ivanovitch, but the other – Savva Gavrilovitch, our Ivan Ivanovitch, Yelevfery Yelevferievitch, Makar Nazaryevitch, Foma Grigoryevitch . . . I cannot go on! It is too much for me! My hand is tired with writing! And how many ladies there were! Dark and fair, and long and short, stout as Ivan Nikiforovitch, and so thin that it seemed as though one could hide each one of them in the scabbard of the police-captain's sword. What caps! What dresses! Red, yellow, coffee-coloured, green, blue, new, turned and re-made – fichus, ribbons, reticules! Goodbye to my poor eyes! They will be no more use after that spectacle. And what a long table was drawn out! And how everybody talked; what an uproar there was! A mill with all its clappers, grindstones and wheels going is nothing to it! I cannot tell you for certain what they talked about, but it must be supposed that they discussed many interesting and important topics, such as the weather, dogs, ladies' caps, wheat, horses. At last Ivan Ivanovitch – not *the* Ivan Ivanovitch but the other one who squinted – said: 'I am very much surprised that my right eye' (the squinting Ivan Ivanovitch always spoke ironically of himself) 'does not see Ivan Nikiforovitch.'

'He would not come!' said the police-captain.

'How is that?'

'Well, it's two years, thank God, since they had a quarrel, that is Ivan Ivanovitch and Ivan Nikiforovitch, and wherever one goes the other won't come on any account!'

'What are you telling me!' At this the squinting Ivan Ivanovitch turned his eyes upwards and clasped his hands together.

'Well now, if men with good eyes don't live in peace, how am I to see eye to eye with anyone!'

At these words everyone laughed heartily. We were all very fond of the squinting Ivan Ivanovitch, because he used to make jokes that were precisely in the taste of the day. Even a tall lean man in a wadded overcoat with a plaster on his nose who had hitherto been sitting in the corner without the slightest change in the expression of his face, even when a fly flew up his nose – even this gentleman rose from his seat and moved nearer to the crowd surrounding the squinting Ivan Ivanovitch.

'Do you know what,' the latter said when he saw a goodly company standing round him, 'instead of gazing at my cross-eye, as you are now, let us reconcile our two friends! At this moment Ivan Ivanovitch is conversing with the ladies – let us send on the sly for Ivan Nikiforovitch and bring them together.'

All unanimously fell in with Ivan Ivanovitch's suggestion and decided to send at once to Ivan Nikiforovitch's house to beg him most particularly to come to dine with the police-captain. But the important question to whom to entrust this weighty commission puzzled everyone. They discussed at length who was most capable and most skilful in the diplomatic line; at last, it was unanimously resolved to confide the task to Anton Prokofyevitch Golopuz.

But we must first make the reader a little acquainted with this remarkable person. Anton Prokofyevitch was a perfectly virtuous man in the full meaning of that word; if any of the worthy citizens of Mirgorod gave him a neck-handkerchief or a pair of breeches, he thanked them; if any gave him a slight flip on the nose, he thanked them even then. If he were asked: 'Why is it your frock-coat is brown, Anton Prokofyevitch, but the sleeves are blue?' He almost always answered: 'And you haven't one at all! Wait a bit, it will soon be shabby and then it will be all alike!' And in fact the blue cloth began, from the effect of the sun, to turn brown, and now it goes perfectly well with the colour of the coat. But what is strange is that Anton Prokofyevitch has the habit of wearing cloth clothes in the summer and cotton in the winter. He has no house of his own. He used to have one at the end of the town, but he sold it and with the money he got for it he bought three bay horses and a small chaise, in which he used to ride about visiting the neighbouring landowners. But as the horses gave him a great deal of trouble, and besides he needed money to buy them oats, Anton Prokofyevitch swopped them for a fiddle and a serf-girl, receiving a twenty-five-rouble note into the bargain. Then Anton Prokofyevitch sold the fiddle and swopped the girl for a morocco purse set with gold, and now he has a purse the like of which no one else possesses. He pays for this gratification by not being able to drive about the countryside, and is forced to remain in town and to spend his nights at different houses, especially those of the gentlemen who derive pleasure from flipping him on the nose. Anton Prokofyevitch is fond of good fare and plays pretty well at 'Fools' and 'Millers.' Obedience has always been his natural element, and so, taking his cap and his stick, he set off immediately.

But as he went, he began thinking how he was to move Ivan Nikiforovitch to come to the reception. The somewhat harsh character of that otherwise estimable individual made his task almost an impossible one. And, indeed, how could he be induced to come when even to get out of bed was a very great effort for him? And even supposing that he did get up, was he likely to go where – as he undoubtedly knew – his irreconcilable enemy was to be found? The more Anton Prokofyevitch considered the subject, the more difficulties he found. The day was sultry; the sun was scorching; the perspiration poured down him in streams. Anton Prokofyevitch, though he was flipped on the nose, was rather a wily man in many ways. It was only in barter that he was rather unlucky. He knew very well when he had to pretend to be a fool, and sometimes knew how to hold his own in circumstances and cases in which a clever man can not often steer his course.

While his resourceful mind was thinking out means for persuading Ivan Nikiforovitch, and he was going valiantly to face the worst, an unexpected circumstance somewhat disconcerted him. It will not be amiss at this juncture to inform the reader that Anton Prokofyevitch had, among other things, a pair of trousers with the strange peculiarity of attracting all the dogs to bite his calves whenever he put them on. As ill-luck would have it, he had put on those trousers that day, and so he had hardly abandoned himself to meditation when a terrible barking in all directions smote on his hearing. Anton Prokofyevitch set up such a shout (no one could shout louder than he) that not only our friend the serving-woman and the inmate of the immense overcoat ran out to meet him, but even the urchins from Ivan Ivanovitch's courtyard raced to him, and, though the dogs only succeeded in biting one leg, this greatly cooled his ardour, and he went up the steps with a certain timidity.

7

And Last

'Ah, good day! What have you been teasing my dogs for?' said Ivan Nikiforovitch, on seeing Anton Prokofyevitch; for no one ever addressed the latter except jocosely.

'Plague take them all! Who's teasing them?' answered Anton Prokofyevitch.

'That's a lie.'

'Upon my soul, it isn't! Pyotr Fyodorovitch asks you to dinner.'

'Hm!'

'Upon my soul! I can't tell you how earnestly he begs you to come. "What's the meaning of it," he said, "Ivan Nikiforovitch avoids me as though I were an enemy; he will never come for a little chat or to sit a bit." '

Ivan Nikiforovitch stroked his chin.

" 'If Ivan Nikiforovitch will not come now," he said, "I don't know what to think: he must have something in his mind against me! Do me the favour, Anton Prokofyevitch, persuade Ivan Nikiforovitch!" Come, Ivan Nikiforovitch, let us go! There is a delightful company there now!'

Ivan Nikiforovitch began scrutinising a cock, who was standing on the steps crowing his loudest.

'If only you knew, Ivan Nikiforovitch,' the zealous delegate continued, 'what oysters, what fresh caviare has been sent to Pyotr Fyodorovitch!'

At this Ivan Nikiforovitch turned his head and began listening attentively. This encouraged the delegate.

'Let us make haste and go; Foma Grigoryevitch is there, too! What are you doing?' he added, seeing that Ivan Nikiforovitch was still lying in the same position. 'Well, are we going or not?'

'I don't want to.'

That 'I don't want to' was a shock to Anton Prokofyevitch; he had already imagined that his urgent representations had completely prevailed on this really worthy man; but he heard instead a resolute 'I don't want to.'

'Why don't you want to?' he asked almost with annoyance, a feeling he very rarely displayed, even when he had burning paper put on his head, which was a trick the judge and the police-captain were particularly fond of.

Ivan Nikiforovitch took a pinch of snuff.

'It's your business, Ivan Nikiforovitch, but I don't know what prevents you.'

'Why should I go?' Ivan Nikiforovitch brought out at last. 'The ruffian will be there!' That was what he usually called Ivan Ivanovitch now . . . Merciful heavens! And not long ago . . .

'Upon my soul, he won't! By all that's holy he won't! May I be struck dead on the spot with a thunderbolt!' answered Anton Prokofyevitch, who was ready to take his oath a dozen times in an hour. 'Let us go, Ivan Nikiforovitch!'

'But you are lying, Anton Prokofyevitch, he is there, isn't he?'

'Indeed and he's not! May I never leave the spot if he is! And think yourself what reason have I to tell a lie! May my arms and legs be withered! . . . What, don't you believe me even now? May I drop here dead at your feet! May neither father nor mother nor myself ever see the kingdom of heaven! Do you still disbelieve me?'

Ivan Nikiforovitch was completely appeased by these assurances, and bade his valet in the enormous overcoat to bring him his trousers and his nankeen Cossack coat.

I imagine that it is quite superfluous to describe how Ivan Nikiforovitch put on his trousers, how his cravat was tied, and how, finally, he put on his Cossack coat which had split under the left sleeve. It is enough to say that during that time he maintained a decorous composure and did not answer one word to Anton Prokofyevitch's proposition that he should swop something with him for his Turkish purse.

Meanwhile the assembled company were, with impatience, awaiting the decisive moment when Ivan Nikiforovitch would make his appearance, and the universal desire that these worthy men should be reconciled might at last be gratified. Many were almost positive that Ivan Nikiforovitch would not come. The police-captain even offered to take a wager with squinting Ivan Ivanovitch that he would not come, and only gave it up because the latter insisted that the police-captain should stake his wounded leg and he his cross-eye – at which the police-captain was mightily offended and the company laughed on the sly. No one had yet sat down to table, though it was long past one o'clock – an hour at which people have got some way with their dinner at Mirgorod, even on grand occasions.

Anton Prokofyevitch had hardly appeared at the door when he was instantly surrounded by all. In answer to all questions he shouted one decisive phrase: 'Won't come!' . . . He had scarcely uttered this, and a shower of reproaches and abuse and possibly flips, too, was about to descend on his head for the failure of his mission, when the door opened suddenly and – Ivan Nikiforovitch walked in.

If Satan himself or a corpse had suddenly appeared he would not have produced such amazement as that into which Ivan Nikiforovitch's entrance plunged the whole company; while Anton Prokofyevitch went off into guffaws of laughter, holding his sides with glee that he had so taken them in.

Anyway, it was almost incredible to everyone that Ivan Nikiforovitch could, in so short a time, have dressed as befits a gentleman. Ivan Ivanovitch was not present at this moment; he had left the room. Recovering from their stupefaction, all the company showed their interest in Ivan Nikiforovich's health and expressed their pleasure that he had grown stouter. Ivan Nikiforovitch kissed everyone and said: 'Much obliged.'

Meanwhile the smell of beetroot soup floated through the room and agreeably tickled the nostrils of the fasting guests. All streamed into the dining-room. A string of ladies, talkative and silent, lean and stout, filed in ahead, and the long table was dotted with every hue. I am not going to describe all the dishes on the table! I shall say nothing of the cheese-cakes and sour cream, nor of the sweetbread served in the beetroot soup, nor of the turkey stuffed with plums and raisins, nor of the dish that looked very much like a boot soaked in kvass, nor of the sauce which is the swan-song of the old cook, the sauce which is served in flaming spirit to the great diversion, and, at the same time, terror of the ladies. I am not going to talk about these dishes because I greatly prefer eating them to expatiating on them in conversation.

Ivan Ivanovitch was very much pleased with the fish prepared with horseradish sauce. He was entirely engrossed in the useful and nutritious exercise of eating it. Picking out the smallest fish-bones, he laid them on the plate, and somehow chanced to glance across the table. Heavenly Creator! How strange it was! Opposite him was sitting Ivan Nikiforovitch!

At the very same instant Ivan Nikiforovitch looked up, too . . . ! No . . . ! I cannot! Give me another pen! My pen is feeble, dead; it has too thin a nib for this picture! Their faces were as though turned to stone with amazement reflected on them. Each saw the long-familiar face, at the sight of which, one might suppose, each would advance as to an unexpected friend, offering his snuffbox with the words: 'Help yourself,' or, 'I venture to ask you to help yourself'; and yet that very face was terrible as some evil portent! Drops of sweat rolled down the faces of Ivan Ivanovitch and of Ivan Nikiforovitch.

All who were sitting at the table were mute with attention and could not take their eyes off the friends of days gone by. The ladies, who had till then been absorbed in a rather interesting conversation on the method of preparing capons, suddenly ceased talking. All was hushed! It was a picture worthy of the brush of a great artist.

At last Ivan Ivanovitch took out his handkerchief and began to blow his nose, while Ivan Nikiforovitch looked round and rested his eyes on the open door.

The police-captain at once noticed this movement and bade the servant shut the door securely. Then each of the friends began eating, and they did not once glance at each other again.

As soon as dinner was over, the two old friends rose from their seats and began looking for their caps to slip away. Then the police-captain gave a wink, and Ivan Ivanovitch – not *the* Ivan Ivanovitch but the other, the one who squinted – stood behind Ivan Nikiforovitch's back while the police-captain went up behind Ivan Ivanovitch's back, and both began shoving them from behind so as to push them towards each other and not to let them go till they had shaken hands. Ivan Ivanovitch, the one who squinted, though he shoved Ivan Nikiforovitch a little askew, yet pushed him fairly successfully to the place where Ivan Ivanovitch was standing; but the police-captain took a line too much to one side, because again he could not cope with his unruly member which, on this occasion, would heed no command, and, as though to spite him, lurched a long way off in quite the opposite direction (this may possibly have been due to the number of liqueurs on the table), so that Ivan Ivanovitch fell against a lady in a red dress who had been compelled by curiosity to thrust herself into their midst. Such an incident boded nothing good. However, to mend matters, the judge took the police-captain's place and, sniffing up all the snuff from his upper lip, shoved Ivan Ivanovitch in the other direction. This is the usual means of bringing about a reconciliation in Mirgorod; it is not unlike a game of ball. As soon as the judge gave Ivan Ivanovitch a shove, the Ivan Ivanovitch who squinted pushed with all his strength and shoved Ivan Nikiforovitch, from whom the sweat was dropping like rainwater from a roof. Although both friends resisted stoutly, they were yet thrust together, because both sides received considerable support from the other guests.

Then they were closely surrounded on all sides and not allowed to go until they consented to shake hands.

'God bless you, Ivan Nikiforovitch and Ivan Ivanovitch! Tell us truthfully now: what did you quarrel about? Wasn't it something trifling?

Aren't you ashamed before men and before God!'

'I don't know,' said Ivan Nikiforovitch, panting with exhaustion (it was noticeable that he was by no means averse to reconciliation). 'I don't know what I have done to Ivan Ivanovitch; why did he cut down my goose-pen and plot my ruin?'

'I am not guilty of any such evil designs,' said Ivan Ivanovitch, not looking at Ivan Nikiforovitch. 'I swear before God and before you, honourable gentlemen, I have done nothing to my enemy. Why does he defame me and cast ignominy on my rank and name?'

'How have I cast ignominy on you, Ivan Ivanovitch?' said Ivan Nikiforovitch. Another moment of explanation – another moment of reconciliation – and the long-standing feud was on the point of dying out. Already Ivan Nikiforovitch was feeling in his pocket to get out his snuff-horn and say: 'Help yourself.'

'Was it not damage,' answered Ivan Ivanovitch without raising his eyes, 'when you, sir, insulted my rank and name with a word which it would be unseemly to repeat here?'

'Let me tell you as a friend, Ivan Ivanovitch!' (At this Ivan Nikiforovitch put his finger on Ivan Ivanovitch's button, which was a sign of his complete goodwill.) 'You took offence over the devil knows what, over my calling you a "gander" . . . '

Ivan Nikiforovitch was instantly aware that he had committed an indiscretion in uttering that word; but it was too late: the word had been uttered. All was ruined! Since Ivan Ivanovitch had been beside himself and had flown into a rage, such as God grant one may never see, at the utterance of that word in private – think, dear readers, what it was now when this murderous word had been uttered in a company among whom there were a number of ladies, in whose society Ivan Ivanovitch liked to be particularly punctilious. Had Ivan Nikiforovitch acted otherwise, had he said 'bird,' and not 'gander,' the position might still have been saved. But – all was over!

He cast on Ivan Nikiforovitch a glance – and what a glance! If that glance had been endowed with the power of action it would have reduced Ivan Nikiforovitch to ashes. The guests understood that glance, and of their own accord made haste to separate them. And that man, a paragon of gentleness, who never let one beggar-woman pass without questioning her, rushed out in a terrible fury. How violent are the tempests aroused by the passions!

For a whole month nothing was heard of Ivan Ivanovitch. He shut himself up in his house. The sacred chest was opened, from the chest were taken – what? Silver roubles! Old ancestral silver roubles! And these silver roubles passed into the inky hands of scribblers. The case was transferred to the higher court. And when Ivan Ivanovitch received the joyous tidings that it would be decided on the morrow, only then he looked out at the world and made up his mind to go out. Alas! For the next ten years the higher court informed him daily that the case would be settled on the morrow!

Five years ago I was passing through the town of Mirgorod. It was a bad time for travelling. Autumn had set in with its gloomy, damp weather, mud and fog. A sort of unnatural greenness – the work of the tedious, incessant rains – lay in a thin network over the meadows and cornfields, on which it seemed no more becoming than mischievous tricks in an old man, or roses on an old woman. In those days weather had a great effect upon me: I was depressed when it was dreary. But in spite of that I felt my heart beating eagerly as I drove into Mirgorod. Goodness, how many memories! It was twelve years since I had seen Mirgorod. Here, in those days, lived in touching friendship two unique men, two unique friends. And how many distinguished persons had died! The judge, Demyan Demyanovitch, was dead by then, Ivan Ivanovitch, the one who squinted, had taken leave of life, too. I drove into the principal street: posts were standing everywhere with wisps of straw tied to their tops: they were altering the streets! Several huts had been removed. Remnants of hurdles and fences remained standing disconsolately.

It was a holiday. I ordered my sack-covered chaise to stop before the church, and went in so quietly that no one turned round. It is true there was no one to do so: the church was deserted; there were scarcely any people about; evidently even the most devout were afraid of the mud. In the dull, or rather, sickly weather the candles were somehow strangely unpleasant; the dark side-chapels were gloomy; the long windows with their round panes were streaming with tears of rain. I walked out into the side-chapel and addressed a venerable old man with grizzled hair. 'Allow me to ask, is Ivan Nikiforovitch living?' At that moment the lamp before the ikon flared up and the light fell directly on the old man's face. How surprised I was when looking closely at it I saw familiar features! It was Ivan Nikiforovitch himself! But how he had changed!

'Are you quite well, Ivan Nikiforovitch? You look much older!'

'Yes, I am older. I have come today from Poltava,' answered Ivan Nikiforovitch.

'Good gracious! You have been to Poltava in such dreadful weather?'

'I was forced to! My lawsuit . . . '

At this I could not help dropping a sigh.

Ivan Nikiforovitch noticed that sigh and said: 'Don't be anxious: I have positive information that the case will be settled next week and in my favour.'

I shrugged my shoulders and went to find out something about Ivan Ivanovitch.

'Ivan Ivanovitch is here!' someone told me: 'he is in the choir.'

Then I caught sight of a thin, wasted figure. Was that Ivan Ivanovitch? The face was covered with wrinkles, the hair was completely white. But the bekesh was still the same. After the first greetings, Ivan Ivanovitch, addressing me with the good-humoured smile which so well suited his funnel-shaped face, said: 'Shall I tell you my agreeable news?'

'What news?' I asked.

'Tomorrow my case will positively be settled; the court has told me so for certain.'

I sighed still more heavily, and made haste to say goodbye – because I was travelling on very important business – and got into my chaise.

The lean horses, known in Mirgorod by the name of the post-express horses, set off, making an unpleasant sound as their hoofs sank into the grey mass of mud. The rain poured in streams on to the Jew who sat on the box covered with a sack. The damp pierced me through and through. The gloomy gate with the sentry-box, in which a veteran was cleaning his grey accoutrements, slowly passed by. Again the same fields, in places black and furrowed and in places covered with green, the drenched cows and jackdaws, the monotonous rain, the tearful sky without one gleam of light in it – It is a dreary world, friends!

PETERSBURG TALES

NEVSKY PROSPECT

THERE IS NOTHING FINER than Nevsky Prospect,[93] not in Petersburg anyway: it is the making of the city. What splendour does it lack, that fairest of our city thoroughfares? I know that no one among the poor clerks that live there would exchange Nevsky Prospect for all the blessings of the world. Not only the young man of twenty-five summers with a fine moustache and a splendidly cut coat, but even the veteran with white hairs sprouting on his chin and a head as smooth as a silver dish is enthusiastic over Nevsky Prospect. And the ladies! Nevsky Prospect is even more attractive to the ladies. And indeed to whom is it not attractive? As soon as you step into Nevsky Prospect you are in an atmosphere of gaiety. Though you may have some necessary and urgent work to do, yet as soon as you are there you forget all about business. This is the one place where people put in an appearance without necessity, without being driven there by the needs and commercial interests that swallow up all Petersburg. A man met on Nevsky Prospect seems less of an egoist than on Morskaya, Gorokhovaya, Lityeinaya, Meshchanskaya[94] and other streets, where covetousness, self-interest, and need are apparent in all those walking by or flying past in carriages and droshkies.[95] Nevsky Prospect is the general channel of communication in Petersburg. The man who lives on the Petersburg or Viborg Side[96] who hasn't seen his friend at Peski[97] or at the Moscow Gate for years may reckon with certainty on meeting him in Nevsky Prospect. No directory list at an Address Enquiry Office gives such accurate information as Nevsky Prospect. All-powerful Nevsky Prospect! Sole place of entertainment for the poor man in Petersburg! How cleanly swept are its pavements, and, my God, how many feet leave their traces on it! The clumsy, dirty boots of the discharged soldier, under whose weight the very granite seems to crack, and the miniature, ethereal little shoes of the young lady who turns her head towards the glittering shop-windows as the sunflower to the sun, and the clanking sabre of the hopeful lieutenant which marks a sharp scratch along it – all print the scars of strength or weakness on it! What rapid transformation scenes pass over it in a single day! What changes it goes through between one dawn and the next! Let us begin with earliest morning when all Petersburg smells of hot, freshly-baked bread and is filled with old women in ragged gowns and pelisses who are making their raids on the churches and on compassionate passers-by. Then Nevsky Prospect is empty: the stout shopkeepers and their assistants are still asleep in their linen shirts or washing their genteel cheeks and drinking their coffee; beggars gather near the doors of the confectioners' shops where the drowsy Ganymede [98] who the day before flew round like a fly with chocolate, crawls out with no cravat on, broom in hand, and thrusts stale pies and scraps upon them. Working people move to and fro about the streets: sometimes peasants cross it, hurrying to their work, in high boots caked with mortar which even the Ekaterinsky canal,[99] famous for its cleanness, could not wash off. At this hour it is not proper for ladies to walk out, because Russian people like to explain their meaning in rude expressions such as they would not hear even in a theatre. Sometimes a drowsy government clerk trudges along with a portfolio under his arm, if the way to his department lies through Nevsky Prospect. It may be confidently stated that at this period, that is, up to twelve o'clock, Nevsky Prospect is for no man the goal, but simply the means of reaching it: it is filled with people who have their occupations, their anxieties, and their annoyances, and are thinking nothing about it. Peasants talk about ten kopecks or seven coppers, old men and women wave their hands or talk to themselves, sometimes with very striking gesticulations, but no one listens to them or laughs at them with the exception perhaps of street boys in homespun smocks, darting like lightning along Nevsky Prospect with empty bottles or pairs of boots from the cobblers in their arms. At that hour you may put on what you like, and even if you wear a cap instead of a hat, or the ends of your collar stick out too far from your cravat, no one notices it.

At twelve o'clock tutors of all nationalities make a descent upon Nevsky Prospect with their young charges in fine cambric collars. English Joneses and French Kocks walk arm in arm with the nurslings entrusted to their parental care, and with becoming dignity explain to them that the signboards over the shops are put there that people may know what is to be found within. Governesses, pale Misses, and rosy Mademoiselles, walk majestically behind their light and nimble charges, bidding them hold themselves more upright or not drop their left shoulder; in short, at this hour Nevsky Prospect plays its pedagogic part. But as two o'clock approaches, the governesses, tutors, and children are fewer; and finally are crowded out by their tender papas walking arm in arm with their gaudy, variegated, and hysterical spouses. Gradually these are joined by all who have finished their rather important domestic duties, such as talking to the doctor about the weather and the pimple that has come out on their nose, enquiring after the health of their horses and their promising and gifted children, reading in the newspaper a leading article and the announcements of the arrivals and departures, and finally drinking a cup of tea or coffee. They are joined, too, by those whose enviable destiny has called them to the blessed vocation of clerks on special commissions, and by those who serve in the Department of Foreign Affairs and are distinguished by the dignity of their pursuits and their habits. My God! What splendid positions and duties there are! How they elevate and sweeten the soul! But, alas, I am not in the service and am denied the pleasure of watching the refined behaviour of my superiors to me. Everything you meet on Nevsky Prospect is brimming over with propriety: the men in long surtouts[100] with their hands in their pockets, the ladies in pink, white, or pale blue satin redingotes[101] and stylish hats. Here you meet unique whiskers, drooping with extraordinary and amazing elegance below the cravat, velvety, satiny whiskers, as black as sable or as coal, but alas! invariably the property of members of the Department of Foreign Affairs. Providence has denied black whiskers to clerks in other departments; they are forced, to their great disgust, to wear red ones. Here you meet marvellous moustaches that no pen, no brush could do justice to, moustaches to which the better part of a life has been devoted, the objects of prolonged care by day and by night; moustaches upon which enchanting perfumes are sprinkled and on which the rarest and most expensive kinds of pomade are lavished; moustaches which are twisted up at night in thick curl-papers; moustaches to which their possessors display the most touching devotion and which are the envy of passers-by. Thousands of varieties of hats, dresses, and kerchiefs, flimsy and bright-coloured, for which their owners feel sometimes an adoration that lasts two whole days, dazzle every one on Nevsky Prospect. A whole sea of butterflies seem to have flown up from their flower-stalks and to be floating in a glittering cloud above the beetles of the male sex. Here you meet waists of a slim delicacy beyond dreams of elegance, no thicker than a bottle-neck, and respectfully step aside for fear of a careless nudge with a discourteous elbow; your heart beats with apprehension lest from an incautious breath the exquisite product of art and nature may be snapped in two. And the ladies' sleeves that you meet on Nevsky Prospect! Ah, how exquisite! They are like two air balloons and the lady might suddenly float up into the air, were she not held down by the gentleman accompanying her; for it would be as easy and agreeable for a lady to be lifted into the air as for a glass of champagne to be lifted to the lips. Nowhere do people bow with such dignity and ease as on Nevsky Prospect. Here you meet with a unique smile, a smile that is the acme of art, that will sometimes melt you with pleasure, sometimes make you bow your head and feel lower than the grass, sometimes make you hold it high and feel loftier than the Admiralty spire.[102] Here you meet people conversing about a concert or the weather with extraordinary dignity and sense of their own consequence. Here you meet a thousand incredible types and figures. Good heavens! what strange characters are met on Nevsky Prospect! There are numbers of people who, when they meet you, invariably stare at your boots, and when they have passed, turn round to have a look at the skirts of your coat. I have never been able to make out why it is. At first I thought they were bootmakers, but not a bit of it: they are for the most part clerks in various departments, many of them are very good at referring a case from one department to another; or they are people who spend their time walking about or reading the paper in restaurants – in fact they are usually very respectable people. In this blessed period between two and three o'clock in the afternoon, which might be called the moving centre of Nevsky Prospect, there is a display of all the finest products of the wit of man. One exhibits a smart overcoat with the best beaver on it, the second – a lovely Greek nose, the third – superb whiskers, the fourth – a pair of pretty eyes and a marvellous hat, the fifth – a signet ring on a jaunty forefinger, the sixth – a foot in a bewitching shoe, the seventh – a cravat that excites wonder, and the eighth – a moustache that reduces one to stupefaction. But three o'clock strikes and the display is over, the crowd grows less dense . . . At three o'clock there is a fresh change. Suddenly it is like spring on Nevsky Prospect; it is covered with government clerks in green uniforms. Hungry titular, lower court and other councillors do their best to quicken their pace. Young collegiate registrars and provincial and collegiate secretaries are in haste to be in time to parade Nevsky Prospect with a dignified air, trying to look as if they had not been sitting for the last six hours in an office. But the elderly collegiate secretaries and titular and lower court councillors walk quickly with bowed heads: they are not disposed to amuse themselves by looking at the passers-by; they have not yet completely torn themselves away from their office cares; in their heads is a regular list of work begun and not yet finished; for a long time instead of the signboards they seem to see a cardboard rack of papers or the full face of the head of their office.

From four o'clock Nevsky Prospect is empty, and you hardly meet a single government clerk. Some sewing-girl from a shop runs across Nevsky Prospect with a box in her hands. Some luckless victim of a benevolent attorney, cast adrift in a frieze overcoat;[103] an eccentric visitor to whom all hours are alike; a tall, lanky Englishwoman with a reticule and a book in her hand; a foreman in a high-waisted coat of cotton-shoddy with a narrow beard, a ramshackle figure, back, arms, head, and legs all twisting and turning as he walks deferentially along the pavement; sometimes a humble craftsman . . . those are all that we meet at that hour on Nevsky Prospect.

But as soon as dusk descends upon the houses and streets and the watchman covered with a sack climbs up his ladder to light the lamp, and engravings which do not venture to show themselves by day peep out of the lower windows of the shops, Nevsky Prospect revives again and begins to be astir. Then comes that mysterious time when the street lamps throw a marvellous alluring light upon everything. You meet a great number of young men, for the most part bachelors, in warm surtouts and overcoats. There is a suggestion at this time of some object, or rather something like an object, something extremely unaccountable; the steps of all are more rapid and altogether very uneven; long shadows flit over the walls and pavement and almost reach the heads on the Police Bridge.[104] Young collegiate registrars, provincial and collegiate secretaries walk up and down for hours, but the elderly collegiate registrars, the titular and lower court secretaries are for the most part at home, either because they are married, or because the German cook living in their house gives them a very good dinner. Here you may meet some of the respectable-looking old gentlemen who with such dignity and propriety walked on Nevsky Prospect at two o'clock. You may see them racing along like the young government clerks to peep under the hat of some lady descried in the distance, whose thick lips and fat cheeks plastered with rouge are so attractive to many, and above all to the shopmen, workmen, and shopkeepers who promenade in crowds, always in German coats, and usually arm in arm.

'Stay!' cried Lieutenant Pirogov on such an evening, nudging a young man who walked beside him in a dress-coat and cloak; 'Did you see her?'

'I did; lovely, a perfect Bianca of Perugino.'[105]

'But which do you mean?'

'The lady with the dark hair . . . And what eyes! Good God, what eyes! Her whole attitude and shape and the lines of the face – Exquisite!'

'I am talking of the fair girl who passed after her on the other side. Why don't you go after the brunette if you find her so attractive?'

'Oh, how can you!' cried the young man in the dress-coat, turning crimson. 'As though she were one of the women who walk Nevsky Prospect at night. She must be a very distinguished lady,' he went on with a sigh, 'why, her cloak alone is worth eighty roubles.'

'You simpleton!' cried Pirogov, giving him a violent shove in the direction in which the brilliant cloak was fluttering, 'Go along, you ninny, why are you lingering? And I will follow the fair one.'

'We know what you all are,' Pirogov thought to himself with a self-satisfied and confident smile, convinced that no beauty could withstand him.

The young man in the dress-coat and the cloak with timid and tremulous step walked in the direction in which the bright coloured cloak was fluttering, at one moment shining brilliantly as it approached a street lamp, at the next shrouded in darkness as it moved further away. His heart throbbed and he unconsciously quickened his pace. He dared not even imagine that he could have a claim on the attention of the beauty who was retreating into the distance, and still less could he admit the evil thought suggested by Lieutenant Pirogov. All he wanted was to see the house, to discover where was the abode of this exquisite creature who seemed to have flown straight down from heaven on to Nevsky Prospect, and who would probably fly away, no one could tell whither. He darted along so fast that he was continually jostling dignified, grey-whiskered gentlemen off the pavement. This young man belonged to a class which is a great exception among us, and he no more belonged to the common run of Petersburg citizens than a face that appears to us in a dream belongs to the world of actual fact. This exceptional class is very rare in the town where all are officials, shopkeepers, or German craftsmen. He was an artist. A strange phenomenon, is it not? A Petersburg artist. An artist in the land of snows. An artist in the land of the Finns where everything is wet, flat, pale, grey, foggy! These artists are utterly unlike the Italian artists, proud and ardent as Italy and her skies. The Russian artist on the contrary is, as a rule, mild, gentle, retiring, careless, and quietly devoted to his art; he drinks tea with a couple of friends in his little room, modestly discusses his favourite subjects, and does not trouble his head at all about anything superfluous. He frequently engages some old beggar woman, and makes her sit for six hours on end in order to transfer to canvas her pitiful, almost inanimate countenance. He draws a sketch in perspective of his studio with all sorts of artistic litter lying about, copies plaster-of-Paris hands and feet, turned coffee-coloured by time and dust, a broken easel, a palette lying upside down, a friend playing the guitar, walls smeared with paint, with an open window through which there is a glimpse of the pale Neva and poor fishermen in red shirts. Almost all these artists paint in grey, muddy colours that bear the unmistakable imprint of the North. For all that, they all work with instinctive enjoyment. They are often endowed with real talent, and if only they were breathing the fresh air of Italy, they would no doubt develop as freely, broadly, and brilliantly as a plant at last brought out from indoors into the open air. They are, as a rule, very timid; stars and thick epaulettes reduce them to such an embarrassment that they ask less for their pictures than they had intended. They are sometimes fond of dressing smartly, but anything smart they wear always looks too startling and rather like a patch. You sometimes meet them in an excellent coat and a muddy cloak, an expensive velvet waistcoat and a coat covered with paint, just as on one of their unfinished landscapes you sometimes see the head of a nymph, for which the artist could find no other place, sketched on the background of an earlier work at which he had once painted with enjoyment. Such an artist never looks you straight in the face; or, if he does look at you, it is with a vague, indefinite expression. He does not transfix you with the vulture-like eye of an observer or the hawk-like glance of a cavalry officer. This is because he sees at the same time your features and the features of some plaster-of-Paris Hercules[106] standing in his room, or because he is imagining a picture which he dreams of producing later on. This makes him often answer incoherently, sometimes quite at random, and the muddle in his head increases his shyness. To this class belonged the young man we have described, an artist called Piskarev, retiring, shy, but bearing in his soul sparks of feeling, ready at a fitting opportunity to burst into flame. With a secret tremor he hastened after the lady who had made so strong an impression on him and seemed to be himself surprised at his audacity. The unknown being who had so captured his eyes, his thoughts, and his feelings suddenly turned her head and glanced at him.

Good God, what divine features! The dazzling whiteness of the exquisite brow was framed by hair lovely as an agate. They curled, those marvellous tresses, and some of them strayed below the hat and caressed the cheek, flushed by the chill of evening with a delicate fresh colour. A swarm of exquisite visions hovered about her lips. All the memories of childhood, all the visions that rise from dreaming and quiet inspiration in the lamplight – all seemed to be blended, mingled, and reflected on her harmonious lips. She glanced at Piskarev and his heart quivered at that glance; her glance was severe, a look of indignation came into her face at the sight of this impudent pursuit; but on that lovely face even wrath was bewitching. Overcome by shame and timidity he stood still, dropping his eyes; but how could he lose his divinity without even finding out the sanctuary in which she was enshrined? Such was the thought in the mind of the young dreamer, and he resolved to follow her. But, to avoid her notice, he fell back a good distance, looked carelessly from side to side and examined the signboards on the shops, at the same time he did not lose sight of a single step the unknown lady took. Passers-by were less frequent, the street became quieter. The beauty looked round and he fancied that her lips were curved in a faint smile. He was in a tremor all over and could not believe his eyes. No, it was the deceptive light of the street lamp which had thrown that semblance of a smile upon her lips; no, his own dreams were mocking him. But he held his breath and everything in him quivered in a vague tremor, all his feelings were in a glow and everything before him was lost in a sort of mist; the pavement seemed moving under his feet, the carriages with trotting horses seemed to stand still, the bridge stretched out and its arch seemed broken, the houses were upside down, a sentry-box seemed reeling towards him, and the sentry's halberd, together with the gilt letters of the signboard and the scissors painted on it, all seemed to be gleaming on his very eyelash. And all this was produced by one glance, by one turn of a pretty head. Hearing nothing, seeing nothing, understanding nothing, he followed the light traces of the lovely feet, trying to moderate the swiftness of his own steps which moved in time with the throbbing of his heart. At moments he was overcome with doubt whether the look on her face was really so gracious; and then for an instant he stood still; but the beating of his heart, the irresistible violence and turmoil of his feelings drove him forward. He did not even notice a four-storeyed house that loomed before him, four rows of windows, all lighted up, burst upon him all at once, and he was brought up suddenly by striking against the iron railing of the entrance. He saw the fair stranger fly up the stairs, look round, lay a finger on her lips, and make a sign for him to follow her. His knees trembled, his feelings, his thoughts were aflame. A thrill of joy, unbearably acute, flashed like lightning through his heart. No, it was not a dream! Good God, what happiness in one instant! What a lifetime's rapture in two minutes!

But was it not all a dream? Could the being for one heavenly glance from whom he was ready to give his life, to approach whose dwelling he looked upon as an unutterable bliss – could she have just been so gracious and attentive to him? He flew up the stairs. He was conscious of no earthly thought; he was not burning with the fire of earthly passion. No, at that moment he was pure and chaste as a virginal youth still aflame with the vague spiritual craving for love. And what would have awakened base thoughts in a dissolute man, in him made them still holier. This confidence, shown him by a weak and lovely creature, laid upon him the sacred duty of chivalrous austerity, the sacred duty to carry out all her commands. All that he desired was that those commands should be as difficult, as hard to carry out as possible, that with more effort he might fly to overcome all obstacles. He did not doubt that some mysterious and at the same time important circumstance compelled the unknown lady to confide in him; that she would certainly require some important service from him, and he felt in himself strength and resolution enough for anything.

The staircase went round and round, and his thoughts whirled round and round with it. 'Be careful!' a voice rang out like a harp string, sending a fresh thrill all through him. On the dark landing of the fourth storey the fair stranger knocked at a door; it was opened and they went in together. A woman of rather attractive appearance met them with a candle in her hand, but she looked so strangely and impudently at Piskarev that he dropped his eyes. They went into the room. Three female figures in different corners of the room met his eye. One was laying out cards; another was sitting at the piano and with two fingers strumming out a pitiful travesty of an old polonaise; the third was sitting before a looking-glass, combing out her long hair and had apparently no intention of discontinuing her toilette on the arrival of an unknown visitor. An unpleasant untidiness, usually only seen in the neglected rooms of bachelors, was everywhere apparent. The furniture, which was fairly good, was covered with dust. Spiders' webs stretched over the carved cornice; through the open door of another room he caught the gleam of a spurred boot and the red edging of a uniform; a man's loud voice and a woman's laugh rang out without restraint.

Good God, where had he come! At first he would not believe it, and began looking more attentively at the objects that filled the room; but the bare walls and uncurtained windows betrayed the absence of a careful housewife; the faded faces of these pitiful creatures, one of whom was sitting just under his nose and staring at him as coolly as though he were a spot on someone's dress – all convinced him that he had come into one of those revolting dens in which the pitiful vice that springs from a tawdry education and the terrible over-population of a great town finds shelter, one of those dens in which man sacrilegiously tramples and derides all that is pure and holy, all that makes life fair, where woman, the beauty of the world, the crown of creation, is transformed into a strange, ambiguous creature, where she loses with purity of heart all that is womanly, revoltingly adopts the swagger and impudence of man, and ceases to be the delicate, the lovely creature, so different from us. Piskarev scanned her from head to foot with perplexed eyes, as though trying to make sure whether this was really she who had so enchanted him and had brought him flying in from Nevsky Prospect. But she stood before him lovely as ever; her eyes were even more heavenly. She was fresh, she was not more than seventeen; it could be seen that she had not long been in the grip of vice: it had as yet left no trace upon her cheeks, they were fresh and faintly flushed with colour; she was lovely.

He stood motionless before her and was ready to sink into the same simple-hearted forgetfulness as before. But the beauty was tired of this long silence and gave a meaning smile, looking straight into his eyes. That smile was full of a sort of pitiful insolence, it was so strange and as incongruous with her face as a sanctimonious air with the brutal face of a bribe-taker or a manual of bookkeeping with a poet. He shuddered. She opened her lovely lips and began saying something, but all she said was so stupid, so vulgar . . . As though intelligence were lost with innocence! He wanted to hear no more. He was extremely absurd and simple as a child. Instead of taking advantage of such graciousness, instead of rejoicing in such a chance, as any one else in his place would probably have done, he rushed headlong away like a wild antelope and ran out into the street.

He sat in his room with his head bowed and his hands hanging loose, like a poor man who has found a precious pearl and at once dropped it into the sea. 'Such a beauty, such divine features! And where? In such a place . . . ' That was all that he could articulate.

Nothing, indeed, moves us to such pity as the sight of beauty touched by the putrid breath of vice. Ugliness may go with it, but beauty, tender beauty . . . In our thoughts it blends with nothing but purity and innocence. The beauty who had so enchanted poor Piskarev really was a rare and marvellous exception. Her presence in those vile surroundings seemed even more marvellous. All her features were so purely moulded, the whole expression of her lovely face wore the stamp of such nobility, that it was impossible to think that vice already held her in its clutches. She should have been the priceless pearl, the whole world, the paradise, the wealth of a devoted husband; she should have been the lovely, gentle star of some quiet family circle, and with the faintest movement of her lovely lips have given her sweet commands there. She would have been a divinity in the crowded drawing-room, on the shining parquet, in the glare of candles surrounded by the silent adoration of a crowd of admirers; but, alas! by some terrible machination of the fiendish spirit, eager to destroy the harmony of life, she had been flung with mocking laughter into this fearful slough.

Wrung by heart-rending pity, he sat on before a candle that was burnt low in the socket. Midnight was long past, the belfry chime rang out half-past twelve, and he sat on without stirring, neither asleep nor fully awake. Sleep, aided by his stillness, was beginning to steal over him, already the room was beginning to disappear, and only the light of the candle still shone through the dreams that were overpowering him, when all at once a knock at the door made him start and wake up. The door opened and a footman in gorgeous livery walked in. Never had a gorgeous livery peeped into his lonely room, and at such an hour of the night! . . . He was amazed, and with impatient curiosity looked intently at the footman who entered.

'The lady,' the footman pronounced with a deferential bow, 'whom you visited some hours ago bade me invite you and sent the carriage to fetch you.'

Piskarev stood in speechless wonder: the carriage, a footman in livery! . . . No, there must be some mistake . . .

'My good man,' he said timidly, 'you must have come to the wrong door. Your mistress must have sent you for someone else and not for me.'

'No, sir, I am not mistaken. Did you not accompany my mistress home? It's in Liteyny Street, on the fourth storey.'

'I did.'

'Then, if so, pray make haste; my mistress is very anxious to see you, and begs you to come straight to her house.'

Piskarev ran down the stairs. A carriage was, in fact, standing in the courtyard. He got into it, the door was slammed, the cobbles of the pavement resounded under the wheels and the hoofs, and the illuminated perspective of houses with lamp-posts and signboards passed by the carriage windows. Piskarev pondered all the way and could not explain this adventure. A house of her own, a carriage, a footman in gorgeous livery . . . He could not reconcile all this with the room on the fourth storey, the dusty windows, and the jangling piano. The carriage stopped before a brightly lighted entry, and he was at once struck by the procession of carriages, the talk of the coachmen, the brilliantly lighted windows, and the strains of music. The footman in gorgeous livery helped him out of the carriage and respectfully led him into a hall with marble columns, with a porter in gold lace, with cloaks and fur coats flung here and there, and a brilliant lamp. An airy staircase with shining banisters, fragrant with perfume, led upwards. He was already mounting it; hesitating at the first step and panic-stricken at the crowds of people, he went into the first room. The extraordinary brightness and variety of the scene completely staggered him; it seemed to him as though some demon had crumbled the whole world into bits and mixed all these bits indiscriminately together. The gleaming shoulders of the ladies and the black dress-coats, the lustres, the lamps, the ethereal floating gauze, the filmy ribbons, and the stout bassoon looking out from behind the railing of the orchestra – everything was dazzling to him. He saw at the same instant such numbers of venerable old or middle-aged men with stars on their evening-coats and ladies sitting in rows or stepping so lightly, proudly, and graciously over the parquet floor; he heard so many French and English words; moreover, the young men in black dress-coats were filled with such dignity, spoke or kept silence with such gentlemanly decorum, were so incapable of saying anything inappropriate, made jokes so majestically, smiled so politely, wore such superb whiskers, so skilfully displayed their elegant hands as they straightened their cravats, the ladies were so ethereal, so steeped in perfect gratification and beatitude, so enchantingly cast down their eyes, that . . . but Piskarev's subdued air, as he leaned timidly against a column, was enough to show that he was completely overwhelmed. At that moment the crowd stood round a group of dancers. They whirled around, draped in the transparent creations of Paris, in garments woven of air itself; carelessly they touched the parquet floor with their gleaming feet, as ethereal as though they trod on air. But one among them was lovelier, more splendid, and more brilliantly dressed than the rest. An indescribable, subtle perfection of taste was apparent in all her attire, and at the same time it seemed as though she cared nothing for it, as though it had come unconsciously, of itself. She looked and did not look at the crowd of spectators crowding round her, she cast down her lovely long eyelashes indifferently, and the gleaming whiteness of her face was still more dazzling when she bent her head and a light shadow lay on her enchanting brow.

Piskarev did his utmost to make his way through the crowd and get a better look at her; but to his intense vexation a huge head of curly black hair was continually screening her from him; moreover, the crush was so great that he did not dare to press forward or to step back, for fear of jostling against some privy councillor. But at last he squeezed his way to the front and glanced at his clothes, anxious that everything should be neat. Heavenly Creator! What was his horror! He had on his every-day coat, and it was all smeared with paint; in his haste to set off, he had actually forgotten to change into suitable clothes. He blushed up to his ears and, dropping his eyes in confusion, would have gone away but there was absolutely nowhere he could go; kammer-junkers[107] in gorgeous attire formed a compact wall behind him. By now his desire was to be as far away as possible from the beauty of the lovely brows and eyelashes. In terror he raised his eyes to see whether she were looking at him. Good God! She stood facing him . . . What did it mean? 'It is she!' he cried almost at the top of his voice. It really was she – the one he had met on Nevsky Prospect and had escorted home.

Meanwhile she lifted her eyelashes and looked at all with her clear eyes. 'Aïe, aïe, aïe, how beautiful! . . . ' was all he could say with bated breath. She scanned the faces around her, all eager to catch her attention, but with an air of weariness and indifference she looked away and met Piskarev's eyes. Oh heavens! What paradise! Oh God, for strength to bear this! Life cannot contain it, such rapture tears it asunder and bears away the soul! She made a sign, but not by hand nor by inclination of the head; no, the sign was a look in her ravishing eyes so subtle, so imperceptible that no one else could see it, but he saw it, he understood it. The dance lasted long; the exhausted music seemed to flag and die away and again it broke out, shrilled and thundered; at last the dance was over. She sat down. Her panting bosom heaved under the light cloud of gossamer, her hand (Oh heavens! what a marvellous hand!) dropped on her knee, rested on her filmy gown which under it seemed breathing music, and its delicate lilac hue made that lovely hand look more dazzlingly white than ever. Only to touch it and nothing more! No other desires – they would be insolence . . . He stood behind her chair, not daring to speak, not daring to breathe. 'You have been bored?' she pronounced. 'I have been bored too. I see that you hate me . . . ' she added, drooping her long eyelashes.

'Hate you? I? . . . I? . . . ' Piskarev, completely overwhelmed, tried to articulate, and he would probably have poured out a stream of incoherent words, but at that moment a kammer-junker with a magnificent curled shock of hair came up making witty and polite remarks. He rather agreeably displayed a row of rather good teeth, and at every jest his wit drove a sharp nail into Piskarev's heart. At last someone fortunately addressed the kammer-junker with a question.

'How unbearable it is!' she said, lifting her heavenly eyes to him. 'I will sit at the other end of the room; be there!' She glided through the crowd and vanished. He pushed his way through the crowd like one possessed, and in a flash was there.

So this was she! She sat like a queen, finer than all, lovelier than all, and her eyes sought him.

'Are you here?' she asked softly. 'I will be open with you: no doubt you think the circumstances of our meeting strange. Can you imagine that I belong to the degraded class of beings among whom you met me? You think my conduct strange, but I will reveal a secret to you. Can you promise never to betray it?' she pronounced, fixing her eyes upon him.

'Oh I will, I will, I will! . . . '

But at that moment an elderly man shook hands with her and began speaking in a language Piskarev did not understand. She looked at the artist with an imploring gaze, and signed to him to remain where he was and await her return: but in an access of impatience he could not obey a command even from her lips. He followed her, but the crowd parted them. He could no longer see the lilac dress; in consternation he forced his way from room to room and elbowed all he met mercilessly, but in all the rooms gentlemen were sitting at whist plunged in dead silence. In a corner of the room some elderly people were arguing about the superiority of military to civil service; in another some young men in superb dress-coats were making a few light remarks about the voluminous works of a poet. Piskarev felt that a gentleman of venerable appearance had taken him by the button of his coat and was submitting some very just observation to his criticism, but he rudely thrust him aside without even noticing that he had a very distinguished order on his breast. He ran into another room – she was not there, into a third – she was not there either. 'Where is she? Give her to me! Oh, I cannot live without another look at her! I want to hear what she meant to tell me!' But all his search was in vain. Anxious and exhausted, he huddled in a corner and looked at the crowd. But everything seemed blurred to his strained eyes. At last the walls of his own room began to grow distinct. He raised his eyes: before him stood a candlestick with the light flickering in the socket; the whole candle had burned away and the melted grease lay on his table . . .

So he had been asleep! My God, what a splendid dream! And why had he awakened? Why had it not lasted one minute longer? She would no doubt have appeared again! The unwelcome dawn was peeping in at his window with its unpleasant, dingy light. The room was in such a grey, untidy muddle . . . Oh, how revolting was reality! What was it beside dreams? He undressed quickly and got into bed, wrapping himself up in the coverlet, anxious to recapture the dream that had flown. Sleep certainly did not tarry, but it presented him with something quite different from what he wanted: at one time, Lieutenant Pirogov with his pipe, then the porter of the Academy, then an actual civil councillor, then the head of a Finnish woman who had sat to him for a portrait, and such foolish things.

He lay in bed till the middle of the day longing to dream again, but she did not appear. If only for one minute she had shown her lovely features, if only for one minute her light step had rustled, if only her hand, shining white as driven snow, had for one minute gleamed before him!

Dismissing everything, forgetting everything, he sat with a crushed and hopeless expression, full of nothing but his dream. He never thought of touching anything; his eyes were fixed in a vacant, lifeless stare upon the windows that looked into the yard, where a dirty water-carrier was slopping water that froze in the air, and the cracked voice of a pedlar bleated like a goat, 'Old clothes for sale.' The sounds of everyday reality rung strangely in his ears. So he sat on till evening and then flung himself eagerly into bed. For hours he struggled with sleeplessness; at last he overcame it. Again a dream, a vulgar, horrid dream. 'God, have mercy! For one minute, just for one minute, let me see her!'

Again he waited for the evening, again he fell asleep. He dreamed of a government clerk who was at the same time a government clerk and a bassoon. Oh, this was insufferable! At last she appeared! Her head and her curls . . . she gazed at him . . . for – oh, how brief a moment, and then again mist, again some stupid dream.

At last, dreaming became his life and from that time his life was strangely turned upside down; he might be said to sleep when he was awake and to come to life when he was asleep. Any one seeing him sitting dumbly before his empty table or walking along the street would certainly have taken him for a lunatic or a man deranged by drink: his eyes had a perfectly vacant look, his natural absent-mindedness developed and drove every sign of feeling and emotion out of his face. He only revived at the approach of night.

Such a condition destroyed his health, and the worst torture for him was the fact that sleep began to desert him altogether. Anxious to save the only treasure left him, he used every means to regain it. He had heard that there were means of inducing sleep – one need only take opium. But where could he get opium? He thought of a Persian who kept a shawl-shop and, whenever he saw Piskarev, asked him to paint a

beautiful woman for him. He resolved to apply to him, assuming that
he would be sure to have the drug he wanted.

The Persian received him, sitting on a sofa with his legs crossed
under him. 'What do you want opium for?' he asked.

Piskarev told him about his sleeplessness.

'Very well, you must paint me a beautiful woman, and I will give you
opium. She must be a real beauty, let her eyebrows be black and her
eyes be as big as olives; and let me be lying near her smoking my pipe.
Do you hear, let her be pretty! Let her be a beauty!'

Piskarev promised everything. The Persian went out for a minute
and came back with a little jar filled with a dark liquid; he carefully
poured some of it into another jar and gave it to Piskarev, telling him to
take not more than seven drops in water. He greedily clutched the
precious little jar, with which he would not have parted for a pile of
gold, and ran headlong home.

When he got home he poured several drops into a glass of water and,
swallowing it, lay down to sleep.

Oh God, what joy! She! She again, but now in quite a different
world! Oh, how charmingly she sat at the window of a bright little
country house! In her dress was the simplicity in which the poet's
thought is clothed. And her hair! Merciful heavens! How simple it was
and how it suited her. A short shawl was thrown lightly around her
graceful throat; everything about her was modest, everything about
her showed a mysterious, inexplicable sense of taste. How charming
her graceful carriage! How musical the sound of her steps and the
rustle of her simple gown! How lovely her hand, clasped by a hair
bracelet! She said to him with a tear in her eye: 'Don't look down upon
me; I am not at all what you take me for. Look at me, look at me more
carefully and tell me: am I capable of what you imagine?' 'Oh no, no!
May he who should dare to think it, may he . . . '

But he awoke, deeply moved, harassed, with tears in his eyes. 'Better
that you had not existed! had not lived in this world, but had been an
artist's creation! I would never have left the canvas, I would have gazed
at you for ever and kissed you! I would have lived and breathed in you,
as in the loveliest of dreams, and then I should have been happy. I
should have desired nothing more, I would have called upon you as my
guardian angel at sleeping and at waking, and I would have gazed on
you, if ever I had to paint the divine and holy. But as it is . . . how
terrible life is! What good is it that she lives? Does a madman's life
rejoice his friends and family who once loved him? My God! What is
our life! An everlasting disharmony between dream and reality!' Such

ideas absorbed him continually. He thought of nothing, he almost gave up eating, indeed, and with the impatience and passion of a lover waited for the evening and his coveted dreams. The continual concentration of his thoughts on one subject at last so completely mastered his whole being and imagination that the coveted image appeared before him almost every day always in positions that were the very opposite of reality, for his thoughts were as pure as a child's. Through these dreams, the subject of them became in his imagination more pure and was completely transformed.

The opium inflamed his thoughts more than ever, and if there ever was a man passionately, terribly, and ruinously in love to the utmost pitch of madness he was that luckless man.

Of his dreams one rejoiced him more than any: he saw himself in his studio. He was in good spirits and sitting happily with the palette in his hand! And she was there. She was his wife. She sat beside him leaning her lovely elbow on the back of his chair and looking at his work. Her eyes were languid and weary with excess of bliss; everything in his room breathed of paradise; it was so bright, so neat. Good God! She leaned her lovely head on his bosom . . . He had never had a better dream than that. He rose after it fresher, less absent-minded than before. A strange idea came into his mind. 'Perhaps,' he thought, 'she has been drawn into vice by some awful chance, through no will of her own, perhaps her soul is disposed to penitence; perhaps she herself is longing to escape from her awful position. And am I to stand aside indifferently and let her go to ruin when I have only to hold out a hand to save her from drowning?' His thoughts carried him further. 'No one knows me,' he said to himself, 'and no one cares what I do, and I have nothing to do with any one either. If she shows herself genuinely penitent and changes her mode of life, I will marry her. I ought to marry her, and no doubt I should do much better than many who marry their housekeepers or sometimes the most contemptible creatures. But my action will be disinterested and very likely a good deed. I shall restore to the world the loveliest of its ornaments!'

Making this light-hearted plan, he felt the colour flushing in his cheek; he went up to the looking-glass and was frightened at his hollow cheeks and the paleness of his face. He began carefully dressing; he washed, smoothed his hair, put on a new coat, a smart waistcoat, flung on his cloak, and went out into the street. He breathed the fresh air and had a feeling of freshness in his heart, like a convalescent who has gone out for the first time after a long illness. His heart throbbed when he turned into the street, which he had not passed through again since that fatal meeting.

He was a long time looking for the house. He walked up and down the street twice, uncertain before which to stop. At last one of them seemed to him like it. He ran quickly up the stairs and knocked at the door: the door opened and who came out to meet him? His ideal, his mysterious divinity, the original of his dream pictures – she who was his life, in whom he lived so terribly, so agonisingly, so blissfully – she, she herself, stood before him! He trembled; he could hardly stand on his feet for weakness, overcome by the rush of joy. She stood before him as lovely as ever, though her eyes looked sleepy, though a pallor had crept over her face, no longer quite so fresh; but still she was lovely.

'Ah!' she cried on seeing Piskarev and rubbing her eyes (it was two o'clock in the afternoon); 'why did you run away from us that day?'

He sat down in a chair, feeling faint, and looked at her.

'And I am only just awake; I was brought home at seven in the morning. I was quite drunk,' she added with a smile.

Oh, better you had been dumb and could not speak at all than uttering such words! She had shown him in a flash the whole panorama of her life. But, in spite of that, struggling with his feelings, he made up his mind to try whether his representations would have any effect on her. Pulling himself together, he began in a shaking but ardent voice depicting her awful position. She listened to him with a look of attention and with the feeling of wonder which we display at the sight of something strange and unexpected. She looked with a faint smile towards her friend who was sitting in a corner, and who left off cleaning a comb and also listened with attention to this new preacher.

'It is true that I am poor,' said Piskarev, at last, after a prolonged and persuasive appeal, 'but we will work, we will do our best, side by side, to improve our position. Yes, nothing is sweeter than to owe everything to one's own work. I will sit at my pictures, you shall sit by me and inspire my work, while you are busy with sewing or some other handicraft, and we shall not need for anything.'

'Indeed!' she interrupted his speech with an expression of some scorn. 'I am not a washerwoman or a seamstress that I should have to work.'

Oh God! In those words the whole of a mean, degraded life was portrayed, the life of the true followers of vice, full of emptiness and idleness!

'Marry me!' her friend who had till then sat silent in the corner put in, with a saucy air. 'When I am your wife I will sit like this!' As she spoke she pursed up her pitiful face and assumed a silly expression, which greatly diverted the beauty.

Oh, that was too much! That was more than he could bear! He

rushed away with every thought and feeling in a turmoil. His mind was clouded: stupidly, aimlessly, he wandered about all day, seeing nothing, hearing nothing, feeling nothing. No one could say whether he slept anywhere or not; only next day, by some blind instinct, he found his way to his room, pale and terrible-looking, with his hair dishevelled and signs of madness in his face. He locked himself in his room and admitted no one, asked for nothing. Four days passed and his door was not once opened; at last a week had passed, and still the door was locked. People went to the door and began calling him, but there was no answer; at last the door was broken open and his lifeless corpse was found with the throat cut. A bloodstained razor lay on the floor. From his arms flung out convulsively and his terribly distorted face, it might be concluded that his hand had faltered and that he had suffered in agony before his soul left his sinful body.

So perished the victim of a frantic passion, poor Piskarev, the gentle, timid, modest, childishly simple-hearted artist whose spark of talent might with time have glowed into the full bright flame of genius. No one wept for him; no one was seen beside his dead body except the regulation police superintendent and the indifferent face of the town doctor. His coffin was taken to Ohta[108] quickly, without even the rites of religion; only a soldier-watchman who followed it wept, and that simply because he had had a glass too much of vodka. Even Lieutenant Pirogov did not come to look at the dead body of the poor luckless artist to whom he had extended his exalted patronage. He had no thoughts to spare for him; indeed, he was absorbed in a very exciting adventure. But let us turn to him. I do not like corpses, and it is always disagreeable to me when a long funeral procession crosses my path and some veteran dressed in a sort of capuchin[109] takes a pinch of snuff with his left hand because he has a torch in his right. I always feel annoyed at the sight of a magnificent catafalque[110] with a velvet pall; but my annoyance is mingled with sadness when I see a cart dragging the red, uncovered coffin of some poor fellow and only some old beggar woman who has met it at the crossways follows it weeping, because she has nothing else to do.

I believe we left Lieutenant Pirogov at the moment when he parted with Piskarev and went in pursuit of the fair-haired charmer. The latter was a lively, rather attractive little creature. She stopped before every shop and gazed at the sashes, kerchiefs, ear-rings, gloves, and other trifles in the shop-windows, was continually twisting and turning and gazing about her in all directions and looking behind her. 'You'll be mine, you darling!' Pirogov said confidently, as he pursued her, turning up the collar of his coat for fear of meeting someone of his acquaintance. It will be as well, however, to let the reader know what sort of person Lieutenant Pirogov was.

But before we describe Lieutenant Pirogov, it will be as well to say something of the circle to which Lieutenant Pirogov belonged. There are officers who form a kind of middle class in Petersburg. You will always find one of them at every evening party, at every dinner given by a civil councillor or an actual civil councillor who has risen to that grade by forty years of service. The group of pale daughters, as colourless as Petersburg, some of them no longer in their first youth, the tea-table, the piano, the impromptu dance, are all inseparable from the gay epaulette which gleams in the lamplight between the virtuous young lady and the black coat of her brother or of some old friend of the family. It is extremely difficult to arouse and divert these phlegmatic misses. To do so needs a great deal of skill, or rather perhaps the absence of all skill. One has to say what is not too clever or too amusing and to bring in the trivialities that women love. One must give credit for that to the gentlemen we are discussing. They have a special gift for making these colourless beauties laugh and listen. Exclamations, smothered in laughter, of 'Oh, do stop! Aren't you ashamed to be so absurd!' are often their highest reward. They rarely, one may say never, get into higher circles: from those regions they are completely crowded out by the so-called aristocrats. At the same time, they pass for well-bred, highly educated men. They are fond of talking about literature; praise Bulgarin,[111] Pushkin,[112] and Gretch,[113] and speak with contempt and witty sarcasm of A. A. Orlov.[114] They never miss a public lecture, though it may be on bookkeeping or even forestry. You will always find one of them at the theatre, whatever the play, unless, indeed, it be one of the farces of the 'Filatka'[115] class, which greatly offend their fastidious taste. They are priceless at the theatre and the greatest asset to managers. They are particularly fond of fine verses in a play, and they are greatly given to calling loudly for the actors; many of them, by teaching in government establishments or preparing pupils for them, arrive at keeping a carriage and pair. Then their circle becomes wider and in the end they succeed in marrying a merchant's daughter who can play the piano, with a dowry of a hundred thousand, or something near it, in cash, and a lot of bearded relations. They can never attain to this honour, however, till they have reached the rank of colonel, at least, for Russian merchants, though there may still be a smell of cabbage about them, will never consent to see their daughters married to any but generals or colonels at the lowest. Such are the leading characteristics of this class of young men. But Lieutenant Pirogov had a number of talents belonging to him individually. He recited verses from *Dimitry Donsky*[116] and *Woe from Wit*[117] with great effect, and possessed the art of blowing smoke out of a pipe in rings so successfully that he could string a dozen of them together in a chain; he could tell a very good story to the effect that a cannon was one thing and a unicorn was another. It is difficult to enumerate all the qualities with which fate had endowed Pirogov. He was fond of talking about actresses and dancers, but not quite in such a crude way as young lieutenants commonly hold forth on that subject. He was very much pleased with his rank in the service, to which he had only lately been promoted, and although he did occasionally say as he lay on the sofa: 'Oh dear, vanity, all is vanity.[118] What if I am a lieutenant?' yet his vanity was secretly much flattered by his new dignity; he often tried in conversation to allude to it in a roundabout way, and on one occasion when he jostled against a copying clerk in the street who struck him as uncivil he promptly stopped him and in few but vigorous words pointed out to him that there was a lieutenant standing before him and not any other kind of officer. He was the more eloquent in his observations as two very nice-looking ladies were passing at the moment. Pirogov displayed a passion for everything artistic in general and encouraged the artist Piskarev; this may have been partly due to a desire to see his manly countenance portrayed on canvas. But enough of Pirogov's good qualities. Man is such a strange creature that one can never enumerate all his good points, and the more we look into him the more new characteristics we discover and the description of them would be endless. And so Pirogov continued to pursue the unknown fair one, from time to time he addressed her with questions to which she responded infrequently with abrupt and incoherent sounds. They passed by the wet Kazan gate into Myeshtchansky Street – a street of tobacconists and little shops, of German artisans and Finnish nymphs. The fair lady ran faster than ever, and scurried in at the gate of a rather dirty-looking house. Pirogov followed her. She ran up a narrow, dark staircase and went in at a door through which Pirogov boldly followed her. He found himself in a big room with black walls and a grimy ceiling. A heap of iron screws, locksmith's tools, shining tin coffeepots and candlesticks lay on the table; the floor was littered with brass and iron filings. Pirogov saw at once that this was a workman's lodging. The unknown charmer darted away through a side-door. He hesitated for a minute, but, following the Russian rule, decided to push forward. He went into the other room, which was quite unlike the first and very neatly furnished, showing that it was inhabited by a German. He was struck by an extremely strange sight: before him sat Schiller.[119] Not the Schiller who wrote *William Tell* and the *History of the Thirty Years' War*, but the famous Schiller the ironmonger and tinsmith of Myeshtchansky Street. Beside Schiller stood Hoffmann – not the writer Hoffmann,[120] but a rather high-class bootmaker who lived in Ofitsersky Street and was a great friend of Schiller's. Schiller was drunk and was sitting on a chair, stamping and saying something with heat. All this would not have surprised Pirogov, but what did surprise him was the extraordinary attitude of the two figures. Schiller was sitting with his head flung up and his rather thick nose in the air, while Hoffmann was holding the nose between his finger and thumb and was brandishing the blade of his cobbler's knife over its very surface. Both individuals were talking in German, and so Lieutenant Pirogov, whose knowledge of German was confined to 'Gut Morgen' could not make out what was going on. However, what Schiller said amounted to this: 'I don't want it, I have no need of a nose!' he said, waving his hands, 'I use three pounds of snuff a month on my nose alone. And I pay in a nasty Russian shop, for a German shop does not keep Russian snuff. I pay in a nasty Russian shop forty kopecks a pound – that makes one rouble twenty kopecks, twelve times one rouble twenty kopecks – that makes fourteen roubles forty kopecks. Do you hear, friend Hoffmann? Fourteen roubles forty kopecks on my nose alone! And on holidays I take a pinch of rappee,[121] for I don't care to use nasty Russian snuff on a holiday. In the year I use two pounds of rappee at two roubles the pound. Six and fourteen makes twenty roubles forty kopecks on snuff alone. It's a robbery. I ask you, my friend Hoffmann, isn't it?' Hoffmann, who was drunk himself, answered in the affirmative. 'Twenty roubles and forty kopecks. I am a Swabian;[122] we have a king in Germany.[123] I don't want a nose! Cut off my nose! Here is my nose.'

And had it not been for Lieutenant Pirogov's suddenly appearing, Hoffmann would certainly, for no rhyme or reason, have cut off Schiller's nose, for he already had his knife in position, as though he were going to cut a sole.

Schiller seemed very much annoyed that an unknown and uninvited person should so inopportunely interrupt him. Although he was in a state of intoxication, he felt that it was rather improper to be seen in the presence of an outsider in such a state and engaged in such proceedings. Meanwhile Pirogov made a slight bow and, with his characteristic agreeableness, said: 'Excuse me . . . !'

'Be off!' Schiller responded emphatically.

Lieutenant Pirogov was taken aback at this. Such treatment was absolutely new to him. A smile which had begun faintly to appear on his face vanished at once. With a feeling of wounded dignity he said: 'I am surprised, sir . . . I suppose you have not observed . . . I am an officer . . .'

'And what's an officer? I'm a Swabian Myself' (at this Schiller banged the table with his fist) 'will be an officer; a year and a half a junker, two years a lieutenant, and tomorrow I shall be an officer at once. But I don't want to serve. This is what I'd do to officers: phoo!' Schiller held his open hand before him and spat into it.

Lieutenant Pirogov saw that there was nothing for him to do but retire. Such a proceeding, however, was quite out of keeping with his rank, and was disagreeable to him. He stood still several times on the stairs as though trying to rally his forces and to think how to make Schiller feel his impudence. At last he decided. That Schiller might be excused because his head was fuddled with wine and beer; besides, he recalled the image of the charming blonde, and he made up his mind to consign it to oblivion.

Early next morning Lieutenant Pirogov appeared at the tinsmith's workshop. In the outer room he was met by the fair-haired charmer, who asked him in a rather austere voice, which went admirably with her little face: 'What do you want?'

'Oh, good-morning, my pretty dear! Don't you recognise me? You little rogue, what charming eyes!'

As he said this Lieutenant Pirogov tried very charmingly to chuck her under the chin; but the lady uttered a frightened exclamation and with the same austerity asked: 'What do you want?'

'To see you, that's all that I want,' answered Lieutenant Pirogov, smiling rather agreeably and going nearer; but noticing that the timorous beauty was about to slip through the door, he added: 'I want to order some spurs, my dear. Can you make me some spurs? Though indeed no spur is needed to make me love you, a curb is what one needs, not a spur. What charming little hands!'

Lieutenant Pirogov was particularly agreeable in declarations of this kind.

'I will call my husband at once,' cried the German, and went out and within a few minutes Pirogov saw Schiller come in with sleepy-looking eyes; he had only just woken up after the drunkenness of the previous day. As he looked at the officer he remembered as though in a confused dream what had happened the previous day. He could recall nothing exactly as it was, but felt that he had done something stupid and so received the officer with a very sullen face. 'I can't ask less than fifteen roubles for a pair of spurs,' he brought out, hoping to get rid of Pirogov, for as a respectable German he was ashamed to look at any one who had seen him in an unseemly condition. Schiller liked to drink without spectators, in company with two or three friends, and at such times locked himself in and would not admit even his own workman.

'Why are they so expensive?' asked Pirogov, genially.

'German work,' Schiller pronounced coolly, stroking his chin; 'a Russian will undertake to make them for two roubles.'

'Well, to show you that I like you and should be glad to make your acquaintance, I will pay fifteen roubles.'

Schiller remained for a minute pondering; as a respectable German he felt a little ashamed. Hoping to put him off the order, he declared that he could not undertake it for a fortnight. But Pirogov, without making any objections, readily assented to this.

The German mused and began pondering how he could best do the work so as to make it really worth fifteen roubles.

At this moment the blonde charmer came into the room and began looking for something on the table, which was covered with coffeepots. The lieutenant took advantage of Schiller's absorption, stepped up to her and pressed her arm, which was bare to the shoulder.

This was very distasteful to Schiller. 'Meine Fraue!' he cried.

'Was wollen Sie doch?' answered the fair charmer.

'Gehen Sie to the kitchen!'[124] The lady withdrew.

'In a fortnight then?' said Pirogov.

'Yes, in a fortnight,' replied Schiller, still pondering. 'I have a lot of work now.'

'Goodbye for the present, I will look in again.'

'Goodbye,' said Schiller, closing the door after him.

Lieutenant Pirogov made up his mind not to relinquish his pursuit, though the lady had so plainly rebuffed him. He could not conceive that any one could resist him, especially as his politeness and the brilliant rank of a lieutenant gave him a full claim to attention. It must be mentioned also that with all her attractiveness Schiller's wife was extremely stupid. Stupidity, however, adds a special charm to a pretty wife. I have known several husbands, anyway, who were in raptures over the stupidity of their wives and saw in it evidence of childlike innocence. Beauty works perfect miracles. All spiritual defects in a beauty, far from exciting repulsion, become somehow wonderfully attractive, even vice has an aroma of charm in the beautiful; but when beauty disappears, a woman needs to be twenty times as intelligent as a man merely to inspire respect, to say nothing of love. Schiller's wife, however, for all her stupidity was always faithful to her duties, and consequently it was no easy task for Pirogov to succeed in his bold enterprise. But there is always a pleasure in overcoming difficulties, and the fair lady became more and more attractive in his eyes every day. He took to enquiring pretty frequently about the progress of the spurs, so that at last Schiller was weary of it. He did his utmost to finish the spurs quickly; at last they were done.

'Oh, what splendid workmanship,' cried Lieutenant Pirogov on seeing the spurs. 'Good Heavens, how well it's done! Our general hasn't spurs like that.'

A feeling of self-complacency filled Schiller's soul. His eyes began to look fairly good-humoured, and he felt inwardly reconciled to Pirogov. 'The Russian officer is an intelligent man,' he thought to himself.

'So, then, you could make a sheath for a dagger or for anything else?'

'Indeed I can,' said Schiller with a smile.

'Then make me a sheath for a dagger. I will bring it you. I have a very fine Turkish dagger, but I should like to have another sheath for it.'

This was like a bomb dropped upon Schiller. His brows were suddenly knitted.

'So that's what you are after,' he thought to himself, inwardly swearing at himself for having praised his own work. To refuse it now he felt would be dishonest; besides, the Russian officer had praised his workmanship. Slightly shaking his head, he gave his consent; but the kiss which Pirogov as he went out impudently printed on the lips of the pretty wife reduced the tinsmith to stupefaction.

I think it will not be superfluous to make the reader better acquainted with Schiller himself. Schiller was a regular German in the full significance of the word. From the age of twenty, that happy time when the Russian lives without a thought of the morrow, Schiller had already mapped out his whole life and did not deviate from his plan under any circumstances. He made it a rule to get up at seven, to dine at two, to be punctual in everything, and to get drunk every Sunday. He set before himself as an object to save a capital of fifty thousand in the course of ten years, and all this was as certain and as unalterable as fate, for sooner would a government clerk forget to look in at the porter's lodge of his chief than a German would bring himself to break his word. Never under any circumstances did he increase his expenses, and if the price of potatoes went up much above the ordinary he did not spend one half-penny more on them but simply diminished the amount they consumed, and although he was left sometimes feeling rather hungry, he soon got used to it. His exactitude was such that he made it his rule to kiss his wife twice in the twenty-four hours but not more, and that he might not exceed the number he never put more than one small teaspoonful of pepper in his soup; on Sunday, however, this rule was not so strictly kept, for then Schiller used to drink two bottles of beer and one bottle of herb-flavoured vodka which, however, he always abused. He did not drink like an Englishman, who locks his doors directly after dinner and gets drunk in solitude. On the contrary, like a German he always drank with inspiration either in the company of Hoffmann the boot-maker or with Kunts the carpenter, who was also a German and a great drunkard. Such was the disposition of the worthy Schiller, who was indeed placed in a very difficult position. Though he was phleg-matic and a German, Pirogov's behaviour excited in him a feeling akin to jealousy. He racked his brains and could not think how to get rid of this Russian officer. Meanwhile Pirogov, smoking a pipe in the company of his brother officers – since Providence has ordained that wherever there is an officer there is a pipe – alluded significantly and with an agreeable smile on his lips to his little intrigue with the pretty German, with whom he was, according to his account, already on the best of terms, though as a matter of fact he had almost lost all hope of winning her favour.

One day he was walking along Myeshtchansky Street looking at the house adorned by Schiller's signboard with coffeepots and samovars on it; to his great joy he caught sight of the fair charmer's head thrust out of window watching the passers-by. He stopped, kissed his hand to her and said: 'Gut Morgen.' The fair lady bowed to him as to an acquaintance.

'I say, is your husband at home?'

'Yes,' she answered.

'And when is he out?'

'He is not at home on Sundays,' said the foolish little German.

'That's not bad,' Pirogov thought to himself. 'I must take advantage of that.'

And the following Sunday he suddenly and unexpectedly stood facing the fair German. Schiller really was not at home. The pretty wife was frightened; but Pirogov on this occasion behaved rather warily, he was very respectful in his manner, and, making his bows, displayed all the elegance of his supple figure in his close-fitting uniform. He made polite and agreeable jests, but the silly little German responded with nothing but monosyllables. At last, having made his attack from all sides and seeing that nothing would entertain her, he suggested that they should dance. The German agreed in a trice, for all German girls are passionately fond of dancing. Pirogov rested great hopes upon this: in the first place it gave her pleasure, in the second place it displayed his figure and dexterity; and thirdly he could get so much closer to her in dancing and put his arm round the pretty German and lay the foundation for everything else; in short, he reckoned on complete success resulting from it. He began humming a gavotte, knowing that Germans must have something sedate. The pretty German walked into the middle of the room and lifted her shapely foot. This attitude so enchanted Pirogov that he flew to kiss her. The lady began to scream, and this only enhanced her charm in Pirogov's eyes. He was showering kisses on her when the door suddenly opened and Schiller walked in, together with Hoffmann and Kunts the carpenter. All these worthy persons were as drunk as cobblers.

But . . . I leave the reader to imagine the wrath and indignation of Schiller.

'Ruffian!' he shouted in the utmost indignation. 'How dare you kiss my wife? You are a scoundrel and not a Russian officer. The devil take you! That's right, isn't it so, friend Hoffmann? I am a German and not a Russian swine.' (Hoffmann gave him an affirmative answer.) 'Oh, I don't want to be made a fool of! Take him by the collar, friend Hoffmann; I won't have it,' he went on, brandishing his arms violently, while his whole face was the colour of his red waistcoat. 'I have been living in Petersburg for eight years, I have a mother in Swabia and an uncle in Nuremberg, I am a German and not a horned ox. Away with him altogether, my friend Hoffmann. Hold him by his arms and his legs, comrade Kunts!'

And the Germans seized Pirogov by his arms and his legs.

He tried in vain to get away; these three tradesmen were among the sturdiest people in Petersburg, and they treated him so roughly and disrespectfully that I cannot find words to do justice to the melancholy incident.

I am sure that next day Schiller was in a perfect fever, that he was trembling like a leaf, expecting from moment to moment the arrival of the police, that he would have given anything in the world for what had happened on the previous day to be a dream. But what has been cannot be changed. No comparison could do justice to Pirogov's anger and indignation. The very thought of such an insult drove him to fury. He thought Siberia and the lash too slight a punishment for Schiller. He flew home to dress himself and go at once straight to the general to paint to him in the most vivid colours the seditious insolence of the Germans. He meant to lodge a complaint in writing with the general staff; and, if the punishment meted out to the offenders was not satisfactory, to carry the matter to higher authorities.

But all this ended rather strangely; on the way he went into a café, ate two jam puffs, read something out of *The Northern Bee*[125] and left the café with his wrath somewhat cooled. Then a pleasant fresh evening led him to take a few turns along Nevsky Prospect; by nine o'clock he had recovered his serenity and decided that he had better not disturb the general on Sunday; especially as he would be sure to be away somewhere. And so he went to spend the evening with one of the directors of the control committee, where he met a very agreeable party of government officials and officers of his regiment. There he spent a very pleasant evening, and so distinguished himself in the mazurka that not only the ladies but even their partners were moved to admiration.

'Marvellously is our world arranged,' I thought as I walked two days later along Nevsky Prospect, and mused over these two incidents. 'How strangely, how unaccountably Fate plays with us! Do we ever get what we desire? Do we ever attain what our powers seem specially fitted for? Everything goes by contraries. Fate gives splendid horses to one man and he drives in his carriage without noticing their beauty, while another who is consumed by a passion for horses has to go on foot, and all the satisfaction he gets is clicking with his tongue when trotting horses are led past him. One has an excellent cook, but unluckily so small a mouth that he cannot take more than two tiny bits; another has a mouth as big as the arch of the Staff Headquarters,[126] but also has to be content with a German dinner of potatoes. What strange pranks Fate plays with us!'

But strangest of all are the incidents that take place in Nevsky Prospect. Oh, do not trust that Nevsky Prospect! I always wrap myself more closely in my cloak when I pass along it and try not to look at the objects which meet me. Everything is a cheat, everything is a dream, everything is other than it seems! You think that that gentleman who walks along in a splendidly cut coat is very wealthy? – not a bit of it. All his wealth lies in his coat. You think that those two stout men who stand facing the church that is being built are criticising its architecture? – not at all; they are saying how queerly two crows are sitting opposite each other. You think that that enthusiast waving his arms about is describing how his wife was playing ball out of window with an officer who was a complete stranger to him? – not so at all, he is talking of Lafayette.[127] You imagine those ladies . . . but ladies are least of all to be trusted. Do not look into the shop-windows, the trifles exhibited in them are delightful but they are suggestive of a fearful pile of notes. But God preserve you from peeping under the ladies' hats! However attractively in the evening a fair lady's cloak may flutter in the distance, nothing would induce me to follow her and try to get a closer view. Keep your distance, for God's sake, keep your distance from the lamp-post! and pass by it quickly, as quickly as you can! It is a happy escape if you get off with nothing worse than some of its stinking oil on your foppish coat. But, apart from the lamp-post, everything breathes deception. It deceives at all hours, Nevsky Prospect does, but most of all when night falls in masses of shadow on it, throwing into relief the white and dun-coloured walls of the houses when all the town is transformed into noise and brilliance, when myriads of carriages roll over bridges, postilions shout and jolt up and down on their horses, and when the demon himself lights the street lamps to show everything in false colours.

THE NOSE

1

A N EXTRAORDINARILY STRANGE incident took place in Petersburg on the 25th of March. The barber, Ivan Yakovlevitch, who lives in the Voznesensky Prospect[128] (his surname is lost, and nothing more appears even on his signboard, where a gentleman is depicted with his cheeks covered with soapsuds, together with an inscription 'also lets blood'[129]) – the barber Ivan Yakovlevitch woke up rather early and was aware of a smell of hot bread. Raising himself in bed he saw his spouse, a rather portly lady who was very fond of drinking coffee, engaged in taking out of the oven some freshly-baked loaves.

'I won't have coffee today, Praskovya Osipovna,' said Ivan Yakovlevitch; 'instead I should like some hot bread with onion.' (The fact is that Ivan Yakovlevitch would have liked both, but he knew that it was utterly impossible to ask for two things at once, for Praskovya Osipovna greatly disliked such caprices.)

'Let the fool have bread, so much the better for me,' thought his spouse to herself; 'there will be an extra cup of coffee left,' and she flung one loaf on the table.

For the sake of propriety Ivan Yakovlevitch put a tail coat over his shirt, and, sitting down to the table, sprinkled with salt and prepared two onions, took a knife in his hand and, making a solemn face, set to work to cut the bread. After dividing the loaf into two halves he looked into the middle of it – and to his amazement saw there something that looked white. Ivan Yakovlevitch scooped at it carefully with his knife and felt it with his finger: 'It's solid,' he said to himself. 'Whatever can it be?'

He thrust in his finger and drew it out – it was a nose! . . . Ivan Yakovlevitch's hand dropped with astonishment, he rubbed his eyes and felt it: it actually was a nose, and, what's more, it looked to him somehow familiar. A look of horror came into Ivan Yakovlevitch's face.

But that horror was nothing to the indignation with which his wife was overcome.

'Where have you cut that nose off, you brute?' she cried wrathfully. 'You scoundrel, you drunkard, I'll go to the police myself to tell of you! You ruffian! Here I have heard from three men that when you are shaving them you pull at their noses till you almost tug them off.'

But Ivan Yakovlevitch was more dead than alive: he perceived that the nose was no other than that of Kovalyov, the collegiate assessor, whom he shaved every Wednesday and every Sunday.

'Stay, Praskovya Osipovna! I'll wrap it up in a rag and put it in a corner. Let it stay there for a bit; I'll return it later on.'

'I won't hear of it! As though I would allow a stray nose to lie about in my room. You dried-up biscuit! To be sure, he can do nothing but sharpen his razors on the strop, but soon he won't be fit to do his duties at all, the gad-about, the good-for-nothing! As though I were going to answer to the police for you . . . Oh, you sloven, you stupid blockhead. Away with it, away with it! Take it where you like! Don't let me set eyes on it again!'

Ivan Yakovlevitch stood as though utterly crushed. He thought and thought, and did not know what to think. 'The devil only knows how it happened,' he said at last, scratching behind his ear. 'Did I come home drunk last night or not? I can't say for certain now. But from all signs and tokens it must be a thing quite unheard of, for bread is a thing that is baked, while a nose is something quite different. I can't make head or tail of it.' Ivan Yakovlevitch sank into silence. The thought that the police might make a search there for the nose and throw the blame of it on him reduced him to complete prostration. Already the red collar, beautifully embroidered with silver, the sabre, hovered before his eyes, and he trembled all over. At last he got his breeches and his boots, pulled on these wretched objects, and, accompanied by the stern up-braidings of Praskovya Osipovna, wrapped the nose in a rag and went out into the street.

He wanted to thrust it out of sight somewhere, under a gate, or somehow accidentally to drop it and then turn off into a side street, but as ill-luck would have it he kept coming upon someone he knew, who would at once begin by asking: 'Where are you going?' or 'Whom are you going to shave so early?' so that Ivan Yakovlevitch could never find a good moment. Another time he really did drop it, but a sentry pointed to it with his halberd from a long way off, saying as he did so: 'Pick it up, you have dropped something!' and Ivan Yakovlevitch was obliged to pick up the nose and put it in his pocket. He was overcome by despair, especially as the number of people in the street was continually increasing as the shops and stalls began to open.

He made up his mind to go to St Isaac's Bridge[130] in the hope of being able to fling it into the Neva . . . But I am rather in fault for not having hitherto said anything about Ivan Yakovlevitch, a worthy man in many respects.

Ivan Yakovlevitch, like every self-respecting Russian workman, was a terrible drunkard, and though every day he shaved other people's chins, his own went for ever unshaven. Ivan Yakovlevitch's tail coat (he never wore any other shape) was piebald, that is, it was black dappled all over with brown and yellow and grey; the collar was shiny, and instead of three buttons there was only one hanging on a thread. Ivan Yakovlevitch was a great cynic, and when Kovalyov the collegiate assessor said to him while he was being shaved: 'Your hands always stink, Ivan Yakovlevitch,' the latter would reply with the question: 'What should make them stink?' 'I can't tell, my good man, but they do stink,' the collegiate assessor would say, and, taking a pinch of snuff, Ivan Yakovlevitch lathered him for it on his cheeks and under his nose and behind his ears and under his beard – in fact wherever he chose.

The worthy citizen found himself by now on St Isaac's Bridge. First of all he looked about him, then bent over the parapet as though to look under the bridge to see whether there were a great number of fish racing by, and stealthily flung in the rag with the nose. He felt as though with it a heavy weight had rolled off his back. Ivan Yakovlevitch actually grinned. Instead of going to shave the chins of government clerks, he repaired to an establishment bearing the inscription 'Tea and refreshments' and asked for a glass of punch, when he suddenly observed at the end of the bridge a police inspector of respectable appearance with full whiskers, with a three-cornered hat and a sword. He turned cold, and meanwhile the inspector beckoned to him and said: 'Come this way, my good man.'

Ivan Yakovlevitch, knowing the etiquette, took off his hat some way off and, as he approached, said: 'I wish your honour good health.'

'No, no, old fellow, I am not "your honour": tell me what you were about, standing on the bridge?'

'Upon my soul, sir, I was on my way to shave my customers, and I was only looking to see whether the current was running fast.'

'That's a lie, that's a lie! You won't get off with that. Kindly answer!'

'I am ready to shave you, gracious sir, two or even three times a week with no conditions whatever,' answered Ivan Yakovlevitch.

'No, my friend, that is nonsense; I have three barbers to shave me and they think it a great honour, too. But be so kind as to tell me what you were doing there?'

Ivan Yakovlevitch turned pale . . . but the incident is completely veiled in obscurity, and absolutely nothing is known of what happened next.

2

Kovalyov the collegiate assessor woke up early next morning and made the sound 'brrrr . . . ' with the lips as he always did when he woke up, though he could not himself have explained the reason for his doing so. Kovalyov stretched and asked for a little looking-glass that was standing on the table. He wanted to look at a pimple which had come out upon his nose on the previous evening, but to his great astonishment there was a completely flat space where his nose should have been. Kovalyov in a fright asked for some water and a towel to rub his eyes: there really was no nose. He began feeling with his hand, and pinched himself to see whether he was still asleep: it appeared that he was not asleep. The collegiate assessor jumped out of bed, he shook himself – there was still no nose . . . He ordered his clothes to be given him at once and flew off straight to the head police-master.

But meanwhile we must say a word about Kovalyov in order that the reader may have some idea of what kind of collegiate assessor he was. Collegiate assessors who receive that title through learned diplomas cannot be compared with those who are created collegiate assessors in the Caucasus. They are two quite different species. The learned collegiate assessors . . . But Russia is such a wonderful country that, if you say a word about one collegiate assessor, all the collegiate assessors from Riga to Kamchatka[131] would certainly take it to themselves; and it is the same, of course, with all grades and titles. Kovalyov was a collegiate assessor from the Caucasus. He had only been of that rank for the last two years, and so could not forget it for a moment; and to give himself greater weight and dignity he did not call himself simply collegiate assessor but always spoke of himself as a major. 'Listen, my dear,' he would usually say when he met in the street a woman selling shirt-fronts, 'you go to my house; I live in Sadovoy Street; just ask, does Major Kovalyov live here? Any one will show you.' If he met some prepossessing little baggage he would give her besides a secret instruction, adding: 'You ask for Major Kovalyov's flat, my love.' For this reason we will for the future speak of him as the major.

Major Kovalyov was in the habit of walking every day up and down

Nevsky Prospect. The collar of his shirt-front was always extremely clean and well starched. His whiskers were such as one may see now-adays on provincial and district surveyors, on architects and army doctors, also on those employed on special commissions and in general on all such men as have full ruddy cheeks and are very good hands at a game of boston: these whiskers start from the middle of the cheek and go straight up to the nose. Major Kovalyov used to wear a number of cornelian[132] seals, some with crests on them and others on which were carved Wednesday, Thursday, Monday, and so on. Major Kovalyov had come to Petersburg on business, that is, to look for a post befitting his rank: if he were successful, the post of a vice-governor, and failing that the situation of an executive clerk in some prominent department. Major Kovalyov was not averse to matrimony, but only on condition he could find a bride with a fortune of two hundred thousand. And so the reader may judge for himself what was the major's position when he saw, instead of a nice-looking, well-proportioned nose, an extremely stupid level space.

As ill-luck would have it, not a cab was to be seen in the street, and he was obliged to walk, wrapping himself in his cloak and hiding his face in his handkerchief, as though his nose were bleeding. 'But perhaps it was my imagination: it's impossible I could have been so silly as to lose my nose,' he thought, and went into a confectioner's on purpose to look at himself in the looking-glass. Fortunately there was no one in the shop: some boys were sweeping the floor and putting all the chairs straight; others with sleepy faces were bringing in hot turnovers on trays: yesterday's papers covered with coffee stains were lying about on the tables and chairs. 'Well, thank God, there is nobody here,' he thought; 'now I can look.' He went timidly up to the mirror and looked. 'What the devil's the meaning of it? How nasty!' he commented, spitting. 'If only there had been something instead of a nose, but there is nothing! . . . '

Biting his lips, he went out of the confectioner's with annoyance, and resolved, contrary to his usual practice, not to look or smile at any one. All at once he stood as though rooted to the spot before the door of a house. Something inexplicable took place before his eyes: a carriage was stopping at the entrance; the carriage door flew open; a gentleman in uniform, bending down, sprang out and ran up the steps. What was the horror and at the same time amazement of Kovalyov when he recognised that this was his own nose! At this extraordinary spectacle it seemed to him that everything was heaving before his eyes; he felt that he could scarcely stand; but he made up his mind, come what may, to await the gentleman's return to the carriage, and he stood trembling all over as though in fever. Two minutes later the nose actually did come out. He was in a gold-laced uniform with a big stand-up collar; he had on chamois-leather breeches, at his side was a sword. From his plumed hat it might be gathered that he was of the rank of a civil councillor. Everything showed that he was going somewhere to pay a visit. He looked to both sides, called to the coachman to open the carriage door, got in and drove off.

Poor Kovalyov almost went out of his mind; he did not know what to think of such a strange occurrence. How was it possible for a nose – which had only yesterday been on his face and could neither drive nor walk – to be in uniform! He ran after the carriage, which luckily did not go far, but stopped before Kazan Cathedral.[133]

He hurried into the cathedral, made his way through a row of old beggar women with their faces tied up and two chinks in place of their eyes at whom he used to laugh so merrily, and went into the church. There were not many worshippers inside the church, and they were all huddled around the door. Kovalyov was so agitated that he was utterly unable to pray, and he looked in every corner of the church trying to catch a glimpse of this gentleman. At last he saw him standing off to one side. The nose was completely covering up his face with a large stiff collar and was praying with an expression of the greatest devoutness.

'How am I to approach him?' thought Kovalyov. 'One can see by everything – from his uniform, from his hat – that he is a civil councillor. The devil only knows how to do it!'

He began by coughing at his side; but the nose never changed his devout attitude and continued to bow very low.

'Sir,' said Kovalyov, inwardly forcing himself to speak confidently. 'Sir . . .'

'What do you want?' answered the nose, turning round.

'It seems . . . strange to me, sir . . . You ought to know your proper place, and all at once I find you, where? . . . You will admit . . .'

'Excuse me, I cannot understand what you are talking about . . . Explain.'

'How am I to explain to him?' thought Kovalyov, and plucking up his courage he began: 'Of course I . . . I am a major, by the way. For me to go about without a nose you must admit is improper. An old woman selling peeled oranges on Voskresensky Bridge may sit there without a nose; but having prospects of obtaining . . . and being besides acquainted with a great many ladies in the families of Tchehtarev the civil councillor and others . . . You can judge for yourself . . . I don't know, sir (at this point Major Kovalyov shrugged his shoulders) . . . excuse me . . . if you look at the matter in accordance with the principles of duty and honour . . . you can understand of yourself . . . '

'I don't understand a word,' said the nose. 'Explain it more satisfactorily.'

'Sir,' said Kovalyov, with a sense of his own dignity, 'I don't know how to understand your words. The matter appears to me perfectly obvious . . . either you wish . . . Why, you are my own nose!'

The nose looked at the major and his eyebrows slightly quivered.

'You are mistaken, sir, I am an independent individual. Moreover, there can be no sort of close relations between us. I see, sir, from the buttons of your uniform, you must be serving in a different department.' Saying this the nose turned away.

Kovalyov was utterly confused, not knowing what to do or even what to think. Meanwhile they heard the agreeable rustle of a lady's dress: an elderly lady was approaching, all decked out in lace, and with her a slim lady in a white dress which looked very charming on her slender figure, in a straw-coloured hat as light as a pastry puff. Behind them stood, opening his snuffbox, a tall footman with big whiskers and quite a dozen collars.

Kovalyov came nearer, pulled out the cambric collar of his shirtfront, arranged the seals on his gold watch-chain, and, smiling from side to side, turned his attention to the ethereal lady who, like a spring flower, faintly swayed forward and put her white hand with its halftransparent fingers to her brow. The smile on Kovalyov's face broadened when he saw under the hat her round, dazzlingly white chin and part of her cheek flushed with the hues of the first spring rose; but all at once he skipped away as though he had been scalded. He recollected that he had absolutely nothing on his face in place of a nose, and tears oozed from his eyes. He turned away to tell the gentleman in uniform straight out that he was only pretending to be a civil councillor, that he was a rogue and a scoundrel, and that he was nothing else than his own nose . . . But the nose was no longer there; he had managed to gallop off, probably again to call on someone.

This reduced Kovalyov to despair. He went back and stood for a minute or two under the colonnade, carefully looking in all directions to see whether the nose was anywhere about. He remembered very well that there was a plume in his hat and gold lace on his uniform; but he had not noticed his greatcoat nor the colour of his carriage, nor his horses, nor even whether he had a footman behind him and if so in what livery. Moreover, such numbers of carriages were driving backwards and forwards and at such a speed that it was difficult even to distinguish them; and if he had distinguished one of them he would have had no means of stopping it. It was a lovely, sunny day. There were masses of people on Nevsky; ladies were scattered like a perfect cataract of flowers all over the pavement from Politseysky[134] to the Anitchkin Bridge.[135] Here he saw coming towards him an upper-court councillor of his acquaintance whom he used to call 'lieutenant-colonel,' particularly if he were speaking to other people. There he saw Yaryzhkin, a head clerk in the senate, a great friend of his, who always lost points when he went eight at boston.[136] And here was another major who had received the rank of assessor in the Caucasus, beckoning to him . . .

'Ah, deuce take it,' said Kovalyov. 'Hi, cab! Drive straight to the police-master's.'

Kovalyov got into a cab and shouted to the driver: 'Drive like a house on fire.'

'Is the police-master at home?' he cried, going into the entry.

'No,' answered the porter, 'he has only just gone out.'.

'Well, I declare!'

'Yes,' added the porter, 'and he has not been gone so long: if you had come but a tiny minute earlier you might have found him.'

Kovalyov, still keeping the handkerchief over his face, got into the cab and shouted in a voice of despair: 'Drive on.'

'Where?' asked the cabman.

'Drive straight on!'

'How straight on? Here's the turning, is it to right or to left?'

This question pulled Kovalyov up and forced him to think again. In his position he ought first of all to address himself to the department of law and order, not because it had any direct connection with the police but because the intervention of the latter might be far more rapid than any help he could get in other departments. To seek satisfaction from the higher officials of the department in which the nose had announced himself as serving would have been injudicious, since from the nose's own answers he had been able to perceive that nothing was sacred to that man and that he might tell lies in this case too, just as he had lied in declaring that he had never seen him before. And so Kovalyov was on the point of telling the cabman to drive to the police station, when again the idea occurred to him that this rogue and scoundrel who had at their first meeting behaved in such a shameless way might seize the opportunity and slip out of the town – and then all his searches would be in vain, or might be prolonged, which God forbid, for a whole month. At last it seemed that Heaven itself directed him. He decided to go straight to a newspaper office and without loss of time to publish a circumstantial description of the nose, so that any one meeting it might at once present it to him or at least let him know where it was. And so, deciding upon this course, he told the cabman to drive to the newspaper office, and all the way never ceased pommelling him with his fist on the back, saying as he did so, 'Quicker, you rascal; make haste, you knave!'

'Ugh, sir!' said the cabman, shaking his head and flicking with the reins at the horse, whose coat was as long as a lapdog's. At last the droshky stopped and Kovalyov ran panting into a little reception-room where a grey-headed clerk in spectacles, wearing an old tail coat, was sitting at a table and with a pen between his teeth was counting over some coppers he had before him.

'Who receives enquiries here?' cried Kovalyov. 'Ah, good-day!'

'I wish you good-day,' said the grey-headed clerk, raising his eyes for a moment and then dropping them again on the money lying in heaps on the table.

'I want to insert an advertisement . . . '

'Allow me to ask you to wait a minute,' the clerk pronounced, with one hand noting a figure on the paper and with the finger of his left hand moving two beads on the reckoning board. A flunkey with braid on his livery and a rather clean appearance, which betrayed that he had at some time served in an aristocratic family, was standing at the table with a written paper in his hand and thought fit to display his social abilities: 'Would you believe it, sir, that the little cur is not worth eighty kopecks; in fact I wouldn't give eight for it, but the countess is fond of it – my goodness, she is fond of it, and here she will give a hundred roubles to any one who finds it! To speak politely, as you and I are speaking now, people's tastes are quite incompatible: when a man's a sportsman then he'll keep a setter or a poodle; he won't mind giving five hundred or a thousand so long as it is a good dog.'

The worthy clerk listened to this with a significant air, and at the same time was reckoning the number of letters in the advertisement brought him. Along the sides of the room stood a number of old women, shop-boys, and house-porters who had brought advertisements. In one it was announced that a coachman of sober habits was looking for a situation; in the next a second-hand carriage brought from Paris in 1814 was offered for sale; next a maid-servant, aged nineteen, experienced in laundry work and also competent to do other work, was looking for a situation; a strong droshky with only one spring broken was for sale; a spirited, young, dappled grey horse, only seventeen years old, for sale;

a new consignment of turnip and radish seed from London; a summer villa with all conveniences, stabling for two horses, and a piece of land that might well be planted with fine birches and pine trees; there was also an appeal to those wishing to purchase old boot-soles, inviting such to come for the same every day between eight o'clock in the morning and three o'clock in the afternoon. The room in which all this company was assembled was a small one and the air in it was extremely thick, but the collegiate assessor Kovalyov was incapable of noticing the stench both because he kept his handkerchief over his face and because his nose was goodness knows where.

'Dear sir, allow me to ask you . . . my case is very urgent,' he said at last impatiently.

'In a minute, in a minute! . . . Two roubles, forty-three kopecks! . . . This minute! One rouble and sixty-four kopecks!' said the grey-headed gentleman, flinging the old women and house-porters the various documents they had brought. 'What can I do for you?' he said at last, turning to Kovalyov.

'I want to ask . . . ' said Kovalyov. 'Some robbery or trickery has occurred; I cannot make it out at all. I only want you to advertise that any one who brings me the scoundrel will receive a handsome reward.'

'Allow me to ask what is your surname?'

'No, why put my surname? I cannot give it you! I have a large circle of acquaintances: Madame Tchehtarev, wife of a civil councillor, Pelageya Grigoryevna Podtatchin, widow of an officer . . . they will find out. God forbid! You can simply put: "a collegiate assessor," or better still, "a person of major's rank." '

'Is the runaway your house-serf, then?'

'A house-serf indeed! that would not be so great a piece of knavery! It's my nose . . . has run away from me . . . my own nose.'

'H'm, what a strange surname! And is it a very large sum this Mr Nosov has robbed you of?'

'Nosov! . . . you are on the wrong tack. It is my nose, my own nose that has disappeared, I don't know where. The devil wanted to have a joke at my expense.'

'But in what way did it disappear? There is something I can't quite understand.'

'And indeed, I can't tell you how it happened; the point is that now it is driving about the town, calling itself a civil councillor. And so I beg you to announce that any one who catches him must bring him at once to me as quickly as possible. Only think, really, how can I get on without such a conspicuous part of my person. It's not like a little toe, the loss of which I could hide in my boot and no one could say whether it was there or not. I go on Thursdays to Madame Tchehtarev's; Pelageya Grigoryevna Podtatchin, an officer's widow, and her very pretty daughter are great friends of mine; and you can judge for yourself what a fix I am in now . . . I can't possibly show myself now . . . '

The clerk pondered, a fact which was manifest from the way he compressed his lips.

'No, I can't put an advertisement like that in the paper,' he said at last, after a long silence.

'What? Why not?'

'Well. The newspaper might lose its reputation. If every one is going to write that his nose has run away, why . . . As it is, they say we print lots of absurd things and false reports.'

'But what is there absurd about this? I don't see anything absurd in it.'

'You fancy there is nothing absurd in it? But last week, now, this was what happened. A government clerk came to me just as you have; he brought an advertisement, it came to two roubles seventy-three kopecks, and all the advertisement amounted to was that a poodle with a black coat had strayed. You wouldn't think that there was anything in that, would you? But it turned out to be a lampoon on someone: the poodle was the cashier of some department, I don't remember which.'

'But I am not asking you to advertise about poodles but about my own nose; that is almost the same as about myself.'

'No, such an advertisement I cannot insert.'

'But since my nose really is lost!'

'If it is lost that is a matter for the doctor. They say there are people who can fit you with a nose of any shape you like. But I observe you must be a gentleman of merry disposition and are fond of having your joke.'

'I swear as God is holy! If you like, since it has come to that, I will show you.'

'I don't want to trouble you,' said the clerk, taking a pinch of snuff. 'However, if it is no trouble,' he added, moved by curiosity, 'it might be desirable to have a look.'

The collegiate assessor took the handkerchief from his face. 'It really is extremely strange,' said the clerk, 'the place is perfectly flat, like a freshly fried pancake. Yes, it's incredibly smooth.'

'Will you dispute it now? You see for yourself I must advertise. I shall be particularly grateful to you and very glad this incident has given me the pleasure of your acquaintance.'

The major, as may be seen, made up his mind on this occasion to resort to a little flattery.

'To print such an advertisement is, of course, not such a very great matter,' said the clerk. 'But I do not foresee any advantage to you from it. If you do want to, put it in the hands of someone with a skilful pen, describe it as a rare freak of nature, and publish the little article in the *Northern Bee*' (at this point he once more took a pinch of snuff) 'for the benefit of youth' (at this moment he wiped his nose), 'or anyway as a matter of general interest.'

The collegiate assessor felt quite hopeless. He dropped his eyes and looked at the bottom of the paper where there was an announcement of an entertainment; his face was ready to break into a smile as he saw the name of a pretty actress, and his hand went to his pocket to feel whether he had a five-rouble note there, for an officer of his rank ought, in Kovalyov's opinion, to have a seat in the stalls; but the thought of his nose spoilt it all.

Even the clerk seemed touched by Kovalyov's difficult position. Desirous of relieving his distress in some way, he thought it befitting to express his sympathy in a few words: 'I am really very much grieved that such an incident should have occurred to you. Wouldn't you like a pinch of snuff? It relieves headache and dissipates depression; even in intestinal trouble it is of use.' Saying this the clerk offered Kovalyov his snuffbox, rather neatly opening the lid with a portrait of a lady in a hat on it.

This unpremeditated action drove Kovalyov out of all patience.

'I can't understand how you can think fit to make a joke of it,' he said angrily; 'don't you see that I am without just what I need for sniffing! The devil take your snuff! I can't bear the sight of it now, not merely your miserable Berezina snuff[137] but even if you were to offer me rappee itself!' Saying this he walked out of the newspaper office, deeply mortified, and went in the direction of the local police superintendent.

Kovalyov walked in at the very moment when he was stretching and clearing his throat and saying: 'Ah, I should enjoy a couple of hours' nap!' And so it might be foreseen that the collegiate assessor's visit was not very opportune. The police superintendent was a great patron of all arts and manufactures; but the paper note he preferred to everything. 'That is a thing,' he used to say, 'there is nothing better than that thing; it does not ask for food, it takes up little space, there is always room for it in the pocket, and if you drop it, it does not break.'

The police superintendent received Kovalyov rather coldly and said that after dinner was not the time to make an enquiry, that nature itself had ordained that man should rest a little after eating (the collegiate assessor could see from this that the sayings of the ancient sages were not unfamiliar to the local superintendent), and that a respectable man does not have his nose pulled off.

This was adding insult to injury. It must be said that Kovalyov was very easily offended. He could forgive anything whatever said about himself, but could never forgive insult to his rank or his calling. He was even of the opinion that any reference to officers of the higher ranks might be allowed to pass in stage plays, but that no attack ought to be made on those of a lower grade. The reception given him by the local superintendent so disconcerted him that he tossed his head and said with an air of dignity and a slight gesticulation of surprise: 'I must observe that after observations so insulting on your part I can add nothing more . . .' and went out.

He went home hardly conscious of the ground under his feet. By now it was dusk. His lodgings seemed to him melancholy or rather utterly disgusting after all these unsuccessful efforts. Going into his entry he saw his valet, Ivan, lying on his dirty leather sofa; he was spitting on the ceiling and rather successfully aiming at the same spot. The nonchalance of his servant enraged him; he hit him on the forehead with his hat, saying: 'You pig, you are always doing something stupid.' Ivan leapt up and rushed headlong to help him off with his cloak.

Going into his room, weary and dejected, the major threw himself into an easy chair, and at last, after several sighs, said: 'My God, my God! Why has this misfortune befallen me? If I had lost an arm or a leg – anyway it would have been better; but without a nose a man is goodness knows what: neither fish nor fowl nor human being, good for nothing but to fling out of window! And if only it had been cut off in battle or in a duel, or if I had been the cause of it myself, but, as it is, it is lost for no cause or reason, it is lost for nothing, absolutely nothing! But no, it cannot be,' he added after a moment's thought; 'it's incredible that a nose should be lost. It must be a dream or an illusion. Perhaps by some mistake I drank instead of water the vodka I use to rub my chin after shaving. Ivan, the fool, did not remove it and very likely I took it.' To convince himself that he was not drunk, the major pinched himself so painfully that he shrieked. The pain completely convinced him that he was living and acting in real life. He slowly approached the looking-glass and at first screwed up his eyes with the idea that maybe his nose would appear in its proper place; but at the same minute sprang back, saying: 'What a caricature.'

It really was incomprehensible; if a button had been lost or a silver spoon or a watch or anything similar – but to have lost this, and in one's own flat too! . . . Thinking over all the circumstances, Major Kovalyov reached the supposition that what might be nearest the truth was that the person responsible for this could be no other than Madame Podtatchin, who wanted him to marry her daughter. He himself liked flirting with her, but avoided a definite engagement. When the mother had informed him directly that she wished for the marriage, he had slyly put her off with his compliments, saying that he was still young, that he must serve for five years so as to be exactly forty-two. And that Madame Podtatchin had therefore made up her mind, probably out of revenge, to ruin him, and had hired for the purpose some peasant witches, because it was impossible to suppose that the nose had been cut off in any way; no one had come into his room; the barber Ivan Yakovlevitch had shaved him on Wednesday, and all Wednesday and even all Thursday his nose had been all right – that he remembered and was quite certain about; besides, he would have felt pain, and there could have been no doubt that the wound could not have healed so soon and been as flat as a pancake. He formed various plans in his mind: either to summon Madame Podtatchin formally before the court or to go to her himself and tax her with it. These reflections were interrupted by a light which gleamed through all the cracks of the door and let him know that a candle had been lighted in the entry by Ivan. Soon Ivan himself appeared, holding it before him and lighting up the whole room. Kovalyov's first movement was to snatch up his handkerchief and cover the place where yesterday his nose had been, that his really stupid servant might not gape at the sight of anything so peculiar in his master.

Ivan had hardly time to retreat to his lair when there was the sound of an unfamiliar voice in the entry, pronouncing the words: 'Does the collegiate assessor Kovalyov live here?'

'Come in, Major Kovalyov is here,' said Kovalyov, jumping up hurriedly and opening the door.

There walked in a police officer of handsome appearance, with whiskers neither too fair nor too dark, and rather fat cheeks, the very one who at the beginning of our story was standing at the end of St Isaac's Bridge.

'You have been pleased to lose your nose, sir?'

'That is so.'

'It is now found.'

'What are you saying?' cried Major Kovalyov. He could not speak for joy. He gazed open-eyed at the police officer standing before him, on whose full lips and cheeks the flickering light of the candle was brightly reflected. 'How?'

'By a strange chance: he was caught almost on the road. He had already taken his seat in the diligence and was intending to go to Riga, and had already taken a passport in the name of a government clerk. And the strange thing is that I myself took him for a gentleman at first, but fortunately I had my spectacles with me and I soon saw that it was a nose. You know I am short-sighted. And if you stand before me I only see that you have a face, but I don't notice your nose or your beard or anything. My mother-in-law, that is my wife's mother, doesn't see anything either.'

Kovalyov was beside himself with joy. 'Where? Where? I'll run at once.'

'Don't disturb yourself. Knowing that you were in need of it I brought it along with me. And the strange thing is that the man who has had the most to do with the affair is a rascal of a barber in Voznesensky Street, who is now in custody. I have long suspected him of drunkenness and thieving, and only the day before yesterday he carried off a strip of buttons from one shop. Your nose is exactly as it was.' With this the police officer put his hand in his pocket and drew out the nose just as it was.

'That's it!' Kovalyov cried. 'That's certainly it. You must have a cup of tea with me this evening.'

'I should look upon it as a great pleasure, but I can't possibly manage it: I have to go from here to the penitentiary . . . How the prices of all provisions are going up! . . . At home I have my mother-in-law, that is my wife's mother, and my children, the eldest particularly gives signs of great promise, he is a very intelligent child; but we have absolutely no means for his education . . . '

For some time after the policeman's departure the collegiate assessor remained in a state of bewilderment, and it was only a few minutes later that he was capable of feeling and understanding again: he was reduced to such stupefaction by this unexpected good fortune. He took the recovered nose carefully in his two hands, holding them together like a cup, and once more examined it attentively.

'Yes, that's it, it's certainly it,' said Major Kovalyov. 'There's the pimple that came out on the left side yesterday.' The major almost laughed aloud with joy.

But nothing in this world is of long duration, and so his joy was not so great the next moment; and the moment after, it was still less, and in the end he passed imperceptibly into his ordinary frame of mind, just as a circle on the water caused by a falling stone gradually passes away into the unbroken smoothness of the surface. Kovalyov began to think, and reflected that the business was not finished yet; the nose was found, but it had to be put on, fixed in its proper place.

'And what if it won't stick?' Asking himself this question, the major turned pale.

With a feeling of irrepressible terror he rushed to the table and moved the looking-glass forward that he might not put the nose on crooked. His hands trembled. Cautiously and circumspectly he replaced it in its former position. Oh horror, the nose would not stick on! . . . He put it to his lips, slightly warmed it with his breath, and again applied it to the flat space between his two cheeks; but nothing would make the nose keep on.

'Come, come, stick on, you fool!' he said to it; but the nose seemed made of wood and fell on the table with a strange sound as though it were a cork. The major's face worked convulsively.

'Is it possible that it won't grow on again?' But, however often he applied it to the proper place, the attempt was as unsuccessful as before.

He called Ivan and sent him for a doctor who tenanted the best flat on the first storey of the same house. The doctor was a handsome man, he had magnificent pitch-black whiskers, a fresh and healthy wife, ate fresh apples in the morning and kept his mouth extraordinarily clean, rinsing it out for nearly three-quarters of an hour every morning and cleaning his teeth with five different sorts of brushes. The doctor appeared immediately. Asking how long ago the trouble had occurred, he took Major Kovalyov by the chin and with his thumb gave him a flip on the spot where the nose had been making the major jerk back his head so abruptly that he knocked the back of it against the wall. The doctor said that that did not matter, and, advising him to move a little away from the wall, he told him to bend his head round first to the right, and feeling the place where the nose had been, said, 'H'm!' Then he told him to turn his head round to the left side and again said 'H'm!' And in conclusion he gave him again a flip with his thumb, so that Major Kovalyov threw up his head like a horse when his teeth are being looked at. After making this experiment the doctor shook his head and said: 'No, it's impossible. You had better stay as you are, for it may be made much worse. Of course, it might be stuck on; I could stick it on for you at once, if you like; but I assure you it would be worse for you.'

'That's a nice thing to say! How can I stay without a nose?' said Kovalyov. 'Things can't possibly be worse than now. It's simply beyond everything. Where can I show myself with such a caricature of a face? I have a good circle of acquaintances. Today, for instance, I ought to be at two evening parties. I know a great many people; Madame Tchehtarev, the wife of a civil councillor, Madame Podtatchin, an officer's widow . . . though after the way she has behaved, I'll have nothing more to do with her except through the police. Do me a favour,' Kovalyov went on in a supplicating voice; 'is there no means of sticking it on? Even if it were not neatly done, so long as it would keep on; I could even hold it on with my hand at critical moments. I wouldn't dance in any case for fear of a rash movement upsetting it. As for remuneration for your services, you may be assured that as far as my means allow . . . '

'Believe me,' said the doctor, in a voice neither loud nor low but persuasive and magnetic, 'that I never work from mercenary motives; that is opposed to my principles and my science. It is true that I accept a fee for my visits, but that is simply to avoid wounding my patients by refusing it. Of course I could replace your nose; but I assure you on my honour, since you do not believe my word, that it will be much worse for you. You had better wait for the action of nature itself. Wash it frequently with cold water, and I assure you that even without a nose you will be just as healthy as with one. And I advise you to put the nose in a bottle, in spirits or, better still, put two tablespoonfuls of sour vodka on it and heated vinegar – and then you might get quite a sum of money for it. I'd even take it myself, if you don't ask too much for it.'

'No, no, I wouldn't sell it for anything,' Major Kovalyov cried in despair; 'I'd rather it were lost than that!'

'Excuse me!' said the doctor, bowing himself out, 'I was trying to be of use to you . . . Well, there is nothing for it! Anyway, you see that I have done my best.' Saying this the doctor walked out of the room with a majestic air. Kovalyov did not notice his face, and, almost lost to consciousness, saw nothing but the cuffs of his clean and snow-white shirt peeping out from the sleeves of his black tail coat.

Next day he decided, before lodging a complaint with the police, to write to Madame Podtatchin to see whether she would consent to return him what was needful without a struggle. The letter was as follows:

DEAR MADAM ALEXANDRA GRIGORYEVNA – I cannot understand this strange conduct on your part. You may rest assured that you will gain nothing by what you have done, and you will not get a step nearer forcing me to marry your daughter. Believe me, that business in regard to my nose is no secret, no more than it is that you and no other are the person chiefly responsible. The sudden parting of the same from its natural position, its flight and masquerading, at one time in the form of a government clerk and finally in its own shape, is nothing else than the consequence of the sorceries practised by you or by those who are versed in the same honourable arts as you are. For my part I consider it my duty to warn you, if the above-mentioned nose is not in its proper place today, I shall be obliged to resort to the assistance and protection of the law.

I have, however, with complete respect to you, the honour to be

Your respectful servant,

PLATON KOVALYOV

DEAR SIR, PLATON KUZMITCH! – Your letter greatly astonished me. I must frankly confess that I did not expect it, especially in regard to your unjust reproaches. I assure you I have never received the government clerk of whom you speak in my house, neither in masquerade nor in his own attire. It is true that Filipp Ivanovitch Potantchikov has been to see me, and although, indeed, he is asking me for my daughter's hand and is a well conducted, sober man of great learning, I have never encouraged his hopes. You make some reference to your nose also. If you wish me to understand by that that you imagine that I meant to make a long nose at you, that is, to give you a formal refusal, I am surprised that you should speak of such a thing when, as you know perfectly well, I was quite of the opposite way of thinking, and if you are courting my daughter with a view to lawful matrimony I am ready to satisfy you immediately, seeing that has always been the object of my keenest desires, in the hope of which I remain always ready to be of service to you.

ALEXANDRA PODTATCHIN

'No,' said Kovalyov to himself after reading the letter, 'she really is not to blame. It's impossible. The letter is written as it could not be written by any one guilty of a crime.' The collegiate assessor was an expert on this subject, as he had been sent several times to the Caucasus to conduct investigations. 'In what way, by what fate, has this happened? Only the devil could make it out!' he said at last, letting his hands fall to his sides.

Meanwhile the rumours of this strange occurrence were spreading all over the town, and of course not without especial additions. Just at that time the minds of all were particularly interested in the marvellous: experiments in the influence of magnetism had been attracting public attention only recently.[138] Moreover, the story of the dancing chair in

Konyushenny Street[139] was still fresh, and so there is nothing to be surprised at in the fact that people were soon beginning to say that the nose of a collegiate assessor called Kovalyov was walking along Nevsky Prospect at exactly three in the afternoon. Numbers of inquisitive people flocked there every day. Somebody said that the nose was in Yunker's shop – and near Yunker's there was such a crowd and such a crush that the police were actually obliged to intervene. One speculator, a man of dignified appearance with whiskers, who used to sell all sorts of cakes and tarts at the doors of the theatres, made purposely some very strong wooden benches, which he offered to the curious to stand on, for eighty kopecks each. One very worthy colonel left home earlier on account of it, and with a great deal of trouble made his way through the crowd; but to his great indignation, instead of the nose, he saw in the shop-windows the usual woollen vest and a lithograph depicting a girl pulling up her stocking while a foppish young man, with a waistcoat with revers and a small beard, peeps at her from behind a tree; a picture which had been hanging in the same place for more than ten years. As he walked away he said with vexation: 'How can people be led astray by such stupid and incredible stories!' Then rumour would have it that it was not on Nevsky Prospect but in the Tavritchesky Park[140] that Major Kovalyov's nose took its walks abroad; that it had been there for ever so long; that, even when Hozrev-Mirza[141] used to live there, he was greatly surprised at this strange freak of nature. Several students from the Academy of Surgery made their way to the park. One worthy lady of high rank wrote a letter to the superintendent of the park asking him to show her children this rare phenomenon with, if possible, an explanation that should be edifying and instructive for the young.

All the gentlemen who invariably attend social gatherings and like to amuse the ladies were extremely thankful for all these events, for their stock of anecdotes was completely exhausted. A small group of worthy and well-intentioned persons were greatly displeased. One gentleman said with indignation that he could not understand how in the present enlightened age people could spread abroad these absurd inventions, and that he was surprised that the government took no notice of it. This gentleman, as may be seen, belonged to the number of those who would like the government to meddle in everything, even in their daily quarrels with their wives. After this . . . but here again the whole adventure is lost in fog, and what happened afterwards is absolutely unknown.

3

What is utterly nonsensical happens in the world. Sometimes there is not the slightest resemblance to truth about it: all at once that very nose which had been driving about the place in the form of a civil councillor, and had made such a stir in the town, turned up again as though nothing had happened, in its proper place, that is, precisely between the two cheeks of Major Kovalyov. This took place on the seventh of April. Waking up and casually glancing into the looking-glass, he sees – his nose! Puts up his hands, actually his nose! 'Aha!' said Kovalyov, and in his joy he almost danced a jig barefoot about his room; but the entrance of Ivan checked him. He ordered the latter to bring him water at once, and as he washed he glanced once more into the looking-glass – the nose! As he wiped himself with the towel he glanced again into the looking-glass – the nose!

'Look, Ivan, I fancy I have a pimple on my nose,' he said, while he thought: 'How dreadful if Ivan says "No, indeed, sir, there's no pimple and, indeed, there is no nose either!"'

But Ivan said: 'There is nothing, there is no pimple: your nose is quite clear!'

'Good, dash it all!' the major said to himself, and he snapped his fingers.

At that moment Ivan Yakovlevitch the barber peeped in at the door, but as timidly as a cat who has just been beaten for stealing the bacon.

'Tell me first: are your hands clean?' Kovalyov shouted to him while he was still some way off.

'Yes.'

'You are lying!'

'Upon my word, they are clean, sir.'

'Well, mind now.'

Kovalyov sat down. Ivan Yakovlevitch covered him up with a towel, and in one instant with the aid of his brushes had smothered the whole of his beard and part of his cheek in cream, like that which is served at merchants' name-day parties.[142]

'My eye!' Ivan Yakovlevitch said to himself, glancing at the nose and then turning his customer's head on the other side and looking at it sideways. 'There it is, sure enough. What can it mean?' He went on pondering, and for a long while he gazed at the nose. At last, lightly, with a cautiousness which may well be imagined, he raised two fingers to take it by the tip. Such was Ivan Yakovlevitch's system.

'Now, now, now, mind!' cried Kovalyov. Ivan Yakovlevitch let his hands drop, and was flustered and confused as he had never been confused before. At last he began circumspectly tickling him with the razor under his beard, and, although it was difficult and not at all handy for him to shave without holding on to the olfactory portion of the face, yet he did at last somehow, pressing his rough thumb into his cheek and lower jaw, overcome all difficulties, and finish shaving him.

When it was all over, Kovalyov at once made haste to dress, took a cab, and drove to the confectioner's shop. Before he was inside the door he shouted: 'Waiter, a cup of chocolate!' and at the same instant peeped at himself in the looking-glass. The nose was there. He turned round gaily and, with a satirical air, slightly screwing up his eyes, looked at two military men, one of whom had a nose hardly bigger than a waistcoat button. After that he set off for the office of the department, in which he was urging his claims to a post as vice-governor or, failing that, the post of an executive clerk. After crossing the waiting-room he glanced at the mirror; the nose was there. Then he drove to see another collegiate assessor or major, who was much given to making fun of people, and to whom he often said in reply to various sharp observations: 'There you are, I know you, you are as sharp as a pin!' On the way he thought: 'If even the major does not split with laughter when he sees me, then it is a sure sign that everything is in its place.' But the sarcastic collegiate assessor said nothing. 'Good, good, dash it all!' Kovalyov thought to himself. On the way he met Madame Podtatchin with her daughter; he was profuse in his bows to them and was greeted with exclamations of delight – so there could be nothing amiss with him, he thought. He conversed with them for a long time and, taking out his snuffbox, purposely put a pinch to each nostril while he said to himself: 'So much for you, you petticoats, you hens! But I am not going to marry your daughter all the same. Just simply *par amour* – I dare say!'

And from that time forth Major Kovalyov promenaded about, as though nothing had happened, on Nevsky Prospect, and at the theatres and everywhere. And the nose, too, as though nothing had happened, sat on his face without even a sign of coming off at the sides. And after this Major Kovalyov was always seen in a good humour, smiling, resolutely pursuing all the pretty ladies, and even on one occasion stopping before a shop in Gostiny Dvor[143] and buying the ribbon of some order, I cannot say with what object, since he was not himself a cavalier of any order.

So this is the strange event that occurred in the Northern capital of our spacious empire! Only now, on thinking it all over, we perceive that there is a great deal that is improbable in it. Apart from the fact that it certainly is strange for a nose supernaturally to leave its place and to appear in various places in the guise of a civil councillor – how was it that Kovalyov did not grasp that he could not advertise about his nose in a newspaper office? I do not mean to say that I should think it too expensive to advertise: that is nonsense, and I am by no means a mercenary person: but it is unseemly, awkward, not nice! And again: how did the nose come into the loaf, and how about Ivan Yakovlevitch himself? . . . no, that I cannot understand, I am absolutely unable to understand it! But what is stranger, what is more incomprehensible than anything is that authors can choose such subjects. I confess that is quite beyond my grasp, it really is . . . No, no! I cannot understand it at all. In the place, it is absolutely without profit to the fatherland; in the second place . . . but in the second place, too, there is no profit. I really do not know what to say of it . . .

And yet, with all that, though of course one may admit the first point, the second and the third . . . may even . . . but there, are there not inconsequences everywhere? – and yet, when you think it over, there really is something in it. Whatever any one may say, such things do happen – not often, but they do happen.

THE PORTRAIT

1

NOWHERE did so many people pause as before the little picture-shop in Shtchukinui Dvor.[144] This little shop offered, in fact, the most varied collection of curiosities. The pictures were principally in oil, covered with dark-green varnish, in tinsel frames of a dull yellow. Winter scenes with white trees; very red sunsets, like raging conflagrations; a Flemish boor, with pipe and crippled hand, more like a turkey-cock in cuffs than a human being – these were the prevailing subjects. To these must be added a few engravings – a portrait of Khozreff-Mirza in a sheepskin cap, and portraits of some generals or other with three-cornered hats and hooked noses. Moreover, the doors of such booths are usually festooned with bundles of publications,[145] printed on large sheets of bark, which bear witness to the native talent of the Russian.

On one was the Tzarevna Miliktrisa Kirbitievna;[146] on another the city of Jerusalem, over whose houses and churches spread red paint, embracing in its sweep a part of the ground, and two praying Russian muzhiks in their shirt-sleeves. There are usually but few purchasers of these productions, but the gazers were many. Some truant lackey probably yawned before them, holding in his hand the dishes containing dinner from the cook-shop for his master, who would doubtless not get his soup very hot. Before them, too, would probably be standing a soldier wrapped in his cloak – that cavalier of the old-clothes' mart, with two penknives for sale – and Okhtenka, the huckstress, with her basketful of shoes. Each expresses his admiration in his own fashion. The muzhiks generally touch them with their fingers; the cavaliers gaze seriously at them; serving-boys and apprentices laugh, and tease each other with the coloured caricatures; old lackeys in frieze mantles look at them merely for the sake of yawning away their time somewhere; and the hucksters, young Russian women, halt by instinct to hear what people are gossiping about, and to see what they are looking at.

At the time when our story opens, the young painter, Tchartkoff, paused involuntarily as he passed the shop. His old cloak and un-dandified attire showed him to be a man who was devoted to his art with self-denying zeal, and who had no time to trouble himself about clothes, which always have a secret attraction for young men. He paused before the little shop, and at first enjoyed an inward laugh over the monstrosities of pictures. At length he sank unconsciously into a reverie, and began to ponder on the question, What sort of people wanted these productions? It did not seem remarkable to him that the Russian people should gaze with rapture upon *Eruslanoff Lazarevitch*, on *The Glutton* and *The Carouser*, on *Thoma and Erema*. The delineations of those subjects were sufficient and very easily intelligible to the masses. But where were there purchasers for those streaky, dirty oil-paintings? Who needed those Flemish boors,[147] those red and blue landscapes, which put forth some claims to a higher stage of art, but which expressed all the depths of its degradation? They did not appear in the least like the works of a self-taught child. In that case, in spite of the intentional caricature of the design, a sharp distinction would have manifested itself. But here were visible only simple dulness, weak, faltering incapacity, which stood, through self-will, in the ranks of art, while its true place was among the lowest trades – an incapacity which was true, never-theless, to its vocation, and dragged its trade into art. The same colours, the same manner, the same driving, practised hand, belonging rather to a manufactured automaton than to a man!

He stood long before the dirty pictures, thinking not at all of them at length; but meanwhile the proprietor of the stall, a little grey man, in a frieze cloak, with a beard which had not been shaved since Sunday, had been nudging him for some time, bartering and settling on prices, without even knowing what pleased him, or what he wanted. 'Here, I'll take a silver piece for these peasants and this little landscape. What painting! it fairly puts your eyes out; only just received from the factory; the varnish isn't dry yet. Or, here is a winter scene – take the winter scene; fifteen roubles; the frame alone is worth it. What a winter scene!' Here the merchant gave a light fillip to the canvas, as if to demonstrate all the merits of the winter scene. 'Pray have them done up and sent to your house. Where do you live? Here, boy, give me some string!'

'Hold, brother, not so fast!' said the painter, coming to himself, and perceiving that the brisk dealer was beginning in earnest to do them up. He was rather ashamed not to take any thing after standing so long at the stall; and he said, 'Here, stop! I will see if there is anything I want here'; and, bending over, he began to pick up from the floor, where they were thrown in a heap, worn, dusty old paintings, which evidently commanded no respect. There were old family portraits, whose descendants, probably, could not be found on earth; totally unknown pictures, with torn canvas; frames minus their gilding; in a word, all sorts of old trash. But the painter began his search, thinking to himself, 'Perhaps I may find something.' He had often heard stories about pictures of the great masters having been found among the rubbish at the cheap print-sellers' shops.

The dealer, perceiving what he was about, ceased his importunities, and, assuming his usual attitude and the accompanying expression, took up his post again at the door, hailing the passers-by, and pointing to his stall with one hand. 'Hither, friends, here are pictures; enter, enter; just received from the makers!' He shouted his fill, and generally in vain: he had a long talk with a rag-merchant standing opposite, also at the door of his stall; and finally, recollecting that he had a customer in his shop, he turned his back on the public, and went inside. 'Well, my friend, have you chosen anything?' But the painter had already been standing for some time immovable before a portrait in a large, originally magnificent, frame, but upon which hardly a trace of gilding now remained.

It represented an old man, with a thin, bronzed face and high cheek-bones; it seemed as if the features were depicted in a moment of convulsive agitation, and bespoke an un-northern power; the burning south was stamped upon them. He was muffled in a voluminous Asiatic costume. Dusty and defaced as the portrait was, when he had succeeded in removing the dirt from the face, he saw traces of the work of a great artist. The portrait appeared to be unfinished, but the power of the handling was striking. The eyes were the most remarkable of all: it seemed as though the full power of the artist's brush and all his care had been lavished upon them. They fairly looked, gazed, out of the portrait, destroying its harmony with their strange liveliness. When he carried the portrait to the door, the eyes glanced even more penetratingly. They produced nearly the same impression on the public. A woman standing behind him exclaimed, 'He looks, he looks!' and jumped back. He experienced an unpleasant feeling, inexplicable even to himself, and put the portrait on the floor.

'How? You take the portrait?' said the dealer.

'How much is it?' said the painter.

'Why chaffer over it? Give me seventy-five kopecks.'

'No.'

'Well, how much will you give?'

'Twenty kopecks,' said the painter, preparing to go.

'What a price! Why, you couldn't buy the frame for that! Perhaps you will decide to purchase tomorrow. Sir, sir, turn back! Add ten kopecks. Take it, take it! give me a white note.[148] To tell the truth, you are my first customer, and that's the only reason.' Then he made a gesture, as if to signify, 'So be it; let the picture go!'

Thus Tchartkoff quite unexpectedly purchased the old portrait, and at the same time reflected, 'Why have I bought it? What is it to me?' But there was nothing to be done. He pulled the twenty-kopeck piece from his pocket, gave it to the merchant, took the portrait under his arm, and carried it home. On the way thither, he remembered that the twenty-kopeck piece he had given for it was his last. His thoughts at once grew dark. Vexation and careless indifference took possession of him at one and the same moment. 'Devil take it! This world is disagreeable enough!' he said, with the feeling of a Russian whose affairs are going wrong. And almost mechanically he went on at a quickened pace, filled with indifference to everything. The red light of sunset still lingered in half the sky; the houses facing that way still almost gleamed with its warm light; and meanwhile the cold blue light of the moon grew brighter. Light, half-transparent shadows fell in bands upon the ground, broken by the houses and the feet of the pedestrians. The painter began by degrees to glance up at the sky, flushed with a thin, transparent, dubious light; and nearly at the same moment from his mouth fell the words, 'What a delicate tone!' and the words, 'What a nuisance! Deuce take it!' and, readjusting the portrait, which slipped from under his arm incessantly, he quickened his pace.

Weary, bathed in perspiration, he dragged himself to the fifteenth line, on Vasilievsky Island.[149] With difficulty and much panting he made his way up the stairs flooded with soapsuds, and adorned with the tracks of dogs and cats. To his knock on the door, there was no answer: there was no one at home. He leaned against the window, and disposed himself to wait patiently, until at last there resounded behind him the footsteps of a boy in a blue blouse – his servant, model, colour-grinder, and scrubber of floors, who also dirtied them with his boots. The boy was called Nikita, and spent all his time in the streets when his master was not at home. Nikita tried for a long time to get the key into the lock, which was quite invisible, by reason of the darkness.

Finally the door was opened. Tchartkoff entered his ante-room, which was intolerably cold, as painters' rooms always are, which fact, moreover, they do not notice. Without giving Nikita his coat, he went into his studio, a large, square, but low apartment, with frozen windows, and fitted up with all sorts of artistic rubbish – bits of plaster hands, canvas stretched on frames, sketches begun and discarded, and draperies thrown over chairs. He was very tired: he threw off his cloak, placed the portrait abstractedly between two small canvases, and threw himself on the narrow divan, of which it was impossible to say that it was covered with leather, because a row of brass nails, which had formerly fastened it, had long been left alone by themselves, and the leather remained above by itself; so that Nikita was in the habit of stuffing dirty stockings, shirts, and all the soiled linen, under it. Having seated himself, and stretched himself, as much as it was possible to stretch, on the narrow divan, he finally called for a light.

'There are no candles,' said Nikita.

'How, none?'

'And there were none last night,' said Nikita. The artist recollected that, in fact, there had been no candles the previous evening, quieted down, and became silent. He let himself be undressed, and put on his old, much-worn dressing-gown.

'There has been a gentleman here,' said Nikita.

'Well, he came for money, I know,' said the painter, waving his hand.

'Yes, and he was not alone,' said Nikita.

'Who else?'

'I don't know – some policeman or other.'

'But why a policeman?'

'I don't know why: he says because your rent is not paid.'

'Well, what will come of it?'

'I don't know what will come of it: he said, "If he won't pay, why, let him leave the rooms." They are both coming again tomorrow.'

'Let them come,' said Tchartkoff, with sad indifference; and that gloomy mood took full possession of him.

Young Tchartkoff was an artist of talent, which promised great things: by fits and starts his work gave evidence of observation, thought, and a strong inclination to approach nearer to nature.

'Look here, my friend,' his professor said to him more than once, 'you have talent; it will be a shame if you waste it: but you are impatient; you have but to be attracted by a thing, to fall in love with a thing – you are all engrossed with it, and everything else is rubbish, all else goes for nothing, you won't even look at it. See to it that you do not become a fashionable artist: at present your colours begin to assert themselves too loudly; your drawing is not strong; at times it is quite weak – no lines are to be seen: you are already striving after the fashionable light, because it strikes the eye at once . . . See, you fall into the English style[150] as if on purpose. Have a care! the world already begins to attract you: I have already seen you with a shiny hat, a foppish neckerchief . . . It is seductive; it is possible to allow one's self to paint fashionable little pictures and portraits for money; but talent is ruined, not developed, by that means. Be patient; think out every piece of work; discard your foppishness; let others amass money, your own will not fail you.'

The professor was partly right. Our artist sometimes wanted to carouse, to play the fop, in a word, to exhibit his youth in some way or other; but he could control himself withal. At times he could forget everything, when he had once taken his brush in hand, and could not tear himself from it except as from a delightful dream. His taste perceptibly developed. He did not as yet understand all the depths of Raphael,[151] but he was attracted by Guido's[152] broad and rapid handling, he paused before the portraits by Titian,[153] he delighted in the Flemish masters. The dark veil enshrouding the ancient pictures had not yet passed away from before them; but he already saw something in them, though in private he did not agree with the professor that the old masters are irremediably lost to us: it seemed to him that the nineteenth century had improved upon them considerably, that the delineation of nature had become clearer, more vivid, nearer; in a word, he thought on this point as youth does think, having already accomplished something, and recognising it with internal pride. It sometimes vexed him when he saw how a strange artist, French or German, sometimes not even a painter by profession, but only a skilful dauber, produced, by the celerity of his brush and the vividness of his colouring, a universal commotion, and amassed in a twinkling a funded capital. This did not occur to him when, fully occupied with his own work, he forgot food and drink and all the world: but when dire want arrived, when he had no money wherewith to buy brushes and colours, when his implacable landlord came ten times a day to demand the pay for his rooms, then did the luck of the wealthy artists present itself to his hungry imagination; then did the thought which so often traverses Russian minds, traverse his – to give up altogether, and go down hill, and utterly to the bad. And now he was almost in this frame of mind.

'Yes, be patient, be patient!' he exclaimed with vexation; 'but there is an end to patience at last. Be patient! but what money am I to dine with tomorrow? No one will lend me any. If I bring myself to sell all my pictures and sketches, they would give me twenty kopecks for the whole of them. They are useful; I feel that not one of them was undertaken in vain; I learned something from each one. Yes, but of what use? Studies, trial-sketches – and all will be studies, trial-sketches – and there will be no end to them. And who will buy, knowing me not even by name? Yes, and who wants drawings from the antique, or the life class, or my unfinished love of a Psyche, or the perspective of my chamber, or the portrait of my Nikita, though it is better, to tell the truth, than the portraits by any of the fashionable artists? In fact, what does it mean? Why do I worry, and toil like a learner over the alphabet, when I might shine as brightly as the rest, and have money, too, like them?'

Thus speaking, the artist suddenly shuddered, and turned pale: a convulsively distorted face gazed at him, peeping forth from the surrounding canvas; two terrible eyes were fixed straight upon him, as if preparing to devour him; on the mouth was written a menacing command of silence. Frightened, he tried to scream and summon Nikita, who had already succeeded in setting up a gigantic snoring in his ante-room; but he suddenly paused and laughed; the sensation of fear subsided in a moment; it was the portrait he had bought, and which he had quite forgotten. The light of the moon, illuminating the chamber, fell upon it, and lent it a strange likeness to life. He began to examine and wipe it off. He moistened a sponge with water, passed it over the picture several times, washed off nearly all the accumulated and encrusted dust and dirt, hung it on the wall before him, and wondered yet more at the remarkable workmanship: almost the whole face had gained new life, and the eyes gazed at him so that he shuddered at last; and, springing back, he exclaimed in a voice of surprise, 'It looks, it looks, with human eyes!' Then suddenly there came to his mind a story he had heard long before from his professor, of a certain portrait by the renowned Leonardo da Vinci,[154] upon which the great master laboured several years, and still held it incomplete, and which, according to Vasari,[155] was nevertheless deemed by all the most complete and finished product of his art. The most finished thing about it was the eyes, which amazed his contemporaries: the very smallest, barely visible veins in them were not omitted, but committed to the canvas. But here, in the portrait now before him, there was something singular. This was no longer art: it even destroyed the harmony of the portrait; they were living, human eyes! It seemed as though they had been cut from a living man, and inserted there. Here was none of that high enjoyment which takes possession of the spirit at the sight of an artist's production, no matter how terrible the subject he may have chosen: there was a painful, fatiguing sensation here. 'What is it?' the artist asked himself involuntarily; 'but this is nature, nevertheless, living nature. Whence this strangely unpleasant feeling? Is a slavish, literal copy of nature a crime which proclaims itself in a shrill, discordant shriek? If you take an unsympathetic subject, one void of feeling, having no sympathy with it yourself, will it infallibly stand forth, in its fearful realism, unillumined by any intangible, hidden light, to the thoughts of all? Will it stand forth in such realism as is displayed, when, wishing to understand the secret of a very handsome man, you arm yourself with an anatomical knife, cut to his heart, and behold a hideous man? Why does simple, lowly Nature reveal herself in the works of one artist in such a light that you experience no sensation of degradation – on the contrary, you seem to enjoy it for some reason, and things seem to flow more quietly and smoothly around you after it? And why does this same Nature seem, in the hands of another artist, low and vile? Yet he was true to Nature too. But, no, there is nothing illuminating in her. It makes no difference what aspect Nature wears: however magnificent she may be, there is always something wanting, unless the sun is in the sky.'

Again he approached the portrait, in order to view those wondrous eyes, and perceived with terror that they were gazing at him. This was no copy from Nature: it was life, the strange life which might have lighted up the face of a dead man, who had risen from the grave. Whether it was the effect of the moonlight, which brought with it fantastic thoughts, and transformed things into strange likenesses, opposed to those of matter-of-fact day, or from some other cause, it suddenly became frightful to him, he knew not why, to sit alone in the room. He retreated softly from the portrait, turned aside, and tried not to look at it; but his eye involuntarily, of its own accord, glanced sideways, and watched it. Finally, he became afraid to walk about the room: it seemed as though someone were on the point of stepping up behind him; and every time he turned, he glanced timidly back. He had never been cowardly; but his imagination and nerves were sensitive, and that evening he could not explain his involuntary fear. He seated himself in the corner, but even then it seemed to him that someone was peeping over his shoulder into his face. Even Nikita's snores, resounding from the ante-room, did not chase away his fear. At length he rose from his seat, timidly, without raising his eyes, went behind his screen, and lay down on his bed. Through the cracks of the screen he saw his room illuminated by the moon, and saw the portrait hanging stiffly on the wall. The eyes were fixed upon him in a still more terrible and significant manner, and it seemed as if they would not look at anything but him. Overpowered with a feeling of oppression, he decided to rise from his bed, seized a sheet, and, approaching the portrait, covered it up completely.

Having done this, he lay down more quietly on the bed, and began to meditate upon the poverty and pitiful lot of the artist, of the thorny path before him in the world; but, meanwhile, his eye glanced involuntarily through the joint of the screen, at the portrait muffled in the sheet. The light of the moon heightened the whiteness of the sheet, and it seemed to him as though those terrible eyes shone through the cloth. With terror he fixed his eyes more steadfastly on it, as if wishing to convince himself that it was all nonsense. But at length, in fact . . . he sees, sees clearly: there is no longer a sheet . . . the portrait is quite uncovered, and gazes past everything around it, straight at him; gazes fairly into his heart . . . His heart grows cold. And he sees: the old man has moved, and suddenly, supporting himself on the frame with both arms, has raised himself by his hands, and, putting forth both feet, has leaped out of the frame . . . Through the crack of the screen, the empty frame alone was now visible. Footsteps resounded in the room, and they approached nearer and nearer to the screen. The poor artist's heart began to beat harder. He expected every moment, his breath failing for fear, that the old man would look round the screen at him. And lo! he did look behind the screen, with the very same bronzed face, and with his big eyes roving about. Tchartkoff tried to scream, and felt that his voice was gone; he tried to move, to make a gesture; his limbs refused their office. With open mouth, and failing breath, he gazed at the terrible, tall phantom, in some sort of a voluminous Asiatic robe, and waited for what it would do. The old man sat down almost on his very feet, and then pulled out something from among the folds of his wide garment: it was a purse. The old man untied it, seized it by both ends, and shook it. Heavy rolls of money, like long pillars, fell out with a dull thud upon the floor: each was wrapped in blue paper, and on each was marked, '1,000 ducats'. The old man extended his long, bony hand from his wide sleeves, and began to undo the rolls. The gold glittered. Great as was the artist's unreasoning fear, and feeling of oppression, he bent all his attention upon the gold, gazing motionless, as it made its appearance in the bony hands, gleamed, rang lightly or dully, and was wrapped up again. Then he perceived one packet which had rolled farther than the rest, to the very leg of his bedstead, near his pillow. He grasped it almost convulsively, and glanced in fear at the old man to see if he perceived it. But the old man appeared very much occupied: he collected all his rolls, replaced them in the purse, and went outside the screen without looking at him. Tchartkoff's heart beat wildly as he heard the rustle of the retreating footsteps sounding through the room. He clasped his roll more closely in his hand, quivering in every limb; and suddenly he heard the footsteps approaching the screen again . . . Apparently the old man had recollected that one roll was missing. And lo! again he looked round the screen at him. The artist in despair grasped the roll with all his strength, exerted all his power to make a movement, shrieked – and awoke.

He was bathed in a cold perspiration; his heart beat as hard as it was possible for it to beat; his chest was oppressed, as though his last breath was about to fly from it. 'Was it a dream?' he said, seizing his head with both hands. But the terrible life-likeness of the apparition did not resemble a dream. As he woke, he saw the old man step into the frame: the skirts of the voluminous garment even fluttered, and his hand felt plainly that a moment before it had held something heavy. The moonlight illumined the room, bringing out from the dark corners, here a canvas, there the model of a hand; a drapery thrown over a chair; trousers and uncleaned boots. Then he perceived that he was not lying in his bed, but standing upright, directly before the portrait. How he had come there, he could not in the least comprehend. Still more surprised was he, to find the portrait quite uncovered, and there actually was no sheet over it. Motionless with terror, he gazed at it, and perceived that the living, human eyes were fastened upon him. A cold perspiration started out upon his face. He wanted to move away, but felt that his feet had in some way become rooted to the earth. And he saw – that this was not a dream. The old man's features moved, and his lips began to project towards him, as though he wanted to suck him in ... With a yell of despair he jumped back – and awoke.

'Was it a dream?' With his heart beating to bursting, he felt about him with both hands. Yes, he was lying in bed, and in precisely the position in which he had fallen asleep. Before him stood the screen. The moonlight flooded the apartment. Through the crack of the screen, the portrait was visible, covered with the sheet, as it should be, just as he had covered it. And so this, too, was a dream? But his clenched fist still felt as though something had been in it. The beating of his heart was violent, almost terrible; the weight upon his breast, intolerable. He fixed his eyes upon the crack, and stared steadfastly at the sheet. And lo! he sees plainly how the sheet begins to open, as though hands were pushing from underneath, and trying to throw it off. 'Lord God, what is it!' he shrieked, crossing himself in despair – and awoke.

And was this also a dream? He sprang from his bed, frantic, half mad, and could not comprehend what had happened to him: was it the oppression of a nightmare, or *domovoi*,[156] the raving of fever, or a living apparition? Striving to calm, as far as possible, his mental tumult, and wildly rushing blood, which beat with straining pulses in every vein, he went to the window, and opened the pane. The cool, fragrant breeze revived him. The moonlight lay on all the roofs and white walls of the houses, though small clouds passed frequently across the sky. All was still: from time to time there struck the ear, the distant rumble of a drozhky, whose driver was sleeping in some obscure alley, lulled to slumber by his lazy nag, as he awaited a belated passenger. He put his head out of the pane, and gazed long. Already the signs of approaching dawn were spreading in the sky. At last he felt drowsy, clapped to the pane, stepped back, lay down in bed, and quickly fell, like one exhausted, into a deep sleep.

He awoke late, and with the disagreeable feeling of a man who has been choked with coal-gas: his head ached painfully. The room was dim: an unpleasant humidity pervaded the air, and penetrated the cracks of his windows, stopped with pictures and grounded canvas. Dissatisfied and depressed as a wet cock, he seated himself on his dilapidated divan, not knowing what to do, what to undertake, and at length remembered all his dream. As he recalled it, the dream presented itself to his mind as so oppressively real that he even began to wonder whether it were a dream, and simple delirium, whether there were not something else here, whether it were not an apparition. Removing the sheet, he looked at the terrible portrait by the light of day. The eyes were really striking in their extraordinary liveliness, but he found nothing particularly terrible in them; yet an indescribably unpleasant feeling lingered in his mind. Nevertheless, he could not quite convince himself that it was a dream. It struck him that there must have been some terrible fragment of reality in the midst of the dream. It seemed as though there were something in the old man's very glance and expression which said that he had been with him that night: his hand felt the weight which had so recently lain in it as if someone had but just snatched it from him. It seemed to him, that, if he had only grasped the roll more firmly, it would have remained in his hand, even after his awakening.

'My God, if I had only a portion of that money!' he said, breathing heavily; and in his fancy, all those rolls, with their fascinating inscription, '*1,000 ducats*', began to pour out of the purse. The rolls opened, the gold glittered, was wrapped up again; and he sat motionless, with his eyes fixed on the empty air, as if he were incapable of tearing himself from such a sight, like a child who sits before a plate of sweets, and beholds, with watering mouth, other people devouring them.

At last there came a knock on the door, which recalled him unpleasantly to himself. The landlord entered with the constable of the district, whose presence, as is well known, is even more disagreeable to poor people than is the presence of a beggar to the rich. The landlord of the little house in which Tchartkoff lived resembled the other individuals who own houses anywhere in the fifteenth line of Vasilievsky Island, on the Petersburg side, or in the distant regions of Kolomna[157] – individuals of which there are many in Russia, and whose character is as difficult to define as the colour of a threadbare surtout. In his youth he had been a captain and a braggart, had served in the civil service, was a master in the art of flogging, was skilful and foppish and stupid; but in his old age he combined all these various qualities into a kind of dim indefiniteness. He was a widower, already on the retired list, no longer boasted, nor was dandified, no longer quarrelled, and loved only to drink tea and talk all sorts of nonsense over it; he walked about his room, and arranged the ends of the tallow candles; punctually at the end of each month he called upon his lodgers for his money; went out into the street, with the key in his hand, to look at the roof of his house, and sometimes chased the *dvornik* (porter) out of his kennel, where he had hidden himself to sleep; in a word, he was a man on the retired list, who, after the turmoils and wildness of his life, had only his old-fashioned habits left.

'Please to see for yourself, Varukh Kuzmitch,' said the landlord, turning to the officer, and throwing out his hands, 'this man does not pay his rent, he does not pay.'

'How can I when I have no money? Wait, and I will pay.'

'I can't wait, my good fellow,' said the landlord angrily, making a gesture with the key which he held in his hand. 'Lieutenant-Colonel Potogonkin has lived with me seven years, seven years already; Anna Petrovna Buchmisteroff hires the carriage-house and stable, except two stalls, and has three household servants . . . that is the kind of lodgers I have. I will say to you frankly, that this is not an establishment where people do not pay their rent. Pay your money at once, if you please, or else clear out.'

'Yes, if you hired the rooms, please to pay,' said the constable, with a slight shake of the head, as he laid his finger on one of the buttons of his uniform.

'Well, what am I to pay with? That's the question. I haven't a groschen just at present.'

'In that case, satisfy the claims of Ivan Ivanovitch with the fruits of your profession,' said the officer: 'perhaps he will consent to take pictures.'

'No, thank you, my good fellow, no pictures. Pictures of holy subjects, such as one could hang upon the walls, would be well enough; or some general with a star, or Prince Kutusoff's portrait:[158] but this fellow has painted that muzhik, that muzhik in his blouse, his servant who grinds his colours! The idea of painting his portrait, the hog! I'll thrash him well: he took all the nails out of my bolts, the scoundrel! Just see what subjects! Here he has drawn this room. It would have been well enough if he had taken a clean, well-furnished room; but he has gone and drawn this one, with all the dirt and rubbish which he has collected. Just see how he has defaced my room! Look for yourself. Yes, and my lodgers have been with me seven years, the lieutenant-colonel, Anna Petrovna Buchmisteroff ... No, I tell you, there is no worse lodger than a painter: he lives like a pig; simply – God have mercy!'

And the poor artist had to listen patiently to all this. Meanwhile the officer had occupied himself with examining the pictures and studies, and showed that his mind was more advanced than the landlord's, and that he was not insensible to artistic impressions.

'Heh!' said he, tapping one canvas, on which was depicted a naked woman, 'this subject is – lively. But why so much black under her nose? Did she take snuff?'

'Shadow,' answered Tchartkoff gruffly, without looking at him.

'But it might have been put in some other place: it is too conspicuous under the nose,' observed the officer. 'And whose likeness is this?' he continued, approaching the old man's portrait. 'It's too terrible. Was he really so dreadful? Ah! why, he actually looks! What a Gromoboy![159] From whom did you paint it?'

'Ah! it is from a –' said Tchartkoff, and did not finish his sentence: he heard a crack. It seems that the officer had pressed too hard on the frame of the portrait, thanks to the axelike build of his constable's hands: the small boards on the side caved in, one fell on the floor, and with it fell, with a heavy clash, a roll in blue paper. The inscription caught Tchartkoff's eye – '1,000 ducats'. Like a madman, he sprang to pick it up, grasped the roll, and gripped it convulsively in his hand, which fell down with the weight.

'Wasn't there a sound of money?' enquired the officer, hearing the noise of something falling on the floor, and not catching sight of it, by reason of the rapidity of the movement with which Tchartkoff had hastened to pick it up.

'What business is it of yours what is in my room?'

'It's my business because you ought to pay your rent to the landlord at once, because you have money, and won't pay – that's why it's my business.'

'Well, I will pay him today.'

'Well, and why wouldn't you pay him before, instead of making trouble for your landlord, and bothering the police to boot?'

'Because I did not want to touch this money. I will pay him all this evening, and leave the rooms tomorrow, because I will not stay with such a landlord.'

'Well, Ivan Ivanovitch, he will pay you,' said the constable, turning to the landlord. 'But in case you are not satisfied in every respect this evening, then you must excuse me, Mr Painter.' So saying, he put on his three-cornered hat, and went into the ante-room, followed by the landlord hanging his head, and apparently engaged in meditation.

'Thank God, Satan has carried them off!' said Tchartkoff, when he heard the door of the ante-room shut. He looked out into the ante-room, sent Nikita off on some errand, in order to be quite alone, fastened the door behind him, and, returning to his room, began with wildly beating heart to undo the roll.

In it were ducats, all new, and bright as fire. Almost beside himself, he sat down beside the pile of gold, still asking himself, 'Is not this all a dream?' There were just a thousand in the roll: the exterior was precisely like what he had seen in his dream. He turned them over, and looked at them for some minutes, without coming to his senses. His imagination conjured up all the tales of hoards, cabinets with secret drawers, left by ancestors for their spendthrift descendants, with firm belief in the extravagance of their life. He pondered thus: 'Did not some grandfather, in the present instance, leave a gift for his grandchild, shut up in the frame of the family portrait?' Filled with romantic fancies, he began to think: had not this some secret connection with his fate? Was not the existence of the portrait bound up with his own existence, and was not his acquisition of it a kind of predestination? He began to examine the frame with curiosity. On one side a cavity was hollowed out, concealed so skilfully and neatly by a little board, that, if the massive hand of the constable had not effected a breach, the ducats might have remained hidden to the end of time. On examining the portrait, he marvelled again at the exquisite workmanship, the extraordinary treatment of the eyes; they no longer appeared terrible to him; but, nevertheless, each time, a disagreeable feeling involuntarily lingered in his mind. 'No,' he said to himself, 'no matter whose grandfather you were, I'll put a glass over you, and get you a gilt frame.' Then he laid his hand on the golden pile before him, and his heart beat faster at the touch. 'What shall I do with them?' he said, fixing his eyes on them. 'Now I am independent for at least three years: I can shut myself up in my room and work. I have money for colours now; for dinner, tea, my food and lodging – no one will annoy and disturb me now. I will buy myself a first-class manikin, I will order a plaster torso, I will model feet, I will have a Venus, I will buy engravings of the best pictures. And if I work three years to satisfy myself, without haste, not for sale, I shall surpass them all, and I may become a distinguished artist.'

Thus he spoke in solitude, with his good judgement prompting; but louder and more distinct sounded another voice within him. And as he glanced once more at the gold, it was not thus that his twenty-two years and fiery youth spoke. Now everything was within his power on which he had hitherto gazed with envious eyes, which he had viewed from afar with longing. How his heart beat when he thought of it! To wear a fashionable coat, to feast after long abstinence, to hire handsome apartments, to go, on the instant, to the theatre, to the confectioner's, to . . . other places; and seizing his money, he was in the street in a moment.

First of all he went to the tailor, clothed himself anew from head to foot, and began to look at himself incessantly, like a child. He bought perfumes, pomades; hired the first elegant suite of apartments with mirrors and plate-glass windows which he came across in Nevsky Prospect, without haggling about the price; bought, on the impulse of the moment, in a shop, a costly opera-glass; bought, also on impulse, a quantity of neckties of every description, many more than he needed; had his hair curled at the hairdresser's; rode through the city twice without any object whatever; ate an immense amount of candy at the confectioner's; and went to the French Restaurant, of which he had heard rumours as indistinct as though they had concerned the Empire of China. There he dined, with his arms akimbo, casting proud glances at the other visitors, and continually arranging his curls in the glass. There he drank a bottle of champagne, which had been known to him hitherto only by hearsay. The wine rather affected his head; and he emerged into the street, lively, pugnacious, ready to raise the Devil, according to the Russian expression. He strutted along the sidewalk, levelling his opera-glass at everybody. On the bridge he caught sight of his former professor, and slipped past him neatly, as if he did not see him, so that the astounded professor stood stock-still on the bridge for a long time, with a face suggestive of an interrogation-point.

All his things, everything he owned – easels, canvas, pictures – were transported that same evening to his elegant quarters. He arranged the best of them in conspicuous places, threw the worst into a corner, and promenaded up and down the handsome rooms, glancing constantly in the mirrors. An unconquerable desire to seize fame by the tail, and show himself to the world at once, had arisen in his mind. He already heard the shouts, 'Tchartkoff! Tchartkoff! Have you seen Tchartkoff's picture? How rapidly Tchartkoff paints! How much talent Tchartkoff has!' He paced the room in a state of rapture, unconscious whither he went. The next day he took ten ducats, and went to the publisher of a popular journal, asking his charitable assistance. He was joyfully received by the journalist, who called him on the spot, '*Most respected sir*,' squeezed both his hands, made minute enquiries as to his name, birthplace, residence; and the next day there appeared in the journal, below a notice of some newly invented tallow candles, an article with the following heading:

TCHARTKOFF'S IMMENSE TALENT

We hasten to delight the cultivated inhabitants of the capital with a discovery which we may call splendid in every respect. All are agreed that there are among us many very handsome physiognomies and faces, but hitherto there has been no means of committing them to the wonder-working canvas for transmission to posterity. This want has now been supplied: an artist has been found who unites in himself all desirable qualities. The beauty can now feel assured that she will be depicted with all the grace of her spiritual charms, airy, fascinating, wondrous, butterfly-like, flitting among the flowers of spring. The stately father of a family can see himself surrounded by his family. Merchant, warrior, citizen, statesman – hasten one and all, come from your promenade, your expedition to your friend, your cousin, to the glittering bazaar; hasten, wherever you may be. The artist's magnificent establishment [Nevsky Prospect, such and such a number] is all hung with portraits from his brush, worthy of Van Dyck or Titian. One knows not which to admire most, their truth and likeness to the originals, or the wonderful brilliancy and freshness of the colouring. Hail to you, artist! you have drawn a lucky number in the lottery. Long live Andrei Petrovitch!' (The journalist evidently liked familiarity.) 'Glorify yourself and us. We know how to prize you. Universal popularity, and with it money, will be your meed, though some of our brother journalists may rise against you.

The artist read this article with secret satisfaction: his face beamed. He was mentioned in print; it was a novelty to him: he read the lines over several times. The comparison with Van Dyck and Titian flattered him extremely. The phrase, 'Long live Andrei Petrovitch,' also pleased him greatly: being called by his Christian name and patronymic in print was an honour hitherto utterly unknown to him. He began to pace the chamber briskly, to tumble his hair; now he sat down in an armchair, then sprang up, and seated himself on the sofa, planning each moment how he would receive visitors, male and female; he went to his canvas, and made a rapid sweep of the brush, endeavouring to impart a graceful movement to his hand.

The next day, the little bell at his door rang: he hastened to open. A lady entered, followed by a lackey in a furred livery-coat; and with the lady entered an eighteen-year-old girl, her daughter.

'You are Monsieur Tchartkoff?'

The artist bowed.

'A great deal is being written about you: your portraits, it is said, are the height of perfection.' So saying, the lady raised her glass to her eyes, and glanced rapidly over the walls, upon which nothing was hanging. 'But where are your portraits?'

'They have been taken away,' replied the artist, somewhat confusedly: 'I have but just moved into these apartments; so they are still on the road . . . they have not arrived.'

'You have been in Italy?' asked the lady, levelling her glass at him, as she found nothing else to point it at.

'No, I have not been there; but I wish to go . . . and I have deferred it for a while . . . Here is an armchair, Madame: you are fatigued?' . . .

'Thank you: I have been sitting a long time in the carriage. Ah, at last I behold your work!' said the lady, running to the opposite wall, and bringing her glass to bear upon his studies, programmes, perspectives, and portraits which were standing on the floor. 'C'est charmant, Lise! Lise, venez-ici. Rooms in the style of Teniers.[160] Do you see? Disorder, disorder, a table with a bust upon it, a hand, a palette; here is dust . . . see how the dust is painted! C'est charmant. And here on this canvas is a woman washing her face. Quelle jolie figure![161] Ah! a little peasant, a muzhik in a Russian blouse! See – a little muzhik! So you do not devote yourself exclusively to portraits?'

'Oh! that is rubbish. I was trying experiments . . . studies.'

'Tell me your opinion of the portrait painters of the present day. Is it not true that there are none now like Titian? There is not that strength of colour, that – that . . . what a pity that I cannot express to you in Russian.' (The lady was fond of paintings, and had gone through all the galleries in Italy with her eyeglass.) 'But Monsieur Nohl . . . ah, how he paints! What remarkable work! I think his faces have even more expression than Titian's. You do not know M. Nohl?'

'Who is Nohl?' enquired the artist.

'Monsieur Nohl. Ah, what talent! He painted her portrait when she was only twelve years old. You must certainly come to see us. Lise, you shall show him your album. You know, we came expressly that you might begin her portrait immediately.'

'What? I am ready this very moment.' And in a trice he pulled forward an easel with a piece of canvas already prepared, grasped his palette, and fixed his eyes on the daughter's pretty little face. If he had been acquainted with human nature, he might have read in it the dawning of a childish passion for balls, the dawning of sorrow and misery at the length of time before dinner and after dinner, of a desire to go to walk in her dress only, the heavy traces of uninterested application to various arts, insisted upon by her mother for the elevation of the sentiments of her soul. But the artist perceived only the tender little face, a seductive subject for his brush, the body almost as transparent as porcelain, the slight attractive fatigue, the delicate white neck, and the aristocratically slender form. And he prepared beforehand to triumph, to display the delicacy of his brush, which had hitherto had to deal only with the harsh features of coarse models, with severe antiques and copies of classic masters. He already saw in fancy how this delicate little face would turn out.

'Do you know,' said the lady with a positively touching expression of countenance, 'I should like . . . she is dressed up now; I confess, that I should not like her in the costume to which we are accustomed: I should like her to be simply attired, and seated among green shadows, like meadows, with a flock or a grove in the distance . . . so that it could not be seen that she goes to balls or fashionable entertainments. Our balls, I confess, so murder the intellect, so deaden all remnants of feeling . . . Simplicity, would there were more simplicity!' Alas! it was stamped on the faces of mother and daughter, that they had so overdanced themselves at balls, that they had become almost wax figures.

Tchartkoff set to work, seated the original, reflected a bit, fixed upon the idea, waved his brush in the air, settling the points mentally, screwed his eyes up a little, retreated, looked off in the distance, and then began and finished the sketching in, in an hour. Satisfied with it, he began to paint: the work fascinated him; he forgot everything, forgot the very existence of the aristocratic ladies, began even to display some artistic tricks, uttering various odd sounds; humming to himself now and then, as artists do when immersed heart and soul in their work. Without the slightest ceremony, with one wave of his brush, he made the sitter lift her head, which finally began to turn in a very decided manner, and express utter weariness.

'Enough, for the first time, enough,' said the lady.

'A little more,' said the artist, forgetting himself.

'No, it is time to stop. Lise, three o'clock!' said the lady, taking out a tiny watch, which hung by a gold chain from her girdle. 'Ah, how late it is!' she cried.

'Only a minute,' said Tchartkoff innocently, with the pleading voice of a child.

But the lady appeared to be not at all inclined to yield to his artistic demands on this occasion: she promised instead to sit longer the next time.

'It is vexatious, all the same!' thought Tchartkoff to himself: 'I had just got my hand in;' and he remembered that no one had interrupted him or stopped him when he was at work in his studio on Vasilievsky Ostroff. Nikita sat motionless in one place – you might paint him as long as you pleased: he even went to sleep in the attitude prescribed to him. And, dissatisfied, he laid his brush and palette on a chair, and paused in irritation before the picture.

The woman of the world's compliments awoke him from his reverie. He flew to the door to show them out: on the stairs he received an invitation to dine with them the following week, and returned with a cheerful face to his apartments. The aristocratic lady had completely charmed him. Up to that time he had looked upon such beings as unapproachable – born solely to ride in magnificent carriages with liveried footmen and stylish coachman, and to cast indifferent glances on the poor man travelling on foot in a cheap cloak. And now, all of a sudden, one of those beings had entered his room: he was painting her portrait, was invited to dinner in an aristocratic house. An unusual feeling of pleasure took possession of him: he was completely intoxicated, and rewarded himself with a splendid dinner, an evening at the theatre; and afterwards he took a ride through the city in a carriage without any necessity whatever.

But during all these days, his ordinary work did not fall in with his mood at all. He did nothing but prepare himself, and wait for the moment when the bell should ring. At last the aristocratic lady arrived with her pale daughter. He seated them, pulled forward the canvas, with skill, and some efforts at fashionable airs, and began to paint. The sunny day and bright light aided him not a little: he saw in his dainty sitter much, which, caught and committed to the canvas, would give great value to the portrait; he perceived that he might bring forth something rare if he could reproduce, with accuracy, all which nature then offered to his eyes. His heart even began to beat faster when he felt that he was expressing something which others had not even seen as yet. His work engrossed him completely: he was entirely taken up with his painting, and again forgot the aristocratic origin of the sitter. With heaving breast he saw the delicate traits and the almost transparent body of the eighteen-year-old maiden appear under his hand. He had caught every shade, the slight sallowness, the almost imperceptible blue tinge under the eyes – and was already preparing to put in the tiny pimple on the brow, when he suddenly heard the mother's voice behind him.

'Ah! why do you paint that? It is not necessary: and you have made it here . . . in several places, rather yellow . . . and here quite so, like dark spots.' The artist undertook to explain that the spots and yellow tinge would turn out well, that they brought out the delicate and pleasing tones of the face. He was informed that they did not bring out tones, and would not turn out well at all, and that it merely seemed so to him. 'But permit me to touch up just this one place, here, with yellow,' said the simple-minded artist. But he was not permitted. It was explained to him that just today Lise did not feel quite well; that she never was sallow, and that her face was distinguished for its fresh colouring. Sadly he began to erase what his brush had produced upon the canvas. Many a nearly invisible trait disappeared, and with it vanished also a portion of the resemblance. He began indifferently to give it that commonplace colouring which can be painted mechanically, and which lends to a face, even when taken from nature, the sort of cold ideality observable on school programmes. But the lady was satisfied when the objectionable colour was quite banished. She merely expressed surprise that the work lasted so long, and added that she had heard that he finished a portrait completely in two sittings. The artist could not think of any answer to this. The ladies rose, and prepared to depart. He laid aside his brush, escorted them to the door, and then stood disconsolate for a long while in one spot, before his portrait.

He gazed stupidly at it; and meanwhile there passed before his mind those delicate feminine features, those shades, and airy tints which he had copied, which his brush had annihilated. Engrossed with them, he set the portrait on one side, and hunted up the head of Psyche,[162] which he had long before thrown on canvas in a sketchy manner. It was a pretty little face, well painted, but entirely ideal, cold, consisting of the common features not assumed by a living being. For lack of occupation, he now began to go over it, imparting to it all he had taken note of in his aristocratic sitter. Those features, shadows, tints, which he had noted, made their appearance here in the purified form in which they appear when the painter, after closely observing nature, subordinates himself to her, and produces a creation equal to her own.

Psyche began to live; and the scarce dawning thought began, little by little, to clothe itself in a visible form. The type of face of the fashionable young lady was unconsciously communicated to Psyche, and nevertheless she had an expression of her own which gave it claims to be considered in truth, an original creation. It seemed as if he made use of some things and yet of all that the original suggested to him throughout, and gave himself up entirely to his work. For several days he was engrossed by it alone. And the ladies surprised him at this work on their arrival. He had not time to remove the picture from the easel. Both ladies uttered a cry of amazement, and clasped their hands.

'Lise, Lise! Ah, how like! Superbe, superbe! What a happy thought to drape her in a Greek costume! Ah, what a surprise!'

The artist could not see his way to disabusing the ladies of their pleasant mistake. Shamefacedly, with drooping head, he murmured, 'This is Psyche.'

'In the character of Psyche? C'est charmant!' said the mother, smiling, upon which the daughter also smiled. 'Confess, Lise, does it not please you to be painted in the character of Psyche better than any other way? Quelle idée délicieuse!¹⁶³ But what treatment! It is Correggio¹⁶⁴ himself. I must say, that, although I had read and heard about you, I did not know you had so much talent. You positively must paint me too.' Evidently, the lady wanted to be portrayed as some sort of Psyche also.

'What am I to do with them?' thought the artist. 'If they will have it so, why, let Psyche pass for what they choose:' and he said aloud, 'Pray sit a little longer: I will touch it up here and there.'

'Ah! I am afraid you will . . . it is such a likeness now!'

But the artist understood that the difficulty was with the sallowness, and so he reassured them by saying that he only wished to give more brilliancy and expression to the eyes. But, in truth, he was ashamed, and wished to impart a little more likeness to the original, lest any one should accuse him of actual barefaced flattery. And, in fact, the features of the pale young girl at length appeared more clearly in Psyche's countenance.

'Enough,' said the mother, beginning to fear that the likeness might become too decided. The artist was remunerated in every way – with smiles, money, compliments, cordial pressures of the hand, invitations to dinner: in a word, he received a thousand flattering rewards.

The portrait created a furore in the city. The lady exhibited it to her friends: all admired the skill with which the artist had preserved the likeness, and at the same time conferred more beauty on the original.

The last remark, of course, was prompted by a slight tinge of envy. And the artist was suddenly overwhelmed with work. It seemed as if the whole city wanted to be painted by him. The door-bell rang incessantly. From one point of view, this might be considered advantageous, as presenting to him endless practice in variety and number of faces. But, unfortunately, they were all people who were hard to get along with, busy, hurried people, or belonging to the fashionable world, consequently more occupied than any one else, and therefore impatient to the last degree. In all quarters, the demand was merely that the likeness should be good and quickly done. The artist perceived that it was a simple impossibility to finish his work; that it was necessary to exchange the power of his treatment for lightness and rapidity – to catch only the general, palpable expression, and not waste labour on delicate details – in a word, to copy nature in her finish was utterly out of the question. Moreover, it must be added that nearly all his sitters made many stipulations on various points. The ladies required that mind and character chiefly should be represented in their portraits: that he should make a point of nothing else; that all angles should be rounded, all unevenness smoothed away, and even removed entirely if possible; in a word, that their faces should be such as to cause every one to stare with admiration, if not fall in love with outright. And in consequence of this, when they sat to him, they sometimes assumed expressions which greatly amazed the artist: one tried to express melancholy; another, meditation; another wanted to make her mouth small on any terms, and puckered it up to such an extent that it finally looked like a spot about as big as a pinhead. And in spite of it all, they demanded of him good likenesses and unconstrained naturalness. And the men were no better than the ladies: one insisted upon being painted with an energetic, muscular turn to his head; another, with upturned, inspired eyes; a lieutenant of the guard demanded that Mars[165] should be visible in his eyes, without fail; an official in the civil service drew himself up to his full height in order to express his uprightness, his nobility, in his face, and so that his hand might rest upon a book bearing the words in plain characters, 'He always stood up for the right.' At first such demands threw the artist into a cold perspiration: he had to think it over, to consider; and there was but very little time for that. Finally he acquired the knack of it, and never troubled himself at all about it. He understood at a word how each wanted himself portrayed. If a man wanted Mars in his face, he put in Mars; he gave a Byronic turn and attitude to those who aimed at Byron.[166] If the ladies wanted to be Corinne,[167] Undine,[168] or Aspasia,[169] he agreed with great readiness, and threw in a sufficient measure of good looks from his own imagination, which, as is well known, does no harm, and for the sake of which an artist is even forgiven a lack of resemblance. He soon began to wonder himself at the rapidity and dash of his brush. And of course those who sat to him were in ecstasies, and proclaimed him a genius.

Tchartkoff became a fashionable artist in every sense of the word. He began to dine out, to escort ladies to the galleries and even to walk, to dress foppishly, and to assert audibly that an artist should belong to society, that he must uphold his profession, that artists dress like shoe-makers, do not know how to behave themselves, do not preserve the highest tone, and are lacking in all polish. At home, in his studio, he carried cleanliness and spotlessness to the last extreme, set up two superb footmen, took foppish pupils, dressed several times a day in various morning costumes, curled his hair, practised various manners of receiving his callers, busied himself in adorning his person in every conceivable way, in order to produce a pleasing impression on the ladies: in a word, it would soon have been impossible for any one to recognise in him the modest artist who had formerly toiled unknown in his miserable quarters in the Vasilievsky Island. He now expressed himself decidedly concerning artists and art; declared that too much credit had been given to the old masters; that they all, down to Raphael, painted not figures, but herrings; that the idea that there was any holiness about them existed only in the minds of the spectators; that even Raphael did not always paint well, and that fame attached to many of his works, simply by force of tradition; that Michael Angelo[170] was a braggart because he could boast only a knowledge of anatomy; that there was no grace about him, and that real brilliancy and power of treatment and colouring were to be looked for only in the present century. And there, naturally, the question touched him personally. 'No, I do not understand,' said he, 'how others toil and work with difficulty: a man who labours for months over a picture is a dauber, and no artist in my opinion; I don't believe he has any talent: genius works boldly, rapidly. Here,' said he, turning generally to his visitors, 'is this portrait which I painted in two days, this head in one day, this in a few hours, this in little more than an hour. No, I . . . I confess I do not recognise as art that which adds line to line: that is a trade, not art.' In this manner did he lecture his visitors; and the visitors admired the strength and boldness of his works, even uttered exclamations on hearing how fast they had been produced, and then said to each other, 'This is talent, real talent! See how he speaks, how his eyes gleam. Il y a quelque chose d'extraordinaire dans toute sa figure!'[171]

It flattered the artist to hear such reports about himself. When printed praise appeared in the papers, he rejoiced like a child, although this praise was purchased with his money. He carried the printed slips about with him everywhere, showed them to friends and acquaintances as if by accident, and it pleased him to the extent of simple-minded naïveté. His fame increased, his works and orders multiplied. Already the same portraits over and over wearied him with the same attitudes and turns, which he had learned by heart. He painted them now without any great interest in the work, trying to make some sort of a head, and giving them to his pupils to finish. At first he had tried to devise a new attitude each time, to surprise with his power and the effect. Now this had grown wearisome to him. His brain was tired with planning and thinking. It was out of his power, then or ever: his fast life, and society, where he tried to play the part of a man of the world, all this bore him far away from labour and thought. His work grew cold and dim; and he betook himself with indifference to monotonous, set, well-worn forms. The uniform, cold, eternally spick and span, and, so to speak, buttoned-up faces of the government officials, soldiers, and statesmen, did not offer a wide field for his brush: it forgot superb draperies, and powerful emotion and passion. Of groups, artistic drama and its lofty connections, there was nothing to be said. Before him was only a uniform, a corsage, a dress-coat, in the face of which the artist feels cold, and before which all imagination vanishes. Even his own peculiar merits were no longer visible in his works, yet they continued to enjoy renown; although genuine connoisseurs and artists merely shrugged their shoulders when they saw his latest productions. But some who had known Tchartkoff before, could not understand how the talent of which he had given such clear indications in the beginning, could have so vanished; and they strove in vain to divine by what means genius could be extinguished in a man just when he had attained to the full development of his powers.

But the intoxicated artist did not hear these criticisms. He began to attain to the age of dignity, both in mind and years: he began to grow stout, and increase visibly in flesh. He read in the papers phrases with adjectives, 'Our most respected Andrei Petrovitch; our worthy Andrei Petrovitch.' He began to receive offers of distinguished posts in the service, invitations to examinations and committees. He began, as is usually the case in maturer years, to advocate Raphael and the old masters, not because he had become thoroughly convinced of their transcendent merits, but in order to snub the younger artists. He began, according to the universal custom of those who have attained maturity, to accuse all young men, without exception, of immorality and a vicious turn of mind. He began to believe that everything in the world simply happens, that there is no higher inspiration, and that everything should of necessity be brought under one strict rule in the interests of accuracy and uniformity. In a word, his life already was approaching the verge of the years when everything which suggests impulse, contracts within a man; when a powerful chord appeals more feebly to the spirit, and weaves no piercing strains about the heart; when the touch of beauty no longer converts virgin strength into fire and flame, but all the burnt-out sentiments become more vulnerable to the sound of gold, hearken more attentively to its seductive music, and, little by little, permit themselves to be completely lulled to sleep by it. Fame can give no pleasure to him who has stolen it, not won it: it produces a permanent shock only in the breast of him who is worthy of it. And so all his feelings and impulses turned towards gold. Gold was his passion, his ideal, his fear, his delight, his aim. The bundles of bank-bills increased in his coffers; and, like all to whose lot falls this fearful gift, he began to grow miserly, inaccessible to every sentiment except the love of gold, a causeless miser, an extravagant amasser, and on the point of becoming one of those strange beings of whom there are many in this unfeeling world, on whom the man full of life and heart gazes with horror, who regards them as walking stony sepulchres with dead men inside, instead of hearts. But something occurred which gave him a powerful shock, and disturbed the whole tenor of his life.

One day he found upon his table a note, in which the Academy of Painting begged him, as a worthy member of its body, to come and give his opinion upon a new work which had been sent from Italy by a Russian artist who was perfecting himself there. The artist was one of his former comrades, who had been possessed with a passion for art from his earliest years, had given himself up to it with his whole soul, estranged himself from his friends, from his relatives, from his pleasant habits, and had hastened there, where, under a magnificent sky, flourishes a splendid hot-bed of art, to wonderful Rome, at whose very name the artist's heart beats wildly and hotly. There, like an exile, he buried himself in his work and in toil from which he permitted nothing to entice him. He cared not whether his character were talked about, or not, or his ignorance of the art of getting on with people, or his neglect of polite usages; nor of the discredit which he cast upon his calling of artist by his poor, old-fashioned dress. It was nothing to him if his brother artists were angry. He neglected everything, and devoted himself wholly to art. He visited the galleries unweariedly, he stood for hours at a time before the works of the great masters, seizing and studying their marvellous methods. He never finished anything without revising his impressions several times before these great teachers, and reading in their works silent but eloquent counsels. He entered into no noisy conversations or disputes. He neither advocated nor opposed the purists. He gave each impartially his due, appropriating from all only that which was most beautiful, and finally became the pupil of the divine Raphael alone – as a great poet-artist, after reading many works of various kinds, full of many charms and splendid beauties, at last made Homer's *Iliad*[172] alone his breviary, having discovered that it contains all one wants, and that there is nothing which is not expressed in it, in deep and grand perfection. And so he brought away from his school the grand conception of creation, the mighty beauty of thought, the high charm of that heavenly brush.

When Tchartkoff entered the room, he found a great crowd of visitors already collected before the picture. The most profound silence, such as rarely settles upon a throng of critics, reigned over all, on this occasion. He hastened to assume the significant expression of a connoisseur, and approached the picture; but, O God! what did he behold!

Pure, faultless, beautiful as a bride, stood the picture before him. Modest, reverent, innocent, and simple as a guardian angel, it rose above them all. It seemed as though the divine figures, embarrassed by the many glances directed at them, had dropped their beautiful eyelashes in confusion. The critics regarded the new, hitherto unknown work, with a feeling of involuntary wonder. All seemed united in it – the art of Raphael, which was reflected in the lofty grace of the grouping; the art of Correggio, breathing from the finished perfection of the work-manship. But more striking than all else was the evident power of creation, still contained in the artist's mind. The very minutest object in the picture was informed with it; everything was done with order and inward power; he had caught that melting roundness of outline which is visible in nature only to the artist creator, and which comes out as angles with a copyist. It was plainly to be seen how the artist, having drawn it all from the visible world, had first stored it in his mind, and then had drawn it thence, as from a spiritual source, into one harmonious, triumphant song. And it was evident, even to the uninitiated, how vast a gulf was fixed between creation and a mere copy from nature. It was almost impossible to describe that rare silence which unconsciously overpowered all who cast their eyes on the picture – not a rustle, not a sound: and the picture seemed more and more noble with every moment that passed; more brilliantly and wonderfully stood forth at length in one instant – the fruit which had descended from heaven into the artist's mind – the instant for which all human life is but the preparation.

Involuntary tears stood ready to fall in the eyes of those who surrounded the picture. It seemed as though all tastes, all bold, irregular errors of taste, even, joined in a silent hymn to the divine work.

Motionless, with open mouth, Tchartkoff stood before the picture; and at length, when by degrees the visitors and critics began to murmur and comment upon the merits of the work, and when at length they turned to him, and begged him to express an opinion, he came to himself once more; he tried to assume an indifferent, everyday expression; tried to make some of the commonplace, everyday remarks of hardened artists, in the following style: 'Yes, in fact, to tell the truth, it is impossible to deny the artist's talent; there is something to it; he evidently tried to express something; but as to the chief point' . . . and then as a conclusion to this, of course follow praises to such an effect that no artist would have felt flattered by them: he tried to do this; but the speech died upon his lips, tears and sobs burst forth uncontrollably for answer, and he rushed from the room like one beside himself.

In a moment he stood, deprived of sense and motion, in the middle of his magnificent studio. All his being, all his life, had been aroused in one instant, as if youth had returned to him, as if the dying sparks of his talent had blazed forth afresh. The bandage suddenly fell from his eyes. Heavens! to think of having mercilessly wasted the best years of his youth, of having extinguished, trodden out perhaps, the spark of fire, which, cherished in his breast, might perhaps have been developed now into magnificence and beauty, and have extorted, too, its meed of tears and admiration! And to have ruined it all, ruined it without pity! It seemed as though suddenly and all together there revived in his soul those impulses, that devotion, which he had known in other days. He seized a brush, and approached his canvas. The perspiration started out upon his face with his efforts: one thought possessed him wholly, one desire consumed him; he tried to depict a fallen angel. This idea was most in harmony with his frame of mind. But alas! his figures, attitudes, groups, thoughts, arranged themselves stiffly, disconnectedly. His hand and his imagination had been too long confined to one groove; and the powerless effort to escape from the bonds and fetters which he had imposed upon himself, showed itself in irregularities and errors. He had despised the long, wearisome ladder to knowledge, and the first fundamental law of the future great man. He gave vent to his vexation. He ordered all his last productions to be taken out of his studio, all the fashionable, lifeless pictures, all the portraits of hussars, ladies, and councillors of state.

He shut himself up alone in his room, would order no food, and devoted himself entirely to his work. He sat toiling like a youth, like a scholar. But how pitifully ignoble was all which proceeded from his hand! He was stopped at every step by his ignorance of the very first principles: the simple ignorance of the mechanical part chilled all inspirations, and formed an impassable barrier to his imagination. His brush returned involuntarily to hackneyed forms: the hands folded themselves in a set attitude; the heads dared not make any unusual turn; the very folds of the garments turned out commonplace, and would not subject themselves or drape themselves to any unaccustomed posture of the body. And he felt, he felt and saw it all himself.

'But had I really any talent?' he said at length: 'did not I deceive myself?' And, uttering these words, he turned to his early works, which he had painted so purely, so unselfishly, in former days, in his wretched cabin yonder in lonely Vasilievsky Island, far from people, luxury, and every indulgence. He turned to them now, and began attentively to examine them all; and all the misery of his former life came back to him. 'Yes,' he cried despairingly, 'I had talent: the signs and traces of it are everywhere visible . . . '

He paused suddenly, and shivered all over: his eyes encountered eyes fixed immovably upon him. It was that remarkable portrait which he had bought in Shtchukinui Dvor. All this time it had been covered up, concealed by other pictures, and had utterly gone out of his mind. Now, as if by design, when all the fashionable portraits and paintings had been removed from the studio, it looked forth, together with the productions of his early youth. As he recalled all the strange story; as he remembered that this singular portrait had been, in a manner, the cause of his errors; that the hoard of money which he had obtained in such peculiar fashion had given birth in his mind to all the wild caprices which had destroyed his talent – madness was on the point of taking possession of him. On the instant he ordered the hateful portrait to be removed. But his mental excitement was not thereby diminished. Every feeling, his whole being, was shaken to its foundation; and he suffered that fearful torture which is sometimes exhibited in nature, as a striking anomaly, when a feeble talent strives to display itself on a scale too great for it, and cannot display itself – that torture which in youth gives birth to greatness, but, when reverie is carried to too great an extent, is converted into unquenchable thirst – that fearful torture which renders a man capable of terrible things. A horrible envy took possession of him, envy which bordered on madness. The gall flew to his face when he beheld a work which bore the stamp of talent. He gnashed his teeth, and devoured it with the glare of a basilisk.[173] He conceived the most devilish plan which ever entered into the mind of man, and he hastened with the strength of madness to carry it into execution. He began to purchase the best which art produced, of every kind. Having bought a picture at a great price, he transported it to his room with care, and flung himself upon it with the ferocity of a tiger, cut it, tore it, chopped it into bits, and stamped upon it, accompanying these proceedings with a grin of delight. The incalculable riches which he had amassed, enabled him to gratify this devilish desire. He opened his bags of gold, and unlocked his coffers. No monster of ignorance ever destroyed so many superb productions of art as did this raging avenger. At any auction where he made his appearance, every one despaired at once of obtaining any work of art. It seemed as if an angry heaven had sent this fearful scourge into the world expressly to destroy all harmony. This terrible passion communicated to him a horrible colour: the gall abode permanently in his face. Blame of the world, and scorn of it, were expressed in his countenance. It seemed as though that awful demon were incarnate in him, which Pushkin has described[174] in an ideal manner. His tongue uttered nothing except biting and censorious words. He swooped down like a harpy[175] into the street; and all, even his acquaintances, catching sight of him in the distance, sought to turn aside and avoid a meeting with him, saying that it poisoned all the rest of the day.

Fortunately for the world and art, such a strained and forced life could not last long: the measure of his passions was too abnormal and colossal for his feeble strength. The attacks of madness began to appear more frequently, and ended at last in the most frightful illness. A violent fever, combined with galloping consumption, seized upon him with such force, that in three days there remained only a shadow of his former self. To this was added indications of hopeless madness. Sometimes several men were unable to hold him. The long-forgotten, living eyes of the remarkable portrait began to torment him, and then his madness became dreadful. All the people who surrounded his bed seemed to him horrible portraits. The portrait doubled and quadrupled itself in his eyes; all the walls seemed hung with portraits, which fastened their living, motionless eyes upon him; horrible portraits glared at him from the ceiling, from the floor; the room widened and lengthened endlessly, in order to make room for more of the motionless eyes. The doctor who had undertaken to attend him, having learned something of his strange history, strove with all his might to fathom the secret connection between the visions of his fancy and the occurrences of his life, but without the slightest success. The sick man understood nothing, felt nothing, except his own tortures, and gave utterance only to frightful yells and unintelligible gibberish.

At last his life ended in a final attack of unutterable suffering. His corpse was horrible. Nothing could be found of all his great wealth; but when they beheld the mutilated fragments of all the grand works of art, the value of which exceeded a million, they understood the terrible use which had been made of it.

2

A throng of carriages, droschkie, and calashes[176] stood at the entrance of a house in which an auction sale was going on of the effects belonging to one of those wealthy art-lovers who have dreamed their lives sweetly away, engrossed with Loves and Zephyrs, have innocently passed for Maecenases,[177] and in a simple-minded fashion expended, to that end, the millions amassed by their thrifty fathers, and frequently even by their own early labours. As is well known, there are no such Maecenases in existence now; and our nineteenth century long ago acquired the aspect of a parsimonious banker, rejoicing in his millions only in the form of figures jotted down on paper. The long saloon was filled with the most motley throng of visitors, collected like birds of prey swooping down upon an unburied corpse. There was a whole squadron of Russian shop-keepers from Gostinnui Dvor, and even from the old-clothes mart, in blue coats of foreign make. Their faces and expressions were a little more sedate here, more natural, and did not display that fictitious desire to serve which is so marked in the Russian shop-keeper when he stands before a customer in his shop. Here they stood upon no ceremony, although the saloons were full of those very aristocrats before whom, in any other place, they would have been ready to sweep, with reverences, the dust brought in by their feet. Here they were quite at their ease, handled pictures and books without ceremony, desirous of ascertaining the value of the goods, and boldly disarranged the prices attached by the connoisseur-Counts. There were many of the infallible attendants of auctions who make it a point to go to one every day as regularly as to take their breakfast; aristocratic connoisseurs, who look upon it as their duty not to miss any opportunity of adding to their collections, and who have no other occupation between twelve o'clock and one; finally those noble gentlemen, with garments and pockets very threadbare, who make their daily appearance without any selfish object in view, but merely to see how it all goes off – who will give more, who less, who will outbid the other, and who will get it. A quantity of pictures were lying about in disorder: with them were mingled furniture, and books with possibly the cipher of the former owner, who never was moved by any laudable desire to glance into them. Chinese vases, marble slabs for tables, old and new furniture with curving lines, with griffins, sphinxes, and lions' paws, gilded and ungilded, chandeliers, sconces – all were heaped together, and not in the order of the shops. It presented a perfect chaos of art. The feeling we generally experience at an auction is a strange one: everything about it bears some likeness to a funeral procession. The room in which it takes place, is always rather dark – the windows, piled up with furniture and pictures, admit but scant light: the silence expressed in the faces, and the funereal voice of the auctioneer, the tapping of the hammer and the requiem of the poor arts, met together so strangely here; all this seems to heighten still further the peculiar unpleasantness of the impression.

The auction appeared to be at its height. A whole throng of respectable people had collected in a group, and were discussing something eagerly. On all sides resounded the words, *roubles, roubles*, giving the auctioneer no time to repeat the added price, which had already reached a sum four times as great as the price announced. The surging throng was competing for a portrait which could not but arrest the attention of all who possessed any knowledge of art. The skilled hand of an artist was plainly visible in it. The portrait had apparently been several times restored and renovated, and presented the dark features of an Asiatic in voluminous garments, with a strange and remarkable expression of countenance; but what struck the buyers more than all else, was the peculiar liveliness of the eyes. The more the people looked at them, the more did they seem to pierce into each man's heart. This peculiarity, this strange illusion of the artist, attracted the attention of nearly all. Many who had been bidding for it, withdrew because the price had risen to an incredible sum. There remained only two well-known aristocrats, amateurs of painting, who were unwilling to forgo such an acquisition. They grew warm, and would, probably, have raised the price to an impossible sum, had not one of the lookers-on suddenly exclaimed, 'Permit me to interrupt your competition for a while: I, perhaps, more than any other, have a right to this portrait.'

These words at once fixed the attention of all upon him. He was a tall man of thirty-five, with long black curls. His pleasing face, full of a certain bright nonchalance, indicated a soul removed from all wearisome, worldly excitement; his garments made no pretence to fashion: all about him indicated the artist. He was, in fact, B. the painter, personally well known to many of those present.

'However strange my words may seem to you,' he continued, perceiving that the general attention was directed to him, 'yet, if you consent to listen to a short story, you may possibly see that I was right in uttering them. Everything assures me that this is the portrait which I am looking for.'

A very natural curiosity illumined the faces of nearly all; and even the auctioneer paused as he was opening his mouth, and with hammer uplifted in the air, prepared to listen. At the beginning of the story, many glanced involuntarily towards the portrait; but later on, all bent their attention solely on the narrator, as his tale grew gradually more absorbing.

'You know that portion of the city which is called Kolomna,' he began. 'There everything is unlike anything else in Petersburg: there it is neither capital nor provinces. It seems, you know, when you traverse those streets, as though all youthful desires and impulses deserted you. Thither the future never comes, all is peace and desolation, all that has fallen away from the movement of the capital. Retired tchinovniks remove thither to live; widows; people not very well off, who have acquaintance in the senate, and therefore condemn themselves to this for nearly the whole of their lives; retired cooks, who gossip all day at the markets, talk nonsense with the muzhiks in the petty shops, purchasing each day five kopecks' worth of coffee, and four of sugar; and, in short, that whole list of people who can be described by the one word *ash-coloured* – people whose garments, faces, hair, eyes, have a sort of troubled, ashy surface, like a day when there is in the sky neither cloud nor sun, but it is simply neither one thing nor the other: the mist settles down, and robs every object of its distinctness. Among them may be reckoned retired theatrical servants, retired titular councillors, retired sons of Mars, with ruined eyes and swollen lips. These people are utterly passionless. They walk along without glancing at anything, and maintain silence without thinking of anything. There are not many possessions in their chambers – sometimes merely a stoup of pure Russian vodka, which they absorb monotonously all day long, without its having any marked tendency to affect their heads, caused by a strong dose such as the young German mechanic loves to treat himself to on Sundays – that bully of Myeshtchanskaya Street, sole controller of all the sidewalks after twelve o'clock at night.

'Life in Kolomna is terribly lonely: rarely does a carriage appear, except, perhaps, one containing an actor, which disturbs the universal stillness by its rumble, noise, and jingling. There all are – pedestrians: the driver frequently loiters along, carrying hay for his shaggy little horse. You can get lodgings for five roubles a month, coffee in the morning included. Widows with pensions are the most aristocratic families there; they conduct themselves well, sweep their rooms often, chatter with their friends about the dearness of beef and cabbage; they frequently have a young daughter – a taciturn, quiet, sometimes pretty creature – an ugly little dog, and wall-clocks which strike in a melancholy fashion. Then come the actors whose salaries do not permit them to desert Kolomna, an independent folk, living, like all artists, for pleasure. They sit in their dressing-gowns, cleaning their pistols, glueing together all sorts of things out of cardboard, which are useful about a house, playing checkers and cards with any friend who chances to drop in, and so pass away the morning, doing pretty nearly the same in the evening, with the addition of punch now and then. After these great people and aristocracy of Kolomna, come the rank and file. It is as difficult to put a name to them as to number the multitude of insects which breed in stale vinegar. There are old women who get drunk, who make a living by incomprehensible means, like ants, drag old clothes and rags from the Kalinkin Bridge[178] to the old-clothes mart, in order to sell them there for fifteen kopecks – in a word, the very dregs of mankind, whose condition no beneficent, political economist has devised any means of ameliorating.

'I have enumerated them in order to show you how often such people find themselves under the necessity of seeking immediate temporary assistance, of having recourse to borrowing; and there settles among them a peculiar race of money-lenders who lend small sums on security at an enormous percentage. These petty usurers are sometimes more heartless than the great ones, because they penetrate into the midst of poverty, and sharply displayed beggarly rags, which the rich usurer, who has dealings only with carriage-customers, never sees – and because every feeling of humanity, too, soon dies within them. Among these usurers was a certain . . . but I must not omit to mention that the occurrence which I have undertaken to relate, refers to the last century; namely, to the reign of our late Empress Ekaterina the Second. You will understand that the very appearance and life of Kolomna must have changed materially. So, among the usurers was a certain person – an extraordinary being in every respect, who had settled in that quarter of the city long before. He went about in voluminous Asiatic attire; his dark complexion pointed to a Southern origin; but to what particular nation he belonged – India, Greece, or Persia – no one could say with certainty. Of tall, almost colossal stature, with dark, thin, glowing face, and an indescribably strange colour in his large eyes of unwonted fire, with heavy, overhanging brows, he differed sharply and strongly from all the ash-coloured denizens of the capital.

'His very dwelling was unlike the other small wooden houses. It was of stone, in the style of those formerly much affected by Genoese merchants, with irregular windows of various sizes, with iron shutters and bars. This usurer differed from other usurers also in that he could furnish any required sum, from that desired by the poor old beggar-woman to that demanded by the extravagant court grandee. The most gorgeous equipages often showed themselves in front of his house, and from their windows sometimes peeped forth the head of an elegant lady of society. Rumour, as usual, reported that his iron coffers were full of untold gold, treasures, diamonds, and all sorts of pledges, but that, nevertheless, he was not the slave of that avarice which is characteristic of other usurers. He lent money willingly, stipulating very favourable terms of payment, so it appeared, but, by some curious method of reckoning, made them amount to an incredible percentage. So said rumour, at least. But what was strangest of all, and could not fail to strike many, was the peculiar fate of all who received money from him: all ended their lives in some unhappy way. Whether this was simply the popular opinion, stupid, superstitious rumours, or reports circulated with an object, is not known. But several instances which happened within a brief space of time before the eyes of all, were vivid and striking.

'Among the aristocracy of that day, the one who speedily attracted to himself the eyes of all was a young man of one of the best families, distinguished also in his early years in court-circles, a warm admirer of all true and noble things, zealous for all which art or the mind of man produced, and giving promise of becoming a Maecenas. He was soon deservedly distinguished by the Empress, who conferred upon him an important post, fully proportioned to his desires – a post in which he could accomplish much for science and the general welfare. The youthful dignitary surrounded himself with artists, poets, and learned men. He wished to give work to all, to encourage all. He undertook, at his own expense, a number of useful publications; gave many orders; proclaimed many prizes for the encouragement of different arts; spent a great deal of money, and finally ruined himself. But, full of noble impulses, he did not wish to relinquish his work, sought a loan every-where, and finally betook himself to the well-known usurer. Having effected a considerable loan from him, the man changed completely in a short time: he became a persecutor and oppressor of budding talent and intellect. He saw the bad side in every publication, and every word he uttered was false. Then, unfortunately, came the French Revolution. This furnished him with an excuse for every sort of suspicion. He began to discover a revolutionary tendency in everything: he encountered hints in everything. He became suspicious to such a degree, that he began, finally, to suspect himself; began to concoct terrible and unjust accusations, made scores of people unhappy. Of course, such conduct could not fail, in time, to reach the throne. The kind-hearted Empress was shocked; and, full of the noble spirit which adorns crowned heads, she uttered words which, although they could not descend to us in all their sharpness, have yet preserved the memory of their deepest meaning engraven on many hearts. The Empress remarked, that not under a monarchical government were the high and noble impulses of souls persecuted; not there were the creations of intellect, poetry, and art contemned and oppressed; that, on the other hand, monarchs alone were their protectors; that Shakspeare[179] and Molière[180] flourished under their magnanimous protection, while Dante[181] could not find a corner in his republican birthplace; that true geniuses arise in the period of brilliancy and power of emperors and empires, but not in the time of monstrous political apparitions and republican terrorism, which, up to that time, had never given to the world a single poet; that poet-artists should be marked out for favour, for peace, and divine quiet alone compose their minds, not excitement and tumult; that learned men, poets, and all producers of art, are the pearls and diamonds in the imperial crown: by them is the epoch of the great ruler adorned, and from them it receives yet greater brilliancy. In a word, when the Empress uttered these words, she was divinely beautiful for the moment. I remember old men who could not speak of it without tears. All were interested in the affair. It must be remarked, to the honour of our national pride, that in the Russian's heart there always beats a fine feeling that he must adopt the part of the persecuted. The dignitary who had betrayed his trust was punished in an exemplary manner, and degraded from his post. But he read a much more dreadful punishment in the faces of his fellow-countrymen: this was a sharp and universal scorn. It is impossible to describe what that vainglorious soul suffered: pride, betrayed self-love, ruined hopes, all united, and he died in a terrible attack of raving madness.

'Another striking example occurred also in view of all: among the beauties in which our Northern capital is assuredly not poor, one decidedly surpassed all the rest. Her loveliness was a combination of our Northern charms with the charms of the South – a brilliant such as rarely makes its appearance on earth. My father admitted that he had never beheld anything like it in the whole course of his life. Everything seemed to be united in her – wealth, intellect, and spiritual charms. She had throngs of admirers; and the most distinguished of them all was

Prince R., the most noble-minded, the best, of all young men, the finest in face, and in his magnanimous and knightly sentiments the grand ideal of romance and women, a Grandison[182] in every acceptation of the term. Prince R. was passionately and desperately in love: he was requited by a like ardent passion. But the match seemed unequal to the parents. The prince's family estates had not been in his possession for a long time, his family was out of favour, and the sad state of his affairs was well known to all. Of a sudden the prince quitted the capital, as if for the purpose of arranging his affairs, and after a short interval reappeared, surrounded with luxury and incredible splendour. Brilliant balls and parties made him known at court. The beauty's father began to relent, and a most interesting wedding took place in the city. Whence this change in circumstances, this unheard-of wealth of the bridegroom, came, no one could fully explain; but it was whispered that he had entered into a compact with the mysterious usurer, and had borrowed money of him. However that may have been, the wedding was a source of interest to the whole city, and the bride and bridegroom were the objects of general envy. Every one knew of their warm and faithful love, the long persecution they had had to endure from every quarter, the great personal worth of both. Ardent women at once sketched out the heavenly bliss which the young couple would enjoy. But it turned out very differently.

'In the course of a year a frightful change came over the husband. His character, up to that time so fine and noble, became poisoned with jealous suspicions, irritability, and inexhaustible caprices. He became a tyrant and persecutor to his wife – something which no one could have foreseen – and indulged in the most inhuman deeds, even in blows. In a year's time, no one would have recognised the woman who such a little while before had shone, and drawn about her throngs of submissive adorers. Finally, no longer able to endure her heavy lot, she proposed a divorce. Her husband flew into a rage at the very suggestion. In the first burst of passion, he chased her about the room with a knife, and would doubtless have murdered her then and there, if they had not seized him and prevented him. In a burst of madness and despair he turned the knife against himself, and ended his life amid the most horrible sufferings.

'Besides these two instances which occurred before the eyes of all the world, stories circulated of a great number which took place among the lower classes, nearly all of which had tragic endings. Here an honest, sober man became a drunkard; there a shop-keeper's clerk robbed his master; again, a driver who had conducted himself properly for a number of years, cut his passenger's throat for a groschen. It was impossible that such occurrences, related, too, sometimes not without embellishments, should not inspire a sort of involuntary horror in the sedate inhabitants of Kolomna. No one cherished any doubt as to the presence of an evil power in this man. They said that he imposed conditions which made the hair rise on one's head, and which the miserable wretch never afterward dared reveal to any other being; that his money possessed a power of attraction; that it grew hot of itself, and that it bore strange marks . . . In short, many were the silly stories in circulation. And it is worthy of remark, that all this colony of Kolomna, this whole race of poor old women, petty officials, petty artists, and, in a word, all the insignificant people whom we have just recapitulated, agreed that it was better to endure anything, and to suffer the extreme of misery, rather than to have recourse to the terrible usurer: old women were even found dying of hunger, who preferred to kill their bodies rather than lose their souls. Those who met him in the street felt an involuntary fear. Pedestrians took care to turn aside from his path, and gazed long after the extremely tall, receding figure. In his face alone, there was enough that was uncommon to cause any one to ascribe to him a supernatural nature. The strong features, so deeply chiselled, not seen in many men; the glowing bronze of his complexion; the incredible thickness of his brows; the intolerable, terrible eyes; even the wide folds of his Asiatic garment – everything seemed to indicate that all passions of other people were pale compared to the passions raging in that body. My father stopped short every time he met him, and could not refrain each time from saying, "A devil, a perfect devil!" But I must introduce you as speedily as possible to my father, who, with others, is the chief character in this story.

'My father was a remarkable man in many respects. He was an artist of rare ability, a self-taught artist, seeking in his own soul, without teachers or schools, principles and rules, carried away only by the thirst for perfection, and treading a path indicated by his own instincts, for reasons unknown, perchance, even to himself – one of those natural marvels whom their contemporaries often honour with the insulting title of *fools*, and who are chilled neither by blame nor their own lack of success, who gain only fresh vigour, and, in their own minds, have gone far beyond those works on account of which they have received the name of fools. Through some lofty and secret instinct he perceived the presence of a soul in every object; he embraced, by his unaided mind, the true significance of the words, *historical painting*; he comprehended why a simple head, a simple portrait by Raphael, Leonardo da Vinci,

Titian, Correggio, can be considered an historical painting, and why a huge picture with historical subject remains, nevertheless, a *genre* picture, in spite of all the artist's pretensions to historical painting. And this secret instinct and personal conviction turned his brush to Christian subjects, grand and lofty to the last degree. He had none of the vanity or irritability so inseparable from the character of many artists. His was a strong character: he was an honourable, upright, even rough man, covered with a sort of hard rind without, not entirely lacking in pride, and given to expressing himself both sharply and scornfully about people. "What are they looking at?" he generally said. "I am not working for them. I don't carry my pictures to the tavern. He who understands me is grateful. The man of the world is not to blame that he understands nothing about painting; but he does understand cards, and he knows good wine and horses; – why should a gentleman know more? Observe, if you please, how he tries one, and then another, and then begins to consider, when his living does not depend upon it. Let every man attend to his own affairs. To my mind, that man is the best of all who says frankly that he does not understand a thing, rather than the man who pretends, talks as though he knew a thing he does not know, and is simply disgusting and intolerable." He worked for very small pay; that is to say, for just enough to support his family, and obtain the tools to work with. Moreover, he never, under any circumstances, refused to aid any one, or to lend a helping hand to a poor artist: he believed with the simple, reverent faith of his ancestors; and from that cause, it may be, that noble expression which even brilliant talents cannot acquire, showed itself in the faces he painted. At length, by his unintermitting labour, and perseverance in the path he had marked out for himself, he began to win the approbation of those who honoured his folly and his self-taught talent. They gave him constant orders for churches, and he never lacked employment. One of his paintings possessed a strong interest for him. I no longer recall the precise subject: I only know that he needed to represent the Spirit of Darkness in it. He pondered long what form to give him: he wished to concentrate in his face all that weighs down and oppresses a man. In the midst of his meditations, there suddenly occurred to his mind the image of the mysterious usurer; and he thought involuntarily, "That's what I ought to paint for the Devil!" Imagine his amazement when one day, as he was at work in his studio, he heard a knock at the door, and directly after there entered that very same terrible usurer. He could not repress an inward shudder, which involuntarily traversed every limb.

' "You are an artist?" he said to my father abruptly.

' "I am," answered my father in surprise, waiting for what should come next.

' "Good! Paint my portrait. I may possibly die soon. I have no children; but I do not wish to die completely, I wish to live. Can you paint a portrait that shall be as though it lived?"

'My father reflected, "What could be better? He offers himself for the Devil in my picture.' He promised. They agreed upon a time and price; and the next day my father took palette and brushes, and went to his house. The lofty courtyard, dogs, iron doors and locks, arched windows, coffers draped with strange covers, and, last of all, the re-markable owner himself, seated motionless before him, all produced a strange impression on him. The windows seemed intentionally barred, and so encumbered below that they admitted the light only from the top. "Devil take him, how well his face is lighted!" he said to himself, and began to paint assiduously, as though afraid that the favourable light would disappear. "What strength!" he repeated to himself. "If I make half a likeness of him, as he is just now, it will surpass all my other works: he will simply start from the canvas if I am only partly true to nature. What remarkable features!" he kept repeating, redoubling his energy; and he began himself to see how some traits were making their appearance on the canvas. But the more closely he approached him, the more conscious he became of an aggressive, uneasy feeling, which he could not explain to himself. But, notwithstanding this, he set himself to copy with literal accuracy every slightest trait and expression. First of all, however, he busied himself with the eyes. There was so much force in those eyes, that it seemed impossible to reproduce them exactly as they were in nature. But he resolved, at any price, to seek in them the most minute characteristics and shades, to penetrate their secret . . . But as soon as he approached them, and began to redouble his exertions, there sprang up in his mind such a terrible feeling of repulsion, of inexplicable oppression, that he was forced to lay aside his brush for a while, and begin anew. At last he could bear it no longer: he felt as if those eyes were piercing into his soul, and causing intolerable emotion. On the second and third days this became still stronger. It became horrible to him. He threw down his brush, and declared abruptly that he could paint him no longer. You should have seen how the terrible usurer changed countenance at these words. He threw himself at his feet, and besought him to finish the portrait, saying that his fate and his existence in the world depended on it; that he had already caught his prominent features; that if he could reproduce them accurately, his life would be preserved in his portrait, in a supernatural manner; that by that means he would not die completely; that it was necessary for him to continue to exist in the world.

'My father was frightened by these words: they seemed to him strange and terrible to such a degree, that he threw down his brushes and palette, and rushed headlong from the room.

'The memory of it troubled him all day and all night; but the next morning he received the portrait from the usurer, brought by a woman who was the only creature in his service, who announced that her master did not want the portrait, would pay nothing for it, and had sent it back. On the evening of the same day he learned that the usurer was dead, and that preparations were in progress to bury him according to the rites of his religion. All this seemed to him inexplicably strange. But from that day a marked change showed itself in his character. He was possessed by a troubled, uneasy feeling, of which he was unable to explain the cause; and he soon committed a deed which no one could have expected of him. For some time the works of one of his pupils had been attracting the attention of a small circle of connoisseurs and amateurs. My father had perceived his talent, and manifested a particular liking for him in consequence. Suddenly he became envious of him. The general interest in him and talk about him became unendurable to my father. Finally, to complete his vexation, he learned that his pupil had been asked to paint a picture for a recently built and wealthy church. This enraged him. "No, I will not permit that fledgling to triumph!" said he: "it is early, friend, to think of consigning the old men to the gutters. I still have powers, God be praised! We'll soon see which will put down the other." And the straightforward, honourable man employed intrigues and plots which he had hitherto abhorred. He finally contrived that there should be a competition for the picture which other artists were permitted to enter into with their works. Then he shut himself up in his room, and grasped his brush with zeal. It seemed as if he were striving to summon all his strength for this occasion. And, in fact, it turned out to be one of his best works. No one doubted that he would bear off the palm. The pictures were placed on exhibition, and all the others seemed to his as night to day. Then, of a sudden, one of the members present, an ecclesiastical personage if I mistake not, made a remark which surprised every one. "There is certainly much talent in this artist's picture," said he, "but no holiness in the faces: there is even, on the contrary, a sort of demoniacal look in the eyes, as though some evil feeling had guided the artist's hand." All looked, and could not but acknowledge the truth of the words. My father rushed forward to his picture, as though to verify for himself this offensive remark, and perceived with horror that he had bestowed the usurer's eyes upon nearly all the figures. They had such an annihilatingly diabolical gaze, that he involuntarily shuddered. The picture was rejected; and he was forced to hear, to his indescribable vexation, that the palm was awarded to his pupil. It is impossible to describe the state of rage in which he returned home. He almost killed my mother, he drove the children away, broke his brushes and easels, tore down the usurer's portrait from the wall, demanded a knife, and ordered a fire built in the chimney, intending to cut it in pieces and burn it. A friend, an artist, caught him in the act as he entered the room – a jolly fellow, like my father, always satisfied with himself, inflated by no unattainable wishes, doing daily anything that came to hand, and taking still more gaily to his dinner and little carouses.

' "What are you doing? What are you preparing to burn?" he asked, and stepped up to the portrait. "Why, this is one of your very best works. This is the usurer who died a short time ago: yes, it is a most perfect thing. You did not stop until you had got into his very eyes. Never in life did eyes look as these of yours do now."

' "Well, I'll see how they look in the fire!" said my father, making a movement to fling the portrait into the grate.

' "Stop, for Heaven's sake!" exclaimed his friend, restraining him: "give it to me, rather, if it offends your eyes to such a degree." My father began to insist, but yielded at length; and the jolly fellow, well pleased with his acquisition, carried the portrait home with him.

'When he was gone, my father felt more calm. The burden seemed to have disappeared from his soul together with the portrait. He was surprised himself at his evil feelings, his envy, and the evident change in his character. Reviewing his acts, he became sad at heart; and not without inward sorrow did he exclaim, "No, it was God who punished me! My picture, in fact, brought disgrace. It was meant to ruin my brother-man. A devilish feeling of envy guided my brush, and that devilish feeling must have made itself visible in it." He set out at once to seek his former pupil, embraced him warmly, begged his forgiveness, and endeavoured as far as possible to excuse his own fault. His labours continued, as before, undisturbed; but his face more frequently was thoughtful. He prayed more, grew more taciturn, and expressed himself less sharply about people: even the rough exterior of his character was modified to some extent. But a certain occurrence soon disturbed him more than ever. He had seen nothing for a long time of the comrade who had begged the portrait of him. He had already decided to hunt him up, when the latter suddenly made his appearance in his room. After a few words and questions on both sides, he said, "Well, brother, it was not without cause that you wished to burn that portrait. Devil take it, there's something horrible about it! . . . I don't believe in sorcerers; but, begging your pardon, there's an unclean spirit in it . . . "

' "How so?" asked my father.

' "Well, from the very moment I hung it up in my room, I felt such depression . . . just as if I wanted to murder someone. I never knew in my life what sleeplessness was; but now I suffer not from sleeplessness alone, but from such dreams! . . . I cannot tell whether they are dreams, or what; it is as if a *domovoi* were strangling one: and the old man appears to me in my sleep. In short, I can't describe my state of mind. I never had anything of the sort before. I have been wandering about miserably all the time: I have had a sensation of fear, of expecting something unpleasant. I have felt as if I could not speak a cheerful or sincere word to any one: it is just as if a spy were sitting over me. And from the very hour that I gave that portrait to my nephew, who asked for it, I felt as if a stone had been rolled from my shoulders: I immediately felt cheerful, as you see me now. Well, brother, you made the very Devil!"

'During this recital, my father listened with unswerving attention, and finally enquired, "And your nephew now has the portrait?"

' "My nephew, indeed! He could not stand it!" said the jolly fellow: "do you know, the soul of that usurer has migrated into it; he jumps out of the frame, walks about the room; and what my nephew tells of him is simply incomprehensible. I should take him for a lunatic, if I had not undergone a part of it myself. He sold it to some collector of pictures; and he could not stand it either, and got rid of it to someone else."

'This story produced a deep impression on my father. He became seriously pensive, fell into hypochondria, and finally became fully convinced that his brush had served as a tool of the Devil; that a portion of the usurer's life had actually passed into the portrait, and was now troubling people, inspiring diabolical excitement, beguiling painters from the true path, producing the fearful torments of envy, and so forth, and so forth. Three catastrophes which occurred afterwards, three sudden deaths of wife, daughter, and infant son, he regarded as a divine punishment on him, and firmly resolved to leave the world. As soon as I was nine years old, he placed me in an academy of painting, and, paying all his debts, retired to a lonely cloister, where he soon afterwards took the vows. There he amazed every one by the strictness of his life, and his untiring observance of all the monastic rules. The prior of the monastery, hearing of his skill in painting, ordered him to paint the principal ikon in the church. But the humble brother said plainly that he was unworthy to touch a brush, that his was contaminated, that with toil and great sacrifice must he first purify his spirit in order to render himself fit to undertake such a task. They did not care to force him. He increased the rigours of monastic life for himself as much as possible. At last, even it became insufficient, and not strict enough for him. He retired, with the approval of the prior, into the desert, in order to be quite alone. There he constructed for himself a cell from branches of trees, ate only uncooked roots, dragged about a stone from place to place, stood in one spot with his hands lifted to heaven, from the rising until the going-down of the sun, reciting prayers without cessation: in short, he underwent, it seemed, every possible degree of suffering and of that pitiless self-abnegation, of which instances can perhaps be found in some Lives of the Saints. In this manner did he long – for several years – exhaust his body, invigorating it, at the same time, with the strength of fervent prayer. At length, one day he came to the cloister, and said firmly to the prior, "Now I am ready. If God wills, I will finish my task." The subject he selected was the Birth of Christ. A whole year he sat over it, without leaving his cell, barely sustaining himself with coarse food, and praying incessantly. At the end of the year the picture was ready. It was a really wonderful work. You must know, that neither prior nor brethren knew much about painting; but all were struck with the marvellous holiness of the figures. The expression of reverent humility and gentleness in the face of the Holy Mother, as she bent over the Child; the deep intelligence in the eyes of the Holy Child, as though he saw something afar; the triumphant silence of the Magi, amazed by the Divine Miracle, as they bowed at his feet; and finally, the indescribable peace which informed the whole picture – all this was presented with such even strength and powerful beauty, that the impression it made was magical. All the brethren threw themselves on their knees before the new ikon; and the prior, deeply affected, exclaimed, "No, it is impossible for any artist, with the assistance only of earthly art, to produce such a picture: a holy, divine power guided thy brush, and the blessing of Heaven rested upon thy labour!"

'By that time I had completed my education at the academy, received the gold medal, and with it the joyful hope of a journey to Italy – the fairest dream of a twenty-year-old artist. It only remained for me to take leave of my father, from whom I had been separated for twelve years. I confess that even his image had long faded from my memory. I had heard somewhat of his grim saintliness, and rather expected to meet a hermit of rough exterior, a stranger to everything in the world, except his cell and his prayers, worn out, dried up, by eternal fasting and penance. But how great was my surprise, when a handsome, almost divine, old man stood before me! And no traces of exhaustion were visible on his countenance: it beamed with the light of a heavenly joy. His beard, white as snow, and his thin, almost transparent hair of the same silvery hue, fell picturesquely upon his breast, and upon the folds of his black gown, and even to the rope with which his poor monastic garb was girded. But most surprising to me of all, was to hear from his mouth such words and thoughts about art, as, I confess, I long shall bear in mind, and I sincerely wish that all my comrades would do the same.

' "I expected you, my son," he said, when I approached for his blessing. "The path awaits you, in which your life is henceforth to flow. Your path is pure – desert it not. You have talent: talent is the most priceless of God's gifts – destroy it not. Search out, learn all you see, subject all things to your brush; but in all, see that you find the hidden soul, and most of all, strive to attain to the grand secret of creation. Blessed is the elect one, who masters that! There is for him, no mean object in nature. In lowly themes, the artist creator is as great as in great ones: in the despicable, there is nothing for him to despise; for the glorious mind of the creator penetrates it, and the despicable has received a lofty significance, for it has passed through the purifying fire of his mind. An intimation of God's heavenly paradise is contained for the artist, in art, and by that alone is it higher than all else. But by as much as triumphant rest is grander than every earthly emotion; by as much as the angel, pure in the innocence of its bright spirit, is above all invisible powers and the proud passions of Satan – by just so much is the lofty creation of art higher than everything else on earth. Sacrifice everything to it, and love it with passion – not with the passion breathing with earthly desire, but a peaceful, heavenly passion. Without it a man is not capable of elevating himself above the earth, and cannot produce wondrous sounds of soothing; for the grand creations of art descend into the world in order to soothe and reconcile all. It cannot plant discord in the spirit, but ascends, like a resounding prayer, eternally to God. But there are moments, dark moments" . . . he paused, and I observed that his bright face darkened, as though some cloud crossed it for a moment. "There is one incident of my life," he said. "Up to this moment, I cannot understand what that terrible figure was, of which I painted a likeness. It was certainly some diabolical apparition. I know that the world denies the existence of the Devil, and therefore I will not speak of him. I will only say that I painted him with repugnance: I felt no liking for my work, even at the time. I tried to force myself, and, stifling every emotion in a hard-hearted way, to be true to nature. It was not a creation of art: and therefore the feelings which overpower every one who looks at it, are feelings of repulsion, disturbing emotions, not the feelings of an artist; for an artist infuses peace into commotion. I have been informed that this portrait is passing from hand to hand, and sowing unpleasant impressions, inspiring artists with feelings of envy, of dark hatred towards their brethren, with malicious thirst for persecution and oppression. May the Almighty preserve you from such passions! There is nothing more terrible. It is better to endure the bitterness of all possible persecution than to subject any one to even the shadow of persecution. Preserve the purity of your mind. He who possesses talent should be purer than all others. Much is forgiven to another which is not forgiven to him. A man who has emerged from his house in brilliant, festive garments, has but to be spattered with a single drop of mud from a wheel, and people surround him, and point the finger at him, and talk of his want of cleanliness; while the same people do not perceive the multitude of spots upon other passers-by, who are clothed in ordinary garments, for spots are not visible on ordinary garments."

'He blessed and embraced me. Never in my life was I so grandly moved. Reverently, rather than with the feeling of a son, I leaned upon his breast, and kissed his scattered silver locks.

'Tears shone in his eyes. "Fulfil my one request, my son," said he, at the moment of parting. "You may chance to see the portrait I have mentioned, somewhere. You will know it at once by the strange eyes, and their peculiar expression. Destroy it at any cost . . . "

'Judge for yourselves whether I could refuse to promise, with an oath, to fulfil this request. In the space of fifteen years, I had never succeeded in meeting with anything which in any way corresponded to the description given me by my father, until now, all of a sudden, at an auction . . . '

The artist did not finish his sentence, but turned his eyes to the wall in order to glance once more at the portrait. The whole throng of his auditors made the same movement, seeking the wonderful portrait with their eyes. But, to their extreme amazement, it was no longer on the wall. An indistinct murmur and exclamation ran through the crowd, and then was heard distinctly the word, *stolen*. Someone had succeeded in carrying it off, taking advantage of the fact that the attention of the spectators was distracted by the story. And those present remained long in a state of surprise, not knowing whether they had really seen those remarkable eyes, or whether it was simply a dream, which had floated for an instant before their vision, strained with long gazing at old pictures.

THE OVERCOAT

IN THE DEPARTMENT of . . . but I had better not mention in what department. There is nothing in the world more readily moved to wrath than a department, a regiment, a government office, and in fact any sort of official body. Nowadays every private individual considers all society insulted in his person. I have been told that very lately a petition was handed in from a police-captain of what town I don't recollect, and that in this petition he set forth clearly that the institutions of the State were in danger and that its sacred name was being taken in vain; and, in proof thereof, he appended to his petition an enormously long volume of some work of romance in which a police-captain appeared on every tenth page, occasionally, indeed, in an intoxicated condition. And so, to avoid any unpleasantness, we had better call the department of which we are speaking a certain department.

And so in a certain department there was a government clerk; a clerk of whom it cannot be said that he was very remarkable; he was short, somewhat pockmarked, with rather reddish hair and rather dim, bleary eyes, with a small bald patch on the top of his head, with wrinkles on both sides of his cheeks and the sort of complexion which is usually associated with haemorrhoids . . . no help for that, it is the Petersburg climate. As for his grade in the service (for among us the grade is what must be put first), he was what is called a perpetual titular councillor, a class at which, as we all know, various writers who indulge in the praiseworthy habit of attacking those who cannot defend themselves jeer and jibe to their hearts' content. This clerk's surname was Bash-matchkin. From the very name it is clear that it must have been derived from a shoe (*bashmak*); but when and under what circumstances it was derived from a shoe, it is impossible to say. Both his father and his grandfather and even his brother-in-law, and all the Bashmatchkins without exception wore boots, which they simply re-soled two or three times a year. His name was Akaky Akakyevitch. Perhaps it may strike the reader as a rather strange and far-fetched name, but I can assure him that it was not far-fetched at all, that the circumstances were such that it was quite out of the question to give him any other name. Akaky Akakyevitch was born towards nightfall, if my memory does not deceive me, on the twenty-third of March. His mother, the wife of a government clerk, a very good woman, made arrangements in due course to christen the child. She was still lying in bed, facing the door, while on her right hand stood the godfather, an excellent man called Ivan Ivanovitch Yeroshkin, one of the head clerks in the Senate, and the godmother, the wife of a police official, and a woman of rare qualities, Arina Semyonovna Byelobryushkov. Three names were offered to the happy mother for selection – Moky, Sossy, or the name of the martyr Hozdazat. 'No,' thought the poor lady, 'they are all such names!' To satisfy her, they opened the calendar at another place, and the names which turned up were: Trifily, Dula, Varahasy. 'What an infliction!' said the mother. 'What names they all are! I really never heard such names. Varadat or Varuh would be bad enough, but Trifily and Varahasy!' They turned over another page and the names were: Pavsikahy and Vahtisy. 'Well, I see,' said the mother, 'it is clear that it is his fate. Since that is how it is, he had better be called after his father, his father is Akaky, let the son be Akaky, too.' This was how he came to be Akaky Akakyevitch. The baby was christened and cried and made wry faces during the ceremony, as though he foresaw that he would be a titular councillor. So that was how it all came to pass. We have recalled it here so that the reader may see for himself that it happened quite inevitably and that to give him any other name was out of the question. No one has been able to remember when and how long ago he entered the department, nor who gave him the job. However many directors and higher officials of all sorts came and went, he was always seen in the same place, in the same position, at the very same duty, precisely the same copying clerk, so that they used to declare that he must have been born a copying clerk in uniform all complete and with a bald patch on his head. No respect at all was shown him in the department. The porters, far from getting up from their seats when he came in, took no more notice of him than if a simple fly had flown across the vestibule. His superiors treated him with a sort of domineering chilliness. The head clerk's assistant used to throw papers under his nose without even saying: 'Copy this' or 'Here is an interesting, nice little case' or some agreeable remark of the sort, as is usually done in well-behaved offices. And he would take it, gazing only at the paper without looking to see who had put it there and whether he had the right to do so; he would take it and at once set to work to copy it. The young clerks jeered and made jokes at him to the best of their clerkly wit, and told before his face all sorts of stories of their own invention about him; they would say of his landlady, an old woman of seventy, that she beat him, would enquire when the wedding was to take place, and would scatter bits of paper on his head, calling them snow. Akaky Akakyevitch never answered a word, however, but behaved as though there were no one there. It had no influence on his work even; in the midst of all this teasing, he never made a single mistake in his copying. Only when the jokes were too unbearable, when they jolted his arm and prevented him from going on with his work, he would bring out: 'Leave me alone! Why do you insult me?' and there was something strange in the words and in the voice in which they were uttered. There was a note in it of something that aroused compassion, so that one young man, new to the office, who, following the example of the rest, had allowed himself to mock at him, suddenly stopped as though cut to the heart, and from that time forth, everything was, as it were, changed and appeared in a different light to him. Some unnatural force seemed to thrust him away from the companions with whom he had become acquainted, accepting them as well-bred, polished people. And long afterwards, at moments of the greatest gaiety, the figure of the humble little clerk with a bald patch on his head rose before him with his heart-rending words: 'Leave me alone! Why do you insult me?' and in those heart-rending words he heard others: 'I am your brother.' And the poor young man hid his face in his hands, and many times afterwards in his life he shuddered, seeing how much inhumanity there is in man, how much savage brutality lies hidden under refined, cultured politeness, and, my God! Even in a man whom the world accepts as a gentleman and a man of honour . . .

It would be hard to find a man who lived in his work as did Akaky Akakyevitch. To say that he was zealous in his work is not enough; no, he loved his work. In it, in that copying, he found a varied and agreeable world of his own. There was a look of enjoyment on his face; certain letters were favourites with him, and when he came to them he was delighted; he chuckled to himself and winked and moved his lips, so that it seemed as though every letter his pen was forming could be read in his face. If rewards had been given according to the measure of zeal in the service, he might to his amazement have even found himself a civil councillor; but all he gained in the service, as the wits, his fellow-clerks expressed it, was a buckle in his buttonhole and a pain in his back. It cannot be said, however, that no notice had ever been taken of him. One director, being a good-natured man and anxious to reward him for his long service, sent him something a little more important than his ordinary copying; he was instructed from a finished document to make some sort of report for another office; the work consisted only of altering the headings and in places changing the first person into the third. This cost him such an effort that it threw him into a regular perspiration: he mopped his brow and said at last, 'No, better let me copy something.'

From that time forth they left him to go on copying for ever. It seemed as though nothing in the world existed for him outside his copying. He gave no thought at all to his clothes; his uniform was – well, not green but some sort of rusty, muddy colour. His collar was very short and narrow, so that, although his neck was not particularly long, yet, standing out of the collar, it looked as immensely long as those of the plaster kittens that wag their heads and are carried about on trays on the heads of dozens of foreigners living in Russia. And there were always things sticking to his uniform, either bits of hay or threads; moreover, he had a special art of passing under a window at the very moment when various rubbish was being flung out into the street, and so was continually carrying off bits of melon rind and similar litter on his hat. He had never once in his life noticed what was being done and going on in the street, all those things at which, as we all know, his colleagues, the young clerks, always stare, carrying their sharp sight so far even as to notice any one on the other side of the pavement with a trouser strap hanging loose – a detail which always calls forth a sly grin. Whatever Akaky Akakyevitch looked at, he saw nothing anywhere but his clear, evenly written lines, and only perhaps when a horse's head suddenly appeared from nowhere just on his shoulder, and its nostrils blew a perfect gale upon his cheek, did he notice that he was not in the middle of his writing, but rather in the middle of the street.

On reaching home, he would sit down at once to the table, hurriedly sup his soup and eat a piece of beef with an onion; he did not notice the taste at all, but ate it all up together with the flies and anything else that Providence chanced to send him. When he felt that his stomach was beginning to be full, he would rise up from the table, get out a bottle of ink and set to copying the papers he had brought home with him. When he had none to do, he would make a copy expressly for his own pleasure, particularly if the document were remarkable not for the beauty of its style but for the fact of its being addressed to some new or important personage.

Even at those hours when the grey Petersburg sky is completely overcast and the whole population of clerks have dined and eaten their fill, each as best he can, according to the salary he receives and his personal tastes, when they are all resting after the scratching of pens and bustle of the office, their own necessary work and other people's, and all the tasks that an over-zealous man voluntarily sets himself even beyond what is necessary, when the clerks are hastening to devote what is left of their time to pleasure; some more enterprising are flying to the theatre, others to the street to spend their leisure, staring at women's hats, some to spend the evening paying compliments to some attractive girl, the star of a little official circle, while some – and this is the most frequent of all – go simply to a fellow-clerk's flat on the third or fourth storey, two little rooms with an entry or a kitchen, with some pretensions to style, with a lamp or some such article that has cost many sacrifices of dinners and excursions – at the time when all the clerks are scattered about the little flats of their friends, playing a tempestuous game of whist, sipping tea out of glasses to the accompaniment of farthing rusks, sucking in smoke from long pipes, telling, as the cards are dealt, some scandal that has floated down from higher circles, a pleasure which the Russian can never by any possibility deny himself, or, when there is nothing better to talk about, repeating the everlasting anecdote of the commanding officer who was told that the tail had been cut off the horse on the Falconet monument[183] – in short, even when every one was eagerly seeking entertainment, Akaky Akakyevitch did not give himself up to any amusement. No one could say that they had ever seen him at an evening party. After working to his heart's content, he would go to bed, smiling at the thought of the next day and wondering what God would send him to copy. So flowed on the peaceful life of a man who knew how to be content with his fate on a salary of four hundred roubles, and so perhaps it would have flowed on to extreme old age, had it not been for the various calamities that bestrew the path through life, not only of titular, but even of privy, actual court and all other councillors, even those who neither give counsel to others nor accept it themselves.

There is in Petersburg a mighty foe of all who receive a salary of four hundred roubles or about that sum. That foe is none other than our northern frost, although it is said to be very good for the health. Between eight and nine in the morning, precisely at the hour when the streets are full of clerks going to their departments, the frost begins giving such sharp and stinging flips at all their noses indiscriminately that the poor fellows don't know what to do with them. At that time, when even those in the higher grade have a pain in their brows and tears in their eyes from the frost, the poor titular councillors are sometimes almost defenceless. Their only protection lies in running as fast as they can through five or six streets in a wretched, thin little overcoat and then warming their feet thoroughly in the porter's room, till all their faculties and qualifications for their various duties thaw again after being frozen on the way. Akaky Akakyevitch had for some time been feeling that his back and shoulders were particularly nipped by the cold, although he did try to run the regular distance as fast as he could. He wondered at last whether there were any defects in his overcoat. After examining it thoroughly in the privacy of his home, he discovered that in two or three places, to wit on the back and the shoulders, it had become a regular sieve; the cloth was so worn that you could see through it and the lining was coming out. I must observe that Akaky Akakyevitch's overcoat had also served as a butt for the jibes of the clerks. It had even been deprived of the honourable name of overcoat and had been referred to as the 'dressing jacket.' It was indeed of rather a strange make. Its collar had been growing smaller year by year as it served to patch the other parts. The patches were not good specimens of the tailor's art, and they certainly looked clumsy and ugly. On seeing what was wrong, Akaky Akakyevitch decided that he would have to take the overcoat to Petrovitch, a tailor who lived on a fourth storey up a back staircase, and, in spite of having only one eye and being pockmarked all over his face, was rather successful in repairing the trousers and coats of clerks and others – that is, when he was sober, be it understood, and had no other enterprise in his mind. Of this tailor I ought not, of course, to say much, but since it is now the rule that the character of every person in a novel must be completely drawn, well, there is no help for it, here is Petrovitch too. At first he was called simply Grigory, and was a serf belonging to some gentleman or other. He began to be called Petrovitch from the time that he got his freedom and began to drink rather heavily on every holiday, at first only on the chief holidays, but afterwards on all church holidays indiscriminately, wherever there is a cross in the calendar. On that side he was true to the customs of his forefathers, and when he quarrelled with his wife used to call her 'a worldly woman and a German.' Since we have now mentioned the wife, it will be necessary to say a few words about her too, but unfortunately not much is known about her, except indeed that Petrovitch had a wife and that she wore a cap and not a kerchief, but apparently she could not boast of beauty; anyway, none but soldiers of the Guards peeped under her cap when they met her, and they twitched their moustaches and gave vent to a rather peculiar sound.

As he climbed the stairs leading to Petrovitch's – which, to do them justice, were all soaked with water and slops and saturated through and through with that smell of spirits which makes the eyes smart, and is, as we all know, inseparable from the back stairs of Petersburg houses – Akaky Akakyevitch was already wondering how much Petrovitch would ask for the job, and inwardly resolving not to give more than two roubles. The door was open, for Petrovitch's wife was frying some fish and had so filled the kitchen with smoke that you could not even see the black-beetles. Akaky Akakyevitch crossed the kitchen unnoticed by the good woman, and walked at last into a room where he saw Petrovitch sitting on a big, wooden, unpainted table with his legs tucked under him like a Turkish Pasha. The feet, as is usual with tailors when they sit at work, were bare; and the first object that caught Akaky Akakyevitch's eye was the big toe, with which he was already familiar, with a misshapen nail as thick and strong as the shell of a tortoise. Round Petrovitch's neck hung a skein of silk and another of thread and on his knees was a rag of some sort. He had for the last three minutes been trying to thread his needle, but could not get the thread into the eye and so was very angry with the darkness and indeed with the thread itself, muttering in an undertone: 'It won't go in, the savage! You wear me out, you rascal.' Akaky Akakyevitch was vexed that he had come just at the minute when Petrovitch was in a bad humour; he liked to give him an order when he was a little 'elevated,' or, as his wife expressed it, 'had fortified himself with fizz, the one-eyed devil.' In such circumstances Petrovitch was as a rule very ready to give way and agree, and invariably bowed and thanked him, indeed. Afterwards, it is true, his wife would come wailing that her husband had been drunk and so had asked too little, but adding a single ten-kopeck piece would settle that. But on this occasion Petrovitch was apparently sober and consequently curt, unwilling to bargain, and the devil knows what price he would be ready to lay on. Akaky Akakyevitch perceived this and was, as the saying is, beating a retreat, but things had gone too far, for Petrovitch was screwing up his solitary eye very attentively at him and Akaky Akakyevitch involuntarily brought out: 'Good-day, Petrovitch!' 'I wish you a good-day, sir,' said Petrovitch, and squinted at Akaky Akakyevitch's hands, trying to discover what sort of goods he had brought.

'Here I have come to you, Petrovitch, do you see . . . !'

It must be noticed that Akaky Akakyevitch for the most part explained himself by apologies, vague phrases, and particles which have absolutely no significance whatever. If the subject were a very difficult one, it was his habit indeed to leave his sentences quite unfinished, so that very often after a sentence had begun with the words 'It really is, don't you know . . . ' nothing at all would follow and he himself would be quite oblivious, supposing he had said all that was necessary.

'What is it?' said Petrovitch, and at the same time with his solitary eye he scrutinised his whole uniform from the collar to the sleeves, the back, the skirts, the buttonholes – with all of which he was very familiar, they were all his own work. Such scrutiny is habitual with tailors, it is the first thing they do on meeting one.

'It's like this, Petrovitch . . . the overcoat, the cloth . . . you see everywhere else it is quite strong; it's a little dusty and looks as though it were old, but it is new and it is only in one place just a little . . . on the back, and just a little worn on one shoulder and on this shoulder, too, a little . . . do you see? That's all, and it's not much work . . .'

Petrovitch took the 'dressing jacket,' first spread it out over the table, examined it for a long time, shook his head and put his hand out to the window for a round snuffbox with a portrait on the lid of some general – which precisely I can't say, for a finger had been thrust through the spot where a face should have been, and the hole had been pasted up with a square bit of paper. After taking a pinch of snuff, Petrovitch held the 'dressing jacket' up in his hands and looked at it against the light, and again he shook his head; then he turned it with the lining upwards and once more shook his head; again he took off the lid with the general pasted up with paper and stuffed a pinch into his nose, shut the box, put it away and at last said: 'No, it can't be repaired; a wretched garment!' Akaky Akakyevitch's heart sank at those words.

'Why can't it, Petrovitch?' he said, almost in the imploring voice of a child. 'Why, the only thing is it is a bit worn on the shoulders; why, you have got some little pieces . . .'

'Yes, the pieces will be found all right,' said Petrovitch, 'but it can't be patched, the stuff is quite rotten; if you put a needle in it, it would give way.'

'Let it give way, but you just put a patch on it.'

'There is nothing to put a patch on. There is nothing for it to hold on to; there is a great strain on it, it is not worth calling cloth, it would fly away at a breath of wind.'

'Well, then, strengthen it with something – upon my word, really, this is . . . !'

'No,' said Petrovitch resolutely, 'there is nothing to be done, the thing is no good at all. You had far better, when the cold winter weather comes, make yourself leg wrappings out of it, for there is no warmth in stockings, the Germans invented them just to make money.' (Petrovitch was fond of a dig at the Germans occasionally.) 'And as for the overcoat, it is clear that you will have to have a new one.'

At the word 'new' there was a mist before Akaky Akakyevitch's eyes, and everything in the room seemed blurred. He could see nothing clearly but the general with the piece of paper over his face on the lid of Petrovitch's snuffbox.

'A new one?' he said, still feeling as though he were in a dream; 'why, I haven't the money for it.'

'Yes, a new one,' Petrovitch repeated with barbarous composure.

'Well, and if I did have a new one, how much would it . . . ?'

'You mean what will it cost?'

'Yes.'

'Well, three fifty-rouble notes or more,' said Petrovitch, and he compressed his lips significantly. He was very fond of making an effect, he was fond of suddenly disconcerting a man completely and then squinting sideways to see what sort of a face he made.

'A hundred and fifty roubles for an overcoat,' screamed poor Akaky Akakyevitch – it was perhaps the first time he had screamed in his life, for he was always distinguished by the softness of his voice.

'Yes,' said Petrovitch, 'and even then it's according to the coat. If I were to put marten on the collar, and add a hood with silk linings, it would come to two hundred.'

'Petrovitch, please,' said Akaky Akakyevitch in an imploring voice, not hearing and not trying to hear what Petrovitch said, and missing all his effects, 'do repair it somehow, so that it will serve a little longer.'

'No, that would be wasting work and spending money for nothing,' said Petrovitch, and after that Akaky Akakyevitch went away completely crushed, and when he had gone Petrovitch remained standing for a long time with his lips pursed up significantly before he took up his work again, feeling pleased that he had not demeaned himself nor lowered the dignity of the tailor's art.

When he got into the street, Akaky Akakyevitch was as though in a dream. 'So that is how it is,' he said to himself. 'I really did not think it would be so . . . ' and then after a pause he added, 'So there it is! so that's how it is at last! and I really could never have supposed it would have been so. And there . . . ' There followed another long silence, after which he brought out: 'So there it is! well, it really is so utterly unexpected . . . who would have thought . . . what a circumstance . . . ' Saying this, instead of going home he walked off in quite the opposite direction without suspecting what he was doing. On the way a clumsy sweep brushed the whole of his sooty side against him and blackened all his shoulder; a regular hatful of plaster scattered upon him from the top of a house that was being built. He noticed nothing of this, and only after he had jostled against a sentry who had set his halberd down beside him and was shaking some snuff out of his horn into his rough fist, he came to himself a little and then only because the sentry said: 'Why are you poking yourself right in one's face, haven't you the pavement to yourself?' This made him look round and turn homeward; only there he began to collect his thoughts, to see his position in a clear and true light and began talking to himself no longer incoherently but reasonably and openly as with a sensible friend with whom one can discuss the most intimate and vital matters. 'No, indeed,' said Akaky Akakyevitch, 'it is no use talking to Petrovitch now; just now he really is . . . his wife must have been giving it to him. I had better go to him on Sunday morning; after the Saturday evening he will be squinting and sleepy, so he'll want a little drink to carry it off and his wife won't give him a penny. I'll slip ten kopecks into his hand and then he will be more accommodating and maybe take the overcoat . . .'

So reasoning with himself, Akaky Akakyevitch cheered up and waited until the next Sunday; then, seeing from a distance Petrovitch's wife leaving the house, he went straight in. Petrovitch certainly was very tipsy after the Saturday. He could hardly hold his head up and was very drowsy: but, for all that, as soon as he heard what he was speaking about, it seemed as though the devil had nudged him. 'I can't,' he said, 'you must kindly order a new one.' Akaky Akakyevitch at once slipped a ten-kopeck piece into his hand. 'I thank you, sir, I will have just a drop to your health, but don't trouble yourself about the overcoat; it is not a bit of good for anything. I'll make you a fine new coat, you can trust me for that.'

Akaky Akakyevitch would have said more about repairs, but Petrovitch, without listening, said: 'A new one now I'll make you without fail; you can rely upon that, I'll do my best. It could even be like the fashion that has come in with the collar to button with silver claws under appliqué.'

Then Akaky Akakyevitch saw that there was no escape from a new overcoat and he was utterly depressed. How indeed, for what, with what money could he get it? Of course he could to some extent rely on the bonus for the coming holiday, but that money had long ago been appropriated and its use determined beforehand. It was needed for new trousers and to pay the cobbler an old debt for putting some new tops to some old boot-legs, and he had to order three shirts from a seamstress as well as two specimens of an undergarment which it is improper to mention in print; in short, all that money absolutely must be spent, and even if the director were to be so gracious as to assign him a gratuity of forty-five or even fifty, instead of forty roubles, there would still be left a mere trifle, which would be but as a drop in the ocean beside the fortune needed for an overcoat. Though, of course, he knew that Petrovitch had a strange craze for suddenly putting on the devil knows what enormous price, so that at times his own wife could not help crying out: 'Why, you are out of your wits, you idiot! Another time he'll undertake a job for nothing, and here the devil has bewitched him to ask more than he is worth himself.' Though, of course, he knew that Petrovitch would undertake to make it for eighty roubles, still where would he get those eighty roubles? He might manage half of that sum; half of it could be found, perhaps even a little more; but where could he get the other half? . . . But, first of all, the reader ought to know where that first half was to be found. Akaky Akakyevitch had the habit every time he spent a rouble of putting aside two kopecks in a little locked-up box with a slit in the lid for slipping the money in. At the end of every half-year he would inspect the pile of coppers there and change them for small silver. He had done this for a long time, and in the course of many years the sum had mounted up to forty roubles and so he had half the money in his hands, but where was he to get the other half, where was he to get another forty roubles? Akaky Akakyevitch pondered and pondered and decided at last that he would have to diminish his ordinary expenses, at least for a year; give up burning candles in the evening, and if he had to do anything he must go into the landlady's room and work by her candle; that as he walked along the streets he must walk as lightly and carefully as possible, almost on tiptoe, on the cobbles and flagstones, so that his soles might last a little longer than usual, that he must send his linen to the wash less frequently, and that, to preserve it from being worn, he must take it off every day when he came home and sit in a thin cotton-shoddy dressing-gown, a very ancient garment which Time itself had spared. To tell the truth, he found it at first rather hard to get used to these privations, but after a while it became a habit and went smoothly enough – he even became quite accustomed to being hungry in the evening; on the other hand, he had spiritual nourishment, for he carried ever in his thoughts the idea of his future overcoat. His whole existence had in a sense become fuller, as though he had married, as though some other person were present with him, as though he were no longer alone, but an agreeable companion had consented to walk the path of life hand in hand with him, and that companion was no other than the new over-coat with its thick wadding and its strong, durable lining. He became, as it were, more alive, even: more strong-willed, like a man who has set before himself a definite aim. Uncertainty, indecision, in fact all the hesitating and vague characteristics vanished from his face and his manners. At times there was a gleam in his eyes, indeed, the most bold and audacious ideas flashed through his mind. Why not really have marten on the collar? Meditation on the subject always made him absent-minded. On one occasion when he was copying a document, he very nearly made a mistake, so that he almost cried out 'ough' aloud and crossed himself. At least once every month he went to Petrovitch to talk about the overcoat, where it would be best to buy the cloth, and what colour it should be, and what price, and, though he returned home a little anxious, he was always pleased at the thought that at last the time was at hand when everything would be bought and the overcoat would be made. Things moved even faster than he had anticipated. Contrary to all expectations, the director bestowed on Akaky Akakyevitch a gratuity of no less than sixty roubles. Whether it was that he had an inkling that Akaky Akakyevitch needed a greatcoat, or whether it happened so by chance, owing to this he found he had twenty roubles extra. This circumstance hastened the course of affairs. Another two or three months of partial fasting and Akaky Akakyevitch had actually saved up nearly eighty roubles. His heart, as a rule very tranquil, began to throb. The very first day he set off in company with Petrovitch to the shops. They bought some very good cloth, and no wonder, since they had been thinking of it for more than six months before, and scarcely a month had passed without their going to the shop to compare prices; now Petrovitch himself declared that there was no better cloth to be had. For the lining they chose calico, but of a stout quality, which in Petrovitch's words was even better than silk, and actually as strong and handsome to look at. Marten they did not buy, because it certainly was dear, but instead they chose cat fur, the best to be found in the shop – cat which in the distance might almost be taken for marten. Petrovitch was busy over the coat for a whole fortnight, because there were a great many buttonholes, otherwise it would have been ready sooner. Petro-vitch asked twelve roubles for the work; less than that it hardly could have been, everything was sewn with silk, with fine double seams, and Petrovitch went over every seam afterwards with his own teeth imprinting various figures with them. It was . . . it is hard to say precisely on what day, but probably on the most triumphant day of the life of Akaky Akakyevitch that Petrovitch at last brought the overcoat. He brought it in the morning, just before it was time to set off for the department. The overcoat could not have arrived more in the nick of time, for rather sharp frosts were just beginning and seemed threatening to be even more severe. Petrovitch brought the greatcoat himself as a good tailor should. There was an expression of importance on his face, such as Akaky Akakyevitch had never seen there before. He seemed fully conscious of having completed a work of no little moment and of having shown in his own person the gulf that separates tailors who only put in linings and do repairs from those who make up new materials. He took the greatcoat out of the pocket-handkerchief in which he had brought it (the pocket-handkerchief had just come home from the wash), he then folded it up and put it in his pocket for future use. After taking out the overcoat, he looked at it with much pride and, holding it in both hands, threw it very deftly over Akaky Akakyevitch's shoulders, then pulled it down and smoothed it out behind with his hands; then draped it about Akaky Akakyevitch with somewhat jaunty carelessness. The latter, as a man advanced in years, wished to try it with his arms in the sleeves. Petrovitch helped him to put it on, and it appeared that it looked splendid too with his arms in the sleeves. In fact it turned out that the overcoat was completely and entirely successful. Petrovitch did not let slip the occasion for observing that it was only because he lived in a small street and had no signboard, and because he had known Akaky Akakyevitch so long, that he had done it so cheaply, but on Nevsky Prospect they would have asked him seventy-five roubles for the work alone. Akaky Akakyevitch had no inclination to discuss this with Petrovitch, besides he was frightened of the big sums that Petro-vitch was fond of flinging airily about in conversation. He paid him, thanked him, and went off on the spot, with his new overcoat on, to the department. Petrovitch followed him out and stopped in the street, staring for a good time at the coat from a distance and then purposely turned off and, taking a short cut by a side street, came back into the street and got another view of the coat from the other side, that is, from the front.

Meanwhile Akaky Akakyevitch walked along with every emotion in its most holiday mood. He felt every second that he had a new overcoat on his shoulders, and several times he actually laughed from inward satisfaction. Indeed, it had two advantages, one that it was warm and the other that it was good. He did not notice the way at all and found himself all at once at the department; in the porter's room he took off the overcoat, looked it over and put it in the porter's special care. I cannot tell how it happened, but all at once every one in the department learned that Akaky Akakyevitch had a new overcoat and that the 'dressing jacket' no longer existed. They all ran out at once into the porter's room to look at Akaky Akakyevitch's new overcoat, they began welcoming him and congratulating him so that at first he could do nothing but smile and afterwards felt positively abashed. When, coming up to him, they all began saying that he must 'sprinkle' the new overcoat and that he ought at least to stand them all a supper, Akaky Akakyevitch lost his head completely and did not know what to do, how to get out of it, nor what to answer. A few minutes later, flushing crimson, he even began assuring them with great simplicity that it was not a new overcoat at all, that it was just nothing, that it was an old overcoat. At last one of the clerks, indeed the assistant of the head clerk of the room, probably in order to show that he was not proud and was able to get on with those beneath him, said: 'So be it, I'll give a party instead of Akaky Akakyevitch and invite you all to tea with me this evening; as luck would have it, it is my name-day.' The clerks naturally congratulated the assistant head clerk and eagerly accepted the invitation. Akaky Akakyevitch was beginning to make excuses, but they all declared that it was uncivil of him, that it was simply a shame and a disgrace and that he could not possibly refuse. However, he felt pleased about it afterwards when he remembered that through this he would have the opportunity of going out in the evening, too, in his new overcoat. That whole day was for Akaky Akakyevitch the most triumphant and festive day in his life. He returned home in the happiest frame of mind, took off the overcoat and hung it carefully on the wall, admiring the cloth and lining once more, and then pulled out his old 'dressing jacket,' now completely coming to pieces, on purpose to compare them. He glanced at it and positively laughed, the difference was so immense! And long afterwards he went on laughing at dinner, as the position in which the 'dressing jacket' was placed recurred to his mind. He dined in excellent spirits and after dinner wrote nothing, no papers at all, but just took his ease for a little while on his bed, till it got dark, then, without putting things off, he dressed, put on his overcoat, and went out into the street. Where precisely the clerk who had invited him lived we regret to say that we cannot tell; our memory is beginning to fail sadly, and everything there is in Petersburg, all the streets and houses, are so blurred and muddled in our head that it is a very difficult business to put anything in orderly fashion. However that may have been, there is no doubt that the clerk lived in the better part of the town and consequently a very long distance from Akaky Akakyevitch. At first the latter had to walk through deserted streets, scantily lighted, but as he approached his destination the streets became more lively, more full of people, and more brightly lighted; passers-by began to be more frequent, ladies began to appear, here and there, beautifully dressed, beaver collars were to be seen on the men. Cabmen with wooden trelliswork sledges, studded with gilt nails, were less frequently to be met; on the other hand, jaunty drivers in raspberry-coloured velvet caps with varnished sledges and bearskin rugs appeared, and carriages with decorated boxes dashed along the streets, their wheels crunching through the snow.

Akaky Akakyevitch looked at all this as a novelty; for several years he had not gone out into the streets in the evening. He stopped with curiosity before a lighted shop-window to look at a picture in which a beautiful woman was represented in the act of taking off her shoe and displaying as she did so the whole of a very shapely leg, while behind her back a gentleman with whiskers and a handsome imperial on his chin was putting his head in at the door. Akaky Akakyevitch shook his head and smiled and then went on his way. Why did he smile? Was it because he had come across something quite unfamiliar to him, though every man retains some instinctive feeling on the subject, or was it that he reflected, like many other clerks, as follows: 'Well, upon my soul, those Frenchmen! It's beyond anything! If they try on anything of the sort, it really is . . . !' Though possibly he did not even think that; there is no creeping into a man's soul and finding out all that he thinks. At last he reached the house in which the assistant head clerk lived in fine style; there was a lamp burning on the stairs, and the flat was on the second floor. As he went into the entry Akaky Akakyevitch saw whole rows of goloshes. Amongst them in the middle of the room stood a samovar hissing and letting off clouds of steam. On the walls hung coats and cloaks, among which some actually had beaver collars or velvet revers. The other side of the wall there was noise and talk, which suddenly became clear and loud when the door opened and the footman came out with a tray full of empty glasses, a jug of cream, and a basket of biscuits. It was evident that the clerks had arrived long before and had already drunk their first glass of tea. Akaky Akakyevitch, after hanging up his coat with his own hands, went into the room, and at the same moment there flashed before his eyes a vision of candles, clerks, pipes, and card tables, together with the confused sounds of conversation rising up on all sides and the noise of moving chairs. He stopped very awkwardly in the middle of the room, looking about and trying to think what to do, but he was observed and received with a shout and they all went at once into the entry and again took a look at his overcoat. Though Akaky Akakyevitch was somewhat embarrassed, yet, being a simple-hearted man, he could not help being pleased at seeing how they all admired his coat. Then of course they all abandoned him and his coat, and turned their attention as usual to the tables set for whist. All this – the noise, the talk, and the crowd of people – was strange and wonderful to Akaky Akakyevitch. He simply did not know how to behave, what to do with his arms and legs and his whole figure; at last he sat down beside the players, looked at the cards, stared first at one and then at another of the faces, and in a little while began to yawn and felt that he was bored – especially as it was long past the time at which he usually went to bed. He tried to take leave of his hosts, but they would not let him go, saying that he absolutely must have a glass of champagne in honour of the new coat. An hour later supper was served, consisting of salad, cold veal, a pasty, pies, and tarts from the confectioner's, and champagne. They made Akaky Akakyevitch drink two glasses, after which he felt that things were much more cheerful, though he could not forget that it was twelve o'clock and that he ought to have been home long ago. That his host might not take it into his head to detain him, he slipped out of the room, hunted in the entry for his greatcoat, which he found, not without regret, lying on the floor, shook it, removed some fluff from it, put it on, and went down the stairs into the street. It was still light in the streets. Some little general shops, those perpetual clubs for house-serfs and all sorts of people, were open; others which were closed showed, however, a long streak of light at every crack of the door, proving that they were not yet deserted, and probably maids and menservants were still finishing their conversation and discussion, driving their masters to utter perplexity as to their whereabouts. Akaky Akakyevitch walked along in a cheerful state of mind; he was even on the point of running, goodness knows why, after a lady of some sort who passed by like lightning with every part of her frame in violent motion. He checked himself at once, however, and again walked along very gently, feeling positively surprised himself at the inexplicable impulse that had seized him. Soon the deserted streets, which are not particularly cheerful by day and even less so in the evening, stretched before him. Now they were still more dead and deserted; the light of street lamps was scantier, the oil was evidently running low; then came wooden houses and fences; not a soul anywhere; only the snow gleamed on the streets and the low-pitched slumbering hovels looked black and gloomy with their closed shutters. He approached the spot where the street was intersected by an endless square, which looked like a fearful desert with its houses scarcely visible on the further side.

In the distance, goodness knows where, there was a gleam of light from some sentry-box which seemed to be standing at the end of the world. Akaky Akakyevitch's light-heartedness grew somehow sensibly less at this place. He stepped into the square, not without an involuntary uneasiness, as though his heart had a foreboding of evil. He looked behind him and to both sides – it was as though the sea were all round him. 'No, better not look,' he thought, and walked on, shutting his eyes, and when he opened them to see whether the end of the square were near, he suddenly saw standing before him, almost under his very nose, some men with moustaches; just what they were like he could not even distinguish. There was a mist before his eyes and a throbbing in his chest. 'I say the overcoat is mine!' said one of them in a voice like a clap of thunder, seizing him by the collar. Akaky Akakyevitch was on the point of shouting 'Help' when another put a fist the size of a clerk's head against his very lips, saying: 'You just shout now.' Akaky Akakyevitch felt only that they took the overcoat off, and gave him a kick with their knees, and he fell on his face in the snow and was conscious of nothing more. A few minutes later he came to himself and got on to his feet, but there was no one there. He felt that it was cold on the ground and that he had no overcoat, and began screaming, but it seemed as though his voice could not carry to the end of the square. Overwhelmed with despair and continuing to scream, he ran across the square straight to the sentry-box, beside which stood a sentry leaning on his halberd and, so it seemed, looking with curiosity to see who the devil the man was who was screaming and running towards him from the distance. As Akaky Akakyevitch reached him, he began breathlessly shouting that he was asleep and not looking after his duty not to see that a man was being robbed. The sentry answered that he had seen nothing, that he had only seen him stopped in the middle of the square by two men, and supposed that they were his friends, and that, instead of abusing him for nothing, he had better go the next day to the superintendent and that he would find out who had taken the overcoat. Akaky Akakyevitch ran home in a terrible state: his hair, which was still comparatively abundant on his temples and the back of his head, was completely dishevelled; his sides and chest and his trousers were all covered with snow. When his old landlady heard a fearful knock at the door she jumped hurriedly out of bed and, with only one slipper on, ran to open it, modestly holding her shift across her bosom; but when she opened it she stepped back, seeing what a state Akaky Akakyevitch was in. When he told her what had happened, she clasped her hands in horror and said that he must go straight to the superintendent, that the police constable of the quarter would deceive him, make promises and lead him a dance; that it would be best of all to go to the superintendent, and that she knew him indeed, because Anna the Finnish girl who was once her cook was now in service as a nurse at the superintendent's; and that she often saw him himself when he passed by their house, and that he used to be every Sunday at church too, saying his prayers and at the same time looking good-humouredly at every one, and that therefore by every token he must be a kind-hearted man. After listening to this advice, Akaky Akakyevitch made his way very gloomily to his room, and how he spent that night I leave to the imagination of those who are in the least able to picture the position of others. Early in the morning he set off to the police superintendent's, but was told that he was asleep. He came at ten o'clock, he was told again that he was asleep; he came at eleven and was told that the superintendent was not at home; he came at dinner-time, but the clerks in the ante-room would not let him in, and insisted on knowing what was the matter and what business had brought him and exactly what had happened; so that at last Akaky Akakyevitch for the first time in his life tried to show the strength of his character and said curtly that he must see the superintendent himself, that they dare not refuse to admit him, that he had come from the department on government business, and that if he made complaint of them they would see. The clerks dared say nothing to this, and one of them went to summon the superintendent. The latter received his story of being robbed of his overcoat in an extremely strange way. Instead of attending to the main point, he began asking Akaky Akakyevitch questions, why had he been coming home so late? Wasn't he going, or hadn't he been, to some house of ill-fame? So that Akaky Akakyevitch was overwhelmed with confusion, and went away without knowing whether or not the proper measures would be taken in regard to his overcoat. He was absent from the office all that day (the only time that it had happened in his life). Next day he appeared with a pale face, wearing his old 'dressing jacket' which had become a still more pitiful sight. The tidings of the theft of the overcoat – though there were clerks who did not let even this chance slip of jeering at Akaky Akakyevitch – touched many of them. They decided on the spot to get up a subscription for him, but collected only a very trifling sum, because the clerks had already spent a good deal on subscribing to the director's portrait and on the purchase of a book, at the suggestion of the head of their department, who was a friend of the author, and so the total realised was very insignificant. One of the clerks, moved by compassion, ventured at any rate to assist Akaky Akakyevitch with good advice, telling him not to go to the district police inspector, because, though it might happen that the latter might be sufficiently zealous of gaining the approval of his superiors to succeed in finding the overcoat, it would remain in the possession of the police unless he presented legal proofs that it belonged to him; he urged that far the best thing would be to appeal to a Person of Consequence; that the Person of Consequence, by writing and getting into communication with the proper authorities, could push the matter through more successfully. There was nothing else for it. Akaky Akakyevitch made up his mind to go to the Person of Consequence. What precisely was the nature of the functions of the Person of Consequence has remained a matter of uncertainty. It must be noted that this Person of Consequence had only lately become a person of consequence, and until recently had been a person of no consequence. Though, indeed, his position even now was not reckoned of consequence in comparison with others of still greater consequence. But there is always to be found a circle of persons to whom a person of little consequence in the eyes of others is a person of consequence. It is true that he did his utmost to increase the consequence of his position in various ways, for instance by insisting that his subordinates should come out on to the stairs to meet him when he arrived at his office; that no one should venture to approach him directly, but all proceedings should be by the strictest order of precedence; that a collegiate registration clerk should report the matter to the provincial secretary, and the provincial secretary to the titular councillor or whomsoever it might be, and that business should only reach him by this channel. Every one in Holy Russia has a craze for imitation, every one apes and mimics his superiors. I have actually been told that a titular councillor who was put in charge of a small separate office, immediately partitioned off a special room for himself, calling it the head office, and set special porters at the door with red collars and gold lace, who took hold of the handle of the door and opened it for every one who went in, though the 'head office' was so tiny that it was with difficulty that an ordinary writing table could be put into it. The manners and habits of the Person of Consequence were dignified and majestic, but not complex. The chief foundation of his system was strictness, 'strictness, strictness, and – strictness!' he used to say, and at the last word he would look very significantly at the person he was addressing, though, indeed, he had no reason to do so, for the dozen clerks who made up the whole administrative mechanism of his office stood in befitting awe of him; any clerk who saw him in the distance would leave his work and remain standing at attention till his superior had left the room. His conversation

with his subordinates was usually marked by severity and almost confined to three phrases: 'How dare you? Do you know to whom you are
speaking? Do you understand who I am?' He was, however, at heart a
good-natured man, pleasant and obliging with his colleagues; but the
grade of general had completely turned his head. When he received it,
he was perplexed, thrown off his balance, and quite at a loss how to
behave. If he chanced to be with his equals, he was still quite a decent
man, a very gentlemanly man, in fact, and in many ways even an
intelligent man, but as soon as he was in company with men who were
even one grade below him, there was simply no doing anything with
him: he sat silent and his position excited compassion, the more so
as he himself felt that he might have been spending his time to in-
comparably more advantage. At times there could be seen in his eyes
an intense desire to join in some interesting conversation, but he was
restrained by the doubt whether it would not be too much on
his part, whether it would not be too great a familiarity and lowering
of his dignity, and in consequence of these reflections he remained
everlastingly in the same mute condition, only uttering from time to
time monosyllabic sounds, and in this way he gained the reputation of
being a very tiresome man.

So this was the Person of Consequence to whom our friend Akaky
Akakyevitch appealed, and he appealed to him at a most unpropitious
moment, very unfortunate for himself, though fortunate, indeed, for
the Person of Consequence. The latter happened to be in his study,
talking in the very best of spirits with an old friend of his childhood who
had only just arrived and whom he had not seen for several years. It was
at this moment that he was informed that a man called Bashmatchkin
was asking to see him. He asked abruptly, 'What sort of man is he?' and
received the answer, 'A government clerk.' 'Ah! He can wait, I haven't
time now,' said the Person of Consequence. Here I must observe that
this was a complete lie on the part of the Person of Consequence: he
had time; his friend and he had long ago said all they had to say to each
other and their conversation had begun to be broken by very long
pauses during which they merely slapped each other on the knee, saying,
'So that's how things are, Ivan Abramovitch!' – 'There it is, Stepan
Varlamovitch!' but, for all that, he told the clerk to wait in order to
show his friend, who had left the service years before and was living at
home in the country how long clerks had to wait in his ante-room. At
last after they had talked, or rather been silent to their hearts' content
and had smoked a cigar in very comfortable armchairs with sloping
backs, he seemed suddenly to recollect, and said to the secretary, who

was standing at the door with papers for his signature: 'Oh, by the way, there is a clerk waiting, isn't there? Tell him he can come in.' When he saw Akaky Akakyevitch's meek appearance and old uniform, he turned to him at once and said: 'What do you want?' in a firm and abrupt voice, which he had purposely practised in his own room in solitude before the looking-glass for a week before receiving his present post and the grade of a general. Akaky Akakyevitch, who was overwhelmed with befitting awe beforehand, was somewhat confused and, as far as his tongue would allow him, explained to the best of his powers, with even more frequent 'ers' than usual, that he had had a perfectly new overcoat and now he had been robbed of it in the most inhuman way, and that now he had come to beg him by his intervention either to correspond with his honour the head policemaster or anybody else, and find the overcoat. This mode of proceeding struck the general for some reason as taking a great liberty. 'What next, sir,' he went on as abruptly, 'don't you know the way to proceed? To whom are you addressing yourself? Don't you know how things are done? You ought first to have handed in a petition to the office; it would have gone to the head clerk of the room, and to the head clerk of the section, then it would have been handed to the secretary and the secretary would have brought it to me . . .'

'But, your Excellency,' said Akaky Akakyevitch, trying to collect all the small allowance of presence of mind he possessed and feeling at the same time that he was getting into a terrible perspiration, 'I ventured, your Excellency, to trouble you because secretaries . . . er . . . are people you can't depend on . . .'

'What? what? what?' said the Person of Consequence, 'where did you get hold of that spirit? Where did you pick up such ideas? What insubordination is spreading among young men against their superiors and betters.' The Person of Consequence did not apparently observe that Akaky Akakyevitch was well over fifty, and therefore if he could have been called a young man it would only have been in comparison with a man of seventy. 'Do you know to whom you are speaking? Do you understand who I am? Do you understand that, I ask you?' At this point he stamped and raised his voice to such a powerful note that Akaky Akakyevitch was not the only one to be terrified. Akaky Akakyevitch was positively petrified; he staggered, trembling all over, and could not stand; if the porters had not run up to support him, he would have flopped upon the floor; he was led out almost unconscious. The Person of Consequence, pleased that the effect had surpassed his expectations and enchanted at the idea that his words could even deprive a man of consciousness, stole a sideways glance at his friend to see how he was taking it, and perceived not without satisfaction that his friend was feeling very uncertain and even beginning to be a little terrified himself.

How he got downstairs, how he went out into the street – of all that Akaky Akakyevitch remembered nothing, he had no feeling in his arms or his legs. In all his life he had never been so severely reprimanded by a general, and this was by one of another department, too. He went out into the snowstorm, that was whistling through the streets, with his mouth open, and as he went he stumbled off the pavement; the wind, as its way is in Petersburg, blew upon him from all the points of the compass and from every side street. In an instant it had blown a quinsy[184] into his throat, and when he got home he was not able to utter a word; with a swollen face and throat he went to bed. So violent is sometimes the effect of a suitable reprimand!

Next day he was in a high fever. Thanks to the gracious assistance of the Petersburg climate, the disease made more rapid progress than could have been expected, and when the doctor came, after feeling his pulse he could find nothing to do but prescribe a fomentation,[185] and that simply that the patient might not be left without the benefit of medical assistance; however, two days later he informed him that his end was at hand, after which he turned to his landlady and said: 'And you had better lose no time, my good woman, but order him now a deal coffin,[186] for an oak one will be too dear for him.' Whether Akaky Akakyevitch heard these fateful words or not, whether they produced a shattering effect upon him, and whether he regretted his pitiful life, no one can tell, for he was all the time in delirium and fever. Apparitions, each stranger than the one before, were continually haunting him: first, he saw Petrovitch and was ordering him to make a greatcoat trimmed with some sort of traps for robbers, who were, he fancied, continually under the bed, and he was calling his landlady every minute to pull out a thief who had even got under the quilt; then he kept asking why his old 'dressing jacket' was hanging before him when he had a new overcoat, then he fancied he was standing before the general listening to the appropriate reprimand and saying 'I am sorry, your Excellency,' then finally he became abusive, uttering the most awful language, so that his old landlady positively crossed herself, having never heard anything of the kind from him before, and the more horrified because these dreadful words followed immediately upon the phrase 'your Excellency.' Later on, his talk was a mere medley of nonsense, so that it was quite unintelligible; all that could be seen was that his incoherent words and thoughts were concerned with nothing but the overcoat. At last poor Akaky Akakyevitch gave up the ghost. No seal was put upon his room nor upon his things, because, in the first place, he had no heirs and, in the second, the property left was very small, to wit, a bundle of goose-feathers, a quire of white government paper, three pairs of socks, two or three buttons that had come off his trousers, and the 'dressing jacket' with which the reader is already familiar. Who came into all this wealth God only knows, even I who tell the tale must own that I have not troubled to enquire. And Petersburg remained without Akaky Akakyevitch, as though, indeed, he had never been in the city. A creature had vanished and departed whose cause no one had championed, who was dear to no one, of interest to no one, who never even attracted the attention of the student of natural history, though the latter does not disdain to fix a common fly upon a pin and look at him under the microscope – a creature who bore patiently the jeers of the office and for no particular reason went to his grave, though even he at the very end of his life was visited by a gleam of brightness in the form of an overcoat that for one instant brought colour into his poor life – a creature on whom calamity broke as insufferably as it breaks upon the heads of the mighty ones of this world . . . !

Several days after his death, the porter from the department was sent to his lodgings with instructions that he should go at once to the office, for his chief was asking for him; but the porter was obliged to return without him, explaining that he could not come, and to the enquiry 'Why?' he added, 'Well, you see: the fact is he is dead, he was buried three days ago.' This was how they learned at the office of the death of Akaky Akakyevitch, and the next day there was sitting in his seat a new clerk who was very much taller and who wrote not in the same upright hand but made his letters more slanting and crooked.

But who could have imagined that this was not all there was to tell about Akaky Akakyevitch, that he was destined for a few days to make a noise in the world after his death, as though to make up for his life having been unnoticed by any one? But so it happened, and our poor story unexpectedly finishes with a fantastic ending. Rumours were suddenly floating about Petersburg that in the neighbourhood of the Kalinkin Bridge and for a little distance beyond, a corpse had taken to appearing at night in the form of a clerk looking for a stolen overcoat, and stripping from the shoulders of all passers-by, regardless of grade and calling, overcoats of all descriptions – trimmed with cat fur, or beaver or wadded, lined with racoon, fox and bear – made, in fact, of all sorts of skin which men have adapted for the covering of their own. One of the clerks of the department saw the corpse with his own eyes and at once recognised it as Akaky Akakyevitch; but it excited in him such terror, however, that he ran away as fast as his legs could carry him and so could not get a very clear view of him, and only saw him hold up his finger threateningly in the distance.

From all sides complaints were continually coming that backs and shoulders, not of mere titular councillors, but even of upper court councillors, had been exposed to taking chills, owing to being stripped of their greatcoats. Orders were given to the police to catch the corpse regardless of trouble or expense, alive or dead, and to punish him in the cruellest way, as an example to others, and, indeed, they very nearly succeeded in doing so. The sentry of one district police station in Kiryushkin Place snatched a corpse by the collar on the spot of the crime in the very act of attempting to snatch a frieze overcoat from a retired musician, who used in his day to play the flute. Having caught him by the collar, he shouted until he had brought two other comrades, whom he charged to hold him while he felt just for a minute in his boot to get out a snuffbox in order to revive his nose which had six times in his life been frostbitten, but the snuff was probably so strong that not even a dead man could stand it. The sentry had hardly had time to put his finger over his right nostril and draw up some snuff in the left when the corpse sneezed violently right into the eyes of all three. While they were putting their fists up to wipe them, the corpse completely vanished, so that they were not even sure whether he had actually been in their hands. From that time forward, the sentries conceived such a horror of the dead that they were even afraid to seize the living and confined themselves to shouting from the distance: 'Hi, you there, be off!' and the dead clerk began to appear even on the other side of the Kalinkin Bridge, rousing no little terror in all timid people.

We have, however, quite deserted the Person of Consequence, who may in reality almost be said to be the cause of the fantastic ending of this perfectly true story. To begin with, my duty requires me to do justice to the Person of Consequence by recording that soon after poor Akaky Akakyevitch had gone away crushed to powder, he felt something not unlike regret. Sympathy was a feeling not unknown to him; his heart was open to many kindly impulses, although his exalted grade very often prevented them from being shown. As soon as his friend had gone out of his study, he even began brooding over poor Akaky Akakyevitch, and from that time forward, he was almost every day haunted by the image of the poor clerk who had succumbed so completely to the befitting reprimand. The thought of the man so worried him that a week later he actually decided to send a clerk to find out how he was and whether he really could help him in any way. And when they brought him word that Akaky Akakyevitch had died suddenly in delirium and fever, it made a great impression on him, his conscience reproached him and he was depressed all day. Anxious to distract his mind and to forget the unpleasant impression, he went to spend the evening with one of his friends, where he found a genteel company and, what was best of all, almost every one was of the same grade so that he was able to be quite free from restraint. This had a wonderful effect on his spirits, he expanded, became affable and genial – in short, spent a very agreeable evening. At supper he drank a couple of glasses of champagne – a proceeding which we all know has a happy effect in inducing good-humour. The champagne made him inclined to do something unusual, and he decided not to go home yet but to visit a lady of his acquaintance, one Karolina Ivanovna – a lady apparently of German extraction, for whom he entertained extremely friendly feelings. It must be noted that the Person of Consequence was a man no longer young, an excellent husband, and the respectable father of a family. He had two sons, one already serving in his office, and a nice-looking daughter of sixteen with a rather turned-up, pretty little nose, who used to come every morning to kiss his hand, saying: 'Bon jour, Papa.' His wife, who was still blooming and decidedly good-looking, indeed, used first to give him her hand to kiss and then would kiss his hand, turning it the other side upwards. But though the Person of Consequence was perfectly satisfied with the kind amenities of his domestic life, he thought it proper to have a lady friend in another quarter of the town. This lady friend was not a bit better looking nor younger than his wife, but these mysterious facts exist in the world and it is not our business to criticise them. And so the Person of Consequence went downstairs, got into his sledge, and said to his coach-man, 'To Karolina Ivanovna,' while luxuriously wrapped in his warm fur coat he remained in that agreeable frame of mind sweeter to a Russian than anything that could be invented, that is, when one thinks of nothing while thoughts come into the mind of themselves, one pleasanter than the other, without the labour of following them or looking for them. Full of satisfaction, he recalled all the amusing moments of the evening he had spent, all the phrases that had set the little circle laughing; many of them he repeated in an undertone and found them as amusing as before, and so, very naturally, laughed very heartily at them again. From time to time, however, he was disturbed by a gust of wind which, blowing suddenly, God knows whence and wherefore, cut him in the face, pelting him with flakes of snow, puffing out his coat-collar like a sack, or suddenly flinging it with unnatural force over his head and giving him endless trouble to extricate himself from it. All at once, the Person of Consequence felt that someone had clutched him very tightly by the collar. Turning round he saw a short man in a shabby old uniform, and not without horror recognised him as Akaky Akakyevitch. The clerk's face was white as snow and looked like that of a corpse, but the horror of the Person of Consequence was beyond all bounds when he saw the mouth of the corpse distorted into speech and, breathing upon him the chill of the grave, it uttered the following words: 'Ah, so here you are at last! At last I've . . . er . . . caught you by the collar. It's your overcoat I want, you refused to help me and abused me into the bargain! So now give me yours!' The poor Person of Consequence very nearly died. Resolute and determined as he was in his office and before subordinates in general, and though any one looking at his manly air and figure would have said: 'Oh, what a man of character!' yet in this plight he felt, like very many persons of athletic appearance, such terror that not without reason he began to be afraid he would have some sort of fit. He actually flung his overcoat off his shoulders as fast as he could and shouted to his coachman in a voice unlike his own: 'Drive home and make haste!' The coachman, hearing the tone which he had only heard in critical moments and then accompanied by something even more rousing, hunched his shoulders up to his ears in case of worse following, swung his whip and flew on like an arrow. In a little over six minutes the Person of Consequence was at the entrance of his own house. Pale, panic-stricken, and without his overcoat, he arrived home instead of at Karolina Ivanovna's, dragged himself to his own room and spent the night in great perturbation, so that next morning his daughter said to him at breakfast, 'You look quite pale today, Papa': but her papa remained mute and said not a word to any one of what had happened to him, where he had been, and where he had been going. The incident made a great impression upon him. Indeed, it happened far more rarely that he said to his subordinates, 'How dare you? Do you understand who I am?' and he never uttered those words at all until he had first heard all the rights of the case.

What was even more remarkable is that from that time the apparition of the dead clerk ceased entirely: apparently the general's overcoat had fitted him perfectly, anyway nothing more was heard of overcoats being snatched from any one. Many restless and anxious people refused, however, to be pacified, and still maintained that in remote parts of the town the ghost of the dead clerk went on appearing. One sentry in

Kolomna, for instance, saw with his own eyes a ghost appear from behind a house; but, being by natural constitution somewhat feeble – so much so that on one occasion an ordinary, well-grown pig, making a sudden dash out of some building, knocked him off his feet to the vast entertainment of the cabmen standing round, from whom he exacted two kopecks each for snuff for such rudeness – he did not dare to stop it, and so followed it in the dark until the ghost suddenly looked round and, stopping, asked him: 'What do you want?' displaying a fist such as you never see among the living. The sentry said: 'Nothing,' and turned back on the spot. This ghost, however, was considerably taller and adorned with immense moustaches, and, directing its steps apparently towards Obuhov Bridge,[187] vanished into the darkness of the night.

THE CARRIAGE[188]

THE LITTLE TOWN OF B. has grown much more lively since a cavalry regiment began to be stationed in it. Till then it was fearfully dull. When one drove through it and glanced at the low-pitched, painted houses which looked into the street with an incredibly sour expression . . . well, it is impossible to put into words what things were like there: it is as dejecting as though one had lost money at cards, or just said something stupid and inappropriate – in short, it is depressing. The plaster on the houses has peeled off with the rain, and the walls instead of being white are piebald; the roofs are for the most part thatched with reeds, as is usual in our Southern towns. The gardens have long ago, by order of the police-master, been cut down to improve the look of the place. There is never a soul to be met in the streets; at most a cock crosses the road, soft as a pillow from the dust that lies on it eight inches thick and at the slightest drop of rain is transformed into mud, and then the streets of the town of B. are filled with those corpulent animals which the local police-master calls Frenchmen; thrusting out their solemn snouts from their baths, they set up such a grunting that the traveller can do nothing but urge on his horses. It is not easy, however, to meet a traveller in the town of B. On rare, very rare occasions, some country gentleman, owning eleven souls of serfs and dressed in a full nankeen[189] coat, jolts over the road in something between a chaise and a cart, and peeps out from behind piled-up sacks of flour, as he lashes his solemn mare behind whom runs a colt. Even the marketplace has rather a melancholy air: the tailor's shop stands out very foolishly with one corner to the street instead of the whole shop-front; facing it, a brick building with two windows has been in the course of construction for fifteen years: a little further, standing all by itself, there is one of those paling fences so fashionable, painted grey to match the mud, and erected as a model for other buildings by the police-master in the days of his youth, before he had formed the habit of sleeping immediately after dinner and drinking at night a beverage flavoured with dry gooseberries. In other parts the fences are all of hurdle.[190] In the middle of the square, there are very tiny shops; in them one may always see a bunch of bread-rings, a peasant woman in a red kerchief, a hundredweight of soap, a few pounds of bitter almonds, small shot for sportsmen, some cotton-shoddy material, and two shopmen who spend all their time playing a sort of quoits near the door.

But as soon as the cavalry regiment was stationed at the little town of B. everything was changed: the streets were full of life and colour, in fact, they assumed quite a different aspect; the low-pitched little houses often saw a graceful, well-built officer with a plume on his head passing by on his way to discuss promotion or the best kind of tobacco with a comrade, or sometimes to play cards for the stake of a chaise, which might have been described as the regimental chaise for, without ever leaving the regiment, it had already gone the round of all the officers: one day the major rolled up in it, the next day it was to be seen in the lieutenant's stable, and a week later, lo and behold, the major's orderly was greasing its wheels again. The wooden fence between the houses was always studded with soldiers' caps hanging in the sun; a grey military overcoat was always conspicuous on some gate; in the side streets soldiers were to be seen with moustaches as stiff as boot-brushes. These moustaches were on view everywhere; if work-women gathered in the market with their tin mugs, one could always get a glimpse of a moustache behind their shoulders. The officers brought life into the local society which had until then consisted of a judge, who lived in the same house with a deacon's wife, and a police-master, who was a very sagacious person, but slept absolutely the whole day from dinner-time until evening and from evening until dinner-time. Society gained even more in numbers and interest when the headquarters of the general of the brigade were transferred to the town. Neighbouring landowners, whose existence no one would previously have suspected, began visiting the district town more frequently to see the officers and sometimes to play a game of 'bank,'[191] of which there was an extremely hazy notion in their brains, busy with thoughts of crops and hares and their wives' commissions.

I am very sorry that I cannot recall what circumstance it was that led the general of the brigade to give a big dinner; preparations for it were made on a vast scale; the clatter of the cooks' knives in the general's kitchen could be heard almost as far as the town gate. The whole market was completely cleared for the dinner, so that the judge and his deaconess had nothing to eat but buckwheat cakes and cornflour-shape. The little courtyard of the general's quarters was packed with chaises and carriages. The company consisted of gentlemen – officers and a few neighbouring landowners. Of the latter, the most noteworthy was Pifagor Pifagorovitch Tchertokutsky, one of the leading aristocrats of the district of B., who made more noise than any one at the elections and drove to them in a very smart carriage. He had once served in a cavalry regiment and had been one of its most important and conspicuous officers, anyway he had been seen at numerous balls and assemblies, wherever his regiment had been stationed; the young ladies of the Tambov and Simbirsk[192] provinces, however, could tell us most about that. It is very possible that he would have gained a desirable reputation in other provinces, too, if he had not resigned his commission owing to one of those incidents which are usually described as 'an unpleasantness'; either he had given someone a box on the ear in old days, or was given it, which I don't remember for certain; anyway, the point is that he was asked to resign his commission. He lost nothing of his importance through this, however. He wore a high-waisted dress-coat of military cut, spurs on his boots, and a moustache under his nose, since, but for that, the nobility of his province might have supposed that he had served in the infantry, which he always spoke of contemptuously. He visited all the much-frequented fairs, to which those who make up the heart of Russia, that is, the nurses and children, stout landowners and their daughters, flock to enjoy themselves, driving in chaises with hoods, gigs, waggonettes, and carriages such as have never been seen in the wildest dreams. He had a special scent for where a cavalry regiment was stationed, and always went to interview the officers, very nimbly leaping out of his light carriage in view of them and very quickly making their acquaintance. At the last election he had given the nobility of the provinces an excellent dinner, at which he had declared that, if only he were elected Marshal, he 'would put the gentry on the best possible footing.' Altogether he lived like a gentleman, as the expression goes in the provinces; he married a rather pretty wife, getting with her a dowry of two hundred souls and some thousands in cash. This last was at once spent on a team of six really first-rate horses, gilt locks on the doors, a tame monkey, and a French butler for the household. The two hundred souls, together with two hundred of his own, were mortgaged to the bank for the sake of some commercial operations.

In short, he was a proper sort of landowner, a very decent sort of landowner . . .

Apart from this gentleman, there were a few other landowners at the general's dinner, but there is no need to describe them. The other guests were the officers of the same regiment, besides two staff-officers, a colonel, and a rather stout major. The general himself was a thick-set, corpulent person, though an excellent commanding officer, so the others said of him. He spoke in a rather thick, consequential bass. The dinner was remarkable: sturgeon of various sorts, as well as sterlet,[193] bustards, asparagus, quails, partridges, and mushrooms testified to the fact that the cook had not had a drop of anything strong between his lips since the previous day, and that four soldiers had been at work with knives in their hands all night, helping him with the fricassee[194] and the jelly. A multitude of bottles, tall ones with Lafitte[195] and short ones with Madeira;[196] a lovely summer day, windows wide open, plates of ice on the table, the crumpled shirt-fronts of the owners of extremely roomy dress coats, a crossfire of conversation drowned by the general's voice and washed down by champagne – all was in keeping. After dinner they all got up from the table with an agreeable heaviness in their stomachs, and, after lighting pipes, some with long and some with short mouth-pieces, went out on to the steps with cups of coffee in their hands.

'You can look at her now,' said the general; 'if you please, my dear boy,' he went on, addressing his adjutant, a rather sprightly young man of agreeable appearance, 'tell them to bring the bay mare round! Here you shall see for yourself.' At this point the general took a pull at his pipe and blew out the smoke, 'she is not quite well-groomed: this wretched, accursed little town! She is a very' – puff–puff – 'decent mare!'

'And have you' – puff-puff – 'had her long, your Excellency?' said Tchertokutsky.

'Well . . . ' puff–puff–puff . . . 'not so long; it's only two years since I had her from the stud-stables.'

'And did you get her broken in, or have you been breaking her in here, your Excellency?'

Puff–puff–pu — ff pu—ff, 'Here,' saying this the general completely disappeared in smoke.

Meanwhile a soldier skipped out of the stables, the thud of hoofs was audible, and at last another soldier with huge black moustaches, wearing a white smock, appeared, leading by the bridle a trembling and frightened mare, who, suddenly flinging up her head, almost lifted the soldier together with his moustaches into the air.

'There, there, Agrafena Ivanovna!' he said, leading her up to the steps.

The mare's name was Agrafena Ivanovna. Strong and wild as a beauty of the south, she stamped her hoof upon the wooden steps, then suddenly stopped.

The general, laying down his pipe, began with a satisfied air looking at Agrafena Ivanovna. The colonel himself went down the steps and took Agrafena Ivanovna by the nose, the major patted Agrafena Ivanovna on the leg, the others made a clicking sound with their tongues.

Tchertokutsky went down and approached her from behind, the soldier, drawn up to attention and holding the bridle, looked straight into the visitor's eyes as though he wanted to jump into them.

'Very, very fine,' said Tchertokutsky, 'a horse with excellent points! And allow me to ask your Excellency, how does she go?'

'Her action is very good, only . . . that fool of a doctor's assistant, the devil take the man, gave her pills of some sort and for the last two days she has done nothing but sneeze.'

'Very fine horse, very; and have you a suitable carriage, your Excellency?'

'A carriage? . . . But she is a saddle-horse, you know.'

'I know that, but I asked your Excellency to find out whether you have a suitable carriage for your other horses.'

'Well, I am not very well off for carriages I must own; I have long been wanting to get an up-to-date one. I have written to my brother who is in Petersburg just now, but I don't know whether he'll send me one or not.'

'I think, your Excellency, there are no better carriages than the Viennese.'

'You are quite right there,' puff–puff–puff —

'I have an excellent carriage, your Excellency, of real Vienna make.'

'What is it like? Is it the one you came here in?'

'Oh no, that's just for rough work, for my excursions, but the other . . . It is a wonder! Light as a feather, and when you are in it, it is simply, saving your Excellency's presence, as though your nurse were rocking you in the cradle!'

'So it is comfortable?'

'Very comfortable indeed: cushions, springs and all looking like a picture.'

'That's nice.'

'And so roomy! As a matter of fact, your Excellency, I have never seen one like it. When I was in the service I used to put a dozen bottles of rum and twenty pounds of tobacco in the boxes, and besides that I used to have about six uniforms and under-linen and two pipes, the very long ones, your Excellency, while you could put a whole ox in the pockets.'

'That's nice.'

'It cost four thousand, your Excellency.'

'At that price it ought to be good; and did you buy it yourself?'

'No, your Excellency, it came to me by chance; it was bought by my friend, the companion of my childhood, a rare man with whom you would have got on perfectly, your Excellency; we were on such terms that what was his was mine, it was all the same, I won it from him at cards. Would you care, your Excellency, to do me the honour to dine with me tomorrow, and you could have a look at the carriage at the same time?'

'I really don't know what to say . . . for me to come alone like that . . . would you allow me to bring my fellow-officers?'

'I beg the other officers to come too. Gentlemen! I shall think it a great pleasure to see you in my house.'

The colonel, the major, and the other officers thanked him with a polite bow.

'What I think, your Excellency, is that if one buys a thing it must be good, if it is not good there is no use having it. When you do me the honour to visit me tomorrow, I will show you a few other things I have bought in the useful line.'

The general looked at him and blew smoke out of his mouth. Tchertokutsky was highly delighted at having invited the officers: he was inwardly ordering pasties and sauces while he looked very good-humouredly at the gentlemen in question, who for their part, too, seemed to feel twice as amiably disposed to him, as could be discerned from their eyes and the small movements they made in the way of half-bows. Tchertokutsky put himself forward with a more free-and-easy air, and there was a melting tone in his voice as though it were weighed down with pleasure.

'There, your Excellency, you will make the acquaintance of my wife.'

'I shall be delighted,' said the general, stroking his moustache.

After that Tchertokutsky wanted to set off home at once that he might be beforehand in preparing everything for the reception of his guests and the dinner to be offered them; he took up his hat, but, strangely enough, it happened that he stayed on for some time. Meanwhile card tables were set in the room. Soon the whole company was divided into parties of four for whist and sat down in the different corners of the general's rooms. Candles were brought; for a long time Tchertokutsky was uncertain whether to sit down to whist or not, but as the officers began to press him to do so, he felt that it would be a breach of the rules of civility to refuse and he sat down for a little while. By his side there appeared from somewhere a glass of punch which, without noticing it, he drank off instantly. After winning two rubbers

Tchertokutsky again found a glass of punch at hand and again without observing it emptied the glass, though he did say first: 'It's time for me to be getting home, gentlemen, it really is time,' but again he sat down to the second game.

Meanwhile conversation assumed an entirely personal character in the different corners of the room. The whist players were rather silent, but those who were not playing sat on sofas at one side and kept up a conversation of their own. In one corner the staff-captain, with a cushion thrust under his back and a pipe between his teeth, was recounting in a free and flowing style his amatory adventures, which completely absorbed the attention of a circle gathered round him. One extremely fat landowner with short hands rather like overgrown potatoes was listening with an extraordinarily mawkish air, and only from time to time exerted himself to get his short arm behind his broad back and pull out his snuffbox. In another corner a rather heated discussion sprang up concerning squadron drill, and Tchertokutsky, who about that time twice threw down a knave instead of a queen, suddenly intervened in this conversation, which was not addressed to him, and shouted from his corner: 'In what year?' or 'Which regiment?' without observing that the question had nothing to do with the matter under discussion. At last, a few minutes before supper, they left off playing, though the games went on verbally and it seemed as though the heads of all were full of whist. Tchertokutsky remembered perfectly that he had won a great deal, but he picked up nothing, and getting up from the tables stood for a long time in the attitude of a man who has found he has no pocket-handkerchief. Meanwhile supper was served. It need hardly be said that there was no lack of wines and that Tchertokutsky was almost obliged to fill up his glass at times, since there were bottles standing on the right and on the left of him.

A very long conversation dragged on at table, but it was rather oddly conducted. One colonel who had served in the campaign of 1812[197] described a battle such as had certainly never taken place, and then, I am quite unable to say for what reason, took the stopper out of the decanter and stuck it in the pudding. In short, by the time the party began to break up it was three o'clock, and the coachmen were obliged to carry some of the gentlemen in their arms as though they had been parcels of purchases, and in spite of all his aristocratic breeding Tchertokutsky bowed so low and with such a violent lurch of his head, as he got into his carriage, that he brought two burrs home with him on his moustache.

At home every one was sound asleep. The coachman had some difficulty in finding a footman, who conducted his master across the drawing-room and handed him over to a maid-servant, in whose charge Tchertokutsky made his way to his bedroom and got into bed beside his young and pretty wife, who was lying in the most enchanting way in snow-white sleeping-attire. The jolt made by her husband falling upon the bed awakened her. Stretching, lifting her eyelashes and three times rapidly blinking her eyes, she opened them with a half-angry smile, but seeing that he absolutely declined on this occasion to show any interest in her, she turned over on the other side in vexation, and laying her fresh little cheek on her arm soon afterwards fell asleep.

It was at an hour which would not in the country be described as early that the young mistress of the house woke up beside her snoring spouse. Remembering that it had been nearly four o'clock in the morning when he came home, she did not like to wake him, and so, putting on her bedroom slippers which her husband had ordered for her from Petersburg, with a white dressing-gown draped about her like a flowing stream, she washed in water as fresh as herself and proceeded to attire herself for the day. Glancing at herself a couple of times in the mirror, she saw that she was looking very nice that morning. This apparently insignificant circumstance led her to spend two hours extra before the looking-glass. At last she was very charmingly dressed and went out to take an airing in the garden. As luck would have it, the weather was as lovely as it can only be on a summer day in the South. The sun, which was approaching the zenith, was blazing hot; but it was cool walking in the thick, dark avenue, and the flowers were three times as fragrant in the warmth of the sun. The pretty young wife quite forgot that it was now twelve o'clock and her husband was still asleep. Already she could hear the after-dinner snores of two coachmen and one postilion sleeping in the stable beyond the garden, but she still sat on in a shady avenue from which there was an open view of the highroad, and was absent-mindedly watching it, stretching empty and deserted into the distance, when all at once a cloud of dust appearing in that distance attracted her attention. Gazing intently, she soon discerned several carriages. The foremost was a light open carriage with two seats. In it was sitting a general with thick epaulettes that gleamed in the sun, and beside him a colonel. It was followed by another carriage with seats for four in which were the major, the general's adjutant, and two officers sitting opposite. Then came the regimental chaise, familiar to every one, at the moment in the possession of the fat major. The chaise was followed by a *bon-voyage*,[198] in which there were four officers seated and a fifth on their knees, then came three officers on excellent, dark bay dappled horses.

'Then they may be coming to us,' thought the lady. 'Oh, my goodness, they really are! They have turned at the bridge!' She uttered a shriek, clasped her hands and ran right over the flower-beds straight to her husband's bedroom; he was sleeping like the dead.

'Get up! Get up! Make haste and get up!' she shouted, tugging at his arm.

'What?' murmured Tchertokutsky, not opening his eyes.

'Get up, poppet! Do you hear, visitors!'

'Visitors? What visitors?' . . . Saying this he uttered a slight grunt such as a calf gives when it is looking for its mother's udder, 'Mm . . . ' he muttered: 'stoop your neck, precious! I'll give you a kiss.'

'Darling, get up, for goodness' sake, make haste! The general and the officers! Oh dear, you've got a burr on your moustache!'

'The general! So he is coming already, then? But why the devil did nobody wake me? And the dinner, what about the dinner? Is everything ready that's wanted?'

'What dinner?'

'Why, didn't I order it?'

'You came back at four o'clock in the morning and you did not say one word to me, however much I questioned you. I didn't wake you, poppet, because I felt sorry for you, you had had no sleep . . . '

The last words she uttered in an extremely supplicating and languishing voice.

Tchertokutsky lay for a minute in bed with his eyes starting out of his head, as though struck by a thunderbolt. At last he jumped out of bed with nothing but his shirt on, forgetting that this was quite unseemly.

'Oh, I am an ass!' he said, slapping himself on the forehead; 'I invited them to dinner! What's to be done? Are they far off?'

'I don't know . . . I expect they will be here every minute.'

'My love . . . hide yourself . . . Hey, who's there? You wretched girl, come in; what are you afraid of, silly? The officers will be here in a minute: you say that your master is not at home, say that he won't be home at all, that he went out early in the morning . . . Do you hear? And tell all the servants the same; make haste!' Saying this, he hurriedly snatched up his dressing-gown and ran to hide in the carriage-house, supposing that there he would be in a position of complete security, but, standing in the corner of the carriage-house, he saw that even there he might be seen. 'Ah, this will be better,' flashed through his mind, and in one minute he flung down the steps of the carriage standing near, leapt in, closed the door after him, for greater security covering himself with the apron and the leather, and lay perfectly still, curled up in his dressing-gown.

Meanwhile the carriages drove up to the front steps. The general stepped out and shook himself; after him the colonel, smoothing the plume of his hat with his hands, then the fat major, holding his sabre under his arm, jumped out of the chaise, the slim sub-lieutenants skipped down from the *bon-voyage* with the lieutenant who had been sitting on the others' knees, and, last of all, the officers who had been elegantly riding on horseback alighted from their saddles.

'The master is not at home,' said a footman, coming out on to the steps.

'Not at home? He'll be back to dinner, I suppose?'

'No. His Honour has gone out for the whole day. He won't be back until tomorrow about this time perhaps.'

'Well, upon my soul,' said the general. 'What is the meaning of this?'

'I must own it is queer,' said the colonel, laughing.

'No, really . . . how can he behave like this?' the general went on with displeasure. 'Whew! . . . the devil . . . why, if he can't receive people, what does he ask them for?'

'I can't understand how any one could do it, your Excellency,' a young officer observed.

'What, what?' said the general, who had the habit of always uttering this interrogative monosyllable when he was talking to an officer.

'I said, your Excellency, that it is not the way to behave!'

'Naturally . . . why, if anything has happened, he might let us know at any rate, or else not have asked us.'

'Well, your Excellency, there is no help for it, we shall have to go back,' said the colonel.

'Of course, there is nothing else for it. We can look at the carriage though without him; it is not likely he has taken it with him. Hey, you there! Come here, my man!'

'What is your pleasure?'

'Are you the stable-boy?'

'Yes, your Excellency.'

'Show us the new carriage your master got lately.'

'This way, sir; come to the carriage-house.'

The general went to the carriage-house together with the officers.

'Shall I push it out a little? It is rather dark in here.'

'That's enough, that's enough, that's right!'

The general and the officers stood round the carriage and carefully examined the wheels and the springs.

'Well, there is nothing special about it,' said the general. 'It is a most ordinary carriage.'

'A very ugly one,' said the colonel; 'there is nothing good about it at all.'

'I fancy, your Excellency, it is not worth four thousand,' said the young officer.

'What?'

'I say, your Excellency, that I fancy it is not worth four thousand.'

'Four thousand, indeed! Why, it is not worth two, there is nothing in it at all. Perhaps there is something special about the inside . . . Unbutton the leather, my dear fellow, please.'

And what met the officers' eyes was Tchertokutsky sitting in his dressing-gown curled up in an extraordinary way. 'Ah, you are here!' . . . said the astonished general.

Saying this he slammed the carriage door at once, covered Tchertokutsky with the apron again, and drove away with the officers.

A MADMAN'S DIARY

OCTOBER 3

TODAY an extraordinary event occurred. I got up rather late in the morning, and when Mavra brought me my cleaned boots I asked her the time. Hearing that it was long past ten I made haste to dress. I own I wouldn't have gone to the department at all, knowing the sour face the chief of our section will make me. For a long time past he has been saying to me: 'How is it, my man, your head always seems in a muddle? Sometimes you rush about as though you were crazy and do your work so that the devil himself could not make head or tail of it, you write the title with a small letter, and you don't put in the date or the number.' The damned heron! To be sure he is jealous because I sit in the director's room and mend pens for his Excellency. In short I wouldn't have gone to the department if I had not hoped to see the counting-house clerk and to find out whether maybe I could not get something of my month's salary in advance out of that wretched Jew. That's another creature! Do you suppose he would ever let one have a month's pay in advance? Good gracious! The heavens would fall before he'd do it! You may ask till you burst, you may be at your last farthing, but the grey-headed devil won't let you have it – and when he is at home his own cook slaps him in the face; everybody knows it. I can't see the advantage of serving in a department; there are absolutely no possibilities in it. In the provincial government, or in the civil and crown offices, it's quite a different matter: there you may see some wretched man squeezed into the corner, copying away, with a nasty old coat on and such a face that it nearly makes you sick, but look what a villa he takes! It's no use offering him a gilt china cup: 'That's a doctor's present,' he will say. You must give him a pair of trotting horses or a droshky or a beaver fur worth three hundred roubles. He is such a quiet fellow to look at, and says in such a refined way: 'Oblige me with a penknife just to mend a pen,' but he fleeces the petitioners so that he scarcely leaves them a shirt to their backs. It is true that ours is a gentlemanly office, there is a cleanliness in everything such as is never seen in provincial offices, the tables are mahogany and all the heads address you formally . . . I must confess that if it were not for the gentlemanliness of the service I should have left the department long ago.

I put on my old greatcoat and took my umbrella, as it was raining in torrents. There was no one in the streets; some women pulling their skirts up to cover themselves, and some Russian merchants under umbrellas and some messengers met my eye. I saw none of the better class except one of ourselves. I saw him at the crossroads. As soon as I saw him I said to myself: 'No, my dear man, you are not on your way to the department; you are running after that girl who is racing ahead and looking at her feet.' What sad dogs clerks are! Upon my soul, they are as bad as any officer: if any female goes by in a hat they are bound to be after her. While I was making this reflection I saw a carriage driving up to the shop which I was passing. I recognised it at once. It was our director's carriage. 'But he can have nothing to go to the shop for,' I thought; 'I suppose it must be his daughter.' I flattened myself against the wall. The footman opened the carriage door and she darted out like a bird. How she glanced from right to left, how her eyes and eyebrows gleamed . . . Good God, I am done for, done for utterly! And why does she drive out in such rain! Don't tell me that women have not a passion for all this frippery. She didn't know me, and, indeed, I tried to muffle myself up all I could, because I had on a very muddy greatcoat of an old-fashioned cut. Now people wear cloaks with long collars while I had short collars one above the other, and, indeed, the cloth was not at all rainproof. Her little dog, who had been too late to dash in at the door, was left in the street. I know the dog – her name is Madgie. I had hardly been there a minute when I heard a thin little voice: 'Good-morning, Madgie.' 'Well, upon my soul! Who's that speaking?' I looked round and saw two ladies walking along under an umbrella: one old and the other young; but they had passed already and again I heard beside me: 'It's too bad of you, Madgie!' What the devil! I saw that Madgie was sniffing at a dog that was following the ladies. 'Aha,' I said to myself, 'but come, surely I am drunk! Only I fancy that very rarely happens to me.' 'No, Fido, you are wrong there,' said Madgie – I saw her say it with my own eyes. 'I have been, wow, wow, I have been very ill, wow, wow, wow!' 'Oh, so it's you, you little dog! Goodness me!' I must own I was very much surprised to hear her speaking like a human being; but afterwards, when I thought it all over, I was no longer surprised. A number of similar instances have as a fact occurred. They say that in England a fish popped up and uttered two words in such a strange language that the learned men have been for three years trying to interpret them and have not succeeded yet. I have read in the papers of two cows also who went into a shop and asked for a pound of tea. But I must own I was much more surprised when Madgie said: 'I did write to you, Fido; I expect Polkan did not take my letter.' Dash it all! I never in all my life heard of a dog being able to write. No one but a gentleman born can write correctly. It's true, of course, that some shopmen and even serfs can sometimes write a little; but their writing is for the most part mechanical: they have no commas, no stops, no style.

It amazed me. I must confess that of late I have begun seeing and hearing things such as no one has ever seen or heard before. 'I'll follow that dog,' I said to myself, 'and find out what she is like and what she thinks.' I opened my umbrella and set off after the two ladies. They passed into Gorohovy Street, turned into Myeshtchansky and from there into Stolyarny Street; at last they reached Kokushin Bridge[199] and stopped in front of a big house. 'I know that house,' I said to myself. 'That's Zvyerkov's Buildings. What a huge edifice! All sorts of people live in it: such lots of cooks, of visitors from all parts! And our friends the clerks, one on the top of another, with a third trying to squeeze in, like dogs. I have a friend living there, who plays capitally on the horn.' The ladies went up to the fifth storey. 'Good,' I thought, 'I won't go in now, but I will note the place and I will certainly take advantage of the first opportunity.'

OCTOBER 4

Today is Wednesday, and so I was in our chief's study. I came a little early on purpose and, sitting down, began mending the pens. Our director must be a very clever man. His whole study is lined with bookshelves. I have read the titles of some of them: they are all learned, so learned that they are quite beyond any one like me – they are all either in French or in German. And just look into his face! Ough! What importance in his eyes! I have never heard him say a word too much. Only sometimes when one hands him the papers he'll ask: 'What's it like out of doors?' 'Damp, your Excellency.' Yes, he is a cut above any one like me! He's a statesman. I notice, however, he is particularly fond of me. If his daughter, too, were . . . Ah, you rascal! . . . Never mind, never mind, silence! I read *The Bee*. They are stupid people, the French! What do they want? I'd take the lot of them, upon my word I would, and thrash them all soundly! In it I read a very pleasant description of a ball written by a country gentleman of Kursk. The country gentlemen of Kursk write well. Then I noticed it was half-past twelve and that our chief had not come out of his bedroom. But about half-past one an event occurred which no pen could describe. The door opened, I thought it was the director and jumped up from my chair with my papers, but it was she, she herself! Holy saints, how she was dressed! Her dress was white as a swan – ough, how sumptuous! And the look in her eye – like sunshine, upon my soul, like sunshine. She bowed and said: 'Hasn't Papa been here?' Aïe, aïe, aïe, what a voice! A canary, a regular canary. 'Your Excellency,' I was on the point of saying, 'do not bid them punish me, but if you want to punish, then punish with your own illustrious hand.' But dash it all, my tongue would not obey me, and all I said was: 'No, madam.' She looked at me, looked at the books, and dropped her handkerchief. I dashed forward, slipped on the damned parquet and almost smashed my nose but recovered myself and picked up the handkerchief. Saints, what a handkerchief! The most delicate batiste [200] – amber, perfect amber! You would know from the very scent that it belonged to a general's daughter. She thanked me and gave a faint smile, so that her sugary lips scarcely moved, and after that went away. I stayed on another hour, when a footman came in and said: 'You can go home, Aksenty Ivanovitch, the master has gone out.' I cannot endure the flunkey set: they are always lolling about in the vestibule and don't as much as trouble themselves to nod. That's nothing: once one of the beasts had the effrontery to offer me his snuffbox without even getting up from his seat. Doesn't the fellow know I am a government clerk, that I am a gentleman by birth! However, I took my hat and put on my greatcoat myself, for these gentry never help me on with it, and went off. At home I spent most of the time lying on my bed. Then I copied out some very good verses:

> My love for one hour I did not see,
> And a whole year it seemed to me.
> My life is now a hated task,
> How can I live this life, I ask.

It must be written by Pushkin. [201] In the evening, wrapping myself up in my greatcoat, I went to the front door of her Excellency's house and waited about for a long time on the chance of her coming out to get into her carriage, that I might snatch another glimpse of her.

NOVEMBER 6

The head of our section was in a fury today. When I came into the department he called me into his room and began like this: 'Come, kindly tell me what you are doing?' 'How do you mean?' I said. 'I am doing nothing.' 'Come, think what you are about! Why, you are over forty. It's time you had a little sense. What do you imagine yourself to be? Do you suppose I don't know all the tricks you are up to? Why, you are dangling after the director's daughter! Come, look at yourself; just think what you are! Why, you are a nonentity and nothing else! Why, you haven't a penny to bless yourself with. And just look at yourself in the looking-glass – how could you think of such a thing!' Dash it all, because his face is rather like a medicine bottle and he has a shock of hair on his head curled in a tuft, and pomades it into a kind of rosette, and holds his head in the air, he imagines he is the only one who may do anything. I understand, I understand why he is in such a rage with me. He is envious: he has seen perhaps signs of preference shown to me. But I spit on him! As though a court councillor were of so much consequence! He hangs a gold chain on his watch and orders boots at thirty roubles – but deuce take him! Am I some plebeian – a tailor or a son of a non-commissioned officer? I am a gentleman. Why, I may rise in the service too. I am only forty-two, a time of life in which a career in the service is really only just beginning. Wait a bit, my friend! We too shall be a colonel and perhaps, please God, something better. We shall set up a flat, and better maybe than yours. A queer notion you have got into your head that no one is a gentleman but yourself. Give me a fashionably cut coat and let me put on a cravat like yours – and then you wouldn't hold a candle to me. I haven't the means, that's the trouble.

NOVEMBER 8

I have been to the theatre. It was a performance of the Russian fool Filatka. I laughed very much. There was a vaudeville too, with some amusing verses about lawyers, and especially about a collegiate registrar, very freely written so that I wondered that the censor had passed it; and about the merchants they openly said that they cheat the people and that their sons are debauched and ape the gentry. There was a very amusing couplet about the journalists too; saying that they abused every one and that an author begged the public to defend him against them. The authors do write amusing plays nowadays. I love being at the theatre. As soon as I have a coin in my pocket I can't resist going. And among our dear friends the officials there are such pigs; they positively won't go to the theatre, the louts; unless perhaps you give them a free ticket. One actress sang very nicely. I thought of her . . . ah, you rascal! . . . Never mind, never mind . . . silence!

NOVEMBER 9

At eight o'clock I went to the department. The head of our section put on a look as though he did not see me come in. On my side, too, I behaved as though nothing had passed between us. I looked through and checked some papers. I went out at four o'clock. I walked by the director's house, but no one was to be seen. After dinner for the most part lay on my bed.

NOVEMBER 11

Today I sat in our director's study. I mended 23 pens for him and for her . . . aïe, aïe! For her Excellency 4 pens. He likes to have a lot of pens. Oo, he must have a head! He always sits silent, and I expect he is turning over everything in his head. I should like to know what he thinks most about. What is going on in that head? I should like to get a close view of the life of these gentlemen, of all these *équivoques*[202] and court ways. How they go on and what they do in their circle – that's what I should like to find out! I have several times thought of beginning a conversation on the subject with his Excellency, but, dash it all! I couldn't bring my tongue to it; one says it's cold or warm today and can't utter another word. I should like to look into the drawing-room, of which one only sees the open door and another room beyond it. Ah, what sumptuous furniture! What mirrors and china! I long to have a look in there, into the part of the house where her Excellency is, that's where I should like to go! Into her boudoir where there are all sorts of little jars, little bottles, and such flowers that one is frightened even to breathe on them, to see her dresses lying scattered about, more like ethereal gossamer than dresses. I long to glance into her bedroom, there I fancy there must be marvels . . . a paradise, such as is not to be found in the heavens. To look at the little stool on which she puts her little foot when she gets out of bed and the way she puts a stocking on that little snow-white foot . . . Aïe, aïe, aïe! Never mind, never mind . . . silence.

But today a light as it were dawned upon me. I remembered the conversation between the two dogs that I heard on Nevsky Prospect. 'Good,' I thought to myself, 'now I will learn all. I must get hold of the correspondence that these wretched dogs have been carrying on. Then I shall certainly learn something.' I must own I once called Madgie to me and said to her: 'Listen, Madgie; here we are alone. If you like I will shut the door too, so that no one shall see you; tell me all you know about your young lady: what she is like and how she behaves. I swear I won't tell any one.' But the sly little dog put her tail between her legs, doubled herself up and went quickly to the door as though she hadn't heard. I have long suspected that dogs are far more intelligent than men; I am even convinced that they can speak, only there is a certain doggedness about them. They are extremely diplomatic: they notice everything, every step a man takes. Yes, whatever happens I will go tomorrow to Zvyerkov's Buildings, I will question Fido, and if I am successful I will seize all the letters Madgie has written her.

NOVEMBER 12

At two o'clock in the afternoon I set out determined to see Fido and question her. I can't endure cabbage, the smell of which floats from all the little shops in Myestchansky Street; moreover, such a hellish reek rises from under every gate that I raced along at full speed holding my nose. And the nasty workmen let off such a lot of soot and smoke from their workshops that a gentleman cannot walk there. When I climbed up to the sixth storey and rang the bell, a girl who was not at all bad-looking, with little freckles, came to the door. I recognised her: it was the girl who was with the old lady. She turned a little red, and I said to myself at once: 'You are on the look-out for a young man, my dear.' 'What do you want?' she asked. 'I want to have a few words with your dog.' The girl was silly. I saw at once that she was silly. At that moment the dog ran out barking; I tried to catch hold of her, but the nasty wretch almost snapped at my nose. However, I saw her bed in the corner. Ah, that was just what I wanted. I went up to it, rummaged in the straw in the wooden box, and to my indescribable delight pulled out a packet of little slips of paper. The wretched dog, seeing this, first bit my calf, and then when she perceived that I had taken her letters began to whine and fawn on me, but I said: 'No, my dear, goodbye,' and took to my heels. I believe the girl thought I was a madman, as she was very much frightened. When I got home I wanted to set to work at once to decipher the letters, for I don't see very well by candlelight; but Mavra had taken it into her head to wash the floor. These stupid Finnish women always clean at the wrong moment. And so I went out to walk about and think over the incident. Now I shall find out all their doings and ways of thinking, all the hidden springs, and shall get to the bottom of it all. These letters will reveal everything. Dogs are clever creatures, they understand all the diplomatic relations, and so no doubt I shall find there everything about our gentleman: the portrait and all the doings of the man. There will be something in them too about her who . . . never mind, silence! Towards evening I came home. For the most part I lay on my bed.

NOVEMBER 13

Well, we shall see! The writing is fairly distinct, at the same time there is something doggy about the hand. Let us read:

> DEAR FIDO – I never can get used to your plebeian name. As though they could not have given you a better one? Fido, Rose – what vulgarity! No more about that, however. I am very glad we thought of writing to each other.

The letter is very well written. The punctuation and even the spelling is quite correct. Even the chief of our section could not write like this, though he does talk of having studied at some university. Let us see what comes next.

'It seems to me that to share one's ideas, one's feelings, and one's impressions with others is one of the greatest blessings on earth.'

H'm! . . . an idea taken from a work translated from the German. I don't remember the name of it.

'I say this from experience, though I have not been about the world, beyond the gates of our house. Is not my life spent in comfort? My young lady, whom her papa calls Sophie, loves me passionately.'

Aïe, aïe! Never mind, never mind! Silence!

'Papa, too, often caresses me. I drink tea and coffee with cream. Ah, *ma chère*,[203] I ought to tell you that I see nothing agreeable at all in big, gnawed bones such as our Polkan crunches in the kitchen. The only bones that are nice are those of game, and then only when the marrow hasn't been sucked out of them by someone. What is very good is several sauces mixed together, only they must be free from capers and green stuff; but I know nothing worse than giving dogs little balls of bread. A gentleman sitting at the table who has been touching all sorts of nasty things with his hands begins with those hands rolling up bread, calls one up and thrusts the ball upon one. To refuse seems somehow discourteous – well, one eats it – with repulsion, but one eats it . . . '

What the devil's this! What nonsense! As though there were nothing better to write about. Let us look at another page and see if there is nothing more sensible.

'I shall be delighted to let you know about everything that happens here. I have already told you something about the chief gentleman, whom Sophie calls papa. He is a very strange man.'

Ah, here we are at last! Yes, I knew it; they have a very diplomatic view of everything. Let us see what Papa is like.

' . . . a very strange man. For the most part he says nothing; he very rarely speaks. But about a week ago he was continually talking to himself: "Shall I receive it or shall I not?" He would take a paper in one hand and close the other hand empty and say: "Shall I receive it or shall I not?" Once he turned to me with the question: "What do you think, Madgie, shall I receive it or not?" I couldn't understand a word of it, I sniffed at his boots and walked away. A week later, *ma chère*, he came in in high glee. All the morning gentlemen in uniform were coming to see him and congratulating him on something. At table he was merrier than I have ever seen him; he kept telling stories. And after dinner he lifted me up to his neck and said: "Look, Madgie, what's this?" I saw a little ribbon. I sniffed it, but could discover no aroma whatever; at last I licked it on the sly: it was a little bit salt.'

H'm! This dog seems to me to be really too . . . she ought to be thrashed! And so he is ambitious! One must take that into consideration.

'Farewell, *ma chère*! I fly, and so on . . . and so on . . . I will finish my letter tomorrow. Well, good-day, I am with you again. Today my young lady Sophie . . . '

Oh come, let us see about Sophie. Ah, you rascal . . . Never mind, never mind . . . let us go on.

'My young lady Sophie was in a great fluster. She was getting ready to go to a ball, and I was delighted that in her absence I could write to you. My Sophie is always very glad to go to a ball, though she always gets almost angry when she is being dressed. I cannot understand why people dress. Why don't they go about as we do, for instance? It's nice and it's comfortable. I can't understand, *ma chère*, what pleasure there is in going to balls. Sophie always comes home from balls at six o'clock in the morning, and I can almost always guess from her pale and exhausted face that they had given the poor thing nothing to eat. I must own I couldn't live like that. If I didn't get grouse and gravy or the roast wing of a chicken, I don't know what would become of me. Gravy is nice too with grain in it, but with carrots, turnips, or artichokes it is never good.'

Extraordinary inequality of style! You can see at once that it is not a man writing; it begins as it ought and ends with dogginess. Let us look at one more letter. It's rather long. H'm! And there's no date on it.

'Ah, my dear, how one feels the approach of spring! My heart beats as though I were always expecting someone. There is always a noise in my ears so that I often stand for some minutes with my foot in the air listening at doors. I must confide to you that I have a number of suitors. I often sit at the window and look at them. Oh, if only you knew what ugly creatures there are among them. One is a very ungainly yard-dog, fearfully stupid, stupidity is painted on his face; he walks about the street with an air of importance and imagines that he is a distinguished person and thinks that everybody is looking at him. Not a bit of it. I don't take any notice of him – I behave exactly as though I didn't see him. And what a terrible Great Dane stops before my window! If he were to stand upon his hind legs, which I expect the clumsy fellow could not do, he would be a whole head taller than my Sophie's papa, though he is fairly tall and stout. That blockhead must be a frightfully insolent fellow. I growled at him, but much he cared: he hardly frowned, he put out his tongue, dangled his huge ears and looked up at the window – such a country bumpkin! But can you suppose, *ma chère*, that my heart makes no response to any overture? Ah no . . . If only you could see one of my suitors climbing over the fence next door, by name Trèsor . . . Ah, *ma chère*, what a face he has! . . . '

Ough, the devil! . . . What rubbish! How can any one fill a letter with foolishness! Give me a man! I want to see a man. I want spiritual sustenance – in which my soul might find food and enjoyment; and instead of that I have this nonsense . . . Let us turn over the page and see whether it is better!

'Sophie was sitting at the table sewing something, I was looking out of window because I am fond of watching passers-by, when all at once the footman came in and said "Teplov!" "Ask him in," cried Sophie, and rushed to embrace me. "Ah Madgie, Madgie! If only you knew who that is: a dark young man, a kammer-junker, and such eyes, black as agates!" And Sophie ran off to her room. A minute later a kammer-junker with black whiskers came in, walked up to the looking-glass, smoothed his hair and looked about the room. I growled and sat in my place. Sophie soon came in and bowed gaily in response to his scraping; and I just went on looking out of window as though I were noticing nothing. However, I bent my head a little on one side and tried to hear what they were saying. Oh, *ma chère*, the nonsense they talked! They talked about a lady who had mistaken one figure for another at the dance; and said that someone called Bobov with a ruffle on his shirt looked just like a stork and had almost fallen down on the floor, and that a girl called Lidin imagined that her eyes were blue when they were really green – and that sort of thing. "Well," I thought to myself, "if one were to compare that kammer-junker to Trèsor, heavens, what a difference!" In the first place, the kammer-junker has a perfectly flat face with whiskers all round as though he had tied it up in a black handkerchief; while Trèsor has a delicate little countenance with a white patch on the forehead. It's impossible to compare the kammer-junker's figure with Trèsor's. And his eyes, his ways, his manners are all quite different. Oh, what a difference! I don't know, *ma chère*, what she sees in her Teplov. Why she is so enthusiastic about him . . . '

Well, I think myself that there is something wrong about it. It's impossible that she can be fascinated by Teplov. Let us see what next.

'It seems to me that if she is attracted by that kammer-junker she will soon be attracted by that clerk that sits in papa's study. Oh, *ma chère*, if you knew what an ugly fellow that is! A regular tortoise in a bag . . . '

What clerk is this? . . .

'He has a very queer surname. He always sits mending the pens. The hair on his head is very much like hay. Papa sometimes sends him out instead of a servant . . . '

I do believe the nasty little dog is alluding to me. But my hair isn't like hay!

'Sophie can never help laughing when she sees him.'

That's a lie, you damned little dog! What an evil tongue! As though I didn't know that that is the work of envy! As though I didn't know whose tricks were at the bottom of that! This is all the doing of the chief of my section. The man has vowed eternal hatred, and here he tries to injure me again and again, at every turn. Let us look at one more letter though. Perhaps the thing will explain itself.

'MY DEAR FIDO, – Forgive me for not writing for so long. I have been in a perfect delirium. How truly has some writer said that love is a second life. Moreover, there are great changes in the house here. The kammer-junker is here every day. Sophie is frantically in love with him. Papa is very good-humoured. I have even heard from our Grigory, who sweeps the floor and almost always talks to himself, that there will soon be a wedding because papa is set on seeing Sophie married to a general or a kammer-junker or to a colonel in the army . . . '

Dence take it! I can't read any more . . . It's always a kammer-junker or a general. Everything that's best in the world falls to the kammer-junkers or the generals. If you find some poor treasure and think it is almost within your grasp, a kammer-junker or a general will snatch it from you. The devil take it! I should like to become a general myself, not in order to receive her hand and all the rest of it; no, I should like to be a general only to see how they would wriggle and display all their court manners and *équivoques* and then to say to them: I spit on you both. Deuce take it, it's annoying! I tore the silly dog's letters to bits.

DECEMBER 3

It cannot be. It's idle talk! There won't be a wedding! What if he is a kammer-junker? Why, that is nothing but a dignity, it's not a visible thing that one could pick up in one's hands. You don't get a third eye in your head because you are a kammer-junker. Why, his nose is not made of gold but is just like mine and every one else's; he sniffs with it and doesn't eat with it, he sneezes with it and doesn't cough with it. I have often tried to make out from what all these differences arise. Why am I a titular councillor and on what grounds am I a titular councillor? Perhaps I am not a titular councillor at all? Perhaps I am a count or a general, and only somehow appear to be a titular councillor. Perhaps I don't know myself who I am. How many instances there have been in history: some simple, humble tradesman or peasant, not even a nobleman, is suddenly discovered to be a grand gentleman or a baron, or what do you call it . . . If a peasant can sometimes turn into something like that, what may not a nobleman turn into? I shall suddenly, for instance, go to see our chief in a general's uniform: with an epaulette on my right shoulder and an epaulette on my left shoulder, and a blue ribbon across my chest; well, my charmer will sing a different tune then, and what will her papa, our director, himself say? Ah, he is very ambitious! He is a mason,[204] he is certainly a mason; though he does pretend to be this and that, but I noticed at once that he was a mason: if he shakes hands with any one, he only offers him two fingers. Might I not be appointed a governor-general this very minute or an intendant, or something of that sort? I should like to know why I am a titular councillor. Why precisely a titular councillor?

DECEMBER 5

I spent the whole morning reading the newspaper. Strange things are going on in Spain. In fact, I can't really make it out. They write that the throne is vacant, and that they are in a difficult position about choosing an heir, and that there are insurrections in consequence. It seems to me that it is extremely queer. How can the throne be vacant? They say that some Donna ought to ascend the throne.[205] A Donna cannot ascend the throne, she cannot possibly. There ought to be a king on the throne. 'But,' they say, 'there is not a king.' It cannot be that there is no king. A kingdom can't exist without a king. There is a king, only probably he is in hiding somewhere. He may be there, but either family reasons or danger from some neighbouring State, such as France or some other country, may compel him to remain in hiding, or there may be some other reasons.

DECEMBER 8

I quite wanted to go to the department, but various reasons and considerations detained me. I cannot get the affairs of Spain out of my head. How can it be that a Donna should be made queen? They won't allow it. England in the first place won't allow it. And besides, the politics of all Europe, the Emperor of Austria and our Tsar . . . I must own these events have so overwhelmed and shaken me that I haven't been able to do anything all day. Mavra remarked that I was extremely absent-minded at table. And I believe I did accidentally throw two plates on the floor, which smashed immediately. After dinner I went for a walk down the hill: I could deduce nothing edifying from that. For the most part I lay on my bed and reflected on the affairs of Spain.

2000 A.D., APRIL 43

This is the day of the greatest public rejoicing! There is a king of Spain! He has been discovered. I am that king. I only heard of it this morning. I must own it burst upon me like a flash of lightning. I can't imagine how I could believe and imagine myself to be a titular councillor. How could that crazy, mad idea ever have entered my head? It's a good thing that no one thought of putting me in a madhouse. Now everything has been revealed to me. Now it is all as plain as possible. But until now I did not understand, everything was in a sort of mist. And I believe it all arose from believing that the brain is in the head. It's not so at all; it comes with the wind from the direction of the Caspian Sea. First of all, I told Mavra who I am. When she heard that the King of Spain was standing before her, she clasped her hands and almost died of horror; the silly woman had never seen a king of Spain before. I tried to reassure her, however, and in gracious words tried to convince her of my benevolent feelings towards her, saying that I was not angry with her for having sometimes cleaned my boots so badly. Of course they are benighted people; it is no good talking of elevated subjects to them. She is frightened because she is convinced that all kings of Spain are like Philip II.[206] But I assured her that there was no resemblance between me and Philip II and that I have not even one Capuchin. I didn't go to the department. The devil take it! No, my friends, you won't allure me there again; I am not going to copy your nasty papers!

MARTOBER 86 BETWEEN DAY AND NIGHT

Our office messenger arrived today to tell me to go to the department, and to say that I had not been there for more than three weeks.

But people are unjust: they do their reckoning by weeks. It's the Jews brought that in because their Rabbi washes once a week. However, I did go to the department for fun. The head of our section thought that I should bow to him and apologise, but I looked at him indifferently, not too angrily and not too graciously, and sat down in my place as though I did not notice anything. I looked at all the scum of the office and thought: 'If only you knew who is sitting among you!' Good gracious! Wouldn't there be an upset! And the head of our section would bow to me as he bows now to the director. They put a paper before me to make some sort of an extract from it. But I didn't touch it. A few minutes later every one was in a bustle. They said the director was coming. A number of the clerks ran forward to show off to him, but I didn't stir. When he walked through our room they all buttoned up their coats, but I didn't do anything at all. What's a director? Am I going to tremble before him – never! He's a fine director! He is a cork, he is not a director. An ordinary cork, a simple cork and nothing else – such as you cork a bottle with. What amused me most of all was when they put a paper before me to sign. They thought I should write at the bottom of the paper, So-and-so, head-clerk of the table – how else should it be! But in the most important place, where the director of the department signs his name, I wrote 'Ferdinand VIII' You should have seen the awe-struck silence that followed; but I only waved my hand and said: 'I don't insist on any signs of allegiance!' and walked out. From there I walked straight to the director's. He was not at home. The footman did not want to let me in, but I spoke to him in such a way that he let his hands drop. I went straight to her dressing-room. She was sitting before the looking-glass; she jumped up and stepped back on seeing me. I did not tell her that I was the King of Spain, however; I only told her that there was a happiness awaiting her such as she could not imagine, and that in spite of the wiles of our enemies we should be together. I didn't care to say more and walked out. Oh, woman is a treacherous creature! I have discovered now what women are. Hitherto no one has found out with whom woman is in love: I have been the first to discover it. Woman is in love with the devil. Yes, joking apart. Scientific men write nonsense saying that she is this or that – she cares for nothing but the devil. You will see her from a box in the first tier fixing her lorgnette. You imagine she is looking at the fat man with decorations. No, she is looking at the devil who is standing behind his back. There he is, hidden in his coat. There he is, making signs to her! And she will marry him, she will marry him. And all these people, their dignified fathers who fawn on everybody and push their way to court and say that they are patriots and one thing and another: profit, profit is all that these patriots want! They would sell their father and their mother and God for money, ambitious creatures, Judases! All this is ambition, and the ambition is because of a little pimple under the tongue and in it a little worm no bigger than a pin's head, and it's all the doing of a barber who lives in Gorohovy Street, I don't remember his name; but I know for a fact that, in collusion with a midwife, he is trying to spread Mahometanism all over the world, and that is how it is, I am told, that the majority of people in France profess the Mahometan faith.

NO DATE. THE DAY HAD NO NUMBER.

I walked incognito along Nevsky Prospect. His Majesty the Tsar drove by. All the people took off their caps and I did the same, but I made no sign that I was the King of Spain. I thought it improper to discover myself so suddenly before every one, because I ought first to be presented at court. The only thing that has prevented my doing so is the lack of a Spanish national dress. If only I could get hold of a royal mantle. I should have liked to order it from a tailor, but they are perfect asses; besides they neglect their work so, they have given themselves up to speculating and for the most part are employed in laying the pavement in the street. I determined to make the mantle out of my new uniform, which I had only worn twice. And that the scoundrels should not ruin it I decided to make it myself, shutting the door that no one might see me at it. I ripped it all up with the scissors because the cut has to be completely different.

I DON'T REMEMBER THE DATE. THERE WAS NO MONTH EITHER. GOODNESS KNOWS WHAT TO MAKE OF IT.

The mantle is completely finished. Mavra gave a shriek when she saw me in it. However, I can't make up my mind to present myself at court, for so far there is no deputation from Spain. It wouldn't be proper to go without deputies: there would be nothing to give weight to my dignity. I expect them from hour to hour.

THE 1ST

I am extremely surprised at the tardiness of the deputies. What can be detaining them? Can it be the machinations of France? Yes, that is the most malignant of States. I went to enquire at the post office whether the Spanish deputies had not arrived; but the postmaster was excessively stupid and knew nothing. 'No,' he said, 'there are no deputies here, but if you care to write a letter I will send it off in accordance with the regulations.' Dash it all, what's the use of a letter? A letter is nonsense. Letters are written by chemists, and even then they have to moisten their tongues with vinegar or else their faces would be all over scabs.

MADRID, FEBRUARY THIRTIETH

And so here I am in Spain, and it happened so quickly that I can hardly realise it yet. This morning the Spanish deputies arrived and I got into a carriage with them. The extraordinary rapidity of our journey struck me as strange. We went at such a rate that within half an hour we had reached the frontiers of Spain. But of course now there are railroads all over Europe, and steamers go very rapidly. Spain is a strange land! When we went into the first room I saw a number of people with shaven heads. I guessed at once that these were either grandees or soldiers because they do shave their heads. I thought the behaviour of the High Chancellor, who led me by the hand, extremely strange. He thrust me into a little room and said: 'Sit there, and if you persist in calling yourself King Ferdinand, I'll knock the inclination out of you.' But knowing that this was only to try me I answered in the negative, whereupon the Chancellor hit me twice on the back with the stick and it hurt so that I almost cried out, but I restrained myself, remembering that this is the custom of chivalry on receiving any exalted dignity, for customs of chivalry persist in Spain to this day. When I was alone I decided to occupy myself with the affairs of state. I discovered that Spain and China are one and the same country, and it is only through ignorance that they are considered to be different kingdoms. I recommend every one to try and write Spain on a bit of paper and it will always turn out China. But I was particularly distressed by an event which will take place tomorrow. Tomorrow at seven o'clock a strange phenomenon will occur: the earth will fall on the moon. The celebrated English chemist Wellington has written about it. I must confess that I experience a tremor at my heart when I reflect on the extreme softness and fragility of the moon. You see the moon is generally made in Hamburg, and very badly made too. I am surprised that England hasn't taken notice of it. It was made by a lame cooper, and it is evident that the fool had no idea what a moon should be. He put in tarred cord and one part of olive oil; and that is why there is such a fearful stench all over the world that one has to stop up one's nose. And that's how it is that the moon is such a soft globe that man cannot live on it and that nothing lives there but noses. And it is for that very reason that we can't see our noses, because they are all in the moon. And when I reflected that the earth is a heavy body and when it falls may grind our noses to powder, I was overcome by such uneasiness that, putting on my shoes and stockings, I hastened to the hall of the Imperial Council to give orders to the police not to allow the earth to fall on the moon. The grandees with shaven heads whom I found in great numbers in the hall of the Imperial Council were very intelligent people, and when I said: 'Gentlemen, let us save the moon, for the earth is trying to fall upon it!' they all rushed to carry out my sovereign wishes, and several climbed up the walls to try and get at the moon; but at that moment the High Chancellor walked in. Seeing him they all ran in different directions. I as King remained alone. But, to my amazement, the Chancellor struck me with his stick and drove me back to my room! So great is the power of national customs in Spain.

JANUARY OF THE SAME YEAR (IT CAME AFTER FEBRUARY)

So far I have not been able to make out what sort of a country Spain is. The national traditions and the customs of the court are quite extraordinary. I can't make it out, I can't make it out, I absolutely can't make it out. Today they shaved my head, although I shouted at the top of my voice that I didn't want to become a monk. But I can't even remember what happened afterwards when they poured cold water on my head. I have never endured such hell. I was almost going frantic so that they had a difficulty in holding me. I cannot understand the meaning of this strange custom. It's a stupid, senseless practice! The lack of good sense in the kings who have not abolished it to this day is beyond my comprehension. Judging from all the circumstances, I wonder whether I have not fallen into the hands of the Spanish Inquisition,[207] and whether the man I took to be the Grand Chancellor isn't the Grand Inquisitor. Only I cannot understand how a king can be subject to the Inquisition. It can only be through the influence of France, especially of Polignac.[208] Oh, that beast of a Polignac! He has sworn to me enmity to the death. And he pursues me and pursues me; but I know, my friend, that you are the tool of England. The English are great politicians. They poke their noses into everything. All the world knows that when England takes a pinch of snuff, France sneezes.

THE TWENTY-FIFTH

Today the Grand Inquisitor came into my room again, but hearing his steps in the distance I hid under a chair. Seeing I wasn't there, he began calling me. At first he shouted 'Popristchin!' I didn't say a word. Then: 'Aksenty Ivanov! Titular councillor! nobleman!' I still remained silent. 'Ferdinand VIII, King of Spain!' I was on the point of sticking out my head, but then I thought: 'No, my friend, you won't take me in, I know you: you will be pouring cold water on my head again.' However, he caught sight of me and drove me from under the chair with a stick. That damned stick does hurt. However, I was rewarded for all this by the discovery I made today. I found out that every cock has a Spain, that it is under his wings not far from his tail.

The Grand Inquisitor went away, however, very wroth, threatening me with some punishment. But I disdain his impotent malice, knowing that he is simply an instrument, a tool of England.

34 ЕЕBRUARY YRAE 349

No, I haven't the strength to endure more. My God! The things they are doing to me! They pour cold water on my head! They won't listen to me, they won't see me, they won't hear me. What have I done to them? Why do they torture me? What do they want of a poor creature like me? What can I give them? I have nothing. It's too much for me, I can't endure these agonies, my head is burning and everything is going round. Save me, take me away! Give me a troika and horses swift as a whirlwind! Take your seat, my driver, ring out, my bells, fly upwards, my steeds, and bear me away from this world! Far away, far away, so that nothing can be seen, nothing. Yonder the sky whirls before me, a star sparkles in the distance; the forest floats by with dark trees and the moon; blue-grey mist lies stretched under my feet; a chord resounds in the mist; on one side the sea, on the other Italy, yonder the huts of Russia can be seen. Is that my home in the distance? Is it my mother sitting before the window? Mother, save your poor son! Drop a tear on his sick head! See how they torment him! Press your poor orphan to your bosom! There is nowhere in the world for him! He is persecuted! Mother, have pity on your sick child! . . .

And do you know that the King of France[209] has a boil just under his nose?

THE GOVERNMENT INSPECTOR

It is no use to blame the looking-glass if your face is awry.

(A Proverb)

Translator's Note

All Gogol's plays were written between 1832 and 1837, in the period of literary fertility when he was still under the happy influence of Pushkin. His first dramatic effort was either 'Marriage' (in its earlier version called 'The Suitors') or a comedy called 'The Order of Vladimir of the Third Class', dealing with the intrigues of an official who goes mad from disappointed ambition. This play he abandoned, recognising that it would inevitably be rejected by the Censor. 'A Lawsuit', 'The Servants' Hall', and 'A Fragment', are all that has survived of it. The central theme reappears in the story 'A Madman's Diary'.

In 1834 the first version of 'The Government Inspector' was written. The plot of this play, the most finished and completely successful of Gogol's works, was, like that of *Dead Souls*, given him by Pushkin, who, while staying at an inn in Nizhny-Novgorod, was mistaken for a great official from Petersburg. That this masterpiece was ever allowed to see the light was due to the good offices of the poet Zhukovsky, who gave it to the Tsar to read. Nicholas was delighted with it, and decreed that it should be produced. It was first performed in 1836, and has held the stage ever since, and not only in Russia.

The one-act sketch, 'The Gamblers', was the latest of the plays, begun in 1836, and only completed in its final shape in 1842.

Characters in the Play

Characters and Costumes

Directions for the Actors

THE MAYOR, an elderly man who has spent his life in the Service, very shrewd in his own way. Though he accepts bribes he is very dignified in his deportment; serious and even a little sententious; he speaks neither loudly nor softly, neither too little nor too much. Every word he utters is significant. His features are coarse and heavy, as is always the case with men who have passed through hardships in the lower ranks of the Service. The transition from fear to joy, from cringing to haughtiness, is somewhat rapid in him, as is common in a man of unrefined instincts. He is usually wearing a uniform adorned with frogs and high boots with spurs. His hair is cut short and streaked with grey.

ANNA ANDREYEVNA, his wife, a provincial coquette, not yet middle-aged, whose life has been spent between novels and albums and the supervision of her stores and maids. Very inquisitive and given to the display of vanity. Sometimes domineers over her husband simply because he is not ready with an answer for her; but this domineering is confined to trifles, and shows itself in scolding and raillery. She wears four different dresses in the course of the play.

HLESTAKOV, a young man of three-and-twenty, thin and slender; rather silly, what is known as scatter-brained – one of those who in their office are called feather-heads. He speaks and acts without the slightest reflection. He is incapable of steady attention to any subject. He speaks jerkily, and the words dart from his lips quite unexpectedly. The more candour and simplicity an actor puts into this part, the more he will succeed in it. He is dressed in the fashion.

OSIP is a servant like most servants who are getting on in years. He speaks gravely, is a little condescending sometimes, and likes to repeat to himself moral reflections intended for his master. His voice is almost always composed, but when talking to his master there is a stern, abrupt, and even rather rude tone in it. He is more intelligent than his master, and so is quicker to grasp things, but is not fond of saying too much, and is a silent knave. He wears a shabby grey or dark blue coat.

BOBCHINSKY and DOBCHINSKY are both short, squat little men; extremely alike and very inquisitive; both rather corpulent; both speak very rapidly, and eke out their words with gesticulations. Dobchinsky is a little taller and more serious than Bobchinsky, but Bobchinsky is livelier and more free and easy.

LYAPKIN-TYAPKIN, the Judge, is a man who has read five or six books, and so is something of a free-thinker. He is given to reading meanings into everything, and so attaches weight to every word he utters. The actor ought to maintain an air of great significance throughout. He speaks in a bass voice with a slow drawl, with a wheeze and a hiss like an old-fashioned clock, which first gives a hiss and then strikes.

ZEMLYANIKA, the Charity Commissioner, is a very stout, stolid, clumsy man, but is, nevertheless, a wily rogue. Very officious and obliging.

THE POSTMASTER is good-natured to the point of simplicity.

The other characters do not need special explanation; their prototypes are continually before us.

The actors must pay special attention to the last scene. The last word ought to give an electric shock to all present at once. The whole group ought to change its position instantly. A cry of astonishment ought to spring from all the women as though from one bosom. Disregard of these instructions may ruin the whole effect.

ACT ONE

A room in the Mayor's house

The Mayor, *the* Charity Commissioner,
the School Inspector, *the* Judge,
the Police Superintendent, *the* Doctor, *two* Policemen

THE MAYOR   I have called you together, gentlemen, to communicate
to you a most unpleasant piece of news: an Inspector is coming to
visit us.

AMMOS FYODOROVITCH   An Inspector?

ARTEMY FILIPPOVITCH   An Inspector?

THE MAYOR   A Government Inspector, from Petersburg, incognito; and
with secret orders.

AMMOS FYODOROVITCH   That's a pleasant surprise!

ARTEMY FILIPPOVITCH   As though we hadn't trouble enough!

LUKA LUKITCH   Good heavens! And with secret orders!

THE MAYOR   I had a sort of foreboding of it: all night long I was
dreaming of two extraordinary rats. I assure you I never saw rats
like them: black and unnaturally large! They came and sniffed
about – and went away. Here, I'll read you the letter I've received
from Andrey Ivanovitch Tchmyhov, whom you know, Artemy
Filippovitch. This is what he writes: 'Dear friend and benefactor!'
(*mutters in an undertone, hastily looking through the letter*) 'and to
inform you' . . . Ah, here it is: 'I hasten to inform you, among
other things, that an official has arrived with instructions to inspect
the whole province, and especially our district (*lifts up his finger
significantly*). I have learned this from the most reliable sources,
though he passes himself off for a private person. As I know
that you have your little failings like everybody else, for you are
a sensible man and don't like to let things slip through your
fingers' . . . (*pausing*) well, we are all friends here . . . 'I advise you
to take steps in time, for he may arrive any minute, if, indeed, he
has not come already and is not living among you incognito . . .
Yesterday I . . .' well, here he goes on to family affairs, 'my sister
Anna Kirillovna and her husband have come to stay with us; Ivan

Kirillovitch has grown much stouter, and is always playing the fiddle' . . . and so on and so on. So that's the position!

AMMOS FYODOROVITCH   Yes, it's an extraordinary position, simply extraordinary. There must be some reason for it.

LUKA LUKITCH   What is it for, Anton Antonovitch, how do you account for it? Why should an Inspector come here?

THE MAYOR   What for! It seems it was to be! (*with a sigh*). Hitherto, and thank God for it, they have pried into other towns, now our turn has come.

AMMOS FYODOROVITCH   I imagine, Anton Antonovitch, that there is a subtle and chiefly political reason. I'll tell you what it means: Russia . . . yes . . . is meaning to go to war, and the ministers, you see, have sent an official to find out whether there is any treason here.

THE MAYOR   Pooh, what next! And you a sensible man, too! Treason in a district town! Is it on the frontier, pray? Why, you might gallop for three years and not reach any foreign country.

AMMOS FYODOROVITCH   No, I tell you, you are wrong there . . . you are . . . they have all sorts of schemes in Petersburg; they may be far away, but they take stock of everything.

THE MAYOR   They may or they may not; anyway, I have warned you, gentlemen. Mind you, I have taken measures in my own department, and I advise you to do the same. And especially you, Artemy Filippovitch! Our visitor is pretty certain to want to inspect the charitable institutions under your supervision first of all, and so you take care that everything is as it should be: see that the nightcaps are clean and that the patients don't look like sweeps, as they do on ordinary days.

ARTEMY FILIPPOVITCH   Oh, that's no great matter. Of course they can put on clean nightcaps.

THE MAYOR   Yes; and over every bed put an inscription in Latin or some other language . . . that's for you to decide, Christian Ivanovitch . . . the name of each disease, when each patient was taken ill, the day of the week and the month . . . It's a pity your patients smoke such strong tobacco that it makes one sneeze when one goes in. And it would be better if there were fewer of them: he will suspect at once that there is something wrong with the management, or that the doctor does not know his business.

ARTEMY FILIPPOVITCH   Oh, as to doctoring, Christian Ivanovitch and I came to the conclusion long ago that the nearer to nature the better – we don't make use of expensive medicines. They are simple people: if they die, they'll die anyhow; if they recover, they recover anyhow. And it would be difficult for Christian Ivanovitch to interview the patients; he does not know a word of Russian.

(HÜBNER *emits a sound intermediate between e and a.*)

THE MAYOR   I should advise you too, Ammos Fyodorovitch, to look after the law-court. In the hall where the applicants come with complaints and petitions the porters have taken to keeping geese with a lot of young goslings, which are always waddling about under one's feet. Of course poultry-keeping is a most laudable pursuit, and why shouldn't the porter keep them? Only it's not the thing, you know, in a public office . . . I meant to mention it to you before, but I always forgot it somehow.

AMMOS FYODOROVITCH   I'll order them all to be taken to my kitchen today. Won't you come to dinner with me?

THE MAYOR   It's a pity, too, that you have all sorts of rubbish hanging up to dry in the court itself, and there's a hunting-whip on the top of the case where deeds are kept. I know you are fond of sport, but it would be better to take it away for a time, and when the Inspector has gone you can hang it up again if you like. And then your Assessor too . . . of course he is a man who understands his business, but he smells as though he had just come out of a distillery – that's not the thing either. I meant to speak about it long ago, but my attention was always called off to something else, I don't know what. Something can be done for it if, as he says, it is his natural smell; he might be advised to try onion or garlic or something. Christian Ivanovitch might give him some drug for it.

(HÜBNER *gives vent to the same inarticulate sound.*)

AMMOS FYODOROVITCH   No, there is no getting over it: he says his nurse dropped him as a baby and he has smelt a little of vodka ever since.

THE MAYOR   Oh well, I only just mentioned it. As for the way that the business of the court is conducted, and what Andrey Ivanovitch in his letter calls 'failings', I can say nothing. And indeed, what is there to say? There is no man entirely free from sin . . . This is ordained by God Himself, and it is no use the Voltairians[210] disputing it.

AMMOS FYODOROVITCH   What do you mean by sin, Anton Antonovitch? There are sins and sins. I tell every one openly that I take bribes, but what bribes? Wolfhound puppies. That's a very different matter.

THE MAYOR   Well, puppies or anything else, it's bribes just the same.

AMMOS FYODOROVITCH   Oh no, Anton Antonovitch. If a man takes a fur coat worth five hundred roubles or a shawl for his wife . . .

THE MAYOR   Well, what of it if the only bribes you take are puppies? You don't believe in God: you never go to church; while I am firm in the faith, anyway, and go to church every Sunday. But you . . . Oh, I know you: when you begin talking about the creation of the world, it makes my hair stand on end.

AMMOS FYODOROVITCH   But I came to my views of myself, by my own thinking.

THE MAYOR   Well, in some cases too much thinking is worse than none at all. I spoke of the district court – but there, to tell the truth it is not likely that any one will peep into it; it's a spot to be envied indeed, it's under the special protection of Providence. But you, Luka Lukitch, as the Inspector of Schools, must be particularly careful about the teachers. Of course they are learned men and have been educated at all sorts of colleges, but they have very strange peculiarities, naturally, inseparable from their vocation. One of them, for instance, the one with a fat face . . . I can't recollect his name, never seems able to go into his desk without making a grimace like this (*makes a grimace*) and then begins smoothing his beard from under his cravat. Of course, if he makes a face like that at one of the boys it does not matter; it may be necessary, I can't judge; but just think if he does it to a visitor – that might be a dreadful thing: the Inspector or some one else might think it was meant for him. Goodness only knows what it might lead to.

LUKA LUKITCH   What am I to do with him? I've spoken to him over and over again. Only the other day, when our marshal of nobility[211] came into the classroom, he made a face worse then anything I've ever seen. He did it with the best intentions, but I got a talking-to for letting free-thinking notions be put into the boys' heads.

THE MAYOR   And I must say a word to you about the history teacher. He is a brainy fellow, one can see, and has any amount of learning, but he lectures with such fervour that he forgets himself. I heard him once: so long as he was talking about the Assyrians[212] and the Babylonians[213] it was not so bad, but when he came to Alexander the Great,[214] I can't describe how he went on. I thought the house was on fire, I did indeed! He jumped out of his desk and banged a chair on the floor with all his might. Of course Alexander the Great was a hero, but why smash the chairs? Its destroying Government property.

LUKA LUKITCH   Yes, he is excitable. I've mentioned it to him several times. He answers: 'You may say what you like, but in the cause of learning I am ready to give my life.'

THE MAYOR Yes, such is the mysterious dispensation of Providence; clever men are either drunkards or they make such faces that you don't know where to look.

LUKA LUKITCH I wouldn't wish my worst enemy to serve in the department of education! One is afraid of every one: every one interferes, every one wants to show what a clever person he is.

THE MAYOR There would be nothing to mind – but it's the damnable incognito! He'll look in all of a sudden: 'Aha! so you are here, my pets! And who is Judge here!' he will say. 'Lyapkin-Tyapkin.' – 'Hand him over! And who is Charity Commissioner!' – 'Zemlyanika.' – 'Hand him over!' That's what's so awful!

(Enter the POSTMASTER.*)*

THE POSTMASTER Do explain, gentlemen, what's this, what official's coming?

THE MAYOR Why, haven't you heard?

THE POSTMASTER I have heard from Pyotr Ivanovitch Bobchinsky. He was in the post office just now.

THE MAYOR Well, what do you think about it?

THE POSTMASTER What do I think? There'll be war with the Turks.[215]

AMMOS FYODOROVITCH My very words! Just what I thought.

THE MAYOR Yes, you're both completely out of it!

THE POSTMASTER Indeed, but it's war with the Turks. It's all those nasty French.

THE MAYOR War with the Turks! It's we who are going to catch it, not the Turks. That's certain – I have a letter.

THE POSTMASTER Oh, in that case, there won't be war with the Turks.

THE MAYOR Well, what do you say, Ivan Kuzmitch?

THE POSTMASTER What do I matter? How about you, Anton Antonovitch?

THE MAYOR Me? Well, I'm not alarmed – but there, just a bit . . . The shopkeepers and townspeople make me uneasy. They say I am the plague of their lives; though God is my witness, if I have taken something here and there, it has been with no ill-feeling. Indeed, I fancy . . . *(takes him by the arm and leads him aside)* . . . I wonder whether there hasn't been some secret report against me. Why should an Inspector be sent to us? Listen, Ivan Kuzmitch, couldn't you, for our common benefit, just unseal and read every letter which reaches your post office, going or coming; just to see whether there is any tale-bearing or correspondence going on. If not, you can seal it up again; or, indeed, you can deliver it open.

THE POSTMASTER I know, I know . . . You need not teach me, I do that already, not so much by way of precaution as from curiosity: I do like to know what's going on in the world. I assure you, it makes capital reading. It is a pleasure to read some letters – all sorts of incidents are so well described . . . and so instructive. Better than the *Moscow News*!

THE MAYOR Well, tell me, haven't you read anything about an official from Petersburg?

THE POSTMASTER No, nothing about a Petersburg one, but a lot about those at Saratov and Kostroma.[216] But it is a pity you don't read the letters: there are fine passages in them. For instance, a lieutenant was writing to a friend the other day, and he described a ball in a most amusing way . . . very, very nice it was. 'My life, dear friend,' he writes, 'is passed in Elysium:[217] young ladies in plenty, bands playing, banners flying.' . . . It's written with great feeling. I have kept it on purpose. Would you like me to read it?

THE MAYOR Oh, it's not the moment for that now. Well then, Ivan Kuzmitch, do me the favour, if any sort of complaint or report comes into your hands, keep it without hesitation.

THE POSTMASTER I shall be pleased.

AMMOS FYODOROVITCH You had better look out; you will get into trouble for that one of these days!

THE POSTMASTER Oh, I dare say!

THE MAYOR Nonsense, nonsense. It would be a very different thing if you made public use of it, but this is a private affair.

AMMOS FYODOROVITCH Yes, there is mischief afoot! And I must tell you, Anton Antonovitch, I was coming to offer you a present – a dog, own sister to the hound that you know. You are aware, of course, that Tcheptovitch is taking proceedings against Varhovinsky, and now I'm in clover. I am coursing hares on the lands of both.

THE MAYOR Holy saints! I don't care about your hares now: I can't get that damned incognito out of my head. One keeps expecting that the door will open – and in will walk . . .

(BOBCHINSKY *and* DOBCHINSKY *enter, breathless*.)

BOBCHINSKY An extraordinary incident!

DOBCHINSKY A surprising piece of news!

ALL What? What is it?

DOBCHINSKY An unforeseen occurrence: we went to the inn . . .

BOBCHINSKY (*interrupting*) Pyotr Ivanovitch and I went to the inn.

DOBCHINSKY (*interrupting*)   Oh, allow me, Pyotr Ivanovitch, I'll tell the
story.

BOBCHINSKY   Oh no, allow me . . . allow me, allow me . . . you will
never find words to tell it . . .

DOBCHINSKY   And you will get muddled and forget something.

BOBCHINSKY   I shan't, upon my soul I shan't. Don't interrupt, let me
tell it, don't interrupt! Gentlemen, do please tell Pyotr Ivanovitch
not to interfere.

THE MAYOR   For goodness, sake, do tell us what has happened! My
heart's in my mouth. Sit down, gentlemen! Take a chair, Pyotr
Ivanovitch, here is a chair. (*They all sit down round the two* PYOTR
IVANOVITCHES.) Well, now, what is it?

BOBCHINSKY   Allow me, I will begin at the beginning. As soon as I had
the pleasure of leaving your company, when you seemed somewhat
perturbed by the letter you had received . . . yes, I ran then . . . Oh,
please don't interrupt, Pyotr Ivanovitch! I know it all perfectly well –
So, you see I ran in to Korobkin's. And not finding Korobkin at
home, I called at Rastakovsky's; and not finding Rastakovsky at home,
I went on to see Ivan Kuzmitch here, so as to tell him the news you
had received, and as I came away I met Pyotr Ivanovitch . . .

DOBCHINSKY (*interrupting*)   Near the stall where they sell pies.

BOBCHINSKY (*waving him aside*)   Near the stall where they sell
pies. Yes, when I met Pyotr Ivanovitch I said to him, 'Have you
heard the news Anton Antonovitch has from a trustworthy corres-
pondent?' And Pyotr Ivanovitch had heard of it already from your
housekeeper, Avdotya, who had been sent to Filip Antonovitch
Potchetchuev's on some errand, I don't know what . . .

DOBCHINSKY (*interrupting*)   To get a keg for French vodka.

BOBCHINSKY (*waving him aside*)   To get a keg for French vodka. So we
went, Pyotr Ivanovitch and I, to Potchetchuev's. Please, Pyotr
Ivanovitch . . . er . . . don't interrupt, please don't interrupt! We
were going to Potchetchuev's, and on the way Pyotr Ivanovitch
said, 'Let us go into the inn. My stomach . . . I've had nothing to
eat all day, and there is a quaking in my stomach.' Yes, in Pyotr
Ivanovitch's stomach . . . 'And they have just got in a new lot of
smoked salmon,' he said, 'so let's have lunch.' No sooner had we
walked into the inn than a young man . . .

DOBCHINSKY (*interrupting*)   Of pleasant appearance, not wearing official
uniform . . .

BOBCHINSKY   Of pleasant appearance, not wearing official uniform, was
walking about the room like this, and in his face such a look of

deliberation, so to speak . . . a physiognomy . . . gestures, and here (*twirls his hand about his forehead*) a vast deal of everything. I had a sort of foreboding and said to Pyotr Ivanovitch, 'There is something behind this.' Yes, and Pyotr Ivanovitch had already beckoned to the innkeeper . . . to Vlass, the innkeeper; his wife was brought to bed three weeks ago, and a smart little baby too, he will keep an inn like his father. Calling Vlass up, Pyotr Ivanovitch asks him on the quiet: 'Who is that young man?' he says, and Vlass answers: 'That,' he says . . . Oh, don't interrupt me, Pyotr Ivanovitch, please don't interrupt me, you can't tell it, you really can't; you lisp, it's one of your teeth, I know, makes you lisp . . . 'That young man,' he says, 'is an official, yes, and has come from Petersburg, and his name,' he says, 'is Ivan Alexandrovitch Hlestakov, and he is going,' he says, 'to the province of Saratov, and he's very strange in his deportment,' he says, 'he has been here nearly a fortnight, he goes on staying in the house, takes everything on tick and won't pay a penny.' As he was saying this, an inspiration dawned upon me. 'Ah!' I said to Pyotr Ivanovitch . . .

DOBCHINSKY No, Pyotr Ivanovitch, it was I who said 'Ah!'

BOBCHINSKY You said it first, and then I said it. 'Ah!' we cried, Pyotr Ivanovitch and I. 'But what is his object in staying here when he has to go to Saratov?' Yes. Why, he is that official, not a doubt of it!

THE MAYOR Who? What official?

BOBCHINSKY The official that you have had warning of – the Government Inspector.

THE MAYOR (*in alarm*) Good God, what are you saying? It can't be!

DOBCHINSKY It is! He pays no money and he does not go away. Who can it be if not he? And his travelling pass is for Saratov.

BOBCHINSKY It is he, upon my word it is. So keenly observant: looked into everything. He saw that Pyotr Ivanovitch and I were eating smoked salmon – chiefly on account of Pyotr Ivanovitch's stomach – yes; so he peeped into our plates. It gave me quite a turn.

THE MAYOR Lord have mercy on us sinners! What room is he in?

DOBCHINSKY Number five, under the stairs.

BOBCHINSKY The very room in which the officers who were here last year had a fight.

THE MAYOR And has he been here long?

DOBCHINSKY A fortnight already. He came on St Vassily's day.[218]

THE MAYOR A whole fortnight! (*Aside*) Saints alive! Holy martyrs, get me out of this! Within this fortnight the sergeant's widow has been flogged! The prisoners have not had their rations! The streets . . . like a regular pot-house! and the filth! Disgrace! Ignominy! (*Clutches his head.*)

ARTEMY FILIPPOVITCH   What do you think, Anton Antonovitch? Should we all go in a body to the inn?

AMMOS FYODOROVITCH   No, no! Let the provost, the clergy, and the merchants go first; in the book of *John the Mason*[219] it says . . .

THE MAYOR   No, no; allow me to decide. I have had difficulties before and they have passed off safely, and I have been thanked into the bargain. Maybe God will pull us through this time too. (*Turning to* BOBCHINSKY) You say he is a young man?

BOBCHINSKY   Yes, he is – not more than twenty-three or twenty-four.

THE MAYOR   That's as well; it is easier to see through a young man. It is hard work with an old devil, but a young man is all on the surface. You see to your own departments, gentlemen, while I'll go round myself, alone, or with Pyotr Ivanovitch here, privately, as though taking a walk, to see that visitors to the town are suffering no inconvenience. Hey, Svistunov?

SVISTUNOV   What is your pleasure?

THE MAYOR   Go at once for the Police Superintendent; but no, I shall want you. Tell some one to fetch the Police Superintendent as quick as he can, and then come here.

(SVISTUNOV *runs off post-haste.*)

ARTEMY FILIPPOVITCH   Come along, come along, Ammos Fyodorovitch. There really may be trouble.

AMMOS FYODOROVITCH   But what have you to fear? Put clean nightcaps on your patients and there is no finding anything amiss.

ARTEMY FILIPPOVITCH   Nightcaps! The patients are ordered clear soup, and there is such a stink of cabbage in all my corridors that you have to hold your nose.

AMMOS FYODOROVITCH   My mind is at rest. When you come to think of it, whoever would look into the district court? And if he does peep into some document, God help him! Here I have been sitting in the Judge's seat for fifteen years, but if ever I look into the statement of a case I chuck it away in despair! Solomon[220] himself could not make out the rights and wrongs of it.

(*The* JUDGE, *the* CHARITY COMMISSIONER, *the* SCHOOL INSPECTOR, *and the* POSTMASTER *go out, and in the doorway run into* SVISTUNOV.)

THE MAYOR   Well, is the chaise there?

SVISTUNOV   Yes, sir.

THE MAYOR　Go into the street . . . but no, stay! Go and fetch . . . But where are the others? Surely you haven't come back alone? I sent word that Prohorov was to be here. Where is Prohorov?

SVISTUNOV　Prohorov is at the police station, but he can't be put to any use.

THE MAYOR　How's that?

SVISTUNOV　Well, he was brought in this morning dead drunk. They have poured two buckets of water over him, but he's not come to himself yet.

THE MAYOR (*clutching his head*)　Oh, my God! my God! Make haste into the street . . . no, run into the other room first and bring me my sword and new hat. Well, Pyotr Ivanovitch, let us be off!

BOBCHINSKY　Me too, me too! Do let me go too, Anton Antonovitch!

THE MAYOR　No, no, Pyotr Ivanovitch, you can't! It would be awkward, and besides, there is not room in the chaise.

BOBCHINSKY　Never mind, never mind, I'll manage: I'll hop along after the chaise. If only I can have a peep through the door or something, to see what he will do and all that . . .

THE MAYOR (*taking his sword from* SVISTUNOV)　Go at once and get the watchmen. Let each one of them take . . . Ah, what scratches there are on the sword! That confounded blackguard Abdulin – sees his Mayor with an old sword and never thinks of sending me a new one from his shop. Ah, deceitful wretches! And I'll be bound the rascals are getting up petitions on the sly. Every one of them is to take a street . . . oh, dash it, street! I mean, a broom – and sweep the street leading to the inn, and sweep it clean too . . . Do you hear? And you mind, now! I know you; you are hand in glove with all sorts of people and slipping silver spoons into your boots – you had better look out, I have a sharp eye! What have you been up to with Tchernyaev, the draper, eh? He was giving you two yards of cloth for your uniform and you walked off with the whole piece! You'd better be careful! You take more than's due to your rank. Go along!

(*Enter* UHOVYORTOV, *the Police Superintendent.*)

THE MAYOR　Ah, Stepan Ilyitch! Kindly tell me, where had you vanished to? It's beyond everything.

UHOVYORTOV　I was just here by the gate.

THE MAYOR　Well, listen, Stepan Ilyitch! The official from Petersburg has arrived. What arrangements have you made?

UHOVYORTOV　According to your instructions, I have sent Constable Pugovitsin with the watchmen to sweep the pavements.

THE MAYOR   And where is Derzhimorda?

UHOVYORTOV   He has gone with the fire-hose.

THE MAYOR   And Prohorov's drunk?

UHOVYORTOV   Yes, sir.

THE MAYOR   How could you allow it?

UHOVYORTOV   Goodness only knows. There was a fight just outside the town yesterday – he went to settle it and came back drunk.

THE MAYOR   I tell you what, you do this: Constable Pugovitsin . . . he is a tall fellow, so let him stand on the bridge to make a good appearance. And look sharp and pull down the old fence beside the cobbler's and stick in a pole with a wisp of straw tied at the top, as though new streets were being laid out. The more destruction there is everywhere, the more it shows the activity of the town authorities. Ah, I forgot that beside that fence there is a rubbish heap it would take forty waggons to shift. What a nasty town it is, to be sure! Wherever you put up a monument, or even a plain fence, people shoot rubbish there of all sorts – I don't know where they get it from! (*Sighs.*) And if the official asks the police whether they are satisfied, they are all to say, 'Perfectly satisfied, your honour'; and if anybody is dissatisfied, I'll give him something to satisfy him afterwards . . . Och, och, och! I am to blame, very much to blame. (*Takes up the hat-box instead of the hat.*) God grant it all goes off well – and soon too, and I'll put up a candle such as no one has ever put up before: I'll make every scoundrelly shopkeeper produce a hundredweight of wax. Oh, my God, my God! Let us go, Pyotr Ivanovitch! (*Is putting the cardboard box on his head instead of the hat.*)

UHOVYORTOV   Anton Antonovitch, that's the box and not your hat.

THE MAYOR (*flinging down the box*)   If it's a box, it's a box, damn it! Oh, and if he should ask why the almshouse church has not been built, though a grant was made for it five years ago, don't forget to say that the building was begun, but it was burnt down. I sent in a report about it. Or some one may forget like a fool and say it was never begun. And tell Derzhimorda not to be too free with his fists; he keeps order by giving every one a black eye – innocent and guilty. Come along, Pyotr Ivanovitch, come along! (*Goes out and comes back.*) And don't let the soldiers go into the street without anything on: those wretched fellows in the garrison put their coats on over their shirts and nothing on their legs.

(*All go out.*)

(ANNA ANDREYEVNA *and* MARYA ANTONOVNA *run on to the stage*.)

ANNA   Where are they, where are they? Oh dear! (*Opening the door*)
Papa! Antosha! Anton! (*Speaking quickly*) And it's all your doing, it's
all because of you. You would be dawdling, first a pin, then a
fichu![221] (*Runs to the window and calls*) Anton, Anton, where are you
off to? Well, has he come? the Inspector? Has he a moustache?
What sort of moustache?

THE MAYOR'S VOICE   Presently, presently, my dear!

ANNA   Presently? That's a nice thing! Presently! I don't want it to be
presently . . . One thing you might tell me, what is he – a colonel?
Eh? (*Scornfully*) He is gone! I won't let him forget it! And it's all
because of her: 'Mamma, mamma, do wait. I'll just pin my fichu
behind, I won't be a minute!' This is what comes of your minute!
Here we have heard nothing! And it's all your confounded vanity:
you heard the Postmaster was here, so you had to go prinking
before the looking-glass, turning this way and that way. She fancies
he is sweet on her, and all the time he is making faces at you behind
your back.

MARYA   Well, it can't be helped, mamma. We shall know all about it in
another hour or two.

ANNA   In an hour or two! Thanks very much. A nice answer! I wonder
you didn't tell me we shall know better still in a month. (*Leans out of
window.*) Hey, Avdotya? Eh? I say, Avdotya, have you heard that
somebody has arrived? . . . You haven't? What a silly girl! He
waved you off? Let him wave; you should have got it out of him all
the same. Couldn't find that out! Her head's full of nonsense, thinks
of nothing but young men. What? They went off so quickly! But
you should have run after the chaise. Run now, run along! Do you
hear, run and ask where they are going: and mind you find out
what kind of gentleman he is, what he is like – do you hear? Look
through the door and find out everything, and what colour his eyes
are, whether they are black – and come back at once, do you hear?
Make haste, make haste, make haste, make haste!

(*Goes on shouting till the curtain falls.*)

(*The curtain falls upon them both standing at the window.*)

ACT TWO

A little room at the inn. A bed, a table, a trunk,
an empty bottle, high boots, a clothes-brush, etc.

Osip *is lying on his master's bed.*

osip Damn it all! How hungry I am! There is a hullaballoo in my
stomach as though a whole regiment were blowing trumpets. We
don't seem any nearer getting home. What is one to do? It's going
on for two months since we left Petersburg! He has frittered away
his money, silly boy, and now he sits looking glum and has nothing
to say for himself. And there'd have been enough, more than enough,
for the journey: but no, he had to cut a dash in every town!
(*Mimicking*) 'Hey, Osip, go and take the best room and order the
very best dinner: I can't eat a bad dinner, I must have the very best.'
Right enough if he were somebody of consequence instead of just a
registry clerk! He makes friends on the way and plays cards – so here
he has lost all his money! Ugh! I am sick of this life! Really, it's better
in the country; there's no publicity, but there's less anxiety; you take
a wife and spend your time lying on the stove and eating pies. Though
who denies it, living in Petersburg is better than anything if you
come to that. Life there's polite and genteel enough, if only you've
money to spend: theatres, dancing dogs, and anything you like. They
all speak as nice and refined as the gentry themselves pretty near;
if you go to the Arcade, the shopmen call out 'Good sir!'; in the
ferryboat you sit next to a Government clerk; if you want company
you go to the shop: there a soldier will tell you about life in camp and
explain what every star in the sky means, so that you see it all as plain
as your hand; some old lady will drop in or a smart servant girl . . .
My eye! (*Smirks and shakes his head.*) It's all polish and civility, dash it
all! You never hear a rude word; every one calls you 'mister.' If you
are tired of walking, you take a cab and sit like a lord – and if you
don't want to pay him, well, you needn't: every house has a gate at
the back as well as in front, and you can whisk through, so that no
devil can catch you. There's only one drawback: sometimes the food
is first-rate and sometimes you are almost starved, as I am now. And
it's all his fault. What is one to do with him? His papa sends him

money, but he does not keep it – not he! . . . He has a fine time, driving about in cabs, and every day I have to get him theatre tickets, and then in a week he sends me to the market to sell his new dress-coat. Sometimes he goes on until he hasn't a shirt left and walks about in nothing but his jacket and overcoat . . . Upon my word, it's a fact! Fine English cloth, too! He gave a hundred and fifty roubles for the coat alone, and he lets it go at the market for twenty roubles; and as for the trousers, they fetch next to nothing. And why is it? It's all because he doesn't do his work: instead of going to the office he walks up and down the Nevsky or plays cards. Ah, if the old master knew! Little he'd care if you are in the Government service, he'd lift up your little shirt and give you such a whipping you'd be rubbing yourself for the next four days. If you've got a job, stick to it. Here the innkeeper says he won't give us anything till we have paid for what we have had; but what if we don't pay? (*With a sigh.*) Oh dear, if I'd only some cabbage soup! I feel I could eat up the whole world. Somebody is knocking; I suppose it is he. (*Hastily jumps off the bed.*)

(*Enter* HLESTAKOV.)

HLESTAKOV   Here, take these. (*Gives him his cap and cane.*) Ah, you have been lolling on my bed again?

OSIP   Why should I loll on it? Have I never seen a bed before?

HLESTAKOV   That's a lie. You've been sprawling on it; you see it is all crumpled.

OSIP   What do I want with it? A bed is nothing new to me. I've got legs, I can stand. Why should I lie on your bed?

HLESTAKOV (*walking up and down the room*)   See whether there is any tobacco in the pouch.

OSIP   How can there be? You smoked the last four days ago.

HLESTAKOV (*walks about pursing up his lips in different ways; at last speaks in a loud and resolute voice*)   I say . . . Osip!

OSIP   Yes, sir?

HLESTAKOV (*in a loud, but not so resolute voice*)   You go there.

OSIP   Where?

HLESTAKOV (*in a voice neither resolute nor loud, but approaching entreaty*)   Downstairs, to the dining-room . . . Tell them to . . . send me up some dinner.

OSIP   Oh no, I don't want to.

HLESTAKOV   How dare you, you fool?

OSIP   Why, nothing will come of it if I do. The landlord says he won't give you any more dinners.

HLESTAKOV   How dare he refuse? What nonsense next?

OSIP   And he says he will go to the Mayor too. 'Your master,' he says, 'has paid nothing for three weeks. You and your master are swindlers,' he says, 'and your master's a rogue.' He says he's seen such scoundrels and cheats before.

HLESTAKOV   And you are pleased, you brute, to repeat all that to me.

OSIP   He says, 'At that rate any one might come, live at my expense and not pay, and there would be no getting rid of him. I won't do things by halves,' he says. 'I'll lodge a complaint and have him taken to the police station and to prison.'

HLESTAKOV   Come, come, you fool, that's enough! Go along, go along, tell him. What a coarse beast it is!

OSIP   I'd better tell the landlord to come to you himself.

HLESTAKOV   What do I want with the landlord? You go and speak to him.

OSIP   But really, sir . . .

HLESTAKOV   There, run along, damn you! Call the landlord.

(OSIP *goes out*.)

(*Alone*.) It's awful how hungry I am! I went for a little walk, I thought my appetite would go off – no, damn it, it hasn't. Yes, if I hadn't had such a spree at Penza[222] there would have been money enough to get home. That infantry captain did me shockingly; how he piled up the tricks! He only sat down for a quarter of an hour, but he cleaned me out. And yet, shouldn't I like another game with him! But there seems no chance of it. What a beastly little town! At the greengrocer's they won't give you anything on tick. It's really mean. (*Begins whistling, first from 'Robert le Diable',*[223] *then 'The Red Sarafan',*[224] *and then nothing in particular*.) There's nobody coming.

(*Enter* OSIP *and the* WAITER.)

WAITER   The master told me to ask you what he can do for you.

HLESTAKOV   Good-day, friend! I hope you are quite well.

WAITER   Yes, thank God!

HLESTAKOV   Well, how are things in your inn? All going well?

WAITER   Yes, think God! All is well.

HLESTAKOV   Many visitors?

WAITER   Yes, a fair number.

HLESTAKOV   Look here, my good fellow, they haven't brought me my dinner yet, so please tell them to make haste – you see, I have got something I must do directly after dinner.

WAITER   But the master says he won't send you up any more. I think he
    meant to go to the Mayor today to lodge a complaint.

HLESTAKOV   What has he got to complain of? Consider for yourself,
    my good man, what am I to do? I must eat, I shall waste away if I go
    on like this. I am frightfully hungry. I am not joking.

WAITER   No, sir. He said, 'I won't give him dinner again till he pays for
    what he has had.' That was his answer.

HLESTAKOV   But you talk to him, reason with him.

WAITER   But what am I to say to him?

HLESTAKOV   You point out to him seriously that I must eat. Money is
    one thing . . . He thinks that if a peasant like himself can go without
    food for a day, other people can do the same. That's news!

WAITER   Very well, I'll tell him.

(WAITER *and* OSIP *go out*.)

HLESTAKOV (*alone*)   It is beastly though if he won't give me anything at
    all to eat. I am hungrier than I have ever been in my life. Shall I
    raise something on my clothes? Sell my trousers? No, I'd rather go
    hungry than not arrive home in my Petersburg suit. What a pity
    Joachim[225] would not let me hire a carriage! It would have been
    fine, dash it all, to arrive in a carriage; think of driving up like a
    swell to a neighbour's, with lamps lighted and Osip in livery
    perched up behind! I can fancy what a flutter it would make! 'Who
    is it? What is it?' And my footman goes up (*drawing himself up and
    acting as footman*): 'Ivan Alexandrovitch Hlestakov from Petersburg;
    are they at home?' And the bumpkins don't even know what 'at
    home' means. If some goose of a landowner comes to see them, he
    pushes straight into the drawing-room like a bear. You go up to a
    pretty daughter: 'Madam, I am delighted' (*rubs his hands and scrapes
    with his foot*). Ugh! (*Spits*.) I feel quite sick, I am so hungry.

(*Enter* OSIP *and* WAITER.)

HLESTAKOV   Well?

OSIP   They are bringing your dinner.

HLESTAKOV (*claps his hands and gives a little skip on his chair*)   Dinner!
    Dinner! Dinner!

WAITER (*with plates and dinner-napkins*)   The landlord is sending you
    dinner for the last time.

HLESTAKOV   The landlord, the landlord . . . Much I care for your
    landlord! What have you got there?

WAITER   Soup and roast meat.

HLESTAKOV What, only two courses?

WAITER That's all, sir.

HLESTAKOV What nonsense! I won't have that. You tell him it's impossible! That's not enough.

WAITER Well, the landlord says it's too much.

HLESTAKOV And why is there no sauce?

WAITER There is no sauce.

HLESTAKOV Why not? I saw them cooking no end of stuff as I passed by the kitchen. And two little chaps were eating salmon and all sorts of good things in the dining-room this morning.

WAITER Well, there is, to be sure, but again there isn't.

HLESTAKOV What do you mean by 'there isn't'?

WAITER Well, there isn't.

HLESTAKOV And salmon and fish and cutlets?

WAITER They are for the better sort, sir.

HLESTAKOV You are a fool!

WAITER Yes, sir.

HLESTAKOV You are a nasty pig . . . What, they are eating it and I'm not. Dash it all, why can't I have it too? Aren't they travellers the same as I am?

WAITER Well, we all know they are not the same.

HLESTAKOV What are they, then?

WAITER They are the usual sort! They pay for what they have, to be sure.

HLESTAKOV I won't discuss it with a fool like you. (*Helps himself to soup and eats.*) Do you call this soup? You have simply filled the tureen with water: there is no taste in it, though it does stink. I won't have this soup, bring me another.

WAITER I'll take it away. The landlord said, 'If he doesn't like it, he needn't have it.'

HLESTAKOV (*protecting the tureen with his hands*) Come, come, come . . . leave it, you ass! I suppose you are accustomed to treat other people like that, but I am not that sort. I don't advise you to try it on with me . . . (*Eats.*) My God, what soup! (*Goes on eating it.*) I don't believe anyone in the world has ever tasted such soup: there are horrid feathers floating in it instead of fat. (*Cuts the fowl.*) My goodness, what a hen! Serve the meat. There is a little soup left there, Osip, you can have it. (*Cuts the meat.*) What sort of meat is this? It's not meat.

WAITER What is it, then?

HLESTAKOV The devil only knows, but it's not meat. You've roasted the chopper instead of the beef. (*Eats it.*) The blackguards, the low beasts! The stuff they give one to eat! Chewing one mouthful makes my jaws ache. (*Picks his teeth with his fingers.*) The sneaks! It's just like the bark of a tree – I can't get it out. My teeth will be black after eating such stuff. Scoundrels! (*Wipes his mouth with his dinner-napkin.*) Is there nothing more?

WAITER   No.

HLESTAKOV   Low beasts! Sneaks! And no sauce or pudding at all. Wretches! Simply fleecing travellers!

(WAITER, *with the help of* OSIP, *clears away the plates and dishes.*)

HLESTAKOV (*Alone.*) Really, I feel as though I had not eaten anything. I've just had enough to make me hungrier. If I'd a penny I'd send to the market and have a bun.

OSIP (*coming in*)   The Mayor has come about something; he is making enquiries and asking questions about you.

HLESTAKOV (*scared*)   Good gracious! That beast of a landlord has sent in a complaint already! What if he hauls me off to prison? Well, if I am treated like a gentleman, perhaps . . . no, no, I won't go! There are officers and all sorts of people lounging about in the town, and, as ill-luck would have it, I've been cutting a dash and winking at a shopkeeper's pretty daughter . . . No, I won't go! What is he thinking about? How dare he? What does he take me for? Am I a shopkeeper or a workman? (*Assuming confidence and drawing himself up.*) I shall say to him outright: 'How dare you? How . . . ' (*The door handle turns;* HLESTAKOV *grows pale and shrinks. The* MAYOR *comes in with* DOBCHINSKY *and stands still. For some moments he and* HLESTAKOV *stare at each other in alarm.*)

THE MAYOR   (*slightly recovering himself and standing at attention*) I humbly wish you good-day.

HLESTAKOV (*bowing*)   I wish you a good-day, sir.

THE MAYOR   Excuse me.

HLESTAKOV   It's all right . . .

THE MAYOR   It is my duty as the head official of the town to concern myself that visitors and all persons of rank should suffer no inconvenience . . .

HLESTAKOV (*at first faltering a little, but speaking more loudly as he goes on*) But what am I to do? It's not my fault . . . I am really going to pay . . . They'll send me money from the country.

(BOBCHINSKY *peeps in at the door.*)

He is more to blame: he gives me beef as hard as a board, and as for the soup, goodness only knows what he puts in it. I had to throw it out of the window. He has been starving me for days . . . the tea is so queer, it smells of fish and not of tea. Why should I . . . It's an odd thing!

THE MAYOR (*intimidated*) Forgive me, it is really not my fault. The beef in the market is always good. It is brought by dealers from Kolmogory,[226] sober men of exemplary behaviour. In fact I don't know where he could get beef like that. But if anything is amiss, then allow me to suggest that I should take you to other apartments.

HLESTAKOV No, I won't go! I know what you mean by other apartments – prison. But what right have you? How dare you . . . Why, I . . . I am in the Service in Petersburg. (*Blustering*) I'll . . . I'll . . . I'll . . .

THE MAYOR (*aside*) O merciful God, what a violent man! He's found out everything, those damned shopkeepers have told him everything!

HLESTAKOV (*bluffing*) I wouldn't go if you came with a whole regiment of soldiers. I'll write straight to the minister! (*Thumping the table with his fist.*) What next? What are you about?

THE MAYOR (*standing at attention and trembling*) Have pity on me, don't ruin me . . . I have a wife, little children . . . don't wreck a man's life!

HLESTAKOV No, I won't go! What next? What do I care? Because you have a wife and little children I am to go to prison, a fine idea! (BOBCHINSKY *peeps in at the door and vanishes in alarm.*) No, thank you very much, I won't go!

THE MAYOR (*trembling*) It was my inexperience, God knows it was my inexperience, the insufficiency of my income . . . only consider: my salary is hardly enough for tea and sugar. If I have taken bribes they are nothing to speak of – something for the table or cloth for a suit. As for the sergeant's widow who keeps a shop and the story of my flogging her, that's a slander, upon my soul it is. It's an invention of my enemies; they wouldn't scruple to take my life.

HLESTAKOV Well, I have nothing to do with them. (*Pondering*) But I don't know why you are talking about enemies and a sergeant's widow . . . A sergeant's wife is a very different matter, but you daren't flog me, that's too big a job for you . . . I dare say! Who has ever heard of such a thing! I'll pay, I'll pay the bill, but I haven't the money now. That's why I am staying on here, because I haven't a farthing.

THE MAYOR (*aside*) Oh, the artful devil! That's a far-fetched device! He is putting us off the scent, you can make what you like of it! There's no knowing how to get at him. Well, I'll try my luck, here goes! What will be will be, I'll chance it. (*Aloud*) If you are really in need of money or anything else, I am at your service this very minute. It is my duty to assist visitors to the town.

HLESTAKOV   Oh yes, do lend me some money! I'll pay the landlord on the spot. I don't want more than two hundred roubles, even less would do.

THE MAYOR (*offering him notes*)   Here are exactly two hundred roubles, don't trouble yourself to count them.

HLESTAKOV (*taking the money*)   I am very much obliged to you. I will send it you back as soon as I am home in the country . . . I was unexpectedly short of money . . . I see you are a real gentleman. Now the position is quite different.

THE MAYOR (*aside*)   Well, thank God, he has taken the money. It will all be plain sailing now, it seems, and I managed to slip four hundred into his hand instead of two.

HLESTAKOV   Hey, Osip!

(OSIP *comes in.*)

Call the waiter! (*To the* MAYOR *and* DOBCHINSKY) But why are you standing? Please sit down. (*To* DOBCHINSKY) Please take a seat.

THE MAYOR   It's quite all right, we can stand.

HLESTAKOV   Oh, please do sit down. I see now how straightforward and hospitable you are; I must own I had thought at first you had come to . . . (*To* DOBCHINSKY) Sit down!

(*The* MAYOR *and* DOBCHINSKY *sit down.*
BOBCHINSKY *peeps in at the door and listens.*)

THE MAYOR (*aside*)   I must be bolder. He wants to be treated incognito. Very good, we'll keep it up, we'll pretend we haven't a notion who he is. (*Aloud*) We, that is, Pyotr Ivanovitch Dobchinsky, a landowner of the district, and I, in the discharge of our duties, called at the inn on purpose to ascertain whether visitors to the town are properly treated, for I am not like some mayors who do not care about anything; apart from my duty, I am prompted by Christian benevolence to desire that every mortal should be well entertained – and here I am rewarded by the opportunity of making such an agreeable acquaintance.

HLESTAKOV   I too am delighted. If it had not been for you, I must own I should have had to stop here a long time; I couldn't think how I was to pay the bill.

THE MAYOR (*aside*)   Um, tell that to others! Couldn't think how he was to pay! (*Aloud*) And may I make so bold as to enquire where you are bound for?

HLESTAKOV   I am going to the Saratov province, to my own estate.

THE MAYOR (*aside, with an ironical expression*)   To the Saratov province! Eh? And not a blush! Oh, you want to be pretty sharp with him. (*Aloud*) An excellent undertaking, though in travelling, of course, there is the unpleasantness of not being able to get horses, but, on the other hand, it is a distraction for the mind. You are travelling, I presume, for your own pleasure chiefly?

HLESTAKOV   No, my father insists on my coming. The old man is in a taking because so far I have not been promoted in the Service. He fancies that as soon as you arrive in Petersburg they stick a Vladimir ribbon in your buttonhole.[227] I'd like to see him knocking about in the office!

THE MAYOR (*aside*)   Just listen! The yarn he is spinning! Dragging in his old father too! (*Aloud*) And shall you make a long stay?

HLESTAKOV   I really don't know. My old father is as stupid and obstinate as a post, the old codger. I shall tell him straight out: I can't live without Petersburg, say what you like. Why on earth should I waste my life among peasants? A man's requirements are different nowadays; my soul thirsts for culture.

THE MAYOR (*aside*)   A fine tangle! He goes on with one lie after another and never breaks down. And he is nothing much to look at, a puny fellow, you could knock him down with a feather. But wait a minute, I'll make you speak out! (*Aloud*) That's a perfectly true remark of yours. What can be done in the wilds? Here, for instance: one spends sleepless nights, doing one's utmost for one's country, sparing nothing, but as for recognition there is no knowing when that will come. (*Takes a look round the room.*) This room seems rather damp?

HLESTAKOV   It's a horrible room, and the bugs are beyond anything I've ever seen: they bite like dogs.

THE MAYOR   Only fancy! Such a cultured visitor, and to suffer from what? From worthless bugs who ought never to have been born into the world! And the room is dark, too, isn't it?

HLESTAKOV   Yes, very dark. The landlord has taken to refusing me candles. Sometimes a fancy takes one to do something: to read, or even, at times, to write, and I cannot – it's dark.

THE MAYOR   May I venture to beg you . . . but no, I am not worthy of the honour.

HLESTAKOV   Why, what?

THE MAYOR   No, no, I am unworthy!

HLESTAKOV   Why, what is it?

THE MAYOR   I would venture . . . I have an excellent room for you at home, light, quiet . . . But no, I feel that it would be too great an honour . . . Don't be angry – believe me, it was in the simplicity of my heart that I offered it.

HLESTAKOV On the contrary, by all means, I shall be delighted. I would much rather be in a private house than in a nasty inn.

THE MAYOR And I shall be delighted! And my wife will be overjoyed! It has always been my way from my earliest childhood to put hospitality before everything, especially if the visitor is a man of culture. Please don't imagine that this is flattery; no, I am free from that vice; I speak out of the fulness of my heart.

HLESTAKOV Very much obliged to you. I am the same myself – I don't like insincere people. I do like your open-heartedness and cordiality, and I must own I ask nothing but devotion and respect, respect and devotion.

(Enter the WAITER, *accompanied by* OSIP.
BOBCHINSKY *peeps in at the door.)*

WAITER You sent for me, sir?

HLESTAKOV Yes, give me the bill.

WAITER I gave it you, for the second time, this morning.

HLESTAKOV I don't remember your stupid bills. Tell me, how much is it?

WAITER You ordered dinner on the first day, and on the second only had some smoked salmon, and after that you had everything put down.

HLESTAKOV Idiot! There's no need to go into the items. Tell me what it all comes to.

THE MAYOR But don't you trouble about it: he can wait. *(To the* WAITER) Be off, the bill shall be settled.

HLESTAKOV Yes, indeed, that's true. *(Puts the money in his pocket.)*

(The WAITER *goes out.* BOBCHINSKY *peeps in at the door.)*

THE MAYOR Wouldn't you like, perhaps, to look at some institutions of our town, charitable and otherwise?

HLESTAKOV Why, what is there to see?

THE MAYOR Oh well, you might see how things are done with us . . . the management . . .

HLESTAKOV Delighted, I am ready.

(BOBCHINSKY pops his head in at the door.)

THE MAYOR And then, if you feel disposed, we might visit the district school and see the methods of instruction in the sciences.

HLESTAKOV Certainly, by all means.

THE MAYOR And then, if you like to visit the prison and the police stations – you can see how criminals are kept in our town.

HLESTAKOV But why the police stations? I'd rather look at the charitable institutions.

THE MAYOR As you prefer. Will you come in your own carriage or in the chaise with me?

HLESTAKOV I would rather come with you in the chaise.

THE MAYOR (*to* DOBCHINSKY) Well, Pyotr Ivanovitch, there will be no room for you now.

DOBCHINSKY Never mind, I shall be all right.

THE MAYOR (*aside to* DOBCHINSKY) Listen: you run along as fast as your legs can carry you, and take two notes: one to Zemlyanika at the hospital and another to my wife. (*To* HLESTAKOV) May I ask your permission to write in your presence a couple of lines to my wife, to tell her to prepare for our honoured guest?

HLESTAKOV Oh, why? . . . Here is the ink, though – but about paper I don't know. Perhaps this bill would do?

THE MAYOR I will write on it. (*Writes, and at the same time murmurs to himself*) We shall see how things will go after lunch and a bottle of something good! And we have some local Madeira – not much to look at, but it would knock an elephant off its legs. If only I could find out what he is like and how far I need be afraid of him.

> (*After writing the note, he hands it to* DOBCHINSKY, *who goes to the door, but at that moment the door comes off its hinges and* BOBCHINSKY, *who has been listening outside, flies into the room with it. Every one utters an exclamation.* BOBCHINSKY *gets up.*)

HLESTAKOV I say, I hope you are not hurt?

BOBCHINSKY No, no, nothing to speak of, not the slightest derangement, only a little bruise on my nose. I'll run to Christian Ivanovitch: he has a plaster that will put it right.

THE MAYOR (*making a reproachful sign to* BOBCHINSKY, *says to* HLESTAKOV) It's of no consequence. Shall we go now? And I will tell your servant to bring your luggage. (*To* OSIP) My good man, bring everything round to my house, to the Mayor's – any one will show you the way. After you! (*Shows* HLESTAKOV *out and follows him, but turning back says, reproachfully, to* BOBCHINSKY) Just like you! Couldn't you find somewhere else to tumble about? Sprawling like the devil knows what!

> (*Goes out.* BOBCHINSKY *follows him.*)

> (*Curtain.*)

ACT THREE

Scene: Same as Act One

Anna Andreyevna *and* Marya Antonovna
stand at the window in the same position.

ANNA Here we have been waiting a whole hour, and it is all you with your silly prinking: she was perfectly ready, but no! she must go on fussing . . . I ought not to have heeded her. How annoying! As though to spite us, not a soul in sight! Every one might be dead.

MARYA But really, mamma, in another two minutes we shall know all about it. Avdotya must be back soon now. (*Looks out of window and shrieks*) Oh, mamma! mamma! somebody's coming, look, at the end of the street.

ANNA Where? You're always fancying something. Oh yes, there is somebody. Who is it? Rather short . . . dressed like a gentleman . . . Who is it? Eh? It's vexing! Whoever can it be?

MARYA It's Dobchinsky, mamma!

ANNA Dobchinsky! You're always imagining things . . . It's no more Dobchinsky! . . . (*Waves her handkerchief.*) Hey, you! Come here, make haste!

MARYA It really is Dobchinsky, mamma.

ANNA You say that just to contradict me. I tell you it's not Dobchinsky.

MARYA What did I say? What did I say, mamma? Now you see it is Dobchinsky.

ANNA To be sure it is Dobchinsky, I see it is now – what do you want to argue about? (*Shouts at the window*) Make haste, make haste! How slow you are! Well, where are they? Eh? Don't wait till you get in, tell me now. What? Very stern? Eh? And my husband, my husband? (*Moving a little away from the window in annoyance.*) What an idiot! Till he gets indoors he won't say a word!

(DOBCHINSKY *comes in.*)

Now, if you please, aren't you ashamed of yourself? I relied upon you as the one man I could trust – all the rest ran off and you went with them! I haven't been able to get a word of sense out of any one so far. Aren't you ashamed? I stood godmother to your Vanitchka and Lizanka, and this is how you treat me!

DOBCHINSKY Upon my word, to show my respect for you I've run till I'm out of breath. How do you do, Marya Antonovna?

MARYA Good-morning, Pyotr Ivanovitch.

ANNA Well, what happened? Come, tell us! How are things going?

DOBCHINSKY Anton Antonovitch has sent you a note.

ANNA Oh, and what sort of man is he? A general?

DOBCHINSKY No, he is not a general, but he is as good as any general: such culture and dignified manners.

ANNA Ah! Then he is the man they wrote to my husband about.

DOBCHINSKY The very one. I was the first to discover it, together with Pyotr Ivanovitch.

ANNA Come, tell us all about it.

DOBCHINSKY Well, thank God, everything went off satisfactorily. At first he did give Anton Antonovitch rather a curt reception, yes; he was angry, and said that everything was wrong at the inn, and that he wouldn't come and stay with him, and that he did not want to go to prison on his account; but later on, when he found that Anton Antonovitch was not to blame and talked a little more to him, he quite changed his mind, and, thank God, every-thing went off well. They've gone now to inspect the charitable institutions ... At first Anton Antonovitch really did suspect there had been a secret report sent in against him; I was a little scared myself too.

ANNA But you have nothing to be afraid of – you are not in the Service.

DOBCHINSKY No, but you know you can't help feeling alarmed when a great man speaks.

ANNA Oh, well ... but that's all nonsense. Tell us what he is like? Is he old or young?

DOBCHINSKY Young, a young man, about three-and-twenty, but he speaks quite like an old man. 'Certainly,' he says, 'I am ready to go there, and there too' ... (*waves his arms*) and all said so nicely. 'I am fond of reading and writing,' he said, 'but it's tiresome that it is rather dark in my room.'

ANNA And what is he to look at? Dark or fair?

DOBCHINSKY No, more of an auburn brown, and his eyes are as quick as squirrels', they make one feel quite uncomfortable.

ANNA What has your father written me here? (*Reads*) 'I hasten to tell you, my love, that my position was truly dreadful; but trusting in God's mercy two salted cucumbers and half a portion of caviare,

one rouble twenty-five copecks . . . ' (*Stops.*) I can't make it out.
What have salted cucumbers and caviare to do with it?

DOBCHINSKY   Anton Antonovitch wrote it in haste on an odd scrap of
paper; it's a bill of some sort.

ANNA   Oh yes, to be sure. (*Goes on reading.*) 'But trusting in God's
mercy I believe that it will all end well. Make haste and get a room
ready for our illustrious guest, the one with the yellow paper; don't
trouble to have anything extra for dinner, for we shall have a meal
with Artemy Filippovitch at the hospital, but have plenty of wine.
Tell Abdulin at the shop to send the best he has, or I'll ransack his
whole cellar. Kissing your little hand, love, I remain your Anton
Skvoznik-Dmuhanovsky.' . . . Oh, my goodness! We must make
haste! Hey, who is there? Mishka!

DOBCHINSKY (*runs towards the door shouting*) Mishka! Mishka! Mishka!

(*Enter* MISHKA.)

ANNA   Listen: run to Abdulin's shop . . . wait a minute, I'll give you a
note. (*Sits down to the table, writes a note, speaking as she writes.*) Give
this note to Sidor, the coachman, and tell him to run with it to
Abdulin's and bring wine from the shop. And you go and get the
room properly ready for a visitor. Put in a bedstead and a washstand
and so on.

DOBCHINSKY   Well, Anna Andreyevna, I'll run along to see how he is
conducting the inspection.

ANNA   Run along, run along! I won't keep you.

(DOBCHINSKY *goes out.*)

Well, Mashenka, now we must think of what we are going to wear.
He is a Petersburg swell: God forbid he should laugh at us. The most
suitable thing for you is the light blue dress with the little flounces.

MARYA   Oh, la! mamma, the blue! I don't like it a bit. The Lyapkin-
Tyapkin girl is always in blue and Zemlyanika's daughter too. No,
I'd better put on my rainbow dress.

ANNA   Your rainbow dress! . . . Really, you'll say anything to contradict;
the blue's much better, for I want to wear my primrose.

MARYA   Oh, mamma, primrose doesn't suit you!

ANNA   Primrose doesn't suit me?

MARYA   It doesn't . . . I'll answer for it, it doesn't: you ought to have
dark eyes to wear primrose.

ANNA   What next! And haven't I dark eyes? As dark as can be. What
nonsense she talks! My eyes not dark, and me always Queen of
Clubs[228] when I tell my fortune!

MARYA   Oh, mamma, you ought to be a Queen of Hearts.

ANNA   Nonsense, absolute nonsense. I have never been a Queen of Hearts.

(*Goes out quickly with* MARYA ANTONOVNA *and speaks outside.*)

What will she think of next! Queen of Hearts! I've never heard of such a thing.

(*A door opens and* MISHKA *sweeps out dust;*
OSIP *comes in at the other door with a portmanteau on his head.*)

OSIP   Which way?

MISHKA   This way, uncle, this way!

OSIP   Stay, let me rest. Ah, what a dog's life! Every burden is heavy when the belly is empty.

MISHKA   I say, uncle, will the general soon be here?

OSIP   What general?

MISHKA   Why, your master.

OSIP   My master? He a general?

MISHKA   Why, isn't he a general?

OSIP   Oh, he is a general right enough – on the other side.

MISHKA   Why, is that more or less than a real general?

OSIP   More.

MISHKA   Well I never! That's why they are kicking up such a fuss.

OSIP   Look here, my lad: I see you are a smart fellow; get me something to eat.

MISHKA   There's nothing ready for you yet, uncle. You won't have just anything ordinary, but when your master sits down to table, they'll give you some of the same.

OSIP   And what have you got in the ordinary way?

MISHKA   Cabbage soup, pudding, and pies.

OSIP   Give me that – cabbage soup, pudding, and pies. It doesn't matter, I can eat anything. Come, let us carry the portmanteau in. Is there another way out of the room?

MISHKA   Yes.

(*The two carry the portmanteau into room at side. The* CONSTABLES
fling open both halves of the door. Enter HLESTAKOV, *after him the*
MAYOR, *followed at a little distance by* ARTEMY FILIPPOVITCH
ZEMLYANIKA, LUKA LUKITCH HLOPOV, DOBCHINSKY, *and*
BOBCHINSKY *with a plaster on his nose. The* MAYOR *points out to the*
CONSTABLES *a piece of paper on the floor – they run and pick it up,*
jostling each other in their haste.)

HLESTAKOV Excellent institutions! I like the way you show visitors everything in your town. In other towns I was shown nothing.

THE MAYOR In other towns, I venture to assure you, the mayors and other functionaries are more anxious about their own interests, so to speak; while here, I may say, we have no other thought but to deserve the attention of our superiors by our good conduct and vigilance.

HLESTAKOV The lunch was very nice; I've really eaten too much. Do you have lunches like that every day?

THE MAYOR On purpose for such a welcome guest.

HLESTAKOV I am fond of good fare. That's what life is for – to gather the flowers of pleasure. What was the fish called?

ARTEMY FILIPPOVITCH (*running up*) Labardan,[229] sir!

HLESTAKOV Very good. Where was it we had lunch? At the hospital, wasn't it?

ARTEMY FILIPPOVITCH Just so, one of our charitable institutions.

HLESTAKOV I remember, I remember; there were beds standing about. And have most of the patients recovered? I don't think there were many there.

ARTEMY FILIPPOVITCH There are about a dozen left, not more, and the others have all recovered. It's the organisation, the management. Ever since I took control there – you may think it incredible – they all get well like flies. No sooner does a patient get into the hospital than he is well, and it is not so much owing to the medicines as through conscientiousness and good management.

THE MAYOR Ah, how brain-racking, I venture to assure you, are the duties of the mayor of a city! So many matters are laid upon him: take cleanliness alone, repairs and reconstruction . . . in fact, the most able man would find himself in difficulties, but, thank God, everything is going well. Another mayor, of course, would be feathering his own nest, but would you believe it, even lying in bed I keep thinking, 'Almighty God, how can I contrive to prove my zeal to my superiors and give them satisfaction?' Whether they bestow a reward, of course, that's for them to decide, but anyway my heart will be at rest. When everything in the town is as it should be, the streets are swept, the convicts are well looked after, and not many drunken people about, then what more do I want? I may say truly I don't care for honours. They, of course, are alluring, but, compared with virtue, all is dust and ashes.

ARTEMY FILIPPOVITCH (*aside*) How the rascal does hold forth! It's a heaven-sent gift!

HLESTAKOV That's true. At times I indulge in such reflections myself; sometimes in prose and sometimes I toss off a poem.

BOBCHINSKY (*to* DOBCHINSKY) That's well said, Pyotr Ivanovitch, very well said! Such observations ... one can see he has studied learned subjects.

HLESTAKOV Tell me, please, have you any entertainments – clubs where one could play cards, for instance?

THE MAYOR (*aside*) Hey, my fine gentleman, I know what you are driving at! (*Aloud*) Heaven forbid! No such clubs have ever been heard of here! I have never held a card in my hand in my life; in fact, I have no notion how you play with them. I could never bear the sight of them; indeed, if I do chance to see a King of Diamonds or anything of the kind, it makes me feel perfectly sick. I once happened to build a house with cards to amuse the children, and I was dreaming of the damned things all night afterwards, confound them! How can people waste precious time on them?

LUKA LUKITCH (*aside*) And he won a hundred roubles from me last night, the rascal!

THE MAYOR I prefer to devote my time to the welfare of the State.

HLESTAKOV Well now, you go too far ... It all depends on the point of view from which you look at it. If you leave off just when you ought to double your stakes ... then of course ... No, I don't agree with you; it is very pleasant to have a game sometimes.

(*Enter* ANNA ANDREYEVNA *and* MARYA ANTONOVNA.)

THE MAYOR I venture to introduce my family: my wife and my daughter.

HLESTAKOV (*bowing*) How happy I am, madam, to have the pleasure, in a sense, of seeing you.

ANNA It is an even greater pleasure to us to see so distinguished a visitor.

HLESTAKOV (*striking an attitude*) Upon my soul, madam, it is quite the opposite: it is a much greater pleasure for me.

ANNA How can you! You are pleased to say that as a compliment. I beg you to be seated.

HLESTAKOV To stand beside you is a happiness; but if you particularly wish it, I will sit down. How happy I am to be sitting at last by your side!

ANNA Indeed, I could never presume to take that to myself. I suppose that after Petersburg your journey must have been very distasteful to you.

HLESTAKOV Extremely distasteful. After being used to living, *comprenez-vous*,[230] in the world, to find oneself on the road: dirty inns, benighted ignorance . . . But for the chance which, I must own (*looks meaningly at* ANNA ANDREYEVNA *and strikes an attitude*), makes up for everything . . .

ANNA Indeed, you must find it unpleasant.

HLESTAKOV At this moment, madam, I find it very pleasant.

ANNA How can you! You do me too much honour. I don't deserve it.

HLESTAKOV Not deserve it! You do deserve it, madam.

ANNA I live in the country . . .

HLESTAKOV Yes, but the country, too, has its hillsides and brooks . . . though, of course, there is no comparing it with Petersburg! Ah, Petersburg! That's something like life. Perhaps you think I am only a copying clerk; no, the head of my section is on friendly terms with me. He slaps me on the shoulder and says, 'Come round to dinner, my boy!' I only look in at the office for two or three minutes, just to say how things must be done. And then the copying clerk, poor rat, goes scratching and scribbling away. They did want to make me a collegiate assessor, but I thought, What's the use? And the porter runs after me up the stairs with a brush in his hand: 'Allow me, Ivan Alexandrovitch,' he says, 'I'll clean your boots.' (*To the* MAYOR) Why are you standing, gentlemen, please sit down.

THE MAYOR ⎫ ⎧ In our rank we can very well stand.
ARTEMY ⎪ ⎪
  FILIPPOVITCH ⎬ (*speaking together*) ⎨ We will stand.
LUKA LUKITCH ⎭ ⎩ Please don't trouble on our account.

HLESTAKOV Never mind rank. I beg you to sit down! (*The* MAYOR *and all the others sit down.*) I don't like standing on ceremony. On the contrary, I do my utmost, my very utmost, to pass unnoticed. But I never can escape observation, it seems impossible! As soon as I appear anywhere people begin saying, 'There's Ivan Alexandrovitch, there he goes!' And once I was actually taken for the Commander-in-Chief: the soldiers all came out of the guardhouse, saluting. And the officer, who is a great friend of mine, said to me afterwards, 'Do you know, old man, we all quite took you for the Commander!'

ANNA Just fancy!

HLESTAKOV I know all the pretty actresses. You see, I have written a few little things for the stage, too. I am often in literary circles . . . on friendly terms with Pushkin. I used often to say to him, 'Well, Pushkin, old man, how are things going?' 'So-so, old man,' he would answer, 'only so-so.' . . . He is quite a character.

ANNA   So you write too? How delightful it must be to be an author!
No doubt you have things in the magazines?

HLESTAKOV   Yes, I send things to the magazines too. I am the author of
lots of works, really: *The Marriage of Figaro*, *Robert le Diable*,
Norma.[231] I can't remember the titles of all of them. And it was all a
mere chance – I had no intention of writing, but the Director of
Theatres said to me, 'Come, old man, write something for us!'
Well, I thought, why not? And on the spot, in one evening I think
it was, I wrote the whole thing, to the surprise of everybody. I have
a wonderfully ready wit. Everything that has been published under
the name of Baron Brambeus,[232] *The Frigate Hope*,[233] and the *Moscow
Telegraph*[234] . . . I wrote them all.

ANNA   Only fancy! So you are Brambeus?

HLESTAKOV   To be sure, I correct all their articles. Smirdin[235] pays me
forty thousand to do it.

ANNA   Then I expect *Yuri Miloslavsky*[236] is your work too?

HLESTAKOV   Yes, I am the author of it.

ANNA   I guessed it at once.

MARYA   Oh, mamma, but it says on the book that it is written by Mr
Zagoskin.

ANNA   There, I knew you would want to be arguing even here.

HLESTAKOV   Oh yes, that's true; that is by Zagoskin, but there is another
Yuri Miloslavsky, and that is mine.

ANNA   Well, I am sure it was yours that I read. So beautifully written!

HLESTAKOV   I must own I live for literature. My house is the finest in
Petersburg. Every one knows it – Ivan Alexandrovitch's house.
(*Addressing the whole company*) Pray, gentlemen, if you come to
Petersburg, I beg that you will all come to see me. I give balls, too.

ANNA   I can fancy the taste and magnificence of the balls you give!

HLESTAKOV   There's no word for it. On the table, for instance, there'll
be a watermelon that cost seven hundred roubles. The soup is
brought in a saucepan straight from Paris on a steamer. As soon as
you lift the lid there is an aroma – you'd never smell anything like
it in nature. I am at a ball every day. We make up a whist party –
the Foreign Minister, the French Ambassador, the English
Ambassador, the German Ambassador, and I. And I get so tired
out with playing that I don't know where I am. I can only run
home to my flat on the fourth storey and say to the cook, 'Take
my greatcoat, Mavrushka.' What nonsense I am talking – I forgot
that I live on the first floor. My staircase alone is worth . . . you
would be interested to see my hall before I am even awake in the

morning: there are counts and princes jostling each other and buzzing away there like bumblebees; you can hear nothing but bz–z–z . . . Sometimes, too, the Minister . . .

(*The* MAYOR *and the others, overcome with awe, get up from their seats.*)

My letters actually come addressed 'your Excellency.' At one time I was head of a Government department. It was a queer business: the director disappeared – no one knew what had become of him. Well, naturally, there was a lot of talk – what was to be done, and who was to fill his place. Many of the generals were eager and took it on – but as soon as they tackled it they saw it was too much for them. You'd think it would be easy enough, but look into it and it is the very devil of a job! They see there is nothing for it – they turn to me. And all at once messengers come racing along the street, messengers and more messengers – would you believe it, thirty-five thousand messengers! What do you say to that, I ask you now! 'Ivan Alexandrovitch, come and take charge of the department,' they say. I must say I was a bit taken aback. I came out in my dressing-gown; I meant to refuse, but there, I thought, it will get to the Tsar, and then there is one's official record to think of . . . 'Very well, gentlemen, I accept the post, I accept,' I said, 'so be it,' I said, 'only with me, gentlemen, you had better look out! You must mind your P's and Q's. You know what I am.' . . . And, as a matter of fact, when I walked through the offices you would have thought there was an earthquake, they were all trembling and shaking.

(*The* MAYOR *and the others tremble with alarm;*
HLESTAKOV *grows more excited.*)

Oh, I am not to be trifled with! I gave them all a good scare. The very Privy Council[237] is afraid of me. And well they might be! I am like that! I don't mind any one . . . I tell them all, 'Don't teach me!' I go everywhere, positively everywhere. I am in and out of the Palace every day. Tomorrow I am to be made a Field Marshal . . . (*Slips and almost falls on the floor, but the officials support him respectfully.*)

THE MAYOR (*approaches, and tries to speak, trembling all over*) Your – your – your – your . . .

HLESTAKOV (*in a sharp, abrupt tone*) What's that?

THE MAYOR Your – your – your – your . . .

HLESTAKOV (*in the same tone*) I can make nothing of it. It's all nonsense.

THE MAYOR Your – your – your . . . cency . . . Excellency, wouldn't you graciously lie down? Here is your room and everything ready for you.

HLESTAKOV Nonsense – lie down! By all means, I don't mind lying down. You gave me a good lunch, gentlemen. I am pleased, quite pleased. (*With a theatrical flourish*) Labardan, labardan! (*Retires to the room at the side, followed by the* MAYOR.)

BOBCHINSKY (*to* DOBCHINSKY) What a man, Pyotr Ivanovitch: that's what one means by a man! Never in my life have I been in the presence of a person of so much consequence. I almost died of fright. What do you think, Pyotr Ivanovitch, what can his rank be?

DOBCHINSKY I fancy he must be a general or something like that.

BOBCHINSKY Why, I think a general would take off his hat to him; and if he is a general he must be the Generalissimo himself. Did you hear how he lords it over the Privy Council? Make haste, let us go and tell Ammos Fyodorovitch and Korobkin. Goodbye, Anna Andreyevna!

DOBCHINSKY (*to* ANNA ANDREYEVNA) Goodbye!

(*Both go out.*)

ARTEMY FILIPPOVITCH (*to* LUKA LUKITCH) I am terrified, there's no other word for it; but what of I really don't know. And we are actually not in uniform. He will wake up sober, and then what if he sends a report to Petersburg?

(*Exit, plunged in thought, together with the* SCHOOL INSPECTOR, *saying as they go out, 'Goodbye, madam!'*)

ANNA Ah, what an agreeable man!

MARYA Oh, the pet!

ANNA Only fancy, what refinement! You can see a man of fashion at once. His manners and everything . . . Oh, how delightful! I am awfully fond of young men like that! I am all in a flutter. He seemed very much attracted, though, didn't he; I noticed he kept looking at me.

MARYA Oh, mamma, he was looking at me!

ANNA Keep your silly nonsense to yourself, please! It's quite out of place here.

MARYA But, mamma, he was, really!

ANNA There! God knows, she must always be arguing! How should he look at you? What should make him look at you?

MARYA Really, mamma, he did keep looking at me. When he began talking about literature he glanced at me, and when he told us how he played whist with the Ambassadors he gave me a look.

ANNA   Oh well, maybe he did give a glance at you, but that did not mean anything. 'Come,' he thought, 'I may as well give her a look!'

THE MAYOR (*enters on tiptoe*)   Sh–sh!

ANNA   Well?

THE MAYOR   I am sorry I made him drunk. What if only one-half of what he said is true! (*Ponders.*) And it must be true. When a man is in liquor he brings it all out; what is in his heart is on his tongue. Of course he did embroider a little; but there, nothing is ever said without a little trimming. He plays cards with the ministers and is in and out of the Palace . . . Upon my soul, the more one thinks about it . . . the devil only knows . . . my head is in a regular whirl; it's as though I were on the edge of a precipice or just going to be hanged.

ANNA   And I did not feel in the least frightened of him; I saw in him simply a man of the highest society and culture, I don't care about his rank.

THE MAYOR   Ugh! these women! The word covers it all. It's all trumpery to them! You never know what a woman will blurt out. She will get off with a whipping, but her husband will be done for. You behaved as freely with him, my love, as though you had been talking to Dobchinsky.

ANNA   I shouldn't worry about that if I were you. We know a thing or two. (*Looks at her daughter.*)

THE MAYOR (*to himself*)   What's the use of talking to them! . . . My God, it is a queer business! It's upset me so, I can't get over it. (*Opens the door and speaks in the doorway.*) Mishka! call Constables Svistunov and Derzhimorda, they are not far off, somewhere at the gate. (*After a brief silence.*) Things are odd nowadays: you would expect people to be something to look at, anyway, but a thin little whipper-snapper like that – who'd guess what he is? In a military uniform a man is presentable, anyway, but put him in a swallowtail and he looks like a fly with its wings cut off; but he did keep it up at the inn this morning – he told us such fine tales and taradiddles that I thought we should never get anything out of him. But he has given in at last. In fact, he said more than he need. You can see he is young.

(*Enter* OSIP. *All run towards him, beckoning.*)

ANNA   Come here, my good man!

THE MAYOR   Sh! Well? . . . Well, is he asleep?

OSIP   Not yet, he is yawning and stretching.

ANNA I say, what is your name?

OSIP Osip, madam.

THE MAYOR (*to his wife and daughter*) That will do, that will do. (*To Osip*) Well, friend, have they given you a good dinner?

OSIP Yes, thank you, sir, a very good dinner.

ANNA Come, tell me; I suppose a great many counts and princes come to see your master?

OSIP (*aside*) What am I to say? They've given me a good dinner already, so maybe they will give me a better one. (*Aloud*) Yes, there are counts too.

MARYA You dear Osip, how pretty your master is!

ANNA And do tell us, Osip, please, how does he . . .

THE MAYOR Hold your tongue! You simply hinder me with your silly questions. Come, my good man . . .

ANNA And what is your master's rank?

OSIP Oh, the usual thing.

THE MAYOR Oh, my God, how you keep on with your silly questions! You won't let one say a word of what matters. Come, my man, what is your master like? Is he strict? Is he fond of finding fault?

OSIP Yes, he likes things done properly. Everything must be just so for him.

THE MAYOR I like your face, friend. I am sure you are a good man. Come, tell me . . .

ANNA I say, Osip, and does your master wear a uniform at home?

THE MAYOR Oh, be quiet, do, you magpies! This is serious: it's a question of life and death . . . (*To Osip*) Well, friend, I really like you. An extra glass of tea does not come amiss on a journey, does it, and it is cold weather too. So here is a couple of roubles for tea.

OSIP (*taking the money*) Very much obliged to you, sir! God give you good health! I am a poor man, you've helped me.

THE MAYOR That's all right, pleased to do it. Well, friend, tell me . . .

ANNA Tell me, Osip, what sort of eyes does your master like best?

MARYA You dear Osip, what a charming little nose your master has.

THE MAYOR Oh, stop, let me speak! (*To Osip*) Come, friend, what does your master take most notice of – I mean, what does he like best when he is travelling?

OSIP It's all according, just as it happens. What he likes best is being well received, well entertained.

THE MAYOR Well entertained?

OSIP Yes, well entertained. Here, I am only a servant, but he sees that I am well entertained too. Yes indeed. Sometimes when we have been to a place, 'Well, Osip,' he will say, 'have you been well looked after?' 'No, sir, very badly!' – 'Ah,' he'd say, 'that's poor hospitality. You remind me when I reach home.' Never mind, I think to myself, I am a plain man. (*Waves his hand.*)

THE MAYOR   You are right there, you are right there, you talk sense. I gave you something for tea, so here is something more for buns.

OSIP   You are very kind, sir. (*Puts the money in his pocket.*) I'll drink your honour's health.

ANNA   Come and talk to me, Osip. I'll give you something too.

MARYA   You dear Osip, take your master a kiss!

(HLESTAKOV *is heard coughing in the next room.*)

THE MAYOR   Hush! (*Walks on tiptoe; the rest of the conversation is in an undertone.*) Don't make a noise whatever you do! Come, run along, you've talked enough!

ANNA   Come, Mashenka! I'll tell you what I have noticed in our visitor, something we can only talk about by ourselves.

THE MAYOR   Oh, they'll talk, you may be sure! If you had to listen you would soon wish you were deaf! (*Turning to* OSIP) Well, friend . . .

(*Enter* SVISTUNOV *and* DERZHIMORDA.)

THE MAYOR   Sh! You clumsy bears, how you tramp with your boots! They thump like some one dropping half a ton out of a cart! Where the devil have you been?

DERZHIMORDA   Acting on instructions, I went . . .

THE MAYOR   Sh–sh! (*puts his hand over his mouth*). How the ass brays! (*Imitating him*) Acting on instructions indeed! Booming like a drum! (*To* OSIP) Go along, friend, and get everything ready for your master. Ask for anything we have in the house.

(*Exit* OSIP.)

And you – stand at the front door and don't move from the spot! And don't allow any outsider into the house, especially any of the shopkeepers! If you let a single one of them in, I'll . . . As soon as you see any one coming with a petition, or even without a petition, but looking like a man who might want to present a petition against me, throw him out by the scruff of the neck! Like this! Give it him! (*indicating a kick with his foot*). Do you hear? Sh–sh!

(*Follows the* CONSTABLES *out on tiptoe.*)

(*Curtain.*)

The same room in the Mayor's house

AMMOS FYODOROVITCH, ARTEMY FILIPPOVITCH, *the* POSTMASTER,
LUKA LUKITCH, *all in full dress uniform, together with*
DOBCHINSKY *and* BOBCHINSKY, *enter cautiously, almost
on tiptoe. The whole scene is conducted in an undertone.*

AMMOS FYODOROVITCH (*arranging them all in a semicircle*)   For goodness'
sake, gentlemen, make haste and form in a circle, and look as
correct as you can! Bless the man, he visits at the Palace and blows
up the Privy Council! Stand in military order, it must be in military
order! You run along over there, Pyotr Ivanovitch, and you, Pyotr
Ivanovitch, stand here.

(*Both the* PYOTR IVANOVITCHES *run on tiptoe.*)

ARTEMY FILIPPOVITCH   You may say what you like, Ammos Fyodorovitch, but we ought to take some steps.

AMMOS FYODOROVITCH   What steps?

ARTEMY FILIPPOVITCH   We all know what.

AMMOS FYODOROVITCH   Slip something into his hand?

ARTEMY FILIPPOVITCH   Well, yes.

AMMOS FYODOROVITCH   It's risky, dash it all! He might make the devil of
a fuss: a great man like that! But maybe in the form of a subscription
from the gentry of the neighbourhood for some memorial?

THE POSTMASTER   Or, I say, what about money that has reached the
post office with no one to claim it?

ARTEMY FILIPPOVITCH   You'd better look out that he doesn't pack you
off by post somewhere. Listen to me: these things are not done like
that in a well-regulated community. Why is there a whole regiment
of us here? We ought to pay our respects one by one, and then,
tête-à-tête . . . you know . . . what's proper – so that no one gets
wind of it! That's the way to do things in well-regulated society!
It's for you to begin, Ammos Fyodorovitch.

AMMOS FYODOROVITCH   Oh, better you: our distinguished visitor has
broken bread in your establishment.

ARTEMY FILIPPOVITCH   It ought to be Luka Lukitch, as representing
enlightenment and education.

LUKA LUKITCH   I can't, I can't, gentlemen! I must own I have been so brought up that if I am addressed by any one who is a single grade above me in the Service, I feel more dead than alive and can't open my lips. No, you must let me off, gentlemen, you really must!

ARTEMY FILIPPOVITCH   Yes, Ammos Fyodorovitch, it must be you and no one else. As soon as you open your mouth it might be Cicero[238] speaking.

AMMOS FYODOROVITCH   What next, what next! Cicero! What an idea! If one does get a bit excited at times talking about hounds or retrievers . . .

ALL (*surrounding him*)   Oh no, not only about dogs, you can talk about the Tower of Babel[239] too . . . No, Ammos Fyodorovitch, don't fail us, be a father to us! No, Ammos Fyodorovitch!

AMMOS FYODOROVITCH   Let me alone, gentlemen! (*At that moment there is a sound of footsteps and a cough in* HLESTAKOV's *room. All rush higgledy-piggledy to the other door, jostling each other and trying to get out, which they do not accomplish without some of them getting jammed in the doorway. Exclamations in an undertone.*)

VOICE OF BOBCHINSKY   Oh, Pyotr Ivanovitch, Pyotr Ivanovitch, you have trodden on my foot!

VOICE OF ARTEMY FILIPPOVITCH   You will be the death of me, gentlemen – I am as flat as a pancake!

(*A few cries of 'Oh! Oh!' At last they all squeeze their way out and the stage is left empty. Enter* HLESTAKOV *looking drowsy.*)

HLESTAKOV   I fancy I've had a pretty long snooze. How did they come by such feather beds and pillows? I am in a regular perspiration. I fancy they must have given me something strong at lunch yesterday, there is a drumming in my head still. One might spend one's time very pleasantly here, I perceive. I do like hospitality, and I must own I like it much better when people try to please me out of pure kindness and not from self-interest. And the Mayor's daughter is not at all bad looking, and the mamma too might still . . . Well, I don't know, but I do like this sort of life.

(*Enter* AMMOS FYODOROVITCH.)

AMMOS FYODOROVITCH (*standing still, to himself*)   O Lord, O Lord preserve me! My knees are giving way under me. (*Aloud, drawing himself up and putting his hand on his sword*) I have the honour to introduce myself: Lyapkin-Tyapkin, Collegiate Assessor, and Judge of the district court.

HLESTAKOV Please sit down. So you are the Judge here?

AMMOS FYODOROVITCH In 1816 I was elected by the nobility for three years, and I have retained the post ever since.

HLESTAKOV It's a profitable job being a Judge, isn't it?

AMMOS FYODOROVITCH After nine years of service I was presented with the Order of Vladimir of the Fourth Class with the commendation of my superiors. (*Aside*) The money is in my fist, and my fist feels as though it were on fire.

HLESTAKOV Oh, I like the Vladimir. The Anna of the Third Class [240] is not nearly as nice.

AMMOS FYODOROVITCH (*gradually advancing his clenched fist. Aside*) Merciful God! I don't know where I am. I feel as though I were sitting on hot coals.

HLESTAKOV What have you got in your hand?

AMMOS FYODOROVITCH (*disconcerted, drops the notes on the floor*) Oh, nothing.

HLESTAKOV Nothing? Why, I see you've dropped some money.

AMMOS FYODOROVITCH (*trembling all over*) Not at all! (*Aside*) O God! Here I am in the dock, and the cart coming to take me to prison!

HLESTAKOV (*picking it up*) Yes, it is money.

AMMOS FYODOROVITCH (*aside*) Well, it is all over! I am lost, I am done for!

HLESTAKOV I tell you what, do you mind lending it to me?

AMMOS FYODOROVITCH (*hurriedly*) To be sure, to be sure . . . with pleasure. (*Aside*) Courage! Courage! Pull me through, Holy Mother!

HLESTAKOV I got cleaned out on the journey, you know: what with one thing and another . . . But I will send it you as soon as I get home.

AMMOS FYODOROVITCH Oh, not at all, it's an honour . . . Of course by zeal and devotion to my superiors . . . I will do my poor best to deserve . . . (*Rises from his chair. Drawing himself up, with his hands to his sides*) I will not venture to trouble you further with my presence. Have you any order to give me?

HLESTAKOV What sort of order?

AMMOS FYODOROVITCH I mean, have you no order to give to the district court?

HLESTAKOV Oh, why? No, I have no need of it at present; no, nothing. Thanks so much.

AMMOS FYODOROVITCH (*bowing himself out. Aside*) Well, the town is ours!

HLESTAKOV (*alone*) The Judge is a good fellow! (*Enter the* POSTMASTER *in uniform, holding himself erect, with his hand on his sword.*)

THE POSTMASTER   I have the honour to introduce myself: Shpekin, Court Councillor, Postmaster.

HLESTAKOV   Ah, pleased to see you! I am very fond of good company. Please sit down. You always live here, I suppose?

THE POSTMASTER   Yes, sir.

HLESTAKOV   I like this town, you know. Of course it is not a very big town – but what of it? It is not Petersburg or Moscow. It isn't, is it?

THE POSTMASTER   Perfectly true.

HLESTAKOV   Of course it is only in the capital that you get *bon-ton*[241] and no provincial boobies. Don't you agree?

THE POSTMASTER   Yes, indeed, sir. (*Aside*) He is not a bit proud: asks one about everything.

HLESTAKOV   But yet you must admit that one can be happy even in a little town, can't one?

THE POSTMASTER   Yes, indeed, sir.

HLESTAKOV   What does one want? To my mind all one wants is to be genuinely liked and respected – isn't it?

THE POSTMASTER   Perfectly true.

HLESTAKOV   I must say I am glad to find you agree with me. People may think me queer, but I am like that. (*Looking into his face, says to himself*) I think I'll ask this postmaster for a loan. (*Aloud*) Such a queer thing happened to me: I got regularly cleaned out on the journey. Could you perhaps lend me three hundred roubles?

THE POSTMASTER   Certainly, I shall consider it an honour. Allow me, here. I am truly glad to be of service.

HLESTAKOV   Thanks so much. I must own I hate going short on a journey – there's no point in it, is there?

THE POSTMASTER   No, indeed, sir. (*Rises. Drawing himself up and holding his sword*) I will not venture to trouble you further with my presence . . . Have you no observation to make with regard to the post office?

HLESTAKOV   No, none.

(THE POSTMASTER *bows himself out.*)

HLESTAKOV (*lighting a cigar*)   I think the Postmaster is a very good fellow too; anyway he is obliging. I like such people.

(*Enter* LUKA LUKITCH, *almost shoved in at the door from behind. A voice is heard almost aloud: 'What are you afraid of?'*)

LUKA LUKITCH (*draws himself up in trepidation, holding his sword*)   I have the honour to introduce myself: Hlopov, School Inspector and Titular Councillor.

HLESTAKOV Am pleased to see you! Sit down, sit down. Won't you have a cigar? (*Offers him a cigar.*)

LUKA LUKITCH (*to himself, irresolutely*) Well I never! That I didn't expect. Ought I to take it or not?

HLESTAKOV Take it, take it; it's not a bad cigar. Of course it's not like what you get in Petersburg. There, my good sir, I smoked cigars at twenty-five roubles a hundred – you feel like licking your lips when you've smoked one. Here's a candle, light it. (*Holds a candle to him.*)

(LUKA LUKITCH *tries to light the cigar, but keeps trembling.*)

HLESTAKOV But that's not the right end!

LUKA LUKITCH (*In his panic drops the cigar, and with a wave of his hand says to himself in disgust*) The devil take it all! My damned timidity has ruined everything!

HLESTAKOV You are not fond of cigars, I see. Now I must own they are one of my weaknesses. And the fair sex, too – I can't resist them. And you? Which do you like best, brunettes or blondes?

(LUKA LUKITCH *is utterly nonplussed and unable to answer.*)

HLESTAKOV Come, tell me frankly, brunettes or blondes?

LUKA LUKITCH I can't venture to have an opinion.

HLESTAKOV Come, come, don't turn it off! I really want to know your preference.

LUKA LUKITCH I venture to lay before you ... (*Aside*) I don't know what I am saying.

HLESTAKOV Ah! ah! You won't say. I believe you are smitten with some pretty little brunette. Own up, you are?

(LUKA LUKITCH *remains dumb.*)

HLESTAKOV Ah! You are blushing! You see, you see! Why won't you say?

LUKA LUKITCH I am overawed, your hon ... rev ... excel ... (*Aside*) My cursed tongue has betrayed me!

HLESTAKOV Overawed? There really is something in my eye, you know, that inspires awe. Anyway, I know there is not a woman who can hold out against it, is there?

LUKA LUKITCH Certainly not.

HLESTAKOV A queer thing has happened to me: I've been absolutely cleaned out on the journey here. Couldn't you perhaps lend me three hundred roubles?

LUKA LUKITCH (*clutching at his pockets, to himself*) How awful if I haven't got it! I have, I have! (*Takes out notes, and gives them, trembling.*)

HLESTAKOV   Thanks so much.

LUKA LUKITCH *(drawing himself up and holding his sword)* I will not venture to trouble you longer with my presence.

HLESTAKOV   Goodbye.

LUKA LUKITCH *(Darts out almost at a run and says aside)* Thank God! maybe he won't look into the schoolroom!

(Enter ARTEMY FILIPPOVITCH, *drawing himself up and holding his sword.)*

ARTEMY FILIPPOVITCH   I have the honour to introduce myself: Zemlyanika, Superintendent of Charitable Institutions and Court Councillor.

HLESTAKOV   How do you do? Please sit down.

ARTEMY FILIPPOVITCH   I had the honour of accompanying you and receiving you in person in the charitable institutions committed to my charge.

HLESTAKOV   Oh yes, I remember. You gave me an excellent lunch!

ARTEMY FILIPPOVITCH   Always glad to do my best for the welfare of my country.

HLESTAKOV   I must own I am fond of good fare – it is my weakness. Do tell me, please, I fancy you were a little shorter yesterday than you are today, weren't you?

ARTEMY FILIPPOVITCH   Quite possibly. *(After a pause)* I may say that I spare nothing and zealously perform my duties. *(Draws his chair up closer and says in a low voice)* Now the Postmaster here does nothing at all: all his work is utterly neglected . . . the despatches are held back . . . Perhaps you would look into it yourself? The Judge, too – who was here just before I came in – does nothing but course hares; he keeps dogs in the public court, and his conduct, to tell the truth – and, of course, it is my duty to do so for the good of my country, although he is a relative and a friend – his conduct is most reprehensible. There is a landowner here, Dobchinsky, whom you have seen, and as soon as that Dobchinsky steps out of his house, the Judge will be sitting with his wife, I am ready to take my oath on it . . . And just look at the children: not one of them is like Dobchinsky, but every one of them, even the little girl, is the very image of the Judge.

HLESTAKOV   You don't say so! I should never have thought it.

ARTEMY FILIPPOVITCH   And the School Inspector, too . . . I cannot think how the authorities came to entrust such a post to him: he is worse than a Jacobin,[242] and the pernicious principles he instils into the young are beyond words. If you instruct me to do so, I can put all this into writing.

HLESTAKOV   Very good, do. I shall be very much pleased. You know I like something amusing to read when I am bored . . . What is your name? I keep forgetting.

ARTEMY FILIPPOVITCH   Zemlyanika.

HLESTAKOV   Oh yes, Zemlyanika. And tell me, please, have you any children?

ARTEMY FILIPPOVITCH   To be sure. Five; and two are grown up.

HLESTAKOV   Grown up! You don't say so! And what are . . . what are they . . .

ARTEMY FILIPPOVITCH   You mean, you wish to enquire what are their names?

HLESTAKOV   Yes, what are their names?

ARTEMY FILIPPOVITCH   Nikolay, Ivan, Elizaveta, Marya, and Perpetua.

HLESTAKOV   Very nice.

ARTEMY FILIPPOVITCH   I will not venture to trouble you with my presence and rob you of time dedicated to sacred duties . . . (*Is bowing himself out.*)

HLESTAKOV (*accompanying him*)   No, it's all right. It's all so funny what you were telling me. Come and talk to me another time . . . I like that sort of thing. (*Turns back, and opening the door calls after him*) Hey, you! What's your name? I keep forgetting what to call you.

ARTEMY FILIPPOVITCH   Artemy Filippovitch.

HLESTAKOV   Do me a favour, Artemy Filippovitch; a queer thing has happened to me: I was completely cleaned out on the way here. Have you any money you could lend me – four hundred roubles or so?

ARTEMY FILIPPOVITCH   Yes.

HLESTAKOV   I say, how lucky! Thanks so much.

(*Exit* ARTEMY FILIPPOVITCH.)

(*Enter* BOBCHINSKY *and* DOBCHINSKY.)

BOBCHINSKY   I have the honour to introduce myself: Pyotr Ivanovitch Bobchinsky, a resident of this town.

DOBCHINSKY   Pyotr Ivanovitch Dobchinsky, landowner.

HLESTAKOV   Ah, I saw you yesterday. You tumbled in at the doorway, didn't you? Well, how is your nose?

BOBCHINSKY   Oh, don't trouble; it's healed, thank God, quite healed now.

HLESTAKOV That's a good thing. I am glad . . . (*Speaking suddenly and abruptly*) You haven't any money on you?

DOBCHINSKY Money? Why?

HLESTAKOV A thousand roubles to lend me.

BOBCHINSKY Oh dear, not a sum like that. Haven't you, Pyotr Ivanovitch?

DOBCHINSKY I haven't it with me, for my money, if you care to know, has been lodged in the hands of the public trustee.

HLESTAKOV Ah well, if you haven't a thousand, let me have a hundred.

BOBCHINSKY (*fumbling in his pockets*) Haven't you a hundred roubles, Pyotr Ivanovitch? I have only forty paper notes.

DOBCHINSKY (*looking in his pocketbook*) Twenty-five roubles is all I have.

BOBCHINSKY Oh, look a little more thoroughly, Pyotr Ivanovitch! I know you have a hole in your right-hand pocket; most likely some have slipped through into the lining.

DOBCHINSKY No, really, there's nothing there.

HLESTAKOV Oh, it doesn't matter. I thought I'd just ask. Very good; sixty-five roubles will do . . . Never mind. (*Takes the money.*)

DOBCHINSKY I make bold to ask your assistance about a very delicate matter.

HLESTAKOV And what is it?

DOBCHINSKY It is a matter of great delicacy: my eldest son was born, you see, before I was married . . .

HLESTAKOV Oh?

DOBCHINSKY Though that's only in a manner of speaking; he was born exactly as though in lawful wedlock, and I made it all right and proper afterwards by the bonds of legitimate matrimony. So now you see I want him to become altogether my legitimate son and to bear my name – Dobchinsky.

HLESTAKOV Very good; let him bear your name, that's all right.

DOBCHINSKY I would not have troubled you, but I am sorry, because he is so gifted. The boy . . . is very promising: he can repeat all sorts of poems by heart, and if he can get hold of a knife he makes a little cart as cleverly as a conjuror. Pyotr Ivanovitch here can tell you.

BOBCHINSKY Yes, he has great talents.

HLESTAKOV Very good, very good! I'll see to that, I'll speak about that . . . I have no doubt it will all be arranged, yes, yes . . . (*Turning to* BOBCHINSKY) And haven't you anything to say to me?

BOBCHINSKY I have, indeed, a very humble request.

HLESTAKOV Well, what about?

BOBCHINSKY I humbly beg you, when you go back to Petersburg, say to all those grand gentlemen – senators, admirals, and such, 'Do you know, your Excellency or your Highness, in such and such a town there lives a man called Pyotr Ivanovitch Bobchinsky?' Say that: 'There lives a man called Pyotr Ivanovitch Bobchinsky.'

HLESTAKOV Very well.

BOBCHINSKY Yes, and if you have a chance of speaking to the Tsar, tell the Tsar, 'Do you know, your Imperial Majesty, in such and such a town lives Pyotr Ivanovitch Bobchinsky?'

HLESTAKOV Very well.

DOBCHINSKY Excuse us for troubling you with our presence.

BOBCHINSKY Excuse us for troubling you with our presence.

HLESTAKOV Oh, it's no matter. It's a pleasure.

(Sees them out.)

HLESTAKOV *(alone)* There are a lot of officials here. But I fancy they take me for some one of importance in the Government. I must have told them a fine yarn yesterday. What a set of fools! I must write to Petersburg and tell Tryapitchkin all about it: he is an author, let him write a skit on them. Hey, Osip! bring me ink and paper! (OSIP *looking in at the door says*, *'In a minute.'*) And if Tryapitchkin gets his knife into any one, it's a bad look-out: he wouldn't spare his own father to adorn a tale, and he is fond of money too. But they are good-natured fellows, these officials: it speaks very well for them that they have lent me money. I'll just look how much I have got. That's three hundred from the Judge, that's three hundred from the Postmaster, six hundred, seven hundred, eight hundred . . . what a dirty note! Eight hundred, nine hundred . . . Oho, more than a thousand . . . Now you can come on, captain! I am ready for you! We'll see who will get the best of it this time!

(Enter OSIP with ink and paper.)

HLESTAKOV Now you see, you stupid, how they receive me and make much of me? *(Begins writing.)*

OSIP Yes, thank God. Only do you know what, Ivan Alexandrovitch?

HLESTAKOV What is it?

OSIP You'd better get away from here! It's high time we were off.

HLESTAKOV *(writing)* What nonsense! Why?

OSIP Well, you'd better. Bless the people! You've enjoyed yourself here for two days, and that's enough. What's the good of lingering on with them? Have done with them! Our luck may turn, and some one else arrive . . . believe me, Ivan Alexandrovitch! And the horses here are first-rate – how we should race along!

HLESTAKOV (*writing*)   No, I want to stay here a bit longer. Tomorrow will do.

OSIP   Tomorrow's no good. Do let us be off, Ivan Alexandrovitch, really! It's a great honour for you, of course, but still we'd better make haste and get away; they've mistaken you for somebody else, you know, really . . . And your papa will be angry with you for dawdling so long on the way. We could race along finely! They'd give us capital horses here.

HLESTAKOV (*writing*)   Oh, very well. Only take this letter to the post first, and you can get my travelling pass at the same time if you like. But mind we have good horses now! Tell the drivers I'll pay them a silver rouble each if they'll drive as though I were a special messenger and sing songs! (*Goes on writing.*) I can fancy how Tryapitchkin will split with laughing . . .

OSIP   I'll give it to the man here to post, sir; I had better be packing, so as not to lose time.

HLESTAKOV (*writing*)   Very good, only bring a candle.

OSIP (*Goes out and says behind the scenes*)   I say, my lad! Take this letter to the post and tell the Postmaster to take it unfranked, and tell them to send round at once the troika,[243] the express ones; and say my master doesn't pay the fare, it's at the Crown expense. And tell them to look sharp, or my master will be angry. Stay, the letter is not ready yet.

HLESTAKOV (*goes on writing*)   It would be interesting to know where he is living now – in Post-Office Street or Gorohovy? He is fond of changing his lodging and not paying his rent. I'll chance Post-Office Street. (*Folds up the letter and addresses it.*)

(OSIP *brings a candle.* HLESTAKOV *seals the letter. At that moment the voice of* DERZHIMORDA *is heard:* 'Where are you shoving to, bushy beard? I tell you, I've orders to admit no one.')

HLESTAKOV (*gives the letter to* OSIP)   Here, take it.

VOICES OF SHOPKEEPERS.   Let us in, sir! You can't refuse: we are here on business.

DERZHIMORDA'S VOICE.   Be off, be off! He is not seeing any one, he is asleep.

(*The uproar grows louder.*)

HLESTAKOV   What's going on, Osip? See what the fuss is about.

OSIP (*looks out of window*) It's some shopkeepers want to come in, and the police constable won't let them. They are waving petitions: most likely they want to see you.

HLESTAKOV (*going to the window*) What is it, friends?

VOICES OF SHOPKEEPERS We appeal to your Excellency. Command them to admit our petitions, honoured sir.

HLESTAKOV Let them in, let them in! Let them come here. Osip, tell them they can come in.

(OSIP *goes out.*)

HLESTAKOV (*takes petitions through the window, opens one and reads.*) 'To his Honourable Excellency the Master of Finances, from Abdulin, shopkeeper . . . ' What on earth does it mean? There's no such rank!

(*The* SHOPKEEPERS *come in with a basket
of wine-bottles and loaves of sugar.*)

HLESTAKOV What is it, friends?

SHOPKEEPERS We humbly ask your gracious kindness.

HLESTAKOV What do you want?

SHOPKEEPERS Do not be our ruin, honoured sir! We are suffering cruel wrong.

HLESTAKOV Who is ill-treating you?

ONE OF THE SHOPKEEPERS It's all the Mayor here. There has never been a mayor like him, sir! There are no words bad enough for the things he does. He has ruined us, billeting soldiers on us. His behaviour is most unmannerly. He will pull one by the beard and shout, 'Ah, you Tatar!' Yes indeed! It isn't as though we had shown him any disrespect, we have always done our duty: as for giving something for the dresses of his good lady and his daughter, we have nothing against that. But mind you, that's not enough for him – my word, no! He walks into the shop and takes anything he can lay his hands on. If he sees a piece of cloth, 'Hey, my dear man,' he will say, 'that's a fine bit of cloth, send that round to me.' Well, one has to send it – and there may be fifty yards in the piece.

HLESTAKOV Is it possible? What a scoundrel!

SHOPKEEPERS Indeed it is true, sir! No one remembers a mayor like him. One has to hide everything in the shop when one sees him coming. And it isn't only the dainties that he goes for, he takes all manner of rubbish: plums that have been lying seven years in the barrel, my shopmen would not touch them, but he will take a whole

handful. St Anthony's is his name-day,[244] and then we take him no
end of things, he can't be short of anything; but no, that's not
enough for him: he says St Onufry's[245] is his name-day too. There's
no help for it: one has to give something for that name-day too.

HLESTAKOV   Why, he is a regular brigand!

SHOPKEEPERS   Yes indeed! But only try refusing, and he will quarter a
whole regiment on you. And if you do anything, he will have the
doors locked. 'I am not going to flog you or torture you,' he says,
'that's forbidden by the law,' he says, 'but you just go on eating red
herring, my friend, without a drop to drink.'

HLESTAKOV   Ah, what a scoundrel! Why, he deserves to be sent to
Siberia!

SHOPKEEPERS   Wherever your Excellency thinks fit to send him, so long
as it's a good way off. Do not despise our humble offerings,
honoured sir: we beg you to accept some sugar and a basket of wine.

HLESTAKOV   No, don't you think of such a thing. I don't take bribes at
all. But if you were to let me have a loan . . . of three hundred
roubles, for instance, that would be another thing: I might take a
loan.

SHOPKEEPERS   By all means, honoured sir! (*Take out money.*) But what's
three hundred – better take five; only help us.

HLESTAKOV   Very well, a loan I have nothing against, I'll take it.

SHOPKEEPERS (*offer him money on a silver dish*)   Please accept the tray
with it.

HLESTAKOV   Well, I might take the tray too.

SHOPKEEPERS (*bowing*)   And you might just as well take the sugar with it.

HLESTAKOV   Oh no, I don't take bribes.

OSIP   Your Excellency, why not accept the sugar? Take it! It will all
come in on a journey. Hand me over the sugar loaves and the
basket. Give it here, it will all come in useful. What have you there?
A cord? Give me the cord too – cord comes in handy on a journey
too: if the chaise or anything else breaks down you can tie it up.

SHOPKEEPERS   Pray do us the favour, your Excellency! If you don't help
us in our trouble we don't know what we are to do: we are in a
desperate case.

HLESTAKOV   Certainly, certainly! I'll do my best.

(*The* SHOPKEEPERS *go out.*)

(*A woman's voice is heard: 'No, you daren't turn me away!*
I'll complain of you to the gentleman himself.
Don't shove like that, you hurt me!')

HLESTAKOV   Who is there? (*Goes to the window.*) What is it, my good
woman?

VOICES OF TWO WOMEN   We crave your kind help! Grant us a hearing,
honoured sir!

HLESTAKOV (*at the window*)   Let her in!

(*Enter the* LOCKSMITH'S WIFE *and the* SERGEANT'S WIDOW.)

THE LOCKSMITH'S WIFE (*bowing down to his feet*)   Graciously help me! . . .

THE SERGEANT'S WIDOW   Graciously help me!

HLESTAKOV   But who are you?

THE SERGEANT'S WIDOW   Ivanovna, widow of a sergeant.

THE LOCKSMITH'S WIFE   Fevronya Petrova Poshlyopkin, wife of a locksmith of the town . . .

HLESTAKOV   Stay, speak one at a time. What do you want?

THE LOCKSMITH'S WIFE   Graciously help me, I seek your protection
against the Mayor! God send him every evil! May neither his
children nor he, the rascal, nor his uncles nor his aunts prosper in
anything they undertake!

HLESTAKOV   What has he done?

THE LOCKSMITH'S WIFE   He sent my husband for a soldier, and it was
not his turn, the rascal! and it is against the law, him being a
married man.

HLESTAKOV   How could he do it?

THE LOCKSMITH'S WIFE   He did it, the villain, he did it, may God smite
him in this world and in the next! May every plague overtake him,
and his aunt too, if he has one, and if his father is living, may he, the
blackguard, choke or split, the dirty sneak! It was the tailor's son
who ought to have been taken, a drunken fellow too, but his parents
gave the Mayor a handsome present. Then he pitched on the son of
Panteleyeva who keeps the draper's shop, but she sent his good lady
three pieces of linen, so then he came to me. 'What do you want
with your husband? He is no more good to you.' Well, I know
whether he is any good or not, it's my business, you scoundrel! 'He
is a thief,' says he; 'though he's stolen nothing yet,' says he, 'it's all
one, he will steal some day, he will be sent for a soldier next year
anyway.' But what am I to do without a husband, you rascal! I am a
weak woman, you wretch! May none of your kindred see the light
of day! And if you've a mother-in-law, I hope she'll . . .

HLESTAKOV   All right, all right. (*Motions her to the door.*) Well, and you?

THE LOCKSMITH'S WIFE (*as she goes out*)   Do not forget, honoured sir! Be
merciful!

THE SERGEANT'S WIDOW　It's to complain of the Mayor I've come, sir.

HLESTAKOV　Why, what for? Tell me in a few words.

THE SERGEANT'S WIDOW　He flogged me, sir!

HLESTAKOV　How was that?

THE SERGEANT'S WIDOW　By mistake, sir! Some of our women were fighting in the market, and the police did not get there in time, so they took me up and gave me such a drubbing I couldn't sit down for two days.

HLESTAKOV　What's to be done now?

THE SERGEANT'S WIDOW　Well, there's no help for it now, but make him pay me damages for the mistake. If luck does come one's way, one doesn't want to miss it, and the money would come in wonderfully handy just now.

HLESTAKOV　Very good, very good! You can go, you can go, I'll see about it. (*Hands holding petitions are thrust in at the window.*) Why, who is there now! (*Goes to the window.*) I don't want them! I don't want them! Take them away! (*Moving away.*) I am sick of them, hang it all! Don't let them in, Osip!

OSIP　(*shouts at the window*) Be off, be off! No time now, come tomorrow!

(*The door opens and a figure appears in a frieze overcoat, with an unshaven chin, a swollen lip, and a bandage round his face; behind him is seen a perspective of other figures.*)

OSIP　Be off, be off! Where are you shoving to? (*Pushes the foremost figure out, laying both hands on his stomach, and passes with him into the anteroom, slamming the door behind him.*)

(*Enter* MARYA ANTONOVNA.)

MARYA　Oh!

HLESTAKOV　Why are you so alarmed, madam?

MARYA　No, I am not alarmed.

HLESTAKOV　(*striking an attitude*) Believe me, madam, it is most agreeable to me that you have taken me for a man who . . . But allow me to ask you, where were you going?

MARYA　Really, I wasn't going anywhere.

HLESTAKOV　And why, may I ask, aren't you going anywhere?

MARYA　I thought mamma was here . . .

HLESTAKOV　No, do explain!

MARYA　I am hindering you. You are engaged in important business.

HLESTAKOV　(*striking an attitude*) But your eyes are worth more than important business . . . You cannot hinder me, you cannot possibly; on the contrary, your presence can only be a pleasure.

MARYA   You talk as they do in smart society.

HLESTAKOV   To such a lovely being as you. May I have the happiness of offering you a chair? But no, you should have not a chair but a throne.

MARYA   Really, I don't know. I ought to be going. (*Sits down.*)

HLESTAKOV   What a lovely fichu!

MARYA   You are mocking, you only say that to make fun of us provincials.

HLESTAKOV   How I should like to be that fichu, madam, to embrace your lily neck.

MARYA   I don't understand what you are talking about . . . a fichu . . . What peculiar weather it is today!

HLESTAKOV   Your lips, madam, are better than any weather.

MARYA   You do say such things . . . I should like to ask you to write a few verses in my album. I expect you know ever so many.

HLESTAKOV   For your sake, madam, I'll do anything you please. Command, what sort of verses would you like?

MARYA   Some sort of . . . you know . . . good ones . . . new.

HLESTAKOV   What are poems! I know ever so many!

MARYA   Oh, tell me the ones you will write for me.

HLESTAKOV   But why repeat them? I know them well enough.

MARYA   I am very fond of poetry.

HLESTAKOV   Oh, I know lots of them of all sorts. Well, if you like, I'll write this one:

'Oh, man who in thy hour of grief
    Vainly doth murmur against God.'[246]

And there are others . . . I can't think of them at the moment; but it does not matter. Instead of that I had much better offer you my love, which your eyes have . . . (*Draws his chair nearer.*)

MARYA   Love! I don't understand love . . . I have never known what love means. (*Edges her chair away.*)

HLESTAKOV   Why do you move your chair away? We are better sitting near each other.

MARYA (*moving her chair farther*)   Why nearer? It may just as well be farther.

HLESTAKOV (*moving nearer*)   Why farther? It may just as well be nearer.

MARYA (*moving away*)   But why?

HLESTAKOV (*moving nearer*)   You only imagine that we are near; you must imagine that we are far apart. How happy I should be, madam, if I might hold you in my embraces!

MARYA (*looking out of window*)   What bird was it flew up just now? A magpie, was it?

HLESTAKOV (*kisses her shoulder and looks out of window*)   It's a magpie.

MARYA (*gets up indignantly*)   No, that's too much . . . What impudence!

HLESTAKOV (*detaining her*)   Forgive me, madam: I did it from love, really, from love.

MARYA   You think I am a provincial girl whom you can . . . (*Tries to get away.*)

HLESTAKOV (*still detains her*)   It was love, it really was. I didn't mean any harm, it was only fun: Marya Antonovna, don't be angry! I am ready to beg your pardon on my knees. (*Falls on his knees.*) Forgive me, forgive me! You see, I am on my knees!

(*Enter* ANNA ANDREYEVNA.)

ANNA (*seeing* HLESTAKOV *on his knees*)   Oh, what a surprise!

HLESTAKOV (*getting up*)   Oh, dash it all!

ANNA (*to her daughter*)   What does this mean, miss? This is nice behaviour.

MARYA   Mamma, I . . .

ANNA   Go out of the room, do you hear! Go along! And don't let me set eyes upon you. (MARYA ANTONOVNA *goes out in tears.*) Excuse me, I must own I am so astounded . . .

HLESTAKOV (*aside*)   She too is a dainty morsel, she is very taking. (*Drops on his knees.*) Madam, you see I am dying with love.

ANNA   What, you are on your knees? Oh, get up, get up! The floor is anything but clean.

HLESTAKOV   No, on my knees, it must be on my knees, I want to know what awaits me: life or death.

ANNA   Pardon me, I don't quite grasp the meaning of your words. If I understand you aright, you are declaring your sentiments for my daughter?

HLESTAKOV   No, I am in love with you. My life is in the balance. If you do not requite my constant love, I am not worthy of earthly existence. With heart aglow I ask your hand.

ANNA   But allow me to observe that I am in a certain sense . . . married.

HLESTAKOV   That doesn't matter! Love knows nought of such distinctions; as Karamzin[247] said: 'The laws condemn it.' We will flee to some happy dale beside a running brook . . . Your hand, I ask your hand . . .

(MARYA ANTONOVNA *runs in suddenly*.)

MARYA Mamma, papa says you are to . . . (*Sees* HLESTAKOV *on his knees*.) Oh, what a surprise!

ANNA What do you want? What is it? How flighty! She runs in like a scalded cat! What do you think so surprising? What nonsense have you got in your head? Why, you might be a child of three. Nobody, nobody would ever think that you were eighteen. I don't know when you will learn sense, when you will learn to behave like a well-brought-up girl, when you will understand what is meant by good principles and propriety.

MARYA (*in tears*) Really, mamma, I didn't know . . .

ANNA Your head is always in a flutter; you model yourself on the Lyapkin-Tyapkin girls. Why copy them? There's no need to copy them! There are other examples for you to follow – you have your mother. That's the example you ought to follow!

HLESTAKOV (*seizes the daughter's hand*) Anna Andreyevna, do not oppose our happiness, give your blessing to our constant love!

ANNA (*in amazement*) So then it's her?

HLESTAKOV Say, is it to be life or death?

ANNA There, you see, you silly, you see: for the sake of a worthless girl like you our distinguished visitor was on his knees – and you ran in as though you were mad. Really, it would serve you right if I refused my consent; you do not deserve such happiness.

MARYA I won't do it again, mamma, I'll never do it again.

(*The* MAYOR *comes in breathless*.)

THE MAYOR Your Excellency, spare me! Spare me!

HLESTAKOV What's the matter?

THE MAYOR The shopkeepers have been complaining to your Excellency. I assure you on my honour that not one-half of what they say is true. It's they who cheat and give short measure. The sergeant's widow was lying when she said I had her flogged; it's a lie, indeed it is. She flogged herself.

HLESTAKOV Oh, hang the sergeant's widow – I have something better to think about.

THE MAYOR Don't believe it, don't believe it! . . . They are such liars . . . Why, a babe would not believe them. They are known all over the town for their lying. And as for swindling, I can assure you there have never been such swindlers on this earth.

ANNA Do you know the honour that Ivan Alexandrovitch is doing us? He is asking for our daughter's hand.

THE MAYOR   What next! What next! You are raving! Do not be angry, your Excellency; she is not very strong in the head, her mother was just the same.

HLESTAKOV   But I really am making an offer. I am in love.

THE MAYOR   I cannot believe it, your Excellency!

ANNA   But when he tells you so!

HLESTAKOV   I am speaking seriously . . . I might go off my head from love.

THE MAYOR   I dare not believe it, I am unworthy of such an honour.

HLESTAKOV   But if you won't consent to give me the hand of Marya Antonovna, God only knows what I may do . . .

THE MAYOR   I can't believe it: your Excellency is pleased to jest!

ANNA   Ah, what a blockhead he is! Why, isn't he telling you so?

THE MAYOR   I can't believe it.

HLESTAKOV   Consent, consent! I am a desperate man, I may do anything: when I shoot myself, you will have to answer for it.

THE MAYOR   Oh, my God! I assure you I am not to blame, neither in thought nor act! Please do not be angry! Do as your Excellency thinks best. My head at this moment . . . I don't know what's the matter with it. I have become a greater fool than I have ever been.

ANNA   Well, give them your blessing! (HLESTAKOV *goes up to him with* MARYA ANTONOVNA.)

THE MAYOR   May God bless you! It's not my fault! (HLESTAKOV *kisses* MARYA ANTONOVNA. *The* MAYOR *stares at them.*) What the devil! It's really true! (*Rubs his eyes.*) They are kissing each other! Holy Saints! Kissing! They are really engaged. (*With a cry and skip of delight*) Hey, Anton! Hurrah for the Mayor! What a turn things have taken!

(*Enter* OSIP.)

OSIP   The horses are ready.

HLESTAKOV   Ah, very good . . . I am coming.

THE MAYOR   What? Your Excellency is going?

HLESTAKOV   Yes.

THE MAYOR   Then, when . . . I mean . . . Your Excellency has deigned yourself to hint at a wedding, I believe?

HLESTAKOV   Ah, it's only for a moment . . . for one day, to see my uncle, a rich old man; and I shall be back tomorrow.

THE MAYOR   We will not venture to keep you in the hope of your happy return.

HLESTAKOV   Of course, of course, I shan't be long. Farewell, my love . . . no, I cannot express my feelings! Farewell, darling! (*Kisses her hand.*)

THE MAYOR   But don't you need anything for the journey? I believe your Excellency was a little short of money?

HLESTAKOV   Oh no, why so? (*After a moment's reflection.*) Very well, though.

THE MAYOR   How much would you like?

HLESTAKOV   Oh, well, you lent me two hundred, that is, not two hundred but four hundred – I don't want to take advantage of your mistake – well, perhaps you could let me have the same sum again, to make it a round eight hundred.

THE MAYOR   Certainly. (*Takes notes out of his pocketbook.*) Luckily, I have just got some new notes.

HLESTAKOV   Ah yes! (*Takes the notes and examines them.*) That is nice. They say it brings good luck to have new notes.

THE MAYOR   Yes indeed.

HLESTAKOV   Goodbye, Anton Antonovitch. Very much obliged for your hospitality: I say it sincerely: nowhere have I had such a warm reception. Goodbye, Anna Andreyevna! Farewell, my darling Marya Antonovna!

(*They go out.*)

HLESTAKOV'S VOICE (*behind the scenes*)   Farewell, angel of my heart, Marya Antonovna!

THE MAYOR'S VOICE   What, you are going in the ordinary public post-chaise?

HLESTAKOV'S VOICE   Yes, that's my habit. Springs make my head ache.

THE DRIVER'S VOICE   Wo–o–o . . .

THE MAYOR'S VOICE   Do, anyway, have something to put on the seat. Wouldn't you like me to give you a rug?

HLESTAKOV'S VOICE   No, why? It's of no consequence; but perhaps you might let them bring a rug.

THE MAYOR'S VOICE   Hey, Avdotya! Go to the storeroom and fetch a rug, the best, the Persian one with the blue ground! Make haste!

THE DRIVER'S VOICE   Wo–o–o . . .

THE MAYOR'S VOICE   When are we to expect your Excellency?

HLESTAKOV'S VOICE   Tomorrow or the next day.

OSIP'S VOICE   Oh, is that the rug? Hand it here, put it there! Now put the hay this side.

THE DRIVER'S VOICE   Wo–o–o . . .

OSIP'S VOICE   Here, this side! Here, some more! That's right! That will be fine! (*Slaps his hand on the rug.*) Now, sit down, your Excellency.

HLESTAKOV'S VOICE   Goodbye, Anton Antonovitch!

THE MAYOR'S VOICE   Goodbye, your Excellency.

WOMEN'S VOICES   Goodbye, Ivan Alexandrovitch!

HLESTAKOV'S VOICE   Goodbye, mamma!

THE DRIVER'S VOICE   Hey, my beauties!

(*Bells ring.*)

(*Curtain.*)

ACT FIVE

The same room

The MAYOR, ANNA ANDREYEVNA *and* MARYA ANTONOVNA

THE MAYOR Well, Anna Andreyevna? Eh? Did you ever expect such a thing? A mighty fine catch, damn it all! Come, own up, in your wildest dreams you never hoped for this – from being just a mayor's wife . . . hang it all! . . . to be allied with a devil like this!

ANNA Not at all; I knew it all along. It seems strange to you because you are just an ordinary man and have never mixed with decent people.

THE MAYOR I am a decent person myself, my dear. But really though, Anna Andreyevna, when one comes to think what fine birds we are now, you and I! Eh, Anna Andreyevna? Right at the top of the tree, dash it all! You wait a bit, I'll give it them hot – all those tale-bearers with their complaints! Hey, who's there? (*Enter a* CONSTABLE.) Ah, it's you, Ivan Karpovitch! Bring those shopkeepers here, my lad. I'll give them a lesson, the brutes! I'll teach them to complain! Regular set of Jews they are! You wait, my pets! I won't let you off so easily this time! Make a list of all those who came to grumble of me, and above all, those scribblers who polished up their petitions for them. And let them all know what an honour has been bestowed on me by the grace of God – tell them the Mayor is marrying his daughter, not to any ordinary man but to some one quite special, there is no one like him in the world, he can do anything, anything, anything! Tell them all, let them all know it. Shout it from the housetops, set the bells ringing, dash it all! It's a great day, make the most of it. (*The* CONSTABLE *goes out.*) So that's how it is, Anna Andreyevna, eh? How is it going to be, where are we going to live – here or in Petersburg?

ANNA Naturally, in Petersburg. How could we stay here!

THE MAYOR Well, if it is to be Petersburg, Petersburg let it be. Though it would be very nice here too. I suppose we'll have done with being a mayor, eh, Anna Andreyevna?

ANNA Naturally; it's not much to be the mayor!

THE MAYOR What do you think, Anna Andreyevna, I might come in for a snug berth in the Service now, mightn't I? For, being so thick with all the ministers and in and out of the Palace, he may get me promoted so that I might be a general before long. What do you think, Anna Andreyevna, can I hope to be a general?

ANNA   I should think so! Of course.

THE MAYOR   Dash it all, it will be glorious to be a general! With decorations on one's breast! And which ribbon do you like best, Anna Andreyevna, the red one or the blue?[248]

ANNA   Of course, the blue is the nicest.

THE MAYOR   Eh, so that's what she has set her heart on! The red is not bad either. What makes one want to be a general? Why, if one drives anywhere, postillions and adjutants gallop ahead everywhere calling for horses. And they won't give them to any one else; at the posting-stations they all have to wait – the titular councillors, captains, and mayors – but you don't care a damn. You dine at a governor's, and there – a mayor has to stand in your presence! Ha–ha–ha! (*Goes off into a roar of laughter.*) That's what's so fetching, dash it all!

ANNA   Your tastes are so coarse. You must remember that our whole life has to be changed; that your friends will be very different from the Judge who thinks of nothing but dogs and goes coursing hares with you or Artemy Filippovitch; quite the contrary: all your friends will be of the most refined manners, counts and people of the highest quality . . . Though I must say I feel uneasy about you: you sometimes blurt out words such as are never heard in good society.

THE MAYOR   What of it? Words do no harm.

ANNA   Yes, that was all very well while you were the Mayor, but there life will be utterly different.

THE MAYOR   Yes, they say there are two sorts of fish there, a speckly and a prickly, which simply make your mouth water.

ANNA   He can think of nothing but fish! I am determined that our house shall be the smartest in Petersburg, and that in my drawing-room there shall be such a perfume that there will be no going into it – one will simply shut one's eyes like this! (*She shuts her eyes and sniffs.*) Ah, how delicious!

(*Enter* SHOPKEEPERS.)

THE MAYOR   Ah, good-morning, my bright birds!

SHOPKEEPERS (*bow*)   We wish you good health, sir!

THE MAYOR   Well, my dears, how are you? How is business going? Why, you tea-drinking counter-jumpers, you bring complaints, do you? You arch-rogues, you sly beasts, you deceitful monsters, bringing complaints? Well, have you gained much by it? So you thought you'd get me clapped into prison? Seven devils and one witch beshrew you . . .

ANNA   Good gracious, Antosha, what expressions you do use!

THE MAYOR (*with vexation*)   It's not a matter of words now. Do you know that that official to whom you brought complaints is going to marry my daughter? Eh? What? What have you to say to that? Now I'll give it to you! . . . You cheat people . . . You take a Government contract and pocket a hundred thousand by supplying rotten cloth, and then you subscribe twenty yards and expect a reward for it! And if you were caught, you'd be . . . He struts about like a turkey-cock: he is a shopkeeper, no one must touch him. 'We are as good as the gentry,' he says. But a gentleman . . . ah, you pig faces! A gentleman studies the sciences: if he is thrashed at school, it's to some purpose, that he may learn something useful. And what are you? You begin by petty cheating, you're beaten by your master if you don't cheat successfully. When you are a small boy, before you can repeat the Lord's Prayer, you give short measure; and when you've grown a corporation and stuffed your pockets full, you give yourself airs! Ough, as though you were of consequence! Because you empty sixteen samovars a day have you anything to be proud of? I don't care a rap for your dignified airs!

SHOPKEEPERS (*bowing*)   We are sorry, Anton Antonovitch!

THE MAYOR   You want to complain? And who helped you in your tricks when you were building a bridge and charged twenty thousand for wood when you did not use a hundred roubles' worth? I helped you, you goat's beard! Have you forgotten it? If I had shown you up, I might have sent you to Siberia! What do you say, eh?

ONE OF THE SHOPKEEPERS   We are terribly to blame, Anton Antonovitch! The devil confounded us. We vow we will never complain again. Ask what you like, only don't be angry!

THE MAYOR   Don't be angry! Here you are grovelling at my feet. Why? Because I've got the upper hand of you; but if the luck had been on your side you would have trampled me in the mud, you low cads, and rolled a log on top of me!

SHOPKEEPERS (*bowing down to his feet*)   Do not be the ruin of us, Anton Antonovitch!

THE MAYOR   Now it's 'Do not be the ruin of us!' But what did you say before? I'll . . . (*With a wave of his hand.*) But God forgive you! That's enough! I am not vindictive; only now you mind and be careful! I am marrying my daughter not to any stray gentleman; mind your congratulations are worthy of the occasion . . . you understand? Don't try to get off with a bit of smoked salmon or a loaf of sugar . . . Well, go along. God be with you!

(*The* SHOPKEEPERS *go out.*
Enter AMMOS FYODOROVITCH *and*
ARTEMY FILIPPOVITCH.)

AMMOS FYODOROVITCH (*in the doorway*) Can it really be true, Anton Antonovitch? Have you really come in for this wonderful stroke of luck?

ARTEMY FILIPPOVITCH I have the honour to congratulate you on your great good fortune. I was genuinely delighted when I heard of it. (*Goes to kiss* ANNA ANDREYEVNA's *hand.*) Anna Andreyevna! (*Goes to kiss* MARYA ANTONOVNA's *hand.*) Marya Antonovna!

(*Enter* RASTAKOVSKY.)

RASTAKOVSKY I congratulate you, Anton Antonovitch! May God give you long life and the same to the new couple, and crowds of grand-children and great-grandchildren! Anna Andreyevna! (*Goes up to kiss her hand.*) Marya Antonovna! (*Goes up to kiss her hand.*)

(*Enter* KOROBKIN *and his wife and* LYULYUKOV.)

KOROBKIN I have the honour to congratulate you, Anton Antonovitch! Anna Andreyevna! (*Goes up to kiss her hand.*) Marya Antonovna! (*Goes up to kiss her hand.*)

KOROBKIN'S WIFE My warmest congratulations, Anna Andreyevna, on your new happiness!

LYULYUKOV I have the honour to congratulate you, Anna Andreyevna! (*Kisses her hand, and then turning to the audience makes a clacking noise with his tongue with an air of swaggering bravado.*) Marya Antonovna, I have the honour to congratulate you! (*Kisses her hand, and turns to the audience with the same swaggering air.*)

(*Numbers of Guests in frock-coats and swallowtails enter,
say 'Anna Andreyevna!' and kiss her hand, and
'Marya Antonovna!' and kiss her hand.*
BOBCHINSKY *and* DOBCHINSKY *push their way to the front.*)

BOBCHINSKY I have the honour to congratulate you!

DOBCHINSKY Anton Antonovitch, I have the honour to congratulate you!

BOBCHINSKY   On the propitious event!

DOBCHINSKY   Anna Andreyevna!

BOBCHINSKY   Anna Andreyevna! (*Both approach to kiss her hand at the same moment and knock their heads together.*)

DOBCHINSKY   Marya Antonovna! (*Kisses her hand.*) I have the honour to congratulate you. You will be very, very happy, you will wear a golden dress and have all sorts of delicate soups and spend your time very divertingly.

BOBCHINSKY (*interrupting*)   Marya Antonovna, I have the honour to congratulate you! God give you all prosperity and wealth and a baby boy no bigger than this (*shows with his hand*), little enough to sit on your hand. He will cry all the time Oo–ah! Oo–ah!

(*Some more Visitors come up to kiss the ladies' hands, with them* LUKA LUKITCH *and his wife.*)

LUKA LUKITCH   I have the honour . . .

LUKA LUKITCH'S WIFE (*runs forward*)   I congratulate you, Anna Andreyevna! (*They kiss.*) I was so delighted. I was told, 'Anna Andreyevna has made a match for her daughter.' Ah, my goodness, I thought, and I was so delighted I said to my husband, 'Luka, darling, have you heard of Anna Andreyevna's good fortune?' Well, I thought to myself, thank God! And I said to him: 'I am so immensely delighted that I am burning with impatience to tell Anna Andreyevna herself.' . . . Ah, my goodness, I thought to myself, Anna Andreyevna always expected a good match for her daughter, and now what a destiny! The very thing she wanted! And I was so overjoyed that I couldn't say a word. I cried and cried, I positively sobbed. Luka Lukitch said, 'What are you crying for, Nastenka?' 'Luka, darling, I really don't know,' I said, 'the tears are simply flowing of themselves.'

THE MAYOR   Please sit down, ladies and gentlemen! Hey, Mishka, bring in some more chairs!

(*Enter the* POLICE SUPERINTENDENT *and the* CONSTABLES.)

THE POLICE SUPERINTENDENT   I have the honour to congratulate your worship and to wish you long life and prosperity!

THE MAYOR   Thanks, thanks! Please sit down, gentlemen! (*The Visitors sit down.*)

AMMOS FYODOROVITCH   But do tell us, Anton Antonovitch, how did all this come about?

THE MAYOR   In a most extraordinary way: his Excellency made the proposal in person.

ANNA   In the most respectful and delicate manner. He expressed himself wonderfully well. 'It's entirely out of regard for your virtues,
Anna Andreyevna,' said he. And he is such a delightful, well-bred
man, of the highest principles! 'Believe me, Anna Andreyevna, life
is not worth a farthing to me,' he said. 'I am simply acting from
regard for your rare qualities.'

MARYA   Oh, mamma, but he said that to me!

ANNA   Hold your tongue, you know nothing about it, don't interfere!
'I am amazed, Anna Andreyevna,' he said . . . And he said such
flattering things. And when I tried to say that we dared not hope
for such an honour, he fell on his knees all at once and said in such
a refined way: 'Anna Andreyevna, do not make me the unhappiest
of mortals! Consent to reciprocate my feelings, or I will put an end
to my life.'

MARYA   Really, mamma, he said that about me . . .

ANNA   Yes, of course . . . it was about you too, I don't deny it.

THE MAYOR   He really frightened us; he said he would shoot himself:
'I'll shoot myself, I'll shoot myself!' he said.

MANY OF THE VISITOR   You don't say so!

AMMOS FYODOROVITCH   Well, I am blessed!

LUKA LUKITCH   It's the hand of destiny!

ARTEMY FILIPPOVITCH   Not destiny, old man, destiny has no hands: it's
the reward of merit. (Aside) These swine come in for all the luck!

AMMOS FYODOROVITCH   I'll sell you that puppy you wanted, Anton
Antonovitch, if you like.

THE MAYOR   No, I've no thoughts for puppies now!

AMMOS FYODOROVITCH   If you don't want that one, you might choose
another dog.

KOROBKIN'S WIFE   Ah, Anna Andreyevna, I am delighted at your good
fortune, you can't imagine!

KOROBKIN   And where is our illustrious guest at the moment, may we
enquire? I was told he had left you for some reason.

THE MAYOR   Yes, he has left us for one day on very important business.

ANNA   To visit his uncle and ask his blessing.

THE MAYOR   To ask his blessing; but tomorrow he will . . . (He sneezes:
a general hum of 'God bless you.') Much obliged! But he will be
back tomorrow . . . (Sneezes: a chorus of blessings, loudest of all are the
voices of)

THE POLICE SUPERINTENDENT   Good health to your honour!

BOBCHINSKY   May you live a hundred years and have a sack of gold!

DOBCHINSKY   May God lengthen your days for ages and ages!

ARTEMY FILIPPOVITCH A plague on you!

KOROBKIN'S WIFE The devil take you!

THE MAYOR I thank you sincerely and wish you the same.

ANNA We are intending to live in Petersburg now. I must own that the atmosphere here is . . . so countrified! I must own it's very distasteful. And my husband too . . . will be made a general there.

THE MAYOR Yes, my friends, dash it all, I must say I should awfully like to be a general.

LUKA LUKITCH Please God you will be!

RASTAKOVSKY For man it is impossible, but with God all things are possible.

AMMOS FYODOROVITCH A big ship sails in deep waters.

ARTEMY FILIPPOVITCH A well-deserved honour.

AMMOS FYODOROVITCH (*aside*) It will be a farce if he is made a general! It will suit him like a saddle on a cow! But there is many a slip 'twixt the cup and the lip. There are better men than you here who are not generals yet.

ARTEMY FILIPPOVITCH (*aside*) Dash it all, what next! But there, there's no saying, he may be made a general. He has quite conceit enough for it, the devil take him. (*Addressing him*) You won't forget us then, Anton Antonovitch!

AMMOS FYODOROVITCH And if anything goes wrong – for instance, if we want any assistance in the Service – grant us your protection!

KOROBKIN Next year I shall be taking my son to Petersburg for the service of the State; be so gracious as to extend your protection to him.

THE MAYOR I am ready for my part, I am ready to do my best.

ANNA You are always ready to make promises, Antosha. To begin with, you won't have time to think of it. And besides, how can you, why should you burden yourself with such promises?

THE MAYOR Oh, why not, my love? One can sometimes be of use.

ANNA Of course, but you can't help all the small fry.

KOROBKIN'S WIFE You hear how she speaks of us?

A LADY VISITOR Yes, she was always like that; I know her: let her sit down to the table and she'll put her feet on it.

(*The* POSTMASTER *comes in breathless, holding an open letter in his hand.*)

THE POSTMASTER An amazing thing, gentlemen! The official we took to be the Inspector is not the Inspector at all!

ALL Not the Inspector?

THE POSTMASTER Not a bit of it – I've discovered it from a letter.

THE MAYOR   Good God! From what letter?

THE POSTMASTER   From his own letter. A letter was brought me to the Post Office. I looked at the address – I saw it was addressed to Post-Office Street. I was flabbergasted. 'There,' I thought, 'no doubt he has found out some irregularities in the Post Office department and is informing the authorities.' I took it and unsealed it.

THE MAYOR   How could you?

THE POSTMASTER   I don't know how I could; some supernatural force prompted me. I was on the point of sending for the courier to despatch it by express delivery; but I was overcome by a curiosity such as I have never experienced before. I couldn't let it go, I couldn't, I felt I couldn't! I was simply drawn to open it. I seemed to hear a voice whispering in one ear, 'Don't open it, you will be done for!' and in the other an imp seemed to be muttering, 'Open it, open it, open it!' And when I touched the sealing-wax I felt as though my blood were on fire, and when I opened it an icy shiver ran over me, yes, an icy shiver. My hands trembled and I felt dizzy.

THE MAYOR   But how dared you open the letter of a personage in such a position of authority?

THE POSTMASTER   But that's just the point, that he is not a personage and not in a position of authority!

THE MAYOR   Then what is he, according to you?

THE POSTMASTER   He is nobody at all; goodness knows what to call him.

THE MAYOR (angrily)   What do you mean by nobody? How dare you say that he is nobody, and goodness knows what he is! I'll put you under arrest . . .

THE POSTMASTER   Who, you?

THE MAYOR   Yes, I!

THE POSTMASTER   That's more than you can do.

THE MAYOR   Do you know that he is going to marry my daughter, that I shall be a great personage myself and can pack you off to Siberia if I like?

THE POSTMASTER   Oh, Anton Antonovitch! Don't talk about Siberia, it's a long way off. I'd better read you the letter. Gentlemen, shall I read it aloud?

ALL   Read it, read it!

THE POSTMASTER (reads)   'My dear Tryapitchkin, I hasten to tell you of my marvellous adventures. I was cleaned out on the way by an infantry captain, so much so that the innkeeper here meant to send me to prison; when all of a sudden my Petersburg countenance and get-up induced the whole town to take me for a Governor-General. And I am now staying at the Mayor's, having a gorgeous time, flirting desperately with his wife and daughter; I can't quite make up my mind yet which to begin with – I think I shall start with the mother, for I fancy she is ready to go all lengths. Do you remember how hard up we used to be, how we dined by our wits, and how a confectioner once took me by the collar for telling him to put down our pies to the King of England? Now things have taken quite a different turn. Every one lends me as much money as I like to ask for. They are queer fishes; you would simply die of laughing. You write sketches, I know; you ought to put them in. First and foremost the Mayor – as stupid as an old grey horse . . . '

THE MAYOR   It can't be, it isn't there!

THE POSTMASTER (*shows him the letter*)   Read it yourself!

THE MAYOR (*reads*)   'As an old grey horse.' It can't be, you wrote it yourself.

THE POSTMASTER   How could I have written it?

ARTEMY FILIPPOVITCH   Read!

LUKA LUKITCH   Read!

THE POSTMASTER (*goes on reading*)   'The Mayor – as stupid as an old grey horse.'

THE MAYOR   Oh, damn it all! You need not repeat it! We all know the words are there.

THE POSTMASTER (*goes on reading*)   Hm . . . hm . . . hm . . . 'old grey horse. The Postmaster too is a good fellow.' . . . (*Pausing.*) Well, here he seems to say something unseemly about me too.

THE MAYOR   No, read it!

THE POSTMASTER   Why?

THE MAYOR   No, hang it all, if you are reading it, read it! Read it all!

ARTEMY FILIPPOVITCH   Allow me to read it! (*Puts on his spectacles and reads*) 'The Postmaster is the very image of our office porter Miheyev; I have no doubt the rascal is a regular drunkard too.'

THE POSTMASTER (*to the audience*)   Well, he is a nasty young scamp who wants a whipping, that's all.

ARTEMY FILIPPOVITCH (*goes on reading*)   'The Superintendent of Charitable Institutions . . . er . . . er . . . ' (*Hesitates.*)

KOROBKIN   Why are you stopping?

ARTEMY FILIPPOVITCH   Oh, it's so badly written . . . you can see he is a scoundrel, though.

KOROBKIN   Let me have it! I think my eyes are better. (*Takes hold of the letter.*)

ARTEMY FILIPPOVITCH (*not giving him the letter*) No, we can leave that part out, it is more legible farther on.

KOROBKIN Come, allow me, I can read it all right.

ARTEMY FILIPPOVITCH I'll read it myself if it comes to that; it is quite legible farther on.

THE POSTMASTER No, read it all! Nothing has been left out so far!

ALL Give it him, Artemy Filippovitch, give it him! (*To* KOROBKIN) Read it!

ARTEMY FILIPPOVITCH In a minute. (*Gives him the letter.*) Allow me, here . . . (*Puts his finger over the letter.*) Begin here. (*They all surround him.*)

THE POSTMASTER Read it, read it! Nonsense, read it all!

KOROBKIN (*reading*) 'The Superintendent of Charitable Institutions, Zemlyanika, is a regular pig in a skullcap.'

ARTEMY FILIPPOVITCH (*to the audience*) It is not even witty! A pig in a skullcap! Who has ever seen a pig in a skullcap?

KOROBKIN (*goes on reading*) 'The School Inspector reeks of onions.'

LUKA LUKITCH (*to the audience*) Upon my soul, I never touch an onion.

AMMOS FYODOROVITCH (*aside*) Thank God there is nothing about me.

KOROBKIN (*reading*) 'The Judge . . . '

AMMOS FYODOROVITCH There you are! (*Aloud*) Gentlemen, I think the letter is tedious. Damn it, what is the use of reading this rubbish!

LUKA LUKITCH No!

THE POSTMASTER No, read it all!

ARTEMY FILIPPOVITCH You must read it!

KOROBKIN (*goes on*) 'The Judge, Lyapkin-Tyapkin, is awfully movayton[249] . . . ' (*Pauses.*) That must be a French word.

AMMOS FYODOROVITCH Goodness knows what it means! It's all right if it is only a scoundrel, but it may be something worse.

KOROBKIN (*goes on reading*) 'But they are a hospitable and good-natured set. Goodbye, Tryapitchkin dear. I want to follow your example and take up literary work. It's dull going on like this, one longs for food for the mind. I see I really ought to devote myself to some higher calling. Write to me to the province of Saratov, address – the village of Podkatilovka.' (*Turns over the letter and reads the address.*) It is addressed to 'Ivan Vassilyevitch Tryapitchkin, Number ninety-seven, Third Floor Flat, turning to the right from the entrance by the yard, Post-Office Street, St Petersburg.'

ONE OF THE LADIES What a painful disappointment!

THE MAYOR It's my death-blow! I am killed entirely! I see nothing; nothing but pigs' snouts instead of faces . . . Bring him back! Bring him back! (*Waves his arm.*)

THE POSTMASTER Bring him back indeed! As luck would have it, I told the superintendent to give him the swiftest horses, and it was the devil's prompting made me send the orders on ahead to the other posting-stations.

KOROBKIN'S WIFE This really is most disconcerting, quite unprecedented!

AMMOS FYODOROVITCH But hang it all, gentlemen, he borrowed three hundred roubles from me!

ARTEMY FILIPPOVITCH Three hundred roubles from me too!

THE POSTMASTER (*sighs*) Oh! And three hundred roubles from me too.

BOBCHINSKY And sixty-five roubles in paper money from Pyotr Ivanovitch and me!

AMMOS FYODOROVITCH (*with a gesture expressive of perplexity*) What is the meaning of it, gentlemen? How can we have made such a blunder?

THE MAYOR (*slapping his forehead*) How could I, how could I, old fool that I am? Silly old sheep, I am in my dotage! Thirty years I have been in the Service; not a single merchant, not a contractor could get the better of me; rogues, first-class rogues, I have beaten at their own game; cheats and scoundrels who could have swindled the whole world I've caught tripping. I've hoodwinked three Governors! . . . Governors indeed! (*Waves his hand.*) Governors are not much to boast of . . .

ANNA But this is impossible, Antosha: why, he is engaged to Mashenka . . .

THE MAYOR (*angrily*) Engaged! Pooh! She throws the silly hoax in my face! (*In a frenzy.*) Come and look, come – all the world, all good Christians, look what a fool the Mayor has been made! Call him a fool, the old rascal! (*Shakes his fist at himself.*) Ah, you blockhead! To take a milksop, a rag like that, for a man of consequence! His bells are ringing along the highroad now! He will spread the tale all over the world. It's not enough to be made a laughing-stock – there will come some scribbler, some inkflinger, and will put you in a farce. That's what's mortifying! He won't spare your rank and your calling, and every one will grin and clap. (*To the audience*) What are you laughing at? You are laughing at yourselves . . . You are a fine lot . . . (*Stamps on the floor in a fury.*) I'd do for all those scribblers, the damned liberals and penny-a-liners! The devil's brood! I'd tie you all in a knot, pound you all to a jelly and into the devil's cap with you! . . . (*Makes a thrust with his fist and stamps on the floor.*)

(*After a brief silence.*) I can't get over it. How true it is – those whom God would punish He first deprives of reason.[250] Why, what was there in the least like a Government Inspector in that scatterbrains? Nothing! Not a trace of resemblance – and yet all at once every one was crying, 'The Inspector, the Inspector!' Who was it first set it going that he was the Inspector? Answer!

ARTEMY FILIPPOVITCH (*with a gesture of perplexity*)   If my life depended on it I could not say how it happened. It's as though our minds were befogged or the devil confounded us.

AMMOS FYODOROVITCH   Who set it going? – Why, they set it going, these gallant fellows here (*pointing to* DOBCHINSKY *and* BOBCHINSKY).

BOBCHINSKY   I declare it wasn't me! I never thought of such a thing . . .

DOBCHINSKY   I had nothing to do with it, absolutely nothing.

ARTEMY FILIPPOVITCH   Of course it was your doing . . .

LUKA LUKITCH   To be sure it was. They ran here like mad from the inn: 'He's come, he's come, he doesn't pay his bill . . . ' A fine bird they picked up!

THE MAYOR   It was certainly you! You're the gossips of the town, you cursed liars!

ARTEMY FILIPPOVITCH   The devil take you with your tales of a Government Inspector!

THE MAYOR   You do nothing but prowl about the town and confuse people's minds, you damned rattles! You scatter gossip, you bobtailed magpies!

AMMOS FYODOROVITCH   You dirty sweeps!

LUKA LUKITCH   You dunces!

ARTEMY FILIPPOVITCH   You pot-bellied little shrimps! (*They all surround them.*)

BOBCHINSKY   Upon my word, it wasn't I, it was Pyotr Ivanovitch.

DOBCHINSKY   Oh no, Pyotr Ivanovitch, you were the first to . . .

BOBCHINSKY   Not at all, you were first . . .

(*Enter a* GENDARME.)

GENDARME   The official who has arrived from Petersburg with instructions from the Government summons you to his presence. He is staying at the inn.

(These words fall like a thunderbolt upon all. An exclamation of astonishment rises simultaneously from the lips of all the ladies; the whole group changing their attitude remains petrified. Dumb show – The MAYOR stands in the middle like a post, his arms outstretched and his head flung back; on his right hand are his wife and daughter leaning forward towards him; beyond them is the POSTMASTER, who is transformed into a note of interrogation addressed to the audience; beyond him is LUKA LUKITCH in a state of innocent bewilderment; beyond him at the farther edge of the stage three Lady Visitors, leaning against each other with the most satirical expression, evidently aimed at the MAYOR's family. On the left side of the MAYOR stands ARTEMY FILIPPOVITCH, his head bent a little on one side as though listening to something; beyond him the JUDGE with his hands flung up, squatting almost to the ground and making a movement with his lips as though he were going to whistle or say 'Here is a nice how-do-you-do!' Beyond him is KOROBKIN facing the spectators with a wink and a bitter sneer at the MAYOR; beyond him at the farther edge of the stage DOBCHINSKY and BOBCHINSKY, their hands stretched towards each other, their mouths open, staring at each other with their eyes starting out of their heads. The other Visitors remain standing like posts. For almost a minute and a half the petrified group retains its position.)

(Curtain.)

ENDNOTES

EVENINGS ON A FARM NEAR DIKANKA – Part One

Preface

1 (p. 5) *stove* Stoves in Russia were large, elaborate affairs, with different levels and recesses that could be used for sitting, lying or sleeping.

2 (p. 6) *kammerherr* gentleman of the bedchamber (see Table of Ranks on p. xxxv)

3 (p. 7) *lovage* herb that grows to more than six feet, the leaves of which are often used in soup

4 (p. 7) *Cast not thy pearls before swine* Christ's warning to his disciples in the Sermon on the Mount, Matthew 7:6

5 (p. 8) *kvass* low-alcohol beverage made from wheat, rye, barley or buckwheat meal

6 (p. 8) *sloes* plum-like fruit of the blackthorn tree

7 (p. 8) *frumenty* special dish usually made of cracked wheat, which is boiled and served with milk, egg yolks, almonds, raisins, liquor or assorted meats.

The Fair at Sorotchintsy

8 (p. 11) *Little Russia* the name of Ukraine from medieval times. As early as the reign of Vassily the Blinded (1425–62) men began taking refuge in the Zaporozhye (the name means: Below the Falls), that is, among the islands in the lower reaches of the Dnieper. There a community gradually grew up, the aim of which was to defend the Ukraine from the Tatars of the Crimea, who made yearly raids into Russia, carrying off thousands of men, women and children for sale in the slave-markets of Asia, and also from the Poles who, especially after the union of Lithuania and Poland in 1659, tried to introduce serfdom and Polish institutions into Little Russia. Great numbers of men from all parts of southern Russia were driven by the Tatar and Polish terrors to join the Zaporozhtsy. The sole condition for doing so was a declaration of belief in the Orthodox Church, and of readiness to defend it and to obey the rules of the community. The

Syetch or Syetcha (from a word meaning a clearing in the forest, hence a stronghold made by piling up felled trees) was based an democratic principles. It was divided into *kurens*, each of which elected its own *atamam*, who managed the provisioning. At the *rada*, the general meeting of all the *kurens*, the Cossacks elected the *koshevoy*, and his assistants, the judge, the secretary and the *esaul*. All these held office for a year, but could be deposed at any time if found unsatisfactory. When the Zaporozhtsy were engaged in warfare, the *koshevoy*'s power was absolute, but in peace he could do nothing without the consent of the *rada*.

Celibacy was the strict rule of life in the Syetch; married men who joined the community left their wives behind. It was forbidden under pain of death to bring a woman into the Syetch, and any offence against chastity was severely punished.

At first the Syetch moved from place to place to avoid attack, and it was only towards the end of the sixteenth century that the Zaporozhtsy had a permanent military post on the islands below the Falls, and even then most of the Cossacks only stayed in camp during the summer, returning to their homes for the winter. The Zaporozhtsy took the oath of allegiance to the Russian crown at the same time as the rest of the Ukraine, but they remained practically independent, and at one time transferred their allegiance to Poland, and at another to the Sultan. In 1708, under Mazeppa, they joined Charles XII of Sweden. After the defeat of the latter at Poltava, Peter the Great broke up the Syetch, and the surviving Zaporozhtsy went into the service of the Crimean khan. But in 1733 they were again recognised by the Russian government, and returned to their old haunts. At that date they consisted of three classes: unmarried Cossacks living in the Syetch and enjoying all its rights and privileges, married cossacks living in the villages, who had to join the forces when called upon but could not vote in the *rada* nor fill any post of authority, and peasants, who had to pay a yearly tribute to the Syetch. The Zaporozhtsy were needed by the Russian government as long as the Crimean Tatars were a source of danger. After the conquest of the Crimea, Catherine the Great finally abolished the Syetch in 1775.

(Translator's Note)

9 (p. 12) *pelisse*   a long coat often trimmed with fur

10 (p. 12) *plahta*   a skirt worn over a longer shirt, which was embroidered along the bottom. It consisted of two long pieces of woolen fabric sewn together lengthwise.

11 (p. 13) *bargee*   bargeman

12 (p. 16) *Kotlyarevsky*   Ivan Kotlyarevsky (1769–1838), Ukrainian writer, soldier and patriot. His burlesque of Virgil's *Aeneid* (1790), quoted here, turns the Trojan heroes into Cossacks, and satirises landowners and clergy.

13 (p. 19) *hagglers*   pedlars

14 (p. 20) *blue note*   five rubles (slang)

15 (p. 23) *tsybulya*   onion

16 (p. 24) *heckling*   a term from the textile trade meaning combing out flax or hemp fibres

17 (p. 28) *it was Monday when we started*   According to Russian superstition, Monday is an unlucky day to begin anything.

18 (p. 30) *Artemovsky-Gulak*   Petro Artemovsky-Gulak (1790–1865), Ukrainian poet, author of 'Master and Dog' (1818), a satire on serfdom quoted here

St John's Eve

19 (p. 36) *distaff*   a tool for holding flax or wool in spinning

20 (p. 36) *Podkova*   Ivan Pokhova (?–1578), Cossack general, beheaded by the Polish king Stephen Báthory for appropriating the throne in Moldova. He died a martyr's death and became a Ukrainian folk hero.

21 (p. 36) *Poltor-Kozhuh*   Karp Poltora Kozhukha (?–1642). He was elected supreme commander of the Cossacks in 1638. During his four years as leader, he organised an uprising against Poland, fought the Turks and helped the Tatars defend themselves against the Kalmyks.

22 (p. 36) *Sagaidatchny*   Pyotr Konashevich Sahaidachny (c.1575–1622) from an early age enjoyed a brilliant career as leader of the Cossacks, conducting many successful campaigns against the Turks and showing great diplomatic as well as military skill in allying himself with the Poles against Moscow.

23 (p. 38) *Saint Panteley* [also Panteleimon]   court physician in Rome, martyred by Emperor Constantine in AD303

24 (p. 40) *the bracken blossoms*   According to legend, the flowering fern has magical powers in matters such as revealing secrets, providing prosperity, bringing good luck and fighting demons. It could only

be picked once a year, on St John the Baptist's Day (24 June), a day associated with fertility rites and pre-Christian rituals involving, *inter alia*, lovers discovering the identity of their future spouses.

25 (p. 43) *bandura*   Ukrainian string folk instrument, a sort of giant mandolin that can have up to 68 strings

A May Night, or The Drowned Maiden

26 (p. 55) *gopak*   social and ceremonial dance dating back to the early seventeenth-century, often referred to as the national dance of Ukraine

27 (p. 56) *when the great Tsaritsa Catherine . . . was going to the Crimea*   Catherine II (1729–96) was one of Russia's most important eighteenth-century rulers. She greatly expanded the Russian Empire, modernised its administration along European lines and presided over its enlightenment as it took its place among the nations of Europe. In 1787, she travelled 6000 miles in 6 months to assert Russian sovereignty over her country's acquisitions in the south.

28 (p. 57) *top-knot*   The Zaporozhe Cossacks shaved their heads but kept a large scalplock. According to legend, their enemies could use this as a handle should they succeed in chopping off a Cossack's head.

29 (p. 59) *hetman*   supreme commander of the Ukrainian Cossacks

30 (p. 60) *Intercession*   The Feast of the Intercession is a religious holy day in the Eastern Orthodox Church and is celebrated on 1 or 14 October.

31 (p. 60) *Bezborodko*   Alexander Bezborodko (1747–99) was one of Catherine's brilliant and indispensable advisors – a polyglot, shrewd diplomat, gifted historian, extremely able minister of foreign affairs and Grand Chancellor of Russia.

32 (p. 73) *chaise*   A two- and four-wheeled, one-horse carriage for one or two persons. It had a folding top and a chassis hung on leather straps.

The Lost Letter

33 (p. 75) *Varvara*   early Christian saint and martyr, beheaded by her own father for converting to Christianity

34 (p. 75) *Fools*   popular card game played with a deck of 36 cards

35 (p. 76) *Baturin*   capital of the Cossack Hetmanate, an autonomous Cossack republic from 1669–1708. It was sacked and rased by the Russian army in 1708 but rebuilt in the 1750s. It has now been established as a important national site of Ukrainian history and culture.

36 (p. 81) *bustard*   a large running bird found in southern Europe

37 (p. 81) *from Konotop to Baturin*   a distance of 17 miles

38 (p. 82) *Herod*   Herod Antipas (*c.*20BC–AD*c.*30), ruler of Galilee when it was part of the Roman Empire. He ordered the deaths of John the Baptist and Jesus.

EVENINGS ON A FARM NEAR DIKANKA – Part Two

Preface

39 (p. 90) *tansy*   herb indigenous to Europe used to treat various ills since the eighth century AD

40 (p. 90) *swine-herb*   another name for nightshade, a plant reputed to cause madness and death in humans

41 (p. 90) *trefoil*   a plant with three leaves

Christmas Eve

42 (p. 91) *Uhlan*   lancer in a light calvary unit

43 (p. 100) *St Peter's feast*   29 June, to commemorate Peter, Christ's apostle, martyred by Nero

44 (p. 106) *Gospel of St Luke, chapter thirt . . . thirt . . .*   In Luke 13, Christ reminds his followers in a series of famous parables how a Christian must live in order to be saved.

45 (p. 106) *haycock*   a cone-shaped pile of hay

46 (p. 122) *Potyomkin*   Prince Grigory Aleksandrovich Potyomkin-Tavricheski (1739–91) was a military commander, diplomat, nobleman, and Catherine the Great's lover and confidant. A soldier in the regiment that helped her come to power, he became the governor of Russia's southern provinces (where he annexed the Crimea), was responsible for the construction of many important buildings and served as a skilful negotiator and intriguer at court.

47 (p. 123) *you mean to turn us into carbineers*   a carabineer (the word is variously spelled) is a calvary soldier with a carbine (short rifle).

During Catherine's reign, sixteen regiments of carabineers were indeed created, but they were decommissioned after her death.

48 (p. 123) *Wherein are . . . Tatars in the Crimea?* For hundreds of years Cossack settlements were the object of fierce raids by the Tatars. In response, with the aid of the Russian army, they attacked the Crimea in a war that lasted from 1735–8. Here the reference is to a battle in May 1736, during which the Cossacks helped the Russians cross the Perekop, an elaborate fortification composed of ramparts and a massive ditch.

49 (p. 124) *La Fontaine* Jean de la Fontaine (1621–95) was a seventeenth-century French poet, best known for his *Fables*, collections of subtly comic, incisively satiric, superbly written verse destined to be admired, memorised and cited by generations of French readers.

50 (p. 124) *Brigadier* The *Brigadier-General*, a comedy by Denis Fonvizin (*c.*1744–92), Russia's most important eighteenth-century playwright

51 (p. 125) *Get thee behind me, Satan* the words that Christ used (Matthew 16:23) to rebuke his disciple Peter for worldliness

52 (p. 129) *What a fright!* Gogol has something much earthier here: 'What a shit he painted there!' ('Yaka kaka namelevana!')

A Terrible Revenge

53 (p. 133) *the two days' fight with the Tatars at the Salt Lake* According to legend, the Zaporozhian Cossacks were caught in an ambush and killed by the Tatars. Their bodies were left to rot near a salt lake. Come morning, the corpses, miraculously restored to life, fought again and destroyed their enemies, thus illustrating the healing powers of one's native soil.

54 (p. 137) *Uniats* term for those who accepted the integration of the Eastern Orthodox believers into the Catholic Church. They retained their own rites, language (Church Slavonic) and codes of canon law.

55 (p. 150) *Cracovienne* a lively Polish ballroom dance, usually in 2/4 time. Associated with Cracow, it dates back to the sixteenth-century.

56 (p. 156) *Lemberg* [L'vov in Russian] an ancient city, founded in 1256, important in Galician and Polish history. Since the nineteenth century it has been a major centre for Ukrainian culture.

57 (p. 156) *Wallachia* region in present-day Romania, north of the Danube and south of the Carpathian mountains

58 (p. 156) *Sedmigradsky region* present-day Transylvania, in north-west Romania

59 (p. 157) *Krivan* 8,200-foot mountain in present-day Slovakia

60 (p. 159) *Sivash* system of lagoons on the Sea of Azov, a natural border for Crimea

61 (p. 159) *Galician land* Galicia is an area in western Ukraine (not to be confused with the region in north-west Spain). Its name dates from the early thirteenth-century.

62 (p. 161) *Kanev . . . Tcherkassy* towns in western Ukraine on the Dnieper River

63 (p. 161) *Shumsk* A Polish city from the sixteenth to the end of the eighteenth century, Shumsk became part of Russia and is now populated almost entirely by ethnic Ukrainians.

64 (p. 161) *Galitch* ancient Ukrainian town, annexed by the Poles in 1349

65 (p. 163) *Sagaidachny* See note 21.

66 (p. 163) *Hmelnitsky* Bogdan Khmelnitsky (*c.*1595–1657) led an uprising against the Polish-Lithuanian Commonwealth and liberated Ukraine, paving the way for the Cossack Helmanate of 1648. He negotiated and signed a treaty with Russia in 1654, hoping to guarantee thereby Ukrainian independence.

67 (p. 163) *King of the Poles* Stephen Báthory (1533–1586), King of Poland for ten years, fought successfully for Polish independence and lives on as a national hero, memorialised in literature and art.

Ivan Fyodorovitch Shponka and his Aunt

68 (p. 168) *shoving the other boys off the form* a children's game called *tesnaya baba* in Russian, *ticha baba* in Ukrainian (literally 'squeezed old woman'), involving repeated attempts to push one's competitors off a bench while staying on oneself

69 (p. 169) *scit* Latin for 'he knows [his lesson]'

70 (p. 169) *mazurka* popular Polish folk dance, usually in 3/4 or 3/8 time

71 (p. 170) *Mogilyev* province of present-day Belarus

72 (p. 182) *Travels of Korobeynikov in the Holy Land* an account of a journey made in Egypt and Jerusalem in 1583 by Trifon Korobeynikov, a Moscow merchant. It was published in the eighteenth century and became very popular.

MIRGOROD

73 (p. 197) *Mirgorod* Although its name means city of peace, this Ukrainian town near Poltava was the scene of many battles and a base for important uprisings against the Polish nobility in the seventeenth century.

74 (p. 197) *Zyablovsky* an imaginary author of an imaginary textbook

Old World Landowners

75 (p. 200) *Philemon and Baucis* Characters from a legend recorded in Ovid's *Metamorphoses*. According to Ovid, Zeus and Hermes, in disguise, were turned away when they sought shelter with the rich but welcomed with open arms by Philemon and his wife Baucis. As a punishment, their neighbours were drowned in a flood, but the hospitable couple were granted immortality by being turned into trees when they died. Works by many writers – Shakespeare, Dryden, Swift, Hawthorne – and painters – Jordaens, Rubens and Rembrandt – have represented this myth.

76 (p. 200) *camlet* fabric made of goat's hair

77 (p. 200) *solemnly add v to surnames ending in o* The reference is to Ukrainians seeking to disguise their origins by Russianising their names.

78 (p. 202) *Peter III* Russian Emperor for six months in 1762, Peter III, grandson of Peter the Great and Charles XII of Sweden, is a controversial figure. He has been dismissed as an idiot and a drunkard, yet during his brief reign he attempted some far-reaching reforms – of the Church and the treasury, for example – and he made peace with Prussia. In June 1762, he was deposed by his wife, who became the Empress Catherine the Great, and died three weeks later. Many believe that she gave orders to have him killed.

79 (p. 202) *La Vallière* Françoise Louise de La Baume Le Blanc (1644–1710). A devout Catholic with whom Louis XIV became enamoured, she was his mistress for six years and was the mother of four children by him. She was replaced in the king's affections by

the Marquise de Montespan in 1667 and, appalled by the notoriety she had acquired, left his court to join a nunnery.

80 (p. 203) *jelly*   The Russian word here is *kissel*, a dish made from fresh fruit, thickened with corn starch or potato starch.

81 (p. 208) *the French had a secret agreement with the English to let Bonaparte out again in order to attack Russia*   Napoleon was exiled to the island of Elba in the Mediterranean in April 1814. He escaped and returned in a whirlwind campaign that ended with his defeat by the British and the Prussian armies in June 1815. Sent to St Helena, an island in the south Atlantic, Napoleon continued to be the subject of various conspiracy theories and escape plots.

82 (p. 214) *petit ouvert*   French card-playing expression signifying a weak hand

Viy

83 (p. 221) *Herodias*   wife (and niece and sister-in-law) of Herod Antipas, mother of Salome, and one of the most hateful women in the Bible. Herodias was responsible for the execution of John the Baptist.

84 (p. 221) *Potiphar's wife*   Potiphar is identified in Genesis as the captain of the palace guard. When Joseph is sold into slavery by his brothers and taken to Egypt, Potiphar's wife tries to seduce him and accuses him of attempted rape when he repels her advances.

85 (p. 222) *trepak*   Ukrainian folk dance

86 (p. 226) *Circassian racer*   horse found in southern Russia and Georgia (also known as Karbarda)

The Tale of How Ivan Ivanovitch Quarrelled with Ivan Nikiforovitch

87 (p. 254) *Horol . . . Koliberda*   small Ukrainian towns 65 miles west and 56 miles south-west of Poltava respectively

88 (p. 266) *Lyubiy, Gariy, and Popov*   booksellers at University Publishers, a publishing house responsible for editions of Diderot, Rousseau and Voltaire in the eighteenth century and a clutch of important science books in the nineteenth

89 (p. 274) *santurin or nikopol wine*   Santorini is an island in the Cyclades, 120 miles south-east of the Greek mainland. It is best known for its Vin Santo and very dry white wines. Nikopol is a

town on the Dnieper River, in an intensely cultivated area, but not particularly known for its wine growing.

90 (p. 277) *St Philip's Eve* St Philip's feast day is celebrated by the Eastern Orthodox Church on 6 June.

91 (p. 279) *the campaign of 1807* the war with Napoleon, in which the Russians suffered heavy losses. It ended with the signing of the Treaty of Tilsit in July 1807, leaving Napoleon at the height of his power.

92 (p. 281) *in 1801 I was in the 42nd regiment of light calvary* When Alexander I came to the throne in March 1801, Russia was not fighting an actual war but was in hostile relations with much of Europe.

PETERSBURG TALES

Nevsky Prospect

93 (p. 297) *Nevsky Prospect* the main street of St Petersburg and the most famous street in Russia. Designed by Peter the Great, it runs from the Admiralty Arch to the Alexander Nevsky monastery. Its buildings are a hymn to architectural genius and it occupies a special place in Russian literature and in the national imagination.

94 p. 297) *Morskaya, Gorokhovaya, Lityeinaya, Meshchanskaya* streets in the historic centre of St Petersburg

95 (p. 297) *droshky* four-wheeled open carriage with a long bench for passengers

96 (p. 297) *Viborg Side* municipal district in north-west part of St Petersburg, named after the Swedish city 81 miles north that was conquered and claimed by Peter the Great

97 (p. 297) *Peski* the name of the historical centre of St Petersburg, between the Neva River, Nevsky Prospect and Ligovsky Avenue. It means 'sands', a reference to the nature of the soil.

98 (p. 298) *Ganymede* a boy carried off by Zeus, made cupbearer of the gods, and granted immortality. Ganymede (Catamitus in Latin) became the mythical symbol of the beautiful young male who attracts homosexual love.

99 (p. 298) *Ekaterinsky Canal* A waterway about 5 km long, joining the Moyka and the Fontanka Rivers, the Ekaterinsky Canal was built in 1739. It was made deeper during the reign of Catherine the Great.

100 (p. 299) *surtout* a man's overcoat

101 (p. 299) *redingote*   A French borrowing of 'riding coat', meaning long coat or greatcoat. Originally used for riding, the redingote evolved into a elaborate article of high fashion for both men and women.

102 (p. 300) *Admiralty Spire*   Built mainly of wood in its original form, the central gate tower with its copper-clad spire was designed by Ivan Korobov in 1730. It adorns the Admiralty building, which celebrates naval themes and the greatness of Russia in its elaborate empire style.

103 (p. 301) *frieze overcoat*   long, loose coat, made of coarse wool

104 (p. 301) *Police Bridge*   Also known as Green Bridge and People Bridge, Police Bridge crosses the Moyka Canal and dates from 1716. The original wooden structure was built and painted green in 1730. It was renamed Police Bridge in 1768 because of its proximity to the house of the city police chief, and became St Petersburg's first cast-iron bridge in 1806.

105 (p. 301) *Perugino*   Pietro Vannucci (1450–1523), one of the great painters of the Umbrian school based in Perugia, was commissioned to decorate the Sistine Chapel. A student of Leonardo da Vinci and one of Raphael's teachers, he is famous for his fresco cycles. One candidate for his 'Bianca' is the Virgin Mary in the fresco of the Adoration of the Magi in Santa Maria dei Bianchi in Pieve. Another is the Virgin in a Perugino painting owned by one of Gogol's acquaintances in St Petersburg.

106 (p. 303) *Plaster of Paris Hercules*   Statues of Hercules (Greek Heracles), famous for his feats of strength, were well known in Russia. Particularly popular were representations of his 'Twelve Labours', slaying the Nemean lion, cleaning the Augean stables, capturing the Cretan bull, and so on.

107 (p. 309) *kammer-junker*   chamberlain, title of courtier in Table of Ranks introduced by Paul I (German for 'young lord')

108 (p. 315) *Ohta*   area of St Petersburg on the right bank of the Neva, famous for its cemetery

109 (p. 315) *dressed in a sort of capuchin*   that is, wearing the type of hooded cloak favoured by Capuchin Friars

110 (p. 315) *catafalque*   raised structure on which the coffin of the deceased lies in state

111 (p. 316) *Bulgarin* Faddey Bulgarin (1789–1859) was a Russian writer, editor of *The Northern Bee* and reactionary apologist for the policies of Alexander I and Nicholas I. Pushkin mocked him in a series of brilliant epigrams.

112 (p. 316) *Pushkin* Alexander Pushkin (1799–1837), poet, novelist, dramatist, critic, the founder of modern Russian literature and the most beloved of Russian writers

113 (p. 316) *Gretch* Nikolay Gretch (1789–1869), grammarian, philologist and journalist who collaborated with Bulgarin as an editor on various literary journals and polemicised with Pushkin

114 (p. 316) *Orlov* Alexander Orlov (1791–1840), virulent anti-aristocrat, the author of various satirical novels and fairy tales. The juxtaposition of these names, comparing Pushkin, a national icon who bestrides Russian literature like a colossus, with three relative nonentities, is the point of Gogol's joke.

115 (p. 316) *Filatka* stock folk character in vaudeville

116 (p. 317) *Dimitry Donsky* a tragedy by Vladislav Ozerov (1769–1816), staged in 1807 and designed to stir up Russia's patriotic fervour immediately after a bloody and inconclusive battle (Eylau) during the Napoleonic Wars

117 (p. 317) *Woe from Wit* This is the title of a comedy by Alexander Griboyedov (1795–1829) that first appeared in 1825. It is now considered a classic, particularly because its epigrammatic brilliance and witty exchanges have found their way into the language. See also note 136.

118 (p. 317) *all is vanity* Ecclesiastes 1:2

119 (p. 318) *Schiller* Friedrich Schiller (1759–1805), influential German poet, playwright, historian and critic

120 (p. 318) *Hoffmann* Ernst Theodor Amadeus Hoffmann (1776–1822), gifted writer, musician, poet and painter, chiefly remembered for his superb short stories

121 (p. 318) *rappee* strong snuff made from very dark tobacco leaves

122 (p. 318) *Swabia* region that once included Alsace, Switzerland, Austria and Bavaria, as well as Baden-Würtemburg in the German south-west. It played an important role in the historical, cultural and linguistic development of Germany.

123 (p. 318) *a king in Germany* Francis I, President of the German Confederation, ruled from 1815 to 1835.

124 (p. 320) *Meine Fraue . . . Was wollen Sie doch? . . . Gehen Sie . . . !*
My wife . . . What do you want then? . . . Go . . . !

125 (p. 324) *The Northern Bee*   a political and literary newspaper that
begin publication in 1825 and lasted for almost 40 years. Those
who wrote for it were extremely conservative and pro-government,
which made its opponents dismiss its content as hack journalism.
Both Pushkin and Gogol were criticised in its pages for the lack of
clear moral direction in their work.

126 (p. 324) *Staff Headquarters*   an immense building with a façade of
580m, situated in front of the Winter Palace in St Petersburg. It was
built to commemorate Russia's victory in the Patriotic War of 1812.

127 (p. 325) *Lafayette*   Gilbert du Motier, Marquis de La Fayette
(1757–1834), French military commander and statesman. He
fought under George Washington in the Revolutionary War and
was a leader of the Garde Nationale during the French Revolution.

The Nose

128 (p. 327) *Voznesensky Prospect*   one of three major thoroughfares
that meet at the Admiralty Spire

129 (p. 327) *also lets blood*   Until the end of the eighteenth-century, it
was common for barbers to perform surgery, particularly on
soldiers wounded in battle.

130 (p. 329) *St Isaac's Bridge*   erected in 1727, the first St Petersburg
bridge over the Neva River

131 (p. 330) *Riga to Kamchatka*   from the capital of present-day Latvia
to the easternmost point of Siberia, the full expanse of Russia

132 (p. 331) *Cornelian*   a glassy, reddish-brown translucent stone;
member of the quartz family

133 (p. 332) *Kazan Cathedral*   The Cathedral of our Lady of Kazan
was constructed between 1801 and 1811 by the architect Andrei
Voronikhin (1759–1814). Its design was inspired by the Basilica of
St Peter's in Rome. The censors made Gogol change the venue of
this encounter to an arcade.

134 (p. 334) *Politseysky*   police headquarters

135 (p. 334) *Anitchkin Bridge*   The Anichkov Bridge, part of Nevsky
Prospect where it crosses the Fontanka, was built in 1715 by order

of Peter the Great and named after its engineer. It has been rebuilt multiple times.

136 (p. 334) *boston*	an eighteenth-century card game derived from whist and quadrille that anticipates bridge and hearts. Kovalyov's friend loses points when he does not make the 8 tricks (of 13) that he contracts for.

137 (p. 338) *Berezina snuff*	from tobacco grown on the banks of the Berezina River in present-day Belarus

138 (p. 344) *experiments in the influence of magnetism had been attracting public attention only recently*	In 1819 links between electricity and magnetism were discovered and important experiments with magnetic fields were carried out in 1820.

139 (p. 345) *dancing chair in Konyushenny Street*	a supposedly supernatural event, mentioned in Pushkin's 1833 diary

140 (p. 345) *Tavritchesky Park*	gardens first laid out in 1783 surrounding the magnificent Tauride Palace commissioned by Potyomkin

141 (p. 345) *Hozrev-Mirza*	A Persian prince and grandson of the Shah, Hozrev-Mirza came to St Petersburg to apologise formally for the murder of Alexander Griboyedov (see note 113) in a massacre that followed the seizure of the Russian Embassy in Tehran in 1829. Hozrev-Mirza gave Nicholas I an 88-carat diamond that became known as the Shah diamond.

142 (p. 346) *name-day parties*	Since the Middle Ages, Russians have celebrated their name day, the day associated with their given name, usually that of a saint. Name-days are still fêted more often than birthdays.

143 (p. 347) *Gostiny Dvor*	Designed by Jean Baptiste Vallin de la Mothe (1729–1800), Gostiny Dvor became an elaborate indoor market, St Petersburg's largest and most famous shopping centre and one of the first arcades in the world.

The Portrait

Translated from the Russian by Isabel F. Hapgood, in *St John's Eve and Other Stories*, Freeport, New York, 1971

144 (p. 349) *Shtchukinui Dvor*	a large market, part of the Apraxin Dvor in St Petersburg and named after the merchant who bought it in

the mid eighteenth century. Its wooden buildings burnt to the ground in 1783 and it has been restored a number of times since.

145 (p. 349) *publications* the reference is to popular depictions called *lyubki*. They featured religious stories and fairy tales, both woodcuts and engravings. There was a series of chapbooks associated with these stories as well.

146 (p. 349) *Tsarevna Miliktrisa Kirbitievna* a character from a popular fairy tale, 'Bova Korolevich' or 'The Story of Prince Bova', often depicted in the *lyubki*

147 (p. 350) *Flemish boors* imitations of painters from Flanders, whose work was central to the development of Western painting: in the fifteenth century, figures such as Jan van Eyck and Hans Memling; in the sixteenth, Pieter Brueghel; in the art of 'the Golden Age', Rubens and Anthony van Dyck

148 (p. 352) *white note* slang for 20 rubles

149 (p. 352) *to the fifteenth line on Vasilievsky Island* Thirty of these lines run north-south on the island. They are designated by number and represent not streets but sides of streets.

150 (p. 354) *The English style* The reference is to Sir Joshua Reynolds (1723–92), who brought together the styles of the Italian Renaissance and the fashions of his time. He became particularly well known as a painter of portraits of the rich and famous, and changed pictorial art for ever as a result.

151 (p. 354) *Raphael* Raffaello Sanzio da Urbino (1483–1520), Italian painter, architect and designer. Along with Michelangelo and Leonardo da Vinci, Raphael was a great master of the Italian Renaissance and a legend in his own time. He is best known for the frescoes in the *Stanze* named after him in the Vatican.

152 (p. 354) *Guido* Guido Reni (1575–1642) created easel paintings and large-scale decorations in major cities all over Italy. His work combines a classical style and a remarkable subtlety in the ways he represents flesh tones and emotion.

153 (p. 354) *Titian* Tiziano Vecelli (*c.*1488–1576), one of the most versatile and influential of Italian painters, is well known for his portraits, particularly those of princes, doges, cardinals, artists and writers. He also painted many landscapes and religious subjects.

154 (p. 355) *Leonardo* Leonardo da Vinci (1452–1519), one of the most famous painters of the Italian Renaissance (*The Last Supper*, the *Mona Lisa* – almost certainly the portrait referred to here), was

also the epitome of the Renaissance man, inventor, naturalist, engineer and political adviser.

155 (p. 355) *Vasari* Italian painter, architect and historian, Giorgio Vasari (1511–1574) published in 1550 *Lives of the Most Excellent Painters, Sculptors and Architects*, the most influential history of art ever written.

156 (p. 358) *domovoi* figure from Slavic folklore, variously described as a sprite, goblin, poltergeist and kobold

157 (p. 360) *Kolomna* largest of the seven islands that make up St Petersburg. It is south of the Neva and is a district traditionally associated with many great Russian writers.

158 (p. 361) *Prince Kutusoff's portrait* Mikhail Kutuzov, one of Russia's greatest generals, fought in three Russo-Turkish wars and extensively against Napoleon, most famously in the 1812 campaign in which he brilliantly counter-attacked after ceding Moscow to the French.

159 (p. 361) *Gromoboy* the hero of *Twelve Sleeping Maidens*, a ballad by Vasily Zhukovsky (1783–1852). Gromoboy sells his soul to the devil, imperilling his twelve daughters, but the redemptive power of love assures them a happy ending.

160 (p. 365) *rooms of the style of Teniers* probably David Teniers the Younger (1610–90), a painter known for his startlingly evocative scenes from peasant life. His father, David Teniers the Elder (1582–1649), also had a gift for representing homely, rustic settings.

161 (p. 365) *C'est charmant, Lise! . . . venez-ici . . . Quelle jolie figure!* This is lovely, Lise! . . . come here . . . What a pretty face!

162 (p. 368) *Psyche* In Greek mythology, a beautiful young girl who inadvertently offends Venus, the goddess of love. Cupid falls in love with her and, after many trials, including a visit to the Underworld, they are united in eternal love.

163 (p. 369) *Quelle idée delicieuse!* What a wonderful idea!

164 (p. 369) *Correggio* Antonio Allegri da Correggio (1489–1534) was an Italian Renaissance painter known for his startling compositions, his play with perspective and the erotic character of his mythological scenes. Nineteenth-century tourists in Italy helped re-establish his reputation.

165 (p. 370) *Mars* Roman god of war and agriculture

166 (p. 370) *Byron* George Gordon Byron, 6th Baron Byron (1788–1824), a leading figure in the Romantic movement and the most famous poet of the nineteenth century. He invented the Byronic hero, an exiled figure who is isolated, aloof and attractive.

167 (p. 370) *Corinne* Corinne is the eponymous heroine of a picaresque romance (1807) by Mme de Staël (1766–1817). It is a love story, a homage to the literature and art of Italy, and an allegorical account of the French Revolution.

168 (p. 370) *Undine* Undine is the eponymous heroine of a poem by Zhukovsky (1783–1852), based on the fairy tale of that name by Friedrich de La Motte-Fouqué (1777–1843).

169 (p. 370) *Aspasia* Aspasia (*c.*470–400BC) was born in present-day Turkey and received an excellent education despite her marginal status. Renowned for her beauty and intelligence, she eventually became the mistress of the statesman Pericles, whom she advised on affairs of state.

170 (p. 371) *Michael Angelo* Michelangelo di Lodovico Buonarrotti Simoni (1475–1564), Italian painter, sculptor, architect, poet and engineer, whose greatest achievements include the 400-plus life-size figures on the ceiling of the Sistine Chapel in the Vatican, the statue of David in Florence and the design of St Peter's Basilica in Rome

171 (p. 371) *Il y a quelque chose extraordinaire dans toute sa figure!* There's an extraordinary expression on his face!

172 (p. 374) *Homer's Iliad* epic poem from ancient Greece recounting the Siege of Troy and its consequences. Written by Homer (seventh or eighth century BC), it is the oldest extant work in Western literature.

173 (p. 376) *basilisk* monster of legend, whose glance could cause death. In some versions of the story, it could be killed by the crowing of the cock.

174 (p. 377) *It seemed . . . Pushkin has described* Pushkin's poem *The Demon* depicts the effects of a visitation by an evil genius and his refusal to acknowledge the existence of beauty, inspiration, freedom or love.

175 (p. 377) *harpy* evil creature from classical mythology, half-woman, half-bird

176 (p. 378) *calash* a light carriage with a collapsible top, for two or four passengers

177 (p. 378) *Maecenases*   Gaius Maecenas (70–8BC) was an adviser to the Roman Emperor Augustus and a patron of important Roman poets. His name is now a noun meaning supporter of the arts.

178 (p. 381) *Kalinkin Bridge*   Built across the Griboyedov Canal, the (Staro-)Kalinkin bridge joins Kolomna Island and Pokrovsky Island where it crosses the Fontanka. It was completed in 1787. The four large granite towers on the central span make it particularly distinctive.

179 (p. 383) *Shakspeare*   Queen Elizabeth I and James I were interested in every aspect of the arts and variously involved in Shakespeare's career as a playwright.

180 (p. 383) *Molière*   Molière's great benefactor was Louis XIV, who put him in charge of entertainment at Versailles.

181 (p. 383) *Dante*   Bitterly opposed political factions in Dante's native Florence made for dramatic shifts in his circumstances there, and he was eventually exiled and barred from return on pain of death.

182 (p. 384) *Grandison*   Sir Charles Grandison is the hero of the novel of that name, published in 1753 by Samuel Richardson (1689–1761). Asked by his readers to create a hero as morally exemplary as his female characters, Richardson obliged with this novel about the life of a moral paragon.

The Overcoat

183 (p. 399) *the horse on the Falconet monument*   Commissioned by Empress Catherine II to make a monument to Peter the Great, French sculptor Etienne Falconet (1716–91) created the *The Bronze Horseman*, one of the most famous works in the history of sculpture. Its base is reputed to be the largest stone every moved by man. Peter sits on a rearing horse facing westwards towards the Neva River, a symbol of Russia's desire to westernise.

184 (p. 416) *quinsy*   an abscess in the throat accompanied by painful swallowing, headache, fever and altered speech

185 (p. 416) *fomentation*   a warm medicinal compress

186 (p. 416) *deal coffin*   deal is a piece of sawn softwood, the cheapest material for making a coffin

187 (p. 421) *Obuhov Bridge*   A stone bridge named after its builder, it crosses the Fontanka and was completed in 1786. (Not to be confused with Big Obukhov Bridge, first opened in 2004.)

The Carriage

188 (p. 423) *The Carriage*   Gogol uses 'kolyaska', the word for a four-wheeled carriage with a folding top. It sat four inside and there was a place in front for the driver.

189 (p. 423) *nankeen*   a yellow cotton cloth

190 (p. 424) *hurdle*   a framework used for temporary fencing

191 (p. 424) *play a game of 'bank'*   Gogol's word here is *banchik*, a card game derived from baccarat (Italian 'banco').

192 (p. 425) *Tambov and Simbirsk*   Built in the seventeenth-century as a defence against the Crimean Tatars and nomadic tribes, they became important trade and administrative centres in Gogol's time.

193 (p. 426) *sterlet*   a species of sturgeon found in Europe and parts of Asia

194 (p. 426) *fricassee*   a French stew made from meat cut up and fried in a white sauce

195 (p. 426) *Lafitte* (more normally Lafite)   wine from a 107-hectare estate in the Bordeaux region. The estate dates from 1234 and produces some of the most expensive and sought-after wines in the world.

196 (p. 426) *Madeira*   a fortified Portuguese wine made on the islands of Madeira

197 (p. 429) *the campaign of 1812*   France invaded Russia in June of 1812. Pursuing a scorched-earth policy, the Russian army retreated, avoiding pitched battles. Although Napoleon eventually captured and entered Moscow, he was forced to retreat because his supply lines were hopelessly over-extended, incurring the loss of most of his half-million men in appalling winter weather conditions.

198 (p. 430) *bon-voyage*   a low-slung four-wheel carriage designed for longer journeys

A Madman's Diary

199 (p. 437) *Kokushkin Bridge*   Bridge across the Griboyedov Canal dating from 1786. Gogol lived in this neighbourhood in 1830.

200 (p. 438) *batiste*   a fine, plain weave cloth made from cotton, often used for handkerchiefs

201 (p. 438) *written by Pushkin*   The lines cited were actually written by Nikolay Nikolev (1758–1815), a versatile and much admired poet and playwright.

202 (p. 440) *équivoques*   possibilities of interpreting something in a number of different ways

203 (p. 442) *ma chère*   my dear

204 (p. 446) *mason*   member of a fraternal organisation that traces its ancestry back to stonemasonry. The special handshake referred to is one of the signs that this society's members can use to identify each other.

205 (p. 446) *They say that some Donna ought to ascend the throne*   Isabella II of Spain (1830–1904). Elder daughter of Ferdinand VII and his fourth wife (and niece), Isabella became Queen at the age of three. Her uncle, Carlos, disputed her claim, which caused a civil war.

206 (p. 447) *Philip II*   Philip II (1527–98) was King of Spain, Portugal, Naples and Sicily, as well as Duke of Milan and even King of England for four years while married to Queen Mary I.

207 (p. 451) *Spanish Inquisition*   In 1478, King Ferdinand II and Queen Isabella I got permission from the Pope to 'purify' Spain by seeking out heretics, making them confess and name others, and then punishing them with torture, imprisonment or death. The best known chief inquisitor was Tomas de Torquemada (1420–1498).

208 (p. 451) *Polignac*   Prince Jules de Polignac (1780–1847) was a French statesman and strong royalist supporter in the aftermath of the 1789 Revolution. He served as prime minister under Charles X just before the 1830 Revolution, which overthrew the Bourbon dynasty and ushered in the reign of Louis Philippe.

209 (p. 452) *King of France*   The censorship forced Gogol to change this reference to the King of France, which they apparently saw as a slight on the recently deposed Charles X. Gogol substituted the Bey of Algiers, whom the French had recently deposed.

THE GOVERNMENT INSPECTOR

210 (p. 461) *Voltairians*   followers of François-Marie Arouet (1694–1778), known by his nom de plume Voltaire, the foremost figure in the French Enlightenment. He believed in the existence of a Supreme Being, but was harshly criticised by religious figures for his scepticism and his satiric critiques of belief systems and their absurdities.

211 (p. 462) *marshal of nobility*   Figures elected by the nobility to assist in municipal, judicial and educational affairs, they often served as leaders on local boards, and representatives at the court of the Tsar.

212 (p. 462) *Assyrians* The Assyrian Empire existed in present-day Turkey, Syria, Iran and Iraq for thousands of years before Christ. In its final incarnation it was probably the largest and most powerful empire the world had yet seen, as well as being the cradle of civilisation and the acme of Middle-Eastern culture.

213 (p. 462) *Babylonians* Babylonians were citizens of Babylon, a Semitic city more than 4000 years old. It flourished as an independent city state for a time but was consistently dominated by invaders from throughout the Middle East.

214 (p. 462) *Alexander the Great* Alexander III of Macedon (356–323BC) at his height ruled an empire that stretched from the Adriatic to the Indus. He is generally acknowledged to be the greatest military commander who ever lived (he was never defeated in battle), and he imposed his name, his armies and Greek civilisation on most of the known world before he died at thirty-three.

215 (p. 463) *War with the Turks* Russia went to war with Turkey nine times between 1568 and 1829.

216 (p. 464) *Saratov . . . Kostroma* Saratov is a city on the Volga River founded in 1590. As a series of forts, it enabled the Tsar to control adjacent territory, and in Gogol's time it became an important shipping port. Kostroma, another town in the Grand Duchy of Moscow, served as a retreat for the Grand Dukes in times of war, and the Romanovs regarded it as their protectorate. It was burned down and rebuilt during the reign of Catherine the Great.

217 (p. 464) *Elysium* in classical mythology, the place where the souls of the blessed go

218 (p. 466) *St Vassily's day* 28 February

219 (p. 467) *the book of John the Mason* As Leonard Kent and Richard Peace have pointed out, following E. L.Voytolovskaya, the reference is to a work called *Self Knowledge: A treatise, showing the nature and benefit of that important science, and the way to attain it* (London, 1745). Peace adds, 'Its author, John Mason, was a nonconformist minister. It was translated into Russian as *Poznaniya samogo sebya* by Ivan Turgenev, a well-known mason, and published by N. Novikov in 1783.' In his book on Gogol, Vladimir Nabokov suggests that the reference is rather to a book of adventures concerning John Mason, a sixteenth-century English diplomat travelling on the continent.

220 (p. 467) *Solomon* Israelite king *c.*970–931BC, builder of the First Temple in Jerusalem and noted for his great wisdom

221 (p. 470) *fichu* square or triangular kerchief worn to cover shoulders and a low neckline

222 (p. 473) *Penza* A city 390 miles south-east of Moscow, Penza had a population of 13,000 by the beginning of the nineteenth century.

223 (p. 473) *Robert le Diable* *Robert the Devil*, an opera by Giacomo Meyerbeer (1791–1864), was first performed in 1831 and enjoyed a huge success.

224 (p. 473) *The Red Sarafan* popular folksong, composed by Alexander Varlamov (1801–48)

225 (p. 474) *Joachim* [also Yokhim] well-known horse-and-carriage dealer in St Petersburg

226 (p. 477) *Kholmogory* region in north-west Russian near Archangel, known for the quality of its beef since the seventeenth century

227 (p. 479) *a Vladimir ribbon in your buttonhole* The Order of St Vladimir was established in 1782 by Catherine the Great for meritorious service. The award was divided into four classes.

228 (p. 484) *Queen of Clubs* in fortune-telling, this card is associated with a dark-haired, confident woman

229 (p. 486) *labardan* salted cod

230 (p. 488) *comprenez-vous* French for 'you understand'

231 (p. 489) *The Marriage of Figaro*, *Robert le Diable*, *Norma* operas by Mozart (1756–91), Meyerbeer (see note 213) and Vincenzo Bellini (1801–35)

232 (p. 489) *Baron Brambeus* pseudonym of Osip Senkovsky, journalist, essayist, polyglot and romancer. He is best known for his accounts of fantastic voyages (to the centre of the earth, to Mount Etna), his championing of popular periodicals and his studies of various Eastern languages.

233 (p. 489) *The Frigate Hope* a novel about the Decembrists' revolt, a military uprising against the Tsar in December 1825. The novel was written by Alexander Bestuzhev, pseudonym Marlinsky (1797–1837), a Romantic and revolutionary who sympathised with the officers' grievances.

234 (p. 489) *Moscow Telegraph* journal established in 1825 by Nikolay Polevoy (1796–1846) and his brother Ksenofont, which supported liberal ideas, skirmished with Pushkin and his circle and attacked

conservative writers. It was closed by the government in 1834, for criticising a jingoistic play.

235 (p. 489) *Smirdin* Alexander Smirdin (1795–1857), a publisher responsible for excellent editions of Pushkin, Gogol, Zhukovsky and others, and a crucial figure in the popularisation of Russian literature

236 (p. 489) *Yuri Miroslavsky* historical novel by Mikhail Zagoskin (1789–1852), published in 1829, that became the first Russian bestseller

237 (p. 490) *Privy Council* a legislative body designed to advise Alexander I, created as part of the reforms initiated by Mikhail Speransky in 1810

238 (p. 496) *Cicero* Marcus Tullius Cicero (106–43BC), statesman, scholar, philosopher, politician, lawyer, consul and political theorist. He is generally considered one of Rome's greatest orators and prose stylists.

239 (p. 496) *Tower of Babel* According to Genesis 11:1–9, after the flood, the 'children of men' tried to build a tower as high as heaven, for which God punished them by 'confounding' their languages, thus making it impossible for them to communicate with each other.

240 (p. 497) *Anna of the Third Class* Originally founded in commemoration of Anna Petrovna, daughter of Peter the Great, this order for distinguished civil or military service was re-established by Paul I of Russia in 1797, and named after St Anne, mother of the Virgin Mary.

241 (p. 498) *bon-ton* French for 'good breeding'

242 (p. 500) *Jacobin* name for the most radical group during the French Revolution, and subsequently used to describe those involved in left-wing, revolutionary politics more generally

243 (p. 504) *troika* three-horse team harnessed side by side

244 (p. 506) *St Anthony's is his name day* in this case 30 January

245 (p. 506) *St Onufry* 12 June

246 (p. 509) *Oh, man . . . against God* the opening lines of 'Ode, adapted from Job', a poem by Mikhail Lomonosov (1711–65)

247 (p. 510) *Karamzin* Nikolay Karamzin (1766–1826) essayist, reviewer, poet and historian. The quotation is from a collection called *Bornholm Island*.

248 (p. 516) *which ribbon do you like best, Anna Andreyevna, the red one or the blue?* The order of St Alexander Nevsky, first awarded by Catherine I, features a red sash; the order of St Andrew, established by Peter the Great in 1698, features a blue one. The latter is the more prestigious.

249 (p. 524) *movayton* for *mauvais-ton*, French for 'ill bred'

250 (p. 526) *those whom God would punish He first deprives of reason* ancient Greek proverb, sometimes attributed to Euripides (*c.*480-406BC), a famous Greek dramatist